PENGUIN BOOKS

G L O V E   P U P P E T

Neal Drinnan was born in 1964 in Melbourne, and was dubiously educated at various (now defunct) high schools and Camberwell Boys' Grammar. At the age of seventeen, he abandoned his education and suburban family home life for the lure of Chapel Street and life's more ephemeral things. He has worked in publishing for many years, has been a frequent contributor to *OUTRAGE* magazine and is a regular columnist for Sydney's *Capital Q*. This is his first book.

GLOVE puppet

NEAL DRINNAN

PENGUIN BOOKS

Penguin Books Australia Ltd
487 Maroondah Highway, PO Box 257
Ringwood, Victoria 3134, Australia
Penguin Books Ltd
Harmondsworth, Middlesex, England
Viking Penguin, A Division of Penguin Books USA Inc.
375 Hudson Street, New York, New York 10014, USA
Penguin Books Canada Limited
10 Alcorn Avenue, Toronto, Ontario, Canada M4V 3B2
Penguin Books (NZ) Ltd
Cnr Rosedale and Airborne Roads, Albany, Auckland, New Zealand

First published by Penguin Books Australia Ltd 1998

10 9 8 7 6 5 4 3 2 1

Design by Sandy Cull, Penguin Design Studio
Photography by Maikka Trupp
Puppet handmade by Justine Philip
Author photograph by Brett Monaghan
Quote from *I Had Trouble in Getting to Solla Sellew* by Dr Seuss on page ix
    © Dr Seuss Enterprises, L.P. 1965, 1993 All rights reserved
Typeset in 9pt Stone Serif by Midland Typesetters, Maryborough, Victoria
Printed in Australia by Australian Print Group, Maryborough, Victoria

National Library of Australia
Cataloguing-in-Publication data:

Drinnan, Neal.
  Glove puppet.

  ISBN 0 14 026789 1.

  I. Title.

A823.3

This project has been assisted by the Commonwealth Government
through the Australia Council, its arts funding and advisory body.

FOR TIM

Acknowledgements

I would like to acknowledge Bryony Cosgrove,
Helen Pace, James Bradley, Lyn Amy, David
Nair, Michael West, Kirk Drinnan and David
Wills for all their support and encouragement

I learned there are troubles
Of more than one kind.
Some come from ahead
And some come from behind.

But I've bought a big bat
I'm ready, you see
Now my troubles are going
To have trouble with *me*!

from **I Had Trouble in Getting to Solla Sellew**
DR SEUSS

PROLOGUE

Victoria Station yawned like a cavernous mouth, signalling the end of our journey. My first journey and my mother's last.

Mum was shivering and edgy, scared to disembark. I was jumping in and out, back and forth, as if to show her it was no big deal – train, platform, train, platform. I was mocking her indecision, limbre and lithely.

'Fucken' knock it off Johnny or I'll belt ya . . .'

Her voice caught in her throat, like she was going to be sick.

The man who'd said he was a doctor caught our eye as he stepped from another carriage. We both watched him slink out through one of the exits. I with relief, Mum with poisoned despair. His dirty vinyl bag full of nasty tricks hung awkwardly across his shoulder, making of him a grotesquely degenerate schoolboy. His beady little eyes were darting all over the joint, but he never looked at us again. He had the cowering manner of a guilty dog who'd just snaffled up a dirt-poor family's supper. If I'd been big enough, I'd have beaten him with a stick, a good, thick nursery rhyme faggot barbed with a crooked rusty nail. The train doors finished their clatter of opening and slamming. I was impatient, 'C'mon Ma, let's go.'

It was just us now, frail and forlorn on a dim platform in a vast grey space. A posh, recorded voice offered monotonous information about trains, trains going places that meant nothing to us. A chubby guard, keen to be knocking off for the night, passed by, cursing the sloppy mess from a pie he'd just spilled down his front. 'All bloody gravy, not an ounce of meat,' he muttered.

I fancied some of that pie, meat or gravy, but Mum, she couldn't look at it. She was feeling sick. Sometimes it was like that after she'd had her needle. We trudged across the deserted platform to a dingy alcove where she slid onto the grotty wooden bench, and groaned with relief as she weighed into its cold, hard comfort. 'Mum needs a rest, Love – 'ere's a pound, go get yourself a pie.'

There was no one around except for a man in another alcove nearby. He was huddled into his coat reading the paper, a single suitcase between his legs. When he noticed I was staring as I dawdled past he said, 'Hello.'

I was watching him because he looked like the host on a nightly game show Mum used to watch. I think she was keen on that man on TV. She'd laugh and say, ''Ere Johnny, you's al'ays on about wantin' to know who ya father is, well it's 'im, 'im on telly.' I wondered if this man was the same one. I'd never seen anyone off the telly before.

'Are you on the telly?' I asked.

He sort of cocked his head and smiled in a funny way.

'I've been on the telly, if that's what you mean.'

'Oh, me Mum likes you'n'all.'

He looked over at Mum, who'd slid sideways and was sleeping.

'Is your Mum alright?'

'She's a bit sick, s'all.'

'Perhaps we ought to get her some help. Is she very sick?'

'She's awright, she jus' gets sick wi' someat in 'er stomach 'at's all.'

He didn't seem convinced. I wandered off in search of my pie.

I left the platform and went into the vast entrance hall, gasping at its size. The queen would live somewhere like this, I thought. Most of the shops were closed. I passed an old bag lady who was talking to herself, a slumped, sleeping man who'd wet his trousers and another man cuddling an ancient dog with hardly any fur. I asked the lady at a kiosk for a pie. She gave it to me while scanning the concourse for an adult I might be attached to.

'Love, where's your Mum or Dad?'

'Oh, me Dad's out there.' I gestured towards the platforms. ''E's on the telly me Dad is.'

'Well now there's a thing,' she said, reassured by the knowledge of guardians unseen.

I stood, looking around, eating my lukewarm pie, then, having fingered out the cold part with a dirty splat onto the

3

tiled floor, I headed back to Mum, pastry crust and change in hand.

I wandered slowly past the handsome man again, flaunting my pie crust as if it were worthy of envy, a priceless coronet plucked and flaunted from our family jewels. I squeezed the coins in my other hand, hoping Mum would forget about the change. I was hoping maybe he'd talk to me some more.

'Was that a nice pie?'

'Nah, it was bleedin' cold.'

'Are you sure your Mum's okay?'

'I told ja, she's jus' a bit sick.'

I headed back to Mum, annoyed by all these questions. I remembered what she'd said back home about police, social workers and the like: 'World's full of nosy bloody Parkers.' I looked at the man again. No one understood about when she got sick; soon she'd be up wanting a cup of tea. I looked in my palm and closed it again. I didn't know how much a cup would cost but it didn't look like enough in there to buy her one, not enough for chips or anything.

I finished the pie and sat awhile watching Mum. She looked like a doll, no colour in her face except the make-up she was wearing. She was sweating and cold. Since I'd been away she'd vomited onto the ground. I was very tired by then, so I curled myself near her, my back against the cold drafts, my head near the vague warmth of her lap. I didn't like our chances in London so far.

'What's that you got, Johnny?' It was a hot day, warmer than the warmest day on Brighton Beach, and Mum was all better. She had on her dressing-gown, the silky summer one with big flowers on it. She was smiling and squinting in the sun's glare. 'It's a flower Mum, a big white 'n' yellow flower, smells nice 'n' all.' I went to give it to her but she shook her head. 'You keep it Love, there's plen'y 'ere.' I looked around and she was right; flowers just like it were everywhere. 'You'll be awright ya hear?' She was going somewhere I couldn't follow. I looked deep into the flower and breathed its perfume. A warm smell, a clean smell.

I woke with a start; the TV man was lifting me in his arms. 'We've got to get your Mum to hospital. I've rung for an ambulance,' he said.

Mum was cold. I tried to grab her leg as he lifted me but it was limp. As he drew me to him I smelt that same warm, clean smell.

Real things, by then, had taken on a dreamlike quality. Ambulance men came and a stretcher was wheeled in while a couple of bleary-eyed hobos and the crazy bag lady I'd spotted out on the concourse had begun to gather for what promised to be a show. The bag lady began to shout. 'It's drugs what does it to 'em, I've seen more 'n' one go that way with the drugs.'

She sidled up to us like some pantomime dame, her bottle of sherry ready to fall from her open bag, her vile breath silencing me in the man's arms.

''Ere, don't you let your littl'un look at that, 's not right at his age, all them tarts come to same end with drugs nowadays, not like in the war.'

His brow furrowed and he whispered something to me, something that kept me quiet, about getting out of there safely, about being saved and about a game.

'Just imagine we're on a bridge miles above a cold and stormy sea.'

I thought of Brighton Beach in the dead of winter and shivered.

'I am the bridge, my arms are the supports and when I put you down again you'll know we're safe, so keep quiet and I'll get you across.'

I wasn't scared. In some way the bridge seemed to make sense. I knew something very bad had happened but I didn't move. There was magical strength in those arms, a benevolence in his eyes that hypnotised me, inspired hope somehow. Perhaps he really was my father; he'd already paid me more attention than the thousand other men who might have been my dad. I half wanted to yell out to Mum, but I think I knew she was dead. The muscly arms formed a parapet, a real protection from all that strife, from all those waiting freaks, which I would have been forced to join had he not picked me up.

An ambulance attendant came over and asked the man if he knew Mum.

The bag lady interrupted, 'I was just saying to the nice gent'y'man he shouldn't let his boy see that, them tarts fillin' 'emselves wi' drugs, I 'spect you've seen it all before, but 's not for kids to be seeing.' She was coming at me, trying to touch my face. The man kept turning me so I wouldn't have to endure her inquisitive prods.

'No,' he said calmly in answer to the ambulance attendant. As he did so the bag lady sent her sherry bottle smashing to the ground. 'We were on our way to the tube when I noticed the state she was in.' The man gestured towards Mum, not to the bag lady, who was now on her knees assessing the shattered bottle.

I was distracted by the woman, who had managed to salvage a small quantity of sherry in the jagged remains of the bottle and was trying to work out which angle was safest to drink it from without cutting her lips.

The man was holding my bag, a plastic one from Sainsburys with spare clothes and a toy lorry in it. It suddenly dawned on me that 'we' meant him and me. I asked whether on the bridge I was safe from witches. He told me I was. I asked if the woman was a witch. 'I fear so, I fear so very much.' The bag lady eyed me suspiciously and I decided I'd stay on the bridge a while longer. I felt if he dropped me, I would fall into a coldness and blackness from which I could never return.

The ambulance attendant seemed relieved this was a straight pick-up. No lifesaving required; just midnight in the meat wagon, another dead junkie. 'All aboard – let's move 'er out.' They hauled my Mum onto a stretcher. I watched, silently, and wondered who this man was and what he might do to me. Would he be like the man in the black anorak who gave the other boys on the estate a whole pound one day? He'd gotten cross when they wriggled. What had made them wriggle, I wondered, and was it worth a pound? This man seemed different. I might like him, and as the moment for me to yell out came and went I thought about myself without a mother. There was no reason to think I was any better off with those ambulance attendants than I was with this nice-smelling man. Besides, I knew everyone had to wriggle somewhere along the line if they wanted to survive. Mum taught me that much.

It wasn't until after they'd loaded her onto the trolley, strapped her onto a stretcher, pulled the sheet over her and wheeled her off into the night that my sobbing began. The man carried his tearful child and his suitcase down into the tiled, eerie silence of the London underground. I felt so tired and weak a breeze could have carried me off. Crying never did much good with Mum – why should he have been fussed by it any more than her?

one

L O S T
B O Y

I don't even try wishing for things to be the way they used to be. That's the first rule of growing up. All that wishing shit I left behind. But some residues just won't go away. I still wake up in a sweat; I am jolted from my subconscious by the impact of colliding cars. I am in the car, but am I the driver? I never know.

Brigitte helps me with my dreams. She tells me it will emerge one day and when it does, it will be a breakthrough. 'Was I driving? Was I driving?' I chant to myself as I lie clutching the damp French knot of sheets that have gathered beneath me. Cars cruise past my window, the beams from their headlights casting strange shadows and rare illuminations on my peeling walls. I shudder, cringing like a child afraid of the dark, a boy who might still need Mum or Dad to protect him from the bogeyman. But the bogeyman has already come for them, delivered them to their own private darknesses, and I lie shivering silently, waiting for my turn.

My heart thunders inside me like a galloping horse on hard, dusty turf. I feel as though I am about to have a heart attack. Other times it's a kind of swoon I feel, waking out of something heavenly, something deliriously pleasurable and desperately erotic. Something perfect yet tainted by an underlying and ever-attendant menace. I sense that something very bad would come of my dream had I not woken.

'You can't have a heart attack at 20,' I tell myself. I am young, strong, and my life is nowhere near over yet. I remember what Brigitte said: 'Go back into the dreams, take them all on, fight them, fuck them, do whatever they want if it's the same as what you want, but learn in your dreams that the terms are yours. Your dreams are your freedom and you've every right to demand your freedom.'

The drugs don't help, especially acid, K, MDA and ecstasy. Even the mind-deadening tranquillisers I take to counter them have their dark side. It's not the same bedroom either, not as grand as the one in Paddington with its billowing white curtains, polished boards and huge bed in the centre of the room. How sturdy a vessel that bed proved on balmy summer nights; it sighed, it grunted while we moaned or wept. It seemed to float on the ether of the night. Our magic carpet over Sydney.

The city in all its glittering splendour pulsed outside the full-length sash windows, breathing and gasping in time with its children. Flesh dollies, only minutes away, danced on balconies just like ours, swinging their hips like trashy neon advertisements for warm, moist flesh pockets. Who will buy? Who will buy? How slick, how tempting is sex without love. And all about us, penis pushers, drug pedlars and party people searched for something cold to drink, something hot to fuck. Yet sin wasn't what I yearned for from the city's dark-wall streets or its hole-in-the-wall sleaze clubs. Sin was as vague a notion as I could ever have.

I was the answered prayer, the orphaned child, the victim. I was the bottled rage of the primly dressed woman who wants to have her say on *Oprah*. I was the one we would all love and take in to our hearts and homes if only we could get him out of the telly, out of the institution, out of the abusive family.

Strange how the drugs make me feel – as though I can conjure him up again, as if my imagination can turn air into matter, emptiness into rapture, nervousness into security. Other times they do the opposite, making the past come back.

You probably want to know what Glove Puppet means and who the fuck I am. Well no one calls me that any more, or not to my face. You probably wonder why I'm writing a biography at the age of 20. I'm not famous, I'm not a supermodel, nor am I a former child star from a popular TV series. But I was famous three years ago. That's why I have to write about what happened. Everyone read the papers, they all had opinions, but there's a lot of stuff that no one knows.

Brigitte reckons I should write everything down, including my dreams. Maybe she's right and maybe if I could get my shit together I could sell the real story about what happened to some magazine; maybe the very same ones that made our lives hell. 'Think of writing as a form of exorcism,' Brigitte says. I haven't got too much to lose and I'd love to lift 25,000 dollars out of the coffers of some of those magazines. I've heard that's how much they'd pay me for a story like mine. Maybe even more.

I don't stay in all the time. I prefer the night for going out. Sometimes with my posse, which seems to change from month to month, or sometimes just on my own. It only takes me five minutes to get to Oxford Street, and these days I command a little bit of respect even if I'm still whispered about. Of course people are as nice as pie if they want something from you – an E, some speed or a trip. I don't handle the H one though – not after what happened to my Mum – and even the others I just dabble in a little bit, you know, for friends or acquaintances. Trouble is, once people get stuff from you, they never leave you alone. You've got to be careful too; there is some serious trash in this town and nobody is particularly discreet. Most of these fucking 18-year-olds are just trying to make the scene. They'll talk about having you as their dealer as quickly as they'll say Anaesthezïa from Dizztopia is their hairdresser.

Things have been pretty scary lately. This guy – and I'm not naming names – he went to RENTBaa on one of their big party nights, and he was selling trips to a whole lot of people who were already really shit-faced. Well, he thought it would be a bit of a lark to cut up those cardboard roach mats which are profoundly toxic and sell them as trips, cheap trips, 10 bucks each. That price alone would have set alarms ringing with me but some of the punters in those clubs are total airheads; they would buy anything just to be cool and wasted. The upshot of that particular night of enterprise was that the only trip people got was to St Vincent's Hospital. There were eight casualties. These things tasted so bad that no one would have sucked them for any length of time no matter how out of it they were.

Estelle (the girl from the moon) was around here the next day with her space cadet girlfriend, *Marie Claire* (she named herself after the magazine), and they reckoned one chick died from them. She was found in the lane round the back, but there are other rumours that she was murdered. Estelle says the reason she died from it was because she stuck the roach mat up her arse like a suppository. According to *Marie Claire*, any person tasteless enough to carry a Chanel handbag down Oxford Street is asking for trouble.

I look at her multiple piercings, her pink leatherette hot pants and her torn 70s lime green halter-neck held together with nappy pins and wonder where the true definition of taste resides. 'Those suburban slags come in here of a Saturday night, all of them thinking their cunts are sweet enough to turn those gay boys straight. Next Mardi Gras they should just get a whole train of hoppers packed full of dead slags and all those straight boys can jump 'em as they trundle past.'

There was a picture in the *Telegraph* of the hopper they found this girl in but all you could see in the grainy photo was a pathetic patent leather platform shoe and the Chanel handbag. I'm no detective but you don't usually find the Chanel-handbag-brigade sticking drugs up their arses. Her

Mum's doing a story in *Who* next week. It'll be the usual '*She was just out for a night with her girlfriends, they never usually drink that much and they certainly don't take drugs.*' She'll probably turn out to be a nurse or some other icon of goodness and hope.

The way I see it, if you were dying from poisoning, why would you throw yourself in a hopper down a lane? I reckon someone done her in. I did ring the police – anonymously – to say who I thought sold those trips. He's totally out there, that guy. If he knew I'd told, he'd kill me for sure.

The problem with all these murders is no one ever finds out the truth. The papers run all these stories about people who are dumped on the Cahill Expressway or promising models who disappear from service stations. The media loves freshly damaged or dead meat. They love deciding posthumously that some two-bit waif-cum-model was going to be the next Elle Macpherson or Linda Evangelista, but it's no use getting hooked on the stories because they never get followed up. Drug-related, prostitution-related, thrill kill or just good ol' kiss the girls and make them die. You never find out.

I should concentrate on the real source of my troubles. How things turned very bad for me and nightmarish for my Dad. If it's all going to come out I have to go back to where it started – where I started.

Mum and I lived somewhere near Brighton – Brighton in England. She was a hard-working whore with five or six tattoos and blonde hair, though I'm sure it wasn't naturally blonde.

We lived in a three-room council flat, and somehow she avoided the social workers who would have taken me away if they'd known what went on. Mum was 16 when she had me. I had no father, or perhaps I had a thousand – depends how you view it. Whatever the case, I doubt she could have told you who he was any more than I can. She was on the pension, but that wasn't enough, not for the smack as well.

Mum wasn't your model parent; my earliest memories were of her lying on the bed trying to zip up her jeans with a coat-hanger then clomping around in ferociously high platform shoes. Her tits always seemed as if they were just about to fall out of her top, and on her left breast she had a tat of a heart being carried off by a bird. I loved that tattoo, perhaps in my subconscious it related to breastfeeding; as I sucked, the breast bobbed, the bird seemed to fly. Feeding and movement. It seemed strange that she'd go to such trouble to get those jeans on when they were always being taken off, but I suppose that was the fashion for tarts then and there was no mistaking Mum for anything else.

We had a vague routine of events each day – I remember the hollow clomp of those vinyl shoes along the balcony of our tenement and down our road. I guess because of the smack Mum didn't eat much herself, so in the shop she just bought things for me: cheesesticks, crisps, little plastic containers of jelly or mousse, baby food (even though I was far too old for it), chocolate, Bakewell tarts, sweets with cheap plastic toys attached. Anything bright or trippy that caught her eye. When we got home from the shops I would play with all the food and coloured toys on the kitchen floor. If Mum hadn't met someone down the street who wanted to come back and fuck her then there would probably be someone who just turned up at the door. The winter used to be busier than the summer. Strange, you'd think it'd be the other way around. I remember warm days down on the pier, going on the big candy-coloured slippery dip.

I played on the dirty lino floor by the radiator, breaking or chewing off the plastic wheels on the sherbet train, trying to get the last of the processed cheese out of the cheesestick wrapper. Each day's stuff piled up. I hated any of yesterday's things and the day before's I loathed even more. I watched the telly on the kitchen table while Mum was shagged senseless in the next room or pumped full of smack. Sometimes she would get knocked around a bit but you don't feel it so much on smack, or so they tell me. Some days, four or five of them would come through, so I couldn't tell which one had given her the bruise. Besides, she wore so much mascara and eyeliner that by the end of the day she looked like she had black eyes anyway.

To be fair to her she must have loved me in her own way. She kissed me and played with me between 'clients', but she treated me more like a dream she was having than a child. She used to love Stevie Nicks; sometimes when she got quite out of it she'd play 'Rhiannon' on this old cassette player we had. She'd dance about in her dressing-gown like Kate Bush, a scarf draped, shawl-like, around her and platform boots like the ones Stevie wore. She would pretend to be that gipsy-hearted witch. Mum probably dreamt of having witches' powers, of having any power at all. I would clap when she finally curled, foetus-like, on the floor, the tape warbling to an end.

The sound of shagging was the muzak of my childhood. I made a close study of those sounds, time and movement, good and bad. Bad was when they wanted things Mum wouldn't give them, when she yelled at them, told them to 'sod off'. Good was when she stayed 'in character' for the whole performance, when their demands were simple, when she was compliant. I would think about the different amount of time it took each of them to go to the toilet in Mum. Often I ate a crisp for each grunt made by the man. Once I was doing just this when the man grunting, farted. Did I eat a crisp for this sound also? And if I did would I fall out of step with the grunts which were continuing, quite oblivious to the fart?

Sometimes Mum left the door ajar. I could peek in if I wanted but I didn't always like looking – it was often the hairy arse of some bloke pointing at me, pounding madly into her. I didn't like the hairy ones, nor the fat ones, but some were slim and smooth. There was something I yearned for from those; perhaps it was envy that flickered like a snake's tongue in my heart as Mum danced to a wild beat I could only imagine, a rhythm both exciting and repellent.

There were occasions when the movements varied. Some liked to get slightly different thrusting angles, perhaps to favour one part of their cock or maybe they wanted to try positions with Mum that they weren't allowed with their girlfriends or their wives or the retarded lady in the next Close who did it for free while her own mother was at Bingo. On her good days Mum moaned a bit as if she liked it. Maybe she did. Other times she'd just be quiet, preferring to let them make all the noise. I peered in, crisps or cheesestick in hand and took it all in, the endless parade of arses, the smell of semen and body odour – you'd think it would put you off sex, wouldn't you?

I went to school, in the end. I was 6 when I started; I should have gone the previous year but it must have slipped past Mum until a social worker came and chided her for not sending me. Once I was at school she tried to do most of her work during the day but there were always some who preferred the evening.

I would get fish and chips for supper, or sometimes Mum cooked me egg and bacon with toast. I don't think she knew what a vegetable was. On her days of relative clarity we had oranges and apples from the greengrocer, but Mum preferred never to go anywhere but the corner shop. I walked to school each day and probably got the best food I'd ever had as school dinners.

Around the tenements after school I mucked about with urchins like myself; grubby, dough-faced boys raised on potatoes and lard or sharp-faced, street-smart kids used to dodging their father's drunken backhands. The sea, at least, was not far away. There was a playground down there where a man in a black anorak sometimes went. He would give us 20 pence, or more, if we showed him our doodles. We would go to that park, hoping he'd be there so we could buy some sweets or a big greasy mess of chips with the doodle money. We'd huddle around the broken swings, squabbling like seagulls over our steaming hot reward. Smelling and eating chips was always a treat. Sitting huddled on the ground, clenching my bottom, which was often a little hot and sore from Anorak Man's meddling inquisitiveness. Each boy hungry and quiet, keeping his fingers warm in the oily news-paper as our burning breath sent silent, vaporous SOS rings up into a freezing, colourless sky.

After the chips we wandered around, breaking the things we were strong enough to break, trying to break the things we weren't. We terrorised old ladies at the bus stop who, at first, would try to be sweet to us but who quickly realised we were not the type of children worth being sweet to. The other kids usually got called in for their supper, but Mum wasn't a 'come on Love, your supper's on the table' sort of Mum, nor was she a 'What time do you call this?' sort of Mum when I came in at 8 or 9 of an evening.

In the winter it seemed to be dark all the time. Kids stayed in more and I didn't get invited around to other kids' flats. 'Our Ma says you can't come to our house, she says you're common and you i'nt got a proper Dad or nuffink and your Mum's bad.' Well the other families were hardly what you'd call blue bloods, scarcely qualifying as working class most of them because social security isn't work afterall. Once the girls heard the taunts about Mum and me at school, their skipping ropes quickly whipped rumours into a song. A song Mum refused to ever hear. A song I still remember.

> Knock knock who's at the door
> dirty Johnny Smith whose Mum's a whore
> Knock knock what's that sound
> she's even dirtier for five pound
> Knock knock make that ten
> she'll drop her knickers down and do it all again

I knew that all those groans from the other room were the source of that badness. I never had anyone to our flat, either. Even then I was ashamed of the mess in our place, and the smell. Heroin leaves a sweet smell on the skin of the user.

A couple of times blokes moved in for a while but moved out just as quickly. They were all junkies and each one real-ised, pretty fast, that Mum's 'relative prosperity' came from between her legs; that unless they went out to work she would have to keep doing what she was doing to keep the smack coming in and to keep me in fish and chips.

They argued about smack; about whose turn it was to go to the shop, whose turn to score, who was going to 'cook up'. They lived on Coca-Cola and cups of tea, occasionally having some chocolate or chips while I ate baby food out of crusty plastic bowls with one of many blackened spoons.

When we got new neighbours next door – Mum called the woman a nosy bloody Parker – that must have been the beginning of the end. One night the bloke who came around was pretty drunk. The door was ajar and I looked in because of the commotion. This bloke was laying into Mum good and proper. She had been giving him oral, which cost 10 pounds extra (I had heard these things negotiated). His dick was limp; I suspect he was too pissed to get it up, either that or he was impotent anyway. He was yelling, 'You really are a filfy old slapper injcha, you's just a filfy whore what's more full o'drugs van full o' cock.' He hit her a couple of times across the face and I ran in screaming. She turned on him, shrieking like a banshee, 'You can't even get'cha useless fuckin' prick up ya' pratt, fuck off outa here why don'cha.' And amidst my screams and hers he did.

The nosy Parker from next door came and got in on the act: 'Don't think I don't know what sort o' discustin' business goes on in here you filthy tart, it's nowt more than a knock-up shop and I'm reporting you to the DSS. You're not fit to bring up a little'un in that pigsty and I can't be doing with all this noise not with the baby asleep ——'

Mum went at her with a broom (it was the only time I ever saw her pick it up). It was a terrible fight, and someone must have phoned the police. I guess Mum tried to think fast. She threw stuff into a bag, told me to put clothes on over my pyjamas and said we had to go. We went to the station and got on a late train to London. Perhaps things would be different there. Perhaps the streets were paved with gold, or at least paved with smack.

Mum started to sweat and shiver on the train. She needed her medicine. A vile-looking bloke sitting near us started watching her and finally came over.

'You awright Love?' He was looking at the developing bruise under her left eye.

'Yeah, me old man and I just had a bit of a fallin' out s'all.'

'Sure you did Love, and what sort a' bloke'd knock a lovely piece o' skirt like you around?' Mum sort of smiled, but even I could see that 'lovely piece of skirt' was not an apt description. I also knew that the smile was not the modest smile of a grateful lady. Mum was desperate and anything could happen on this trip to London. No Buckingham Palace or changing of the guard would this Johnny see.

''Ere, Love, I reckon I got a bit o' someat you might fancy.' He fished around in a dirty old vinyl airline bag and pulled out a white plastic sachet.

Her eyes lit up a little. 'What you want for that, then?'

'Nuffink too demandin.' Just a little bit of 'vem comforts what your old man won't be gettin' tonight.'

He looked at me and smiled. 'Don't you worry young lad, I'm a doctor and I wanna get your lovely Mum all nice and well again.'

I had seen some nasty-looking doctors down at the clinic where Mum went intermittently, but never had they looked as wretched as this one. Greasy hair, yellow teeth. He was Fagin on drugs.

Mum needed her medicine, however, and whether it was smack, icing sugar, rat poison or dishwasher powder she was going into the toilet on that train to earn it. I waited outside. We were only 15 minutes from London but I had seen her earn money in much less than 15 minutes.

He came out first, tucking in his shirt. He looked sheepishly at me then slunk off down the other end of the train. Mum came out holding her arm. She was in pain, and there was blood on her jumper. She was still shaking a little and something seemed wrong, by wrong I mean more than usually wrong – wrong, for me, was right.

CURE

I was abducted. Adopted. The man at the station was the most handsome man I'd ever seen. If he had said he was a doctor I might have believed him. He wore a long, dark coat. I suspected him of being magical in some way. He carried me down to the tube station at Victoria and sat with me. He talked quietly about how we were safe from the witch, how my Mum was safe from everything and how there was still a way to go before we were completely safe. He waited patiently until my sobbing had ceased. Then he began talking in that same voice that had so mesmerised me before.

'Do you have a Dad anywhere?'

I shook my head. He sounded like one of the posh people on the telly.

'Do you know your Dad's name?'

'I just told ya I 'int got a Dad.'

'Perhaps you'd like to have one,' he said.

I started to cry again. Mum was, after all, the only person in the world I could call family. Hers was the only care I'd experienced and however dubious that care had been it was the only thing I'd ever taken for granted.

'I better have someone or I'll get meself lost. If you is takin' me some'ere you better not do nuffink bad to me,' I said, mustering all the council estate bravado I could. He bit his bottom lip and his eyes took on a tearful shine. He put his hand on my head and pulled me towards him. I wrapped my arms around him and held on. I did the destitute child perfectly. The poignancy was not lost on my new benefactor. I think that was when I realised I would go with him. What else would I have done? I'd missed my chance at turning myself in to the vagaries of State benevolence. If I didn't go with him what would I do? Who or what would I get instead?

'I know how I could make you safe. I have a bit of a plan.' He took two booklets from his coat pocket. 'Passports,' he said, and looked at a picture in one of them. He looked at me, then at the passport again. He seemed to smile for a second, then he looked panicked for a bit, running his hand through his heavy dark fringe. He glanced about nervously; there was no one around. A cold gust of wind blasted out of the tunnel, reminding me of the coming winter. A wasted-looking punk was arguing with his heavily made-up girl-friend. They had a cassette player and were listening to The Cure; it echoed bleakly down the platform on that same chill November wind. Once the man was sure they weren't inter-ested in us, he began talking to me in a hushed, forthright and serious tone:

'If you want to have a Dad, someone to get you away from here safely, I could pretend it was me, but you'd have to do what I say. If I give you to the police they will take you to some home full of other children. Do you want to go there?'

I thought about a home full of other children, children even poorer than me and the girl at school who lived with another family and had to pretend it was hers because her own parents were dead or didn't want her or something. At least my Mum put up a fight when the welfare lady came around to our place every few months. 'Stupid fat cow,' Mum'd say after she'd been. 'Al'ays picken on us what 'aven't got blokes. *"What do ya' give 'im for 'is tea, are you seein' a fella at the moment?"* All bloody hoity-toity them welfare cows, they'd lock you up at Borstal Johnny if I let 'em 'ave their bloody way. Just cos I don't work at Little Chef like 'er downstairs. Well I do better 'n 'er. My boy's fed I'll 'ave ya know. 'E's better fed than some whats fathers spend every bloody penny they get on lager.' She declared these things as addendums to no one in particular and always after the lady had gone. She never got cross while the woman was visiting. I wondered what this man might have to offer; it was at least worth finding out.

'If you come with me, I could help you to make a happier new life and I will look after you very well. If you come with me now we will get on an aeroplane and live in Australia. It's a long journey and we'll have to play another game to get there, but we will get away from all this cold. I could take you to the welfare people but if you do want to come with me I have an aeroplane ticket for you, a special ticket for a boy your age. We can't help your Mummy anymore. It's very sad I know but you have to leave her behind. Wherever you go, God is looking after her now.'

I knew nothing of God; I had no concept of what sort of thing he/she/it was. But the aeroplane had already done it; to go on an aeroplane I would have done anything.

'Awright, jus' remember what I said before, you promise you won't do nuffink bad to me.'

He took my hand. 'I would never hurt you. I had a little boy your age who died just a couple of weeks ago. You look rather like him, you look the same age and if you really think there is no one else who would look after you or miss you, then we could pretend you were him, but you'll have to do as I say or we'll never get past all of the police.'

I had inherited my mother's distrust of the 'filth'. I already had a sense that authority in general was out to get Mum and me in one way or another. Suddenly the idea of such deception seemed like a very exciting idea, like one of those TV shows where the kids get away with all sorts of pranks. And I had my heart set on that aeroplane ride. I knew my choices were desperately limited. Somewhere beneath all the fear, exhaustion and grief, excitement stirred. I imagined telling all the boys on the estate about going on a plane. Not one of them had been on a plane. For me it was adventure on a grand scale. Poor Mum, her memory being traded in for a plane ticket as quickly as she might have traded me for a much needed hit.

He said I was to call him Dad and that he would call me Vas from then on.

'Vas?' I asked. 'What sor' o' name is 'at?'

He showed me 'my' British passport. 'It's short for Vaslav.' There was a photograph of a woman and a child in it – a mother and son passport. 'Posh git,' I said. I could not remember ever having possessed a bowtie like the boy in the photo, but I did look like him a bit. We both had longish hair. The passport was two years old, and kids grow and change quickly. I looked at 'Dad'. I said, 'Is he dead?' The man nodded sadly. I wanted to know how he had died. I only ever knew of one kid who died. He was a thin, pale kid who went home sick from school and never came back. Miss had come in one day and said that Mickey Macmasters had died from leukemia. I never even knew what the word meant. I asked if this 'Vas' boy had died of leukemia, and the man said no.

I didn't ask any more questions, I didn't want to jeopardise that plane ride. And even if I had to run away from this man when we got to Australia I couldn't see how it could be worse than where I was. If the boy who I was had nothing, why not turn into another boy, even if it meant having a stupid name.

Somewhere warm on a plane. Australia. That was the promise. We caught the train to Heathrow. It all happened so fast. 'Dad' at a counter saying he hadn't had a chance to reconfirm or something, but, yes his son was now travelling with him. I had my bag of clothes and my truck. I suppose it looked better for me to have something; I must have looked like a bit of an urchin. He organised everything. He was saying things to people about how sad it was that my mother had passed away. I didn't realise they were talking about someone else, not my real mother, no one would mourn her. I thought I was going through some procedure that must just happen if your mother dies; someone else could simply take you on. Then I remembered we were tricking these people, that even though they didn't look like police, that was effectively what they all were. People to be tricked.

'Dad' scarcely looked old enough to have a 7-year-old son, but he was confident: he had the passports, the tickets and they never looked closely at me in my tracksuit with pyjamas poking out from underneath. I suppose that is what kids travel in, not bowties like in 'my' picture. My accent wasn't like his, but I never spoke to anyone. Perhaps his clipped and refined voice intimidated the officials, or perhaps the papers just seemed so in order that there was no drama. The last thing officials want late at night is a complex problem like a kidnapped child who no one wants anyway. It's the little things they like to flex their muscles over: dates, incorrect forms, uncertain, non-English-speaking foreigners who are easily unnerved and frightened, shy sari-clad Indian women whose packages may look suspicious. There were softer targets around that night for those passport controllers; they weren't interested in a boy and his Dad.

'You must be tired, Vas,' he smiled. 'Why don't you go to sleep while we wait to get on the plane.'

I did this without hesitation, and when I woke he was carrying me down the walkway. His arms were incredibly strong and I felt I didn't ever want to do anything for myself again. Once on board, he curled me up on some cushions and stroked my forehead. 'We're taking off now,' he whispered. I tried to stay awake, but once we were in the air I drifted off to sleep again. The hum of the aircraft, the constant shshshshsh, the smell of the food and my sleepy head in his lap conspired to make me feel like some modern-day *Oliver Twist*, an escapee from the workhouse who could be saved by love. He could be my Dad, he could be my anything.

On that long flight he talked to me lots, told me some of 'the secrets' that I was soon to know off by heart. He reminded me that he was my Dad, that my name was Vas. We dealt with all the 'police' at the Australian end. I looked so tired and crumpled from the trip, my long hair almost obscuring my face, that no one really observed me anyway. By miracle or providence I got to Sydney. Then I went to 'Dad's' house in Paddington and the real story began.

Vaslav Usher. Not bad for council estate white trash. Poor Johnny's surname was Smith – John Smith can you believe. Mum either had no imagination or a very black sense of humour. I suppose I was named for all my real fathers after all. I became Vaslav, named for Nijinsky. Alas, I have failed in the ballet department; I did try but it really wasn't in the blood. I'm okay on the podium of a nightclub but that's about the extent of it.

And my new father? 'Dad' was never really a suitable title. I preferred Shamash. Shamash is an ancient Babylonian God; son of sin, God of Sun, protector of the poor, the wronged and the traveller. It was a title given to him after his portrayal of that very god on a Mardi Gras float, the first float I ever helped on. He was a veteran of many Mardi Gras. That's who I pray to, that's what he was to me.

CHANGELING

Sydney in late spring appeared to me how Disneyland might appear to any child who'd known nothing but poverty – a fabulous impossibility. On one hand I had embarked on a dangerous adventure, losing what precious little I had. On the other, my life turned into a glorious antipodean fairytale. The problem with happy endings in the real world is you can't shut the book on them or put them in a box when things turn nasty.

It was the flowers on the frangipani trees that really sealed my fate. They were the same white and yellow flowers I had seen in my dream, my dream of saying goodbye to Mum.

Sunshine on Vaslav, fresh food and a bedroom specially for me with an *Empire Strikes Back* quilt cover. 'How come? How come?' I'd whisper to myself in the privacy of my room. I'd giggle at how crazy it was, then feel sad that I couldn't show off to anybody. I couldn't show off to my grubby English mates, and kids in Paddington went on planes all the time. I didn't know anyone, so I decided to watch and listen for as long as it took. I hid food and small amounts of money, just in case my dream turned into a nightmare, just in case my handsome prince proved to be an evil sorcerer and the sweet-smelling flowers grew bitter.

There was a nasty loneliness at first, trapped as I was by the knowledge of things beyond me and secrets I was too young to be burdened with. Fables were more real to me than to most kids, who enjoyed their story time in the warm, loving safety of their cashed-up Paddington palaces.

Paddington was like a storybook kingdom: hills and dales, a topsy-turvy of pretty terraces, some huge, some tiny. Houses of every variety on winding one-way streets, secret lanes offering sudden, blinding glimpses of the sunlit harbour and the brightly coloured boats it coddled. Flowers and trees spilling and pushing into any vacant space – a tropical profusion unlike anything I'd seen. Neighbours seemed to be nice to each other and everyone had cars. People knocked gently on the door and asked if a car could be moved or music turned down. Nothing like, 'I've had enough of ya racket ya noisy bloody cow.'

I see it differently now, its wealth and its beauty. Those houses are fortresses these days; bourgeois bunkers, their facades brindled with iron bars, their interiors trip-wired with elaborate alarms. Now I see them as nervous safety zones where neat, athletic women in costly clothes and new BMWs ferry their precious only children to expensive schools, fathers seldom seen. Families who nervously hope the chaos from the next suburb won't venture beyond the Cutler Footway. Perceptions change as we grow, but I loved that momentary perception when I first arrived.

I woke in the mornings with hot sun streaming in on me. I began to eat the strange things prepared for me in the wood-lined kitchen, and abundance mated with greed to put extra pounds on my wiry carcass. With eager curiosity I picked at fruits, green and orange things I'd never seen like kiwi fruit, mangoes, avocado and strong-tasting cheeses not at all like my processed, heat-sealed favourite, which had to be added to the shopping list. Shamash said the kitchen was like a disco because I opened and closed the fridge so often. He had to explain to me that it wasn't proper to eat a little of something and put it back in the fridge. I didn't understand this for quite some time. I was accustomed to doing just that. He said I must cut off a piece, put it on a plate or go in the yard to eat it if I didn't want to use a plate. I could have all I wanted but I was no longer allowed to sit on the floor and eat like a dog. He felt relieved, however. My hunger I'm sure indicated my acquiescence to his proposal of parenthood, and my nervous little body began enjoying the eager offerings of plenty that were being proffered by everyone I came into contact with.

Staging my 'recovery' meant Shamash had to learn to lie thoroughly and convincingly, time and time again. He must have felt like a politician. We defied bureaucracy. Bureaucracy doesn't always work; it may prove a safety net for some and a snare for others. It's a sleepy old web, spun by incumbents who grow used to the 'rule' and who would just as soon process the rare exception as waddle out to the filing room for a different form. You may slip through the net once but when it picks you up further down, there'll be hell to pay from the net above.

Shamash, however, was a brilliant raconteur, able to charm anyone. He told me the story of his real son, and together we wove our own story from it.

Shamash was a dancer. When he was 16 he had won a scholarship to the Royal Academy of Classical Ballet in London. During his time at the Academy, he had an affair with another student, Angelique. She too had great ambitions to dance on the stage at Covent Garden – until she became pregnant. She and Shamash were barely 18 when they became parents, both living in London away from their own parents, and for a time they fooled themselves that they were grown up enough to look after a child.

Angelique, alone with a new baby for much of the day, became obsessed with her weight and would not eat. Her widowed mother refused to help unless Angelique came home to York with the baby, without Shamash. He was dancing, getting better parts with each production, and she resented his success.

There was something else unsettling Shamash – the gradual realisation that he was gay. Poor Angelique was heartbroken. She went back to her mother in York while Shamash stayed a while in London, depressed but dancing still. Ballet was his rise-above-it-all.

After being refused any contact with his son, Shamash

returned to Australia at the beginning of 1977. He was the same age then as I am now.

He joined the Australian Ballet for a few seasons then married his fortunes with David Bergdorf, now one of Sydney's most successful promoters. Together they formed the Bushka Contemporary Dance Company. Following that, Shamash's parents helped him to start 'Potts En Pointe'. It did very well and has continued to do so 'long after our erstwhile corrupt government withdrew their funding for more sinister enterprises' as David would say. He and Shamash were lovers for a while after Shamash came back from London, and they remained best friends through everything that happened.

Life for Angelique became terribly unhappy. She struggled to overcome her anorexia and spent a lot of time in therapy. Then her mother got cancer. Angelique's father had died when she was a child, and though the family had money her mother didn't leave everything to her only daughter. Instead she left a trust fund for Vaslav's education and a small annuity for Angelique. She had been spending her mother's money like there was no tomorrow, which there turned out not to be. She and Vaslav went to Spain and Portugal whenever they could, and because she said she was too ill to stay in England during winter, they spent it in Florida. She finally wrote to Shamash telling him she couldn't cope with Vaslav on her own, that she was suicidal. She wanted him to come and get their child.

Shamash dropped everything, told her he was coming, and booked a return flight. No one knew what she was planning – she had few close friends by then – but as

Shamash was flying over, Angelique and Vaslav drove into Lake Windermere.

The verdict was accidental death, even though relatives in England whispered that it had been intentional. Shamash never wanted to believe that. He was devastated, and he hoped that it had been an accident, though late October was not the time of year to go to Lake Windermere for a picnic, neither was it en route from York to Manchester airport, which had supposedly been Angelique's destination. Angelique's aunt was left to make all the funeral arrangements. Even she didn't know the story.

Over the years, when I asked and was old enough, Shamash would tell me these terrible tales. Fairytales, parables of fogs and autumn leaves, dimly lit country roads with perilously concealed bends. The lady of the lake, an ice maiden always waiting for a clumsy gear change and the sedative-impaired breaking from a ballet-crippled foot that had never graced the stage. In the Autumn stillness the lake had turned screams into gargles; it waited patiently while a small boy struggled vigorously, his roof-thumping and clawing easing into twitching, his soul departing leaving nothing but the fixed gaze of terror, he, alone with his dead mother in a flotsam of cigarette butts from the brimming ashtray.

I dream about that car accident from time to time. I see those white faces trapped behind the cracked glass of the car windows. I swim down beneath that murky, icy water and when I finally glimpse the boy's face, it's mine. He's smiling. I gasp, forgetting I'm in water and then I, too, start to drown, awakening with a horrible start. It's an obvious enough dream for me to have but I hate it. Like many of my horrible dreams, I never know when it's going to strike. I can never save them because I was born from those deaths and their deaths were of pivotal import to my/our story. Brigitte calls it 'residual psychic etching'. I said I don't care what the fuck you call it, I don't like it. She says 'etchings' are the first and easiest dreams to change because they are linked to the past not to the future. She says she'll have me saving them in no time. I can't wait to see how she's going to get me to do that.

Shamash was only in England for a week. Angelique's aunt met him at the airport, where he had been waiting for three hours, and she told him the news. He travelled to York with her and stayed for the funeral, where he received a fair degree of cold-shouldering from the few family members in attendance. The aunt gave him some photos of Vaslav as a baby, set aside with his birth certificate and passport. They were the only things Shamash took.

No family ties there. No mail or photos of Vaslav from Angelique, not many questions from Shamash's parents over those first few years, either. Perhaps they were relieved he escaped England unhitched and without a bastard child to mar their family tree. They never referred to Angelique or the child in all those missing years. It wasn't until Shamash told them that he was gay that they wished they'd taken a little more interest in his former het incarnation. As for me, I was probably beyond the pale. To Shamash's parents I was living proof of Angelique's unsuitability. They didn't know me long enough to ever think otherwise.

Shamash used to say, 'When I saw you with your mother at Victoria Station you must understand how I felt. It was as if God had given me another child; it was too ridiculous a coincidence to be anything else. I have never seen anything like that since, someone just dying like she did. It was a genuine nightmare that whole trip. I was too afraid to phone Mother and Father and tell them about what happened to Angelique and Vaslav. I kept putting it off and putting it off until you were there, offering me the chance to rewrite the rules, change history a fraction, make it just a little more kind, not just to me but to Johnny/Vaslav too. I must have been mad to try it, but we pulled it off didn't we?' We both marvelled at what we'd done; it seemed a miracle.

Probably the most remarkable thing about my being 'reinvented' was dealing with my utter ignorance. I was illiterate, I'd never seen a shower except on telly, had no idea about how to use cutlery, spoke with an almost unintelligible accent. Shamash seemed to understand me okay. He'd lived there, though I doubt he'd got about with anyone quite like Mum and me.

I was a sullen child for quite some time and barely spoke. What utterances people heard from my constantly hung head must have made them wonder what Angelique had been like and if I had such a thick accent it technically ought to have been northern, which it wasn't. When it became apparent that I was illiterate and a year behind at school Shamash would brush it off to his mother with comments like 'Oh Angelique had strange ideas, sent him to the local school which was probably a bad choice, she wasn't with it for the last couple of years, she kept him out of school because she felt too insecure without him' – that sort of thing.

There was always a perplexed aspect to Grandma's dealings with me. I think she favoured the notion that Shamash had been hoodwinked into believing I was his son. The day she had it out with him, in the living room of the Paddington house, I listened, fascinated, behind the door.

'What would you have me do Mum, drown him in his bath and pretend he went down with Angelique? What bloody difference does it make whether he is my son or not? I believed he was mine when she had him, I was there when he was born, I'm on the birth certificate. I rescued him from that crazy family. I don't see your point!'

'All I'm saying Darling is maybe he has special needs, maybe ——'

'Maybe what, Mum? Maybe he won't turn out "right", maybe he won't be "our kind" of Usher? Just leave me to love and bring him up. If you want to help, fantastic, but if you're ashamed of him, like you seem to be of me and my lifestyle half the time, then leave us to it. It's that bloody simple.'

'Nothing is ever *that bloody simple*, Martin. What do you know about bringing up a child?'

'What does anyone ever know before they have them?'

'Most people mix with other married couples who have young families and can discuss the experience – share some of the burdens. I wonder how many of those sort of friends you and that David Bergdorf have?'

'Let's have a go at David, too, will we?'

'All I'm saying is you have a child who's nearly 8, and mark my words most of the behavioural patterns are set by that age, and you're going off half-cocked to bring him up all on your own.'

'Mum, I can only see how I go. I'll get some help if I need it. I've got Thelma. Maybe now I've got a son who'll be at school, I'll meet some of those precious heterosexual couples. Vas's got no real choice; neither do I. I'll join the Gay and Lesbian parenting network.'

'Oh I can just imagine how much use they'll be. You'll be on the phone to your sister and me looking for help long before you get any from that lot. Those women all live on communes and use their own children as social guinea pigs. They won't let the girls wear pink or have dolls, I've read about all these "experiments" – single mothers with no idea what they're getting into, having babies they can't afford on taxpayers' money, bringing up children who will be tormented at school and maladjusted in later life all because the parents were selfish abusers of a system that gives too much leeway ——'

'For Christ's sake, shut up! We're talking about my son, Vaslav. What possible help can this do him? You're like a bloody broken record Mum. If I've heard your views once I've heard them a thousand times. They just bore me, but most of all THEY DON'T HELP ANYONE! What use is anything that doesn't help people? You've tried to teach me that kindness and caution are synonymous, that you can only ever be generous to people who have exactly the same amount of everything as yourself. I don't understand this tough enclave mentality – this wealth you somehow deserve but no one else should be able to access.'

'Your father and I have worked for years to ensure you

41

and Rosie had everything. You wouldn't have this house in Paddington if your father hadn't organised ——'

'Let's just forget it. The least I can do is try and give Vaslav as many opportunities as I can.'

Grandma made an effort after that, and conceded I was a 'dear little chap'. She seemed to get used to my being around on Shamash's rare visits to the North Shore.

Grandpa, when he wasn't reading the financial papers, would look up and say, 'How's the young fella?' as I wandered past on the way to the pool in the back garden. I desperately wanted to learn to swim, and to everyone's surprise I had no fear of water. I wanted to go in that pool whenever we went to Grandma's. Even when it was cold I'd beg to go in. Grandma would say, 'It's freezing', meaning it was 18 degrees or something. Shamash would say, 'He's from England Mum, this'd be a hot day in England, hey Vas.' I'd giggle, not because it was true but because my life had done this somersault, and there I was with people fussing over my needs, my opinions and my care. And although I had a huge amount of changing to do, there was no doubt in my mind, even after a couple of weeks, that I had landed on my feet, that Shamash was everything he'd seemed, that I was to be looked after and life would be better.

I suppose no matter what Shamash's parents thought of me, their sympathies were with me as I had lost my mother – in both versions of the story. My tale, Angelique's tale and Vaslav's tale were told and told; they were our secrets and there is intimacy in that sort of secret. I always knew the truth but Shamash wove it into both myth and secret, and somehow I became the guardian of both. It is possible to learn a lie, to actually believe it, to rewrite history. Somehow I have a memory of that car going into Lake Windermere, of the jaws-of-life descending to save me but alas not my 'mother'. Shamash and I went there on our last trip back to England. He took me so he could finally lay Angelique and the real Vaslav to rest. From then I was able to mentally picture my second birth as it were. We never went back to Brighton though, to the estate. Shamash offered to take me but I had no interest. Lake Windermere is a prettier place, both to die and to be born; it has worked its way into my 'dreaming'.

Shamash talked to me for hours, trying to work out my interests. He'd take me to book shops and let me have whatever books I wanted. If I showed any interest in trucks, then he'd buy me lots of trucks. If I wanted fish and chips we'd go up to Oxford Street, sit in the park and have them. We'd look in shops which had better things in them than I'd ever seen and because I was with Shamash the shop ladies were nice to me as well: 'How's he liking Australia?' 'Would you like some cake, Vaslav?' None of your 'Get out o' here ya thieving rascal.' I didn't even need to thieve; I could have whatever I liked. It was a true precinct for the privileged, Paddington was, an eye-opener to this little guttersnipe.

Shamash organised private tutors to come to the house. To his great surprise (and mine) I wasn't an imbecile or even especially slow, and let's face it I was hardly what you'd call a winning ticket in the gene pool lottery. Who knows, maybe Mum shagged one of the great minds of England when she was 16 or just, momentarily, snagged herself a cabinet member nosing around the council estate. Perhaps some brainy social commentator was checking the garbage disposal facilities around the back and she happened to be lurking near the piles of old *Sunday Sports* and *Daily Mirrors*. Bingo, an IQ over a hundred, a few brain cells that didn't get clogged up with the fat from the chips. My Mum never got to be a page three girl but perhaps she conceived me on top of one.

It hardly matters now what my seminal source was. I exist, and my slow but absolute foray into Sydney society was under way. Shamash was very popular socially; he had influence, he knew all the 'right' people: curators, actors, artisans. It was names, Darling, names, at our place. None of them meant anything to me back then of course but our house was always full of music, dance and beautiful women with red lipstick and husky voices; alive with the jangle of heavy jewellery, the billowing of extravagant white curtains and clinking of ice in glasses. Expensive, exotic perfumes and *après rasages* mixed with the jasmine and frangipani that blew in from the garden. A spell was cast on all who entered. The golden dancing boys, waxed and polished, with faces to torture the gods, bodies to punish the saints. Theatre directors and their entourages of thespian hangers-on, the voices of the exquisite and the effete echoing through the halls of the Shadforth Street house. I hid from all the grand, urbane confidence that visitors delighted in displaying. It was scary, at first.

People came and went; there was always champagne, always delicious things to eat and always pampering for me. '*Poucet*' became my nickname. 'His father's son,' people would say in big, mock-macho voices. 'A chip off the old block, wouldn't you say, Shamash?' Shamash would laugh discreetly. But I'm jumping ahead.

Thelma, the housekeeper, came in two or three days a week. She always complained cheerfully about the mess she had to clean up, but she was matronly and kind, and wended her way around the banter that used to chortle through the place. 'Thelly,' David Bergdorf would say, 'you've been drinking all the gin again. Shamash, you'll have to fire Thel, she's suckin' down all your gin, mate.'

Thel would stand in the hall with her hands on her hips, smiling dryly. 'We all know who drinks all the gin around here, Mr Bergdorf. My God, when I think about the sort of tax write-offs humble charwomen like me are subsidising with your gin. Martin writes it all off on entertainment, and your gin consumption would form the better part of the national deficit I should say.'

Shamash would dash past, half-dressed, and give her a peck on the cheek. 'We all know Thelly only likes a sherry, don't we Thel? And never more than two a night, isn't that right? And once in a while when there's a *cause célèbre* we can tempt her with a glass of bubbly. I would trust Thelma with my last drop of gin, not so, you, my dear friend.'

Thelma quickly took on the mantle of 'nanny'. It wasn't originally part of her job but Shamash was glad of her help. 'You know my kids are just about big enough to look after themselves and now I get a new boy to start on. We'll have to be friends, Vaslav, because Martin's out at all hours and you'll be stuck with me.'

It was typical of Thel to see a need, roll up her sleeves and get involved. She loved kids, and I'm glad she took to me and that she loved me as she did. If Thel didn't like you she made no secret of it. She had two kids herself: Jeff was already grown up, but Dianne used to play with me when she occasionally came to work with her Mum. She was four years older than me, so she could boss me around a bit. She'd ask me about England and I had to be careful what I said. She also made it clear to me that my Dad was different from other Dads. 'I bet you don't know what a homosexual is,' she'd say teasingly. If she'd said poofter, I might have guessed, but then I accepted everything. Poofter was not a term to be scared of yet.

After my first year of adjusting, I enjoyed my Sydney childhood. From the Paddington house I would go over the Bridge to play for hours in my grandparents' pool, having painstakingly learnt to swim. I had one aunt and uncle who had no children. They were not close to Shamash at that stage, he being a little too arty, I think, for his stockbroker brother-in-law. Rosie was two years older than Shamash, and somehow I don't think she thought it was right, him having a son. She wanted kids but was never able to have them. She was nice to me and looked after me sometimes, but I preferred to go to Thelly's in Homebush or David's in Elizabeth Bay. David always spoilt me, and he had a dog. Homebush reminded me more of where I came from, and I could smell the biscuit factory from Thel's house.

I was okay at school, although the other kids in my class were a year younger than me. There was a tiny stigma attached to this because it may have meant I was dumb. The teacher in my first year had judiciously explained to my class that this was because English school terms were different:

'Vaslav, would you like to tell the other boys and girls about your school in England?' 'Vey're just like 'em ones you got 'ere Miss.' The entire class would erupt with laughter. I spoke as little as possible until I'd got rid of my accent, helped by coaching from Shamash. Sometimes I'd get angry at people trying to change me but then I didn't like the teasing at school.

Shamash was affectionate, though cautiously at first. He would give me a kiss and a cuddle, he'd tousle my hair and sometimes pick me up by my feet and hang me upside down, saying, 'Vaslav the rascal wants hanging out to dry.' We discovered wizzies, and there was just enough room in the back garden for him to do them without scattering the pots of geraniums.

He bought me ballet shoes so I could go into the front room, which was fully equipped with a mirror and barre, and try to copy his steps. I watched him each day like most boys watch their dads shave. Shamash could do extraordinary things with his legs. He'd show off. 'C'mon Vas let's work on your *demi-plié*. Get those legs up to the barre.' It was too high of course; apart from stints on nightclub podiums years later, none of that early training amounted to much. I'm sure the only reason I've been invited to dance in Mardi Gras shows is because I am the son of 'the great one'; everyone says it's not what you know but who you know. I liked watching him; he was a sight to behold. My favourite thing was when he picked me up and twisted me around his head, just as he did with the girls on stage.

When the movie *Flashdance* came out, he used to sneer at it but he could do the dance to 'Maniac'. I'd beg him to do it; I'd bring in water so he could flick it off his head like Jennifer Beals did in the movie. He used to tickle me and say, 'You're just a little steel town girl on a Saturday night aren't you?' I'd squeal and say, 'I'm not a girl, I'm not.'

'A steel town Vas tickled half to death, that's what you'll be when I've finished with you.' He'd tickle and tickle, singing 'What a Feeling' until I was flushed and exhausted on the couch, feeling a little bit like heaven, feeling I was adored. Shamash would leap off down the hall on those legs of his, swollen musculature bulging out of the leotard every which way, singing the theme to *Fame*.

At night Shamash would read stories to me. Sometimes he'd take me to the ballet, often carrying me up to bed from the car, me, already asleep. I loved the luxury of the Opera House and the State Theatre. I decided I wanted to do something in the theatre, and Shamash bought me puppets and a toy theatre. I thought I was too shy to have ever acted or performed, and I imagined painting sets, doing lights or pulling the cords that opened the curtain. I was so disappointed when I discovered they were mechanised. The one in my puppet theatre would lift with one string or draw open with the other.

It was from my private puppet shows that Shamash came to know some of my earlier childhood. I could show him things I would never have told him as my knobbly-headed wooden Punch gave himself injections and drank beer in order to beat and hump Judy. Those were the secret shows that only Shamash saw. They were bedtime shows I'd put on when only he and I were home. He understood the importance of these confessions and never stopped them, even when the Johnny puppet was getting 20 pence from Anorak Man. He'd squirm but he knew better than anyone that shows must go on.

The theatre breathed imagination into me, the colours, the sheer spectacle of it. I begged Shamash to take me to everything, even when he had a date. Of course they had performances to put on too. Their shows were much more sophisticated than mine.

Shamash would go out looking fantastic, dressed in fishnet singlets for nightclubs, torn jeans and cowboy boots. For the Opera House it would be an expensive linen suit, or sometimes a dinner suit. He was very vain, I suppose, but he was also exceptionally beautiful.

The dates had their ultimate destinations, too. Often they would come back to our place, the babysitter (usually Thelly) would go home, and the dates, drinks in hand, would be led up to Shamash's room. He would put on some music in there – Yello was always a favourite, or Grace Jones – and they would do what dates do. Sounds of this sort were familiar. Somehow they represented safety to little *Poucet*. Shamash always closed the door, but he had an old-fashioned lock, without a key. Trembling, I would view his nighttime choreography, and I grew to love it as much as the morning work out. I liked the sudden, secret things the men in there said to each other, words like fuck, cock, arse. Rude words Shamash would never have said to me. In there he'd say them in a different voice, his special voice. Mum had one of those voices, too. She had only used it once in a while, but I remembered the tone; the whore's child's lullaby. The men with Shamash would whisper back, in even lower voices, and I pined for that hotness, that secretness, that nakedness. I wanted my body to grow quickly; I no longer wanted to be a child with toys and books and dumb old things. I, too, wanted to be a *slave to the rhythm*.

Those were hot times in Sydney, the early eighties, just before AIDS. People got pretty carried away in bedrooms in Paddington and Darlinghurst, and Shamash was no puritan when it came to the nocturnal ballet of the flesh. Nor did he shy away from the powders that enhanced the dance. He snorted amyl, sometimes coke, and I learned, through the keyhole, that those smooth arses I had early memories of could be pounded into just as easily as they pounded in. I also learned that drugs were not necessarily a staple diet, not necessarily addictive, not wholly undesirable. I knew that the 'best people' did them as well as the 'worst'. Monkey see, monkey do. If it happens at the bottom you can be sure they're doing it at the top.

MELTING
ICE

Oxford Street. An escape from the suburbs or a ghetto for local inhabitants? A crowded, stacked hierarchy of venues. Not just physically, but socially. It starts underground with sex clubs, dark cavernous gobs that breathe a fetid promise of sordid excitement or drunken relief onto the busy street. Stained chipboard partitions offer yawning holes, the faceless thrill of hot, uvular sensations from the other side. A lucky dip or a game of Russian roulette, indiscriminate mouths offering indifferent supplication. It's a sport not for the faint-hearted, a TAB where all patrons are punters and all cats are grey. Upstairs peep shows proffer bleary-eyed boys with bad skin and reluctant erections. They are yours momentarily for a coin through the cloudy glass divide.

Golden boys from yesteryear wearily dispense condoms and lube carelessly wrapped in Payless paper napkins, tattooing you with a rubber stamp of Bart Simpson as you enter, should you wish to return later, should the current selection prove too grim and a few more drinks be required before carnal agendas can be met. Dry venues, wet venues, peep shows and dingy bars compete like sideshows in a fairground while ATMs that have never known deposits pump out the cash that oils the cogs of this crazy ferris wheel.

At street level the bars purvey the internal lubricants necessary to keep the endless carnival alive. Each bar, pulsating with the flashing of strobes, the constant doof, doof, doof of complex remixes. Songs you know, but you can never remember who sings them. Old favourites redone by some forgettable new studio outfit wearing impossible fashions and sped up until they sound like chipmunks. Songs about following the rules of life, about trying me out or strapping me on, about the rhythm of the night, about swearing on the Bible or about the real me coming alive. Sometimes they're about missing someone like a desert misses rain. I can't help it if, after a few drinks, some of the songs seem to be speaking to me.

At the top of the hierarchy, looking down on it all, are the cocktail bars. Precincts of the most posed and beautiful men, the most worked out, tanned, waxed, designer-singlet-clad bodies you could see. Girls who look like they've just walked off the set of an Aaron Spelling production, heels as high as you like, personas they've invented, beauty at play, sex awaiting consent and jewellery that looks cheap but isn't. They all drink the prettiest, most luridly coloured, most expensive and most alcoholic drinks. The price of one of those drinks would get them into two of those dark clubs.

Three of those cocktails usually ensures that punters end up at one or more of them and that the next day will see the DKNY T-shirt and the Frontier Aviator trousers in the wash or off to the drycleaners. The street seems to know this, it feeds off it and at 3 in the morning attitude seems to vanish. The girls have gone home or to dyke bars or straight venues, and with a carnal flourish from the gods of depravity, a tenuous egalitarianism returns. Then, quietly, unified desires foster a momentary brotherhood in some dark nether world.

The street's glamour is its people, not its architecture – girls and boys strutting, preening and drinking. The boys roam from bar to bar, every muscle of their beefcake bodies accentuated by their child-sized T-shirts. Wind-up boy dolls who know instinctively how to move when they hear the doof, doof of that music. Boys who go to great lengths to look gorgeous and masculine only to throw all 'manhood' away when they mouth the words of campy songs like tribes of drunken high school girls. They are pornography going somewhere to happen. Love them or hate them, come Saturday night, gay or straight, no one wants to miss out on the show.

When you're one of them, you want to stay that way. You don't want to grow old, maybe you don't even want to grow up. But if it is, like some of those 'experts' say, an arrested stage of development, I wish it could have been me who was arrested, not Shamash. You see, no one knew he wasn't really my father, and we both knew it wouldn't have helped matters if they had.

Brigitte knows. Even though I started out just another client of Brigitte's, she doesn't charge me for my visits any more. She says, 'You just come and visit me whenever you feel like it, Darl.' Her house, Misty Rise, is just around the corner in Forbes Street. She's got wind chimes on her balcony, and whenever I go there I feel relaxed. She's very mystical, Brigitte; she knows heaps of weird stuff that she goes on about all the time. It doesn't make all that much sense to me mostly, but sometimes she says things that do. She analyses dreams and seems to know what you're thinking. I don't want to do any of that past life regression – no way – but she did plot my astrological chart, and what she said about me from that made me think there was some order to things. She's quite psychic; she says forget about God and all those other concepts. Before I can even imagine such things I've got to start with learning to love myself. All that stuff sounds wanky, and to be honest it freaks me out a bit.

'Vaslav if you don't clean up that bedroom of yours I'm going to tell Martin I'm resigning, and then where will you be?'

I'd be sitting in there with more toys and books than most other kids, and Thelly'd say I was spoilt.

'You shouldn't keep buying him things, Martin, until he learns how to put them away. It's like a foxes' lair in there.'

'Did you hear what Thel said, Vas? No more books, toys or clothes for you until it's all cleaned up. Now scoot.'

We were sitting in the lounge with the TV on. Shamash was doing some book work and I was watching *Dark Crystal* on video. Already I wanted to watch *Dallas* or Shamash's tape of *Whatever Happened to Baby Jane?* Thelly must have wondered about my tastes. She'd heard David's Bette Davis impersonations and never failed to chuckle at them. 'I was never a Bette Davis fan, even back in the fifties. I always thought she was a battleaxe. I was more your Grace Kelly or Janet Leigh fan,' Thel would say when they started talking about movies. Shamash would smile. 'See David, Thel's got style. She was a Hitchcock girl not a B-grade-fifties-anything-to-save-Bette's-failing-career type movie goer.'

'Style shmile. Give me a woman who can smoke 60 fags a day, drink a bottle of bourbon and still handle one of those huge black Buicks with tears in her eyes while the wipers beat off torrential rain.'

'Well, off you go David. She's holed up somewhere in America. She's in her 80s, had a couple of heart attacks and as many strokes but I believe she's single,' said Thel. 'She might have been an idol to "your lot", but she wasn't someone we girls modelled ourselves on back then. Perhaps I should have been a tougher bird in the bad old days. Could have saved myself considerable grief.'

David and Shamash would look at each other. They loved Thelma's secret, tragic, past. David was always trying to find out more, but they both loved her too much to ever really push her for details.

Shamash wasn't particularly censorious about television but would get 'proper' kids' films for me which I also liked sometimes. I'd put up such a fight over *Dallas*, which was on after my bedtime, that Shamash had started to tape it for me. Thel didn't particularly approve of a child coming home from school to watch such an adult show. She never said anything to Shamash, however, until the day she discovered an explicit magazine under my bed. Thel confronted us both with it in a way that embarrassed Shamash. I could see the colour rise in his cheeks.

'You'd better put these away more carefully, Martin. They're appearing in other quarters.'

He grabbed the magazine from her, and they went into the kitchen. 'Jesus, Thel, a quiet word might have done, don't you think?'

'You're going to have to watch that one, Martin. He's got the makings of a right terror.'

'Have not!' I yelled from the living room.

'And big ears, too,' continued Thelly over the din from the TV.

After she'd gone for the day Shamash said to me, 'Vaslav the snoop should play with his own toys, in his own room, thank-you very much. What do you want with these magazines at your age?'

'Nothing.'

'Well then, why steal them?'

'Dunno, the pictures I s'pose.'

He left the discussion there and wandered out of the room. His face wore an expression that seemed to say, 'I'd laugh if this wasn't for real.'

It took quite some time after that before I found his stash again. He'd pulled out the drawers in his built-in robe and hidden the magazines underneath. I'd wondered, late at night, why I could hear him fiddling with the wardrobe, trying to get the drawers back in. A hiding place, I concurred during one such nocturnal disturbance.

I turned 10 in 1984. AIDS was a whisper then – a rumour, a monster we hoped lurked only in America, like UFOs, trailer parks and serial killers. But it turned out to be real, and by 1984 people could be tested for it. David and Shamash talked about having a test. Both, miraculously according to them, were negative. I hardly knew what it was all about, just that it had to do with sex, and that it was dangerous.

The champagne and gin still flowed at parties, the marijuana smoke still wafted through the house, but the chatter turned to more serious things. To viruses and contagion, to fear, to conversations about 'staying off the scene for a while', then black laughter when someone's voice answered, 'I think that might be a case of too little too late, Love. Talk about closing the stable gate after the horse has bolted.'

The big party event at Shadforth Street that year was the surprise bash Shamash insisted on organising for his parents' thirtieth wedding anniversary. He got caterers in and had a huge ice sculpture of a swan made. Inside the ice sculpture was their present, and no one could depart until it was revealed.

There were dozens of phone calls to plan everything, and I was under the strictest orders to keep the event a secret. Shamash and Rosie revealed their true socialite natures when these sorts of preparations were called for.

'What do you mean waterlilies are not in season? Mum had them for her bouquet thirty years ago. If she could get them then I don't see why we can't have them now . . . If I can't get them in Double Bay where else should I bloody well try? Hopeless, hopeless.'

Shamash was facing a similar *dénouement* with the ice sculpture, which he couldn't store anywhere cool. The caterers wanted to deliver it at 5, he didn't want it until after 7. Thelly muttered to me, 'They're worse than both their parents put together.' Rosie and Shamash, walking past carrying the leaf for the dining table, laughed, 'We are both our parents put together.'

They did their parents proud that night. Shamash stopped bitching about all the North Shore bigots he had to put up with for his parents' sake ('They hate Asians but they love Asian food, they love expensive labels but hate the faggots who design them'), and Rosie finally got her flowers after another round of phone calls. When the guests arrived it was charm, charm and more charm. All Shamash's threats to do an Auntie Mame and serve pickled rattlesnake never came to fruition. As Rosie said, 'If we can't get lilies in Double Bay, I don't like your chances with rattlesnake.'

Surrounded by all the food and decadence, the guests relaxed and enjoyed themselves. Shamash always said apparent wealth was the best antidote to North Shore prejudice, anyway: 'Put 'em in a dinner suit or a Carla Zampatti frock and they usually keep themselves nice.' For a lot of them, visiting the Eastern Suburbs was quite a bohemian adventure. Even if 'parking was a nightmare'.

'Paddington is gorgeous, but we could never give up our view of the Spit,' said one heavily made up 'old friend' as she winked at me.

'Well you know Martin, he was always the arty one, always drawn to the East, weren't you Darling. I thought that anthem of yours used to say "Go west".'

'It did, Mum. They meant San Francisco. You want me to move to Perth or Parramatta?'

'I want you to stay right here in Paddington with Vaslav.'

Grandma drew us both to her as her eyes became dewy. She was getting a bit drunk and sentimental. Shamash refilled her glass shamelessly, and Grandpa said, 'What are you doing to your mother?' Rosie laughed. 'Martin can still do it. He was the only one who could ever get Mum pissed when we were on holidays or out. You used to top up her glass all the time, you horror.'

'Always best to get drunk at the hands of a man who's not going to take advantage of you.' Grandma paused for a second, realising the implications of this, then shrugged and smiled.

'I remember that bottle of Pimms your father took out when we first met. We were just going out for a picnic, and he brought "hard liquor". He pretended it was chivalrous that he remembered to bring a lady's drink. There was I, Miss Post-War Picture Perfect with my home-cooked cold cuts in a basket and a trifle for God's sake, and he's pouring me Pimms and lemonade – more Pimms than lemonade mind you – from this ancient ice box his mother had stored out in the garage.'

Grandpa was laughing too, his eyes lighting up in his foxy old face as I'd never seen them before. 'The best part is poor old Mum thought I was being a real gent "taking a picnic". I told her I'd been down to the grocers and bought everything we needed for a picnic and I'd strapped the old icebox on the back of the car. "Let me have a look, Love," she said. "I'll see what you've left out. You can't leave packing a picnic to a fella." Well, I wouldn't show her. I said she'd either like what I bought or she'd do without.'

'We shouldn't go on,' said Grandma. 'Rosie and Martin have heard this a dozen times.'

'A million times, Mum,' said Rosie. 'But we love it all the same.'

'And there's a tiny bit more revealed with each new telling,' said Shamash, who was swirling his wine in his glass like some arch troublemaker, his father's foxiness somehow reflected in his own eyes.

'Well, Bob had that useless old Austin that you had to crank start – we're talking 1951 mind you,' she said as a general aside, 'and this great icebox strapped on the back. He'd put a huge lump of dry ice in there so every time it was opened we were engulfed in a cloud. I thought it was madly romantic, and before I knew it I was quite tiddly.'

'Oh Love, you were pissed.'

'Bob! Vaslav's here,' Grandma said in mock rebuke.

'He'll hear worse than that if he lives in this house, won't you young fella?'

I nodded, smiling like a reborn angel who'd never heard dirty talk. 'Dad and David say worse on the phone.'

'That's enough, Mr Tattle Tale,' said David.

Grandma was settling back in to the memory. 'A girl had to know how to handle herself on the Pimms.'

Everyone laughed and stared at the light refracted through the dripping centrepiece as I watched grown-ups toasting the years – years I couldn't imagine. Shamash played the handsome, successful son and Rosie, the pretty, well-to-do daughter. I finally got to wear the bowtie I'd never had before, and the family photo taken on the balcony that night looked, for all the world, like a royal one. It could have appeared in *Harpers*.

I loved the clothes and colour of Shamash's world. I may have been trash once but my value had gone up beyond my wildest dreams. I was like those over-valued houses in Paddington, the ones that ended up having mortgages worth more than their resale value when the recession came. Shamash was over-capitalising on me.

The anniversary present that was finally revealed when the ice sculpture melted was two first-class tickets on an exclusive chartered flight to Antarctica, a flight that took only 50 passengers. Grandma and Grandpa had talked of taking one of these trips, and Shamash had thought that to give the present in such a fashion would be ingenious.

It would have been if that flight hadn't crashed.

How strange are some of the twists in Shamash's life – how he found me, how he made me his son, and how he lost his parents against similar odds. He and Rosie had to come to terms with the devastating fact that it was they who had bought the tickets that killed their own Mum and Dad.

Shamash was quite religious in his own way. He seemed to rage against God; it was like opera. I felt strangely remote from the grief, as if it were a nuisance. I felt angry that the crash upset Shamash so much, but I couldn't feel that I'd lost real grandparents. A pall settled over the Shadforth Street house that summer. Shamash lost interest in his dancing and David cast shows without him. Rosie phoned him often: 'For God's sake, Martin, it was an accident. You know they wouldn't blame us. You can't keep doing this to yourself. We'll have to manage somehow. I thought you were the strong one.'

I couldn't count on Shamash's moods then, not for quite a while. He was never cruel to me, though he was sometimes distant. I would go into his room at night and cuddle him. When he was crying he would wrap himself around me and rock me, or himself, to sleep (I was never sure whom the rocking was for). 'Don't you ever leave me, Vas,' he'd say. 'Don't you get yourself killed. If anything happened to you I don't think it would be worth it anymore, do you know what I'm saying?'

He'd come good sometimes: 'I don't suppose a proper dad's meant to cry like I do.'

'So what if you do? It doesn't matter.'

'You don't think I'm an old sook?'

'Nah, I was pretty sad when my Mum died. You're the best person I ever got.'

'You think so?'

'Course. Reckon I was a lucky kid to get the best dad ever – 'specially on a railway station.'

He'd cuddle me close and tell me I was the one sure thing in his life. I don't think I understood the depth of his misery then. Childhood refuses to know misery, it floats above, wondering what it must be like, waiting, one day, to find out.

Shamash was probably too consumed by his own grief to know how much I needed him. When we lay together like that, sometimes all night, he didn't notice how absorbed I was by him. He didn't notice how I stroked his back, how I buried my face in his chest, how the deep breaths I took when I was so close to him were to smell him, not to breathe. Big smells of Shamash, taking some of him inside me. It wasn't just the Eau Sauvage in Summer, the Jazz in winter, it was the essence of him, the mannish smell I didn't produce yet.

How do we know exactly the right way to love someone? What is childish sensuality and sexuality? We imagine that somehow it just comes into being some time, conveniently, around the age of consent. But we all know that the cool and naughty kids start bonking as soon as someone else is prepared to do it with them. The whole world is turned on by young lovers. What's wrong with exploring the parameters a bit earlier?

By the time I was 11 my hormones were working overtime. I was deeply in love with Shamash, deeply in lust. I would bury my head in his clothes, especially his more intimate garments like leotards, underwear. He had a G-string, and the mere look of it excited me. The smell of him in the toilet brought on 'grown up feelings', and a tissue he had masturbated onto and been careless about disposing of I sniffed and tasted. When I lay with him, when I was sure he was asleep and the warm nights kept us uncovered, I could sneak my tongue under his arm and, if I was very bold, I could taste other parts as well. I suppose even if he had woken up he would have been too embarrassed, too incredulous to comment on this sort of behaviour. He would have put it down to an untameable wildness.

As that sad summer came to an end, Mardi Gras suddenly became a focal point as it did each year. This time David wanted me on the Potts En Pointe float. Shamash objected at first.

'He's already getting teased at school about all the ballet shit, and if he goes on the float it'll be worse. Why don't we wait a couple of years, Dave, then see if he wants to?'

'A couple of years! He will be positively adolescent. I know adolescence is not without its charms but we must have the child, the son of Sun and Sky, Quetzalcoatl. They're all characters from the Americas this year, Shamash. Won't the Festival of Light adore a 10-year-old child adorned only in a glorious sheath of gold and magenta with feathers. We need a child to lend a *Satyricon* decadence to the whole shebang.'

Shamash didn't take too much convincing, and I didn't care if I got teased at school. I was sure the other kids would envy me riding on a float like that.

'You'll have to dress him in silver. He's too pale to wear gold.'

'Nonsense,' said David. 'We'll put fake tan on him, and he will ride on the highest point of the float. Gods and princes can get away with lamé at any hour. And Vaslav is a prince, aren't you, Hon?' David pinched my cheek.

Shamash picked me up and hung me over his shoulder, saying, 'Prince of messes and half-full bowls of Rice Bubbles in the dishwasher is what he's prince of this week. I'm trying to teach him to fly, Dave, but can't quite get the take-off happening.' He had me suspended on both arms and was turning around like an amusement park ride.

'Perhaps he's broken,' offered David.

'That'd be right, and the warranty's just expired. Isn't that always the way?'

'You could put him in the dishwasher, that might fix him,' said David, his finger to his mouth as if he were nutting out scientific possibilities.

'You're absolutely right! It said something in the manual about cleaning boys in preparation for flight – *A clean boy offers less particle resistance and can thereby soar at much higher altitudes.'*

'Boys can't fly, you dicks,' I said, giggling and pummelling Shamash's back. 'And I don't want to go in the dishwasher.'

'How do you know? You've never even tried. You could try to catch all those Rice Bubbles that are still in there.'

'Yuk, all soggy mush.'

'Not true Vaslav, they bake on hard as porcelain in the final cycle, and we know how Thelly likes that, don't we?'

And on it would go, he and David treating me more like a kid brother than a son. 'You take the ankles, I'll take the wrists – whoever gets the biggest bit can make a wish.' I can't remember who got the biggest bit; it felt so good being tickled and 'pulled apart' that I hoped the tug of war would never end. They wished for the biggest float ever as I lay writhing on the floor, all giggles, flush and erection.

When it came time for the float it was all hands on deck, and I was old enough by then to get some important jobs like painting and *papier mâché* while all those gorgeous boys and girls from the 'dance factory' made a fuss of me. I have photographs of the float, of me waving to an effigy of Fred Nile. I am making the Indian powowowowow noise with my mouth, although I was an Aztec Indian God technically. But I only knew the wild west ones at the time so I behaved as one. Shamash was Lord Con Ticci Viracocha, Prince and Creator of All Things.

I had been to previous Mardi Gras, sometimes with Thelly, sometimes with Rosie. Because Shamash and David were always on board their float, I had always needed minders. This time I was to take my own place. I loved the parade and I loved the drinks at Shadforth Street afterwards. They were a riot of booze, drugs, music and colour.

I guess that year there would have been Madonna's 'Into The Groove'; there was always Heaven 17, Yello and no party went off without serious dance interpretations of Duran Duran's 'Girls on Film'. I was getting a little bold by then, sneaking small glasses of champagne, which I'm sure Shamash turned a blind eye to. A couple of the girl dancers from the company got me up for 'Girls on Film', prancing about pretending they were lipstick cherry models (which they could have been) until I, light-headed from the champagne, started cat-walking too. Shamash, floating on Mardi Gras high spirits and, no doubt, other substances, would pick me up sometimes and give me a huge 'European kiss'. He always said European kisses were more generous than our WASPy little English pecks, our frigid little smackers: 'The mouth is the mark of generosity, it's the initial source of love in all its forms.' A European kiss meant two, and traditionally they landed on each cheek. Shamash always kissed with his mouth open a bit, leaving a touch of wetness on your cheek afterwards. Because I was special, I was a son, I got the most generous kisses of all. He would press his open mouth to my cheeks for seconds that seemed like minutes, and he would whisper into my ear, 'You know which boy I love most in the whole world don't you? You know who is the most beautiful boy?'

They were rhetorical questions, of course, but they were wonderful affirmations, not only of love but of beauty. It must be said, Shamash's world favoured the fair; it celebrated beauty in all its forms.

I don't know that I would be described as beautiful now. At 20 I don't have Shamash's physical grace nor his break-your-heart cheekbones, but had I stayed in the slums I dare say I would have no beauty at all. Perhaps a momentary bout of cuteness, that sort of disposable, use-up-able, cheap sexual beauty that is so ephemeral. The sort of beauty that is fucked out of you very promptly by the urging of hormones and the demands of addiction. It is fucked out even quicker from whores like my Mum, or like I probably would have been had I stayed, had she lived. I suppose somewhere in my twisted aesthetic this idea controls me. The idea that if someone is beautiful inside you've got to fuck it out of them or fuck into them to get to it. The problem is the more we hammer at whatever it is we want to take from each other, the less it is there.

Shamash and I knew we were perched on the most dangerous of social precipices; we knew what was forbidden. If you'd loved Shamash, if you'd known him like I did, if you were a child as hungry as I was, you would have destroyed him too.

I think it happened during a Blancmange song that I was dancing to with the girls. Shamash was swanning around, kissing people, grinding his hips against them, being generous and pretentious. He was still sporting some of his feathers from the parade but had changed into a one-piece garment that looked like a 1920s bathing suit. It was black and white. I still had on my little gold shorts and a feather necklace. Under the fake tan I was flushed from dancing and from the champagne.

Amidst this oom pah pah Shamash incorporated me into his round of affection pouring. He swept me off the floor as only he could and kissed me, wetly, on each cheek. To my surprise, I kissed him back, first on the cheeks as he had done, then on the mouth. Because we were moving, I was suspended in mid-air. I don't think anyone noticed, but I held the kiss on his mouth for a second or two, my mouth open a little as was his. Suddenly I got really bold and stuck my tongue into his mouth. Shamash shrieked, then laughed. He quickly put me down and smacked my bottom, but as I went back to the girls, back to Blancmange, I saw a flicker of concern pass, almost imperceptibly, over his face.

KIDDIE
PORN

Some politician was on the teev last night crapping on about drugs and 'young people'. It was a current affairs program that kept cutting to the parents of some 20-year-old like me, only this dude had gone to the point of no return on a 'lethal cocktail of narcotics'. The scene was a 'modest' Pymble home (modesty in Pymble starts at about 350K). The family was tearfully huddled on their pastel green sofa – Mum, clinging for dear life to a china-framed picture of her boy, her fingers nervously rubbing the little ceramic rosettes on the corner, her eyes yielding up big drops of ratings rain. Dad sat deadpan, holding her hand – the stoic rock that backs family values. They're trying to come to terms (on national television) with their son's wasted life.

The voice-over kept using terms like 'cut off prematurely' and 'a tragic ending to a promising young life'. A vicar who had worked with teenage drug addicts had his ten cents' worth too: 'We don't blame the parents, all too often "these kids" are displaying warning signs which most parents haven't had the experience or education to recognise.' Blah blah blah, and he finished with some purler about the restlessness of youth and its social consequences, 'which more than ever before are pervading all strata of society'. From this they cut to the stock footage of prostitutes and drunks in Kings Cross. Never mind that half the prostitutes up there are old enough to be the vicar's mother and have lived through AIDS and two world wars – well, Vietnam at least.

So they're panning along the street, showing those sad photocopies on poles and in windows – 'Debbie, please come home, we miss you and so do the kids'. The posters are torn, flapping in the breeze like garage sale notices weeks after the event, leaving viewers with the impression that 'Debbie' never has gone home. The picture is of a birthday girl in happier times. Never mind that she could be living in Newtown and has probably changed her name to Ginger or Chinois. Perhaps she has a well-paid job as a receptionist for a leading international airline. Maybe she works as a sales assistant for Priceline and never had to turn one trick when her train arrived from Orange or Dubbo or wherever the fuck.

During this segment they panned the fountain area and who should be sitting there looking out of it but my mate Owen. He looks up, like hey man and then goes to block the camera. I rang him at his rat nest in Glebe and said, 'Man, you were just on TV as a junkie in the Cross.'

'Hey, I know – wicked wasn't it. They gave me 50 bucks to do that a couple of months ago. Man, I needed that money. This guy who was filming couldn't find any junkies. They're all drunks in the Cross – no smack there – so they got me to do that far-out-man look.'

'What if your Mum sees it?'

'She's in Fiji or Vanuatu or some fuckin' place with Dad. Fifty bucks is 50 bucks, eh Vas? Probably one of their friends'll tell 'em. Hey, you got any weed man? How about I come 'round to your house and play? Watcha say we visit Cone Land?'

I looked at the few sprigs I had left in my mull bowl. Knowing Owen, he'd suck them down in one cone. 'Haven't got much,' I say, 'but come if you want. Bring a vid, the TV's crap.'

They shit me these TV shows, but I can't help watching. It's like they think that somehow they could just stop people experimenting with stuff. As if suddenly everyone who lives on the edge – or even people who experiment with drugs or use them for parties and fun – doesn't have a clue what they're doing. That all of a sudden we'll all be saved and safe and aspiring to that 'modest' house on the harbour.

My theory is that there used to be explorers, places to live dangerously in and as human beings we demand a certain dangerous and exploratory terrain. Drugs allow us to do these things in our heads. Sadly these endeavours are not recognised by the powers that be so we don't get highways and mountains named after us. Also, people have to sell what they've got – get out the hairy chequebook. Or sell a story like mine. Right now that's all I've got to sell. Sympathy? I don't need it. Who's going to put me in gaol? It's not me I seek to vindicate. I don't think I need to worry about film rights either, because until there are robot children for movies, no one will touch this story with a barge pole.

Eleven, 12 were crucial ages for me. Hormonally I developed early in that white trashy way that really was my genetic inheritance. I could masturbate and actually ejaculate. Sure, the amount of sperm was negligible, but it was accompanied by that ancient sting, the sensation that drains and somehow saddens us yet must be done again and again. We all become slaves to it, animals for it, and often we are ruined by it. When at last it came for me, I could finally put reason to a life of unexplained depravity. All that grunting and shagging, all those drawers full of lubricant, condoms and stimulants, all my mother's dressing and undressing; everything made sense.

It was for this that people were dying, this was the rhythm of life, this was why some people were 'bad'. Good people tamed it, hid it, offered it up to God or worked it off in the gym. Not me. I knew as soon as I felt it that badness was in the genes, and while this masturbation thing might have been pleasurable and compelling in its own right, the involvement of someone else in the scenario would be heaven. Or hell.

There were other Mardi Gras, and there was the scandal, the unfinished urban myth about Shamash and me. It's a good one, comparable to Lindy Chamberlain and that baby of hers. But ours is more hush-hush. I've been at things where people have been talking about it without knowing who I was. I've watched breathy would-be socialites whisper about me whenever I pass them. People seem to think you don't notice or hear, or they just don't care. 'Look, that's Vaslav Usher. He's still around can you believe it.' Yeah, I'm still around. What do they expect? Should I be dead at 20? Is my mere presence a reminder of an outdated bit of tabloid titillation? Am I supposed to just vanish as soon as they tire of my story?

No one ever mentions it to my face, no one asks me about it. A whole room might be buzzing with Chinese whispers about what 'used to happen', getting more and more lurid with each drink and each telling. Negligent jurors, these, both condemning me and fantasising about me at the same time, all at my expense. They don't care about protecting victims, if that's what I am supposed to be. They just want another freak in the circus, something to recoil at when they read their Sunday papers over a latte in Victoria Street.

I was a sleazy-snoop-about sort of kid. I knew where Shamash kept his pornography. He did try to hide stuff from me but I could sniff out secret spots like a dog. I wonder if he ever guessed that I snooped like I did? He kept drugs hidden too (not that I stole them then, except perhaps a sniff now and again of the amyl). I remembered how I'd been fascinated by some of Mum's more handsome clients and now I could see dozens of even more desirable men in full colour carnal extravaganzas, I began to think that 'this' was the sex for me.

At primary school a girl sparked my het interest for a while. Even at 12 she hinted constantly at seduction; at secret girl mysteries and pleasures, her chest already pushing forward to accentuate the tiny swellings that would become her breasts. In the playground she'd twist herself around metal poles, suspend herself from monkey bars, fidget in ways that would have her dress riding up or catching between her narrow thighs.

In her back garden after school her legs refused to stay still – they drew constant attention to themselves, knees knocking together as if to say, 'Guess what we've got between us?'

'Vas, has your Dad got a girlfriend?'

'Nah.'

'He doesn't like girls, does he?'

'He likes girls enough.'

'My Mum has a boyfriend.'

'So?'

'I've seen them doing – you know – it.'

'I've seen "that" before.'

'Do you like touching girls?'

'S'alright,' I said, thinking it might be worth a try.

'Come with me,' she demanded one afternoon, dragging me down to the garage at the back of the garden. Her skirt dropped to the concrete floor. 'You'll have to pull your trousers down, too.'

We both stood there behind her Mum's car, her white blouse parting like a theatre curtain to reveal a suprisingly swollen little vulva. It pouted in angry contrast to the precocious, delicate frosting of hair, so new, I'm sure it was still astonishing her. At least I had a couple of hairs of my own for her to touch.

I felt inside her and she pulled me close, touching my hard willy. It was meaty and clammy. She started moaning, moistening and going all weird. I tried to imagine what it must feel like. I guess I envied her a bit; I was starting to wonder if she'd let me put my dick in. 'Go on, what are you afraid of?' she growled with startling urgency. I tried to push my dick in, but it was awkward, what with her skirt around her ankles and my trousers and undies. I moved closer, nearly falling on her, then her ankle touched the exhaust pipe on the car, which was still hot. She squealed from the burn and we were forced apart.

Anyway, her Mum called out to us, 'Vaslav, your Dad's on the phone.' We had to dress quickly and go inside before we got sprung. Her secret wetness was still on my fingers when I picked up the phone, her smell adding strange dimensions to a perfunctory phone conversation with Shamash.

I can't relate to all that gay space, men-only, women-only shit. I guess in sexual terms I took the path of least resistance, but I've always gravitated to those sorts of 'bad girls', those sorts of people.

Heterosexuality may have intrigued me, it still does. I guess that's why I'm more queer than anything else because pornography can be any kind and still turn me on so long as the people in it are sexy. I don't like those fat, 50-year-old women with cunts like badly opened tins of sardines, but neither do I like those overweight, balding Scandinavian men, those warty 'cancer Charlies' with hair on their backs and almost visible bad breath, whose only apparent assets are their huge red schlongs which look like they've been scalded in boiling fat and promise all the STDs under the sun. I've got nothing against old people but I wish they wouldn't do porn movies.

Pornography haunted me as a kid. With the help of Shamash's magazines I knew everything I wanted to do was actually possible. I showed them to a boy at school. He said my Dad was weird but he still came to the Paddington house, still looked at the pictures, still had a snort of the amyl and still let me work my finger into his arsehole before the dull, thumping flush of the amyl had dissipated. He still uttered in that moment of drugged, slightly masculine and strangely fey passivity, the one word that says it all – *cool*. If you'd ever sniffed amyl you'd know *cool* is the wrong word. *Hot*, I would say, is a more apt description. That was one way of taming other boys, get them to have some sex with you and they'd never turn against you at school again. It's the safest form of childhood blackmail. If I qualify for a PhD in anything in this world, blackmail would be it. When sexuality awakens it refuses to be put back down.

Shamash was no angel; he too was a slave. He took the drugs that made the city look more beautiful, made nights last longer, made boys more desirable and turned strong, almost controllable lusts into ones that must be satisfied at all costs. More so after his parents died. There were more young men brought home, more sheet changes, more signs of disapproval from Thel. Damage alters people that way. It shifts our understanding of justice and sends people to war with God.

The Sleaze Ball is an annual spring rite in Sydney. A Bacchanalian fest of diabolical proportions, an occasion for thousands to frock-up as their wildest fantasy. I was well and truly 12 according to Johnny's (non-existent) birth certificate but only just according to Vaslav's. (People often say I'm more like an Aries than a Virgo; that's because I'm a 'secret Aries' but freakishly I have this Virgo ascendant. Brigitte said the cosmos knew I'd be living most of my life as a Virgo.)

I think that was the first time Shamash went out without me having a babysitter. He must have come in at about 3 in the morning (he never stayed out all night like some). He was buzzing, breathing deeply from some designer drug that had mellowed out. I had been asleep on the floor by his wardrobe drawers, his pornography collection strewn around me. He shook me gently.

'Vaslav, what have you been up to? You shouldn't be going through my drawers mate, they're private. And you oughtn't be pouring over all that shit either, not at your age ... there are reasons why you shouldn't be looking at that stuff, good reasons which unfortunately escape me at this precise moment.'

I did my head-hanging bit. 'I was just ——'

'I know what you were just, you were just having a wank but you've got your own room in which to wank. Kiddo, I'm not going to get mad about it, God knows this is a degenerate enough house in a city that is a moral cesspool, and you my darling boy do not hail from a puritanical background. Far be it for me to try to tame your wild spirit, and I'm certainly not the Festival of Light's model father. Now put them away and call it a night.'

'Can I have a cuddle?'

'Oh Kiddo, I've just been to Sleaze. I'm knackered.'

'Just a little one, Shamash.'

'Alright'.

He had taken off his boots and only had a pair of Lycra shorts on. He collapsed onto the bed and closed his eyes. I cuddled him, and whispered, 'I love you Shamash.'

'I know you do, Kiddo. I love you'n'all, now sleep.'

I didn't, though. He sighed long and deep, like you do on drugs. I saw what those drugs did long before I had them myself. I saw their magic. I was sometimes a victim of the snappiness they produced in the ensuing days but Shamash was a happy man that night. He was smiling like an angel, and he smelt of sweat from dancing, exuding the metallic smell of fake tan. I remember how the fragrance of his deodorant lingered on him, with just a faint hint of Jazz.

There lay my saviour, my Dad, my Shamash; there before me was that physique he seemed almost blasé about. He was smiling because he was tripping, dreaming, enjoying the momentary bliss we all try to get a hold of once in a dance-party while. I knew the way he was feeling he wouldn't resist me running my fingers up and down his back. That wasn't a sexual thing; we did that all the time. That's what tactile, affectionate dads do with their boys.

I did it and he groaned a little, he smiled even more, his eyes staying closed. I did it for a long time, gradually moving to his arms then down to his legs. I gently traced his buttocks and he didn't stop me. As I drew with my fingers down the insides of his legs I noticed them move, ever so slightly, apart.

Gently, he angled one leg out, bending it as he did but remaining on his stomach. He was trying to make it look like a natural adjustment but I knew with a flutter of visceral excitement that he was trying to accommodate an erection under there. If he had opened his eyes, my erection would have been visible to him, straining like a grotesquely adult thing from my child-sized Jockettes. But he didn't; he let me keep stroking him, he pretended he was asleep. I moved to the front of the exposed leg and gently up to the Lycra shorts, then ever so slowly to the bulge that was there. He groaned and so did I. It was drenched, and at my touch a fresh discharge seemed to pour forth. He wasn't smiling any more, he seemed to be bracing himself.

His eyes opened, and it was a different Shamash. There was lust in those eyes, there was anger, and pity and desperation. 'It's not going to be enough to have a dad is it, Johnny. You want more than that, don't you.' He tore his shorts down and his erection slung itself free, glistening like some monstrous prize. 'There, that's it, that's what you want to see, isn't it.' Then, before I could do anything, he choreographed a movement so quick, so beautiful that it remains the most exquisite memory of my childhood. He stood, swung me off the bed and twice around his body, and wrapped me around his head. My dick was in his mouth. I must have cum from that sensation in about five seconds. Shamash coughed as I did, sucked hard one last time, and gave a deep, operatic plea: 'Now will the child be stilled.' And the child was.

He took me to my room, to bed, saying quietly, 'We must talk tomorrow. Privately.' I lay sleepily, almost rapturously in my bed, only half aware of the sobs from the next room. The thing that had happened, the secret danger that excited me most of all was his utterance. He had called me 'Johnny'. He'd never called me that before, and I'd half forgotten about Johnny. He could be someone else, he could be anyone at all. Unlike Vaslav, he could never be tamed or cultured. He was like his mother, hardly a person at all, just someone to do stuff to, something to fuck, a disembodied fantasy, a wordless image in one of Shamash's magazines. Could I do those faces the boys in the mags do while they're being fucked? I was consumed by the desire to 'be pornography', to begin cultivating long lost Johnny. I'd had a glimpse of him in my mind's eye; slouching around the council estate wiv' nuffink better t' do 'van suck a bit o' cock and give it nice ol' bit up the jacksy.

Sunday morning arrived. Shamash never slept late after he had done drugs. He never drank much on those nights and was usually in quite good spirits; it was never until Mournful Monday or Eckie Tuesday that that he got moody. Breakfast was a sombre event that morning though.

'You know we can't talk to anyone about what happened last night, Vas. I shouldn't have done that.'

'Doesn't bother me, what happened, Shamash. I'm glad,' I said. 'I won't tell.'

'You will tell, that's just the thing. Perhaps not next week, not next year, perhaps not for several years but all sorts of betrayals await you; sometimes it seems that's what life is all about. You're trying to get hold of every adult thing you can – too soon. If you do everything too early you'll be sorry, things will seem empty when you're older. It's the nature of being a kid, and I'm not trying to patronise you, honestly. The balance is all wrong for us to have anything like what I think you're fantasising.'

'Didn't you like what I was doing last night? Wasn't it nice?'

'Oh come on, Vas, you're a kid. I'm supposed to be your bloody father. Nice is not a word to use for a situation like this. Not everything I get up to is "nice" for Christ's sake. I want to bring you up right, not let you become some sort of freak, and that's what you would become if I let you grow up at the break-neck speed you seem determined to.'

I refused to look up from my cereal.

He went on, 'It's an awful thing to have to tell you, but the world views what we did last night more harshly than almost anything. And the fact that I can't adequately explain why to you is central to the reason for that taboo. This isn't Ancient Greece, and no offence Vas but I've never gone for kids in the past.' He put his arm around me and tried to pretend everything was okay.

I hung my head, shame mingled with unrequited love. But I also began to realise my power. I was a 12-year-old monster. I was a spoilt brat.

two

CHEESE
STICKS

I went to see Brigitte today. She thinks I should record all my dreams, but I'm on Prozac these days so I don't dream very often. I tend to think that the dreams you have on tranquillisers don't really count anyway, and I've been on one thing or another for the last two years. I was taking heavier things for a while – Rohypnols, Valium and various other non-prescription, non-legal shit as well. Brigitte says I shouldn't be on sedatives at my age; she says that if I really was the architect of everything that happened then why is it that I can't cope? Maybe Shamash was right about doing everything so young.

The thing is that sex – the real get-addicted-to-it, have-as-much-of-it-as-you-can-and-use-up-your-youth-because-it's-the-best-sex-asset-you'll-ever-have sex – is a marginal activity. It's seen as delinquent, but there ain't no cure. If I'm a nymphomaniac then fuck the lot of them. It's a victimless crime. I might be marginal, criminal in some ways, but I'm the only victim of my crimes and I'm getting damn tired of everyone's endless interference. 'Get off my case!' I shout to no one in particular and everyone at the same time.

Brigitte's different. She is never shocked by anything. She says, 'I know what you boys are like', with a glint of wickedness flickering in her eye. She's the sort of woman people might call a fag hag if she weren't a dyke. She hasn't got a girl right now, though she reckons she's looking. She's quite old, about 45 or something, but she doesn't look it. Not that that's really old or anything, but she's the first older friend I've made for myself.

Somehow she's beyond all the politics of sexuality. She's not like some of those Newtown dykes, but she's not a bullshit dyke either. She's flying out there in the cosmos somewhere, but still has her feet firmly planted on the ground. She says men are by far the more fragile of the sexes egotistically: 'Their mothers put one foot wrong during childhood and all womankind pays for it the rest of our lives, God help us.'

She sounds like Thel sometimes. Thel had this husband who used to hit the bottle and really knocked her around from time to time: 'I was a fool to love him as long as I did but I had two young kids, and you men'll never understand what that's like. Ten years where I had no choices. I had to stick with him until the kids were both at school and I could get a job and give him his marching orders.'

Brigitte's more mysterious. It's no use asking her how she got enough money to own Misty Rise; she'll just tell you some bullshit about channelling it out of the cosmos or something. But there are pictures of her with an older man, and she refuses to adhere to the reigning lesbian philosophy that rules men out completely as lovers: 'When you get to my age love needs to be more spiritual, the body ain't what it used to be.' When I press her for her history she just says it's another land in which she doesn't travel.

She has theories about everything, and sometimes I like to hear them: 'A lot of promiscuous men pretend they're fetishising masculinity, celebrating the "wholeness" of there being other males like them. They imagine for themselves a fraternity of endless male companionship and eroticism, not realising that the very structure of that society is its own downfall. It becomes like some endless hunting trip – the weather turns cold, it rains, the tent leaks, they run out of cartridges and want to go home, but it's too late.'

I think about some of the old queens who hang out in bars all the time; it's hard to imagine they were ever my age.

I don't know why Brigitte tells me all this, it's not like her lectures are going to make me turn around and behave myself. And I'm not political at all. I don't think I'm a misogynist either, but it's like how everyone thinks all queers are child molesters, or how they think gay men are misogynists and all dykes are man haters or ball breakers. I suppose it's just because we don't fuck girls. I've never thought of myself as a misogynist but I remember Shamash coming back from an all-male dinner party one time and saying to someone on the phone that he'd commented at the table, 'What I hate most about Sydney is all the misogynistic queens.' Apparently there was an embarrassed silence and

Shamash realised suddenly he was not with like minds. When no one said anything he added, 'Tonight's hosts and any future Potts En Pointe financiers excepted, of course.' They'd all laughed after that. I remember him saying to Rosie that the nastiest bitches in this town have got balls, and she'd answered, 'You haven't worked for some of the women.'

Shamash used to go on about all the problems of 'coalitionist politics'. I didn't even know what he meant at first. He said poofs and dykes move further and further apart: 'You might get young gays agreeing with young dykes about issues like pornography and censorship at university but give them a decade and you'll find gay men are just too caught up with the rigours and demands of their sexuality to be really focused on lesbian agendas. Ours (gay and lesbian) is an arranged marriage, but that's as it should be. For all the leftist politics you'll hear espoused from gay and lesbian social advocates, at the end of the day gays and lesbians, like all subcultures and minority groups, are necessarily xenophobic. We need each other for protection if nothing else.' He said good things come from that need.

It's weird when I think about stuff he was involved in, stuff that went right over my head, apart from one line that made sense: 'Don't ever think the world would be a better place if it were run by fags and dykes, Vas. Power works out the same whoever gets it. It is far too hard to acquire and too intoxicating, when obtained, not to corrupt.'

Well I've got fuck-all power though I'm often intoxicated, and it seems to me that it was people who had the power that decided I was corrupted. All these theories don't seem to count for much when I look at the shambles Yours Truly Prince of Messes has made for himself.

Sometimes it seems like everything is to do with sex, but Brigitte says that's specifically my dilemma. I just want out of thinking a lot of the time. With Prozac you can't get quite as out of it; you can't take two or three if you want to go out to a party or a rave or something. What I tend to do is go off it for a few days then take something substantial like an E or two and follow them up later with a Rohy. That way I can have a wild old time without spoiling the 'normalising effects' of the Prozac. I think what most of these medical specialists don't realise is that not everyone wants to be normal, to be saved from depravity. There are certain urges in you from very early on which I suspect are with you until the end, whenever that is.

There is one dream I've had, I keep having: it's about this lane, this walk. I loved it when I was a kid, really a kid. Shamash and I used to go on this walk to David's house in Elizabeth Bay, or Betty Bay as they called it. It was just off Macleay Street, a brick lane that went to all these gorgeous little bridges and gardens with ponds full of fish and stairways that looked too ancient to be in Australia. I used to beg Shamash to let me go to David's on my own but he wouldn't permit it. 'Too close to the Cross for a child,' he'd say. Well, this little walk appears, somewhat differently, in my dreams. It's night and instead of being full of sweet childish things it's chock-full of sex stuff; sexual activities that it's quite difficult for me to negotiate my way past. The thing is, I get quite excited by it but I am trying not to be distracted; I'm on my way somewhere. Then, sometimes my Mum's there too and even though all the other sex is just like men in a beat, she's there and a couple of blokes are giving it to her as well. This doesn't disturb me, but I try to go over 'cos she's waving to me, and then I look in the pond where the fish used to be but they aren't fish any more, they're condoms. I go to reach for one and then I realise they're not condoms but cheesestick wrappers. I start looking for a full one (by full I mean full of cheese not cum) because I'm sure there should be some full ones in there but I never can find one.

Brigitte sighs. 'Oh, Darl, that's sad, that's your childhood you're mourning, that's all the things that are gone.' She's very sentimental, Brigitte, she takes it all mega seriously, deeply, and she's got no time for cynics when it comes to dream interpretation.

'Think about it, Vas, the place where Martin wouldn't let you go on your own, the place where you went anyway, if not literally then metaphorically in terms of the sex. You know what I'm saying, Darl? And the cheesesticks, your Mum, and a life that you have designed mostly around sex, you admit that much yourself. But you know what I think, Vas, what I really think is that if you are invited back into the dream (with Brigitte you have to be 'invited' back into dreams) I think you may very well find a full cheesestick there. This may sound a little kooky to you but if it were me I'd go down to Macleay Street in my waking life, buy a chee-sestick from the corner shop and put it in that pond down there in Elizabeth Bay. It sounds crazy I know but it will help your subconscious mind to know there really is one in there, that your childhood is alive and well inside you, that nothing is ever truly lost forever.'

So I did it. I went into The Mixed Business of Babylon and bought a cheesestick. You'd have to be on Prozac to follow that sort of advice wouldn't you? A grown man putting cheesesticks in a pond in Elizabeth Bay Park. Well I've done worse things than that in parks. With Brigitte I feel I have to do what she says, superstition if you like, but even having done it I get anxious, anxious that when I am invited back into the dream, I will go to that pond with deliberate knowledge and still fail to get the damn cheesestick. It is these types of neuroses that I hope Prozac will help combat. Of course I then worry that the drug itself will repress my 'dream mechanism' so I won't 'receive'; it'll come but I won't be 'taking calls'. Does the brain have a poste restante where later I can claim the 'invitation' I apparently need to go back and reclaim my childhood?

Maybe I just go to Brigitte because she calls me Darl.

Responsibility for one's self. This seems to be my recurring stumbling block; at 20, I seem to be having difficulty reconciling myself to a life spent taking that very responsibility. Perhaps there's a loneliness now that I can't deal with, that burnt-out-ness I was warned about again and again. Maybe it's 'allowed' for me to admit I didn't always know what I was doing, because I didn't. Shamash will forgive me for failing in some ways but we'll always be freaks. It's the love bit that bothers me; I've damaged 'love' somehow, lost its definition, its demarcation lines.

MYSTERY

I haven't been out today. I could use some coffee and I'm out of bread, but some days I can't stand it. I don't feel like 'greeting my public'. There's a woman around the corner in the incredibly overpriced supermarket who calls everyone 'Love' and has the most elaborate 'do' for her hair every day – she's a bit like Mrs Slocombe on that Pommy show. She wears bright purple eye shadow and smokes Holiday 50s.

One of my neuroses is that I can't work out why people are looking at me. I know why they look at her, and believe me, it takes some effort in Darlinghurst to be noticed just for what you look like. I hope when they stare it could be because I'm cute and guys of my age are often admired for that very reason. Oxford Street is surely the Mecca for boy-watching in this town. Sometimes I wonder whether people are watching me because they're homophobes who have come to Oxford

Street just to gawk at the freaks. Then of course there is the other reason, that I'm exactly who I am, that dangerous (former) teenager who made faces at the cameras during one of the decade's biggest legal storms in a teacup.

Brigitte has been nosing around to find me an agent who might sell my story for top dollar. She's talking to a group called Q.U.I.M. (Queer Ultra-Integrity Management). They came up with an immediate offer from *New Weekly* of ten thousand.

'Not enough,' I said. 'God we were in the news plenty. Lindy Chamberlain got more than that.'

I don't know much about these things, not about magazine rights and shit. I'll wait for a better offer. I am, was, news and I want to give them all the secret 'filth' they were hankering for. I want to pull down my 13-year-old's undies and let them see what's there during the forbidden years. I want them to see me confident, clear-skinned at 15, 16; they can see me do all sorts of grown-up stuff at those ages. You see I'm the one who owns me at all those ages. They tried to tell me I didn't back then, but now, at 20, they can't tell me that. Shamash and I have paid and paid for our stolen, not uncomplicated pleasures. It's a user-pays world; I want some of their consumer dollars, I want them to pay for the 'perverse' pleasure we've given them. If it's true as the papers said back then that 'Sydney's Art World Was Rocked To Its Bohemian Foundations' then let's rock it again, let this be a scandalous exposé of those 'paedophile rings' that Shamash supposedly headed.

Lets snare them into the orgies of underage sex that apparently went on in Shadforth Street – 'Choreography For

Kids' as the *Port Jackson Courier* put it. But let them be led and teased slowly, give them almost enough prosaic foreplay to be ready for the literary 'fucking' they're going to get; then just before they're ready fuck'em anyway, without lube or amyl. Get 'em by surprise and fuck'em good I say.

After the Sleaze Ball seduction, Shamash was nervous about being demonstratively affectionate, to say the least. We became a little more distant with each other, and he involved himself with work.

In that last year of primary school I sat the entrance exam for Savant Grammar and passed. For a Bohemian like Shamash, it was a conservative choice, and possibly a little unkind, full of well-bred future bankers and stockbrokers already in an ambitious frenzy to get into the eighties yuppie boom that was going on in the 'real world' outside. Shamash thought I should board. I think our 'incident' had created the need for me to be elsewhere for some of the time.

I guess it gave him more space in his life, too. He was 31 by then, more of a director than a dancer. He was the public face of the company, often being interviewed for arts programs, always going to cocktail parties, charity AIDS dos. He was a typical Sydney socialite in many ways; warm, charismatic, approachable yet secretive, cool, a little flippant and very non-committal. People who knew him socially loved him straight off, but to work with he was apparently difficult, disorganised and a little vague. 'A dizzy North Shore fugitive,' David would say, 'possessed of a capricious artistic temperament.'

Thelly gave him a serve about boarding school too, about sending me to another predominantly male world. I sulked about it, but I went.

What he sought to do when he sent me away (apart from take the heat off himself) was perhaps temper my exploding sexual appetite. Boarding school was not the best place for that. I'm not saying it was an orgy any more than Shadforth Street was, but there were more opportunities where some sort of sexual contact could be engaged in. With my stolen amyl bottle and advanced stage of pubescence, I proved a popular tutor to some of the others in the art of masturbation. The stolen pornography was only ever shown to my 'graduate students'. At boys' schools there are also sure to be one or two masters with a penchant for young fellows. If my advances towards Shamash turned out to be in vain, I could still manage to supplicate a couple of masters, both to my knowledge still at large, still educating the children of paid-up establishment members. I bet they were sweating during the trial, dirty old fuckers.

So there I was, snatched from the heart of Sydney to that dull place, which boasted fresh air, hearty military food and lots of sports. Of course it had a splendid pass rate and really was a 'fine place for young men' – yeah, yeah, yeah. It was old-fashioned and promoted values I know Shamash would have hated – though perhaps he was possessed of a North Shore reactionary streak. In such schools those values are subliminal; you can never put your finger on their wrongness. At Savant it was all about achievement, all about how lucky we were to have the opportunity to be there, how thousands of hungry, capable boys apparently lurked, virtually outside the gates, eager to take our places should we squander our extraordinary opportunity.

That was bullshit. I got in and I wasn't that smart. The school had hopes that I would do things theatrical, as my name suggested, but I didn't show much interest and boys' schools don't particularly encourage interpretive dance unless it's the more violent type on the football field. I hated all those things. Cricket bored me senseless and I could only imagine it being tolerable if matches were played in England next to an ancient church, not next to a Caltex service station in Sydney's north west. You see, if my life were to resemble a Dickens novel, as it does to some extent, I often felt I would like to have risen class wise and found myself once more in the green and pleasant land. For all my grumbling and bitter proletariat background there is a hint of the nouveau riche in me now. England would be a more delightful place to be if one were offering the vicar more tea than it would be offering a pox-ridden wharfie a blow job for 10 quid: ''Ere an' no funny business ni'ver y'ear? Cum in me mouf an' I'll sting ya for anuver fiver.'

It was at Savant that other boys started to give me shit about my Dad being a poof. With the adolescent fascination for reproduction, my origins became a source of the grossest speculation. Travis Cornell was the big bully for a couple of years (until he pushed some little kid off the train, leaving him a paraplegic, and got expelled). He'd heard about fist-fucking somewhere and loved to make up ways in which that activity may have resulted in my conception. A boy on the end of a fist is rather like a glove puppet; hence my nickname. He mastered the fisting gesture as an abusive greeting, the fist turning into a painful punch for me at the end. Cornell used to pin me down and try to fist me. I could tell he loved the idea of this. Even through my trousers he could manage to get two fingers up my arse. Puppet Show became the war cry for this particular playground performance, an event staged weekly, then monthly, then, thankfully, less and less. The first year I was there I went through a dozen pairs of pants. Sometimes both my pairs of trousers would be torn before I could replace them or before Thel could sew them up. I heard a rumour that Cornell got bashed really badly at the beat at Obelisk beach a couple of years back. If only all bashings could be administered with such karmic judiciousness.

When I went home from school on weekends things gradually got better. Shamash started confiding in me again, started letting me back in his room so we could loll about on his bed as we'd always done. But I was getting to be much more 'grown up', my voice quavering from time to time. I didn't tell him about the school brutality; I didn't want him up there making it worse. And I didn't want to embarrass him with the stories the kids told about him. I wanted to revive some toughness from my own childhood. Inside me, Johnny was there accusing me of getting soft, of forgetting what the real world was like, forgetting that what lay inside my torn trousers was of value. It was just ripening and it was gear that could get me things. If I could be handsome, if I could look like some of those boys from Potts En Pointe, I could have whatever I wanted.

Thelly never seemed to be concerned that Shamash and I were so tactile with each other. She never commented except to say she wished her husband had been as good with their kids as Shamash was with me. 'A family is as good as the love that's in it,' she'd say. 'I don't care what you call "a family" but I do know I had to do all the loving in our house. There's plenty of your traditional nuclear families that leave a lot to be desired.' I didn't really know how 'ordinary' fathers were with their sons, but Shamash always said he hoped I would grow up knowing how to cuddle him, a knowledge his father never passed on to him. We had always touched each other, massaged each other, lain around the house together. It was just something beautiful we did, something I treasured. Maybe Grandpa was right to keep his distance, maybe Stoic, Spartan affection as far as dads are concerned is the way to go in order to keep male society at a nervous arm's length from itself. But I loved our cosy calm before the storm.

At school I made friends with Owen, a wiry sort of guy with sandy hair who always wore way oversized jeans and baseball caps when he wasn't in 'Savant Row' (our name for the 'fabulous' designer range launched by our school the year we started). His Dad went to the States all the time and got a different baseball cap each trip. Owen wasn't interested in baseball but was pretty into rap and stuff so he wore them for that. His Dad was really into American sports and constantly tried to foster an interest in his son. Owen was much more interested in the Beastie Boys or L.A. gang warfare, and he seemed disappointed we didn't have crack here yet. Owen was shaping up to be a faggot as well – I think we saw that in each other straight away. He was the first person I told about my Dad being gay, and I guess Owen wasn't as discreet about that disclosure as I hoped. Owen didn't admit he was gay then, I don't suppose I really had either, but he was very interested in my Dad. He was particularly interested in the amyl as well; he was keen on getting wrecked, more keen even than I.

We'd sit in the back of the stables snorting it, not having sex, just giggling, making up these stupid stories about masters masturbating with brooms up their arses or fucking Ms Smedley while she said all this shit in French: *'Ma tante est sur la mer.'* It's not funny now but you piss yourself about that sort of crap at school.

'How big do you reckon Smedley's cunt would be?' Owen would say.

'Oh, about the same size as Mr McCrede's arsehole,' I'd say.

'What would she keep up there?'

'Heaps and heaps of stuff, a portable CD player.'

'Which would be wrecked from all the cunt juice.'

'Oh for sure it'd be wrecked. It'd be fucked I reckon.'

We'd nearly be sick laughing, our heads throbbing, faces flushed from the chemicals. Once we got one of the horses, Mystery, to snort the stuff. She went spastic and kicked a paling out of the stable. We got caught for that but lied about why she did it. The teachers thought we were smoking down there, burning her with a cigarette. They never turned up any cigarettes when they searched my room. They did, however, find a *Hung* magazine.

'Young Vaslav Usher seems to be under some dubious

moral guidance,' I could imagine them saying in the staffroom as they shifted from one foot to another. 'What's the world coming to when kids can find this sort of filth titillating?' I can just see them adjusting their glasses to look at some beautiful blond piece of trash who's sweating cos he's got so much cock crammed up his arse. 'It's just not natural.'

Perhaps rolled up, or even loosely folded, that magazine might have fitted nicely up old McCrede's arsehole.

CHERRY

They say Prozac's not good for creativity, but some days I tend to disagree – besides, there's nothing really new under the sun to say is there? We're just programmed flesh puppets with a limited repertoire of words and responses. Sometimes I say as little as possible. SILENCE = PEACE as well as DEATH.

For example, just as Shamash had all those problems with his mother and acceptance and shit, *Marie Claire*'s mother couldn't care less about her being a lesbian. I know this disappoints her because her mother's always been too busy with her job to pay her the attention she apparently needs. *Marie Claire* puts on all her weird outfits and shows her Mum. Her Mum just shrugs and says, 'If you don't mind looking ridiculous that's up to you – at least I don't have to worry about you getting raped in that gear, you look like some teenage bag lady dragging that stupid Estelle around instead of a shopping jeep.'

'Can you believe that?' *Marie Claire* says to me over the phone. 'Estelle, a fucking shopping jeep, and *rape*. Heaps of really hip girls get raped, raped because breeder scum from the suburbs resent their individuality. She is so self-obsessed, my mother, and so mindlessly suburban. I've had to put up with all her different boyfriends all my life. One of them, I know, would have sexually abused me if he'd had the chance. He came into the bathroom once when I was in the bath then pretended like it was a mistake. *Hullo*. Anyway, I fixed him with a stare like come one step closer and your balls are bubblebath. If the latest one wasn't sooo gross I'd be tempted to seduce him just to teach her a lesson. Do you know what she said to me after the show? The second one, not the first one. Do you know what she said? "I couldn't see that much new in the second show, Allie." She insists on calling me that even though I no longer answer to it. All that genderfuck stuff in the second show just went right over her head. Estelle and I are thinking about just doing women-only shows because the het crowd is so fucked but even in the dyke scene it's not your talent but who you know – or root – that gets your show on. When I get into NIDA they'll be begging for my shows.'

I hold the phone away from my head, noticing how Estelle has dropped out of *Marie Claire*'s future theatrical plans. I wish to myself that NIDA would take her. I don't tell her that the 'genderfuck' in the second show went over my head also, and I have never even lived in the suburbs: 'Well at least your Mum accepts you as a dyke,' I say, hopefully.

'Accepts! Accepts! She doesn't accept shit because she doesn't care – you have to care before you can accept, Vas. God, don't you know anything?'

Apparently not. If she manages to get into NIDA I'll go to UNSW and do Medicine. No I'll do Pharmacology – there's more money in it and more scope for creativity.

Not much happened at Savant about my stolen *Hung* magazine. I was given a punitive assignment to be done on Friday afternoon instead of playing sport, which didn't bother me. The magazine was seized before the nature of the pornography was revealed to any of the other kids, and nothing was reported to 'Dad'. I think the staff were all too aware of Shamash's sexual orientation, of his AIDS involvement and of the probable source of my pornography. The whole situation seemed to be one that they were quite incapable of negotiating. I hadn't even shown the magazine to Owen, but you've got to be very cautious at that age. If my feelings about Owen were wrong, it would have been diabolical to show him, especially as we shared a room. Also, he got to be more like a brother than a sex playmate. We did muck around once or twice but it was more for his benefit than mine. He wanted to see what the 'stuff' looked like when you had a wank, I showed him and he quickly went on to produce his own.

The important thing about that magazine is that although nothing was said at the time, the occurrence was registered then stored somewhere, and it became a nail in the coffin further down the track. But let's dally a little longer on those salad days, jolly boating weather on the Hawkesbury and all that:

'Boys, boys, yes Mr Usher that means you, too. You are a boy, aren't you?'

'Yes sir, I was last time I looked.'

'He was the last time Owen Henley looked too, sir,' added one of my fellow students.

'That's enough of that Bilbury, get those boats cleaned and put away. Usher, see me for a minute when you're back in your uniform.'

It was my 14th birthday. I'd been at Savant for twelve months, almost, and Shamash was going to Amsterdam with the dance company. He wanted to take me as a belated birthday present, which meant my leaving school two weeks before the end of term. Of course it wasn't the sort of interruption Savant usually approved of, but the school 'understood that education had other sides as well, travel being one of them'. Besides, not much happened at the end of term. Wank wank wank. I hate that ponderous seriousness adults have. Like they have so much power, movers and shakers. 'Get a life,' I would have liked to say to those teachers. 'I'm going to Amsterdam, what could be more interesting or important than that?' As if Savant Grammar was Oxford or Cambridge when in fact it was a shit hole with only one building that was a hundred years old, and that had been moved there to give the place character. 'Good-fucking-bye Mr Chips-head.'

I felt very important getting whisked away by Shamash, who arrived looking so cool in his Ray-Bans. 'Well, my darling boy, it's a white Christmas for us this year.

Amsterdam and perhaps Ye Olde England. How about that?'

'I don't care about England. I don't really wanna go there.'

'C'mon Kiddo, we should go there. I want to go back over stuff for myself, too, you know.'

'Shamash, do we have to?'

'What are you scared of?'

'I don't know.'

We were in Hornsby by then. I was feeling better and better the closer we got to Sydney and McDonalds. Truth was I didn't care where we went.

'How many shows in Amsterdam, Shamash?'

'Just three, but I want to go on to London to see about some shows there for next year. If the reviews in the Dutch papers are good, that should clinch it. Mind you, I always get a little nervous in England.'

'Why do you think I don't want to go? Someone's bound to have known Angelique. I'm scared of something weird happening.'

'We'll see how the reviews go. You don't have to come with me to any of my London engagements. David can do that or Ashley.'

'Who's Ashley?'

'This guy I've met whom I like.'

'Is he a dancer?'

'No, a make-up artist, actually.'

'For Potts?'

'He is now. Rachel left in a huff about something so we've put him on. He's good.'

'Was he put on *pre* or *aprés* affair?'

'*Pre*. You'll like him, he's fun. You're not jealous are you, Vas?'

'Nah, you haven't had a boyfriend in ages. Is he young?'

'Twenties.'

'Good looking?'

'Of course, but he's mine you hear.'

'Mirror mirror on the wall. One day, Shamash, the mirror will say, "Shamash yours is beauty true, but beauty more I see afar, imprisoned in Ar-ca-dia."'

'Well Kiddo, all that rowing seems to be doing your arms and chest good. That fabulous pale English skin's lookin' good, too, but I think I've still got a year or two before I have to slip you the poisoned apple. And what's so bad about Savant, that Mr McCrede seemed okay.'

'Doof, my God Shamash, do you realise how daggy and just like a typical parent that sounds? Can't you remember how teachers were always like that to your parents, how they are one way to kids and another to the parents? Don't you ever get like those bourgeois turd-parents other kids have.'

'Bourgeois! So we're using that word now.'

'Yes, and a lot of other words besides, like fuck and cunt. And they're all words I've heard in Shadforth Street. It's just I know what bourgeois means now, and if I keep going to Savant I guess I'll be using it quite a bit.'

'I dare say you will.'

'Will I have my own room in Amsterdam?'

'Well we've got a two-bedroom apartment. It looks quite lavish and tacky in the brochure. But I want you to be nice to Ashley, I want y'all to get along now.'

'Yes, Dad.'

I was just so pleased to be out of that shit hole for six weeks I didn't care about anything. I knew I would be spoilt rotten on that trip.

Ashley seemed okay. He mucked around a lot, which was good, and not in that daggy way either like some people do when they're trying to be 'in with the kids'. His was more a 'couldn't give a shit' type attitude, and he had that twinkle in his eye that told me he was BAD. He told me what the mile high club was, and I asked Shamash if they were going to join it on the plane. They both looked askance, sort of smiling. 'Well, we already have,' said Shamash. 'That trip to Perth last month, it was a night flight and boring. Best to do it on those shorter flights. These big ones are a bit too long to be sexy.' Ashley said, 'Oh, I dunno, depends what sort of medication you have for the flight.' Shamash scowled at him with his 'not in front of the child' scowl.

My sexuality was becoming a worry to Shamash. He felt nervous about divulging too much to me and guilty if he didn't include me. With Ashley there it was easier. Ashley had no responsibilities and didn't pretend to have. I could tell he thought it was wild to be going out with someone who had such an unusual family set-up.

The Amsterdam apartment was in Ruysdaelstraat. It was indeed very tacky, with a huge spa bath. Ashley and Shamash joked that it had an 'international gay bath-house style of decor', but I thought it was pretty cool; the mirrors on the bedroom ceiling were the crowning glory.

107

I went sightseeing with Dove, one of the dancers. She and I went to Anne Frank's house, which I really wanted to see. We were both disappointed that only one room was furnished and how it wasn't such a trick concealment after all. Still, my teachers at Savant would be impressed. Dove took me down all these streets where prostitutes worked from inside their own front windows. I thought about my Mum, and how these tarts had it made compared to her.

There were endless sex shops, one displaying a faded photo of a black man with the largest penis ever. I wanted to go into these places, see all these 'things' they supposedly had. 'Wow, this would be great to tell about at school. Can we go in, Dove?'

'You're too young. Besides, what would your father say?'

In one window was a female dummy on a mechanised bicycle. As she peddled she sent a huge black dildo up and down through a hole in her bicycle seat. In and out this thing went, up into her cunt, and she had this ooohlala expression on her face. Dove grimaced: 'I'd hate to go over a bump on a contraption like that.'

The show wasn't going on until 20th December, but there were rehearsals for Shamash to attend. I stayed at the apartment with Ashley when I wasn't sightseeing. He would sit around, smoking joints, letting me have a few drags on the joint because I kept hassling him. With his shoulder-length hair tied back he looked a bit like a surfie, but in a more poofy and manicured way.

'Martin said you're not that keen on Savant or whatever that school's called.'

'It's a shit hole, I can't wait to be finished school.'

'He told me you were pretty eager to grow up fast.'

'What'd he mean by that?' The hairs on the back of my neck began to rise a bit.

'He reckons every way – sexually, the whole bit.'

I felt a flush of betrayal at this, that Shamash had told this still-new boyfriend so much about me but as my anger rose so did a certain amount of relief, a relief that he had perhaps given me the poisoned apple already. Unbeknown to him. Ashley was bad, just as I intuited, and Shamash didn't even realise.

I considered my answer. 'Yeah, he can't keep me out of trouble, poor old Shamash.'

'Well at least there'd be a few choice opportunities at a boarding school.'

'Not as many as you might think, and it's definitely not encouraged.'

'Not like Amsterdam, hey.'

'Not at all like here.'

'I've got this Dutch porn vid if you want to watch it.'

'Cool with me.'

'They're pretty hot some of these Dutch boys.'

He put it on. Even before the credits had finished I had a raging stiffy. I was determined however to be totally seduced. After all, if you can't get someone to do all the work when you're 14, then when can you? At that age I knew there was something pretty serious about sex, whether with someone my own age or with someone older, but at the same time I didn't have a full understanding of what it was I was trading, what I was giving to get.

What I was trading was danger, absolute freshness, odours that are criminal and intoxicating to imbibe, and an irresistible feyness. The last thing more than anything was the lure. For Ashley it was a hunt, a search for truffles; the sexually hungry adolescent somehow fighting the inevitable descent into adult appetites and grown-up depravity. Brigitte says it is the original sin, the ancient fear that as we squirm beneath our first victor, as we give ourselves to the pleasures he offers, we are losing something irrecoverably; we fear it's our soul, but it's not. It's just our innocence.

But back to that moment, when the hobbledehoy is squirming, saying yes without uttering a word, feeling a confident finger pushing inside him. It is the beginning of some sort of ruin, but he knows not what. He knows that whatever the ruin is he's helpless to stop it. The seducer knows that he will 'give', eventually.

'Is that okay? Am I hurting you?'

'No, doesn't hurt.'

'You like it?'

'Yeah.'

'A lot?'

'Yeah, a lot.'

And he's working the hobbledehoy, gently, hotly, and with increasing certainty about the result. But he must be careful. Hobbledehoy is like a kitten or a puppy, squirming, charged with excesses of youthful electricity, smelling like sweet milk but getting dirtier by the minute. He must be nursed, led gently so his mind doesn't change, so he doesn't get a rush of hormones that make him sullen and contrary. The dotard hates that, that would be a failing, a source of guilt and rage. The cherry, still moist in its glorious chamber, the innocence, not yet lost.

I was lying on the gaudy red and black carpet, my dick already pushing into its cheap acrylic pile. Ashley was sitting on the chair with a Heineken in one hand. And I, feeling Ashley's foot ever so gently brushing the inside of my ankle, did what I'd seen Shamash do; ever so slightly, I parted my legs.

'Hot stuff, hey Vas?'

I nodded. He pushed his foot further up my inside leg and I lifted my hips just enough for him to get his foot under the front of my bicycle shorts if he wanted to. He did want to.

The Dutch boys were getting very carried away, fucking without condoms, cumming from various angles in the blurry pastel shades of a European summer afternoon. And wetness was making its way all over the front of my shorts. Ashley sat beside me, his fly already opened (you can't hear buttons being undone). He looked at his dick, reaching to pull my shorts down a little. I was breathing heavily, I just wanted him to do it all, show me all. His looked big next to mine, more threatening perhaps, but also more exciting.

'Which things out of the movie would you like to do, Vas?'

'I dunno, whatever's fine with me.'

'Whatever it is then.' He kissed me, his beery, smoky breath unlocking memories, and a fresh emission surged forth. 'Horny boy.' It was true enough. He lay me back down and pulled off my shorts and jocks in one go. I felt relieved, taken care of. He licked all the wetness from the end of my cock and I groaned. I put on that fey expression, lifted my legs as his tongue went under and between them, flickering gently over my almost hairless virgin arse.

'Is this okay what we're doing Vas? Are you happy about it?'

'Yeah,' I said pushing aside images of Shamash coming back early.

'What about that, then?' he said, glancing down at his own erection.

'You want me to suck it?'

'I wouldn't say no.'

So I did. I lunged onto it. He lay back on the floor with a loud moan while trying to kick his trousers off. I dare say it wasn't the most stylishly performed fellatio, but he had Shamash for that. He wet his finger and gently started to work it into me while I tested how much of his dick I could get into my mouth without gagging.

We broke for a minute, and he went and grabbed some poppers.

'Have you had these? I believe a bottle or two have gone missing.'

I sniffed the bottle, feeling the familiar rush as his finger tickled my now wet arsehole. 'Phew,' he gasped. 'Your Dad was right – you're on fire pretty early buddy.'

My head throbbed. I was feeling stupid from the amyl and carelessly said between gasps of sensation, 'Did he tell you about us?'

'Us? You and him? He hasn't has he? My God!'

The sensation got to me then – the anger, the dope, the sex, the amyl. I felt sick. I had to run to the bathroom.

'I don't believe it,' Ashley said, rolling on his back, half laughing, half choking. 'This is too twisted – this is wild.'

ACCOMMODATION

The sickness I felt. The loss of innocence without even having Ashley steal my cherry. I still feel sick about that betrayal, about how right Shamash was in his warnings. Worse still was the danger, the danger in the BADNESS I saw in Ashley. For all my pretensions I was not in his grown-up league as far as games and manipulation were concerned. I thought just the sex itself was the limit of being BAD. How little I knew.

I went to bed shaking and crying, and contemplated my tear-streaked face in the mirrored ceiling. I wondered what would happen. What unimaginable, monstrous demon had I unleashed? Myriad possibilities filed through my mind as the infinite nature of grown-up treachery first dawned on me.

Ashley left me alone that night. He probably thought it was more empowering to him to let me contemplate the horrors. For me to gradually realise how important he could be to me, how 'good' he could be, if I played my cards right. But that night I cried for my Dad, I cried for the childhood I had been so careless with, so eager to discard. I was grief-stricken when I finally flushed innocence down the toilet with the vomit and the toilet paper I'd used to wipe away Ashley's saliva from my bottom, the tiny piece of my anatomy that was soon going to seem like my *raison d'être*.

I knew I'd be needing Johnny real soon. He was winking at me from where he slouched by the garbage dump in the council estate. In my mind's eye he was making lewd gestures just like those trashy boys in the porn movies, his hand outlining the erection in his torn jeans, his other hand fingering his mouth for saliva, for lube. He was mustering his strength, weighing his sex because that's all he had to sell, that was his only ticket out of the council estate and at that stage his only ambition.

I slept finally, fitfully, not knowing what Ashley might say. He said nothing to Shamash, calculating the best uses he could make of my tiny slip. Ashley had work to do for the show, though you would never have thought so the way he lolled about like some expensive porn diva. Spending his time drinking, smoking joints, waxing himself and going off at all hours to the solarium. David secretly called Ashley 'Nancy Spungen'. I don't know whether the others liked him; I got the impression from Dove that she thought he was a creep, but he was 'married' to the director so no one said too much.

There were no further advances from Ashley until after Christmas. Everything was set for the trip to England. I was supposed to fly over with Shamash and David while Ashley waited in Amsterdam, but I got sick. Probably part guilt, part something I ate and part fear of going. Shamash couldn't cancel any of the London engagements; there were some big deals involved. I assured him I'd be fine. Ashley said he'd look after me, feed me chicken soup. He winked at me and I thought, Let the Devil in, I am the chicken soup.

My illness vanished as soon as they departed; I guess I was more scared of England than anything else. Ashley seemed to know what I'd done and why. He let the thought of more sex hang in the air, his every move suggesting it; he watched me, touched me, then withdrew. He forced me to go to him for further instruction, my eyes begging him to finish what he'd started.

He and I seemed to have already formed some sort of contract of silence; he wouldn't tell if I didn't. More importantly, he wouldn't mention what I'd said if I played his game. Already I was starting to hate him but I was so excited at the prospect of sex – of him being in a power position over me – that I tried to imagine it as some sort of *Dynasty* set-up. I'd work my butt off to buy his silence, to not have Shamash ever know how I had betrayed him. If I wanted to be a grown-up so much I had to start work right away, in the bedroom, where all grown-ups earn their keep, forge bonds and conflicts. The bed was the performance space of adulthood, the ideal location for an X-rated puppet show. We had nearly six days to play Ashley's game, and what a game that was.

'You're not scared of getting into all this stuff are you, Vas?' he said, as he gently pushed an extra finger into me and rubbed lube down the length of his cock. He'd already tried graduated dildos up there and it seemed that I had finally reached the point of offering him the accommodation he sought.

'If we're going to do it we should use a condom, though.'

'It's alright, I'm clean. I've been tested for AIDS and I'm only doing it like this so you get to start off, at least, with the "real thing". I wouldn't put you at risk any more than your own Dad would. Trust me.' He smiled, one of his department store catalogue smiles, a smile remembered from when he used to model in them. His mention of Shamash hung like cigarette smoke in the air.

How well I'd been educated about safe sex and how easily he got into me without a condom. Of course there were the unspoken things, like 'Shut up freak, you're not in a position to make deals', but it takes maturity to articulate what's going on between those unuttered lines.

'You're going to love this, mate,' he said, as he prepared to enter me, 'but you've got to relax, breathe deeply and very slowly. Then I'll start. We can take as long as we want 'cos the whole idea is that you end up liking it just as much as me.'

Johnny was kept at bay to some extent by Ashley's patience, and I suppose I was lucky to be initiated by someone so considerate. In the days that followed I was transformed from uncertain adolescent to carnal virtuoso.

We had sex two or three times a day in the apartment then rushed about doing other things so we could at least appear to have been usefully employing our time when the others returned. Ashley's desired objectives were met when

I began coming to him, already lubricated; hunger fighting modesty as the child metamorphosed into the freak Shamash had warned me about. Ashley loved the freak he had created. I was channelled by then, my rampant hormones and premature sexual appetite anaesthetising me to the phenomenal guilt I felt about Shamash. I was betraying him in one sense but I hoped saving him in another. I felt wet inside all the time, full of Ashley's cum. How easy and safe for him to have a fresh, undiseased boy–child to download into.

Was I the victim? What about the raw sexual pleasure that accompanied the quite extensive sexual apprenticeship I served those few days in Amsterdam. Am I to retrospectively go back and un-enjoy whatever it was I mistakenly thought was pleasure at the time?

I'm not saying Ashley was right to do what he did, and he revealed himself as being even worse later on. But I did enjoy that sex; I got right into it, stayed into it. Teen sex equalled great sex, at the time. Problem is you have to grow up unless you are a teen suicide.

Shamash must have picked up something of what was going on when he got back. You can't have that much sex without people smelling it or sensing it. Ashley's answer was, 'Martin, how could you say such a thing? I would no more touch the boy than you would in that way.'

Shamash was terrified, of course, but never said anything to me at that stage. I was explosive, contrary and manipulative then. I knew Shamash was praying that we would get through my adolescence without some catastrophic incident; he feared that my behaviour could derail our entire existence. Perhaps he feared me as the enemy despite all the love he had for me, when the real enemy was the man beneath him, snorting amyl as Shamash fucked him, Ashley getting off on sex with Shamash knowing that in the next room lay the son he'd been giving it to the day before. What could Shamash have done had he known his own boyfriend was cheating on him with me? He might have guessed that I probably had not been unresponsive to the advances made, he didn't know what I had said, the extent of my revelation about our encounter. I know what I would have done – I would have said 'This is not happening.' What else could he do without opening gaol gates and institution doors, and with every other conceivable type of hell breaking loose?

The race for me to get to 18 was on. And I didn't mind returning to Savant for the time being. At least I could pick on someone my own size.

S E X
D W A R F

So it was *ciao* to Amsterdam and all its canals, goodbye to innocence and modesty and hello to Vas the monster, abuzz with hormones, desire and guilt. Real guilt for the first time in my life. A new Vas with a glint in his eye. The sort of 14-year-old boy who frightens men in the changing room at the pool, frightens them with undeniable sexuality, self-possession and erections that make it indecent to shed Speedos in the shower. A boy who scares them with the knowledge that they just might put themselves in a situation that could land them in prison, that could wreck the safety of their otherwise decent lives.

We took a train trip to Paris via Austria and spent a few days there. Ashley and Shamash seemed to be going at it a fair bit in the bedroom of the apartment, as if Ashley had to make up for what they'd missed out on while Shamash had been away from Amsterdam. We were right in Le Marais, and

I went walking on my own when the bedroom door shut. I'd had more than enough sex to quieten me down but I still felt aroused by the sound of them, doing heavier stuff than what the hobbledehoy was ready for yet.

We flew back to Sydney, and I discovered that Ashley had already moved in with Shamash before we went to Amsterdam, which I thought was a sneaky thing for Shamash to do without consulting me. What had started out as a temporary arrangement had turned sort of permanent, and I couldn't go into Shamash's bedroom like I used to. When Ashley had the chance to fuck me he did it in my room. He said it was kind of cute on a single bed. My appetite was such that I wasn't too concerned where it happened, and my guilt was adequately suppressed by hormones and desire. It was after, and between times, that I felt the distance grow between Shamash and me. I didn't really want to do it with Ashley anymore, but my libido was such that I seemed unable to say no.

Late one Saturday afternoon Ashley was fucking me in my room when Thel came to Shadforth Street to drop something off; she wasn't usually there on weekends. Thel was not keen on Ashley, you could tell. He was all over her like they were ancient friends, which wasn't Thelly's style, but anyone could tell she hated him grabbing her. She tried to be civil and he tried to pretend he was part of the furniture. Ashley got his trousers on in time and headed out the door; I only had shorts to pull back on. Her eyes narrowed when he sauntered out of my room.

'What are you doing in there?'

'Helping Vas with his homework.'

'I can't imagine what you'd be able to help him with.'

'Well pardon me Thelma, you coach him and you're just the help. I'm sure I can shed a little light on an Anne Tyler novel he's read – and can't understand.'

'He's reading *Tales of the City* at the moment.'

My heart was thumping like you wouldn't believe. I was so scared of Thelly finding out. She called me, and I came out trying to look like I had been reading and had not heard a thing. She asked me what book I was reading. I held up *Tales of the City* and she glared at Ashley. He looked up and said, 'What's that report you're writing for school?' '*Dinner at the Homesick Restaurant,*' I said as a gesture to him. I thought, I'll bail him out this time, because I would be ashamed for Thel to know.

She looked flustered for a second, then turned to Ashley and said, 'You just stay out of his room, you hear?'

Ashley said, 'Yes *Mum*,' and did one of his vile facial expressions. No sooner had she gone than he was bouncing back up the stairs saying, 'Where were we? Ah yes, the cumming part, my favourite bit.'

'Not now Ashley. I don't feel like it anymore.' That's one thing about being fucked, you've got to feel like it. This was the first time I'd held out on him – I felt strangely elated about that.

Thelma must have said something to Shamash because he made sure he didn't leave Ashley alone with me after that. They were starting to niggle at each other a bit, and I guessed that other things were going on. Late at night they would come home with an occasional third party. Perhaps Shamash thought if they got into other weird stuff the pressure would be off me. Youth as fresh as mine was, is, a special attraction all of its own, exciting enough just for its decadence and illegality to not require handcuffs, dildos or any of the other assorted accessories that become standard distractions in the drawers of an increasingly jaded homosexual male's boudoir.

Back at Savant Owen and I shared a reasonably normal year 8. We talked filth all the time, farted and did all those healthy boy things. I didn't confide in him about my 'summer adventures' but I did start eyeing off a particular teacher whose gaze tended to linger too long on boys in the change room. I studied the way he fidgeted from time to time, the proximity he seemed to like having with some boys. I became one of those boys.

I didn't move my arm away from him when he leaned close to me over a prac assignment. I made it clear I wasn't going to move away from him at all. I didn't fancy him that much; he was over 30 and balding a little, though his body was in good shape. The excitement was in the thrill, the danger. A danger far greater for him than for me.

I'd learned a new frequency of communication from Ashley. I was suddenly aware that if I looked someone in the eye a certain way and they returned that look, there was no mistaking what it was about. It was an exciting discovery to be able to convey adult depravity through my teenage eyes, to meet my 'superiors' with a gaze that eliminated the years separating us. To at once be an adult alongside them with a shared agenda and the question, 'Do you dare?'

Sir was keen to play the game. It took him months of exchanging those glances before he suggested I stay back to work on an assignment I was having problems with. Thanks to this incident, I achieved a pass for the next two terms at least.

He was more nervous than I when push came to shove, which irritated me a little. Hobbledehoys can start to get a little cocky once they think they've got some power. So after he'd played the standing too close game, the accidental rubbing game, and finally the game was given away by the bulge in his trousers, we went into the prep lab where he, with far less coolness than Ashley, got all hot and clumsy and knelt before my prick.

He sucked it while he pulled his own stiff, but disappointingly small, dick. I asked him if he did other stuff as well. He looked up from the object of his study, and with a perplexed and ridiculous expression on his face proceeded to ejaculate on the floor. I was sort of disgusted at him by that stage; he was so unsophisticated. I quickly zipped myself into my trousers and left him nearly prostrate on the floor. He looked pathetic, and suddenly I felt incredibly powerful. I hadn't cum and I could tell that he would soon be going into a state of near catatonic fear. I smiled to myself at how inadequate grown-ups could be, how immoral and worthless. I laughed at Savant, with all its bullshit about reputation, employing a man like that who could be hoodwinked into criminal activity by a 14-year-old and live in constant fear. A repulsive dotard – subservient to *me*.

I had wanted him to perform well if he was going to do it; I wanted him to control me in some patriarchal way but he wasn't up to it. It wasn't Vaslav who left him in the prep lab of the science room. It was Johnny. Johnny expected better than that. Johnny didn't suffer fools lightly. If there's such a thing as a moral-free playground where pleasure's to be taken without consequence, then he wants a man with the guts to take his pleasure as he finds it. He's got no time for bourgeois fretting and nervy safety checks.

Owen and I were considered sort of cool that year despite us 'possibly' being faggots. The coolness came from the fact that I would steal small amounts of grass from Shamash and roll joints – not very strong ones – to sell for 10 or 15 dollars each. Neither of us needed the money, but we loved the power and reverence we obtained through doing it. We quickly found ourselves surrounded by boys who were destined to be the 'bad ones' when they grew up. Those invited could come to our room and listen to Stone Roses or Depeche Mode if I was in charge or Beastie Boys and the soundtrack to *Colors* if Owen was. He had a portable CD player his Dad had got him in Japan and we hooked it up to the ghetto-blaster we had in there. CDs were still pretty new then, and that *Colors* soundtrack had us all using the phrase 'move over to the side of the road asshole'. We used it as a code for calling someone an asshole:

'Did you go and see Mr Greenland about your late history assignment Usher?'

'No Sir. He's moved over to the side of the road.'

The whole class would go ballistic with laughter and the masters could only wonder what brand of neo-speak they were being excluded from that year.

In Paddington Shamash's love affair had soured. Ashley had been living there for nine months and he fancied that he was entitled to some sort of financial settlement. He'd done pretty well, picking up a 14-year-old's cherry, which surely you don't do every year of your life, and living in the lap of luxury with a beautiful lover. All this because he could do some fancy work with eyeliner and grease paint.

Shamash had retreated into a textbook-Dad niceness with me, telling me on the phone about the break-up as if he were a mother telling a child that 'Mum and Dad need some time apart, to sort things out'. I tried to hide my joy at their separation, not wanting to look like I was scheming in any way. However trashy I may have been, Ashley was the living end. He got 25,000 dollars out of Shamash. I never knew the exact extent of the blackmail, but if it was paid for 'silence' Shamash never got his end of the bargain. Ashley gossiped, he played Chinese whispers – Sydney whispers is probably a better name for it. He told people that the relationship failed because 'Martin's more interested in his own produce – if you know what I mean', and 'How can a jaded old queen like me at 26 compete with a 14-year-old for youth or 'tightness'? He created a whirlwind of rumours then vanished to New Zealand where he worked for some television station, I think. By the time we were in trouble, he was nowhere to be found.

Sometimes I wonder about all this new age crap, about people telling themselves that they're beautiful loving people, trying to harness within themselves some fucking inner angel, goddess, hero or wolf that a book told them they had. Instead, why don't they just allow themselves to acknowledge that really they are deeply corrupted, hopelessly flawed pieces of cosmic space junk. Not that you can't love junk, but what if 'God' just made you that way? Made you a porn star or a junkie. And maybe he made you that way because he likes to watch you being those things. You might enjoy being those things yourself from time to time.

Once on the council estate the kids got a dog to drink some lager. We all laughed like crazy when the dog got pissed and staggered all over the place. We stopped laughing when it wandered out onto the road then got itself skittled. It just lay there twitching and yelping because its back was broken. No one had the money for a vet so it had to be clubbed to death by some kid's brute of a brother. He bashed it and bashed it with a cricket bat, glad of the excuse for some compassionate violence. 'Die you fuck, die!' he shouted. It didn't seem to want to. The boy it belonged to screamed like his throat was cut while his mother cursed us to hell from the landing, told us we were evil, while looking at me the whole time.

Perhaps we're all like that dog, lurching about until we wander out onto the road and get hit by a bus or something. Maybe 'God' finds it endearing or empowering to see his kids blundering about all flesh and blood and guts – each one a divine little fiasco floundering at happenstance's beck and call.

Brigitte says I see everything in such a bleak way. She says there are dark angels, too: 'They count for just as much – life would be pretty damn dull without its darker side. For sins and allegories to be catalogued, illustrated and contextualised they must be perpetrated by someone and I hardly think the creator would be so churlish as to not allow his/her perpetrators a flicker of completion or enlightenment as they feel the impact of that speeding bus or the twilight consciousness of a fatal heroin overdose.'

Brigitte has a car so she doesn't know there's no such thing as a speeding bus on Oxford Street.

This week I'm trying to have a 'proper Brigitte week'. That means following as much of her advice as possible. I've stayed off Prozac and had no other drugs, either. I'm trying to stay away from the dance clubs and sleaze shops that are distracting and sapping me of my energy. I've got to get out of dead-end behaviour, of blameless, aimless wandering. I'm nearing the end of an age where I can continue to just kill time the way adolescents do in their bored despondent way. And I am aware that a lot of my more seedy behaviour is the ultimate inheritance of gays considerably older than myself.

Brigitte says, 'You'll leave yourself nothing to explore when you really are old and depraved. You're not a prisoner of any particular type of behaviour you know, you don't look older than 20 but you worry all the time that you do, don't you?'

She's right about that. She came around, suggested that instead of sitting cramped in my lounge room with all my books (and mess), we go out and have lunch in the sun in Oxford Street – the Paddington end.

'But people might see us,' I laugh.

'Well you don't seem to mind people seeing you at night, and they get to see a good deal more of you than anyone's going to see today.'

I sniggered. She's too much sometimes, Brigitte. 'Why not Victoria Street, or Roy's? It's more groovy and I might see a cute German or French backpacker.'

Brigitte finally dragged me out into that gorgeous sunny day. I was getting a bit pissed on wine as we sat at a table out the front of Roy's. I'd drunk three glasses to Brigitte's one. I felt like I was getting sunburnt, but she said it was wine-burnt. Brigitte was eating her vegetarian Pad Thai while I toyed with some potato wedges that were all crusty with that MSG shit they put on them. She was going off about the hidden talismans in dreams and karmic reflux or some other thing of hers. I was thinking about Kylie Minogue's latest hairstyle and about how I'll never get a six-pack stomach if I keep eating food that's full of fat. I was looking at myself in the reflection from the window, wondering if the creases of shirt across my stomach could be mistaken for a paunch. I was trying to catch my reflection by surprise – you know, see if I could see myself like I was someone else.

I decided that with my hair like it is, bleached and cropped, and with my tight black T, skin-tight F.A. dacks, Italian boots and trashy ultra-silver sunnies, that I did actually cut a pretty damn sexy image. I'm sure the wine helped me to start feeling so positive, but it was a good feeling. I suddenly felt like I was this ageing movie star but kind of still in my prime at the same time. Anyone who recognised me would think, Wow, Vas looks like sex. He's hot, he's a survivor.

Brigitte's probably right when she says I'm paranoid, but when your whole reputation is based on sex, well you can't help feeling like you've got to look desirable all the time. I've got to look like I'm worth going to prison for. Stupid really, but I'd hate people to go off gossiping and saying 'I saw that Vaslav Usher in Victoria Street today and he looked seriously wasted, he's so sad.' That's why sometimes it's better to think about Kylie or Madonna. Both, I tend to think, look better as brunettes.

So while I'm crapping on inside my head like that what should startle me back into the real world but the trundling sound of some sort of trolley.

'What on earth ——?' said Brigitte peering past me. I looked over my shoulder only to see Estelle heading towards us on roller blades with a child's little red wagon in tow. I could see three supermarket bags on the back and a puppy or dog with one of those circus collars that looks like a tutu. She was out of control and the dog was yapping at every person they passed. I was just preparing to ignore her, hoping she wouldn't see me when she passed by, but it was too late.

'Help, Vaslav!' she cried.

Before I could do anything she'd reached out and grabbed hold of a No Standing sign and managed to stop. The problem was she'd picked up so much momentum that the red wagon swung over towards the gutter and ran side-long into a red BMW that was parked there. The dog's yelping partially obscured the sound of the paint being scratched off the car, but there was no hiding the scratch itself.

Estelle looked around. 'Help me!' she hissed through clenched teeth. Brigitte was pretending to read the menu even though I knew she didn't want anything else. The dog had got out of the wagon and was taking a shit under the next table and one of the grocery bags had split, revealing five frozen TV dinners and nine rolls of unbleached toilet paper. Estelle was squatting on her roller blades looking at the scratch on the car while simultaneously trying to obscure it from view. Even Estelle knew a car like that would belong to some rich cunt. Brigitte whispered across the table to me 'What's the bet that car belongs to some Double Bay estate agent or a crime boss.' I thought the red was more in keeping with an estate agent.

I watched Estelle, thinking, She truly is mad. She'd crouched down to fossick through her backpack for lipsticks. She had three in her hand and I couldn't work out what she was doing, then I realised she was matching them up with the paint on the car. She decided on a pinky-red one, which didn't quite work.

'There's nothing I can do Estelle,' I said to her.

'Well you could fucking well save *Marie Claire*'s dinner for a start.'

I looked over at the wagon and could see the dog already starting to tear open one of the TV dinners. I was really annoyed with her but I went and sealed up the bag anyway. Brigitte looked at the dinners and said, 'You don't want to be buying those things, Darl. They cost a fortune, especially at Delphine's Del' Dell.'

Estelle clenched her teeth and looked at Brigitte. 'They are the only things I can get *Marie Claire* to eat while she's sick, as if it's any of your business.' Brigitte looked away, she can't stand hostility and lets it wash over her without ever taking it to heart. '*Marie Claire*'s sick and we're supposed to do a show tonight. That's why I've got Zsa Zsa with me and the only thing she can do is shit and piss.'

'Where did you get her from?' I asked.

'Some stupid trannie in Surry Hills let us rent her for 25 dollars but she can't do any of the things she's supposed to so I'm taking her and her fuckin' wagon back for a refund.'

Estelle and *Marie Claire* are both would-be performance artists in search of funding. At the moment they are pretending to be dykes in the hope of getting a development grant from the Sydney Gay & Lesbian Mardi Gras for a piece entitled 'Kiss Me Pink Lips and Milk Me Like a Cow'. *Marie Claire* is a lesbian but Estelle isn't. I've promised not to tell anyone in case it affects their submission.

Estelle scribbled something on one of the cafe's free postcards in purple Texta. 'I will leave this under the windscreen wiper for the person who owns the car – best to do the right thing,' she said, wrinkling up her nose. I was in shock that she'd ever do the right thing. Perhaps *Marie Claire* is the evil one.

Finally, she gathered up everything and headed off on her calamitous way. I was amazed the dog even got on board the wagon, but it only did because Estelle stole two chips from my plate and put them in there along with the ashtray from our table.

'I don't know what you see in those girls.'

'Neither do I half the time Brigitte.'

As we left I grabbed the note:

Sorry to trouble you
Mr B.M.W.
You've got a scratch
But I've got a snatch

I put it back and looked at the smears of lipstick on the side of the car. I sniggered. Fancy me thinking she would ever do 'the right thing'.

COLT

It would have been the Christmas after my 15th birthday. I felt really grown up when I was 15; I was getting confident about the shape of my body. I was much more confident than I am now and I couldn't say I've really slipped into decay just yet. It was all the rowing up at Shitsville Savant. I guess I was toughening up physically and emotionally.

I sort of languished like a porn star in Paddington. I felt I'd pulled something off (no pun intended). Shamash started calling me 'the prince'.

'Is Vaslav the prince going to join Dad and Dave for breaky or is some nymph going to come and feed him peeled grapes?'

'I don't want to go down there and fight for one of those stupid milk crates to sit on while some bloody dog eats my focaccia.'

'One dog, one time, got one-quarter of your toasted sandwich. I thought you liked going out for breakfast?'

'It's just a lot of pretentious old wankers down there.'

David took over. 'So Vaslav is now charging Sydney's supposedly beautiful people with being not only wankers but, horror of horrors, *old*.'

Shamash laughed. 'Leave him. He's been at that boarding school so long he doesn't even realise "old" has been deleted from the Eastern suburbs vocabulary. *We are not old* you vile ingrate. Time shall soon plant its hideous blooms on your fair skin, Sonny Jim.'

'Why don't you two just go, for fuck's sake.'

'Such language in our sacred home, Vas,' said Shamash as they slammed the door behind them.

I studied the angles from which I lay on the couch while I ate crisps or bowls of cereal. That always turned Shamash's friends' heads that did. I was a distraction to guests, and I liked it. The irresistible image of a pumped-up adolescent eating a bowl of cereal, food for food's sake, the hunger of a nubile man. Hobbledehoy no longer.

Moody though, perhaps also a studied mannerism. I'd be lying there watching D-Gen or some shit, going ballistic with laughter. Talking to Owen on the phone. We'd do impersonations in mental voices. But I was always eyeing off the people Shamash had around for one reason or another and they all kept their distance. I was still a kid in their eyes.

After they got back from breakfast that day David went home and Shamash and I were left alone.

'I haven't had a hug for the longest time. I miss my boy, you know.' It must have been then he asked me, did I want to talk about Ashley; about what had gone on. I sort of resisted at first, denied anything really happened, but in the end he got serious.

'This is not some trivial urbane little thing we're talking about here. It's getting worse and a bloody sight more complicated as time goes on. I am to blame every bit as much as you, more than you in any legal sense, but for God's sake talk to me. I can't think how anything could be better if you didn't go to boarding school. I don't know whether you're punishing me for making you keep all those secrets. I know it has been difficult, but we haven't done too badly have we? I've given you as much as I can Vas. What would make you happy, Kiddo? I don't know.'

I started to cry then. Really cry. You know what it's like when you try to say stuff when you're crying, you can hardly say the words and then they come out feeling like they've come from another dimension inside you. It's like when you're a baby. I tried to say, 'I'm so sorry Shamash. I was so bad and I know how I hurt you and I don't know how I could hurt you, the only person in the world I love. I'm probably just bad, really bad inside like Mum.' I would have gone on but he came and hugged me and rocked me like I was a baby. I cried and cried while he just kept rocking me. His eyes had tears too but he was stronger. He had a stern look on his face; he had suffered himself. If a heap of bad things happen to you in a row, you can't give them all the same number of tears.

In the end I quietened down to sobs, and he said, 'You

shouldn't say your Mum was bad, Hon. She got you to me, she passed you from one pair of arms to another. That's not bad in this rough and ready world. Tell me what happened. It started in Amsterdam, I know that, so please tell the truth, Vas. Just do me that honour will you?'

So I did tell him everything, almost everything. He told me that it wasn't my fault, blah blah blah, but of course at that age you don't like 'I told you so'. You want things to be your fault but can't cope when they are. I couldn't bear to think I'd fallen into the scenario he'd already warned me about, so I started to be cool about it. Talk man to man, Johnny to Martin:

'Ashley was a cunt, Shamash. I'm not saying that he wasn't sexy – in some ways, he was.'

'Perhaps cunt is the wrong word. Arsehole would be more appropriate.'

'For you perhaps he was an arsehole, to me he was a prick. I was the arsehole. How could you get sucked in by someone like him?' I asked Shamash, as if I were somehow more knowledgeable about these things. 'You could have got something better.'

'If one more person says that to me I'm going to scream. I didn't get someone "better", and don't I know it now. But I'm not perfect, I make big mistakes, too. You want me to have some clean-looking doctor or solicitor like the ones they always seem to have in those American films – the Ken doll in *Parting Glances* perhaps? Life's not like that, Vas. I didn't think he'd try it on with you, or I at least thought there'd be a little warning if he did. I can't be everywhere at once and perhaps I needed to see how predatory you might be getting. I never asked him what he did to – with – you. Do you want to tell?'

'He did pretty much everything. But Shamash, one thing, he never used a condom on me, and I never fucked him, either.'

Shamash started crying then, kind of weeping. He had this sort of gutted, horrified look on his face.

'Ashley said he'd been tested and everything.'

This was difficult for Shamash because he didn't want me to worry unnecessarily about being HIV positive, but he didn't want to sanction or underplay the diabolicalness of what I'd done, either. 'You must never let anyone do that to you! Jesus, Vas, have I not got that message across in the last five years?'

'I bet you did it without condoms sometimes.'

'That's not the point, or it shouldn't be.'

'Well it makes me feel better if you did. That shits me about all these gays – they're not even honest with themselves. I don't think I had much choice in the matter anyway, he kind of tricked me 'cos I said something about you and me.'

'How do you feel now about it?'

I was a teenager so my stock answer to that was a shrug and, 'I dunno.' I suppose I didn't know.

Shamash seemed older that day. Crying does that, but there was something else, too. The worry and the fear. And he was right to be afraid, not of Vaslav his darling boy who would love him 'til he died, but of Johnny whom he hadn't even

138

come face to face with yet. Johnny already knew from which positions he could be best penetrated. He was already sticking things into himself for want of the real thing, he was getting past farting with the other boys and he was already over embarrassment in the change rooms. He was body obsessed, doing stuff to himself for hours in front of the mirror, chafing at the bit for more of the 'real action'. He'd been left in the lurch too. There were Shamash and me sitting together like sex junkies going cold turkey. Father and son, boy and man, both loving and needing each other, and he with his maturity and knowledge was justifiably more scared than me.

He decided that I should go for a blood test just to make sure everything was okay. I said I didn't want to, but eventually we agreed. Our doctor, Andrew, was a friend of Shamash's, but even so, we had to make up a story. We didn't want to have anything more to do with Ashley, and Shamash wasn't sure how Andrew would deal with the truth. Instead we concocted a tale about me and another boy at school who had done 'it', properly, but with no condom. I could hear Andrew saying to Shamash, 'Look, they're 15, it's their first time. Do you really want to worry him about it now? I can't believe he told you he'd done it. Gay kids are usually just as closed with gay parents as straight kids.'

Andrew saw me on his own and asked me a few questions. He was talking about 'the fuck' as if it were only almost a fuck. I said, 'Look, we did the business, he came in there and I shat it out. That was it.'

'Was there much to shit out?' he asked in a medical sort of way.

139

'Nah, it's no big deal. Dad made me come here.' I was trying to sound worldly about it all.

'Well I don't think I need to lecture you on the safe sex bit. Your father's a champion of the cause and I'm sure you'll be fine, but you do have to wait two weeks before we know for sure.'

I did get nervous those two weeks, but the test was negative and it had been months since my last rendezvous with Ashley. What did show up though, and it was of no great medical concern, was cytomeglovirus, which is harmless enough but is not usually found in a young, sexually naive schoolboy doing it for the first time with a similarly naive chum. Its record on my medical card was another drop of mercury in the barometer of our demise. Fair was changing to stormy.

If I'd stayed on the council estate would anyone have made a national hullabaloo over my cheap honour? I would have been raking in the rent without a second thought about how fragile I was, how tender and young. Mum never had anyone there for her when she began her downward spiral. Poor Mum, what a ghastly life she had. If I hadn't been removed I wouldn't have even thought it ghastly, just ordinary. Most people's lives are shit I reckon but the richer we are the more entitled we think we are to having a code of protection around us. The problem is sometimes the rich are trapped by the very same nets they cast.

Shamash spent years working for AIDS groups, rolling up his sleeves and putting together benefits that cost him money. Then because of my 'complicated' childhood all that was as nothing. Forget the false memory syndrome crap; I remember everything. Move over Laura Palmer, you're not the only one who ever led a double life.

In Paddington I could sneak out at night if I wanted to. Shamash would have been horrified if he'd known I was wandering around Taylor Square some nights. I had to be careful, too. Plenty of people could have identified me. Mostly though, at 3 in the morning they were desperados, junkies, drunks and hookers. I was intoxicated just at being out. I didn't need anything, not at the start. It must have been just before I went back to school when I met this guy only a year or two older than me. Colt, he called himself – a roughish kind of dude from the western suburbs. He was good looking in a slutty, peroxide way and I got sort of addicted to him. He was a prostitute and he'd show off to me how he picked guys up along the Wall: the swagger, indifference and confidence as he sauntered over to a car that had slowed. He showed me how to catch your face in the lights in a way that makes you immediately desirable.

'Always say you're 18,' he said, as if I were 'in training'. I guess I pretended I was. He thought I sounded posh. 'Haven't you got rich folks you can nick some money from dude? Better than having these cunts ramming in and out o' you all fuckin' night. Fuck 'em and rob the cunts I say, or do trick sex – make 'em wanna get rid of ya as soon as they get you back to their place. I'm gunna get enough money together to go up to Surfers. I reckon its full of Jap cunts up there. Don't much fancy havin' fuckin' slap heads rootin' me all night but they have loads o' cash and little dicks. Ya just lie on the beach and enjoy the sun and the drugs. That's what I wanna do.'

Colt excited me because he was like Johnny. I found it hard to imagine that the Japanese would have lined up to have a turn at 'sticking it to him' but I was fascinated by the naivete of his dream. I really wanted to have sex with him but he didn't seem to pick that up; I suppose sex was probably the last thing he wanted to do. I was turned on by the fact that he had had so much sex already. I wanted to put my finger or mouth where so many worthless others had been, that was my fantasy. I imagined that after being fucked by all those tricks he'd be grateful if I offered him the opportunity to fuck me. I thought it would be really romantic and cool in a totally grungy sort of way.

But my subtle advances went largely unnoticed. It became apparent that the way for me to 'get wiv' him' would be to do a trick, a threesome with some punter. So I did one night. I was scared when we got into that Commodore, but Colt had a knife and he seemed to know what he was doing. I worried about my inexperience; I felt green and a little shy about sex for cash, about doing it with someone I'd never seen before. I didn't realise that was the whole point, that was my value, that is exactly what they want – still fey enough to squirm, so young that no lighting could reveal decay; perfect, almost ripe, a delicacy. Exquisite human contraband. I'm ready for my close-up, Mr De Mille.

The threesome was an eye-opener. We snuck into the Hyde Park Plaza and went with this old guy in his 40s up to his suite on the eighth floor. He wanted me and Colt to get off together. This pleased me no end; I was going to finally have a crack at Colt. We had to follow his directions, like 'You start kissing him now and you're getting hornier now so you lie on the bed, now you undo his fly, now you suck his cock', and on it went. He was choreographing a sexual scenario which he only wanted to watch. I was getting quite into it. I tried to ignore the old guy masturbating while he watched us and I could tell with Colt that he wasn't nearly as excited by me as I was by him. For him it was more like mundane work, like going to the toilet, remembering where you left your keys or fixing a household appliance.

While all this was going on, the old guy started taking photographs. This seemed to irritate Colt but it encouraged me to do some of the faces I'd liked in mags. I never thought for a minute about them being developed. I had no sense of them having any consequence. The old guy was saying to Colt, 'Now I want you to fuck the little fella. He's got a tight, hungry little arse which wants fucking, so you fuck him good now.' Colt put on a condom and without ever really looking at me, he fucked me. It hurt a bit more than it had with Ashley, mainly because I was under-lubed and the whole thing was taking place at such a fast pace. The old guy gave me some amyl and I was able to at least imagine that Colt was enjoying it. He made noises as if he was cumming but he never did. The old dude sort of groaned, came and rushed into the bathroom.

As soon as he was in there Colt got the film out of the camera and hid it in his pocket. 'That cunt's not gunna get any souvenirs for his money.'

Colt gave me 40 of the 80 dollars he had negotiated with the old dude and we left. I never saw Colt again after that night. Perhaps he went to Surfers. I don't know, but I saw those pictures a couple of years later. I don't know where the prosecution got them from and they were dismissed as evidence, theoretically, but they got into other hands. One thing's for sure, the media didn't dismiss them as evidence.

'Who, we ask, was holding the camera that took these pictures?' said that ponce in the courtroom as Shamash looked at me across the room with an expression of such grief and confusion that it still features in my worst dreams. Those pics were said to be evidence of the child pornography racket Shamash was rumoured to be running. I don't doubt that Colt would have sold them for a price. He may have seen me in the paper – or on the telly more likely.

I could be Johnny at night, on the beat, and still be Vas in his teen-retreat at Shadforth Street, in the kitchen talking to Thelly:

'Does Dianne like it at Sydney Uni, Thel?'

'Yes, she does and she managed to get in there just fine from a state school. I don't know why Martin thinks he has to send you off to that fancy joint when there's a perfectly good school in Woollahra, which is free.'

'Thelly should you be so outspoken about your employer?'

'Employer indeed. How would he run this house without me? Besides I've said as much to his face. Remember, I've brought up two of my own kids, and Jack was never any help even when he was there. In fact it was like having three kids when he came home sozzled. Dianne wants to move out into some shared house in the inner-west and I guess I'll be on my own then.'

'It's a big house just for you.'

'I know. I'd like to sell it and move up to the mountains, but it is too far to come down here. Homebush is enough of a drive for me, especially at night. At least you're big enough and ugly enough to look after yourself.'

'I'm not ugly."

'That's half your problem. If you weren't so damn full of yourself you might not be such a handful for the rest of us.' She always used to pass me some of whatever she was cutting up in the kitchen – usually a bit of ham or cheese. This time she handed me the neck out of a chicken.

'Yuck,' I said.

'I used to make soup out of those when I was young. We never used to waste anything in those days. Now everyone just buys breasts or throws the rest away. When I started working in Paddington you could hear birds, now all you hear is car alarms and those phones people are starting to get. It all changes so fast; what have people got to say now that can't wait I wonder? Dianne wants one and she's still a student. I'm happy for her to get one when they get cheaper, I won't worry so much when she's out at night . . .'

I thought about my own night adventures. If Thel only knew.

'I 'spose Martin pays you too much to give up this job.'

'You are an impertinent little brat, Vaslav, but you're right. Anyway, are you going to cook the pots of bolognaise that keep you two alive? Neither of you eat enough vegies when I'm not here. You should learn to cook. I'll be 55 next birthday, I should think about retirement one day.'

'You could write a book on the things you've seen in Shadforth Street.'

'There'd be a book in that all right, but I don't think Martin would be too pleased. And I don't think I've got the vocabulary for some of the things. I'd be like one of those royal family servants coming out with the dirt and getting a million dollars for it.'

'Well you'd have two queens to write about, three if you include the brat.'

That was the day I actually confessed to Thel I was gay. She paused for a while and went on stuffing the chicken for dinner.

If Thelly ever wondered about what might have been going on she chose to turn a blind eye. She certainly didn't approve of everything but she wasn't a prude. She displayed the same degree of displeasure to whites being washed with coloureds as she did to David's tales of threesomes.

'David Bergdorf, I've lead the life of a nun for years now and I do not need to be subjected to the sordid details of your life. Tell me about a big win on the pokies or a 200,000-dollar trifecta if you want my pulse to race.' She never liked Ashley: 'Don't get me started on him. The day that one left was the best bit of cleaning this house has ever had. He never lifted a finger around this house and he walked away with more money in nine months than I get in two years. I'm in the wrong business or I'm the wrong sex.'

'Or you're too old.' She looked daggers at me, pointing the knife as she did. I hadn't realised what I was saying and I looked away.

'You said it Vas, not me.'

I can still feel the blush I felt that time. So shameless and so ashamed.

I went back to Savant for year 9. Owen was still rooming with me and he was getting more into bands like 'The Cult'. These days he's a real Seattle boy, too macho in his taste to be the poof he is. I saw him a couple of nights ago at the Shift. He hates any of that 'queenie dance shit'; moshing however hasn't become quite the dance style in gay clubs that he would like. 'Find yourself a grungy little Courtney,' I said. 'Marry the bitch, conceive a gutter child while you're both on smack and that would be well cool.'

'Yeah, make sure she's really twisted, too, hey Vas. Stick all different stuff up her man, yeah? Like Courtney does with stilettos. 'Hey baby, you're too fucking out of it to stop me sticking this beer bottle to you aren't you and she'd say fuck off and I'd say fuck you and she wouldn't really make an effort to stop me putting stuff in her shaved little twat, and I'd say you're just a smack head Doll, doll hair, doll eyes.'

There were a few sexual encounters that year with other boys but I was apt to shock them with the sophistication of my tastes, especially fucking. My generation seems not to be as into it as much as Shamash's; it's one of those things either you get a taste for or you don't. I would find homo-sexuality quite inadequate as a sexuality if it didn't involve fucking, but that's just my opinion and fortunately it is one shared by enough of my brothers, as long as I remain comely I should be able to find boys with whom to do it.

147

Savant had me rowing up at the Hawkesbury most weekends and practising each day after school. Shamash would come up and watch some Saturdays then take me back to Paddington in the afternoon. I'd pig out on McDonalds all the way back from Hornsby: milkshake, two quarter pounders with cheese and large fries. Shamash would always sneer at McDonalds and complain about the smell in the car but still ended up eating half the fries.

'Why don't you get your own fucking fries, you always eat mine and I'm starving after rowing.'

'You know I don't like McDonalds, just the fries now and again, and my cruel child denies me a little sustenance after a long drive to pick him up.'

'Yeah, well, I don't come into the Bayswater Brasserie do I, and try and steal your "sauteed rack of dog's bollocks" or whatever they have there, besides which I have to eat all that shit at Savant all week. My God, the poshness ends with the food Shamash, you should try it.'

'I went to boarding school too you know.'

'Not Shitsville though.'

'I bet our food was just as bad. It says in Savant's brochure they have trained nutritionists come in to help plan the menus. We never had that. Why do you think I wanted to get that scholarship to the Academy in London? How was I to know that the food would be even worse there?'

'Dancing had nothing to do with it then, just food hey? As for nutritionists at Savant – I don't think so. I think they just pump the shit back up from the toilets and serve it to us at room temperature, a totally self-sufficient environmentally sound school. I should just get a hose and stick it from my bum to my mouth, save 'em the prep.'

'Oh, Vas stop it. That's off.'

'Well, you should o' come down to Brighton and had tea with Mum and me, egg an' chips on a good night, greasy as old fuck, an' me Ma would o' shagged you an' all.'

'Vas don't talk about her like that mate, she was your Mum.'

'So I can say what I want. She never liked taking it up the arse though I recall.'

'Vaslav stop it.'

''Ere, I 'int Vas no fuckin' more I'm Johnny, HERE'S JOHNNY.'

Shamash hated it, hated me starting to be someone he had no control over, someone who only revealed himself when it was just the two of us. He hated it but I started to find it compelling. I began doing it all the time; it excited me. I was struck by the notion, at 15, that I was really a very interesting character, full of secrets, just waiting to be revealed, Mr Bloody Sophistication. I'd shock Shamash by talking normally while Thel was in the room then I'd notice her leave out of the corner of my eye and I'd answer the next question as Johnny: 'I don't want nuffink for me tea.'

It was like punishing Shamash for forcing me into a secret all those years ago, and it was a type of seduction, it was saying you're not my Dad, I'm something that's not looking for a Dad. It was just a game at first but it began to be a manipulative tool as well. Johnny wasn't fragile; he was the darker side and I was drawn to that side. At the time I yearned for darkness and intrigue and I still wanted to see Shamash's darkness.

He became concerned about my behaviour but once again didn't feel he could safely do anything so he became tense. He would ask me if I wanted to hurt him and I would always slip back into Vas and hug him and say of course I don't. I don't think 'hurt' was what I had in mind either, it was manipulation. I wanted to manipulate the safety out of my life.

I think I knew then that it was only a matter of time, a matter of wine, a project of mine.

JAMBALAYA

I got whisked out of school again. Savant made more of a fuss this time. I was already exhibiting signs that indicated education was not my top priority. I was 16 and starting to talk about leaving school, working in a shop. Shamash wasn't going to have a bar of that. He was rapt that he could afford to take me on the dance tours and hell, I wasn't likely to turn them down. He agreed I could start doing some work for Potts when we got back from the trip; that was the deal to keep me in school.

So it was Europe again and New York and London, and a couple of gigs in Rio at the last minute; five weeks in all. I was very nervous in England. I was also very bad. The cocaine was cheaper and more available. Shamash seldom had it in Australia but all the darlings of Bohemia over there never seemed in short supply. I was beginning to experiment with drugs; Vas did it in secret, but Johnny celebrated their discovery. That trip, that drug, was our real undoing.

The shows were brilliant fiery events. War was brewing in the Middle East, tanks could be seen on highways in the UK and Union Jacks hung patriotically in the windows of the council estates as we sped past in the car. There was something desperate and clichéd about Britain's response to that war. So the stage was set, literally and metaphorically, for the God of Sin to take another lover – a hungry bit of council estate white trash.

Poor Shamash, poor sweet Shamash who needed love so badly. He was sharing hotel rooms with me, we were alone, he no longer had any real control over me. He was being spoiled most nights by his various hosts; whisky and cocaine, expensive hotel suites with Laura Ashley drapery. In his brain that high-pitched coke buzz, in his heart palpitations of success and wellbeing, in his bed a fresh and filthy boy–child. My desires seemed to hang in the air, suspended by the heavy, artificial heat of the rooms.

I was so fucking horny I could have climbed the walls, fucked the floral Austrian blinds, cum all over the duvet. But I didn't have to, not in the end. The cocaine and whisky whispered other things to Shamash, things like, 'Now, now, that's all there is, the moment, the flesh, you've done all you can. Look at him, so hungry for you, nearly out of his mind with lust. There's only one path of action, only one way to calm and soothe him. Shshsh to the white noise in your head, shshsh to all the confusion, only one thing to do, take your reward, your prize – what has been given you.'

'Try not to get worried . . .' That's what I sing to myself on the bad nights; that's what he used to sing when I was little. Lullabies become more savage as you get older. I understand now how, despite our love of gentleness, we want something else that's not so gentle, something that's part gentleness, part savagery. We loved each other, no question about that.

The love started quickly and hotly. Its residues unseemly on the prim English bedding, and we were not careful enough about returning to our separate beds. The housemaids doubtless gossiped.

I'm going to hot things up a bit here. Yeah I'll give you the sex. That's for sale and I was pretty hot. I was fantasy material, gaol bait. Maybe you would have gone to gaol, too. Maybe I was like a mermaid, a siren or just a whore you can't resist after drink and drugs. Vas doesn't get to write this, Johnny can take over. He's good at it, very good at it.

What I hate about the fuckin' Yanks and their porn is they have all this contrived bullshit dialogue, they make macho groans and yabber on in masculine monotones about what they're doing: '*Bug that arse man, fuck it, yeah, you fuck that tight arse.*' Never mind that the arsehole is as big as Texas and yawning like the Grand Canyon. Owen always says with an arse like that you'd have to throw a bone in there, send a dog in after it and fuck the dog before you'd get any service out of it.

You get service easily out of a 16-year-old and that's what I'm leading to. In the French porno films, the good ones, half the boys don't look any older than I was. In some of those, the boys look more like they're having surgery than sex. They get fucked and they yelp, yelp like dogs or moan in really uncontrolled ways. They're not contrived like the

Americans. I can't fathom half of what they say but it sounds better – they don't lie to each other. If they see an arsehole you could park the car in, they find another part of their partner to complement, his cock perhaps or his balls. If you get some piece of trash street hustler to be in a movie, you expect him to be a bit bruised, you don't get some sweet little pink puckered rosebud, you get the Chunnel. If you want convincing Catholic schoolboys with rosy cheeks and pouting perinea you go to a Catholic school. Shit, with the number of priests they charge these days, you'd think they were casting agencies anyway.

European porn is honest porn – unpretentious to boot. Their arseholes work for them. God knows how they do some of the things they do – drugs, I suppose. K is my bet – you could take on the football team after that wicked stuff. Sex is a different ballgame when you're on drugs, especially cocaine, which I had been getting into in London. I'd had some that fateful night, that first real time. Shamash must have known I was high when he came in, but what could he do?

Our sex was more French porn than American. (I prefer to think of myself as one of those Catholic schoolboys rather than the overworked street hustler but I have a place in my heart for both.) If my audience is going to fantasise then I can at least control the fantasy's direction. It was also more like *Endless Love*, the movie, which is a soppy comparison but I have to declare that so all homosexuals aren't eternally accused of being solely consumers of sex, of each other and of ephemeral attributes. But who the fuck isn't attracted to beauty? Owen reckons all arseholes smell the same so why do people bother looking at faces? My answer: Because all arseholes smell the same.

Sure, us men are animals at times, anarchists of desire. Perhaps we frighten the straights by making them think all men 'could' be like this. But Shamash and Vaslav/Johnny did love each other, and when that happens to male homosexuals, even for a moment, they don't walk away from it.

Shamash was more fey than the hobbledehoy. He was faced with losing another type of innocence. He was thinking about legal issues, social implications and his own spiritual failing as a father. Buzz buzz says the cocaine. Carefully, carefully shouts convention. The buzz won out. Johnny won out. Johnny all fresh and showered, all lubed up, reflected exquisitely in the wardrobe mirrors. The hotel, all cosy and flouncy while the December rain beat at the window. The wooden furniture, pot pourri and the metres of unnecessary fabric that covered every possible surface seemed loving and homely, not at all in tune with my desires. Shamash's coat (still the same one I saw that day at Victoria Station) was damp. He shuddered when he came in, and hung up the coat.

'You look rugged up, Vas.'

'I am,' I said, turning *Twin Peaks* down on the telly.

'Did you turn on my electric blanket on the other bed?'

'Forgot, Shamash.'

'You look altogether too carnal for me to give you a cuddle.'

'Pity. I wouldn't mind one.'

He looked puzzled for a second, then tired. Then the buzz from the coke must have kicked in again, and a rush of warmth came over him. Still in his clothes, he pounced on me, tickling me like I was still a kid. I did a laugh that sounded like I still was. He cuddled me for a minute like I was his son. I let him cuddle me as if he were my father. For a minute my ribald calculations failed me; I wanted to be little again. For a thirty-second eternity I longed for my childhood and all its discarded wonders; its cosy security, its storybooks and fragility. But those yearnings passed as easily as the childhood that had treasured them. I had the coke buzz too, and when you're feeling that buzz any sort of physical proximity could turn into sex. Shamash moved to protest when my kiss to his cheek went searching for his mouth. I silenced him with the very kiss he tried to block. He sighed, I think in resignation, in desperation. I did my imitation of Scudder out of that film *Maurice*: 'Now we won't never be parted.' I did that in a Somerset accent, not council estate like Johnny.

There was romance in that line, a romance not lost on Shamash. In his heart of hearts he was always more enchanted by the notion of grand operatic passions, heaven and earth locked in battle with Valkyrian voices raised into a shrill aria that humbled the gods and opened gates to Vall-halla. He was more given to that notion than he was to my vulgar vaudeville of modern homosexuality: the painted faces and board beating, the rowdy show tunes and musty backstages of sex-on-premises venues. From that moment on he believed that line of mine; it signified an embarkation upon HMS *Impossible*, bound for uncharted lands, and the icy storm brewing in the distance was obscured by the ferocity of the heat we felt that night.

After that surrender, after we had both finally abandoned our 'feyness', he started to abandon his role as a parent. He became a lover, a savage one. We had to make every moment a unique one, an ecstatic one, a secret one.

Secrets. We had such a lot of them but this was the one I dreamed of. I longed to see him as a man not a parent. I desperately wanted to have that part revealed to me by him. I ached with joy when I finally whittled him down to it. His so-familiar face, his smell, his occasional awkward mannerisms – so strange in a dancer. I watched as lust overtook the melancholy in his eyes, as his tongue finally accepted my mouth's invitation and his unleashed strength and passion finally made him take me in his arms, like a baby, like Ashley had. At last he dominated me and our drooling cocks battled each other like angry dogs in a pornographic puppet show. His hands travelled down my back. They found the crack of my arse, and he felt the stickiness from the lube:

'You filthy bastard, you had this planned didn't you, Vas?'

'Not Vas, Johnny. I planned it an' all.'

'Don't start on the Johnny bit or that's the end of it, we'll stop here.'

'Sure Mar'in, like you could, ha bloody ha.'

And Johnny was right. He didn't stop.

Shamash fucked me three times that night. Something was being exorcised. I functioned like a well-oiled machine, at that age I was a well-oiled machine – everything worked so well, recovered so quickly.

There was I, a sweet, forbidden duvet delicacy, trained

up real nice by Ashley, used by a teacher and accomplice to a whore. I was a freak, no doubt about that, but there are always sluts, boy sluts, girl sluts. People love sex freaks, trash fucks, dirty young beauty; fresh filth-statutory rape-date rape, boy pussy surprise. The surprise being that the boy lets you have what he is expected to be still guarding, saving, valuing. Surprise is the new currency he's prepared to spend. Spend and spend. An arsehole that yields more than an ATM on a Saturday night. He is always two steps ahead of you in the seduction game. An irresistible nymph, an angel of lust sent down from heaven to provide pleasure to the deserving or an abomination to snare the morally somnambulant.

I could have made a career out of being fucked; perhaps I have. I could have been exploited beyond belief. Shamash could have sold me to some pornographer in Paris and I would have passed the last three years in a drugged stupor making porn movie after porn movie. They could have stuck bigger and bigger things up my arse until I ended up like one of those fist fuckees who almost prolapse when the fist comes out. You can get movies of that; I've seen them.

But that's not what happened. My sex, my uncontrollable libido was treasured by Shamash, kept secret and catered to by him only (for the most part). He let me reveal myself for what I was and he kept it safe. Yes he fucked me as hard as I wanted it. He went to the limits I demanded him to go to. Yes I probably made yelping noises and our lovemaking was full of saliva and lube and bodily smells. We shared extremes of intimacy. He would fuck me and say, 'Christ, Kiddo, what are we doing, this is no good, this is too good.' That trip was like a blur of sex, of reforming our relationship. It was too good; we couldn't stop. I never even thought about stopping and Shamash knew that I was the weakness, that I was the risk. He had to fuck me and fuck me, push me like a wheelbarrow to my 18th birthday. I just wanted more sex, more love, more touching, and he always seemed prepared to bestow it on me, his twisted, monstrous child.

The change in our relationship kept me from going down to Taylor Square, where I could have been murdered, when we returned home. It gave me a new self-esteem. I was suddenly very grown up indeed. Short of slings and harnesses, you don't get much more grown up than we were in the bedroom. And yet we were both like children, too. When lovers reveal themselves to each other to the extent we did there's something archaic and remembered. Some halcyon spiritual recall.

'That's the garden, Darl, memories of the garden. Earth is but heaven seen through a glass darkly.' Brigitte's insights come to me at the strangest times, and of course the glass gets darker still.

I'm going to roll a joint now. I've said enough about that part. I think I could have given more close-up visceral shots, more pink flesh pull-backs as the hard penis enters and withdraws. I could have given you the meat stabbing which they give you in porn movies. That's the total withdrawal of the cock followed by its total re-submergence. Quick, short, sharp jabs, like a sword, in and out of a molten stone, thrusting forward and back accompanied by soft little wails from the one impaled. In and out goes the sword. The grail, the grail can be heard in the wail. But that's a porno technique for the benefit of the cameras and the audience. Once I had it inside I never wanted it to withdraw until it was finished. I would have thrust backwards to foil its escape.

I think about my story and wonder if I could sell it and demand they print it just as I write it. We like to think we're in control – all that shaping of your own destiny and reading the signs as they emerge. All that Brigitte stuff. But I wonder.

As the sexy dope fuzz starts to filter through me I decide it isn't really too late to go out. Not where I have in mind.

COURTNEY

'I never rooted him, he was kissing me, then he started fingering me, that's all.'

'You're a fuckin' slut Mandy, you'd go with any one, you would, bitch.'

On Saturday night these sorts of conversations can be heard clearly from my windows – so clearly that I can't help but get involved. There's a rawness and honesty to people's voices when they're on drugs. I can see them through the blinds; they think this is an unheard, private and ugly moment in their affair, but for me it's like watching a scary movie that I can't just turn off.

She's a pretty little girl with a sexy, heart-shaped face and a *Melrose* hairdo. I'd already be on her side if it were a movie – I always favour forgiveness when it comes to issues of infidelity. Her dress is one of those tiny satin shifts with shoe-string ties on the shoulder, her shoes strappy platform numbers, Joan Crawford style. He's a pumped up 'night wog', probably on steroids, which makes me wonder if he'll go into one of those 'roid rages. Already I can imagine the screams as he flings her about like a rag doll until she breaks.

'You were the one who told me to take that eckie, it just happened. Jesus Stav' can't you just forget about it? I'm still feeling sexy – let's go home, I'm not interested in anyone else. I love my big Greek sex god.'

She's trying to soften him up, her long red nails squeezing his biceps, reminding him of other delicious moments when he's been too caught up in her softness to notice their sharpness. She's rubbing the satin of her dress against his thigh. For a minute I think she'll succeed in taming him – she knows if she can arouse his desire the battle is half won. I feel for this girl, this poor straight girl who gets no scope in her life for any exploration. Love for them is a structured regime which even ecstasy has failed to loosen. Her reputation is at stake. He pushes her away. 'I don't want anyone touching my woman. You got that? You wanna be a whore, I just leave you here, teach you a lesson, slut.'

I hear him bleeping his car, a Mazda RX7 or something. He gets in, starts it up and screeches off down the road, away past all the other Saturday night casualties, past the bottles, vomit, syringes, condoms and dog shit that jostle each other for space on the Darlinghurst streets.

As the car roars off into the distance I am left with the sound of her whimpering on my front steps. Do I ask her in or leave her to the perils of the night? Wait to see a picture of her in a hopper or naked and trampled down one of the many lanes around here, so perfect for rape and murder. I imagine finding her little dress bloodied and smeared with dirt in my rubbish bin or being used as a gag by some brute while she sits shivering in her G-string lace panties, her knees locking together as she tries to protect that place that has already got her in so much trouble tonight. I am putting together an identikit picture of the monster who would turn this perfect-looking semi-durable commodity into fast food and litter. A nasty surprise for the council workers in the morning or an ashen-faced testament to the dangers of itty-bitty dresses, drugs and Oxford Street nightclubs. *Stop*, I scream to myself. I go and open the front door, startling her.

'I just heard all that. You wanna come in for a cup of tea? Can't sit there, you'll get trade.' I try to make my voice sound more poofy than usual so she won't think I'm a sex killer.

'Oh, God, I'm sorry. You forget people live in these places, I'm really embarrassed.'

'Don't be, I've been fingered by dozens of people when I'm on an eckie. He sounds like a right bastard.'

'Oh, he's really sweet sometimes, he's just possessive when he's pissed.'

'Well Hon, anyone who dumps his girlfriend in the middle of the night in these streets ain't worth it. Do you want me to call a cab?'

'No, it's alright, he'll be back – this happens all the time.'

'Fun game,' I say. 'Does anyone ever win?'

'Sometimes.'

So I'm sitting in the lounge at 2.30 in the morning wearing nothing but a sarong with this pretty bimbo who's too cute to really dislike but hardly what I'd call a soulmate.

I make tea, roll another joint when who should roll up but Essie and Macca (my abbreviations for Estelle and *Marie Claire*). Needless to say they don't like their nicknames but bugger them, if they want to turn up at all hours, uninvited, then I'll call them whatever I feel like.

'We saw your light on when we went past – we'd hate to miss any fun.'

They come in, *Marie Claire* dressed in a tight silver pant-suit with angel wings strapped to her back and swimming goggles dangling around her neck. Estelle shocks even me with what she calls her 'Barbie ensemble'. Her hair has been curled and dyed hot pink. On her head she is wearing a pair of baby's pink plastic pants with white lace trims and each leg hole has a pink ponytail pulled through it. She has a peek-a-boo midriff Barbie T-shirt (probably designed to fit a 6-year-old), shimmering with what she calls 'princess span-gles', a shiny Barbie school-daze satchel and powder blue platform boots with pink pedal pushers that have 'Barbie's cunt' hand-stitched into the fly.

They've just been out to Kafae Phuc and performed a new 'piece' called 'Girlie Bitz', which apparently received a mixed reaction. 'It's full of suburban breeders on Saturday night,' says *Marie Claire*. I introduce them to Mandy, who has composed herself a bit, and I try to act like I know her, so she doesn't feel so bad about being dumped on the street like a prossie.

For some reason I've started to feel protective of Mandy, and when I notice she has one of those CC handbags I pretend to plump up a cushion and throw another one on the offending bag. I know how nasty those girls can get, especially when they've had a belly full of cocktails and God knows how much acid. The girls hone in on her, using their cosmetic consultant voices. I can tell she's more than a little intimidated.

'That's such a pretty little dress Mandy, issss that from Sssportsgirl or Portmanssss?'

'Portmans,' says Mandy, unsure whether Portmans is better or worse than Sportsgirl.

I glare at the girls in a 'just watch yourselves' sort of way. 'Mandy's just had a bit of a fight with her boyfriend.'

'He's my husband actually,' she says, as if that mere fact adds dimensions of safety and eons of certainty to her relationship. I think, My God, she couldn't be more than 20. 'This was supposed to be our six-month anniversary but I kind of fucked it up because of that eckie I had.'

'C'mon Mandy, he was being an arsehole,' I say.

'He just gets jealous, it's his insecurity. A lot of guys are really insecure in that way, I shouldn't of let him down like I did, I've just got this bad streak I haven't ironed out.'

'For Christ's sake!' cries *Marie Claire*. 'You're just a child, you shouldn't have to iron anything out, not even his fucking shirts. Girls should be allowed to do whatever they want and bastard men should only be given pleasure by women when it suits them.' She starts flapping her wings in an exaggerated way. 'Even then, stupid men should beg for it – like some dumb old dog for a juicy bone.'

'Juicsssssy juicsssssy,' sings Estelle, stroking her curls and blowing a big pink bubble with her gum. It bursts and I can smell the artificial fruit flavour clear across the room.

Macca's even younger than Mandy. Mandy's looking at her like she's from planet Psycho-Les or something. Macca continues, 'All penetrative relationships are necessarily abusive, the penis knows only plunder.'

Estelle, who has been rocking to some secret music in her head and has hardly said a word so far begins to hiss from the couch. She has just discovered, and is now fingering disdainfully, the gold chain and leather threading of the handbag I'd tried to hide.

'Look *Marie Claire*, a Chanel bag. We love them don't we Puss?' Macca looks over at the bag, her face contorting.

'They look excellent next to a corpse.' Mandy is starting to get agitated and just then we hear the roar of the RX7 as it cruises the street looking for its missing accessory.

'That'll be Stavros,' she says, snatching the purse from Essie who then grabs her hand to look at the ring. '*Marie Claire*, look at the ring, it's beautiful isn't it?'

'Yeah, yeah, whatever,' Macca says, without even turning her head. She's busy peering out the window to see what the noisy black car is about to deliver. Mandy pulls her hand back, still naively unsure whether she's being flattered or insulted.

Mandy opens the door so Stavros can see her. He gets out of the car and lumbers across the street, a perplexed look on his dumb-fuck face. She's acting like nothing has happened earlier, like some sweet little wife with no desires of her own.

They wander back to the car, him muttering, 'Who were them weird chicks?' I can just hear her as she replies, 'I can't remember their names, one of them was called

Vanity Fair or something, I think they're lesbians.'

She's like me a bit – doesn't care so much about the cost, she wanted something and was not going to let her E go to waste. Who knows how long she'll put up with the abuse; perhaps that's their game, he goes off angry, returning to her when the rage subsides. Now she will be able to silence him with her tender little wet mouth, the one that doesn't have a voice of its own yet speaks loud and vulgar at times which don't suit her, times that endanger all of us, well me at least. A genetic weakness that ensures lots of people will want to have us but none will want to keep us. I wonder if people like us ever get control over those desires. Whatever the case, I'm stuck with the Darlinghurst Debutantes until their drugs wear off or until I fall asleep.

'Where'd you find her in that little Miss Fuck-me dress?' asks Macca.

'The storks delivered her to my door. It'll be all wet pussy and eckie talk for those two now they've had their little tiff. She loves him,' I say, mimicking her.

Essie starts singing '*I will hold, cherish and obey . . .*'

'What sort of stupid fuckin' bitch would agree "to obey" for Christ's sake? Not this little black duck that's for sure,' says *Marie Claire*, who orders Essie to get her some water while hunting through my CDs in search of Strawpeople.

I take another toke on the joint, wishing I'd made the most of the night. Essie has emptied her satchel on the floor. She has two Barbies in there, some tampons, cough medicine and several outfits for the dolls ranging from adventurous outdoor wear to glamorous Hollywood evening gowns. She is deliberating over what the dolls' attire should be at 4 in the morning. Macca is trying to untangle the cord that makes her wings flap. 'Angel wings, cunts of things – 80 bucks, too.'

YABBADABBADOO

Sydney is like a prison to me. I can never believe I'm here. Why do I stay? Where else could I go? Selling tickets, programs and taking party bookings for Potts is not much job experience. If I were a waiter I'd go and work on a resort or something. But I am a prisoner. I'd last five minutes on an island; I'd be bored shitless. I need these stone wall streets now, the fuck clubs, the filth. I hate the city because I hate myself, can't live with it, can't live without it.

I'm coming down today, from speed, acid, alcohol and some unidentified sedative fed to me by a dubious acquaintance. I could tell when David came around that he was disappointed to see me hungover and still in bed at 11. Well I'm not his concern anymore and I can do without people fucking well judging me. I've only myself to blame; for everything it seems. Though I never betrayed Shamash again, at least not intentionally.

Last night I had sex with a number of people. I sat in the coffee bar at a sauna looking down through the glass floor at the pool below. I watched people swimming naked; it was like a David Hockney painting come to life. I was very out of it and when you're feeling like that you think everyone else is too. I manage, even shit-faced, to have safe sex (mostly), however I'm constantly amazed at how many people would happily indulge in the old-fashioned sort. You've got to have your wits about you or you'll find someone swallowing up your cock with their arsehole. Conversely you have to make sure none of those lubed-up dicks get up yours without a condom. It's a jungle in there.

At one point I found myself fist-fucking this guy. I've never done it before. He was one of those seriously heavy-duty dudes. I went into a cubicle where he was already displaying himself, amyl in hand. I was sort of getting into it with him but only half-heartedly, and I put two of my fingers into him; well next thing I know he's manoeuvred himself in this trick way and whammo, my whole fucking fist is up there. He hardly seemed to flinch and I sniggered to myself, thinking about Owen and the dog and bone business. The thing that amazed me, once my arm was in there, was how much space there seemed to be; it was like some vast chamber, one of those *Star Trek* black holes – a space–time continuum. I found the whole thing amazing in a really clinical, medical sort of way.

He was snorting amyl, allowing my fist to be the instrument that gave him some sort of isolated head trip, he was somewhere else – head surfing in a parallel universe. I thought how extreme this person's sexuality was, how his arse would be such a dud fuck, it would be like throwing a sausage down a lane. As I swivelled my fist around in there, I thought, He's spoiled himself for fucking, he has changed himself, stretched himself to such an extent that a soft, tight and gentle fuck would be quite out of the question. I twisted the huge loop of steel that pierced his nipple and only then did he groan. The drugs made me laugh; I was thinking, here I am, arm submerged nearly to the elbow in a position so powerful I could probably kill him, turn him inside out, and the only vocal response I get is when I touch his nipple.

I felt scared for that dude, scared by the vulnerability he allowed himself. It was the fist he wanted, not me, probably any fist would have done; fist and amyl were his tickets to nirvana. I withdrew my arm because the fascination passed. I realised that it was not a sexual thing for me, it was like doing an operation. It was the sort of thing Ren and Stimpy would do if they weren't on a kiddies' show. Drugs are bizarre; they turn moments of surrealist revelation, moments of utter debasement and depravity into some zany cartoon caper. Yabbadabbadoo.

I sat engrossed by the blue below, Dante's inferno. Down there a seething morass of lubricated muscle, skin and bone, a grown-up's party, flesh engulfing flesh engulfing flesh, the way *Alien* does, invading and redefining itself as it goes about its terrible business. I was contemplating how I love that sauna, how I love the safety of saunas, how I could stay there in the darkness forever.

I was tripping, thinking how I like this parallel universe that drugs turn on inside my head fuck – believing it was real, which it was at the time. Sometimes I can sit there feeling really sexy. Sometimes feeling like a little kid or an action super hero in a cartoon. One minute my dick feels like it belongs to someone else, next minute it's my actual soul. When that happens I suspect if anyone was to suck it too hard I'd get blasted straight down 'that' tunnel to heaven or hell or some fucking freak-out place. Other times it's different, like with acid when you're seriously shit-faced and some prospective piece of trade's blahing on to you about sex and whadda ya wanna do and d'you like t' fuck, and you're sitting there while they play with your cock and you don't mind but all you can think about is innovative cocktail glass designs or new concepts in semitrailer docking facilities.

That's how it was last night. I was just sitting there in the sauna, lost in ethereal steam not thinking anything, except, you know, buckets and spades, cars and trains, pixies and flowers. Some dude starts wanking me off. I wasn't that fussed but I let him because it felt like he had lube on his hand and that's a kind of nice and easy feeling, like having a little baby angel gently sucking on your soul. Well after a while it started to feel a bit sticky, like when you need more lube and I was thinking of moving on anyway. I pulled his hand away and as I did I looked at it through the mist and saw it was covered in blood. It wasn't lube it was fucking blood! I freaked right out. It was like waking up with a huge spider or snake on you. 'Are you crazy or what?' I shouted at him. He just grinned like an idiot. I headed for the shower. Then I started thinking maybe it was my blood not his.

So I'm trying not to freak right out in the shower, which is on display to everyone. I'm pulling back my foreskin to see if I'm cut in there, trying to see if I'm cut anywhere, on my balls or legs. Inside my head I'm saying 'Cool it, man', but part of me just wants to start crying because I've had such a fright. Other guys are looking at me which means I must be seriously agitated and I wonder if anyone saw the blood. I can't find any cuts and I start to wonder if there really was any blood. It's all gone, washed away down the drain. I look around, trying to see the guy from in the sauna. He's vanished. I shiver, cold and scared. If there was blood, why didn't he go to the shower to wash it off? There are no other showers he could use. I hate that sort of weird stuff, people looking at me like that, like I'm some sort of freak. Blood is not a thing guys want to see at a sauna.

Today I hate saunas, I hate the way they will always be there luring me into acts of sex, sometimes good sex, sometimes bad sex. I hate the fact that I have no control in that regard, that I am incapable of loving anyone new and even if I did, it would end up being in addition to those other things. Would Shamash have saved me from this? Who knows. We might frighten ourselves, us fags, but we are what we are and we do experience some extraordinary sensations in our endless pursuit of whatever it is we are looking for – momentary oblivion or eternal rest.

Hard to go back to school after the London scene. I thought I was hot shit that year; everything was boring, juvenile as far as I was concerned. Even Owen found me a bit up myself;

I was like a spoiled brat, a Texan girl. All the boys would watch *Capital City*, dreaming of their soon-to-be-realised business potential. Even I liked that show, but mostly Owen and I wanted to get stoned down on the oval and come back to our room to listen to music. We had a little bit of an overlap in our tastes so it was mutually agreed CDs we would play: Stone Roses, The Orb and sometimes he allowed Madonna, which we played only if we wanted to do really camp versions of 'Justify My Love'. What was never allowed by Owen was Pet Shop Boys or Kylie. I'd put them on and he'd go ballistic. I'd wrestle him so he couldn't get to the ghetto-blaster, I'd sing the words into his face, 'Better the devil you know, blah blah'. He'd pretend he was in physical pain at the sound of her. I'd prance about doing Pet Shop Boys' songs, 'Being Boring' was my favourite, and whatever else they might have said about me, no one could say I was being boring.

The other boys would bash on the walls. 'Shut up you fuckin' faggot, Usher.' That year the abuse seemed worse. I got bashed a few times. 'Your father's a fucking faggot and so are you Usher.' Faggette they called me. I didn't even deny it by then; in fact I played up to them, camped it up when they abused me: 'Usher, how the fuck did you even get born? You came out of some cunt's arsehole.' I let my work slip and got stoned whenever I could.

It was through this that some other bad business – the worst business – came to pass. One time I went on my own to have a joint at the local park. There is a public toilet block at the far side. I don't think it was a bona fide beat but I would always cast it a sidelong glance just to see if anyone was hanging around. On this occasion a guy was. The dope had made me really horny so I went over to check this bloke out. I was in my Savant tracksuit. That was my excuse if I got caught; I was jogging, 'Training, Sir, for inter-school.' Intercourse on this occasion was more like it. The guy in the toilets was pretty rough, with tats, which I loved, but not that good looking. I thought we'd just have a quickie, which we did, but he was dead keen to fuck me. I said no, just sucking. He wasn't easily discouraged however and twice tried to force himself into me. The second time he got in. I pushed him away and ran off back to the dorms. I really did jog that night.

The next night I wanted to go for a joint and this guy Stewart said he'd come with me. I suspected he might have wanted to kick some game, too. It's like, to do anything at that age you've got to get drunk or stoned so that if something happens there is a sense of diminished responsibility. He wasn't usually one of the dope smokers so I assumed a slight ulterior motive. I didn't particularly fancy this guy but I knew if I were stoned I'd be more keen.

I was more keen. He let me suck his 'famed' big dick and I actually talked him into doing the same to me. The trick was making sure you didn't make them cum; once they'd cum you wouldn't have had a chance. 'GAME OVER', says your internal Timezone. So I used to get them close then push their head down on me. They knew then if they wanted any more they'd have to give a bit of what they got.

We both ended up wanking off together. I could tell with Stewart that the sucking thing was a bit of a freak-out for him. He said quietly, afterwards, 'Is it true you have sex with your Dad?' I thought at the time sarcasm was still 'in' with the dickheads at school. 'Sure,' I sneered. 'All the time.' Perhaps the dope made sarcasm sound somehow earnest, perhaps Stewart was a bit dumb. I think, in retrospect, he was but of course his part in the incident was traumatic for him, too.

A couple of days later I experienced considerable discomfort pissing and a sore arse. I asked the matron if I could see the doctor. I didn't really suspect an STD but I thought if it was doctors had some oath or something that meant they had to keep stuff confidential. At that stage I had not experienced the more unpleasant consequences of sex, and I was woefully ignorant when I arrived at the clinic. I also thought the doctor had seemed okay when I'd visited in the past. A sprained ankle doesn't generate the same sort of inquiry as sore bums and infected urinary tracts.

It was gonorrhoea, and I had it in all three places. That filthy piece of Westie trash must have been ripe with it. Stewart also secretly took himself off to the same doctor, who found it in only two of the places. We should have got together and knocked up a story, nutted something out. The doctor at Savant's clinic was not as open-minded as some in Darlinghurst.

I said I got it from a girl, which of course was stupid considering I had it up the arse. Then I said it was another kid at school. 'You've been having anal sex, haven't you?' demanded the doctor. I didn't know whether he could actually tell or whether he was trying to intimidate me into an admission. He got his admission in the end but I ran out of lies to tell. I couldn't think fast enough and I said I didn't want to talk about it, that it was none of his business. I think that in itself was enough for him to start speculating about sexual abuse. Stewart told the whole story, however, and denied emphatically having fucked me. This left the question, Who did? Stewart probably said something like 'Kids at school reckon he has sex with his Dad', or 'He told me himself he has sex with his Dad', or some shit. Everything got very cloak-and-dagger after that. I didn't find out all the stuff until we were in court.

The doctor contacted my doctor, Shamash's friend Andrew, and discussed the issue with him. Andrew would probably never have been implicated in this whole thing had not one other unfortunate incident occurred. That same week, Shamash had acquired, coincidentally and without any contact with me, the very same complaint. He had gone to Andrew for treatment.

When I went home next weekend Shamash was very cool: 'We need to give it a rest Kiddo, for a little while.' We were both playing the same game. Andrew never told Shamash about me, and he didn't tell the doctor at Savant about Shamash, but all the necessary details were recorded on medical file cards. When required, Shamash's medical records were made available as well as mine. The evidence was all there. As far as the press was concerned, half the gay personalities in the city were allegedly involved in the porn ring. I'd been too vague and indecisive about where I'd contracted my dose of the clap.

Shamash pleaded guilty as years of circumstantial evidence mounted against him. My testimony, short though it was, only made things look more twisted, as though I'd been under some sort of Svengalian influence all those years. I emerged as a cross between Linda Lovelace and Pavlov's dog. 'It's best you say as little as possible,' said Shamash's lawyer.

I talked to Shamash, secretly, on the phone in the two months between the arrest and the arraignment. I stayed at Owen's place when I wasn't at school. Owen's mum was one of three 'temporary carers' who offered to look after me. Thel and David both offered, and I would have preferred either of them, but the court thought Owen's family the least implicated. Owen's mum was pretty spun out, especially since she'd got on alright with Shamash.

He stayed at Shadforth Street on bail until the journalists made it unbearable, until the disgusted neighbours and the empty theatre made it clear to him that Sydney was no longer his. AIDS organisations that he had funded wanted nothing to do with him so he booked into the Sebel under a different name and stayed there until they cottoned on and turfed him out. Down and down he went emotionally. He tried to phone me, but if I didn't answer the phone at Owen's he would just hang up. They suspected him of stalking me.

One Saturday, two weeks prior to the trial, Owen and I said we were going into town. I had managed to speak to Shamash on the Thursday and knew he was at the Hyde Park. I confided to Owen that I was going to see him and that he should wait in the park for me.

'You are so weird, man. If he's been fuckin' you, you should stay away, don't you reckon?'

'You don't understand, Owen. I love him, I'm all he's got.'

'Yeah but if he loved you he wouldn't fuck you, not his own kid. You will have some serious shit in your head after all this Vas, you'll be nutso.'

'Is that what you think, cunt?'

'Hey man, I don't think anything. I always liked your ol' man. I just can't get over all this. How long's he been fucking you? It's gross. Like he's okay looking and that but he's your Dad for Christ's sake. I'd freak if my old man tried it on with me. Barf.'

'I don't want him to go to gaol Owen, but there's nothing I can do. I just want to see him, one last time.'

I guess it was like cinema that meeting, like some tragic war-time romance where the hero was doomed. I suppose I fancied myself as one of those women who was prepared to throw aside conventional morality and fuck him before he died. I thought we could have made love, hugged, cried, held each other desperately. Of course it didn't turn out that way. No last cigarette, no train departing, no parting glances.

I thought how ironic that it was the Hyde Park Plaza again. I went under-cover in one of Owen's baseball caps, the right way around, unlike the way Owen wore them. I couldn't get in the lift fast enough. I got to Shamash's room and he opened the door. He was hideously drunk, his face red and tear-stained. He broke down as soon as he saw me.

'Oh God Vas, what have I done? I just want to die, I'm just going to keep drinking until I do.'

The room was a mess, like some sort of lair, and the do-not-disturb sign had probably been on the door since he arrived.

'I have to plead guilty Vas, there's no way around it. I wish they had the death sentence. I wish I could be hanged.'

'Stop it, stop it,' I wailed through my own sobs. 'I'll testify that I was out of control, that I was a drug addict. I'll say anything that might help.'

He sobered up for a second, though he was swaying. He looked at me with this perplexed expression on his face, this expression of disbelief, of near loathing.

'Are you mad, Vaslav? Johnny? Whoever the fuck you are. It wouldn't make a shit of difference what you said, it wouldn't matter if you said you'd raped me. My life is over, Vas. I'm fucked fucked fucked. I am a piece of living shit, a sarcoma on the face of homosexuality and a blight to father-hood, to man-fucking-kind. Just go, Vas, and try to have a life for my sake. I'm over talking now, I'm drinking to try and get over thinking.'

I tried to hold him but he sort of shook me away.

'No Vas, no cuddles, no more, no more love, no more sex, no more no more.'

And he collapsed and wept as if he might, at any moment, die. He let me hold him then and we both cried and cried until there was a bash at the door.

'We believe the boy is in danger being here Mr Usher. You know a restraining order has been issued against you and you are currently forbidden from having any contact with your son. If anything like this happens again we'll have to take the boy into protective custody and you will no longer be eligible for bail. Do you understand?'

Shamash was still weeping, but sort of laughed. 'Yes

officer, I forgot how dangerous I was, how frightening to young boys, how vile.'

One of the hotel staff had come to investigate and called the police. Of course Shamash was kicked out of there as well after that incident. He ended up somewhere in the Blue Mountains, Leura I think, in a motel. Somewhere he wasn't recognised, somewhere to stay until the trial.

The police took Owen and me back to his place but not before some journo, who had somehow found out about the incident, snapped my picture as I left the hotel with the cops. Everyone knows that photo – my face all blotchy and agro, my fingers doing the 'get fucked' gesture. That picture won some fucking award, ended up on a CD cover for a band I hate, on the cover of a book about child abuse. You can plaster it wherever you like as long as you pay the newspaper for the rights. It made some cunt famous and became my nemesis. These days David tries to make light of it, calls it my 'Jackie O', but I can't make light of that picture even now because that day was, perhaps, the worst day of my life.

Thelly had to reveal things in court that broke her heart. She wasn't up to the fierce questioning she underwent:

'So Mrs Dawson, you never thought it strange that Vaslav continued to sleep with his father, continued to sleep with him even as a teenager?'

'They were very fond of each other. There was quite a bit of tragedy in their pasts.'

'But even so Mrs Dawson, a 15-year-old boy being taken out of school to go abroad each year. Would you have done

181

that with your children at that age?'

'If I'd had the money I dare say I would have.'

I don't think Thel understood. She certainly hadn't known Shamash and I were lovers, but I could see from her face that once she realised he had been 'doing the nasty' with me, she tried to sound as if even that was forgivable. If anyone was to be really disgusted she was the one I could most easily have forgiven, but she wasn't. She knew there was something wrong with the case. She also knew something else.

It got worse and worse for Thel. She said I'd always seemed like I was going to be gay, that I was 'theatrical' like my father. No matter what she said it seemed worse for Shamash. In court he just sat, ashen-faced. He looked so miserable; I watched him thinking he would die from his broken heart. He wouldn't look at me in the courtroom.

Shamash confessed that he had sodomised his own son – he would have pleaded guilty to mass murder by that stage. On the final day he said, 'I'd like to explain something ... no ... there is no point ... it's a monstrous crime.' As he said this he finally looked at me.

B U S H E D

Shamash rang me today. He sounded out of it.

'Hey Vas, remember that night we went to The Fridge in Brixton? Remember how they weren't going to let you in, they didn't think you were 18?'

'Well I wasn't. You said I was a dancer from the company and all "your" dancers were over 18.'

'And that guy at the door said if we were really dancers we should give them a show, and they called other bouncers over to watch, and I said we'd do something from *Hatstand & Codpiece* direct from Adelaide.'

'Direct from Ada-where?' the bouncer had said. I laughed. 'And I got to play the hatstand 'cos I couldn't dance.'

'You could dance, you just never tried. Remember that Celtic proverb I had? *Never give a sword to a man who cannot dance.*'

The line went quiet, and I finally spoke.

'Shamash, do you think things will be alright one day?'
He didn't answer for a long time.

'I don't know, Hon.'

'I still love you for what it's worth. You know David and I will be here for you – Shamash, I'm writing about it all.'

'You're writing a book?'

'I'm sort of just doing it for myself at the moment. Brigitte reckons it would be worth a lot of money to publish.'

'I suppose it would. You should write a book.'

'I could just sell the story to *Who*.'

'Jesus, don't do that. We get that in here.'

'Alright, I'll write a book about it. Maybe when you come out we can launch it?'

'It's not going to take that long to write is it?'

'You'll be out soon.'

'Don't hold your breath. Please not *Who*, whatever you do. Write a book. Or is it the money? You want more money? I'll talk to the solicitor.'

'I don't want more money, I'll write a book instead.'

'Yeah Vas, a book's better. You just stick at it hey and write something thorough. Maybe you can show me first. I don't like what those magazines do. Hey I gotta go, someone's hassling me to use the phone. Maybe you'll come and see me soon?'

'You want me to?'

'Yeah, soon.'

Shamash is 38 now, and if he's lucky he might get out after his 40th birthday, but I've been told not to count on it. He might have to wait until he's 45. He already looks that old anyway, in his face at least. His body he keeps up, he can work out; I think that's the only interest he has anymore. Even that he does out of habit, out of some sort of mechanical need to affirm to himself that he is in fact still alive. I suspect he's on drugs, too. Apparently they get smack in there. I suppose if I were Shamash, if I had as much future as he sees himself as having, I'd be on it too. Smack is perfect, perfect for when there's nothing else. I amaze myself that I haven't dabbled more than once or twice. I've always wondered if I were one of those babies born addicted to the stuff, but I suppose Mum probably didn't get on to it until after she had me.

I rang Owen. Said I wanted to go out drinking. I had the money. There are times when a boy needs to go on a bender, and this was one of them. Owen had been bonking this feral dude called Riz so he dragged him along as well. Riz is the kind of guy who really fucks me off. He's the type of self-professed radical who walks into cafes or bars and picks up people's mobile phones and pretends to talk on them. It was really embarrassing and not the sort of crap I felt like going through. He'd pick them up and say, 'Hello, I'm a big fat capitalist wanker and you're speaking to me on my penis extension.'

Needless to say, the dudes who sit with their phones on the table don't like that sort of thing. They also don't have any respect for dickheads like Riz. We should have gone to Newtown where people still use phone boxes. We mightn't have got kicked out of two cafes that way. I was the one buying their drinks. Owen kept pretending it was cool and funny, the way Riz was going on, but Owen comes from a wealthy family, too. While Riz was taking a piss I said to him, 'The only reason you can afford to slum it is because your folks are loaded. That guy's a dickhead.'

'Well at least he doesn't wax himself and sip cocktails like a girl.'

'He couldn't afford cocktails unless I bought 'em for him – he's fucked, he's a tosspot.'

'Yeah right Mr Together Fuckin' Dude. Excuse me while I just go home and root my old man.'

I walloped him across the face, sort of a slap more than a punch. I knew I was going to punch him up or burst into tears so I ran off, leaving them with a bill to pay, which I knew they couldn't afford. I felt really crappy and thought all I can do is write a fucking book. That's all I've got, that and a bunch of stupid airhead friends who think my childhood is just some elaborate plot device.

About half an hour later Owen turned up with flowers he had stolen from the supermarket around the corner. He sort of hugged me and said sorry. The two of us sat around drinking what was left of some vodka I had in the freezer and smoking dope. We played the mind game we used to do at school called Cardiac Arrest. We would try to talk each other into believing our hearts were slowing down. It used to freak us out when we were stoned. I told him about Mandy and the 'night wog', and Estelle and Macca's reaction.

'That Estelle, she's a fruitcake man, she's like one of those babies born without a brain.'

I sniggered, 'I s'pose she got *Marie Claire* instead.'

'I'd rather my own brain thanks. I wouldn't count on ol' Macca to save the world.'

'Well we're hardly going to save it ourselves, are we,' I muttered into the stinky old bong.

'We're not here to do that, leave that to the mobile phone dudes and dudesses.'

'Maybe them saving the world is like Shamash saving me.'

'How'd he ever save you? he got you in deep shit.'

I didn't answer.

We listened to Stone Roses and it was just like old times. As Owen lay there he said, 'You know, when we were at school and I'd come over to your place I used to think about your Dad, like for sex, I reckon I would'a done it with him.'

'Owen, I guess there are a few things you should know. Number one, he's not really my Dad.'

Owen looked at me in disbelief. 'Whadaya mean?'

And off I went again.

After the court case I lived at Thelly's until school went back. David was deemed an inappropriate guardian and Rosie was relieved at Thel's offer. I was, too. It meant I could go and live in Homebush where I wasn't such a 'celebrity'. I wasn't allowed to see Shamash until I was 18 but I was virtually compelled to see the shrink; even Thel thought it was a good idea. He was like a vulture that man, slick, clever and utterly depraved. When he gave me the tranquillisers, when Johnny emerged to protect Vas from having to expose himself emotionally to the doc, well it was on for young and old. When I told him of my sexual exploits, of my infamous libido, when I told him these things the way Johnny would see them, as lascivious tales to drool over, as phone sex, as 'come on, don't you want to play with those young sticky bits that have been up for grabs for years', when I did that, his Freud and Jung seemed to fly out the window.

Gradually the style of therapy changed too; it became more sedated and more tactile. I didn't even care at the time. I laughed at how perverse this whole arena of behaviour was. It seemed impossible to me that something like that could happen. I guess then I thought, 'Just do what they want, try to enjoy it, be a blameless whore. I couldn't tell Thel about it. I didn't want her to be any more upset than she had been. Besides the easiest thing for me to do was just have sex with people when they required it. I found it easier to have the sex than not to. I still find it easier to have sex than not to, but it is on my terms these days.

When the holidays ended I was supposed to go back to school, this time the local school. I told Thel I didn't want to and she said she couldn't make me. I told her I was going to find a job somewhere, eventually. David had power of attorney for Shamash, which really pissed Rosie off. He was ordered to provide for me from the rent on Shadforth Street. There were provisions made for university, but that never came about; I've already pissed that money up against the wall. I've always had any money I needed. I try not to take very much, just what's required for this dive. I do work when there's a show on. I guess I liked being over in Homebush for a while. Thel went and worked at some gift shop in

Burwood after we left Paddington. She never minded me just hanging around watching vids and getting stoned. She'd nudge me a bit: 'Vas, why don't you get a job a couple of days a week? I'll talk to Dorothea at the shop if you like. She needs someone to unpack stock.'

'I'm not working in some old lady's gift shop.'

'Well a cafe. Go up to Newtown, there's lots of cafes opening up there. Dianne's always on about them.'

After a while I got bored with dope and 'therapy'. I caught the train into Newtown and went into this groovy-looking cafe called Vesuvius on the off-chance. They gave me a job washing dishes straight off. I got into a bit of a scene down there; it was alright. People in Newtown are more laid back. On this side of town people give you about two seconds of smiles and eye contact; they can work out if you're worth their time in less than that. In Newtown they've got a bit more time for you.

Thel had been great but I started to realise I could do whatever I wanted, even move out if I felt like it. She had her film nights and leagues club dos and I wanted more inner-city action. The law had finished with me, processed me, and Shamash was really the only person who had ever given a stuff about me being educated. I'd never put much stock in it myself.

I moved into a share house with all these hippies and neo-punks. I wasn't into all their radical politics but when you're in a house like that you just agree with stuff and have another bong. I think it was my dope they were usually more interested in than their anarchism and revolution, anyway. They were all older than I was.

I ended up waiting at Vesuvius; it was going okay. I'd been there about six months when they accused me of stealing 10 dollars from the tips. It was fucking outrageous. I never stole that money; if I'd wanted money I could have got it easily, I even offered to give them 10 dollars if they wouldn't believe me but they sacked me. Gareth the arsehole manager then went and employed his best friend. I think that was when I really had a breakdown. It was so awful. I just felt like a little kid again, a kid with no Mum or Dad or anything. I walked all the way along King Street crying and shaking. I couldn't stop and people all stared at me. I felt like throwing myself under a bus or something. Destiny, this Goth chick from our share house was coming the other way. She put her arm around me and took me home but it was no good. I felt like I would be depressed forever, like I needed to be put in some sort of home, an asylum or something.

That was when I started really getting into the tranquillisers. I rang David and asked if I could come and stay. He agreed and I packed my bags and came 'home', wherever that was.

The depression continued for months. That was when I tried to top myself. That's when David saved me. I'd have killed myself by now if it weren't for him. It makes you wonder about a psychiatrist who prescribes 'minor tranquilisers' to an 18-year-old who has just been legally orphaned by the authorities, who was clearly quite traumatised by the whole scenario. David was supposed to be away in Melbourne for two days but he came back early and found me.

It's strange but when I took all those pills it didn't seem cataclysmic; I just felt sad and tired. I couldn't see anywhere to go and because he saved me I feel guilty now about what I put him through as well. I didn't want to do that and Shamash, what would my suicide have done to him? I can't think about that; I feel so ashamed now. It becomes apparent that life's not through with me yet, that I, good, bad, responsible or not, am here to stay, for a while at least.

And that brings me to here, where I've been ever since. Near agoraphobic in a three-room flat in Darlinghurst, which is the exact same situation my mother had at the same age. I've come full circle. Even platform shoes are back in. I hear that haunting clomp outside my window, and I think of all the fresh whores out there. All the whores with weighted feet clomping their way to ruin. I think how lucky I am that I'm not dependent on the slickness, the tightness, the currency of my own arsehole to keep me in food and shelter. I don't have to suck old codgers' cocks or give myself injections twice a day. I have been provided for. I am a kept boy. I am a lucky boy.

three

N E W S

Sydney's arts community today mourns the passing of one of its great performers and entrepreneurs, Martin Calvin Usher. The former Director of Potts En Pointe Dance Company and a highly publicised spokesperson for the Sydney gay community died yesterday in the Goldstone Detention Centre.

Prison spokesman Mr Arthur Pembroke said a full investigation of the death would be undertaken, though at this stage there appears to be no suspicious circumstances. In a statement issued to the police last night he concluded by saying, 'Mr Usher had been suffering severe bouts of depression for some months prior to his death and had already withdrawn himself from most prison activities. He was a gentle and popular prisoner with staff here, we are all very shocked and saddened by his sudden death.' Prison officials have decided no further statements will be issued until the

coroner's inquest has been completed and, if necessary, a
hearing surrounding the incident has concluded.

The Usher family have chosen to hold a private funeral
ceremony at an undisclosed church and no statements from
family members have been made at this stage. Martin Usher
will be remembered for his generosity and artistic vision. His
annual KICK-BACK *benefits raised in excess of $700,000 for*
AIDS *charities throughout the 1980s. It is hoped his memory*
will live on through many more performances at Sydney's
much loved Wylde Street Theatre.

Usher's business partner and artistic collaborator, David
Bergdorf, said from the steps of his Elizabeth Bay home, 'We
were the dearest of friends for nearly twenty years. It was the
press who conspired to destroy him three years ago, so I don't
care to dignify any of you with tales and sentiment now.'
Fighting back tears he added, 'I believe in the fullness of time
the people of Sydney will come to understand Martin Usher
the man and truly mourn his tragic and premature demise.
He was a fine man in spite of all the events that culminated
to have him seen as otherwise. That is all I have to say.'

PORT JACKSON DAILY   14/11/94

I don't move from the floor. An exotic-looking arts journo
on the ABC is standing outside the Wylde Street Theatre
looking towards Woolloomooloo. The Bridge and the Opera
House can be seen in the distance. She's talking about Sydney's artistic past, its scandals and misunderstandings.

She had just finished going on about some witch called
Rosaleen Norton whose paintings were banned because they
thought she was a devil worshipper when in fact she was a

pagan and her depictions were of Pan not Beelzebub. She talked about Brett Whiteley's heroin addiction and showed footage of Wendy Whiteley being arrested at customs for drugs or something. Then it was some Danish architect who designed the Opera House and got shitty with the builders because they cut back on the budget for the project and he pissed off back to Denmark. The program's called *Artributes* and the story of Shamash was to be tonight's 'feature':

> *It has been suggested that under current funding legislation, a company like Potts En Pointe would have an uphill battle establishing themselves today. When Martin Usher and David Bergdorf first joined forces, they had plenty of obstacles in their path but as this interview from TDT in June 1981 shows, they were not going to be put off easily.*

They were in flouncy dinner shirts and Shamash looked as if he had eyeliner on; they looked more like Spandau Ballet than entrepreneurs negotiating funding and council permits. Their hair was gelled, their suits expensive and elaborately cut. It was just a few months before he had gone to England to get me. Shamash was first to speak.

> *We have already seen the Woolloomooloo council getting 'matey' with developers. Permits have been consistently granted for enterprises with far less community support than ours. Council has barely stopped short of totally destroying the entire suburb. It has even been suggested people have been done away with so development proposals can proceed unhampered. We're merely trying to get a small liquor licence*

to serve drinks at interval and prior to shows. (A cute, mischievous-looking David butts in. He had a lot more hair then.)

It is quite likely after the Juanita Nielson affair our lives are in danger for coming on this show. (They laugh momentarily, then it was back to the journo.)

Well it wasn't all laughs for Usher and Bergdorf. As the eighties progressed the Sydney gay community felt the full impact of the worsening AIDS crisis. Usher also lost both his parents in the notorious Millionaire's Club flight bound for Antarctica. It was only through the pair's tenacity and innovation that Sydney's leading contemporary dance company weathered the storms of what theatre critic Felicity Duplaix describes as 'the dynamic and unforgiving arena of performance art'.

Usher's life was fraught with tragedy and as one of the country's biggest media scandals was brewing, silently, behind the closed doors of his magnificent Paddington home, the shows just seemed to get bigger and better. (The journo started talking to Felicity Duplaix, leading art critic and editor of *Stage d'Or* magazine.)

As a dancer Martin was one of our best. I saw a great many of his shows here in Sydney and abroad, and the Wylde Street Theatre is the best space in Sydney for contemporary dance of the Potts calibre. I think much of Usher's torment was evident in his dance, and excellence perhaps needs a broader moral meadow, as it were, to manifest itself in. There was a savagery and anarchy in Martin's movement that I haven't seen since on the Australian stage. His other great skills of course were choreography and management. Very few

people had his capacity for fundraising. He was an extraor-
dinary figure, a very kind and generous man. I, like most of
Sydney's arts community, am deeply saddened by his death.

'He never liked you much Flis,' I mumbled to myself. 'Felicity
Duplicity he used to call you. He'd read your editorial *Screen
d'Or* to David in that husky plummy voice.' I started to cry
again.

I tuned out, digesting words until they became abstract
sounds without meaning, floating around in my head –
'brewing behind closed doors'. The telly was skipping from
snippets of different shows to Mardi Gras to David and
Shamash getting a Premier's Award in 1989. Then the camera
followed them back to our table in the Darling Harbour Convention Centre where I was sitting next to Ashley, both of
us kissing both of them.

The camera focused on me kissing Shamash. Then they
froze it and zoomed in. The footage wasn't brilliant quality
to start with so the more they tried to zoom in, the more
pixilated and disturbing the image became. It was as if they
were giving the audience the chance to search my face for
any signs of the corruption that was already 'brewing behind
closed doors'. Even I was looking for signs by the time they
suddenly shattered the still as if it were a family photo that
had been carelessly knocked from its pride of place on the
sideboard. I got a fright when they did it. At the same time
someone kicked my front door, yelling some incomprehen-
sible abuse. I froze where I was, watching the TV version of
my life flash before my eyes. I couldn't turn it off, even
though I knew it would upset me. Now the journalist was

standing outside Goldstone, her red lipstick and trendy clothes completely out of place in that shit hole.

Usher pleaded guilty to four of the charges brought against him and for the last three years this austere penitentiary in Sydney's outer western suburbs has been his sole place of residence. A sombre reminder of one of society's most feared and least tolerated offences. Many questions remain unanswered about the extent to which Vaslav Usher was abused by his father, and allegations of child pornography rings headed by Martin Usher have proven to be largely unfounded.

Questions surrounding the age of consent for homosexuals recur from time to time in the press but one thing is for sure, incest remains taboo and childhood sexual abuse the last frontier of moral transgression. (Suddenly the journalist was in Oxford Street, surrounded by trendies just like herself.) *Here, in Oxford Street, site of the world-famous Sydney Gay and Lesbian Mardi Gras, attitudes seem to be a little more relaxed. In fact several family law specialists say that in cases like that of Martin and Vaslav Usher, there are a number of possible solutions.* (She turned to a smartly dressed lawyer who got to say his bit.)

In a less public case there may have been the possibility of a reconciliation between Usher and his son. The real damage in a scenario like that one was the public nature of the case. Many families have hidden dynamics that aren't easily explained and often fall foul of the law. Where we can we attempt to work with those families. There is often an opportunity to repair or at least reconcile some aspects of the damage that has been done.

The reality is, with many crimes of this nature, the only chance to minimise the damage caused, is through discreet, unpublicised counselling and privately mediated discussions between the parties involved. Neither Usher nor his son were given the remotest opportunity to achieve this; in fact, after Martin Usher's conviction, Vaslav was not even allowed to see his father until he was 18. Needless to say I think it will be a long while before the press are likely to have any concern for the lives they meddle in when it comes to issues as inflammatory as paedophilia and incest. I think the climate of moral panic is far too hot at the moment to let anyone off the hook, and if the press really did have humanitarian concerns for the victims of crime they wouldn't have subjected Vaslav to what they did. (The lawyer looked back to her. She was smiling and nodding in a way that tells us she would never be one of those journalists. We cut to Taylor Square.)

Usher's friends and family have declined to appear, but those who know Vaslav Usher say he is deeply grieved by the loss of his father.

Then 'they' came on and I felt a wave of betrayal and loathing. Those two witches, sitting outside Cafe 191 wearing something halfway between mourning and bondage. Estelle had been pushed into the background as usual by Marie Claire (fuck her italics, the bitch can go without). She looked at the camera.

We haven't known Vas for that long, maybe six months. He's a very sensitive and kind guy but you can always see that hurt – the hurt from what happened to him. We don't know his father but he was still very fond of him. I think they had a bond that challenged even the expanding definition of 'queer', it certainly went beyond the bourgeois sentiments of most current affairs shows, if you know what I mean. (The journo was nodding like she did know what Marie Claire meant.) *It's very hard to establish yourself as a performer when you're gay or lesbian. Estelle and I have both learnt that as performance artists there are a lot of people who can't see past the moral paradigm established by American sitcoms and as Thespian lesbians of the millennium we think that sucks.*

Estelle started to make a sucking sound in the grim residue of her drink and the camera honed in on the straw vacuuming up the murky sludge from some unidentifiable fruit juice. It seemed mine and Martin's life had just been gurgled up a straw into Estelle's mouth. The camera cut back from the journo to the presenter.

Goodbye Martin Usher and hello to the Thespian lesbians of the millennium. To just what extent does art redefine morality? Is it ethically legitimate to reflect on varying forms of moral reality through performative expression? Next week we delve into the sticky questions that surround that very issue in Artributes.

I just lay there exhausted. I bet those girls conned the ABC into getting onto that show. I wished they'd been cut; those idiotic bitches will do anything for attention. Brigitte called and said come over, come and stay for a few days.

I still can't let myself accept the death and how horrible it was. Shamash's death has been accepted as a suicide by the prison but nasty questions surround this 'suicide'. The biggest and most horrific being the fact that something had been inserted into him, anally. If it hadn't been for a careless statement by the coroner when David and I went to see the body, this fact would have been suppressed, too.

Shamash wouldn't do something like that; he wouldn't stick a bottle of fucking hair conditioner up himself and then hang himself. Who for Christ's sake would? David had to give me sedatives when he got me home; I was sick with grief and anger.

I don't mind crying in front of Brigitte. She knows exactly the sort of guilt and fear I'm suffering:

'Yes Darl, horror is real but it's not real for Martin anymore. All the horror is over and done with for him now, and Sweetie you can't take all of this onto yourself. You can't be the one to carry all his guilt as well as your own for the rest of your life. It seems you've had more than your share in this life Darling Heart but that's what life is for. It's a forum for horror, it's a play where we get to explore every type of dynamic and deceit; There is no hell Vas, this is it. You are in hell now and gradually you will rise up out of it. You've got to do that for your Mum who never had the chance, for Martin who loved you and for me and David and Thel.

You see, Darl, we're all just a house of cards really, and

if we fall down we take everyone else with us. You forgive Martin, he forgives you; no one else matters. The law might judge us but I doubt God does, he leaves us to our own devices down here. It's us that have to forgive each other and in that sense we get to play the role of God too. Think of being old and having such a past that you'll be notable as well as notorious – that wicked Vaslav Usher, heir to Sydney's most decadent Bohemian fortune. You'll be more famous than Rosaleen Norton.

You see we need darker heroes, too, Vas. People probably admire them the most secretly. You should aestheticise your life just like your Shamash did with his. The apple's only half-eaten – take another bite, Darl.

PETHIDINE

'Grief and death were born of sin, and devour sin,' Brigitte tells me. It's a quote from St John Chrysostom. She always goes and gets someone else to back her up, even if it's someone who's been dead for five hundred years.

I wonder if anyone has any idea what it would be like being in my situation. I suppose some do. Betrayal is infinite and sin is as random in its selection of perpetrators as HIV is in its selection of infectees. I am a total mess. I feel like the focal point in some vast cosmic enactment of an ancient moral tale that has come to rest. It's as though I'm living out some perpetual myth or scriptural illustration, but I know fuck-all about Scripture and I don't have Brigitte's interpretive skills. Fuck your way out of this one Johnny boy.

I wonder if I should listen to Brigitte. I don't know if she has real messages from the other side – from through that glass that is so dark now it's black. I used to try to visualise it while I was in the bath or stoned. I could see glimmers of movement through the steamed-up mirror or the translucent shower screen. Brigitte taught me that by focusing on things, using the other side of my brain, I could see glimpses of the 'other side'. It seemed to be true, too.

For a while I saw flickers, shadows – possibilities. I couldn't identify them or make them out clearly the way Brigitte does, but it did seem like there was something to the idea. Now I feel locked into myself, forced into some human dimension in which I must endure mental and physical agony for some period of time I know will be longer than I can bear. That's why I've been rocking myself for so long, hugging the pillow. And then it comes again like an attack. The thought of Shamash having to go through whatever it was someone made him go through. And I can't stand to think of a group of them pushing that bottle into him and then making him hang himself. I can't stand thinking about how scared he would have been, how much pain he endured and the dignity he lost. It's like a scenario I have to go through time and time again, each time weeping and rocking; it's like sickness or a fit, imagining his face. Him crying, screaming. Going through his greatest horror some-where else, without me. Like I would have been any help anyway – dream on, Vaslav.

Maybe he was over me. Maybe I'd exhausted him, taken his will away. He may have wondered how he would ever get rid of me, like I was a really bad mistake he made. I was a bad mistake for him. He never got enough good out of me in thirteen years. That's how many years it was when he died. I wonder if I'm some sort of beast. I don't want to be.

Brigitte tries to 'talk me back', tell me I'm loved. But I don't know whether it's true. I don't know who could love me. No one loves you if you don't love yourself, any fool knows that. If I survive all this I wonder what use I'll be to anyone. That's what I keep thinking: What use am I? What good am I? Who will really want me and how?

I feel like I've been born into a nightmare. I see myself as a 7-year-old on Victoria Station, hoping my Mum will wake up. Knowing she won't. Knowing something bad, feeling the weight of my life get heavier and heavier. I never meant to hurt anyone, really I didn't. Ashley hurt me. He shouldn't have messed with me. He should have left me alone even if he saw what I was like. It's like all these people have got inside me and messed around with bits of me and now I don't work properly anymore. Like I'm a person who's not quite right in the head. Then, when I think that, I get really scared because I think I don't have a chance like other people.

And that Johnny is not worth the council estate he slouches about in. He says stuff like 'It's just you and me mate against all 'vem uver cunts', but he's not real and he hasn't done me any good so far. I have to try to believe Brigitte 'cos even if she's wrong she's older. She knows more than me and maybe she is the extra help I need. I guess I love her, too. Right now I need a Valium even though I shouldn't have them with Prozac. Like I give a damn. I am deeply fucked.

We will have the funeral tomorrow at some Anglican church in Mosman. Rosie reckons it's the family church but I can't remember ever going there. I won't argue with her; I can't face her at all. David has organised it with her and I am very scared about going. Shit scared. I want to disappear but I'm not well enough mentally or physically to go anywhere yet. I wish I could just die. Everything is all broken and messy and is fermenting inside my head. Vaslav, Vaslav who is he? Everything's not alright, everything's not fine and I'm not going to sleep well for a very long time.

Miss Ann Thrope's column of Sydney smut

Miss Snitch-I'm a bitch has been down on all fours and had her ear to the ground puntresses, and no, I'm not on my knees to suck cock this time sluts. Well it's a jungle out there at the moment and not a very happy one since Martin Usher died. He was a hunk alright but never did this Miss have the exquisite pleasure of doing a pas de dirt with him. Not like sonny boy, the terror of the Toolshed and the Queen of King's, not even a taxi to Kensington for that one but we must forgive the urgency of youth. In fact he's a bit of a dish himself and a touch more trashy than his Pa. He likes to party just like Dad, perhaps me luck'll change with baby-boy. Usher in the second generation!

Well goss' is that maybe it wasn't suicide like they said. Maybe he was 'done in'. (Please don't cut this Mr Editor, I'm a poor piece o' filth trying to eke out a living in this festering town and any publicity is better than no publicity. I'll battle it out in the courts for the rag – promise!) Well nasties in the pris' comes as no surprise to Miss who's had a vis' herself, and what a sore girl she was après-pris'. 'Know thy enemy'

brothers and sisters, it's still out there and I wouldn't be at
all surprised if we've got a bit of an aboriginal-death-in-
custody if you know what I mean Luvvies.

Messy biz the Usher one and hard to imagine the town
without him but he'll be another candle at the vigil for Miss
Ann Thrope. He was the one who signed the cheque for the
halfway house for girls like myself who arrive from the cunt-
ry with nowt but their arses to pedal. If I were a Sister of
Perpetual Indulgence I'd be thinking about a canonisation for
Mr Usher.

Oh and sit tight you loose-boxed slags, six more ep's of
Ab Fab are on their way next year, let's hope they don't
overlap with Melrose. *I hear that cunt Kimberley's got some-*
thing very nasty up her snatch for next week. I love me Tues-
days, they're a bitch just like me. Kiss Kiss, you're all vile
but I love ya's.

CITY RHYTHM   18/11/94

My phone has gone berserk this week and I have a silent
number. People I haven't spoken to in ages are ringing and
leaving messages. Sherry Brown from Q.U.I.M. has been
talking to both Brigitte and me. Shamash's death has raised
the stakes on everything. She says *Who* have offered 25,000
dollars, and she thinks we can hold out for 32,500. Sherry
seems to be sympathetic, asking me will I be up to it. How
would I know?

'It's going to mean photos Hon, and probably a whole
afternoon of talking. It'll be heavy shit but if you sell them
an exclusive now you can still write your book when everything has died down. They want to use that photo of you

giving the photographers the finger on the cover – you know, the one that won that AJA award.' I said no, if they want a photo it has to be a recent one. I hate that photo; I never want to see it again.

I went to the doctor to get more sleeping pills. There was a woman in there drinking a cask of moselle. Her face was crimson, contorted from years of drinking. I've seen her on Oxford Street many times. I used to even say hi to her but she's gotten so bad these days I don't think she passes the time with anyone anymore. She was just sitting there moaning. Occasionally she'd say, 'I just want me Pethidine or some Panedeine Forte.' Suddenly Oprah came on the TV and she was entranced, hypnotised. There was Oprah on three monitors along the wall; this woman walked up to the TV as if it were really Oprah in the flesh. 'It's me, Oprah. I come in to see ya, Love. You black like me.'

She was rocking back and forth just at the sight of her, as if Oprah were a lullaby to the destitute, a modern Messiah. She spilt a bit of her drink and the receptionist said, 'Shirl you'll have to sit down and behave yourself if you want to watch TV.' This seemed to set her off, interrupting her audience with the omnipotent. She looked back to where she had been sitting and saw an Asian girl in the next chair. She started yelling, delivering a sermon of damnation to everyone in the room.

'I tell you who gets all the money in this country, filthy fuckin' Asian slags. My people get nuthin', it's you cunts, you dirty bitches get everything.'

The receptionist was getting distressed but managed to say, 'Shirl I think it's time to go.'

The receptionist is a Greek girl, even at Shirl's level of inebriation she could ascertain that much. 'Filthy, ugly Greek whore, ugly fuckin' dago scum all of yous, ugliest fuckers in the world . . .'

She was turning, revolving as she ranted, in a rapture of abuse.

The receptionist was at a loss about what to do, not one of the waiting patients was going to say a thing. Shirl was exulted, oblivious to the urine that darkened her tracksuit pants. She was heading towards the closed doors of the doctor's rooms.

'I come for me Pethidine. I just come for me script, you bloody doctors got jobs, I know where all the money in this country goes, to you cunts . . .'

All the doctors were gradually coming out of their rooms, patiently telling her it was time to go. Everyone in the room was pretending to read magazines, safe sex brochures, even their own Medicare cards in order not to look at her. Everyone was ashamed and I could hardly stop myself from crying. I'd been so scared to go out anyway, and then this!

I had to leave; I couldn't even bear waiting to see the doctor so I'd have to just take Brigitte's valerian tablets which is something akin to taking an aspirin for a brain tumour. I was sure I was in hell, which only made me wonder what horrors had befallen that Aboriginal woman. For a moment, in the midst of her tirade, I almost felt a part of it. I imagined dancing with her as we showered the waiting room with tears, urine, racial abuse and cask wine. I realised she, like me, really only hated one person. Herself. It seemed there was no God but Oprah, no refuge but the bottle or the script and heaven was merely phosphorus luminations, trapped beyond the glass of the television screen.

I spoke to Owen today. 'Oh, man, this is serious shit your ol' man dying – fucking heavy nightmare shit. Hey Vas I'm really sorry about what I said back then, you know, about you being fucked in the head from all that stuff. I never meant that dude, you know what I'm saying?'

I almost laughed for the first time since fuck knows when. Today was turning into a carnival of irony and horror.

'Owen,' I said, 'you were right when you said it. I do have serious shit in my head – my head is exploding from all the serious shit that's packed in there.'

'Hey Vas, you're not going to check out are you, like after that Newtown business?'

'Check out?'

'You know man, Kurt Cobain style, better to burn out man not fuck out.'

'Owen, I don't know what I'm gonna do, one minute I want to kill myself the next minute I'm thinking about the 30K I might get for the story. If I can get that much I'll just piss off out of Australia.'

'Just don't do anything stupid.'

'Owen, we've always done stupid things, we've chosen the most stupid and irresponsible paths since we were kids. I, like you, have consistently had no control over doing stupid things – that's why we're friends isn't it?'

He laughed this sort of Beavis and Butthead laugh. 'Oh yeah, I forgot. Hey I saw Estelle and *Marie Claire* yesterday, I told 'em where the church was for the funeral.'

'Fuck, you didn't.'

'I thought those chicks were your friends.'

'"Those chicks" have been talking to every journo in town who'll listen to them – they don't even know anything, all they want is publicity for that cunt lips show of theirs.'

'They seemed really concerned.'

'Owen, they've been on *Artributes* but they haven't even phoned me yet. Unless they're the ones that kicked in my door and left a human turd on the front steps – a choice fucking gift for the bereaved that was.'

'Did someone do that?'

'Yes, that's why I'm at Brigitte's, because I'm scared.'

'Who'd do that?'

'I don't know. It's probably nothing to do with Shamash, just some Darlo dickheads, but right now I feel really vulnerable.'

The funeral lies in wait for us and I worry about how I'll cope at that. I hope the press haven't found out where it is. David and Rosie have invited only a hundred people but many of them will go back to David's house and I know it is staked out. They haven't got their picture of Vaslav the vampire yet, they don't have the society-family-in-mourning photos and the mags are offering big bucks for some glossies. 'Sydney's Scandalous Socialite Suicide' – I can see it already. They'll print anything if I don't give them something soon.

I sat with Brigitte in her lounge room while she played this really mellow Celtic music. She was saying you've got to find somewhere inside yourself that's peaceful. She was lighting candles and burning oils – busy doing what seemed like some ceremonious ritual. Lavinia and Trismegistus (the cats) were rubbing themselves all over me, poking their bums in my face. For a moment I felt like I was under a spell and I saw Shamash as he was, I had this little movie show in my head of him pulling up in that old Volvo of his, parking about a mile out from the curb and running into the Paddo house with arms full of shopping. I saw us on the beach at some indeterminate point in our relationship, just talking. I felt him hugging me after something bad had happened at school, and just as I was doing all this Brigitte said, 'They're the things to hold onto Darl, the good things. You learn from the bad things but you hold on to the good ones.'

I got this bizarre feeling like she knew what I was thinking; it was probably just coincidence or her brilliant intuition. For a moment her whole lounge room seemed to be outside of time and space and I wasn't even stoned. The light from all those candles and lamps fused together into something ethereal; I felt the tiniest sensation of how things could be, how maybe there is a heaven or at least something better than constant bullshit.

'In a way the world isn't even real, it's imagined – a storybook,' she said.

'Yeah, Grimms' Fairytales.'

'Exactly. It's like a school full of children and like in a school, bullies often get the power but even they have their downfall because all fortunes shift. Martin was burned at the stake as surely as those thousands of witches were a few hundred years ago. We can only find the truth in the bones that are left behind Darl. A witch hunt's a witch hunt. People forget they're going to die themselves when they get a bee in their bonnets, they forget they're not already gods and forget about basic things like forgiving. What did Martin ever do to you that couldn't be forgiven by you or anyone else?'

'Nothing,' I said.

I guess it's me I'm worried about. I'm the one who really needs forgiving, and he died without letting me know if I was forgiven. I started to think about Rosie and what she would do when she found out about me not being his son. I wondered if I would still inherit but I figure if I don't get stuff as next of kin I could file a very mean palimony suit. But then I felt guilty thinking that way – money at a time like this.

F O R

S I N C E

I

A M

For since I am
Love's martyr, it might breed idolatry,
If into others' hands these relics came;
As 'twas humility
To afford to it all that a soul can do,
So 'tis some bravery,
That since you would save none of me,
  I bury some of you

John Donne

It was wet and unseasonably cold for the funeral, but the weather was nothing compared to the icy sentiments that surfaced afterwards. I went in one of the mourning cars with

David and Brigitte. She was wearing a purple and gold dress (purple for freedom and gold for the spirit), and with her turban on she looked like Winnie Mandela. I wore this Frontier Aviator suit which David had bought for me. I felt extra strange wearing a suit because I never do. When we got there Owen was wearing a suit, too, one which I have never seen and one I bet he wished he never had. The trousers were too short and it was brown. The fashion victim in me recoiled but the real me was deeply touched by the effort he had made. A whole heap of Potts people were there and then a taxi turned up with Estelle and *Marie Claire*. Just as I would have expected they were in black with veils over their faces, black lipstick and hobnail boots. Estelle had a bunch of trumpet lilies and looked as though she was about to be wedded to death. *Marie Claire* made a beeline for Owen (the only person she knew) and started bitching about not being able to get a bus to this part of Mosman and how they had ended up at the zoo where they had to use some 'breeder's' mobile phone to get a taxi.

'You should have seen him, he gathered the kids around him, he thought we were going to eat them or something. I said in my sweetest voice "Us girls are in a bit of a fix and we need to call a taxi, would you be so kind as to let us use your weeny cancer transmitter?" He said there's a public phone over there and Estelle said – deadpan – "Someone has died and we don't use public phones." That seemed to do it.' Poor Owen, you could tell he didn't want to be associated with them.

Then she came over to me and said she was really sorry,

blah blah blah, and if I needed anything she would be there. I said, 'Yeah, right if it doesn't clash with any of your TV engagements.'

'Oh that, we just overheard that interviewer talking to the lawyer. I thought they might have given a biased view or something so I said we were friends.'

I had sensed the strain between David and Rosie over the last few days; I had opted out of any involvement. David felt that Martin should have his funeral at the Community Church in Darlinghurst. Rosie went so far as to look at it and said it was like a sheltered workshop for people with AIDS: 'He can't have his funeral in a place like that.'

David tried to explain that it was what Shamash would have wanted. He had done work for the mission there and it was his community. According to David, Rosie got impatient and said, 'Where was his community when he was in trouble? I didn't see legions of queens rushing to his defence from the sheltered bloody workshops our parents' money went to run, eckies and frocks is all most of them give two hoots about and then they put up a great bloody fight when they have to have a blood test for insurance. This is a family matter now. Our parents were buried by the vicar at St Oswald's, Martin was christened there and he should be sent off from there.'

David gave in, looked heavenwards and said, 'You'll never escape the North Shore, Shamash. I tried, my Darling.' That seemed to be the start of it all. Rosie looked tired and dour at the funeral. David became increasingly camp. In his speech during the service he employed the word community a number of times; he referred often to Martin's two families, his sister, his parents and his community. There was so much tension something had to give. The vicar skimmed cautiously over the events of the last three years. It was evident by his expression how difficult his whole sermon had been to prepare in a way that appeared impartial on his behalf. David wrote a great eulogy which he read during the service. It had many of us in tears:

For Martin

It is hard to see my friend – how I knew him – in my mind's eye now.

He is still like someone perfect to me but to the world, he has been garbed in filigree layers of shame.

Those who loved him don't see those layers, don't even believe they exist. So I will undress you, Martin, as I did all those years ago and perhaps we will see, once again, your coat of many colours.

I remember you in 76, fresh-faced and firing on all cylinders. Just back from the Academy. How exotic you were, barely 20 and already a much-travelled father. How romantic it all seemed, not so very long ago.

I dream of Shadforth Street, its parties and warmth. I thought you would always be there. It seemed that concrete, that real, but like all the clouds we've pinned our hearts to, it sailed away and is lost from view. We should have cherished it more at the time, laughed more heartily and hugged more closely. We should have known when life was at its best but we dared to hope for more. We were greedy men, greedy for love and for good times. Yet without that greed we'd never have had what we did. I know we'd do it all again.

I thought you'd outlive me; selfishly I hoped you would. You see, we'd already lost half of you – we've already mourned for half of you. We've become used to missing you.

What happened to all the hope? To your generously offered smiles, to your charity – which did begin at home, to your voice on the answering machine and your fingers that would firmly hold the backs of our necks as you planted kisses on us, kisses that felt like they would grow into exotic fruits.

How is it that you came to be so loathed, so attacked by people who never knew you? Why is it that those you were most supposed to have harmed would never have wished you any ill? They never left you, even as the papers tired of you, as the world left you locked away in the too-hard basket. We created a special sad kingdom in our minds, a place in which to try and share some of your horror, carry some of the blame. Perhaps the greatest pain is knowing we were ultimately unable to do that.

We are at sea Shamash, and no one's at the helm. You have carried us, loved us, bedazzled us and we shall doubtlessly sail this ship of fools until we pass over the edge of this flat world. We'll meet you there under the crashing waters of eternity. Perhaps then we will find a kinder justice, a higher mind and a joyous freedom. I am keen to join you if this be the case.

The vicar, to David's surprise, allowed him to play Earth Wind and Fire's 'Fantasy' after the eulogy was read. David had tears running down his face as it played and so did I. It was one of Martin's favourites. He would play it at home from time to time, always trying to reach the high notes at the end. He never could and it was a joke in our place. Both David and I sang, or tried to. A couple of his musical friends joined in as well, wailing the last few bars from the song. I guess it was embarrassing but it just sort of happened. I'm not usually one to sing in public.

Things turned nasty afterwards. Rosie was very distressed. She had no family at all now except her husband. She was having some sort of grief-stricken altercation with David which I couldn't hear, then she came over to where I was standing with Brigitte. I was tensing up but made the effort to say, 'Hi Rosie'. She wasn't coming to pay respects, however. She pulled me away looking very distressed.

'Vaslav, I don't know I'll be able to see you again. Since you came into our family we've had nothing but pain and tragedy. I don't know what you're to blame for and at the moment I don't care, but what I'm left with doesn't feel like a family anymore and if family is such an ill-fated affair I'd do better without it.'

I was speechless. Thel must have heard because she came over. 'Rosie don't, Love. You're very upset and they're not fair things to be saying right now. There are a good many things you don't know my girl, many of which you'll need to keep in touch with Vas to find out. It would break Martin's heart to hear this sort of thing – break his heart, do you hear!' Thel was starting to cry, fishing in her handbag for a tissue. Rosie wandered off in a daze towards her husband.

Brigitte came over and closed her arms around me. We both looked at each other. 'You'll have to forgive that one, Darl. You're both very sad souls right now.' I sniffled and said, 'We never liked each other that much, I never see her anyway – don't want to either.' David looked over and saw tears on my face. He, too, had sensed what Rosie had said. He held up my face in his hands and kissed it. 'Don't listen to her, Vas. She's out of her head, and she is not Shamash. I think deep down she resents him for having been so well loved. Rosie has always tried so hard and Martin did it effortlessly. She doesn't know what she's saying at the moment.'

Rosie left with her husband, even though David tried to get them to his place. It seemed as if she had turned her back on her brother's life. Thelly and Dianne came over. 'You've still got us as family, Vaslav, I want you to know that. You can come and stay with me in Homebush whenever you want.' Thel put her arms around me. 'I'm going to move up to Katoomba soon. Di and I have been looking at houses and we think our offer on one will be accepted. I don't want to live near that Olympic Village when it comes. I'll be too old for all that nonsense. You could come up there to escape Darlinghurst, would you like that?'

'Yes Thelly, I'd like that.'

'I remember how you used to love going up there on that scenic railway, how you would nag your father to take you up there after that time you, Dianne and I had gone. You two loved it but I have no stomach for heights. Martin used to say he never got a moment's peace after that trip. You know I think he might have burned himself out even sooner if he hadn't had you there. It's true Vas, before he brought you back he was far too wild, you calmed him down and made him grow up a lot. You gave him all the respectability he felt he would never have been able to have. His family never really accepted his lifestyle you know. You see, I know more about him and you than you might think. I saw your first passport and I asked Martin a few things, I believe you saved him from a life of melancholy and destructiveness. It's important you see it that way too, Pet. Remember, you're the boy who didn't drown in that crash – so don't drown now.' She winked and I wondered how much Shamash had told her. I would ask her one day soon. She stroked my hair, Dianne gave me a kiss and off they went into the grey North Shore yonder.

The rain began to bucket down, and everything seemed drab. People still stood around with running mascara until finally we headed off to David's. There was no crematorium service and only about thirty people came back. I managed to get rid of Essie and Macca, leaving them gossiping at the bus stop as we cut through the rain in our 'pearl' coloured mourning limo. Estelle had kept one of the trumpet lilies and was rhythmically slapping *Marie Claire*'s face with it. It was annoying her, I could tell. She tore it out of Estelle's hand and threw it into the bushes. As they faded from view I could just see Macca mouthing 'fuck off' to Estelle.

I hid under Shamash's big black coat. I could still smell him in it, I'm sure I could. As we dashed from the car the few photos that were taken would not have shown my face. Inside I began to cheer up for a moment. I almost smiled.

Those cunts weren't going to get another blotchy-faced photo of me. We all got drunk on martinis, not a favourite of mine but quick to work. There seemed to be no other drinks except for Thelly's sherry. David says the one party we'd all like most to attend is our wake. I think what Thel said helped me and so did the drinks.

In the end I asked Owen to come and stay at my place. He was drinking sherry too because the martinis tasted like snake poison to him. I couldn't help taking the piss out of him, Owen, the poo-brown-suited sherry sipper.

'I'll find you something else to wear at my dive.'

'What's wrong with this?'

'A shit-coloured suit that might have fitted you ten years ago? Nothing.'

'You're a cunt, Usher.'

'You're an arsehole, Henley.'

'Glove puppet Usher.'

'Turd-faced Henley.'

We wandered back through Elizabeth Bay, the grown-ups worrying about us. David says I take after my father: 'Three martinis and he's king of the world.'

When we got down the road Owen said, 'Hey dude, you're gunna be rich aren't you?'

'I guess.'

'What'll you do?'

'I dunno, piss off.'

I kicked an empty beer bottle into a waiting styrofoam McDonald's burger box. 'Goal,' I screamed as it hit the wall and splintered into dangerous fragments.

Owen said, 'You need a syringe on either side for points.'

I gave him a dark look. 'You mean for penalties.'

I looked around at all the neon and drizzle; it was like *Blade Runner*. 'That's what I like about inner Sydney. It's a stinking cesspit where no one gives a fuck – there is a constant amnesty on environmentalism and morality here. Shoot, shit and shag where you like. If you don't like this life Owen, you can always get another one. That's what Shamash has done, pissed this joint off. I can feel that he's okay sometimes. Does that sound weird?'

'Yeah, it's weird but I can dig it, he was alright your ol' man.'

'Yeah, I reckon he was alright.'

S P E N D

When my story was printed in the November issue of *ismag* it was their biggest selling edition yet. In the end they offered something like the 30K Q.U.I.M. had been negotiating. Telling the story really was a catharsis for me in a way. The interviewer suspected I was lying; I had to spend two hours going over my abduction in all its detail before she could move on to other things. We did a photo shoot on Brigitte's back balcony – they used one of a sad, ponderous me looking towards Centrepoint as well as some growing-up ones I gave them. According to *ismag*, 'Only the most unscrupulous and immoral of men would eavesdrop on the quiet murmurings of Vaslav's dawning sexuality, seeking to take that which was not yet on offer . . .'

Rosie has been a bit more civil with me since the funeral, allowing me to use a picture of her and me in the article. She was in shock of course, but said she never quite believed

I was Shamash's son. I took that to be a genuine insult but said nothing more about it. Decency got the better of me. I will try to get on with her for Shamash's sake.

The will was easy. I was left the house and a bit of money. Perhaps now that woman who told me I was weird for hanging around and staring at the house might treat me with some respect since I'm her landlord. Everything left for me in the will was left specifically to me. It didn't matter whether I was Shamash's son or not. I sensed that Rosie saw my inheritance as an appalling misplacement of possessions, that I'm somehow not worthy of establishment wealth, but tough for Cosy North Shore Rosie.

No way could I have stayed in Sydney, not with all that publicity at work. I fucked off straight after Christmas and left all the legal matters in David's hands. I'm still abandoning responsibility. Here in Paris I'm enjoying getting tanked up at night on cocaine and Scotch. Warming myself up enough with whisky to face the freezing night outside; coked up enough to negotiate my way socially with the new 'friends' I've met. They're mostly like me – the wrong crowd, transients, Eurotrash, daytime neurotics, night-time in-crowd.

I bought Owen a ticket to come stay with me for a month; I wanted to be with someone I knew for a while. He'll get a real blast living like a king for a spell. I know I should try to save some money but now I have the rent from the house which is $750 a week. David says I should make sure I keep an account for repairs and rates and shit: 'They will be your responsibility now.' Yeah, yeah, I said. A dangerous young man like myself can manage quite well on that much;

besides I'm still living on the magazine money. I bought Brigitte a new computer and she's written to me on it twice already.

I know my way around another little ghetto now, only here I have no past, no scandal. Here I don't mean anything. Here, as long as I pay my hotel bill, as long as *je suis discret* they tolerate me. My money vanishes at an alarming rate; over counters, up my nose and down my throat. At last I feel free to be the slut I was perhaps destined to be. My friend Michel (another gay remittance boy from some province or region I'm unlikely to visit) says *'Mais non, un slut cheri, un courtisane, oui?'*

'Non, un fucking slut.' The French of course don't understand my vulgarity. They don't have to – I won't be troubling them with it for too long.

I told David I'd come back and work at the theatre in April; we both know that I am still good for business even if it's just so people can gawk at me. The trouble is I get nervous, and you can't have coke all the time to give you confidence; we all know where that ends.

I don't seem to really enjoy sex now unless I'm loaded to some extent, but I still have it just the same, more even. I dare say I'll become one of those hard-bitten old queens if I live long enough; even that's in the lap of the gods.

Brigitte said in her first letter, 'I hate to think what you're getting up to over there.' I answered her with, Why don't you come see for yourself Honey Bun? It's just *partie partie partie in Gai Paris pour moi.*

'You just take it easy,' she said in the second. I'm writing to her now to say, 'I do Brigitte, I do.'

She sent me more books – one's called *Manholes to Heaven: Trapdoors to Hell*. I sent her a photo of the catacombs and said, I've already been through the trapdoor. I think she's probably got a different interpretation of what manholes to heaven might mean, and I'm sure she'd find that mine is far too literal.

I have fulfilled one ambition here. I got myself in a porn movie. It wasn't one of Jean Daniel Cadinot's, sadly. He is my favourite pornographer in the whole world. Nor was it as squalid as I'd hoped it might be. My appearance was only a cameo (by cameo I mean I was only fucked once by Bruno Luc, the hero of this *particulaire* tale). I've not seen the finished product but I thought it would be a good addition to my collection of vices. I even thought it could be shrink-wrapped with my book one day – a sort of cross-merchandising Father's Day gift idea. I figure when I get old it'll be good to show the grandkids. Someone else's.

For the film I had to catch a train out to this big old stately home. I was supposed to be a servant boy, and my dialogue was kept to an absolute minimum because my French is so bad. I wore a little bellhop outfit (for a minute), and when they'd done with me they gave me 2000 francs, a vodka and tonic, a line of coke and a limo back into Paris. It wasn't a huge amount of money but at least the film looked classy by porn standards. Also, I stole the bellhop jacket, which looks really cute with my Jean-Paul Gaultier trousers. One thing most people probably don't realise about porn is that some of those camera angles you get require a lot of intrusive manoeuvring. Now I know how women feel when they have to go to a gynaecologist. The French, despite their Catholicism and conservatism, treat sex in a very exciting and matter-of-fact way. It's all about how masculine you are, how strong, how much you can endure.

If I want to live dangerously that is my business. Whatever has happened to me in my 21 years has left me a stranger to safety. Given the choice of a look around Quay-West sauna or Notre Dame Cathedral I think you know where I'd most likely be found. Sure I miss Brigitte, Thel and David, but I also think they heaved a sigh of relief when I took off. They know I've either got to look after myself or not. It's not up to them anymore, and why should it be? They've all done their best with this prodigal varmint. I still wish I'd seen Shamash again. I wish he'd written, even a suicide note, though God knows what the story is there – that could take months to resolve.

I send the folks back home pictures of me drinking Scotch on top of Jim Morrison's grave, smoking a cigarette on Oscar Wilde's fantastic deco death ship, pictures of *me avec une grande baguette* (why a baguette would be feminine I don't know). The monster is loose, making his porn, behaving like trash with all the other dangerous young men, then coming back to the comforts of an expensive hotel. I'm not blaming anyone anymore. I take responsibility for myself, living like I do. That takes a lot of courage. I'm on the edge, sure, but I've got to try to have a good time in the ways I know how. Even Brigitte says debauchery and asceticism can be means to the same end. She just has a clearer idea of that end than I do.

I hope, on my return, I'll be stable enough to pull it off – the job, the wealth, the book even. People will be waiting to see me fall just like they watched Shamash. The world is a butcher's shop and we're all meat for the chopping.

Last night at Quay-West I crossed all the safety barriers. I met this German guy who spoke a little French and no English, but it didn't matter because it wasn't the sort of meeting that required dialogue. He looked dangerous and beautiful, but he turned out to be more dangerous than any-thing else. I was coked, and even though I felt horny I couldn't get a decent erection. He could and was single-minded about wanting to fuck me. We were in a cubicle; he had no intention of using a condom. I got this beautiful body rush from the cocaine, and for a moment I wasn't con-cerned about condoms. I relaxed, totally, as he hammered into me. I felt as though it was someone else down there being fucked. I was in a trance and each thrust seemed to dislodge a memory as if I were undergoing a kind of cerebral colonic irrigation:

In he'd go.

I'd see the swings and slides at the council estate.

Out he'd come.

Once more I'd see the shadowy face of the man in the black anorak, the 20 pence glinting in the pale sunlight.

In he'd go.

I'd see my Mum caught in the dog-like motions of shagging, her face fixed on the ceiling.

Out.

Shamash, totally giving in to me, being there with me and

for me, a distantly remembered fuck that meant something.

In.

The scenic railway with Shamash, and ice-creams.

Out.

Shamash, grey, dead, not the same person, and that bottle
of hair conditioner.

In.

Platform shoes and pusher, neighbours shouting at each
other on the council estate.

I looked up at this dude, who was not particularly interested in me beyond that slick, fleshy tunnel he was plough-
ing with hearty primal devotion. 'Listen, you Kraut bastard,'
I said, 'you're going to cum inside me and you couldn't give
a shit. You'll cum, wipe yourself on a towel and vanish under
the cloud of shame that will descend as soon as you feel *le
petit mort.*' He didn't understand a word of what I said, and
I don't know whether it was a fleeting moment of self-pres-
ervation or a shift in my mood from the cocaine. Whatever
it was, I pushed him off me and left him like a shag on a
rock. You see, I realised something – I realised as much as I
would like to, it is not possible to live life as pornography. I
love pornography but ultimately it doesn't work. It lacks an
enduring philosophy and my life seems based or debased on
its central tenet; an ephemeral ejaculation and its ensuing
void.

I would have liked, on one level, to have abandoned
myself to him, to not have cared, but I couldn't. I'm sure to
many people the whole scenario would be considered appalling, but to me it was an affirmation of worth. It was sad
because it was the death of a belief system but a relief to

realise I still had limits. To me it was a breakthrough. I know the safe-sex brigade would say I'd still taken a shocking risk, but I'm not concerned about that. For me sex has always been as much about death as it has about life, intrinsic to both, preprogrammed, and my programming exists at one end of a preordained polarity with boring pristine celibacy lurking at the other.

Sure, I went and had sex with someone else after that, but it was safer and the images changed too. With the next person I seemed to descend into my subconscious, remembering the dream of the car crash. It was weird – I was being fucked while almost falling asleep. Then, from inside this half sleep, I realised we weren't even in the front of the car, we were both in the back, Shamash and I; it was a taxi and neither of us was driving. I don't know who the driver was or where he was taking us but I'm going to call that driver fate. I don't want to see his face and I don't want to pay his fare.

I'll be home soon – March, April, whenever. Those media people can sharpen their cleavers; Fred Nile can sharpen his wits. I'll get waxed, tanned and detoxed on the way back. I'll be ready. Perhaps I can launch the book and the vid together; it's called *Devinette Devant* (even porn sounds classy in French). Let the French test their filthy bombs – there's something comforting about toxic waste, something funny about how in spite of all the rhetoric in the world no country with any international clout will really lift a finger to save the world we pretend we love. If the law's an ass then morality is a lumberjack. It's all a joke really, and I think Brigitte's right – it's an imagined playground full of bullies, victims and all the inbetweenies. No one grows up; they just fancy they do. Victims turn into bullies or vice versa and all the practice you ever needed was a game of musical chairs as a kid. More and more I hope the world's not real. I'm starting to count on it.

Brigitte says the minute you start counting on it, the less real it will become. 'It'll frighten you, hurt you and thrill you some more but in the end it'll bore you and you'll be looking inside your head for the challenges you need. That's the way it should be. The apple's got a core Darl, and when you've devoured the flesh the seeds still remain. They don't look nearly as tasty but they are where the future lies. Bury them in the ground when you've had enough of eating the flesh and thousands more will grow. The great lie and the worst fear most people have is that somewhere along the way they might have sold their soul. The truth is Darl, that's the part we never owned to begin with.'

When Brigitte writes me all this stuff I think yeah, yeah, but sometimes it's like, with all the blood, guts, needles and buses I go on about or all the trashy DF sex I do, I sense there is something that never gets touched. Something no amount of hammering can knock out. When I feel that way, I get this idea that it's alright to play my shocking part. That this is the only dimension where debauchery is up for exploration. So I explore.

'Bring me another boy, this one is full!'

EPILOGUE

I sit in a bar near Rue St Martin, huddled within the folds of Shamash's big black coat. My chest is sore because I've just had a tattoo carved into it – the same one my Mum used to have. I saw it in the window of a tattoo salon on the Rue de Clichy and took it as an omen.

I've walked past the hotel where I stayed all those years ago with Shamash and Ashley. Now I'm drinking Scotch and coke as well as hot coffee to warm my hands. In my pocket is a cheese pastry thing I bought on the street. I keep taking big greasy chunks off it, and now it's nearly gone. I'm sure this would be considered gauche in here. The Johnny part of me likes to be common, likes to behave like a dero; the Vas part of me indulges him in that. I can smell my own body odour because despite the cold, I was sweating with pain while the tat was being done. Snow has been falling for the first time since I've been here, and I feel good in one of my favourite Vaslavian ways. Owen will be here tomorrow, and that will be excellent.

Two men nearby are talking intimately in that cool, sexy way French people have. I've come to love it since I've been here, though, like everything in Paris, I'll always be ultimately excluded from it. My eyes dart over to them, and I realise they are talking about me. I get that cruise shiver, the feeling of excitement you get when you realise you're being included in something and bypassed at the same time. It's like not knowing whether you might be asked out for dinner or whether you will be dinner. Not speaking much French and not being of any public interest in this part of the world, I wouldn't be so naive as to suppose they were considering me for an enduring friendship or an intellectual discussion. They whisper again while I stuff the last piece of pastry into my mouth. You don't really need to be French to know what they're saying. The spirit of some things speaks for itself:

'*Tu vois ce mec, qu'est-ce que tu crois qu'il serait capable de faire?*'

'*Le mec – là ferait n'importe quoi!*'

Is it that obvious? I ask myself, feeling self-conscious again. I look down at my coffee and feel flakes of the pastry blighting my lips. I drink the last of the Scotch, trying to sink further into the coat as colour rises to my cheeks. It's damp near my tat – it must be bleeding a little. Suddenly, I'm lonely and a little sad, but overall, I think I'm doing fine.

Gay Resort Murder Shock   Phillip Scott

Meet Marc Petrucci. He's just been stood up at the opera. His best friend, Paul, is nearly half his age, with a taste for other people's boyfriends and their champagne. Together they're about to discover that life under the flight path can be deadly, especially if you're in drag.

So when Marc and Paul are offered an expenses-paid island holiday, it seems like a dream come true – until Marc stumbles across a murder . . .

From Oxford Street to the Queensland coast, the Opera House to the inner city, *Gay Resort Murder Shock* is a hilarious adventure with a lethal twist that does for Sydney what *Tales of the City* did for San Francisco.

'Discover Australia's most wonderful wicked wit.'

Wendy Harmer

Quiver   Tobsha Learner

Quiver is twelve interlinked short stories that explore lust and human sexuality in all their sensual manifestations. In her first collection of erotic writing Tobsha Learner transports us into a world of love, power and obsessions, often blurring the line between reality and fantasy, bringing us face-to-face with delicately observed passion and pain.

Experience the angry fearlessness of youth, the pleasure of the new, sexual friction at its most primal, and the lingering fingers of a past that refuses to let go.

Witty and provocative, *Quiver* explores desire in all its complexity.

'A deliciously horny read, inventive and sexy.'

Linda Jaivin

SECOND EDITION

Biochemistry
A Problems Approach

The Benjamin/Cummings Series in the Life Sciences

F. J. Ayala and J. A. Kiger, Jr.
Modern Genetics (1980)

F. J. Ayala and J. W. Valentine
Evolving: The Theory and Processes of Organic Evolution (1979)

M. G. Barbour, J. H. Burk, and W. D. Pitts
Terrestrial Plant Ecology (1980)

L. L. Cavalli-Sforza
Elements of Human Genetics, second edition (1977)

R. E. Dickerson and I. Geis
Proteins: Structure, Function, and Evolution (1982)

L. E. Hood, I. L. Weissman, and W. B. Wood
Immunology (1978)

L. E. Hood, J. H. Wilson, and W. B. Wood
Molecular Biology of Eucaryotic Cells (1975)

A. L. Lehninger
Bioenergetics: The Molecular Basis of Biological Energy Transformations, second edition (1971)

S. E. Luria, S. J. Gould, and S. Singer
A View of Life (1981)

A. P. Spence
Basic Human Anatomy (1982)

A. P. Spence and E. B. Mason
Human Anatomy and Physiology (1979)

G. J. Tortora
Microbiology (1982)

J. D. Watson
Molecular Biology of the Gene, third edition (1976)

I. L. Weissman, L. E. Hood, and W. B. Wood
Essential Concepts in Immunology (1978)

N. K. Wessells
Tissue Interactions and Development (1977)

W. B. Wood, J. H. Wilson, R. M. Benbow, and L. E. Hood
Biochemistry: A Problems Approach, second edition (1981)

SECOND EDITION

Biochemistry

A Problems Approach

William B. Wood
University of Colorado, Boulder

John H. Wilson
Baylor College of Medicine

Robert M. Benbow
The Johns Hopkins University

Leroy E. Hood
California Institute of Technology

The Benjamin/Cummings Publishing Company
Menlo Park, California • Reading, Massachusetts
London • Amsterdam • Don Mills, Ontario • Sydney

Sponsoring Editor: James W. Behnke
Production Editor: John Hamburger
Copy Editor: Gloria Joyce
Book Designer: Paul Quin
Cover Designers: Joan Hargis and Judith Sager
Artist: Cecile Duray-Bito

The cover illustration is a stereo triptych (trip'-tik) showing a DNA double helix. These specially designed three-dimensional graphics are used throughout the book to illustrate a variety of molecular and cellular structures. Techniques for viewing them in stereo are described in the Appendix to Chapter 4. In the cover triptych, phosphate groups are shown in light blue, sugars in blue, purine bases in red, and pyrimidine bases in yellow. (Stereo images courtesy of R. Feldmann, National Institutes of Health.)

Library of Congress Cataloging in Publication Data

Main entry under title:
Biochemistry, a problems approach.

    Includes bibliographies and index.
    1. Biological chemistry—Problems, exercises, etc. I. Wood, William Barry,
1938–   . [DNLM: 1. Biochemistry. QU 4 B6157]
QP518.5.B56 1981   574.19′2′076   81-6124
ISBN 0-8053-9840-6   AACR2

DEFGHIJ-MU-89876543

The Benjamin/Cummings Publishing Company, Inc.
2727 Sand Hill Road
Menlo Park, California 94025

I hear, and I forget,
I see, and I remember,
I do, and I understand.
   Ancient Chinese Proverb

This new edition of *Biochemistry, A Problems Approach,* like the first edition, embodies our conviction that the only way to acquire active familiarity with biochemistry is by doing it. Listening to lectures, reading, and memorizing information are important components of learning, but actively analyzing experimental data and solving concrete problems lead to a deeper understanding. This problem-oriented book is intended to help students of biochemistry experience the third line of the proverb as well as the first two.

Scope of the Book

Biochemistry evolved as a descriptive science. The cataloging of biological compounds by natural product chemists and the elucidation of enzymatic pathways by early physiological chemists presented the biochemistry student of the 1950s with a bewildering diversity of chemical structures and reactions. However, subsequent advances in understanding bioenergetics, metabolic control, heredity, evolution, and the origin of life have transformed biochemistry into a more coherent discipline, with its own simplifying principles.

The central challenge of biochemistry in the 1960s and early 1970s was to provide an organized picture of the cell as a functioning chemical system. This challenge has been met successfully, at least for the simplest cells. The challenge of the future is to comprehend, as completely as possible at the molecular level, the more complex systems we call organisms. To do so, we must understand not only the internal chemistry of cells, but also the chemistry of communication between them. This revised edition is intended to help meet that challenge. The book includes new sections on trans-membrane communication, physiology, cyto-architecture, molecular genetics, and recombinant DNA technology as well as the traditional areas of biochemistry.

Using the Book

This book can be used alone, as the basis for introductory one-semester courses covering macromolecular structure, bioenergetics, metabolism, and gene expression. It also has proven valuable as a complementary text and study aid to more comprehensive biochemistry textbooks in longer courses. The book is designed to encourage self-study and to promote independent exploration, either within or outside a formal course framework.

Each chapter includes presentation of concepts, 15 to 25 problems, and a separate section of answers. The Concepts sections present the material most basic to each topic covered, including all the information necessary to solve the accompanying problems. If the students are encountering this material for the first time, they will benefit from the additional reading suggested in each chapter. At the end of each Concepts section, we provide references to books and articles from the current literature and to four widely used comprehensive biochemistry texts: *Biochemistry* by A. L. Lehninger (second edition); *Biochemistry, The Chemical Reactions of Living Cells,* by D. E. Metzler; *Biochemistry,* by L. Stryer (second edition); and *Principles of Biochemistry,* by A. White, P. Handler, E. Smith, R. Hill, and I. R. Lehman (sixth edition).

The problems relating to each topic are arranged in order of increasing difficulty. The first few are designed to illustrate essential concepts and can be solved by applying the concepts directly. Subsequent problems are more challenging, and may involve analyzing data, designing experiments, or combining basic concepts in a new way. Many important ideas and techniques are presented in the introductions to specific problems in the Problems sections. For reference, these concepts are listed at the end of the corresponding Concepts section.

Solutions to the problems are explained in detail in the Answers sections, wherein lies much of the potential teaching value of the book. Answers to the more challenging problems are written so that the first sentence or two will provide a hint toward the solution, or help steer the student in the right direction. We urge students to work through each answer whether or not they have been able to solve the problem on their own because many ideas not included under Concepts are presented in the Answers sections.

In addition to the answered problems, each chapter includes one to three unanswered problems, marked in the margin with a star (☆). Solutions to these problems are available to instructors on written request from the publisher.

A novel feature of this edition is the expanded use of computer-generated stereo images to illustrate three-dimensional molecular shapes. These striking images, created by Richard Feldmann, are presented as triptychs to allow maximum flexibility in stereo imaging. The triptychs can be used with a conventional stereo viewer, but with a little practice can be viewed in stereo without a viewing aid, as explained in the Appendix to Chapter 4.

Acknowledgments

In preparing this second edition, we have benefited from the experience of many instructors who provided the publishers with suggestions for revisions. We also wish to acknowledge the able assistance of Jim Behnke, sponsoring editor, John Hamburger, production editor, and Gloria Joyce, copy editor, who shepherded the revision through to completion. We are indebted to Cecile Duray-Bito for her knowledgeable rendering of the figures, and to Joan Hargis, Kraig Emmert, Alan Mewbourne, and the staff of the Medical Illustrations Department at Baylor College of Medicine for advice and help in mounting and printing the stereo triptychs. We owe special thanks to Richard J. Feldmann of the Division of Computer Research and Technology, National Institutes of Health, for his patience and generosity in generating and providing the computer images for all the stereo triptychs in the text as well as the color triptych on the cover. Finally, we are grateful to our families and associates for accepting our prolonged involvement with this time-consuming task.

In the course of the revision we have added much new material and have rewritten many sections that required updating. However, we have tried throughout to retain the flavor, format, and general organization of the first edition. We trust that the book will continue to be useful to both students and instructors of biochemistry.

W. B. Wood
J. H. Wilson
R. M. Benbow
L. E. Hood

CONTENTS

PART ONE

Biological Structure and the Chemistry of Proteins

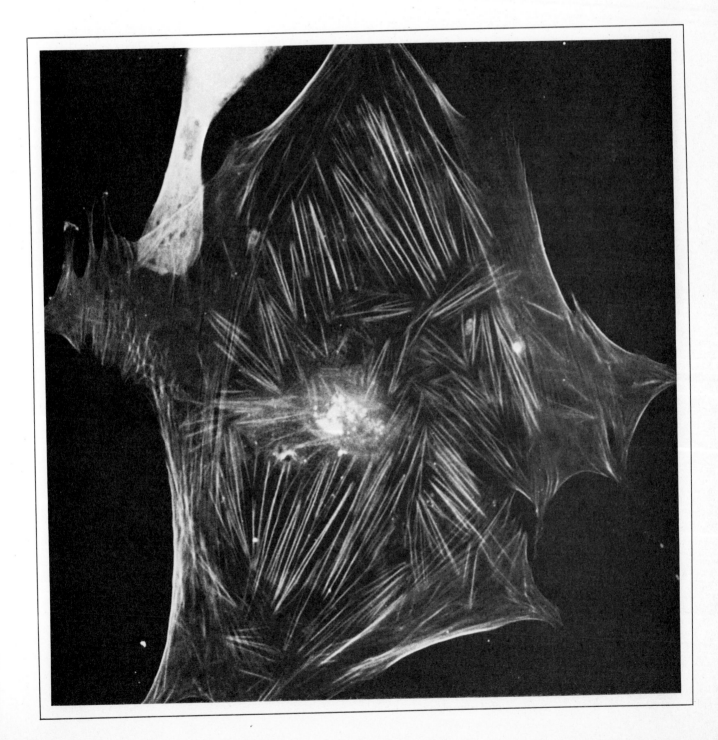

1 Chemical Characteristics of Living Matter

Biochemistry is the study of living organisms at the molecular level. At this level, organisms can be viewed as complex chemical systems that contain all the information necessary to grow and reproduce at the expense of energy and raw materials from the environment. All present-day organisms share common properties in their chemical composition and organization that are the result of natural selection since life began over 3 billion years ago. This chapter considers the chemical makeup of organisms, and the evolutionary rationale for why particular atoms and molecules have been selected over others.

Concepts

1.1 Most organisms are composed of only sixteen chemical elements.

The chemical makeup of organisms appears to have been determined partly by the availability of raw materials in the environment, and partly by the fitness of atoms and molecules for specific roles in life processes. Consequently, the elemental composition of living matter shows both similarities to and distinct differences from the composition of the biosphere—that is, the portion of the earth's crust and atmosphere accessible to organisms. Table 1.1 lists the chemical elements found in organisms, and Table 1.2 compares the elemental composition of living matter to that of the earth's crust. The differences in these compositions can be explained at least partially by the following fitness considerations.

Table 1.1
Elements Found in Organisms

Major covalent-bond-forming elements (all organisms)	Atomic number	Trace elements (all organisms)	Atomic number
H	1	Mn	25
C	6	Fe	26
N	7	Co	27
O	8	Cu	29
P	15	Zn	30
S	16		

Monatomic ions (all organisms)	Atomic number	Trace elements (some organisms)	Atomic number
Na^+	11	B	5
Mg^{2+}	12	Al	13
Cl^-	17	Si	14
K^+	19	V	23
Ca^{2+}	20	Mo	42
		I	53

Table 1.2
Approximate Relative Abundances of Bioelements in All Organisms and in the Earth's Crust (in atoms per 100 atoms)

Element	Organisms[a]	Earth's crust[b]
H	49	0.22
C	25	0.19
O	25	47
N	0.27	<0.1
Ca	0.073	3.5
K	0.046	2.5
Si	0.033	28
Mg	0.031	2.2
P	0.030	<0.1
Na	0.015	2.5
Others	Traces	13.7

[a] From E. S. Deevey, *Scientific American*, September 1970, p. 149.
[b] From E. Frieden, *Scientific American*, July 1972, p. 52.

1.   H, O, N, and C, which make up $>99\%$ by weight of living matter, are the smallest atoms that can attain stable electronic configurations by sharing 1, 2, 3, and 4 electrons, respectively. They form more stable covalent bonds than any other elements with these valences. Moreover, O, N, and C are the only elements that readily form strong multiple bonds. Carbon, with four valence electrons and the ability to form both $C{=}C$ and $C{\equiv}C$ bonds, has the most versatile combining properties of any element. With H, O, and N, carbon can form a tremendous variety of stable molecules. With O_2 it forms CO_2, a stable gas, soluble in water, that is well suited for circulation of carbon between organisms.

O_2 is also soluble in water and therefore is readily available to nearly all organisms. In addition, it is the third most avid electron acceptor among the elements (behind fluorine and chlorine). Consequently, the transfer of electrons from most other molecules to O_2 yields energy. This process (respiration) provides most of the energy available to nonphotosynthetic organisms.

The chemical properties of carbon contrast markedly with those of silicon, which also has four valence electrons and is more abundant in the biosphere, yet is found in living matter as a trace component only. Because of the larger size of the Si atom, Si—Si bonds are weaker than C—C bonds, and polymers of Si are unstable in the presence of water. In striking contrast to C, Si combines with O to form insoluble silicates or network polymers of silicon dioxide (e.g., quartz) and thus tends to remove itself from circulation in an aerobic environment.

2.   Phosphorus and sulfur appear to have been selected for quite different chemical properties. Bonds formed by P and S are often unstable in the presence of water; consequently, considerable energy is required to form them. Because this energy is released when the bonds are hydrolyzed, P- and S-containing molecules such as adenosine triphosphate (ATP) and acetyl coenzyme A are well suited for their roles as the energy carriers of living systems.

3.   Monatomic ions (e.g., Na^+, K^+, Ca^{2+}, and Mg^{2+}) play relatively nonspecific roles in organisms, such as the maintenance of osmotic balance, the formation of ionic gradients in nerve conduction and active transport, and the neutralization of charges on macromolecules. The similar ionic compositions of living matter and seawater suggest that the monatomic ions in organisms may have been selected primarily on the basis of their availability.

4.   By contrast, at least some of the trace elements undoubtedly were selected for their electronic properties. For example, Fe and Cu, which can exist as stable ions in either of two oxidation states, are well suited to their roles in the active sites of cytochrome proteins, where they serve as acceptors and donors in the electron-transfer reactions of respiration.

1.2   Noncovalent bonds are important in biological structure.

In addition to the familiar covalent bonds that link the atoms in a molecule, four kinds of noncovalent interactions are important in biological systems:

1.   **Ionic bonds** result from the electrostatic attraction between two ionized groups of opposite charge, such as carboxyl ($—COO^-$) and amino ($—NH_3^+$) groups in proteins.

2.   **Hydrogen bonds (H-bonds)** result from electrostatic attraction between an electronegative atom (usually O or N) and a hydrogen atom that is bonded covalently to a second electronegative atom. The hydrogen atom is thus shared between two electronegative atoms. Three common H-bonds are shown in Figure 1.1.

3.   **Van der Waals bonds** are short-range attractive forces between chemical groups in contact. These bonds are much weaker than ionic bonds and H-bonds, but they

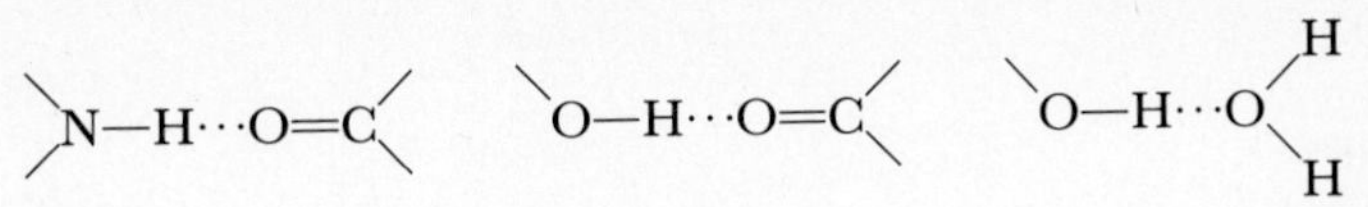

Figure 1.1
Three examples of hydrogen bonding. H-bonds are indicated as dotted lines.

$$\text{N---H}\cdots\text{O=C} \qquad \text{O---H}\cdots\text{O=C} \qquad \text{O---H}\cdots\text{O}\begin{smallmatrix}\text{H}\\\text{H}\end{smallmatrix}$$

contribute significantly to the stability of biological structures that contain many van der Waals contacts.

4. Hydrophobic interactions cause nonpolar groups such as hydrocarbon chains to associate with each other in an aqueous environment. These hydrophobic associations are not bonds in the usual sense, since they result from the solvent properties of water rather than from attraction between associating nonpolar groups. Somehow, in a manner not yet clearly understood, nonpolar groups restrict the normal motion of surrounding water molecules to an energetically unfavorable configuration. Therefore, the association of nonpolar groups with each other is driven by the tendency of water molecules to return to their unrestricted state of lower energy. A familiar result of hydrophobic interactions is that oil droplets suspended in water coalesce to form a separate phase. In living systems, hydrophobic interactions are primarily responsible for the stability of protein molecules, membranes, and most other subcellular structures.

1.3 Organisms are built almost entirely from water and thirty small precursor molecules.

A. Water is by far the most abundant molecule found in organisms. Water not only is readily available in the biosphere, but also possesses unique chemical properties that suit it admirably for biological systems. Most of these properties derive from the polarity and H-bonding ability of water molecules.

1. Because of the electronegativity of oxygen and the bond angle between the two H atoms, the water molecule is polar, with one "end" partially negatively charged and the other "end" partially positively charged, as shown in Figure 1.2. Consequently, water is an excellent solvent for polar substances but is immiscible with nonpolar substances because of the hydrophobic interactions discussed previously.

2. The molecules of liquid water are extensively H-bonded to each other. This bonding results in unusually high heat capacity, heat of vaporization, and heat of fusion compared to most other liquids. (For the importance of these properties to organisms, see Problem 1.7.)

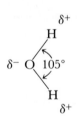

Figure 1.2
Polarity of the H₂O molecule.

B. The overwhelming diversity of molecular structure in organisms is simplified by the generalization that most biomolecules are built from 30 small-molecule precursors, sometimes called the alphabet of biochemistry. These precursor molecules can be grouped into four classes:

1. Twenty L-amino acids are the monomeric units of all proteins. Their structures and chemical properties are considered in detail in Chapter 2.

2. Five aromatic bases—two **purines** (adenine and guanine) and three **pyrimidines** (cytosine, uracil, and thymine)—are linked to the sugars ribose phosphate or deoxyribose phosphate to form **nucleotides,** the monomeric units of RNA and DNA, respectively.

3. A sugar, D-glucose, is the major product of plant photosynthesis and a central intermediate in metabolism. A second sugar, D-ribose, is the precursor of the sugar phosphates in nucleotides.

4. The fatty acid **palmitate,** the tri-alcohol **glycerol,** and the amine **choline** are all constituents of the phospholipid molecules that form the matrix of biological membranes.

Aromatic bases

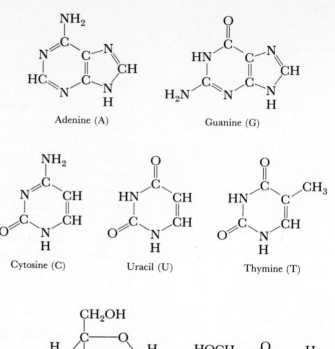

Adenine (A)   Guanine (G)

Cytosine (C)   Uracil (U)   Thymine (T)

Sugars

D-Glucose   D-Ribose

Constituents of lipids

$$CH_3CH_2CH_2CH_2CH_2CH_2CH_2CH_2CH_2CH_2CH_2CH_2CH_2CH_2CH_2COH$$
Palmitic acid

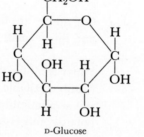

Glycerol

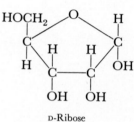

Choline

Figure 1.3
Ten of the 30 basic precursor
molecules of biochemistry. The
remaining 20 are the amino
acids, whose structures are shown
in Table 2.1.

The structures of the aromatic bases, sugars, and constituents of lipids are shown in Figure 1.3.

These 30 molecules, like the bioelements, appear to have been selected according to a combination of their availability and their fitness. They are thought to have been among the most abundant products of prebiotic synthesis in the reducing atmosphere and warm oceans of the primitive earth, prior to the origin of life more than 3 billion years ago. The fitness of these compounds for their roles in living organisms will become clear in the following chapters.

1.4 Macromolecules are polymers of small precursor molecules.

A. More than 90% of the dry weight of most organisms is made up of **macromolecules,** which are large polymers of one or a few similar kinds of precursor molecules linked together into large repeating structures. There are three major classes of macromolecules:

1.   **Proteins** are polymers of amino acids, linked head to tail by amide (peptide) bonds. They play a variety of important roles in organisms, as described in Concept 1.6.

2.   **Nucleic acids,** RNA and DNA, are polymers of nucleotides linked by phosphodiester bonds. The nucleotide sequences of these polymers encode the genetic information that directs growth, development, and reproduction.

3.   **Polysaccharides** are polymers of sugars, linked by glycosidic bonds. They serve primarily as storage sources of energy in plants (starch) and animals (glycogen), and as structural elements in plants (cellulose).

B.   Biopolymers have two common features:

1.   A given kind of polymer contains only one or two types of monomer–monomer bonds. Consequently, polymer synthesis is simplified because it can be catalyzed by one or a few enzymes, with additional machinery when necessary to specify the sequence of monomer addition.

2.   The monomer–monomer bonds in biopolymers are formed by the elimination of water, and can be broken by the addition of water (hydrolysis). The formation of these bonds requires energy. Conversely, hydrolysis is energetically favored, but does not occur at a significant rate in the absence of a catalyst. Therefore, biopolymers are kinetically, but not thermodynamically, stable.

1.5   Larger structures are assembled from macromolecules.

A.   Macromolecules associate specifically with each other to form larger complexes. These in turn are assembled into the subcellular structures and organelles that make up cells themselves. Cells in turn can form tissues, organ systems, and finally whole multicellular organisms. The approximate relative sizes of structures in the subcellular hierarchy are shown in Figure 1.4.

B.   Associations between macromolecules in larger structures are generally noncovalent and thermodynamically stable. As a result, such structures tend to self-assemble, simply by interacting to attain a minimum energy configuration.

1.6   Proteins play a central role in living systems.

Proteins, the most versatile of the macromolecules, are responsible for both the metabolic capabilities and the morphology of organisms. Proteins catalyze the chemical reactions of metabolism, as specific enzymes and carrier molecules. In addition, proteins determine the architecture of organisms, either as enzymes that catalyze the formation of structural elements (e.g., cellulose in plants), as structural elements themselves (e.g., skin, horn, and bone in animals), or as surface elements that determine the specificity of cell–cell interactions. Therefore, the structure and function of proteins is the subject of the next several chapters, as well as a central theme throughout this book.

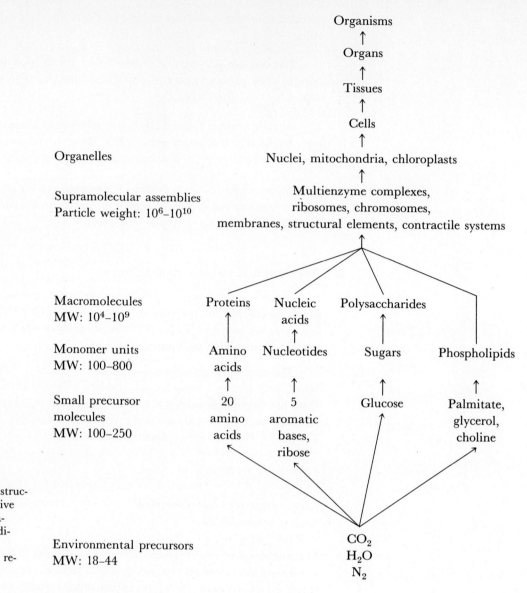

Figure 1.4
The hierarchy of biological structure. The approximate relative sizes of molecules and supramolecular assemblies are indicated as molecular weights (MW) and particle weights, respectively.

References

COMPREHENSIVE TEXTS

Albert L. Lehninger, *Biochemistry,* Worth, New York, 1975, 2nd ed. Introduction and Chapters 1 and 2.

David E. Metzler, *Biochemistry,* Academic Press, New York, 1977. Chapter 2.

Lubert Stryer, *Biochemistry,* W. H. Freeman, San Francisco, 1981, 2nd ed. Chapter 1.

Abraham White, Philip Handler, Emil L. Smith, Robert L. Hill, and I. Robert Lehman, *Principles of Biochemistry,* McGraw-Hill, New York, 1978, 6th ed. Chapter 1.

OTHER REFERENCES

Richard E. Dickerson, Harry B. Gray, and Gilbert P. Haight, Jr., *Chemical Principles,* Benjamin/Cummings, Menlo Park, Calif., 1979, 3rd ed. Chapter 21.

Earl Frieden, "The Chemical Elements of Life," *Scientific American,* July 1972, p. 52.

"Evolution," *Scientific American,* September 1978, entire issue.

George Wald, "The Origins of Life," in *The Scientific Endeavor,* Rockefeller Institute Press, New York, 1964, p. 113. Also published in *Proceedings of the National Academy of Sciences (U.S.)* **52,** 595 (1964).

Problems

1.1   Answer the following with true or false. If false, explain why.

a. The six major covalent-bond-forming elements in living systems are the six most abundant covalent-bond-forming elements in the biosphere.

b. O, N, and C are the elements that most readily form strong multiple bonds.

c. Oxygen is the third most avid electron acceptor of all the elements.

d. The trace elements in organisms probably were selected primarily on the basis of availability.

e. In an H-bond, electrons are shared between a hydrogen atom and two neighboring electronegative atoms.

f. Oil droplets in water coalesce to form a separate phase because of the strong attraction of hydrophobic molecules for each other.

g. Hydrophobic interactions will cause a flexible polymer molecule that carries both hydrophobic and hydrophilic groups to fold spontaneously in aqueous solution so that the hydrophobic groups are inside and the hydrophilic groups are outside.

h. Because of intermolecular H-bonding, water has a higher heat of vaporization than most other liquids.

i. Glucose phosphate combines with aromatic bases to form nucleotides, the monomer units of nucleic acids.

j. Most biological polymers are thermodynamically stable.

1.2   a. The selection of raw materials for biological systems in the course of evolution was determined by _____ and _____.

b. More than 99% by weight of living matter is made up of the four elements _____, _____, _____, and _____.

c. These four elements are also the _____ atoms that can attain stable electronic configurations by accepting, respectively, _____, _____, _____, and _____ electrons to form covalent bonds.

d. Consequently, they form more _____ covalent bonds than any other atoms with these valence electronic configurations.

e. The less stable covalent bonds formed by _____ and _____ suit molecules that contain these atoms for roles as energy carriers.

f. Transfer of electrons from other molecules to _____ provides most of the energy available to nonphotosynthetic organisms.

1.3   a. The monatomic ions in organisms may well have been selected primarily on the basis of their _____.

b. The trace elements _____ and _____ are well suited for roles in electron-transfer processes, because they can exist as stable ions in either of two oxidation states.

c. The three most important types of noncovalent interactions in biological systems are _____, _____, and _____.

d. The weak, short-range attractions between nonpolar groups are called _____ bonds.

e. The unique properties of water are due to the _____ and _____ ability of the H_2O molecule.

f. Compared to other liquids, water has unusually high heat _____, heat of _____, and heat of _____.

1.4   a. Almost all of the innumerable kinds of molecules found in organisms are built up from _____ different small-molecule precursors.

b. The four classes of basic precursor molecules in all organisms are _____, _____, _____, and _____.

c. Nucleic acids are polymers of _____.

d. Biopolymers are _____ unstable, but _____ stable.

e. Larger aggregates, composed of noncovalently associated macromolecules, tend to be _____ stable.

f. As catalysts and structural elements, _____ determine both the metabolic capabilities and the morphology of organisms.

1.5 Protein molecules carry ionized groups, H-bonding groups, and nonpolar groups on their surfaces. Which type of noncovalent interaction—ionic, H-bonding, or hydrophobic—do you suppose is likely to be most important in causing protein molecules in dilute aqueous solution to associate with each other? Why?

1.6 Explain why H-bonding between water molecules should result in a high heat capacity (the quantity of heat required to increase the temperature of 1 g of water 1°; usually expressed in units of calories per degree Celsius or cal/°C).

1.7 Below are some chemical and physical properties of water and a list of possible benefits to organisms. Match each of the properties in the first list with a benefit in the second list, and write a sentence or two explaining your choice.

Properties
_____

a. High heat capacity
b. Higher density than ice
c. High heat of fusion
d. Polarity of water molecules
e. High heat of vaporization

Benefits
_____

1. Organisms are protected against freezing at low temperatures.
2. Land animals can cool themselves by surface evaporation with minimum expenditure of body fluid.
3. Membranes composed of low-molecular-weight, noncovalently bonded lipids are thermodynamically stable.
4. Temperature changes in organisms are minimized.
5. Aquatic environments in cold climates tend to freeze only on the surface rather than freezing solid.

1.8 Where stereoisomers are possible among the 30 basic precursor molecules, only one has been selected for almost exclusive use in organisms; for example, L-amino acids, D-sugars, and so forth. Prebiotic synthesis must have produced D,L mixtures of these compounds, so that both isomers were available in equal abundance to the earliest organisms. Propose a reasonable general explanation for why the use of only one isomer should have prevailed, assuming that there is no intrinsic difference in biological fitness between D and L forms of the same molecule.

☆ 1.9 George Wald has designated the 30 common precursor molecules of biological compounds the "alphabet of biochemistry." Another prominent biologist, attempting an even further simplification, selected seven chemical groups as the primary building blocks of biological molecules. Two of these groups are carbonyl and phosphoryl. What groups would you pick as the other five?

$$-C=O \qquad \begin{array}{c} O \\ \parallel \\ -P-O^- \\ | \\ O^- \end{array}$$

Carbonyl   Phosphoryl

Answers

1.1 a. False. Silicon is more abundant than any of the six except oxygen.
   b. True
   c. True
   d. False. The trace elements undoubtedly were selected on the basis of their specific electronic properties.

    e. False. The H-bond is an electrostatic attraction between an electronegative atom having a partial negative charge, and an H atom that has a partial positive charge because of a covalent attachment to another electronegative atom.

    f. False. Oil droplets coalesce because the energy of water molecules decreases when hydrophobic molecules are removed from the aqueous environment. Because there is little change in the energy of the hydrophobic molecules themselves, the total energy of the system decreases to yield a more stable state when the two phases separate.

    g. True

    h. True

    i. False. Nucleotides are formed from ribose phosphate.

    j. False. The polymerization of monomers involves the removal of water in a process that requires energy. Because the hydrolysis of intermonomer bonds is energetically favorable, polymers are thermodynamically unstable in the presence of water. They are kinetically stable, because spontaneous hydrolysis has a high activation energy (see Chapter 6) and therefore occurs extremely slowly at biological temperatures.

1.2 a. fitness, availability

    b. H, O, N, C

    c. smallest, 1, 2, 3, 4

    d. stable

    e. P, S

    f. O_2

1.3 a. availability (or abundance)

    b. Fe, Cu

    c. ionic bonds, H-bonds, hydrophobic interactions

    d. van der Waals

    e. polarity, H-bonding

    f. capacity, vaporization, fusion

1.4 a. 30

    b. amino acids, aromatic bases, sugars, phospholipid constituents

    c. nucleotides

    d. thermodynamically, kinetically

    e. thermodynamically

    f. proteins

1.5   Because of their polarity and H-bonding properties, water molecules interact strongly with polar groups on solute molecules, thereby shielding them from interaction with other solute groups. Therefore, hydrophobic interactions are likely to be most important in causing protein molecules in dilute aqueous solution to associate.

1.6   To raise the temperature and therefore the kinetic energy of water molecules, some of the H-bonds between them must be broken. When water takes up heat, some of the energy goes into breaking H-bonds rather than increasing the temperature.

1.7   a. 4. The effect of heat production or heat loss is minimized by the high heat capacity of water.

      b. 5. Ice formed on the surface of water floats, and insulates the water below so that it remains liquid.

      c. 1. The higher the heat of fusion (melting), the more heat must be removed from a liquid to freeze it.

      d. 3. The hydrophobic interactions that confer stability on associations of nonpolar groups are dependent on the polarity of water molecules (Concepts 1.2 and 1.3, part A).

      e. 2. The high heat of vaporization means that an animal expends considerable heat to vaporize a small quantity of the water in its body.

1.8   A likely explanation is that standardization on either the D or the L form of each common metabolite is advantageous both for individual organisms and for populations of ecologically related species. All metabolic reactions in organisms are catalyzed by enzymes that are generally specific for either the D or the L form of a substrate. Therefore, for example, if an animal is to digest the starch from a plant and be able to build its own glycogen from the resulting sugar monomers, both the animal and the plant must make their polysaccharides from sugars of the same configuration. Thus the initial selection of each stereoisomer may have been a chance event that was ultimately fixed by the selective advantages of biochemical uniformity among organisms.

2 Amino Acids

Proteins serve as the catalysts for many important reactions in living systems and as structural elements that dictate much of biological architecture. The properties of proteins are determined by the physical and chemical properties of their monomer units, the amino acids. This chapter considers the important chemical characteristics of the 20 common amino acids.

Concepts

2.1 Amino acids form zwitterions.

The general structure for an amino acid is shown in its nonionized and zwitterionic forms in Figure 2.1. The amino group ($-NH_2$), the carboxyl group ($-COOH$), a hydrogen atom (H), and the side chain (R group) are attached to a carbon atom (C) known as the alpha (α) carbon.

In neutral solution (pH = 7), both the α-amino and α-carboxyl groups are ionized. The resulting charged form is called a **zwitterion**. The structures of the 20 common amino acids in neutral solution, their names, abbreviations, pK_a and pI values (Concept 2.2) are given in Table 2.1. The amino acids are grouped in the table according to the chemical properties of their side chains.

2.2 Amino acids behave as acids and bases.

A. The pH of a solution is defined as $-\log [H^+]$, in which $[H^+]$ is the hydrogen-ion concentration.

B. Similarly, the pK_a of a general acid, HA, is defined as $-\log K_a$, in which K_a is the equilibrium constant for the dissociation $HA \rightleftarrows H^+ + A^-$:

$$K_a = \frac{[H^+][A^-]}{[HA]} \tag{2.1}$$

All amino acids have at least two dissociation constants, one for the carboxyl group (K_{a_1}),

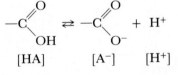

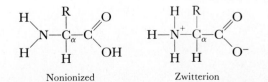

Figure 2.1
Two ionization states of a general amino acid.

Table 2.1
Structures, pK_a Values, and pI Values of the Twenty
Common Amino Acids

Structure	Name	Abbreviation[a]	pK_{a_1} (α-Carboxyl)	pK_{a_2} (α-Amino)	pK_{a_3} (side chain)	pI
Nonpolar side chain						
⁻OOC—C(H)(NH₃⁺)—H	Glycine	Gly (G)	2.3	9.6		6.0
⁻OOC—C(H)(NH₃⁺)—CH₃	Alanine	Ala (A)	2.3	9.7		6.0
⁻OOC—C(H)(NH₃⁺)—CH(CH₃)₂	Valine	Val (V)	2.3	9.6		6.0
⁻OOC—C(H)(NH₃⁺)—CH₂—CH(CH₃)₂	Leucine	Leu (L)	2.4	9.6		6.0
⁻OOC—C(H)(NH₃⁺)—CH(CH₃)—CH₂—CH₃	Isoleucine	Ilu (I)	2.4	9.7		6.1
⁻OOC—C(H)(NH₃⁺)—CH₂—CH₂—S—CH₃	Methionine	Met (M)	2.3	9.2		5.8
⁻OOC—C(H)(NH₃⁺)—CH₂—C₆H₅	Phenylalanine	Phe (F)	1.8	9.1		5.5
⁻OOC—C(H)—(pyrrolidine ring: CH₂ CH₂ CH₂ N H₂⁺)	Proline	Pro (P)	2.0	10.6		6.3
Neutral polar side chain						
⁻OOC—C(H)(NH₃⁺)—CH₂—OH	Serine	Ser (S)	2.2	9.2		5.7
⁻OOC—C(H)(NH₃⁺)—CH(OH)—CH₃	Threonine	Thr (T)	2.6	10.4		6.5
⁻OOC—C(H)(NH₃⁺)—CH₂—SH	Cysteine	Cys (C)	1.7	10.8	8.3 (Sulfhydryl)	5.0
⁻OOC—C(H)(NH₃⁺)—CH₂—C(=O)NH₂	Asparagine	Asn (N)	2.0	8.8		5.4
⁻OOC—C(H)(NH₃⁺)—CH₂—CH₂—C(=O)NH₂	Glutamine	Gln (Q)	2.2	9.1		5.7

Table 2.1 (Continued)

Structure	Name	Abbreviation[a]	pK_{a_1} (α-Carboxyl)	pK_{a_2} (α-Amino)	pK_{a_3} (side chain)	pI
	Tyrosine	Tyr (Y)	2.2	9.1	10.1 (Phenolic hydroxyl)	5.7
	Tryptophan	Trp (W)	2.4	9.4		5.9
Charged polar side chain						
	Aspartate	Asp (D)	2.1	9.8	3.9 (β-Carboxyl)	3.0
	Glutamate	Glu (E)	2.2	9.7	4.3 (γ-Carboxyl)	3.2
	Histidine	His (H)	1.8	9.2	6.0 (Imidazole)	7.6
	Lysine	Lys (K)	2.2	9.0	10.5 (ϵ-Amino)	9.8
	Arginine	Arg (R)	2.2	9.0	12.5 (Guanidino)	10.8

[a] The standard three-letter abbreviation is followed, in parentheses, by the alternative one-letter abbreviation preferred for computer representation of amino acid sequences.

and one for the amino group (K_{a_2}),

$$-NH_3^+ \rightleftharpoons -NH_2 + H^+$$
$$[HA] \qquad [A^-] \quad [H^+]$$

In addition, several amino acids have an ionizable side chain with a third dissociation constant (K_{a_3}). For example, Asp and Glu have a second carboxyl group and Lys has a second amino group. The pK_a values for all ionizable groups of the 20 common amino acids are listed in Table 2.1.

C. The pH of a solution and the dissociation constant, K_a, of an ionizable group in the solution are related by the Henderson–Hasselbalch equation,

$$pH = pK_a + \log\frac{[A^-]}{[HA]} \qquad (2.2)$$

This equation can be used to determine the fraction of ionizable groups found in each of the possible ionization states in solution at a known pH. Note that at pH = pK_a, half of the ionizable groups are dissociated.

D. The pI, or isoelectric point, of an amino acid is the pH at which it carries no *net* charge. For monoamino, monocarboxylic acids, pI is defined by the simple relationship

$$pI = \tfrac{1}{2}(pK_{a_1} + pK_{a_2}) \qquad (2.3)$$

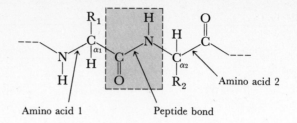

Figure 2.2
The peptide bond joining adjacent amino acids in a protein.

E. The pK_a values of the ionizable groups of amino acids are affected by neighboring chemical groups on the molecule, principally by electron-withdrawing or electron-donating inductive effects. For example, the amino group, the peptide bond (see Figure 2.2) and the carboxyl group attract electrons. Aliphatic groups [e.g., $-CH_3$, $-(CH_2)_n-$] act as weak electron donors.

2.3 In proteins amino acids are linked by peptide bonds.

A. A **peptide bond** is formed when the carboxyl group of one amino acid combines with the amino group of another amino acid, with elimination of water. The structure of the peptide bond is shown in Figure 2.2. A polymer of amino acids joined by peptide bonds is called a **polypeptide**. A protein consists of one or more polypeptides, usually folded into a specific three-dimensional conformation.

B. The peptide bond has partial double-bond character. As a result, the six atoms, C_{α_1} C=O, N—H, and C_{α_2}, lie in the same plane. Successive C_α atoms are always in the *trans* configuration across the peptide bond between them.

2.4 The characteristics of amino acids determine the properties of polypeptides.

A. The planar groups of atoms involved in two adjacent peptide bonds can rotate relative to one another about the C_α—N and C_α—C bonds (Figure 2.2). Steric features of the side chains limit rotation to a few favorable configurations. The restrictions that these factors introduce into polypeptide structure are described in Chapter 4.

B. Both the nitrogen and the oxygen atoms of the peptide bond can participate in hydrogen-bond formation (Concept 1.2):

$$\underset{\diagdown}{N}\overset{\delta^-}{} \overset{\delta^+}{-H} \cdots \overset{\delta^-}{O} = C\diagup$$

A repeating pattern of H-bonding between these atoms leads to ordered polypeptide structures (Chapter 4).

C. The amino acid side chains determine the specific chemical properties and the conformation of a polypeptide. The most important feature of side chains is their polar (hydrophilic) or nonpolar (hydrophobic) character. Polar side chains contain the electronegative atoms N, O, or S. Five of the polar side chains are charged (ionized) at pH = 7. The remainder are neutral, but readily form H-bonds. Hence both classes are soluble in water (hydrophilic). Nonpolar side chains consist only of C and H atoms (except for the S atom in Met). These chains do not form hydrogen bonds and therefore are relatively insoluble in water (hydrophobic).

Cys side chains in proteins usually are linked covalently by disulfide bonds, which form cross-links between two segments of polypeptide:

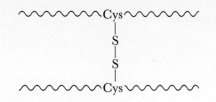

2.5   Amino acids can be separated by paper electrophoresis and paper chromatography.

Paper electrophoresis separates compounds primarily on the basis of their net electrical charge, which can be predicted from the pK_a values of the ionizable groups and the pH of the medium, using the Henderson–Hasselbalch equation. Paper chromatography separates compounds on the basis of their partition coefficients, that is, their relative solubility in polar and nonpolar solvents. Polar molecules are more soluble in polar solvents, whereas nonpolar molecules are more soluble in nonpolar solvents. In paper chromatography the polar phase is stationary (water bound to the cellulose fibers of the paper), and the organic phase (e.g., butanol) is mobile.

Paper electrophoresis and paper chromatography can be used individually or together to separate and analyze mixtures of amino acids, as shown in Figure 2.3. The combination of these two procedures employs paper chromatography in one dimension and (after rotating the paper 90°) paper electrophoresis in the other dimension. This technique, called **fingerprinting,** separates on the basis of both charge and polar character.

2.6   Additional concepts and techniques are presented in the Problems section.

A. Cation-exchange chromatography. Problem 2.8.
B. Amino acids as buffers. Problems 2.13, 2.16, and 2.17.

Origin

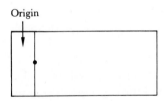

Apply mixture of amino acids.

Paper electrophoresis

Immerse ends of wetted paper
in buffer and apply high-voltage
electrical field at defined pH

Spray with ninhydrin to
visualize amino acids.

Apply mixture of amino acids.

Paper chromatography

Immerse base of paper in tank containing
acetic acid and organic solvent.
Allow solvent to rise to top of paper
by capillary action

Solvent front

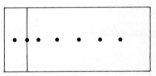

Spray with ninhydrin to
visualize amino acids.

Figure 2.3
Experimental procedures for
paper electrophoresis and paper
chromatography.

References

COMPREHENSIVE TEXTS

Lehninger: Chapter 4   Stryer: Chapter 2

Metzler: Chapter 2   White et al.: Chapter 4

OTHER REFERENCES

R. E. Dickerson and I. Geis, *The Structure and Action of Proteins,* Benjamin/Cummings, Menlo Park, Calif., 1969. Chapter 1.

Problems

2.1   Answer the following with true or false. If false, explain why.

   a. Only at very low or very high pH does the nonionized form of an amino acid predominate.

   b. Leu is more nonpolar than Ala.

   c. At a pH greater than the pK_a of an ionizable group, more than half of such groups are dissociated.

   d. The pI of the tripeptide Lys-Lys-Lys must be greater than any of its individual pK_a values.

   e. There is free rotation about a peptide bond.

   f. Paper electrophoresis separates amino acids on the basis of their polar character.

2.2   By inspection of their structures (Table 2.1), decide which amino acids fit the following descriptions:

   a. _____ alters polypeptide folding because it is not a true amino acid. In the polypeptides of myoglobin and hemoglobin every bend does not have a _____, but every _____ produces a bend. (All three blanks represent the same residue, which is unique in the manner that it forms peptide bonds.)

   b. _____ has a nonpolar side chain and interacts with other aromatic rings. (Aromatic rings have a tendency to stack with other aromatic rings.)

   c. _____ is small, and does not contain sulfur. It can form internal H-bonds in a folded protein.

   d. The lone electron pair at one of the ring nitrogens in _____ makes it, like Met, a potential ligand, important in binding the iron atoms in hemoglobin.

   e. _____ plays a crucial role in stabilizing the structure of many proteins by virtue of the ability of two such residues on different (or the same) polypeptides to form a covalent linkage between their side chains.

   f. The carbons in an amino acid are labeled with Greek letters beginning with the α-carbon and extending out the side chain: $\beta, \gamma, \delta, \epsilon$. If two or three groups other than hydrogen atoms are attached to the β carbon, the molecule is said to branch at the β carbon. Two adjacent residues that branch at the β carbon make the polypeptide structure known as the α helix unstable. By this criterion _____, _____, and _____ should be α-helix breakers when adjacent.

   g. In proteins under normal physiological conditions (near pH = 7), _____ and _____ side chains are almost entirely positively charged, but _____ side chains are only partially positively charged.

2.3   Proteins are long polymers of amino acids joined by peptide bonds. In aqueous solution at pH = 7 most proteins are folded so that the nonpolar amino acid side chains are inside in a nonpolar environment, whereas most of the polar side chains are outside, in contact with water. By inspection of the structures in Table 2.1, answer the following questions:

   a. Are the following amino acids likely to have their side chains on the outside or on the inside of a globular protein in solution: Val, Pro, Phe, Asp, Lys, Ilu, and His?

   b. Why might Gly and Ala be found either inside or outside?

   c. How might Ser, Thr, Asn, and Gln be accommodated inside, even though they are polar?

   d. Where might Cys be found and why?

2.4 Draw the following amino acid or oligopeptide structures and, if possible, build these structures with space-filling molecular models. By convention, the first-named residue is the N-terminal amino acid (i.e., has a free α-amino group).

   a. The dipeptide Ala-His
   b. The tripeptide Glu-Pro-Cys
   c. Show how an oligopeptide of Leu and Lys can be either a branched-chain or a straight-chain structure. (Only straight-chain structures occur in most natural proteins.)

2.5 Each of the ionizable groups in an amino acid has two possible ionization states: charged and uncharged (e.g., —COOH, —COO⁻). Therefore, a molecule with n such groups has 2^n possible ionization states.

   a. Draw the four possible ionization states of the amino acid Ser.
   b. By inspection, indicate which ionization state predominates at pH = 1, pH = 3, pH = pI, pH = 7, and pH = 11.

2.6 a. A mixture of the following amino acids is subjected to paper electrophoresis at pH = 3.9: Ala, Ser, Phe, Leu, Arg, Asp, and His. Which will go toward the anode (+)? Toward the cathode (−)?
   b. Amino acids with identical charges often separate slightly during paper electrophoresis; for example, Gly separates from Leu. Can you suggest an explanation?
   c. Assume that you have a mixture of Ala, Val, Glu, Lys, and Thr at pH = 6.0. Draw the pattern that will be obtained by ninhydrin staining of the amino acids following paper electrophoresis. Indicate the anode (+), cathode (−), origin, and any unresolved amino acids. (Ninhydrin makes the amino acids visible by reacting with free α-amino groups to form colored spots.)

2.7 a. Table 2.2 shows the pK_a values of several peptides. Indicate the direction of migration of the following peptides at pH = 3 and pH = 10 using the pK_a values deduced from a comparison of Tables 2.1 and 2.2: Phe-Ilu; Lys-Lys-Lys; Arg-Asp.

Table 2.2
pK_a Values for Some Peptides (Problem 2.7)

	α-Carboxyl	β-Carboxyl	α-Amino	ε-Amino
Gly-Gly	3.1		8.1	
Gly-Gly-Gly	3.3		7.9	
Ala-Ala	3.2		8.4	
Ala-Ala-Ala-Ala	3.4		7.9	
Ala-Gly-Gly	3.2		8.2	
Gly-Ala	3.2		8.2	
Ala-Gly	3.2		8.2	
Lys-Ala	3.2		7.6	10.7
Ala-Lys-Ala	3.2		7.7	10.4
Ala-Lys-Ala-Ala	3.6		8.0	10.6
Ala-Ala-Lys-Ala	3.6		8.0	10.6
Asp-Gly	2.1	4.5	9.1	

   b. What conclusions can you draw from a comparison of the pK_a's of amino acids and peptides?

2.8 An amino acid analyzer is an instrument that automatically separates amino acids by chromatography on a column of cation-exchange resin and determines their molar ratios (Figure 2.4). The resin contains polystyrene with sulfonic acid groups covalently bonded to the benzene rings as shown in Figure 2.5. Two major kinds of effects act to separate the amino acids: electrostatic interactions with the negatively charged sulfonic acid groups, and hydrophobic interactions with the nonpolar benzene rings.

   a. Explain the elution order shown in Figure 2.4 for the following sets of amino acids (i.e., why does set 1 elute before set 2, etc.?):

   1. Asp
   2. Ser, Thr
   3. Gly, Ala
   4. Val, Met, Leu, Ilu

   5. Tyr, Phe
   6. Lys, His
   7. Arg

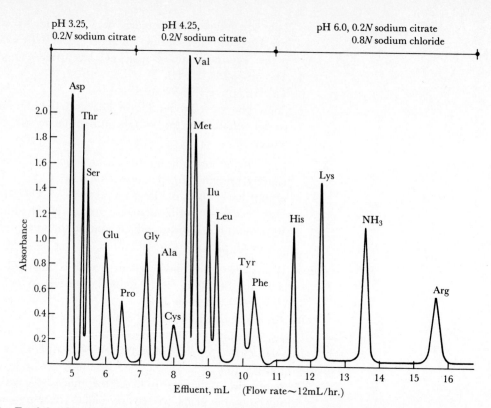

Figure 2.4
Separation of amino acids by cation-exchange chromatography (Problem 2.8). The areas under the peaks are proportional to the amounts of amino acids in the mixture. Three buffers of successively higher pH are used to elute the amino acids from the column.

b. Explain the elution order shown in Figure 2.4 for amino acids within sets 3 and 5. Explain why Asp elutes before Glu.

2.9   How many different polypeptides of 61 residues can be made from the 20 naturally occurring amino acids?

2.10   Indicate the relative mobilities of amino acids in the following mixtures during paper chromatography in a butanol:acetic acid:water system. Assume a pH of 4.5 in the aqueous phase.
   a. Ilu, Lys
   b. Phe, Ser
   c. Ala, Val, Leu
   d. Pro, Val
   e. Glu, Asp
   f. Tyr, Ala, Ser, His

2.11   Indicate which of the following pairs of peptides (or amino acids) could be separated, and which could not, using the conditions of Problem 2.10.
   a. Lys-Lys; Lys
   b. Leu-Leu-Leu; Leu
   c. Trp-Ilu-Phe; Arg-Ilu-Phe
   d. Cys-Cys-Ser; Ala-Ala-Ser

2.12   Which of the following polypeptides is more soluble in water?
   a. Phe_{20} or Gly_{20}
   b. Asp_{20} or Glu_{20} at pH = 6.0
   c. Phe_{20} or Tyr_{20}

2.13   Amino acids occasionally are used as buffers. A buffer is a solution that resists changes

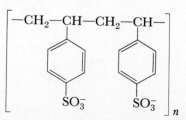

Figure 2.5
Structure of the cation-exchange resin Dowex 50 (Problem 2.8).

in pH when acid or base is added. The pH range over which a buffer is effective is called the buffering range, usually defined as $pK_a + 1$ to $pK_a - 1$.

a. Indicate the buffering range (or ranges) of Gly, His, Asp, and Lys.

b. Choose an amino acid to buffer at pH = 4, pH = 6, pH = 9, and pH = 12.

c. Would you expect a protein containing 100 amino acids to be as good a buffer as its constituent free amino acids at equivalent molar amino acid concentrations? Explain.

2.14 The ϵ-amino group of Lys has a pK_a of 10.5.

a. What fraction of these groups will be protonated (i.e., $-NH_3^+$ rather than $-NH_2$) in a dilute solution of Lys at pH = 9.5?

b. At pH = 11.0?

c. Explain why the pK_a of the ϵ-amino group is higher than that of the α-amino group.

2.15 The γ-carboxyl group of Glu has a pK_a of 4.3.

a. What fraction of these groups will be unprotonated (i.e., $-COO^-$ rather than $-COOH$) in a dilute solution of Glu at pH = 5.0?

b. At pH = 3.8?

c. Explain why this pK_a is higher than the pK_a of the α-carboxyl group.

2.16 a. Assume you have a solution containing 0.1 mol of Ala adjusted to pH = 0.5 with hydrochloric acid. You begin adding $1.0M$ NaOH (a strong base). Sketch the resulting titration curve showing all inflection points. Show your calculations for a few points on the curve. (Pick the pH values to simplify the calculations, rather than simply using pH = 1, = 2, = 3, and so on.) State all your assumptions.

b. Sketch a similar titration curve for a solution containing 0.1 mol of His at pH = 0.5, making the assumptions stated in part a but performing no calculations.

2.17 a. Using the pK_a values in Table 2.1, identify the amino acid that has the titration curve shown in Figure 2.6a.

b. Identify the amino acid that has the titration curve shown in Figure 2.6b. How does this curve differ from the ones you constructed for Problem 2.16?

c. What are the similarities and differences among the four titration curves examined in Problems 2.16 and 2.17a and b?

2.18 From kangaroo-tail collagen you have isolated a series of previously uncharacterized γ-substituted prolines. From their titration curves you determine the pK_a's of the ionizable groups to be as follows:

a. Carboxyproline

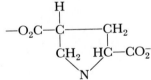

	pK_a
α-Carboxyl	2.0
α-Amino	10.5
γ-Carboxyl	3.8

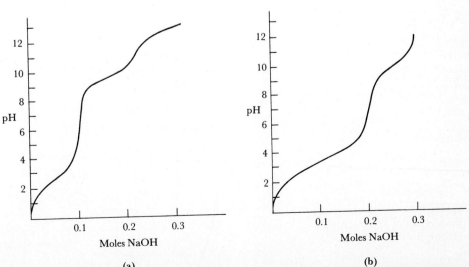

Figure 2.6
Titration curves of two amino acids (Problem 2.17).

(a)   (b)

b. Aminoproline

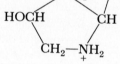

α-Carboxyl	1.9
α-Amino	9.8
γ-Amino	10.0

c. Sulfhydrylproline

α-Carboxyl	1.9
α-Amino	9.9
γ-Sulfhydryl	9.9

Using these pK_a values, calculate the isoelectric point, pI, for each amino acid.

☆ 2.19   Figure 2.4 shows the elution pattern of 16 common amino acids separated by cation-exchange chromatography. If the following amino acids were present in such an experiment, where would you expect them to elute in relation to the 16 amino acids shown in the figure? Briefly explain your answers.

    a. Norleucine: side chain $-CH_2CH_2CH_2CH_3$
    b. Cysteic acid: side chain $-CH_2SO_3^{2-}$
    c. Phosphoserine: side chain $-CH_2OPO_3^{2-}$
    d. Ethanolamine: $H_3^+NCH_2CH_2OH$
    e. Hydroxyproline:

☆ 2.20   Figure 2.7 is a diagram of the fingerprint obtained by subjecting a mixture of 18 amino acids (all but Asn and Gln) to electrophoresis at pH = 6.5 in one dimension and chromatography in the other (butanol : acetic acid : pyridine). Identify the numbered spots. They correspond to the amino acids Arg, Asp, Cys, Pro, Lys, Glu, Ilu, Leu, and His.

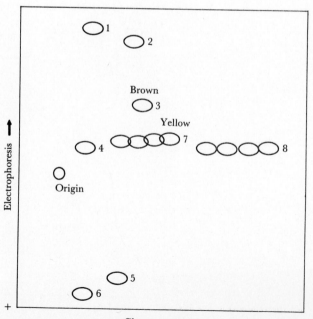

Figure 2.7
Fingerprint of 18 amino acids
(Problem 2.20).

Answers

2.1 a. False. The nonionized form of an amino acid never predominates in aqueous solution.

   b. True

   c. True

   d. True. At its pI the tripeptide will have one full negative charge (α-COO$^-$), one essentially nonionized amino group (α-NH$_2$), and three partially charged amino groups (ϵ-NH$_3^+$). Because the total of the positive charges must equal that of the negative charges at pI, each of the three ϵ-amino groups will be about one-third ionized. The pH at which they will be one-third ionized is higher than their pK_a's.

   e. False. Peptide bonds have partial double-bond character and consequently no free rotation.

   f. False. Paper electrophoresis separates on the basis of net charge.

2.2 a. Pro. Pro is an imino acid; see Figure 2.8b.

   b. Phe

   c. Ser (or Thr)

   d. His

   e. Cys. The bridge is a disulfide bond, —CH$_2$—S—S—CH$_2$—.

   f. Thr, Val, Ilu

   g. Arg, Lys, His

2.3 a. Inside: Val, Pro, Phe, Ilu; outside: Asp, Lys, His.

   b. Gly (—H) and Ala (—CH$_3$) have small side chains and accordingly do not have enough atoms to be strongly hydrophobic. Thus they can be accommodated inside or outside.

   c. Ser, Thr, Asn, and Gln have uncharged polar side chains at pH = 7. They can participate in the formation of internal H-bonds, which neutralize their polar character.

   d. Inside, because two Cys residues often form a —S—S— disulfide bond, which neutralizes the polar character of both residues.

2.4   The complete structures are shown in Figure 2.8.

2.5 a. See Figure 2.9.

   b. By comparing the pH with the pK_{a_1} and pK_{a_2} values of Ser, it is easy to determine which state will predominate. Consider pH = 1. The pK_{a_1} of 2.2 for the reaction —COOH $\rightleftarrows$ —COO$^-$ + H$^+$ indicates that at pH = 2.2 exactly half of the carboxyl groups are in the —COOH state, and half are in the —COO$^-$ state. Below pH = 2.2 the —COOH state predominates. For the amino group, the pK_{a_2} of 9.2 for the reaction —NH$_3^+$ $\rightleftarrows$ —NH$_2$ + H$^+$ indicates that the —NH$_3^+$ state predominates at any pH below 9.2. At pH = 1 the NH$_3^+$, COOH state, or state 4, predominates. (The fraction of molecules in each state could be calculated precisely from equation 2.2.)

   The answers to part b are

pH	Predominant state
1	4
3	3
pI	3
7	3
11	2

2.6 a. The pI's of Ala, Ser, Phe, and Leu are near pH = 6. Because the pI is the pH at which the net charge is 0, at pH = 3.9 these molecules have a net positive charge (i.e., some of their carboxyl groups are in the —COOH state, whereas virtually all of their amino groups are in the —NH$_3^+$ state). Ala, Ser, Phe, and Leu would move toward the cathode and would not separate. His and Arg with pI's of 7.6 and 10.8, respectively, would move toward the cathode, and Asp with a pI of 3.0 would move toward the anode. His and Arg would separate from the other amino acids that move toward the cathode.

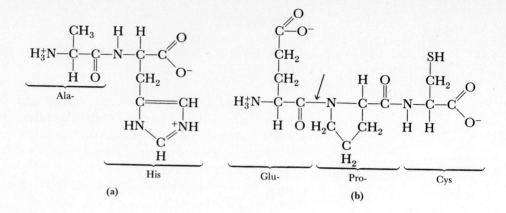

(a)

(b)

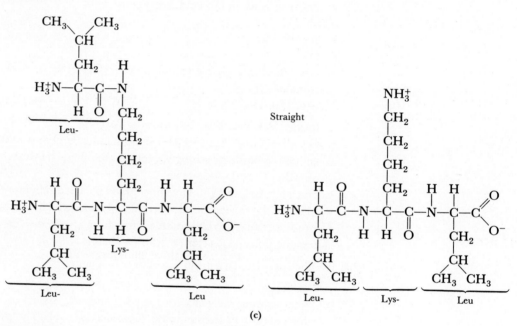

(c)

Figure 2.8
Oligopeptide structures (Answer 2.4). **(a)** Ala-His. **(b)** Glu-Pro-Cys. Note the unique peptide bond of the Pro residue (arrow), which is not a true amino acid, but rather an imino acid. **(c)** A branched tetrapeptide of Leu and Lys, and a straight tripeptide of Leu and Lys.

   b. A larger molecule will move more slowly than a smaller one with the same charge during electrophoresis, because the charge-to-mass ratio is smaller and accordingly the force causing migration is smaller per unit of mass.
   c. See Figure 2.10. A comparison of pI's indicates that Glu, with a net negative charge, will move toward the anode; Lys, with a net positive charge, will move toward the

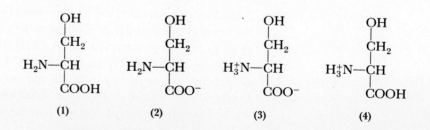

Figure 2.9
The four ionization states of Ser
(Answer 2.5).

Figure 2.10
Electrophoretic separation of
Ala, Glu, Lys, Thr, and Val at
pH = 6.0 (Answer 2.6).

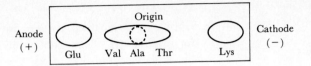

cathode. At pH = 6, Val, Ala, and Thr are near their isoelectric points. Though Thr might be expected to separate from Val and Ala, it does not do so cleanly in practice.

2.7 a.

	pH = 3	pH = 10
Phe-Ilu	Cathode	Anode
Lys-Lys-Lys	Cathode	Cathode
Arg-Asp	Cathode	Anode

b. The pK_{a_1}'s (α-carboxyl) for peptides are higher than for amino acids ($\simeq 3.2$ versus $\simeq 2.2$). The pK_{a_2}'s (α-amino) are lower for peptides than for amino acids ($\simeq 8$ versus $\simeq 9.5$). The pK_{a_3}'s are approximately the same regardless of whether the side chain is attached to an amino acid or to a peptide.

2.8 a. 1. At pH = 3.3 Asp has a net negative charge and accordingly has little charge attraction for the negatively charged sulfonic acid resin. Therefore, it passes most rapidly through the column.

2. Ser and Thr have a slight positive charge and are retained slightly through charge attraction by the column. The hydroxyl groups are polar and accordingly do not interact with the nonpolar polystyrene matrix.

3. Gly and Ala are somewhat positively charged; thus they are retained on the column. In addition, they are more hydrophobic than Ser and Thr and therefore elute somewhat later. At pH = 4.3 Gly and Ala are eluted from the column because their net positive charge is reduced.

4. Val, Met, Leu, and Ilu also are somewhat positively charged. Their very nonpolar side chains cause them to be retained by the nonpolar polystyrene longer than Gly and Ala.

5. Tyr and Phe have properties similar to Val, Met, Leu, and Ilu, and in addition have aromatic rings that interact by "stacking" with the aromatic rings of polystyrene.

6. The remaining amino acids are eluted only after a second pH increase, because their net positive charges require even more titration than any of the previous amino acids.

7. Arg is the most strongly positively charged of the amino acids; thus, it is retained longest.

b. Ala is more hydrophobic than Gly. Tyr is less hydrophobic than Phe. Glu is more hydrophobic and less charged than Asp.

2.9 $20^{61} \simeq 2 \times 10^{79}$. This figure is greater than the estimated number of atoms in the universe!

2.10 The α-NH$_3^+$ and the α-COO$^-$ charges more or less cancel one another at a slightly acidic pH and separation is on the basis of nonpolar character.

a. Ilu is very hydrophobic and Lys is charged. Therefore, Lys would move very slowly and Ilu would move rapidly.

b. Phe is less polar than Ser and moves considerably faster.

c. Leu > Val > Ala. In other words, Leu moves faster than Val, which moves faster than Ala, because Leu is the most hydrophobic and Ala is the least hydrophobic of the three.

d. Val > Pro

e. Glu moves faster than Asp because more of Glu is in the nonionized state (necessary for solubility in the nonpolar solvent) and because the side chain of Glu is more hydrophobic than that of Asp.

f. Tyr > Ala > Ser ≃ His

2.11   The relative mobilities are

a. Lys-Lys ≃ Lys

b. Leu-Leu-Leu > Leu

c. Trp-Ilu-Phe > Arg-Ilu-Phe

d. Ala-Ala-Ser > Cys-Cys-Ser

2.12 a. Gly_{20} > Phe_{20}

b. Asp_{20} ≃ Glu_{20} at pH = 6.0

c. Tyr_{20} > Phe_{20}

2.13 a. As calculated by the Henderson–Hasselbalch equation (equation 2.2), a buffering range of $pK_a \pm 1$ encompasses 82% of the total buffering capacity of an ionizable group. From this definition the buffering ranges are

Gly	1.3 to 3.3	8.6 to 10.6	
His	0.8 to 2.8	8.2 to 10.2	5.0 to 7.0
Asp	1.1 to 3.1	8.8 to 10.8	2.9 to 4.9
Lys	1.2 to 3.2	8.0 to 10.0	9.5 to 11.5

b. Asp or Glu at pH = 4

His at pH = 6

Almost any amino acid at pH = 9 (α-amino group)

Arg at pH = 12

c. Only ionizable groups have buffering capacity. At an equivalent concentration of amino acid residues the protein will be a much poorer buffer, because the α-amino and α-carboxyl groups of all but the terminal amino acids are in peptide linkages and are not charged.

2.14 a. This problem is a simple application of the Henderson–Hasselbalch equation (equation 2.2). The reaction being studied is

$$-NH_3^+ \rightleftarrows -NH_2 + H^+$$

Therefore,

$$[-NH_3^+] = [HA] \quad \text{and} \quad [-NH_2] = [A^-]$$

At pH = 9.5,

$$9.5 = 10.5 + \log \frac{[-NH_2]}{[-NH_3^+]}$$

$$-1 = \log \frac{[-NH_2]}{[-NH_3^+]}$$

$$10^{-1} = \frac{[-NH_2]}{[-NH_3^+]} \quad \text{or} \quad \frac{[-NH_2]}{[-NH_3^+]} = \frac{1}{10}$$

Thus, the fraction of protonated molecules is

$$\frac{10}{10 + 1} = \frac{10}{11} \simeq 91\% \text{ at pH} = 9.5$$

b. At pH = 11.0,

$$11.0 = 10.5 + \log \frac{[-NH_2]}{[-NH_3^+]}$$

$$0.5 = \log \frac{[-NH_2]}{[-NH_3^+]}$$

$$3.2 = \frac{[-NH_2]}{[-NH_3^+]}$$

thus,

$$\frac{[-NH_2]}{[-NH_3^+]} = \frac{3.2}{1}$$

and the fraction of protonated molecules is

$$\frac{1}{4.2} = 24\% \text{ at pH} = 11.0$$

c. The more stable an ionic species, the more the equilibrium will shift to favor it. Delocalization of charge on an ion stabilizes it, whereas concentration of charge destabilizes it. Both $-NH_3^+$ and $-COO^-$ groups tend to withdraw electrons from nearby atoms and become relatively more negatively charged. Since the α-NH_3^+ group must compete with the α-COO^- group for electrons, it carries a greater positive charge than the ϵ-NH_3^+ group. Thus the α-NH_3^+ group is less stable than the ϵ-NH_3^+ group and the equilibrium for its dissociation is shifted away from $-NH_3^+$ toward $-NH_2$ and H^+. Consequently, the K_a is higher and the pK_a is lower for the α-NH_3^+ group.

2.15 a. Using the Henderson–Hasselbalch equation,

$$5.0 = 4.3 + \log \frac{[-COO^-]}{[-COOH]}$$

$$0.7 = \log \frac{[-COO^-]}{[-COOH]}$$

$$5.0 = \frac{[-COO^-]}{[-COOH]}$$

$$\frac{5.0}{6.0} = 83\% \text{ at pH} = 5.0$$

b.

$$3.8 = 4.3 + \log \frac{[-COO^-]}{[-COOH]}$$

$$-0.5 = \log \frac{[-COO^-]}{[-COOH]}$$

$$0.5 = \log \frac{[-COOH]}{[-COO^-]}$$

$$3.2 = \frac{[-COOH]}{[-COO^-]}$$

$$\frac{1}{4.2} = 24\% \text{ at pH} = 3.8$$

c. The electron-withdrawing α-NH_3^+ group exerts an inductive effect, withdrawing electrons from the α-COO^- group, which therefore carries less negative charge than does the γ-COO^- group. Thus the α-COO^- group is more stable than the γ-COO^- group and the equilibrium for α-COOH dissociation is shifted toward α-COO^- and H^+. Consequently, the K_a is higher and the pK_a is lower for the α-COOH group.

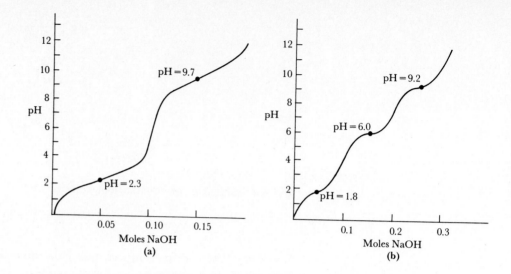

Figure 2.11
Titration curves of **(a)** Ala and
(b) His (Answer 2.16).

2.16   Titration problems can be approached using the Henderson–Hasselbalch equation (equation 2.2). For a given species of a titratable group at pH = pK, [A⁻]/[HA] = 1.0; that is, 50% of the groups are in the A⁻ state. When pH − pK = 1.0, [A⁻]/[HA] = 10, and $\frac{10}{11}$ or $\simeq$ 91% of the groups are in the A⁻ state. When pH − pK = −0.5, 24% are in the A⁻ state, and so on.

   To titrate 0.1 mol of an amino acid will require 0.1 mol of NaOH per titratable group. (Assume that the amount of HCl present is negligible.)

   a. Ala: Inflection points will occur at pH values equal to the pK_{a_1} and pK_{a_2} values of 2.3 and 9.7. These points correspond to 0.05 and 0.15 mol of added NaOH. pH = 1.3 corresponds to 0.09 × 0.10 mol = 0.0090 mol of NaOH added. pH = 3.3 corresponds to 0.91 × 0.10 mol or 0.091 mol added. pH = 4.3 corresponds to 0.99 × 0.10 mol or 0.099 mol of NaOH added. Thus the titration curve for the carboxyl group rises sharply until it meets the titration curve for the amino group (Figure 2.11a). As a general rule, if the pK_a values of titratable groups are separated by more than 2.5 pH units their titration curves can be drawn independently.

   b. His: Inflection points occur at pH values of 1.8, 6.0, and 9.2, corresponding to the three pK_a values. The titration curve is shown in Figure 2.11b.

2.17 a. Arg: The three inflection points are at pH values of 2.2, 9.0, and 12.5. The three titratable groups can be calculated independently.

   b. Asp: The three inflection points are at pH values of 2.1, 3.9, and 9.8. Note that the two lower pK_a values are too close together to be completely independent, as you assumed in Problem 2.16.

   c. Each of the preceding titration curves has similar features resulting from the α-carboxyl and α-amino groups. The curves differ as a result of the absence or presence of a titratable side chain.

2.18 a. At pH = pI the sum of the negative charges must equal the sum of the positive charges. Thus for carboxyproline the sum of the negative charges on the two carboxyl groups must equal 1 to balance the one full positive charge contributed by the α-amino group. The carboxyl groups will carry one negative charge at a pH midway between their pK_a values. Verify this answer for yourself.

$$pI = \frac{pK_a(\alpha\text{-carboxyl}) + pK_a(\gamma\text{-carboxyl})}{2}$$

$$= \frac{2.0 + 3.8}{2}$$

$$pI = 2.9 \text{ for carboxyproline}$$

b. Similarly,

$$pI = \frac{pK_a(\alpha\text{-amino}) + pK_a\,(\gamma\text{-amino})}{2}$$

$$= \frac{9.8 + 10.0}{2}$$

$$pI = 9.9 \text{ for aminoproline}$$

c. The ionization of the sulfhydryl group is $SH \rightleftarrows S^- + H^+$, and $pK_a = 9.9$. At all pH values well below pH $= 9.9$ the sulfhydryl group will be uncharged. Therefore, as a first approximation, its ionization may be neglected.

$$pI = \frac{pK_{a_1} + pK_{a_2}}{2} = \frac{1.9 + 9.9}{2} = 5.9 \text{ for sulfhydrylproline}$$

At pH $= 5.9$ the sulfhydryl group is $> 99\%$ uncharged; therefore, our approximation is valid.

3 Primary Structure
of Polypeptides

The sequence of amino acids in a polypeptide is called its **primary structure.** Sequence analysis provides information on the structural basis of protein function, because the amino acid sequence of a protein determines its three-dimensional conformation (Chapter 4) and resulting functional specificity (Chapters 5 and 6). Sequence analysis is important to the study of gene structure and evolution; the amino acid sequence of a protein can be related through the genetic code (Chapter 21) to the nucleotide sequence of the gene that directed its synthesis (Chapter 20). Small medically useful polypeptides can be synthesized chemically if their sequences are known. This chapter considers the methods currently employed to determine the primary structures of polypeptides.

Concepts

3.1 **A common strategy is employed for analyzing
most amino acid sequences.**

The usual approach to sequencing a polypeptide is as follows:

1. Break all Cys—S—S—Cys disulfide bonds.

2. Determine the amino acid composition.

3. Identify the N-terminal (amino-terminal) and C-terminal (carboxyl-terminal) amino acids. Use a protein sequenator (Concept 3.4) to determine as much of the N-terminal sequence as possible.

4. Break the polypeptide into fragments by internal cleavage at specific amino acid residues. Separate the fragments and determine the amino acid composition of each.

5. Determine the amino acid sequence of each fragment, using a protein sequenator to determine as much of the N-terminal sequence as possible. Repeat steps 4 and 5 if necessary.

6. Order the fragments by repeating steps 4 and 5, using a cleavage procedure of different specificity to generate "overlap peptides." This process yields the complete amino acid sequence.

7. Locate Cys—S—S—Cys disulfide bonds.

The methods employed are described in order in Concepts 3.2 through 3.8. Table 3.1 summarizes the specificities of the various cleavage procedures.

3.2 **Reduction breaks disulfide bonds; alkylation
prevents their re-formation.**

Disulfide cross-links complicate the determination of amino acid sequence and usually are cleaved by reduction before sequence analysis. Alkylation of the resulting

Table 3.1
Specificity of Cleavage Procedures Used in Amino Acid
Sequence Analysis[a]

Procedure	Site	Specificity	Comment
I. Terminal cleavages			
1. Edman degradation	C side of N terminus	R_n = any amino acid	Ineffective for blocked N termini
2. Carboxypeptidase A	N side of C terminus	$R_n \neq$ Arg, Lys, Pro $R_{n-1} \neq$ Pro	Generally removes 1–4 residues sequentially
3. Carboxypeptidase B	N side of C terminus	$R_n =$ Arg, Lys, AECys[b] $R_{n-1} \neq$ Pro	Generally removes 1–4 residues sequentially
4. Hydrazinolysis	Hydrolyzes all peptide bonds and releases free C-terminal amino acid		Used only if procedures I.2 and I.3 fail
II. Internal cleavages			
1. Cyanogen bromide	C side of R_n	$R_n =$ Met	Highly specific
2. Cyanogen bromide, anhydrous	C side of R_n	$R_n =$ Met, Trp	Highly specific
3. Trypsin	C side of R_n	$R_n =$ Lys, Arg, AECys $R_{n+1} \neq$ Pro	Highly specific
4. Chymotrypsin	C side of R_n	$R_n =$ Phe, Trp, Tyr, Leu $R_{n+1} \neq$ Pro	Sometimes effective for $R_n =$ Met, Asn, others
5. Thermolysin	N side of R_n	$R_n =$ Leu, Ilu, Phe, Trp, Tyr, Val $R_{n-1} \neq$ Pro	Sometimes effective for $R_n =$ Ala, others
6. Pepsin	N side of R_n	$R_n =$ Leu, Asp, Glu, Phe, Tyr, Trp $R_{n-1} \neq$ Pro	Other R_n also possible; quite nonspecific
7. Acid phosphatase	C side of R_n	$R_n =$ Asp, Glu	Quite specific

[a] For definition of R_n, R_{n+1}, and R_{n-1}, see Figure 3.4.
[b] AECys = aminoethyl cysteine.

—SH groups prevents disulfide bond re-formation and increases the stability of Cys residues to subsequent acid hydrolysis (Figure 3.1). Reduction is accomplished with an excess of sulfhydryl reagent of general structure RSH, such as β-mercaptoethanol. A commonly used alkylating reagent is iodoacetic acid.

3.3 Amino acid composition is determined after complete hydrolysis of the polypeptide.

Treatment of a polypeptide with $6N$ HCl for 20–24 hr at 110°C in vacuo hydrolyzes (cleaves) all peptide bonds. The resulting amino acids are separated and their molar

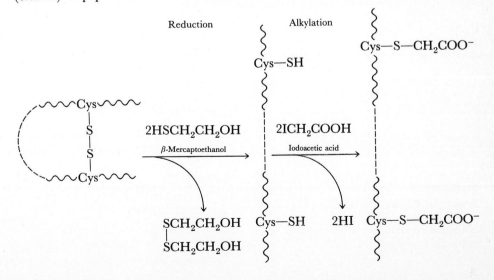

Figure 3.1
Reduction and alkylation of a disulfide bond. Wavy lines symbolize the continuation of a polypeptide. The dashed lines indicate that the cross-linked Cys residues may be in the same or in different polypeptides.

ratios are determined automatically using an amino acid analyzer (Problem 2.8). This procedure destroys Trp and hydrolyzes Asn and Gln to NH_3 plus Asp and Glu, respectively. Trp generally is determined spectrophotometrically in a separate procedure.

3.4 Specific chemical or enzymatic methods are used to identify terminal amino acids.

A. **Edman degradation** is now the preferred method for identification of N-terminal amino acids. Phenylisothiocyanate (PITC, the Edman reagent) reacts with the polypeptide to yield a phenylthiohydantoin (PTH—) derivative of the N-terminal amino acid that can be identified chromatographically. The resulting polypeptide (minus the N-terminal amino acid) can be treated again by the same procedure to identify the next amino acid (Figure 3.2). Various side reactions currently limit the number of successive steps that can be carried out.

The **protein sequenator,** an instrument that automatically performs sequential Edman degradations, can determine N-terminal sequences that range between 30 and 70 residues on large polypeptides. Small polypeptides of less than 30–40 residues often can be sequenced entirely. The protein sequenator has greatly facilitated the determination of complete amino acid sequences.

In some proteins the amino group of the N-terminal amino acid is bonded cova-

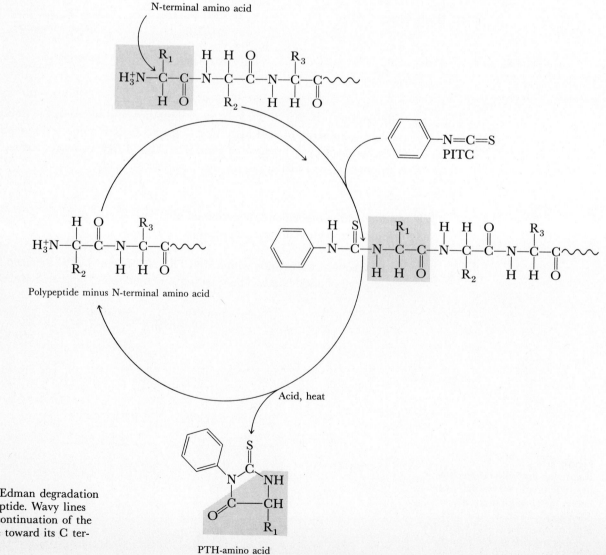

Figure 3.2
Sequential Edman degradation of a polypeptide. Wavy lines symbolize continuation of the polypeptide toward its C terminus.

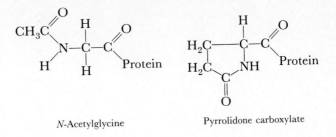

Figure 3.3
Blocked N-terminal amino acids.

N-Acetylglycine   Pyrrolidone carboxylate

lently to another group, which prevents identification by the Edman procedure. Examples of blocked N-termini are *N*-acetylglycine and pyrrolidone carboxylate, formed by cyclization of N-terminal Gln (Figure 3.3).

B. A C-terminal amino acid can be identified using **carboxypeptidases A and B.** These enzymes catalyze sequential hydrolysis of C-terminal amino acids, which then can be identified chromatographically. The usefulness of carboxypeptidases is limited by their specificities (Table 3.1). Carboxypeptidase A will not act if the C-terminal residue is Arg, Pro, or Lys. Carboxypeptidase B will act *only* if the C terminus is Arg or Lys. Furthermore, neither enzyme will act if the penultimate residue is Pro.

    Hydrazinolysis, because it is somewhat unreliable, is used only when neither carboxypeptidase will remove the C-terminal amino acid. Hydrazine cleaves all peptide bonds, thereby forming aminoacyl hydrazides. Only the C-terminal residue is released as a free amino acid, which can be identified chromatographically.

3.5 Internal cleavage at specific amino acid residues breaks a polypeptide into unique fragments.

A. Peptide-bond cleavage can occur on either the N side or the C side of a specific residue (Figure 3.4).

    1.   **Cyanogen bromide (CNBr) treatment** is the most specific internal cleavage procedure (Table 3.1). The reagent attacks only at Met (R_n = Met) residues, cleaving the peptide bond on the C side. In the process, Met is converted to homoserine (Figure 3.5).

    2.   **Trypsin digestion,** the next most specific procedure, cleaves only on the C side of the basic amino acids Arg and Lys (Table 3.1). Trypsin does not catalyze cleavage if the C-side residue is Pro ($R_{n+1} \neq$ Pro).

    It is possible to alter the specificity of trypsin cleavage by chemically modifying the polypeptide substrate. Maleylation with maleic anhydride blocks Lys residues (Figure 3.6a) and allows trypsin to catalyze cleavage only at Arg. Aminoethylation with ethyleneimine (Figure 3.6b) converts Cys to aminoethyl cysteine (AECys). AECys, a Lys analogue, permits trypsin to catalyze cleavage of the adjacent C-side peptide bond.

    3.   Digestions with **chymotrypsin, thermolysin,** and **pepsin** yield less specific cleavages (Table 3.1). Chymotrypsin catalyzes cleavage on the C side of Phe, Trp, Tyr, and Leu. Occasionally, however, it also catalyzes cleavage on the C side of Met, Asn, and

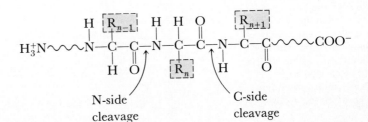

Figure 3.4
Alternative peptide-bond cleavages adjacent to a specific residue (R_n).

N-side cleavage   C-side cleavage

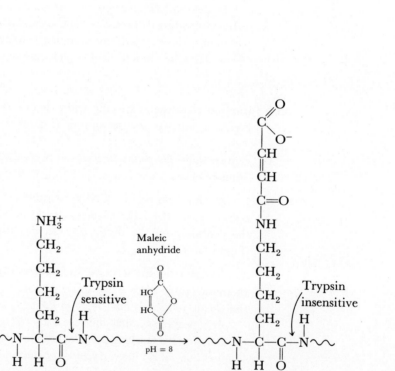

Figure 3.5
Cleavage of a peptide bond adjacent to Met with CNBr.

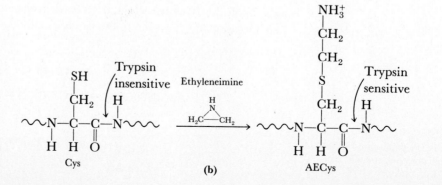

Figure 3.6
Modifications of the polypeptide substrate that alter the specificity of trypsin cleavage. **(a)** Reaction with maleic anhydride (maleylation) blocks trypsin attack at Lys residues. **(b)** Reaction with ethyleneimine (aminoethylation) permits trypsin attack at Cys residues.

other residues. Thermolysin catalyzes cleavage on the N side of a number of hydrophobic residues. Pepsin is quite nonspecific, catalyzing cleavage on the N side of several residues. Cleavage by these enyzmes is blocked if the amino acid adjacent to the cleavage site is Pro.

B. The peptide fragments resulting from cleavage of the polypeptide are separated by chromatography or electrophoresis, and the amino acid composition of each fragment is determined. In preparation for complete sequencing, peptides larger than about 30 residues are subjected to a second internal cleavage procedure, followed by separation of the resulting fragments and determination of their amino acid compositions. Separation of peptide fragments is generally the most difficult step of sequence analysis.

3.6 Overlap peptides are necessary for ordering large peptide fragments.

The initial cleavage is generally made as specific as possible (CNBr or trypsin) in order to generate large peptide fragments. These fragments can be arranged relative to one another after treatment of the original polypeptide by a second cleavage procedure that generates small fragments whose sequences extend across the initial cleavage points (overlap peptides). The amino acid sequence of each overlap peptide orders two (or more) of the original fragments.

3.7 Disulfide bonds are located after cleavage of the unreduced polypeptide.

Cleavage of the intact, unreduced polypeptide produces some fragments of the general structure shown in Figure 3.7. Partial sequence analysis of the two linked peptides is generally sufficient to locate them in the complete structure.

3.8 The protein sequenator is used for microsequence analyses.

Interesting polypeptides often are available only in very small quantities. For example, interferon, a protein that combats viral infections and, apparently, certain types of cancer, was obtainable until recently only in subnanomole amounts. Samples of this size require microsequencing techniques.

There are three general approaches to microsequencing:

1. **Internal label.** Radiolabeled amino acids are incorporated into the polypeptide. The polypeptide is subjected to sequential Edman degradation, and the PTH-amino acid derivatives from each step are separated in the presence of unlabeled carrier PTH-amino acids. The PTH derivatives corresponding to each residue then are counted in a scintillation counter. This method can be used to analyze proteins down to the level of 0.1 micromole (μmol).

2. **External label.** An extrinsic radiolabel such as ^{35}S-PITC can be incorporated into the PTH derivatives during the sequencing procedure. This procedure increases

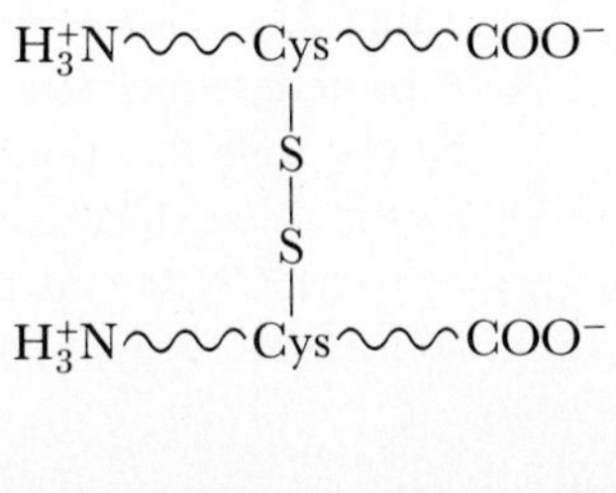

Figure 3.7
Two peptides linked by a disulfide bond.

$$H_3^+N\sim\sim\sim Cys\sim\sim\sim COO^-$$
$$|$$
$$S$$
$$|$$
$$S$$
$$|$$
$$H_3^+N\sim\sim\sim Cys\sim\sim\sim COO^-$$

the sensitivity of the preceding method and can be used to analyze samples in the 500 picomole (pmol) range.

3. **Direct analysis.** A newly developed protein sequenator permits microsamples to be analyzed directly at the 50–100 pmol level. For each of these microsequencing procedures the PTH-amino acid derivatives are separated from one another by high-pressure liquid chromatography.

3.9 Additional concepts and techniques are presented in the Problems section.

A. Distinguishing Gln and Asn from Glu and Asp. Problem 3.12.
B. Sequencing unfractionated mixtures of peptides. Problems 3.13 and 3.15.
C. Analysis of protein sequenator data. Problems 3.17, 3.18, and 3.19.

References

COMPREHENSIVE TEXTS

Lehninger: Chapter 5   Stryer: Chapter 2
Metzler: Chapter 2   White et al.: Chapter 6

OTHER REFERENCES

M. Hunkapiller and L. E. Hood, "New Protein Sequenator with Increased Sensitivity," *Science*, **207**, 523 (1980).

S. Moore and W. H. Stein, "Chemical Structures of Pancreatic Ribonuclease and Deoxyribonuclease," *Science*, **180**, 458 (1973).

Problems

By convention, sequences of amino acids are written with the N terminus to the left. Known sequences are written with dashes (e.g., Ala-Val-Lys) and peptide compositions of unknown sequences are written in parentheses with commas [e.g., (Ala,Lys,Val)]. Assume that the occasional cleavages mentioned in Table 3.1 do not occur unless indicated otherwise. Although acid hydrolysis does not cleave —S—S— bonds, all Cys—S—S—Cys residues are reported as Cys_2 in the problems for convenience. Homoserine residues resulting from CNBr cleavage are reported as the original Met. Destruction by acid hydrolysis has been ignored in reporting Trp. Though the amino acid analyzer does not measure NH_3 content, the appropriate amount is reported with each peptide composition to permit assignment of Glu, Gln, Asp, and Asn.

3.1   Answer the following with true or false. If false, explain why.
   a. In theory, one could use sequential Edman degradation to sequence entirely any unblocked polypeptide.
   b. So long as the penultimate residue of a polypeptide is not Pro, at least one of the carboxypeptidases (A or B) will catalyze removal of the C-terminal residue.
   c. All amino acids except Trp, which is destroyed by acid treatment, can be unambiguously identified with the amino acid analyzer.
   d. A Pro residue adjacent to R_n always blocks cleavage by any of the enyzmes listed in Table 3.1.
   e. A protein sequenator could be used to determine the entire amino acid sequence of a polypeptide 200 residues in length in a single experiment.
   f. Assume that the original treatment of a protein was reduction and alkylation, cleavage with CNBr, separation of the resulting peptide fragments, and digestion of fragments with trypsin. Reduction and alkylation of the intact protein followed by cleav-

age with a mixture of chymotrypsin and trypsin will yield the overlap peptides required to order the original fragments.

   g. By chemical modifications one can obtain a polypeptide that is cleaved by trypsin at Arg and Cys residues only.

3.2 a. Internal cleavage with _____, _____, and _____ is much less specific than that obtained with _____ and _____.

   b. Disulfide bonds are broken by _____ with reagents such as β-mercaptoethanol. _____ of the resulting —SH groups with iodoacetic acid prevents disulfide bond re-formation.

   c. Generally, one would expect thermolysin digestion to yield _____ fragments than trypsin digestion.

3.3   Consider the polypeptide whose primary structure is shown in Figure 3.8.

   a. What fragments are produced by digestion with trypsin?

   b. What fragments are produced by digestion with trypsin after reduction and alkylation of the disulfide bond?

   c. What fragments are produced by digestion with thermolysin?

3.4   Indicate whether and where the following peptides are cleaved by the indicated treatments. Justify your answer.

Peptide	Treatment
a. Phe-Arg-Pro	Trypsin
b. Phe-Met-Leu	Carboxypeptidase B
c. Ala-Gly-Phe	Chymotrypsin
d. Gly-Met-Pro	CNBr
e. Pro-Arg-Met	Trypsin

3.5   Histones, an important class of proteins that bind to the DNA of chromosomes, have very high percentages of Arg and Lys (15–30%). Is it easy to determine histone sequences? Why or why not?

3.6   Deduce the amino acid sequence of a simple polypeptide from the following results:

   A. Acid hydrolysis:
      1. $(Ala_2, Arg, Lys_2, Met, Phe, Ser_2)$

   B. Carboxypeptidase A:
      2. (Ala)

   C. Trypsin:
      3. (Ala,Arg)
      4. (Lys,Phe,Ser)
      5. (Lys)
      6. (Ala,Met,Ser)

   D. CNBr:
      7. $(Ala, Arg, Lys_2, Met, Phe, Ser)$
      8. (Ala,Ser)

   E. Thermolysin:
      9. (Ala,Arg,Ser)
      10. $(Ala, Lys_2, Met, Phe, Ser)$

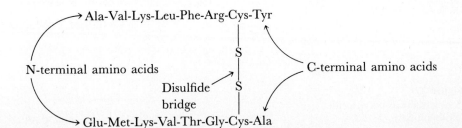

Figure 3.8
A hypothetical polypeptide
(Problem 3.3).

3.7   A polypeptide can be reduced to yield two peptide subunits whose sequences are as follows:

Chain 1: Ala-Cys-Phe-Pro-Lys-Arg-Trp-Cys-Arg-Arg-Val-Cys
Chain 2: Cys-Tyr-Cys-Phe-Cys

The native polypeptide (intact disulfide bonds) is digested with thermolysin and the following peptides are obtained:

1.   (Ala,Cys$_2$,Val)
2.   (Arg,Lys,Phe,Pro)
3.   (Arg$_2$,Cys$_2$,Trp,Tyr)
4.   (Cys$_2$,Phe)

Indicate the positions of the disulfide bonds in the native polypeptide.

3.8   Suppose that you are given a sample of a small polypeptide and are asked to verify that its primary structure is as shown in Figure 3.9. Describe how you could establish the structure in as few steps as possible without using the repetitive Edman procedure. Summarize the results you expect to obtain by indicating the amino acid compositions of the peptides resulting from any cleavage procedure. Also indicate how the disulfide bridge assignments can be determined.

3.9   In the good old days the amino acid sequences of proteins were determined using partial acid hydrolysis. Consider a small polypeptide of amino acid composition (Ala,Arg$_2$,Asp$_2$,Glu$_2$,Gly,Lys,Ser,Thr). Treatment with the Sanger reagent, dinitrofluorobenzene (DNFB) identifies Glu as N-terminal. The following peptides are obtained by partial acid hydrolysis:

(Asp,Glu)   (Ser,Thr)
(Glu,Gly)   (Asp,Lys)
(Asp,Glu,Gly)   (Arg,Thr)
(Ala,Asp)   (Arg$_2$,Thr)
(Ala,Asp,Ser)   (Arg,Lys)
(Asp,Glu,Lys)   (Ala,Asp,Gly)

What is the complete amino acid sequence of the peptide?

3.10   In an attempt to sequence an unknown polypeptide, the following results were obtained. Deduce the amino acid sequence and the placement of the disulfide bridges. The N-acetyl and N-formyl groups indicated in the following compositions would be cleaved from their respective residues during acid hydrolysis. Assume that these linkages have been determined by additional procedures.

A.   Reduction and alkylation:
   1.   (Arg,Cys$_3$,Gly,Lys,Met,N-acetyl-Gly,Pro)
   2.   (Arg$_2$,Cys,Lys$_2$,N-formyl-Met,Phe,Pro$_2$)
B.   Reduction, alkylation, and maleylation followed by trypsin:
   3.   (Arg,Cys,Lys,N-acetyl-Gly)
   4.   (Cys$_2$,Gly,Met,Pro)
   5.   (Arg,N-formyl-Met)
   6.   (Arg,Lys$_2$)
   7.   (Cys,Phe,Pro$_2$)

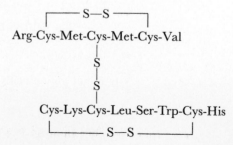

Figure 3.9
A hypothetical polypeptide
(Problem 3.8).

    C.   Trypsin:

        8. $(Cys_4,Gly,Lys,Met,N\text{-acetyl-Gly},Phe,Pro_3)$

        9. 2(Arg)

      10. (Arg,N-formyl-Met)

      11. 2(Lys)

    D.   Reduction and aminoethylation followed by trypsin:

      12. (Cys,N-acetyl-Gly)   16. (Gly,Met,Pro)

      13. 3(Lys)   17. (Arg,N-formyl-Met)

      14. 2(Arg)   18. (Cys,Phe,Pro_2)

      15. 2(Cys)

    E.   Reduction and alkylation followed by CNBr:

      19. $(Arg,Cys_3,Lys,Met,N\text{-acetyl-Gly})$

      20. (Gly,Pro)

      21. (N-formyl-Met)

      22. $(Arg_2,Cys,Lys_2,Phe,Pro_2)$

    F.   Carboxypeptidases A and B:

      23. Nothing

    G.   Hydrazinolysis:

      24. (Pro)

    H.   Chymotryptic digest of peptide 18:

      25. (Cys,Phe,Pro_2)

    I.   Edman degradation of peptide 18:

      26. (Cys)

3.11   Given the following peptides, deduce the amino acid sequence from which they were derived.

    A.   Aminoethylation followed by trypsin:

       1. (Ala,Arg,Gly,Met,Phe)

       2. 2(AECys)

       3. (Ala,AECys,Phe)

       4. (Asp,Lys,Tyr)

    B.   CNBr:

       5. $(Ala_2,Asp,Arg,Cys_3,Gly,Lys,Met,Phe_2,Tyr)$

    C.   Chymotrypsin:

       6. (Ala,Gly,Lys,Met,Phe)

       7. (Asp,Cys,Tyr)

       8. (Ala,Arg,Cys_2,Phe)

    D.   CNBr plus trypsin:

       9. (Gly,Met)

      10. $(Ala,Asp,Cys_3,Lys,Phe,Tyr)$

      11. (Ala,Arg,Phe)

3.12   The dansyl Edman technique, a commonly used modification of the Edman procedure, destroys all amides. Thus any amide or acidic residue must be reported ambiguously as Glx (no decision possible between Glu or Gln) or Asx (no decision possible between Asp or Asn).

    Two procedures commonly are employed for the identification of Glx and Asx:

1.   If the peptide has a single Glx or Asx, it can be compared with a standard of acidic, neutral, and basic amino acids by electrophoresis at pH = 6.5.

2.   The peptide can be hydrolyzed completely using a mixture of enzymes (endopeptidases that generate small fragments and exopeptidases that catalyze sequential cleavage from N termini), followed by amino acid analysis to distinguish the acidic residues from the amides.

    Indicate how you could most easily identify Glx and Asx in the following peptides. Use any cleavage procedures, but remember that dansyl Edman degradation converts Gln and Asn to Glu and Asp, respectively. NH$_3$ cannot be determined on the amino acid analyzer.

  a. Gly-Asx-Val-Ser

  b. Gly-Asx-Glx-Ser

  c. Gly-Asx-Phe-Asx-Ser

  d. Gly-Asx-Asx-Ser

3.13   You are given the following enzymatic digests of a polypeptide. Peptide 8 was produced by chymotrypsin cleavage at Met.

  a. Write as much of the primary structure of this peptide as you can.

  b. Assume that the Arg residues are at positions 7 and 17 (from the N terminus). Suggest an efficient procedure for finishing this sequence. (The repetitive Edman procedure can be used on an unfractionated mixture of peptides.)

  A. Thermolysin:

      1. (Leu,Ser)   4. (Arg,Glx,Gly,Ilu)

      2. (Ilu)   5. (Thr,Val)

      3. (Asx,NH$_3$)   6. (Arg,Ala,Glx,Met,Ser$_2$,Thr,Val)

  B. Chymotrypsin:

      7. (Arg,Glx,Gly,Ilu,Ser,Thr,Val)

      8. (Ala,Arg,Glx,Ilu,Met,Ser$_2$,Thr,Val)

      9. (Asx,Leu,NH$_3$)

3.14   In 1953, Fred Sanger determined the first complete amino acid sequence of a protein. In this problem you will duplicate his efforts with the advantage of more recently developed techniques.

    Given the following results, deduce the amino acid sequence and positions of —S—S— cross-links.

  A. N-terminal analysis:

      1. (PTH-Gly)

      2. (PTH-Phe)

  B. Carboxypeptidase A:

      3. (Ala)

      4. (Asn)

  C. Carboxypeptidase B:

      5. Nothing

  D. Amino acid composition:

      6. (Ala$_3$,Arg,Asx$_3$,Cys$_6$,Glx$_7$,Gly$_4$,His$_2$,Ilu,Leu$_6$,Lys,[NH$_3$]$_6$,Phe$_3$,Pro, Ser$_3$,Thr,Tyr$_4$,Val$_5$)

  E. CNBr:

      7. Same as (6)

  F. Trypsin:

      8. (Ala)

      9. (Gly,Lys,Phe$_2$,Pro,Thr,Tyr)

     10. (Ala$_2$,Arg,Asx$_3$,Cys$_6$,Glx$_7$,Gly$_3$,His$_2$,Ilu,Leu$_6$,[NH$_3$]$_6$,Phe,Ser$_3$, Tyr$_3$,Val$_5$)

  G. Chymotrypsin:

     11. (Ala,Lys,Pro,Thr)

     12. 2(Phe)

     13. 3(Tyr)

     14. (Arg,Asx,Cys$_2$,Glx,Gly$_2$,NH$_3$,Phe,Val)

     15. (Leu)

     16. (Ala,Glx,Leu,Val)

     17. (Asx,Glx,His,Leu,[NH$_3$]$_2$,Val)

     18. (Asx,Glx,NH$_3$,Tyr)

     19. (Ala,Cys$_4$,Glx$_2$,Gly$_2$,His,Ilu,Leu$_2$,NH$_3$,Ser$_3$,Val$_2$)

     20. (Glx,Leu,NH$_3$)

H. Thermolysin:

    21. (Gly)

    22. (Ala,Lys,Pro,Thr,Tyr)

    23. 3(Phe)

    24. (Asx,Glx,His,[NH$_3$]$_2$,Val)

    25. (Arg,Asx,Cys$_2$,Glx,Gly$_2$,NH$_3$,Tyr,Val)

    26. (Asx,Glx,Leu,NH$_3$)

    27. (Ala,Cys$_4$,Glx$_2$,Gly,His,Leu,NH$_3$,Ser$_3$,Val$_2$)

    28. 4(Leu)

    29. (Ala,Glx,Val)

    30. (Tyr)

    31. (Ilu)

    32. (Glx,NH$_3$,Tyr)

I. Reduction and alkylation followed by thermolysin:

    33. (Gly)

    34. (Ala,Lys,Pro,Thr,Tyr)

    35. 3(Phe)

    36. (Asx,Glx,His,[NH$_3$]$_2$,Val)

    37. (Asx,Cys,NH$_3$,Tyr)

    38. (Arg,Cys,Glx,Gly$_2$,Val)

    39. (Asx,Glx,Leu,NH$_3$)

    40. (Cys,Ser,Val)

    41. (Ala,Cys$_2$,Glx$_2$,NH$_3$,Ser,Val)

    42. (Cys,Gly,His,Leu,Ser)

    43. 4(Leu)

    44. (Ala,Glx,Val)

    45. (Tyr)

    46. (Ilu)

    47. (Glx,NH$_3$,Tyr)

J. Reduction and alkylation:

    48. (Ala,Asx$_2$,Cys$_4$,Glx$_4$,Gly,Ilu,Leu$_2$,[NH$_3$]$_4$,Ser$_2$,Tyr$_2$,Val$_2$)

    49. (Ala$_2$,Arg,Asx,Cys$_2$,Glx$_3$,Gly$_3$,His$_2$,Leu$_4$,Lys,[NH$_3$]$_2$,Phe$_3$,Pro, Ser,Thr,Tyr$_2$,Val$_3$)

K. Reduction and aminoethylation followed by trypsin:

    50. (Ala)

    51. (Gly,Lys,Phe$_2$,Pro,Thr,Tyr)

    52. (Asx,NH$_3$)

    53. (Asx,Cys,Glx$_2$,Leu$_2$,[NH$_3$]$_2$,Ser,Tyr$_2$)

    54. (Ala,Cys,Ser,Val)

    55. (Cys)

    56. (Cys,Glx$_2$,Gly,Ilu,NH$_3$,Val)

    57. (Asx,Cys,Glx,His,Leu,[NH$_3$]$_2$,Phe,Val)

    58. (Ala,Cys,Glx,Gly,His,Leu$_3$,Ser,Tyr,Val$_2$)

    59. (Arg,Glx,Gly)

L. Reduction and alkylation followed by pepsin:

    60. (Gly,Ilu,Val)

    61. (Asx,Cys,NH$_3$,Tyr)

    62. 2(Phe)

    63. (Ala,Lys,Pro,Thr,Tyr)

    64. (Ala,Cys$_3$,Glx$_2$,NH$_3$,Ser$_2$,Val)

    65. (Cys,Gly,Leu,Val)

    66. 3(Leu)

    67. (Glx,NH$_3$,Tyr)

    68. (Asx,Glx,NH$_3$)

    69. (Tyr)

    70. (Ala,Glx)

    71. (Leu,Val)

    72. (Cys,Gly,His,Leu,Ser)

    73. (Asx,Glx,His,[NH$_3$]$_2$,Phe,Val)

    74. (Arg,Glx,Gly)

M. Miscellaneous:

    75. Peptide 24 gives His, then Gln, with carboxypeptidase A.

    76. Peptide 42 gives His, then Ser, with carboxypeptidase A.

77. Peptide 41 gives Ser with carboxypeptidase A.

78. Peptide 58 gives AECys, then Val, then Leu, then Tyr with carboxy-peptidases A and B.

3.15   A small protein, containing only 40 amino acid residues, was characterized as follows:

A. Edman degradation gave Asp.

B. The protein was cleaved with CNBr. The resulting *unfractionated mixture* of peptides was analyzed in a protein sequenator. The results are shown in Table 3.2a.

C. The protein was digested with trypsin. The resulting *unfractionated mixture* of peptides was analyzed as in part B. The results are shown in Table 3.2b.

The number at the top of each column in Table 3.2 indicates the position of each amino acid within a peptide. Because the sequenator used in these experiments can determine reliably only the amino acid residues in the first eight positions of the peptide mixture, the data for positions nine or greater have not been included in the table. The residues in each column are arranged alphabetically to indicate that their relationships are unknown.

Given the preceding information, deduce the sequence of the protein. (This method, which eliminates the need for separating peptides, actually is used on small polypeptides.)

3.16   One-letter amino acid abbreviations are becoming widely used, in particular for computer representations of amino acid sequences. The standard one-letter designations have been given in Table 2.1 and are repeated in Table 3.3; they will be used in this and subsequent problems.

Assume that the following protein (a human immunoglobulin light chain) has been (1) reduced and alkylated with iodoacetic acid, (2) reacted with maleic anhydride, and (3) digested with trypsin. Predict the order in which the resulting peptides will be eluted from an anion-exchange column by a gradient of increasing salt concentration. (Peptides with the most negative charge are retained longest.)

```
1          10                20           30
D I V L T Q S P L S L P V T P G Q P A S I S C R S S E D L L E S D G N
      40             50            60
Y L D W Y L Q K P G E S P Q L L I Y L G S N R A S G V P N R F S G S
70          80                90              100
G S G T N F T L K I S R V E A E D V G V Y Y C M Q A L Q T P L T P G
        110            120            130
G G T N V E I K R T V A A P S V F I P P P S D Q E L K S G T A S V V
    140            150            160                170
C L L N N F Y P R E A K V Q W K V D N A L E S G D S N E S V T Q E
              180            190            200
D S K D S T Y S L S S T L T L S K A N Y E K H K V Y A C Q V T H Q G
        210          218
L S S P V T K S F N R G E C
```

Table 3.2
Analysis of Unfractionated Mixtures of Peptides (Problem 3.15)

		1	2	3	4	5	6	7	8
a.	CNBr:	Arg	Gln	Asn	Arg	Asn	Arg	Ala	Ala
	Met	Asp	Pro	Pro	His	Ilu	His	Gly	Lys
		Glu	Thr	Ser	Ilu	Leu	Trp	Phe	Met
		Gly	Tyr	Tyr	Val	Phe	Val	Thr	Tyr
b.	Trypsin:	Asp	Cys	His	Ala	Ilu	Arg	Cys	Glu
		Gly	His	Met	Asn	Leu	Phe	Lys	Leu
	Arg or Lys	Gly	Pro	Thr	Glu	Thr	Ser	Ilu	
		Phe	Pro	Tyr	Val	Trp	Ser		
		Tyr	Tyr						

Table 3.3
One-Letter Amino Acid Abbreviations

A	Alanine	N	Asparagine
B	Aspartic acid or asparagine	P	Proline
C	Cysteine	Q	Glutamine
D	Aspartic acid	R	Arginine
E	Glutamic acid	S	Serine
F	Phenylalanine	T	Threonine
G	Glycine	V	Valine
H	Histidine	W	Tryptophan
I	Isoleucine	X	Unknown amino acid
K	Lysine	Y	Tyrosine
L	Leucine	Z	Glutamic acid or
M	Methionine		glutamine

3.17   The amino acid sequenator is an effective tool if the yield data from its automatic analyses are quantitated carefully. One index of sequenator performance is the **repetitive yield.** This parameter is determined by comparing the recovery of PTH-amino acids for an early and a late step in the sequenator run.

   a. Assume the repetitive yield (average yield *at each step*) in a particular sequenator run is 90%, and that the recovery of PTH-amino acid at the first step is 100 nanomoles (nmol). What would be the recovery, in nanomoles, at steps 5, 10, and 15?
   b. Repeat these calculations for repetitive yields of 80% and of 99%.
   c. What can you conclude about the desirability of obtaining high repetitive yields?
   d. Determine a general formula for repetitive yield in terms of two step-numbers (1 and n) and the recoveries at these steps (r_1 and r_n).

3.18   Consider the following recoveries of PTH-amino acid from a sequenator run:

Step	Recovery (nmol)
1	600
2	500
3	478
4	575
5	437
6	500
7	477
8	416
9	348
10	363

   a. How would you calculate the repetitive yield for this run? (*Hint:* Look at Problem 3.17d and plot log r_n against n.)
   b. What is the repetitive yield?

3.19   Suppose that you are using the sequenator to determine the structure of a protein that reverses the effects of peyote. You discover to your amazement that *two* PTH-amino acids are present at each step of the run. Although disappointed, you forge ahead with the analysis of the recovery data, a portion of which is as follows:

	Recovery (nmol)	
Step 1	Step 5	Step 9
PTH-A(500)	PTH-V(405)	PTH-F(315)
PTH-L(250)	PTH-E(165)	PTH-L(97)

   a. Then, thinking back to Problem 3.18, you realize these results are highly significant. Why?
   b. What are the repetitive yields?
   c. Why might you obtain different recoveries for the two PTH-amino acids?

3.20   A newly developed sequenator allows sequencing of very small quantities of protein, <1 microgram (μg), for many residues. An example of the data obtainable from such

$$
\begin{array}{cccccc}
1 & 5 & 10 & 11 & 15 \\
\end{array}
$$

NH₂- - - - - - -Leu-Lys-Ala-Ilu-Thr-Asp-Met-Leu-Leu-Thr-Glu-Gln-Ilu-

20 21   25   30 31   36
Arg-Glu-Arg-Gln-Arg-Tyr-Leu-Ala-Asp-Leu-Arg-Gln-Arg-Leu-Leu-Glu-Lys-OH

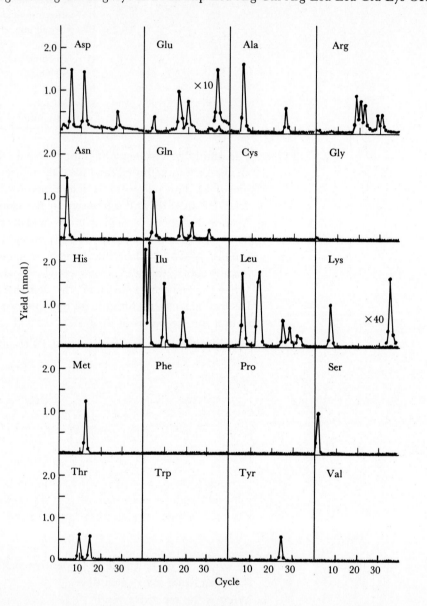

Figure 3.10
Yields of amino acid phenylthiohydantoins from an N-terminal
sequenator analysis of the egg-
laying hormone of *Aplysia californica*.

an analysis is given in Figure 3.10 for the egg-laying hormone of *Aplysia californica*.
Data for each of the 20 PTH-amino acid residues are presented as the yield of each
residue at each cycle or step. The egg-laying hormone is 36 residues in length.

a. What is the amino acid sequence of residues 1–6?
b. Why do two amino acids appear in cycle 5?
c. Calculate the approximate weight of the polypeptide used in this analysis.

☆ 3.21   Suppose that you wish to determine the sequence of a peptide whose composition is
(acetyl,Ala,Asp,Gly,Leu₂,Val,Pro). Which of the following treatments would be the
best choice for the first step in your analysis, and why?

a. Trypsin digestion
b. Chymotrypsin digestion
c. Reduction and alkylation
d. Cyanogen bromide treatment
e. Edman degradation
f. Carboxypeptidase B digestion

☆ 3.22   Given the following analyses of a polypeptide, determine its structure.

  A. Amino acid composition:
     1. (Ala,Cys$_2$,Glu$_2$,Lys,Met,Pro,Ser,Val)
  B. Edman degradation:
     2. (Glu)
  C. Carboxypeptidase A:
     3. (Ser)
  D. Reduction–alkylation plus trypsin:
     4. (Glu,Lys)
     5. (Cys,Val,Pro)
     6. (Ala,Cys,Glu,Met,Ser)
  E. Reduction–aminoethylation plus trypsin:
     7. (Glu,Lys)
     8. (AECys,Pro,Val)
     9. (Ser)
     10. (Ala,AECys,Glu,Met)
  F. CNBr:
     11. (Glu,Met)
     12. (Ala,Cys$_2$,Glu,Val,Lys,Pro,Ser)
  G. Thermolysin:
     No fragments

Answers

3.1   a. True
   b. False. Neither carboxypeptidase will remove a C-terminal Pro.
   c. False. Gln and Asn are hydrolyzed to Glu and Asp.
   d. False. A Pro residue adjacent to R_n blocks cleavage only if it is on the same side as the cleavage.
   e. False. The sequenator could be used to determine the entire sequence, but the polypeptide would have to be cleaved into fragments before sequencing completely.
   f. False. Because trypsin was used in both treatments, there will be no peptides whose sequence overlaps a trypsin cleavage point.
   g. True

3.2   a. chymotrypsin, thermolysin, pepsin, CNBr, trypsin
   b. reduction, Alkylation
   c. more (or smaller)

3.3   a. Ala-Val-Lys
      Leu-Phe-Arg

                 Cys-Tyr
                    |
                    S
                    |
                    S
                    |
      Val-Thr-Gly-Cys-Ala
      Glu-Met-Lys
   b. Ala-Val-Lys
      Leu-Phe-Arg
      Cys-Tyr
      Glu-Met-Lys
      Val-Thr-Gly-Cys-Ala
   c. Ala
      Tyr
      Val-Lys

Glu-Met-Lys

Leu

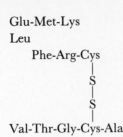

Phe-Arg-Cys
|
S
|
S
|
Val-Thr-Gly-Cys-Ala

3.4 a. No cleavage, because Arg is adjacent to Pro

b. No cleavage, because carboxypeptidase B works only on Arg and Lys

c. No cleavage, because chymotrypsin catalyzes cleavage only on the C side of Phe, Trp, Tyr, and Leu

d. Yes, Gly-Met and Pro. The CNBr reaction is not affected by the presence of Pro.

e. Yes, Pro-Arg and Met. The Pro is not adjacent to the cleaved bond, so it does not prevent cleavage.

3.5   Because of the large number of Lys and Arg residues, trypsin cleavage will generate many small peptides. Unambiguous ordering of these peptides will be difficult. However, if there are few Met residues, or a limited number of thermolysin-sensitive residues, these cleavages can be substituted for the customary first step of trypsin cleavage.

3.6   Ala-Arg-Ser-Phe-Lys-Lys-Met-Ser-Ala

3.7   The amino acid sequence and disulfide bond locations in the polypeptide are shown in Figure 3.11.

3.8   One of the most efficient procedures would be as follows:

A. Reduction and alkylation:

1. (Arg,Cys$_3$,Met$_2$,Val), chain 1

2. (Cys$_3$,His,Leu,Lys,Ser,Trp), chain 2

Thus there are two peptide chains, each with a unique amino acid composition.

B. CNBr:

3. (Arg,Cys$_2$,Met,Val)

4. (Cys$_4$,His,Leu,Lys,Met,Ser,Trp)

In comparing (4) with (2) we see that an extra Cys-Met comes from chain 1. The Met must be C-terminal.

C. Reduction and alkylation followed by CNBr:

5. (Arg,Cys)-Met

6. Cys-Met (see B)

7. (Cys,Val); from (3) this peptide must be joined to (5).

8. (Cys$_3$,His,Leu,Lys,Ser,Trp); this peptide is identical to (2).

D. Reduction and alkylation followed by trypsin:

9. Arg is N-terminal in chain 1; see (1).

10. (Cys$_3$,Met$_2$,Val); remainder of chain 1

11. Cys-Lys

12. (Cys$_2$,His,Leu,Ser,Trp)

E. Reduction and alkylation followed by thermolysin:

13. (Arg,Cys$_3$,Met$_2$)

```
        ┌──────── S—S ────────────────┐
   Ala-Cys-Phe-Pro-Lys-Arg-Trp-Cys-Arg-Arg-Val-Cys
                                 |
                                 S
                                 |
                                 S
                                 |
                      Cys-Tyr-Cys-Phe-Cys
                      └── S—S ───┘
```

Figure 3.11
Primary structure of a polypeptide (Answer 3.7).

14. (Val); this must be C-terminal in chain 1.
15. (Cys$_2$,Lys)
16. Leu-Ser
17. Trp-(Cys,His)

From (5),(6),(7),(9), and (14), chain 1 is

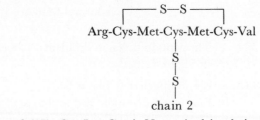

From (11) and (15), Cys-Lys-Cys is N-terminal in chain 2.

F. Thermolysin plus trypsin:
18. (Arg)
19. (Cys$_4$,Met$_2$)
20. (Val)
21. (Cys$_2$,His,Lys,Trp)
22. Leu-Ser

From (19) and (21),

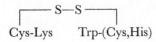

G. Carboxypeptidase A:
23. (Val)
24. (His)

Thus His is C-terminal in chain 2 and peptide 17 must be C-terminal. The thermolysin fragments of chain 2 can be aligned and the sequence is determined.

3.9   Glu-Gly-Asp-Ala-Ser-Thr-Arg-Arg-Lys-Asp-Glu

This sequence can be determined unambiguously, but from the data given it is impossible to determine which end is N-terminal. Thus the reverse of the sequence also is correct.

3.10   The reasoning behind the sequencing of this polypeptide is explained here. For subsequent sequencing problems, only the answers are provided.

A. The polypeptides must consist of two chains linked by —S—S— bonds. The results suggest also that the N-terminal amino acids are blocked.

B. Chain 1: *N*-acetyl-Gly-(Cys,Lys)-Arg
Chain 1: (Cys$_2$,Gly,Met,Pro); no new information
Chain 2: *N*-formyl-Met-Arg
Chain 2: Lys-Lys-Arg
Chain 2: (Cys,Phe,Pro$_2$); no new information

C.
$$\overset{\lceil\text{S—S}\rceil}{} \quad \overset{\lceil\text{—— S—S ——}\rceil}{}$$
N-acetyl-Gly-Cys-Lys(Cys,Cys,Gly,Met,Pro)(Cys,Phe,Pro$_2$)
The remaining fragments convey no new information.

D. *N*-acetyl-Gly-Cys; from (12)
Cys,Cys-(Gly,Met,Pro); from (4), (15), and (16)
The remaining fragments convey no new information.

E. *N*-acetyl-Gly-Cys-Lys-Arg-Cys-Cys-Met-(Gly,Pro); from A, B, D, and E
The remaining fragments convey no new information.

F, G, H, and I.
    Chain 1: Gly-Pro (C-terminal)
    Chain 2: Cys-Pro-Phe-Pro (C-terminal)

Therefore, with the one noted ambiguity, the structure is as shown in Figure 3.12.

Figure 3.12
Primary structure of an unknown polypeptide (Answer 3.10). The locations of the two disulfide bonds are ambiguous in that the adjacent Cys residues in the upper chain cannot be distinguished using the data given.

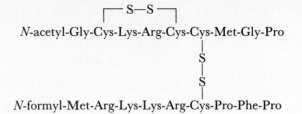

3.11   The peptides given in Problem 3.11 were derived from the circular polypeptide shown in Figure 3.13.

3.12   a. Electrophoresis at pH = 6.5
     b. Enzymatic digestion and amino acid analysis
     c. Thermolysin digestion; then electrophoresis at pH = 6.5. If both peptides are neutral or if both are acidic, the assignments are obvious. If one peptide is neutral and the other is acidic, both could be eluted from paper in water, hydrolyzed, and examined on the amino acid analyzer.
     d. Enzyme digestion and amino acid analysis. If both Asx residues are the same (amide or acid side chains), the assignment is obvious. If one is an acid and the other is an amide, then two steps of the Edman procedure should be carried out. The resulting dipeptide should be examined by electrophoresis at pH = 6.5.

3.13   a.   1   2   3   4   5   7   11   12   13   14   15   17
        Asn-Leu-Ser-Ilu-Val-(Ser,Arg,Thr,Glu,Ala)-Met-Ser-Val-Thr-Ilu-(Glu,Arg,Gly)

     b. 1. Do a trypsin digestion.
        2–4. Do three steps of Edman degradation on the *unfractionated* mixture. This technique is described further in Problem 3.15.

3.14   The amino acid sequences of the two chains of insulin are shown in Figure 3.14. The true locations of the disulfide bonds are as shown. However, the data given in the problem do not distinguish between the alternative bonds Cys_{A6}—S—S—Cys_{B7} and Cys_{A7}—S—S—Cys_{A11}.

3.15   1   2   3   4   5   6   7   8   9   10   11   12   13   14   15   16   17   18   19
        Asp-Pro-Tyr-Val-Ilu-Arg-Gly-Tyr-Met-Glu-Thr-Ser-Ilu-Leu-Val-Ala-Met-Gly-Gln-
        20   21   22   23   24   25   26   27   28   29   30   31   32   33   34   35   36   37
        Asn-Arg-Phe-His-Thr-Ala-Leu-Ser-Cys-Glu-Met-Arg-Tyr-Pro-His-Asn-Trp-Phe-
        38   39   40
        Lys-Gly-Cys

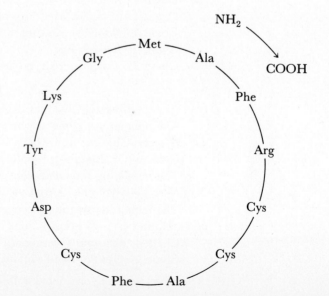

Figure 3.13
Amino acid sequence and polarity of a circular polypeptide (Answer 3.11).

NH₂ termini

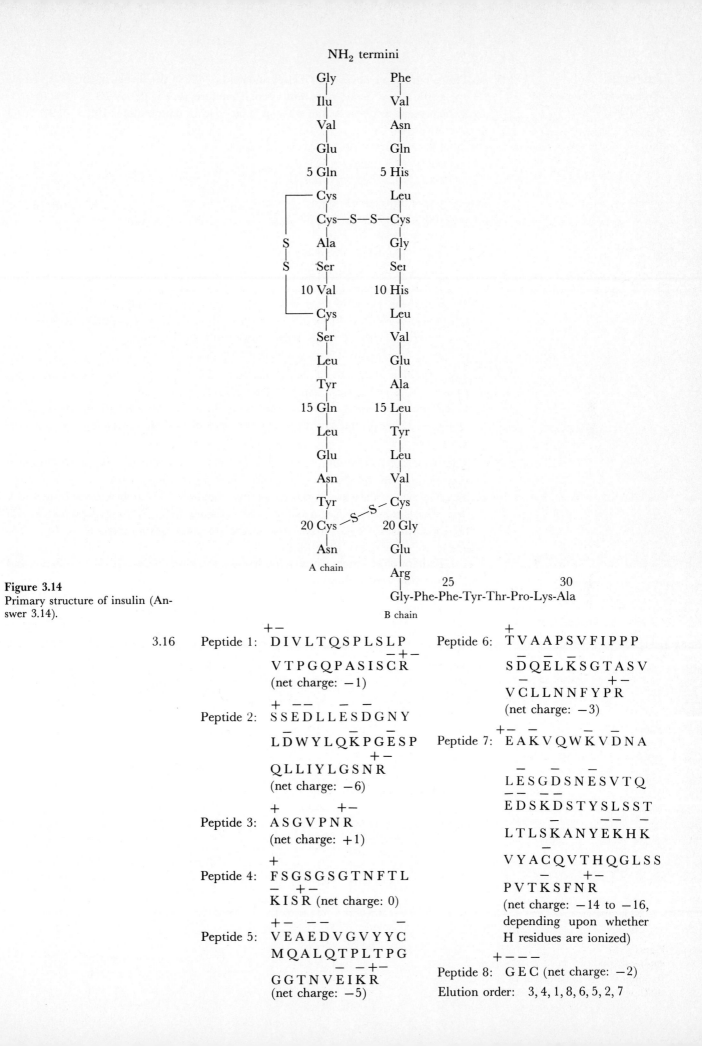

Figure 3.14
Primary structure of insulin (Answer 3.14).

Gly-Phe-Phe-Tyr-Thr-Pro-Lys-Ala

B chain

A chain

3.16

Peptide 1:
$\overset{+-}{\text{D I V L T Q S P L S L P}}$
$\overset{-+-}{\text{V T P G Q P A S I S C R}}$
(net charge: −1)

Peptide 2:
$\overset{+\ --}{\text{S S E D L L E S D G N Y}}$ (with bars)
$\text{L D W Y L Q K P G E S P}$
$\overset{+-}{\text{Q L L I Y L G S N R}}$
(net charge: −6)

Peptide 3:
$\overset{+\ \ \ \ \ +-}{\text{A S G V P N R}}$
(net charge: +1)

Peptide 4:
$\overset{+}{\text{F S G S G S G T N F T L}}$
$\overset{-\ +-}{\text{K I S R}}$ (net charge: 0)

Peptide 5:
$\overset{+-\ --\ \ \ \ -}{\text{V E A E D V G V Y Y C}}$
$\text{M Q A L Q T P L T P G}$
$\overset{-\ -+-}{\text{G G T N V E I K R}}$
(net charge: −5)

Peptide 6:
$\overset{+}{\text{T V A A P S V F I P P P}}$
$\text{S D Q E L K S G T A S V}$
$\overset{-\ \ \ \ \ \ +-}{\text{V C L L N N F Y P R}}$
(net charge: −3)

Peptide 7:
$\overset{+-\ \ -\ \ \ \ \ -\ \ -}{\text{E A K V Q W K V D N A}}$

$\overset{-\ \ \ -\ \ \ -}{\text{L E S G D S N E S V T Q}}$
$\overset{--\ \ --}{\text{E D S K D S T Y S L S S T}}$
$\overset{-\ \ \ \ --\ \ -}{\text{L T L S K A N Y E K H K}}$
$\overset{-}{\text{V Y A C Q V T H Q G L S S}}$
$\overset{-\ \ \ \ +-}{\text{P V T K S F N R}}$
(net charge: −14 to −16, depending upon whether H residues are ionized)

Peptide 8: $\overset{+\ -\ --}{\text{G E C}}$ (net charge: −2)

Elution order: 3, 4, 1, 8, 6, 5, 2, 7

3.17 a. The second-step recovery of PTH-amino acid is 90% of the first step; third-step recovery is 90% of the second step, and so on. Therefore, $(0.9 \times 0.9 \times 0.9 \ldots) = (0.9)^{n-1}$ is the percent recovery at the nth step. The yield in nanomoles is $100 \times (0.9)^{n-1}$, for $n = 5, 10,$ and 15.

$$100 \times (0.9)^4 \simeq 66 \text{ nmol}$$
$$100 \times (0.9)^9 \simeq 39 \text{ nmol}$$
$$100 \times (0.9)^{14} \simeq 23 \text{ nmol}$$

b.
$$100 \times (0.8)^4 \simeq 41 \text{ nmol}$$
$$100 \times (0.8)^9 \simeq 13 \text{ nmol}$$
$$100 \times (0.8)^{14} \simeq 4 \text{ nmol}$$
$$100 \times (0.99)^4 \simeq 96 \text{ nmol}$$
$$100 \times (0.99)^9 \simeq 91 \text{ nmol}$$
$$100 \times (0.99)^{14} \simeq 87 \text{ nmol}$$

c. The higher the repetitive yield, the longer the run that is possible with the sequenator, since background "noise" from random hydrolysis of the polypeptide interferes with the identification of derivatives from steps with low recovery.

d. $r_n = r_1 X^{n-1}$, in which $X =$ the repetitive yield.

3.18 a. The repetitive yield can be calculated from the slope of the line in a plot of log recovery at step n against step n (Figure 3.15).

b. Using the logarithmic form of the equation from Answer 3.17d, $\log r_n = \log r_1 + (n - 1) \log X$, you can determine the slope of this curve, which is the repetitive yield (95%).

3.19 a. The two sets of PTH-amino acids fall on independent repetitive yield plots. Thus, two polypeptides can be sequenced simultaneously in the sequenator.

b. The A, V, and F derivatives give a repetitive yield of $\simeq 95\%$, whereas the L, E, and L derivatives give a repetitive yield of $\simeq 90\%$ (Figure 3.16). Two polypeptides also can be distinguished because their yields at each step are quite different.

c. There are at least two possibilities:

1. Perhaps there are three polypeptides: two identical chains with N-terminal A and one chain with N-terminal L.

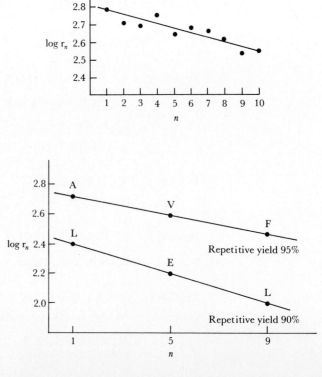

Figure 3.15
Graphical determination of repetitive yield (Answer 3.18).

Figure 3.16
Graphical determination of repetitive yields (Answer 3.19).

2.   In the sequenator the recoveries at the first step are highly variable. Perhaps there are only two polypeptides: one with N-terminal A and the other with N-terminal L, and the difference in initial recoveries is due to chemical differences between the two polypeptides.

3.20 a. Ilu-Ser-Ilu-Asn-Gln-Asp

b. Some Gln loses its amide residue to become Glu. This process is termed **deamidation** and is seen with Asn residues (look at cycle 4) as well as Gln residues.

c. This analysis started with approximately 2 nmol of polypeptide, as can be seen by the Ilu at position 1. Assume that each amino acid has an average molecular weight of 120. Then:

$$\text{Weight of polypeptide} = 120 \times 36 \times 2 \times 10^{-9} = 8.6 \ \mu\text{g}$$

4 Protein Conformation

Proteins consist of polypeptides folded into specific three-dimensional configurations. This chapter considers the interactions that determine these configurations and examines some representative protein structures.

Concepts

4.1 The amino acid sequence of a polypeptide determines its conformation in solution.

Many proteins, after being unfolded artificially (**denatured**), will refold spontaneously to their original (**native**) conformation when incubated at an appropriate temperature, pH, and ionic strength. Thus the information in the amino acid sequence of a polypeptide is sufficient to direct the correct three-dimensional folding under physiological conditions.

4.2 Noncovalent interactions are primarily responsible for maintaining protein conformations.

The forces that determine and maintain protein conformations result primarily from noncovalent interactions of amino acid residues with each other and the surrounding medium. Three principal kinds of noncovalent interactions are involved:

1. **Hydrophobic interactions,** which are quantitatively the most important of the three, lead to a decrease in free energy when hydrophobic side chains are removed from the aqueous environment by folding to the protein interior (Concept 4.3). Van der Waals bonds between hydrophobic groups also contribute to protein stability in molecules where there are many such contacts.

2. **H-bonds** can be formed by the C=O and N—H groups of each peptide bond and the electronegative atoms of polar side chains (Concept 1.2). These groups can H-bond with each other or with water molecules on the exterior of the protein, as shown in Figure 4.1. H-bonds are strongest when the three participating atoms lie in a straight line (Figure 4.1).

3. **Ionic bonds** can form between ionized side chains of opposite charge, such as Asp and Lys (Concept 1.2).

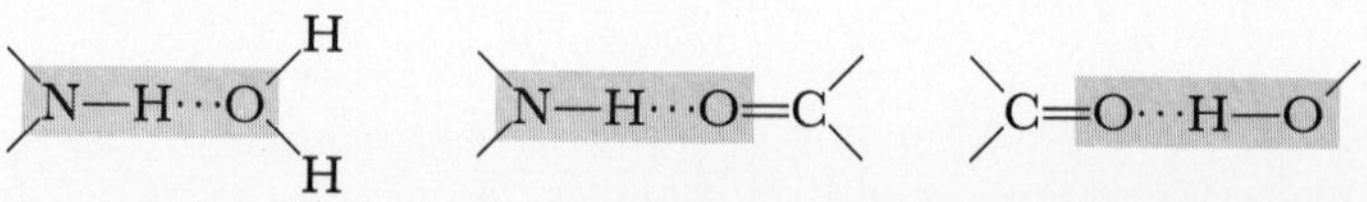

Figure 4.1
Three H-bonds found in proteins. The atoms involved in each H-bond are shaded.

External residue–water   Residue–residue   Residue–residue or residue–water

4.3 Polypeptides in solution fold so as to minimize free energy.

A. The interactions that maintain protein conformation can be explained by considering the thermodynamics of the folding process. A randomly oriented polypeptide will fold to minimize the free energy, G, of the molecule and its immediate surroundings. The resulting free-energy decrease, ΔG, expressed in kilocalories per mole (kcal/mol), is defined by the equation

$$\Delta G = \Delta H - T \Delta S \tag{4.1}$$

in which H is the enthalpy or heat content (kcal/mol), T is the absolute temperature (degrees Kelvin), and S is the entropy or degree of disorder in the system (kcal/mol deg). [*Note:* Most standard references list entropy values in entropy units (e.u.): 1 e.u. = 1 cal/mol deg.] Interactions leading to a decrease in free energy (negative value of ΔG) are thermodynamically favored. Such interactions decrease the enthalpy (negative ΔH) or increase the entropy (positive ΔS) of the system or do both. (For a more detailed explanation of free energy see Concept 9.2.)

B. Hydrophobic interactions are primarily entropy driven. The currently favored explanation is that water molecules surrounding exposed hydrophobic side chains somehow are restricted to ordered configurations. Consequently, folding of hydrophobic groups out of the aqueous phase into the protein interior increases the entropy of the surrounding water. Although the ΔH of this process usually is slightly positive and therefore unfavorable, the large positive ΔS greatly favors folding. Hydrophobic associations, unlike true chemical bonds, increase in stability with increasing temperature as $T \Delta S$ increases. They are relatively nonspecific because they result from solvent properties, rather than from bonding between specific side chains.

C. Formation of internal H-bonds and ionic bonds does not contribute substantially to the ΔG of folding, but does ensure that correct folding occurs. Neutral and charged polar groups inside the protein interact with water molecules before folding and with each other afterward, with little net change in free energy. However, if polar group–water bonds are broken and *not* replaced by internal polar group–polar group bonds, there is a large positive ΔG, which makes incorrect folding highly unfavorable. Structures maintained by H-bonds and ionic bonds decrease in stability as temperature increases.

D. If the environment is changed so that the native configuration is no longer the minimum-free-energy state, proteins will tend to denature. Denaturing reagents such as urea,

$$\begin{array}{c} O \\ \parallel \\ NH_2{-}C{-}NH_2 \end{array}$$

and nonpolar solvents stabilize exposed hydrophobic side chains, thereby lowering the free energy of the unfolded state. Extremes of pH and temperature also denature most proteins. The fully denatured state of a polypeptide is referred to as a **random coil,** implying a lack of ordered structure.

E. The energies of the noncovalent bonds involved in maintaining protein conformation are listed in Table 4.1, together with the energies of two covalent bonds in proteins for comparison. (**Bond energy** is the energy required to break a bond.)

Table 4.1
Bond Energies of Some
Bonds Found in Proteins

Bond	Bond energy[a] (kcal/mol)
Covalent	
C—C (ethane)	83
S—S	50
Noncovalent	
H-bond	3–7
Ionic bond	3–7
Hydrophobic association	(3–5)[b]
Van der Waals bond	1–2

[a] The free energy needed to break the bond.
[b] Here the value represents the free energy that must be supplied to unfold a nonpolar side chain from the protein interior into the aqueous surroundings at 25°C. This energy increases with temperature, unlike other values in the table, and is not really a bond energy, because most of it is not used to break bonds in the unfolding process.

4.4   Native proteins in aqueous surroundings have most nonpolar side chains inside and most polar side chains outside.

To attain minimum-free-energy conformations, proteins must fold so as to shield hydrophobic side chains from the aqueous surroundings while exposing hydrophilic side chains. The few internal polar side chains are in contact with each other through H-bonds or ionic bonds. These important generalizations follow directly from the thermodynamic considerations in Concept 4.3. However, although gross folding is predictable, the interactions determining protein conformation are not yet understood well enough to allow prediction of detailed three-dimensional structure from amino acid sequence.

4.5   Many proteins are stabilized by intramolecular disulfide bonds.

Disulfide bonds can form between Cys residues that become juxtaposed by folding of the polypeptide into a minimum-free-energy configuration. Some proteins undergo internal cleavages following —S—S— bond formation, so that a portion of the polypeptide is removed (e.g., insulin is formed by cleavage of an internal peptide from proinsulin). The three-dimensional structures of such proteins often are no longer minimum-free-energy configurations; they are maintained only by the stability of the disulfide bonds.

4.6   There are four levels of organization in protein structures.

In describing the three-dimensional structure of proteins it is customary to consider four levels of organization. **Primary structure** is the linear sequence of amino acids in a polypeptide (Chapter 3). **Secondary structure** refers to certain repeating conformational patterns, the most common of which are described in Concept 4.7. **Tertiary structure** refers to the overall polypeptide conformation. No clear distinction can be made between secondary and tertiary structure. **Quaternary structure** refers to the spatial relationships between subunits in proteins that consist of two or more polypeptides (**multimeric** proteins; see Chapter 5).

4.7 The α helix and the β sheet are common repeating structural patterns in proteins.

When a polypeptide folds in solution, the backbone polar groups in the interior must interact with each other (Concept 4.3, part C). Two repeating conformations called the **α helix** and the **β sheet** satisfy this condition in many proteins.

1.   The α helix, shown in Figures 4.2 and 4.3, is a regular coiled configuration of the polypeptide chain. There are 3.6 amino acids per helical turn, spanning an axial distance of 0.54 nanometers (nm). The side chains point to the outside of the helix. Each peptide nitrogen is H-bonded to the oxygen of a peptide carbonyl group four residues down the chain. These H-bonds are linear and therefore maximally stable. The α helix is prevented from forming by Pro residues, by two or more consecutive residues with side chains that branch at the β carbon (Val, Ilu, and Thr), or by two or more consecutive residues with ionized side chains of like charge. The α helix is flexible and elastic.

2.   The β sheet, shown in Figures 4.4 and 4.5, is a pleated structure composed of side-by-side polypeptides connected by H-bonds. The two-residue repeat distance is 0.70 nm. The adjacent polypeptides generally run antiparallel to each other, as shown in Figure 4.6. The β sheet is formed most readily by polypeptides with repeating sequences of amino acids with compact side chains, such as (Gly-Ser-Gly-Ala-Gly-Ala)$_n$. The β sheet is flexible, but inelastic.

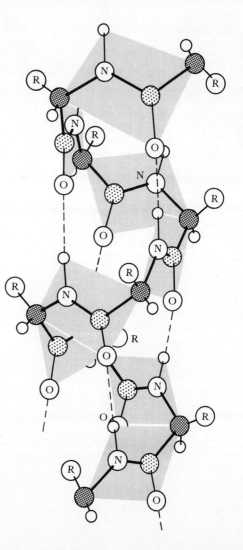

Figure 4.2
The α helix. Only the right-handed form of the helix, shown here, is found in proteins; O atoms, N atoms, and side-chain groups (R) are lettered, and C$_\alpha$ atoms are represented by darker shaded spheres. H-bonds are shown as dashed lines. (Adapted from R. E. Dickerson and I. Geis, *The Structure and Action of Proteins*, Benjamin/Cummings, Menlo Park, Calif. © 1969 Dickerson and Geis.)

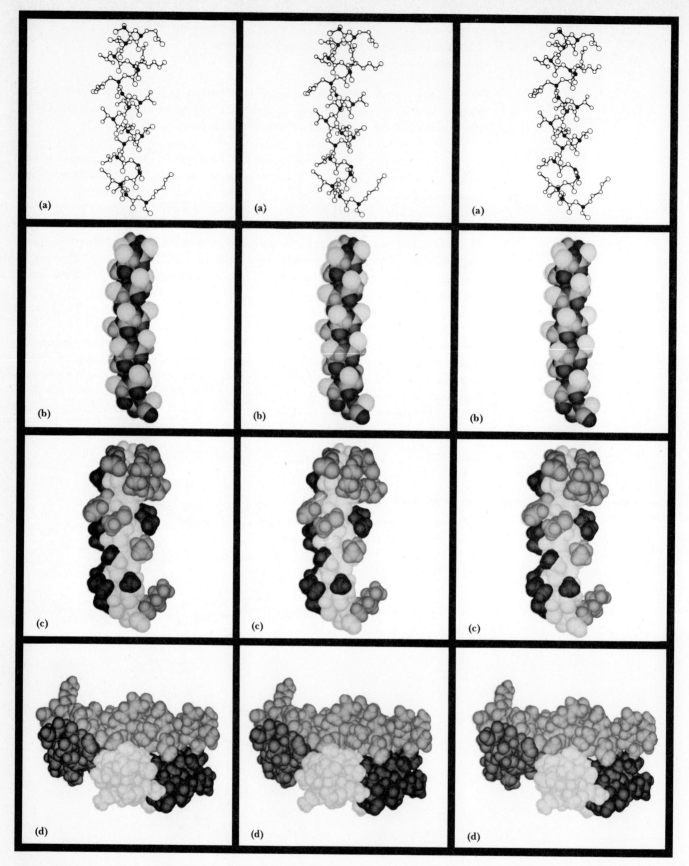

Figure 4.3
Stereo triptychs of α-helices from sperm whale myoglobin. (a) Skeletal model of helix E. C$_\alpha$-atoms are shown in black; H-atoms are not shown. (b) Space-filling model of helix E. Atoms involved in H bonds are shown in black. R groups are shown as light balls. (c) Space-filling model of helix E with R groups included. Black R groups are hydrophobic; gray R groups are hydrophilic. (d) Packing of four α-helices. For stereo viewing, see instructions in the Appendix to Chapter 4. (Stereo figures courtesy of Richard J. Feldmann, NIH.)

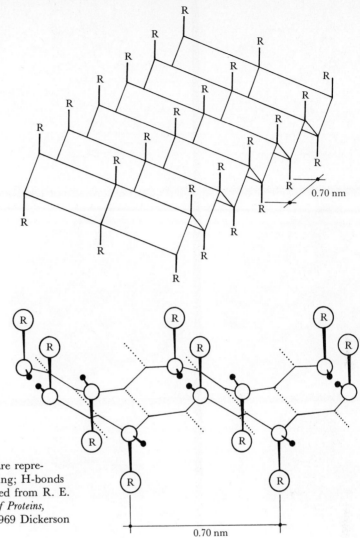

Figure 4.4
Two representations of the β sheet. C_α atoms are represented as unlettered spheres in the lower drawing; H-bonds are shown as dotted lines. (Lower figure adapted from R. E. Dickerson and I. Geis, *The Structure and Action of Proteins*, Benjamin/Cummings, Menlo Park, Calif. © 1969 Dickerson and Geis.)

4.8 The three-dimensional structures of several proteins have been established by x-ray diffraction.

When x-rays pass through a protein crystal, they are diffracted by the atoms of the protein molecules. From the diffraction pattern it is possible to determine the relative positions of these atoms. There is substantial evidence that the native conformations of proteins in crystals and in solution are the same.

The three-dimensional conformations of three proteins are shown in Figures 4.7, 4.9, and 4.10 as computer-generated, stereo triptych diagrams. Viewing these diagrams in three dimensions is a striking and instructive experience, worth the effort it may take to learn how to do so (see viewing instructions in the appendix to this chapter).

1. **Myoglobin** (Figure 4.7) is a single polypeptide of 153 amino acid residues with a molecular weight of 17,500. It functions as an oxygen-storage protein in muscle tissues. Almost all the hydrophobic residues are on the interior of the protein. Within the myoglobin molecule is a heme group, which has the structure shown in Figure 4.8. The heme group also is found in hemoglobin, the oxygen-carrier protein of blood; O_2 is carried on the iron atom of the heme.

2. **Lysozyme** (Figure 4.9) is a single polypeptide of 129 amino acids with a molecular weight of 14,600. It catalyzes the cleavage of certain bacterial polysaccharides.

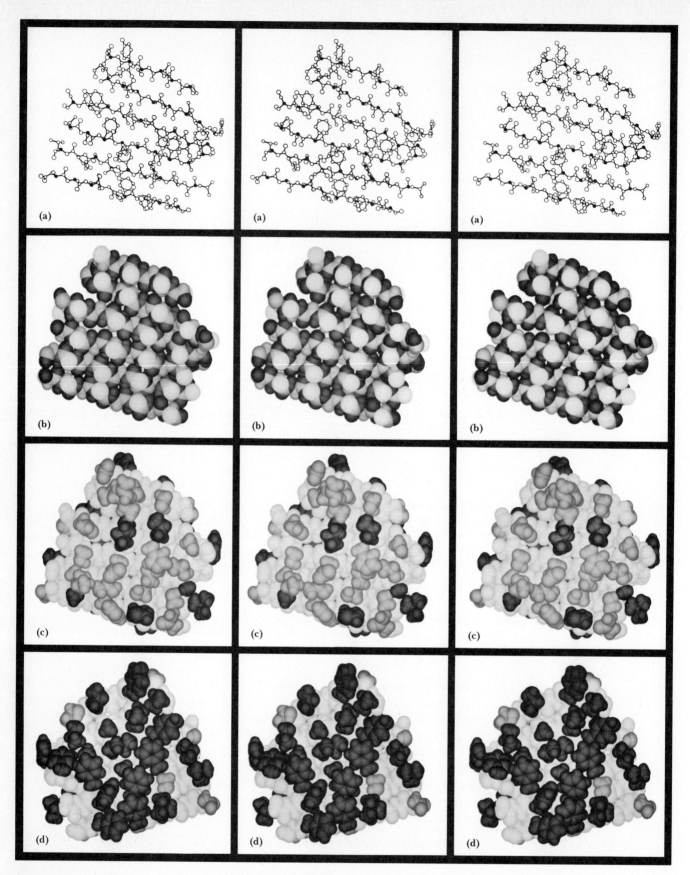

Figure 4.5
Stereo triptychs of a β-sheet structure from Jack bean concanavalin A. **(a)** Skeletal model. C$_\alpha$-atoms are shown in black; H atoms are not shown. **(b)** Space-filling model. Atoms involved in H bonds are shown in black. R groups are shown as light balls. **(c)** Space-filling model with R groups included. Black R groups are hydrophobic; gray R groups are hydrophilic. **(d)** 180° rotation of view C about a vertical axis to show the other side of the β-sheet. Color coding as in **(c)**. The hydrophobic side of the β-sheet faces the interior of the protein; the hydrophilic side faces the solvent. For stereo viewing, see instructions in the Appendix to Chapter 4. (Stereo figures courtesy of Richard J. Feldmann, NIH.)

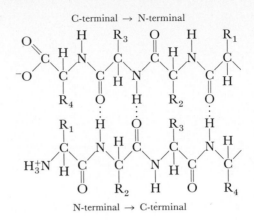

Figure 4.6
Antiparallel polypeptides in a β sheet.

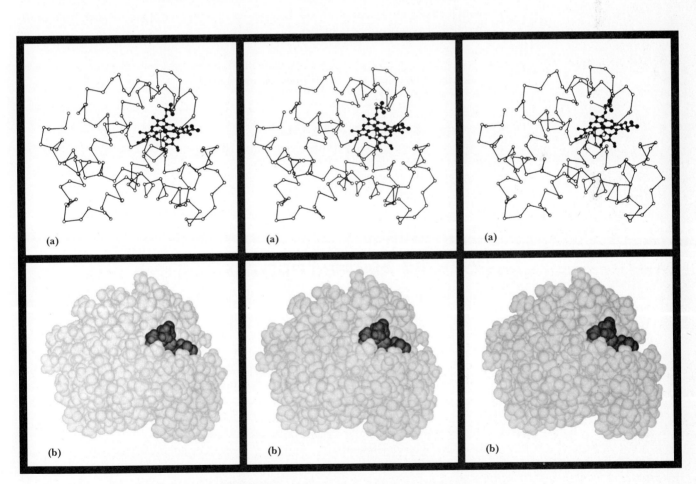

Figure 4.7
Stereo triptychs of sperm whale myoglobin. **(a)** Skeletal model showing only the C_α-atoms of the protein. The atoms in the heme group are shown in black. **(b)** Space-filling model. The atoms in the heme group are shown in black. For stereo viewing, see instructions in the Appendix to Chapter 4. (Stereo figures courtesy of Richard J. Feldmann, NIH.)

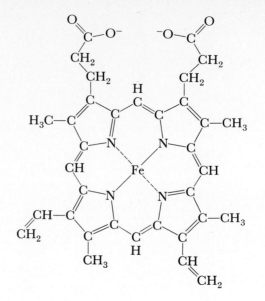

Figure 4.8
Structure of the heme group in
myoglobin and hemoglobin.

3.   **Carboxypeptidase A** (Figure 4.10) is a single polypeptide of 307 amino acids with a molecular weight of 34,600. It catalyzes the cleavage of amino acids from the C termini of polypeptides (Chapter 3).

4.9   Additional concepts and techniques are presented in the Problems section.

A.   Structure of collagen. Problem 4.15.
B.   Optical rotation of polypeptides. Problem 4.18.
C.   Ramachandran diagrams. Problems 4.19 and 4.20.
D.   Helical pitch. Problem 4.21.

Appendix:
Viewing Stereo Triptychs

The stereo triptych (*trip'tik*) is a convenient viewing format suitable for a standard stereoscope or for stereo viewing with unaided eyes using proximal or distal convergence. The most flexible stereo viewing system is a trained pair of eyes, and the training required for stereo viewing is relatively easy. This appendix considers some relevant aspects of normal vision and describes a step-by-step training method for learning to see stereo pictures with unaided eyes.

4A.1   During normal binocular vision, convergence and focus are interdependent.

A.   Convergence describes the coordinated orienting of the two eyes. The orientation of each eye defines a **line of sight** from the object being looked at through the center of the lens to the small differentiated spot on the retina, the **fovea,** which is the point of maximum visual acuity (Figure 4A.1). The lines of sight from the eyes intersect (converge) at the object. This convergence defines your **point of attention**—the point in visual space at which you look. (The degree to which the point of attention behaves as a point is remarkable, as you can observe by scrutinizing a single letter on this page.)

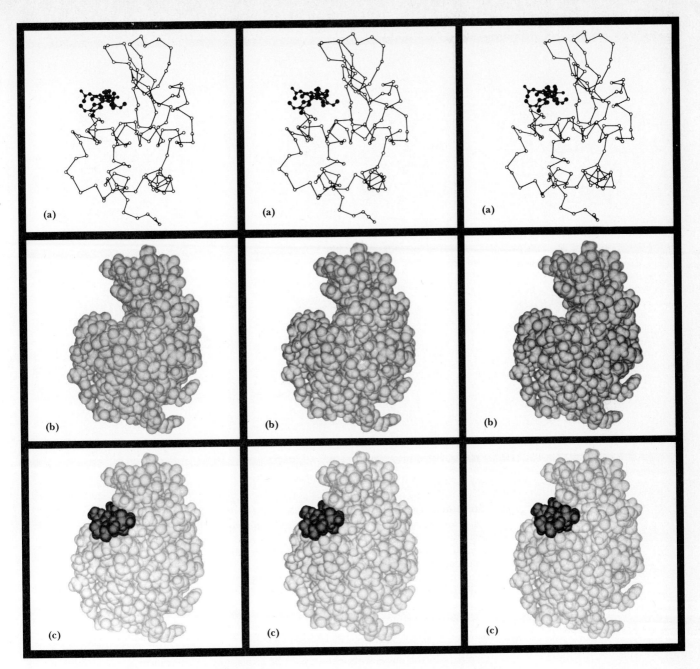

Figure 4.9
Stereo triptychs of chicken lysozyme. **(a)** Skeletal model
showing only the C_α-atoms of the protein. Black spheres
represent the atoms of a trimeric analogue of the polymeric
substrate, positioned in the active site. **(b)** Space-filling
model with the active site open. **(c)** Space-filling model
with the trimeric substrate analogue (black atoms) positioned in the active site. For stereo viewing, see instructions
in the Appendix to Chapter 4. (Stereo figures courtesy of
Richard J. Feldmann, NIH.)

B. Variations in tension on the lens of the eye permit objects at different distances to be
brought into focus. A particular tension on the lens defines a particular plane of focus.
During normal vision, tension automatically adjusts so that the plane of focus always
includes the point of attention (Figure 4A.1). Consequently, the object you are looking
at is seen clearly. (Most prescription glasses shift the focal plane so that aligning it
with the point of attention—that is, focusing—is within the range of the wearer's
natural abilities.)

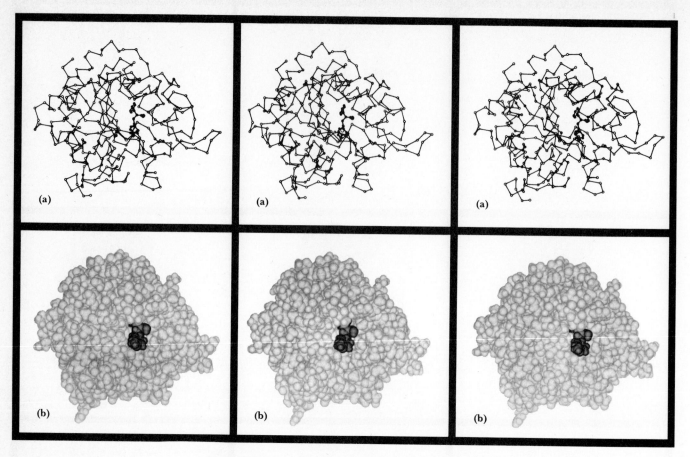

Figure 4.10
Stereo triptychs of bovine carboxypeptidase A. **(a)** Skeletal model showing only the C_α-atoms of the protein. Black spheres represent the atoms of a substrate analogue (carbobenzoxy-Ala-Ala-Tyr) positioned for catalysis in the active site. **(b)** Space-filling model. The atoms of the substrate analogue are shown in black. For stereo viewing, see instructions in the Appendix to Chapter 4. (Stereo figures courtesy of Richard J. Feldmann, NIH.)

C. The three-dimensionality of normal binocular visual perception depends on the slight disparity in the views from each eye. The two slightly different images received by the eyes are fused by the brain into a single percept, which is three-dimensional. This natural fusion mechanism can be defeated by applying gentle pressure below one eye. Do you see a doubling of images? Viewing stereo pictures with unaided eyes uses this natural fusion mechanism in a new way.

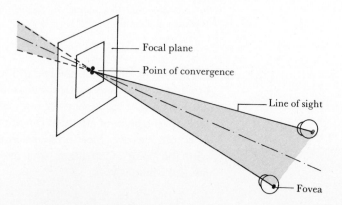

Figure 4A.1
Normal coordination of focus and convergence.

4A.2   **Stereo viewing with unaided eyes requires independence of convergence and focus.**

A.   An artificial three-dimensional image can be produced from two pictures taken from slightly different viewpoints. For a correct three-dimensional image the picture taken from the "right" viewpoint must be seen by the right eye, and that from the "left" viewpoint must be seen by the left eye. There are two ways of viewing such stereo-pair pictures, as illustrated in Figure 4A.2. For viewing with **distal convergence,** the pictures are arranged in the standard manner used with a stereoscope. For viewing with **proximal convergence,** the pictures are switched. In the stereo triptych these two arrangements are combined into a format that can be viewed with a stereoscope or with unaided eyes using proximal or distal convergence (Figure 4A.3). The format shown is standard throughout this book.

B.   Stereo viewing with unaided eyes is unusual in that you must look two places at once. To see both pictures simultaneously, your lines of sight must converge either proximally or distally to the plane of the pictures (Figure 4A.2). However, for the pictures to be in focus, the focal plane must coincide with the plane of the pictures, and not, as normally, with the convergence point. Therefore, you must be able to control focus and convergence independently. Although perhaps difficult to imagine, this skill is relatively easy to learn.

4A.3   **Stereo viewing with unaided eyes is a learned skill.**

A.   The first step in learning to view stereo pictures is to become aware of the visual field beyond your point of attention. Hold a pencil (or finger) about 10 in. in front of your eyes and look fixedly at the tip. Are you aware of one or two images of objects beyond your point of attention? It may help to pick out some relatively isolated and conspicuous object in order to decide. If you see two images, you will be able to learn this viewing method and are ready for the next step. If you are aware of only one image,

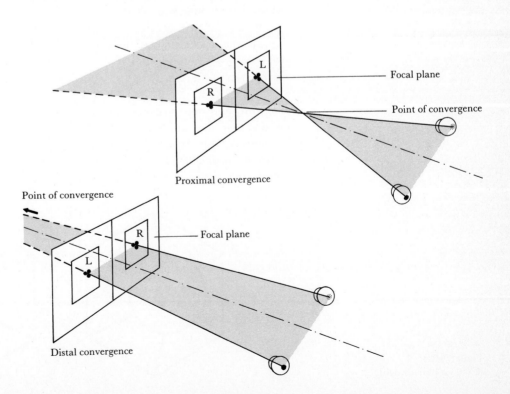

Figure 4A.2
Two arrangements for viewing stereo-pair pictures.

Figure 4A.3
Standard format for stereo triptychs.

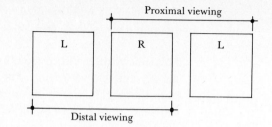

line up your pencil tip with that image and, by blinking your eyes alternately, decide
with which eye you are seeing that image. Most of you in this category are suppressing
the visual information from your weaker eye. It may help you to become aware of the
second image by alternately covering and uncovering your stronger eye while gazing
at the pencil tip, or by dimming the image from your stronger eye by covering it with
a piece of tinted glass that will reduce the entering light without changing its color,
such as a lens from a pair of gray sunglasses (neutral density filter).

B. The second step is to fuse two images using either proximal or distal convergence.
Practice on the stereo pair of images in Figure 4A.4.

For proximal convergence adjust your point of attention to between you and the
stereo pair until you are aware of three separate but out-of-focus images in the background. (It may help to use a pencil tip as a guide or simply cross your eyes slightly.)
Three images will appear when you are looking at a point approximately halfway
between you and the page. (If you see four separate images, your point of attention is
too close to your eyes.) When you see three images, keep your attention on the center
image, disregarding the outer two. The center image, which is a combination of the
two original images, contains the information necessary for a three-dimensional
percept. When the two images are properly overlaid your fusion mechanism will tend
to "lock" onto it. You may need to tilt your head slightly toward one shoulder to bring
the overlaid images to the same level. In any case note the effect of head tilting; proper
head position is essential for comfortable viewing.

For distal convergence, your point of attention must be beyond the stereo pictures. You may find it helpful to look at an object in the distance and then move the
stereo pictures into your field of view. The goal, as before, is to see three images.

When you have obtained three images, you can verify whether you are converging proximally or distally to the page by blinking one eye and observing which of the
two outer images disappears. If your point of attention is proximal to the page, the
right-hand outside image will disappear when you blink your right eye.

C. The third and final step is to focus on the fused image. The image is out of focus
because your eyes are focused proximally or distally, at your point of convergence.
You must now learn to adjust your focus to the plane of the page while maintaining
the three images. The first few times you try this there will be a natural tendency for
the central image to split apart. That is because you have trained yourself since

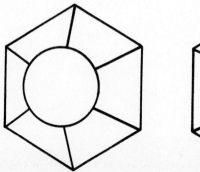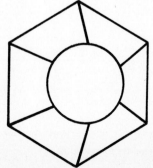

Figure 4A.4
A stereo-pair drawing.

infancy to converge and focus at the same point in space. You may find it useful to move the picture toward or away from your eyes. Once you see the central image in focus you should become aware of a three-dimensional percept within a few seconds. If you are converging proximally, the circle will appear in front of the hexagon; if you are converging distally, the circle will appear behind the hexagon.

It may take you some time to become aware of your ability to control convergence and focus independently. This step is rate-limiting in the overall learning process, and may require considerable effort at first. However, you will find that it becomes easier with practice and that the results will be worth the initial effort.

D. To view a stereo triptych choose the appropriate pair of pictures, depending on whether you prefer proximal or distal convergence, and view them as before. Initially it may help to cover the third picture in the triptych. When the third picture is not covered, note that once you have obtained a three-dimensional image by fusing one pair of adjacent pictures in the triptych, you can shift your gaze to give a three-dimensional image of the other pair without losing fusion or focus. (The surrounding border is designed to aid you in maintaining fusion as you shift your attention, especially in groups of three-dimensional pictures.) The second three-dimensional image is reversed back to front. For wire models this reversal produces a three-dimensional mirror image. For space-filling figures the reversal produces a bizarre effect that has been termed **pseudoscopic.**

4A.4 Stereo viewing differs with proximal and distal convergence.

A. Eye physiology restricts the possible size formats for proximal and distal stereo viewing. The geometry of viewing with proximal convergence can accommodate a large

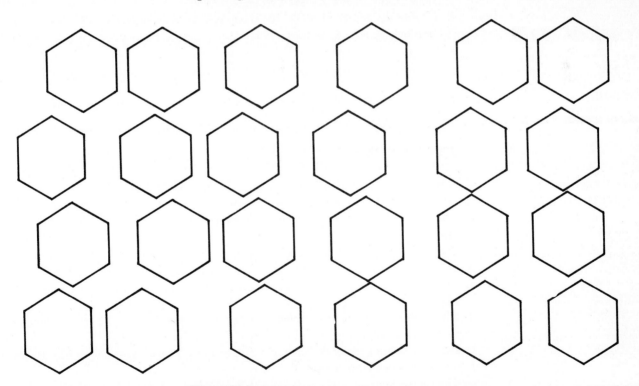

Figure 4A.5
Perceived size as a function of perceived distance. Fuse any adjacent pair of hexagons in the same row. When you have fused one pair you will be able to look around the entire grid and see hexagons at different apparent distances. Compare the sizes of near and distant hexagons.

variety of picture sizes and a corresponding wide range of viewing distances. (Viewing large pictures at a distance represents an additional learning step.) Stereo viewing with distal convergence is more restricted. Because your eyes cannot turn outward, the width of pictures that you can view is limited; their centers cannot be separated by more than the distance between your pupils. This restriction on picture size imposes a corresponding restriction on viewing distance. Fortunately, the size format for standard stereoscopes usually permits them to be viewed with distal convergence. However, the absolute size limit varies with the individual, so you may experience difficulty with some stereo figures.

B. You may notice that the three-dimensional image you perceive is noticeably different in size than the picture on the page. With proximal convergence the image appears smaller, whereas with distal convergence it appears larger. This illusion results from a systematic distortion that is a normal component of visual perception. It may make you curious about how you perceive size (see Figure 4A.5). However, your ability to resolve detail in the picture on the page and in the three-dimensional percept will be the same, because the size of the retinal image remains constant at a given viewing distance, regardless of changes in the point of convergence.

References

COMPREHENSIVE TEXTS

Lehninger: Chapter 6   Stryer: Chapter 2
Metzler: Chapter 2   White et al.: Chapter 6

OTHER REFERENCES

C. B. Anfinsen, "Principles That Govern the Folding of Protein Chains," *Science*, **181**, 223 (1973).

R. E. Dickerson and I. Geis, *The Structure and Action of Proteins,* Benjamin/Cummings, Menlo Park, Calif., 1969. Chapters 2, 3, and 4.

R. J. Feldmann and D. H. Bing, "Teaching Aids for Macromolecular Structure," National Institutes of Health, Bethesda, 1980.

R. Ferragallo, "On Stereoscopic Painting," *Leonardo*, **7,** 97 (1974).

G. E. Schulz and R. H. Schirmer, *Principles of Protein Structure,* Springer-Verlag, New York, 1979.

J. D. Watson, *Molecular Biology of the Gene,* Benjamin/Cummings, Menlo Park, Calif., 1976, 3rd ed. Chapters 4 and 6.

Problems

4.1   Answer the following with true or false. If false, explain why.
  a. H-bonding occurs between hydrogen atoms on the surfaces of proteins in solution.
  b. The thermodynamically most stable conformation of a protein is the structure of lowest free energy.
  c. Formation of internal H-bonds is the major interaction that drives protein folding.
  d. Organic solvents denature proteins primarily by preventing ionic interactions.
  e. Folding of a hydrophobic protein is accompanied by an increase in entropy of the polypeptide.
  f. The term *quaternary structure* refers to protein configuration in the fourth dimension, that is, as a function of time.
  g. Disulfide bonds covalently link Cys residues whose proximity is determined by previous noncovalent interactions.
  h. The amide hydrogen of every peptide bond in an α helix is H-bonded.
  i. From the complete primary structure of a protein, it is possible to calculate its three-dimensional configuration.

4.2 a. Minimum-free-energy configurations of proteins often are reinforced by covalent cross-links between _____ residues.

b. Hydrophobic interactions lead to a _____ in free energy when nonpolar side chains are removed from the aqueous phase.

c. Folding of hydrophobic side chains into the interior of a protein _____ the entropy of the aqueous surroundings.

d. Organic solvents stabilize (decrease the free energy of) _____ groups in an aqueous medium.

e. In an α helix, the H-bonds between C=O and N—H groups are maximally stable because the three atoms involved are _____ .

4.3 Which of the following amino acid residues would you expect to find on the inside, and which on the outside, of a typical globular protein molecule in solution at pH = 7?

Glu	Arg
Val	Phe
Ilu	Met
Asn	Lys
Ser	Thr

4.4 In a nonpolar environment such as the interior of a membrane, the proteins presumably are folded with (a) _____ side chains to the outside and (b) _____ side chains neutralized by interaction with each other.

4.5 Hemoglobin is a tetrameric protein consisting of two α and two β polypeptide subunits. The structure of the α and β subunits is remarkably similar to that of myoglobin. However, at a number of positions, hydrophilic residues in myoglobin have been replaced by hydrophobic residues in hemoglobin.

a. How can this observation be reconciled with the generalization that hydrophobic residues fold into the interior of proteins?

b. In this regard, what can you say about the interactions determining quaternary structure in hemoglobin?

4.6 What would you predict about the ratio of hydrophilic to hydrophobic residues in a series of globular monomeric proteins that range in size from 10,000 to 100,000 daltons?

4.7 As part of an undergraduate biochemistry lab project, you are characterizing three polypeptides of approximately equal molecular weight from human plasma. Using various physical techniques, you have established that in their native states one of the polypeptides is a monomeric, cigar-shaped molecule, the second is monomeric and approximately spherical, and the third is the subunit of a tetramer of identical subunits. Your lab partner has determined the amino acid compositions of the three proteins. However, when he brings you the data, shown in Table 4.2, you are greatly upset to discover that he failed to note which composition corresponds to which protein. A student at the next bench tells you that you should simply deduce which is which from the amino acid compositions themselves. Your partner is sure that the student is trying to trick you into making an error that will lower your grade. Should you take his advice? If you decide to do so, which composition would you assign to which protein, and why?

4.8 Assume the following approximate free-energy changes (ΔG):

1. For folding of hydrophobic residues out of a low ionic strength medium at neutral pH into a nonpolar protein interior: $\Delta G \simeq -4$ kcal/mol residues.

2. For forming an H-bond between any two unbonded polar groups: $\Delta G \simeq -5$ kcal/mol polar groups.

Picture a partially folded protein with an unfolded sequence, still in the aqueous phase, consisting of Ser, Thr, Asn, and two nonpolar residues. What will be the approximate ΔG (in kilocalories per mole of protein molecules) when this sequence is folded into the interior of the structure, under the conditions given in parts a–c?

Table 4.2
Amino Acid Compositions
of Three Hypothetical
Plasma Proteins
(Problem 4.7)

Amino acid	Number of residues per molecule		
	Protein 1	Protein 2	Protein 3
Polar residues			
Arg	12	4	7
Asn	9	6	5
Asp	14	5	9
Cys	7	2	6
Gln	8	7	6
Glu	11	4	6
His	4	2	4
Lys	22	6	15
Ser	20	8	21
Thr	15	5	11
Trp	2	3	3
Tyr	7	7	6
Nonpolar residues			
Ala	14	28	25
Gly	9	9	8
Ilu	5	16	9
Leu	3	19	7
Met	7	11	9
Phe	9	15	11
Pro	8	13	10
Val	16	29	21

a. All its polar groups form internal H-bonds.

b. All but its side-chain polar groups form internal H-bonds.

c. None of its polar groups form internal H-bonds.

d. In which of the preceding three situations will folding occur?

4.9 The following is taken from a 1963 Cold Spring Harbor Symposium paper [*Cold Spring Harbor Symposia on Quantitative Biology*, **28**, 442 (1963)]:

> The only serious challenge to the "thermodynamic" hypothesis (i.e., that primary structure completely determines tertiary configuration) arises from the work of Berson and Yalow. They found that certain antisera can distinguish between sperm whale and pork insulins, proteins that have identical amino acid sequences. On the basis of this evidence they concluded, "It would seem that, *in addition* to amino acid sequence, the precise configuration of folding of the protein molecule is determined by the genetic apparatus."

Propose an alternative explanation that does not challenge the "thermodynamic" hypothesis of protein folding. Describe an experiment to test your proposal. (The structure of insulin is shown in Figure 3.14.)

4.10 An ambitious student decided to test the proposition that many proteins stabilized by covalent —S—S— bonds nevertheless are in minimum-free-energy configurations. He treated a series of proteins containing disulfide bonds with β-mercaptoethanol to reduce the —S—S— linkages, in the presence of $8M$ urea as a denaturant. These reagents gradually were removed by appropriate procedures so that the proteins could refold with re-formation of disulfide bonds. The data obtained are shown in Table 4.3.

Table 4.3
Recovery of Biological
Activity Following
Denaturation and
Refolding of Three
Proteins (Problem 4.10)

Protein	Number of —S—S— bonds	Calculated recovery of biological activity with random joining of —S—S— bonds	Experimental recovery of biological activity
Ribonuclease	4	0.95%	100%
Lysozyme	4	0.95%	80%
Insulin	3	6.7%	7%

a. With four —S—S— bonds show that the expected recovery of biological activity is 0.95% if re-formation of —S—S— bonds occurs randomly.

b. Do the data for ribonuclease and lysozyme support, or contradict, the proposition in the problem?

c. How can you explain the apparent randomness of insulin refolding?

d. Trypsin contains six —S—S— bonds. After subjecting trypsin to the procedure in the problem, only 8% of the enzyme activity was observed experimentally. What is the expected recovery of activity for random —S—S— bond formation? Do the trypsin data support, or contradict, the proposition in the problem?

4.11   Whereas most bacteria are killed by temperatures above 50°C, some thermophilic species thrive at 70–80°C. In what general way(s) might you expect proteins of thermophilic bacteria to differ from the analogous proteins of ordinary bacteria?

4.12   Consider a segment of a polypeptide capable of folding into an α helix. Will it be thermodynamically more likely to do so if the segment is exposed completely to the aqueous surroundings or completely buried in the nonpolar interior of the protein? Explain.

4.13 a. In the middle of a sheet of paper draw an extended polypeptide without side chains. Now draw a second polypeptide in the opposite direction such that maximum hydrogen bonding is achieved between the two polypeptides. Note that successive C_α atoms are always in a *trans* configuration across the peptide bond (Concept 2.3).

b. The structure in part a should be a β sheet. Can additional polypeptides be added to this structure with similar H-bonding?

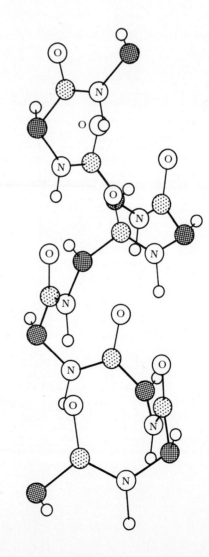

Figure 4.11
The backbone structure of an α helix (Problem 4.14).

c. Why would you expect protein fibers composed of stacked β sheets, such as silk fibroin, to be inelastic?

4.14 Figure 4.11 shows the "backbone" (polypeptide minus side chains) of an α helix. Draw the H-bonds and indicate the positions of the side chains to complete the structure.

4.15 The connective tissue protein **collagen** contains extensive sequences of $(Gly-X-Pro)_n$ or $(Gly-X-Hypro)_n$, in which X is any amino acid. Hypro is the abbreviation for hydroxyproline, a hydroxylated derivative of Pro found in connective tissue proteins (Figure 4.12). The collagen structure consists of three extended left-handed helices that are H-bonded to each other and twisted to form a right-handed superhelix, as shown schematically in Figure 4.13. Only Gly, with no side chain, is able to fit into the interior positions of the superhelix. This unique secondary structure is responsible for the tensile strength of connective tissue proteins.

Suppose that you are given small amounts of three unknown proteins, A, B, and C. Your biochemistry instructor informs you that one protein is predominantly α helix, one is predominantly β sheet, and the third is collagen triple helix. Your laboratory is equipped with an amino acid analyzer, but unfortunately has no x-ray crystallographic equipment. You determine the amino acid composition (in mole percent of

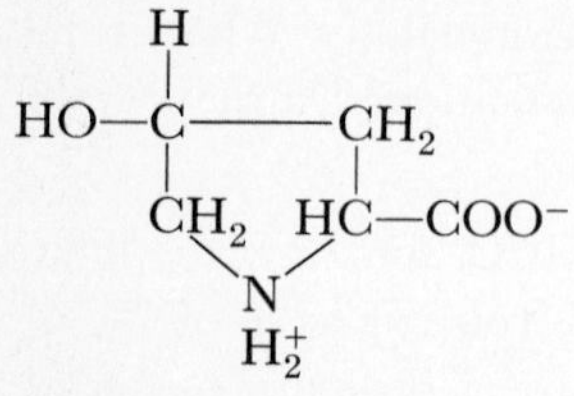

Figure 4.12
Structure of hydroxyproline.
(Problem 4.15)

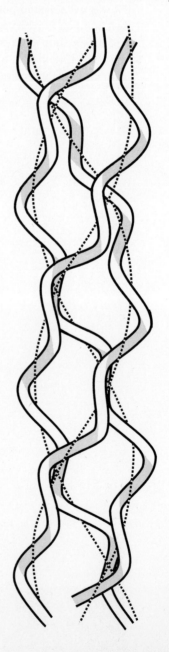

Figure 4.13
The collagen triple-helix structure. (Problem 4.15)

amino acids) of each protein, as shown in Table 4.4. Can you guess the predominant secondary structure of each?

Table 4.4
Amino Acid Composition of Three Proteins (Problem 4.15)

Protein	A	B	C	Protein	A	B	C
Ala	29.4	5.0	10.7	Leu	0.5	6.9	2.4
Arg	0.5	7.2	5.0	Lys	0.3	2.3	3.4
Asp	1.3	6.0	4.5	Met	—	0.5	0.8
Cys	—	11.2	—	Phe	0.5	2.5	1.2
Glu	1.0	12.1	7.1	Pro	0.3	7.5	12.2
Gly	44.6	8.1	33.0	Ser	12.2	10.2	4.3
His	0.2	0.7	0.4	Trp	0.2	1.2	—
Hypro	—	—	9.4	Tyr	5.2	4.2	0.4
Ilu	0.7	2.8	0.9	Val	2.2	5.1	2.3

4.16   The stability of an α helix is determined not only by the formation of interpeptide H-bonds, but also by the nature of its amino acid side chains. Predict which of the following polyamino acids will form α helices, which will form other ordered structures, and which will form no ordered structures in solution at room temperature. Give reasons for your predictions:

a. Polyleucine; pH = 7.0
b. Polyisoleucine; pH = 7.0
c. Polyarginine; pH = 7.0
d. Polyarginine; pH = 13
e. Polyglutamic acid; pH = 1.5
f. Polythreonine: pH = 7.0
g. Polyhydroxyproline: pH = 7.0

4.17   Although it is not yet possible to calculate the precise three-dimensional structure of a protein from its amino acid sequence, some general predictions can be made. Indicate regions in which structures a–d might be present in a protein with the following amino acid sequence. Assume that the protein is in a solution of low ionic strength at pH = 7.

a. α Helix
b. β Sheet
c. Random coil
d. Disulfide bond

```
1                 5                      10                     15
Ilu-Cys-Pro-Val-Gln-His-Tyr-Thr-Ala-Phe-Cys-Trp-Leu-Met-Pro-Gly-Gly-Hypro-
      20                    25                     30                    35
Phe-Gly-Ala-Gly-Ala-Gly-Ser-Gly-Ala-Gly-Ilu-Glu-Asn-Glu-Gln-Asn-Met-Ala-His-
         40                    45                     50                    55
Phe-Trp-Tyr-Lys-Gly-Lys-Lys-Arg-Arg-Cys-Glu-Ilu-Gly-Ser-Gly-Ser-Gly-Ala-
            60                    65
Gly-Ser-Gly-Arg-Arg-Lys-Gly-Arg-Gly-Arg-Pro-Hypro
```

4.18   The optical rotation (a measure of the asymmetry of a polypeptide) of two polyamino acids was measured as a function of pH. The results are given in Figure 4.14.

a. Explain the sharp transitions in optical rotation.
b. How is optical rotation related to secondary structure?

4.19   This problem and the following one introduce you to an elegant tool for the analysis of polypeptide structure called the **Ramachandran diagram.**

The possible structures of a polypeptide are limited by the geometry of the peptide bond and amino acid side chains. The six atoms of a peptide (amide) bond all lie in the same plane (Figure 4.15). With C_{α_1} as a reference point, amide plane 1 can rotate only around the C_α–N axis and amide plane 2 can rotate only around the C_α–C axis. Verify for yourself, using models if necessary, that because of the tetrahe-

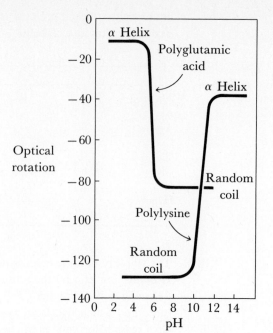

Figure 4.14
Optical rotation of two poly-amino acids as a function of pH (Problem 4.18).

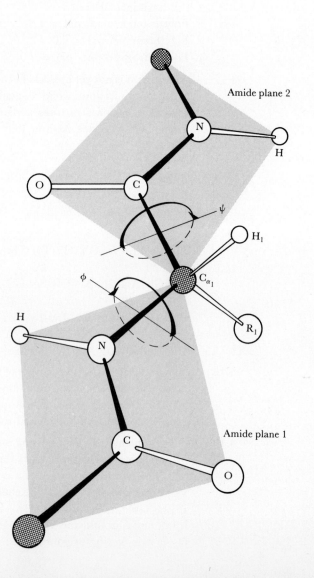

Figure 4.15
Rotation of adjacent amide planes in a polypeptide (Problem 4.19). (From R. E. Dickerson and I. Geis, *The Structure and Action of Proteins,* Benjamin/ Cummings, Menlo Park, Calif. © 1969 Dickerson and Geis.)

dral orientation of the bonds to C_{α_1}, the two planes can be coplanar only when both are perpendicular to a third plane, defined by H_1 and the C_{α_1}–R_1 bond (reference orientation). The angles ϕ and ψ are defined as the degree of clockwise rotation of planes 1 and 2, respectively, away from the reference orientation. When defined for each pair of adjacent residues, the values of ϕ and ψ completely determine the conformation of a polypeptide. Some ϕ and ψ angles are favorable because there is no crowding of atoms, and some are unfavorable because they bring atoms too close together. For example, at $\phi = 180°$ and $\psi = 0°$, the two carbonyl oxygens are crowded into an energetically unfavorable configuration (imagine amide plane 1 rotated 180° from the position shown in Figure 4.15).

When a polypeptide assumes a repeating structure, for example an α helix, every peptide bond in the chain will have the same ϕ and ψ angles. As a consequence, any repeating structure can be defined by characteristic ϕ and ψ angles. These angles are presented in the Ramachandran or ϕ, ψ diagram shown in Figure 4.16.

a. What are the Ramachandran angles for a collagen helix?
b. How does an α helix differ from a collagen helix in terms of Ramachandran angles?
c. How does an antiparallel β sheet differ from a collagen helix?
d. What are the Ramachandran angles for an antiparallel β sheet?
e. What will be the conformation of a random coil in terms of ϕ and ψ? What limitations are imposed?
f. All the common favorable secondary structures fall within the range $\phi = 20°$ to $\phi = 140°$. What advantage does this range have for every amino acid except Gly?

4.20   Examine the Ramachandran diagram of the peptide bonds in lysozyme shown in Figure 4.17.
a. What is the predominant secondary structure?
b. Are any other ordered structures represented by enough peptide bonds to be identifiable?
c. What can you say about the majority of bonds whose ϕ, ψ angles are in highly unfavorable regions?
d. What can you say about the composition of the helical regions of lysozyme?
e. What can you say about the composition of the β-sheet regions of lysozyme?
f. Compare your answers with the actual structure of lysozyme shown in Figure 4.9.

4.21   The pitch (p) of a helix is defined as $p = dn$, in which n is the number of repeating units per turn and d is the distance along the helix axis per repeating unit. Therefore, the pitch is a measure of the distance from any point on the helix to the corresponding point on the next turn of the helix.

Figure 4.16
Ramachandran diagram showing favored rotational angles (ϕ, ψ) for the amide planes in polypeptides (Problem 4.19). White areas enclosed by solid lines represent the most favorable ϕ, ψ angles; light gray areas represent less favorable angles, and dark gray areas represent highly unfavorable angles. The ϕ, ψ angles for antiparallel β sheet (β), collagen triple helix (C), and right-handed α helix (α) fall within favorable regions as shown by circled symbols. (Adapted from R. E. Dickerson and I. Geis, *The Structure and Action of Proteins,* Benjamin/Cummings, Menlo Park, Calif. © 1969 Dickerson and Geis.)

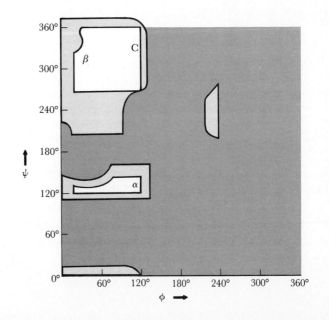

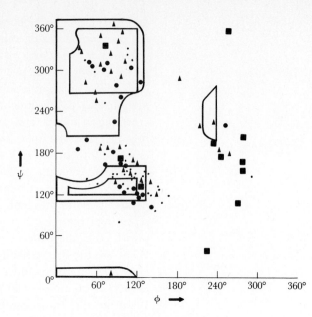

Figure 4.17
Ramachandran diagram of lysozyme (Problem 4.20). The following symbols are used to represent four classes of residues: ·, nonpolar residues; ●, charged polar residues; ▲, neutral polar residues; ■, glycine residues. (Adapted from R. E. Dickerson and I. Geis, *The Structure and Action of Proteins,* Benjamin/Cummings, Menlo Park, Calif. © 1969 Dickerson and Geis.)

   a. What is the pitch of an α helix and the distance per residue?

   b. How long would myoglobin be if it were one continuous α helix?

   c. How long would myoglobin be if it were one strand of a β sheet?

   d. How long would myoglobin be if it were fully extended (distance/residue = 0.36 nm)?

You may find it convenient to do Problems 4.22 through 4.24 with a friend, who can ask you the questions and record or check your answers while you continue to focus on the stereo images.

4.22 Examine the three-dimensional structure of myoglobin in Figure 4.7.

   a. What is the predominant ordered structure in myoglobin?

   b. How many obvious α helices are present? How many β-sheet structures? How many collagen-type helices?

   c. What fraction of the molecule (very roughly) appears to have an ordered structure?

   d. What amino acid residues might you expect at points where α helices are broken or change direction?

4.23 Examine the three-dimensional structure of lysozyme in Figure 4.9.

   a. How does the ordered structure differ from that of myoglobin (Problem 4.22)?

   b. How many clearly distinguishable α helices are present?

   c. The sequences of three peptides within lysozyme are

> Gln-Ala-Thr-Asn-Arg-Asn-Thr
> Gly-Ser-Thr-Asp-Tyr-Gly
> Gln-Ilu-Asn-Ser-Arg

What is the common feature of these amino acids? Where are they located in the molecule?

4.24 Examine the three-dimensional structure of carboxypeptidase A in Figure 4.10.

   a. What is the predominant structure on the exterior of the molecule?

   b. What is the predominant structure in the interior of the molecule?

   c. How many β-sheet structures are present? Are they parallel or antiparallel?

   d. How many obvious α helices do you detect?

   e. How many rows are in the β sheet?

☆ **4.25** a. What is the approximate molecular weight (±20%) of a globular protein molecule consisting of one polypeptide 1000 amino acids in length?

   b. What is the approximate diameter of the molecule (±50%)? The density of protein is 1.3 g/cm^3.

☆ **4.26** How would you expect the ratio of hydrophilic to hydrophobic residues in myoglobin to differ from the ratio in hemoglobin? Explain your answer.

☆ 4.27 A Ramachandran diagram (Figure 4.16), derived from studies of protein models, is useful in predicting the folding pattern of a particular polypeptide if the φ, ψ angles (Figure 4.15) for its constituent amino acids are known. Table 4.5 gives the φ, ψ angles for four stretches of polypeptide in a protein of 80 residues.

Table 4.5
Rotational Angles for Residues in a Hypothetical Protein (Problem 4.27)

Residue		φ	ψ		Residue		φ	ψ
1	. . .					. . .		
5	Arg	113°	+ + 136°		51	Gln	40°	315°
	Cys	130°	127°			Ala	38°	316°
	Glu	128°	125°			Thr	42°	317°
	Leu	120°	127°			Asn	41°	318°
	Ala	115°	135°		55	Arg	40°	316°
10	Ala	125°	126°			Asn	39°	318°
	Ala	130°	126°			Thr	42°	316°
	Met	117°	134°			Asp	40°	315°
	Lys	113°	135°		59	—	278°	168°
	Arg	118°	134°		60	Ser	41°	314°
15	His	132°	123°			Thr	41°	316°
	. . .					Asp	41°	315°
26	Leu	217°	225°			Tyr	39°	316°
	Gly	267°	165°		64	Gly	40°	314°
	Tyr	57°	357°		80	. . .		
29	Gly	267°	210°					

a. From the data in Table 4.5, determine the most likely folding (secondary structure) for the following stretches:

1. Residues 5–15
2. Residues 51–58 and 60–64

b. What is residue 59 most likely to be?
c. What sort of folding might you envision for the peptide 26–31?
d. Is the information in a Ramachandran diagram sufficient to define the three-dimensional configuration of a polypeptide completely?

Answers

4.1 a. False. H-bonding occurs between surface polar groups and water molecules.
   b. True
   c. False. Folding is driven primarily by hydrophobic interactions.
   d. False. Organic solvents denature by lowering the free energy of hydrophobic residues exposed to the solvent, thereby stabilizing the unfolded state.
   e. False. The entropy of the *surroundings* increases. The entropy of the polypeptide, which assumes a more ordered configuration, decreases upon folding.
   f. False. *Quaternary structure* refers to the orientations of the subunit polypeptides in a multimeric protein structure.
   g. True
   h. True
   i. False. Such calculations so far have not been possible.

4.2 a. Cys
   b. decrease
   c. increases
   d. hydrophobic (or nonpolar)
   e. linearly arranged

4.3 Residues with nonpolar side chains are likely to be found inside and those with polar side chains outside. Hence Val, Ilu, Phe, and Met are likely to be inside and Glu, Asn, Ser, Arg, Lys, and Thr are likely to be outside.

4.4 a. hydrophobic (or nonpolar)
   b. hydrophilic (or polar)

4.5 a. Hydrophobic patches occur on the outside of the hemoglobin subunits where the α and β chains fit together. Thus, these patches are on the outside of the subunit, but on the inside of the multimeric protein.
   b. Hydrophobic interactions play an important role.

4.6 As a polypeptide increases in size, the ratio of surface to volume, and hence the ratio of hydrophilic to hydrophobic residues, must decrease. To illustrate this point assume that each of these proteins is a sphere of radius r. As the polypeptide increases in size, the surface area (outside of the protein) increases as r^2, whereas the volume (inside of the protein) increases as r^3.

4.7 The student's advice is sound. Because most of the polar residues in a soluble protein are on the surface of the molecule and almost all the nonpolar residues are folded into the interior, the ratio of polar to nonpolar residues will determine the permissible surface-to-volume ratio, and hence the gross shape of the protein. For any protein molecule of a given molecular weight, some ratio of polar to nonpolar residues will be compatible with a spherical shape. An increase in this ratio, with no change in molecular weight, will necessitate a greater surface-to-volume ratio and lead to a more asymmetric conformation, such as a rod or pancake shape. A decrease in the polar-to-nonpolar ratio requires that the protein exist as a multimer, whose surface-to-volume ratio will be less than that of a monomeric sphere.

If you add the columns in Table 4.2, you will find that the polar-to-nonpolar ratios in the three compositions are about 65 : 35, 30 : 70, and 50 : 50, respectively. Therefore, the surface-to-volume ratios are in the order $1 > 3 > 2$, indicating that 1 is the cigar-shaped protein, 3 is the spherical protein, and 2 is the tetramer subunit.

4.8 a. In the unfolded state, all polar groups will be H-bonded to water molecules. When the sequence folds inside, the released water molecules will H-bond to each other. Therefore, if all polar groups in the sequence re-form H-bonds inside the molecule, they will contribute little to the ΔG of folding, since there will be no net change in the number of H-bonds. Thus the ΔG will result entirely from removal of the two nonpolar side chains from the aqueous phase. It will be approximately $2 \times (-4) = -8$ kcal/mol protein.
   b. If the side-chain polar groups do not form H-bonds internally, four H-bonds will be broken upon folding (one each for Ser and Thr, two for Asn), but the four released water molecules will re-form two H-bonds with each other. Thus, there will be a net loss of two H-bonds, resulting in an unfavorable free-energy contribution of $2 \times (+5) = +10$ kcal/mol. Therefore, the net ΔG will be approximately $+10 - 8 = +2$ kcal/mol protein.
   c. In addition to the side-chain polar groups, each residue in the sequence contributes its peptide-bonded C=O and N—H groups, which also are H-bonded to water in the unfolded state. If none of these groups re-form H-bonds internally, there will be a total of 14 H-bonds broken and 7 re-formed between water molecules. Thus, there will be a net loss of 7 H-bonds and a highly unfavorable contribution to the ΔG for folding of $7 \times (+5) = +35$ kcal/mol. The net ΔG will be approximately $+35 - 8 = +27$ kcal/mol protein.
   d. Spontaneous folding will occur only when ΔG is negative, that is, in the situation described in part a.

4.9 Inactive proinsulin is a single polypeptide that becomes converted to active insulin by excision of an internal 33-residue fragment to produce two polypeptides linked by —S—S— bonds. The proinsulin sequences in the two species could be different, thereby causing differences in tertiary structure that are stabilized by the —S—S— bonds. These differences are preserved after the two proinsulins have been converted by cleavage to the same primary structure. This explanation can be tested by sequence analysis of the two proinsulins.

4.10 a. With eight Cys residues, the first to pair has one chance in seven of selecting the correct partner. Of the six remaining Cys residues, the first to pair has one chance in five to pair correctly. Four Cys residues remain; the first of these to pair has one chance in three of pairing correctly. The final pair is determined by the previous pairings. Therefore, the probability of the three correct choices required to produce an active enzyme is

$$\frac{1}{7} \times \frac{1}{5} \times \frac{1}{3} = \frac{1}{105} = 0.0095 \text{ or } 0.95\%$$

   b. These studies support the proposition because the experimental activities are much greater than that expected from random refolding.

   c. The two chains of insulin result from internal cleavages of proinsulin, as explained in Answer 4.9. Because the noncovalent interactions that directed the initial correct folding are not all present during the refolding process, —S—S— bond formation is random.

   d. $$\frac{1}{11} \times \frac{1}{9} \times \frac{1}{7} \times \frac{1}{5} \times \frac{1}{3} = \frac{1}{10,400} \simeq 0.0001 \text{ or } 0.01\%$$

   An 8% recovery of enzyme activity is far in excess of the random expectation of 0.01%. Thus the proposition is supported.

4.11 Because hydrophobic associations increase in strength with increasing temperature, proteins of thermophilic bacteria might have a higher proportion of hydrophobic residues to increase stability and counteract the denaturing effects of high temperature. A higher content of disulfide bonds also might be found, but keep in mind that although these bonds stabilize finished proteins, they would not assist folding at high temperature. Finally, thermophilic bacteria might contain a high proportion of thermodynamically unstable proteins, produced by folding and disulfide cross-linking of highly hydrophobic precursors, followed by proteolytic removal of excess hydrophobic residues to give kinetically stable proteins with amino acid compositions comparable to those of ordinary bacteria.

4.12 In aqueous surroundings, the C=O and N—H groups of each peptide bond can H-bond either to water or to each other, with little difference in free energy. Consequently, there is relatively little tendency toward α-helix formation. However, in the nonpolar protein interior these polar groups have no alternative but to form H-bonds with each other, and α-helix formation therefore is favored thermodynamically.

4.13 a. See Figure 4.6.
   b. Yes. See Figure 4.6. Each polypeptide would run antiparallel to its two neighbors.
   c. Such fibers are inelastic because their long axes correspond to the backbones of the polypeptides, which are nearly fully extended already.

4.14 See Figure 4.2. Figure 4.11 is turned upside down relative to Figure 4.2.

4.15 A is silk (β sheet). B is wool (α helix). C is collagen (collagen triple helix).

4.16 a. α Helix. Uncharged R groups fit well into an α helix.
   b. No ordered structure. Ilu branches at the β carbon.
   c. No ordered structure. At pH = 7 all Arg residues have positive charges that repel one another more strongly than the H-bonding groups attract one another.
   d. α Helix. No charge and no branching at β carbons.
   e. α Helix. No charge and no branching at β carbons.
   f. No α helix. Thr branches at the β carbon.
   g. Ordered structure. Pro and Hypro fold into a proline helix, which is distinct from the α helix.

4.17 a. α Helix: Val 4 through Met 14
                       Ilu 29 through $\simeq$ Tyr 40
   b. β Sheet: Gly 20 through Gly 28 paired in antiparallel orientation with
                       Gly 58 through Gly 50

c. Random coil: Pro 15 through Phe 19
Lys 41 through Ilu 49 (charged residues)
Arg 59 through Arg 65

d. Disulfide bond: Either Cys 2 or Cys 11 may be joined to Cys 47.

4.18 a. Polyglutamic acid changes from an α helix to a random coil as the carboxyl groups become ionized. Polylysine changes from a random coil to an α helix as amino groups are deprotonated.

b. Optical rotation becomes more positive (dextrorotatory) as polypeptides assume an α-helical configuration.

4.19 a. $\phi = 120°$; $\psi = 320°$.

b. ϕ is identical; ψ for an α helix is about $200°$ less.

c. ψ is nearly identical; ϕ is about $80°$ less.

d. $\phi = 40°$; $\psi = 310°$.

e. The ϕ and ψ angles will be random within the ranges $\phi \simeq 20$–$110°$ and $\psi \simeq 110$–$130°$ and 270–$360°$.

f. The carbonyl group of the peptide bond is rotated away from the side chain of the α carbon.

4.20 a. α Helix

b. Yes. There are about 20 residues in the β-sheet region.

c. Bonds in the highly unfavorable region involve Gly, which has no side chain and thus no ϕ rotation restriction.

d. The helical regions are mainly hydrophobic.

e. The β-sheet regions are mainly hydrophilic.

f. The features deduced from the Ramachandran diagram all are confirmed by the actual structure of lysozyme.

4.21 a. From Concept 4.7, part A, $p = 0.54$ nm and $n = 3.6$ residues per turn. Thus

$$0.54 \text{ nm/turn} = d(\text{nm/residue}) \times 3.6 \text{ residues/turn}$$
$$d = 0.15 \text{ nm}$$

b. 153 residues $\times$ 0.15 nm/residue = 23 nm

c. 153 residues $\times$ 0.70 nm/2 residues = 53 nm

d. 153 residues $\times$ 0.36 nm/residues = 55 nm

4.22 a. α Helix

b. There are eight discrete segments of α helix, no β sheets, and no triple helices.

c. Most of the molecule is clearly α helix. More precisely, 121 of 153 residues, or about 80%, are in helical regions.

d. Pro usually is present. There always is at least one amino acid residue that interferes with α-helix formation.

4.23 a. Lysozyme has much less α-helix and some β-sheet structure.

b. There are four α helices that contain two or more turns and one α helix with a single turn.

c. The one β-sheet structure, which is adjacent to the active site, is composed of three antiparallel chains.

d. Hydrophilic; on the surface of the molecule

4.24 a. α Helix

b. β Sheet

c. Both. Starting from the "bottom" of the molecule: chains 1, 2, and 3 are antiparallel; chains 3, 4, 5, and 6 are parallel; and chains 7 and 8 are parallel in the opposite direction.

d. At least four stretches can be seen clearly: three on the left side and one on the right. Altogether there are eight stretches.

e. There are eight. Six should be obvious; the two rows nearest the "top" of the molecule are shorter than the rest.

5 Principles of Molecular Association

Biological systems employ two distinct levels of association. At one level, molecules are constructed from atoms by strong associations termed **covalent bonds.** Cellular pathways of covalent-bond formation and disruption with attendant utilization and production of energy are described collectively as **metabolism.** At a second level, molecules aggregate because of weak associations termed **noncovalent interactions.** Molecular aggregates may be short-lived, that is, unstable, as is typical of enzyme–substrate complexes, or they may be stable, as is typical of many soluble protein complexes, double-stranded DNA, membranes, and protein fibers. Membranes are important in cells because they enclose space (Chapter 6). The enclosed space is organized and supported by intracellular fibers that make up the cytoskeleton. This chapter considers the general principles of molecular association with emphasis on the symmetry of stable aggregates and cytoarchitectural components.

Concepts

5.1 Biological structures assemble according to a few general principles.

A. Biological structures usually are assembled hierarchically. Small monomeric units are constructed by metabolic pathways; monomers are linked together covalently to form polymers; polymers aggregate to form multimers; multimers assemble into larger complexes. These complexes in turn may combine to form an organelle, a virus particle, or some other subcellular structure. Building by subassembly has two advantages. It minimizes the genetic information required, in that only a few subunit structures must be specified, and it allows rejection of defective substructures at several levels of construction, thereby minimizing waste.

B. The interactions that drive stable supramolecular assembly are primarily hydrophobic; specificity is provided by H-bonds and ionic bonds between polar groups on interacting hydrophobic surfaces. The thermodynamic considerations important to these interactions are identical to those discussed in Concepts 4.2 and 4.3 in connection with the folding of individual protein molecules.

C. Information for assembly may be contained entirely within the subunits, or it may be divided between the subunits and preexisting structure. A structure will self-assemble if the subunits themselves contain all the information required to specify the finished structure. Multimeric enzymes, multienzyme complexes, ribosomes, and simple viruses are examples of complex structures that self-assemble. Each of these structures is simply the minimum-free-energy configuration attainable by subunit interaction. Therefore, self-assembly leads to thermodynamically stable structures. It also minimizes the genetic information required, because subunit structure is sufficient to direct subsequent assembly.

If some information must be supplied by a preexisting structure, an assembly process is said to be **template-directed.** In particular, those processes that involve addition of new subunits to existing structures, such as the building of chromosomes, cell walls, and membranes, may be partially template-directed. For any template-directed assembly process, a change in the template can cause a change in the pattern of subunit association.

Besides templates, some assembly processes involve other accessory proteins that increase the rates of assembly reactions but are not parts of the final structure. Some of these accessory proteins are enzymes that promote covalent modifications of associated subunits, such as the cross-links in collagen fibrils. Other accessory proteins promote the noncovalent association of structural components by mechanisms that are not yet clear.

5.2 Molecular associations obey the principle of molecular complementarity.

Molecules associate across complementary surfaces in van der Waals contact with each other. In general, complementarity of surfaces requires that protrusions on one molecule be matched by cavities on the other, that H-bond donors be situated opposite H-bond acceptors, and that negatively charged groups be located opposite positively charged groups. Complementary surfaces will be referred to here with the general notation A and A′ (Figure 5.1). The region of association defined by A and A′ constitutes the **domain of binding.**

An important consequence of association across complementary surfaces is that each molecule in an aggregate bears a fixed orientation relative to the others. This principle applies to unstable associations such as enzyme–substrate complexes, as well as to the stable associations that characterize larger structures.

5.3 Molecular associations obey symmetry principles.

A. The symmetry properties of an object are defined by the spatial manipulations that permit it to be superimposed on itself. Such manipulations are called **symmetry operations.** Any object can be superimposed on itself by a 360° rotation about any axis. An object that can be superimposed on itself only by this operation is by definition asymmetric. Almost all individual biological molecules, especially macromolecules, are asymmetric. A complex of unlike asymmetric molecules is necessarily also asymmetric (Figure 5.1). Monomeric enzyme–substrate complexes are common examples of pairwise asymmetric complexes. Ribosomes, replication complexes, and transcription complexes are examples of larger asymmetric aggregates. Symmetry is primarily a property of aggregates that contain more than one copy of each different subunit.

B. Symmetric biological structures generally are built from two or more copies of an asymmetric subunit (**protomer**). In multisubunit enzymes the protomer is usually one polypeptide chain. However, a protomer can be an aggregate of two or more unlike polypeptide chains. Hemoglobin, for example, is a symmetric dimer in which each protomer consists of one α and one β globin chain (Figure 5.2).

C. The symmetry of a repeating biological structure is defined with reference to a line called the **axis of symmetry.** Symmetry operations involve movement along a smooth

Figure 5.1
Molecular association across complementary surfaces.

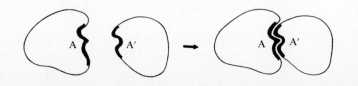

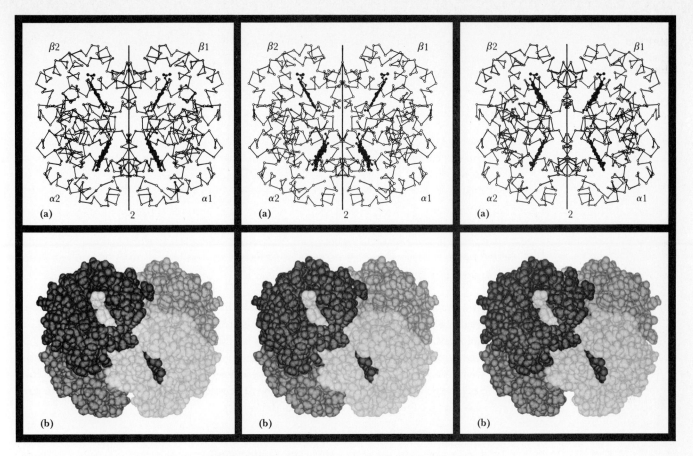

Figure 5.2
Stereo triptychs showing symmetric structure of hemoglobin.
(a) Skeletal model showing only the C_α atoms of the protein. Black spheres represent the atoms of the heme group. The protomers are arranged with 2-fold symmetry about the indicated symmetry axis. **(b)** Space-filling model in the same orientation as **(a)**. The $\alpha_1\beta_1$ protomer is light and the $\alpha_2\beta_2$ protomer is dark. Heme atoms are shown in contrasting shades. For stereo viewing, see instructions in the Appendix to Chapter 4. (Stereo figures courtesy of Richard J. Feldmann, NIH.)

curve that bears a constant relationship to the symmetry axis. There are three related categories of such operations: rotation around the axis, helical motion (screw) around the axis, and translation along the axis (Figure 5.3). Repeating biological structures are thus characterized as having **rotational, screw,** or **translational** symmetry.

5.4 Molecular aggregates whose symmetry is entirely rotational are closed clusters of protomers.

A. Molecular aggregates that possess rotational symmetry superimpose on themselves more than once in a 360° rotation about an axis of symmetry. The number of superpositions in a single rotation defines the "fold" of the axis. An aggregate with a 2-fold axis and one with a 3-fold axis are illustrated in Figure 5.4. Aggregates containing a single axis of rotational symmetry are said to possess **cyclic** (C) point group symmetry (Table 5.1). Protomers in such aggregates are linked by a head-to-tail ring of interactions (Figure 5.4).

B. Because protomers are identical, each must possess both complementary surfaces (A and A′) involved in any pairwise association between them. If the complementary

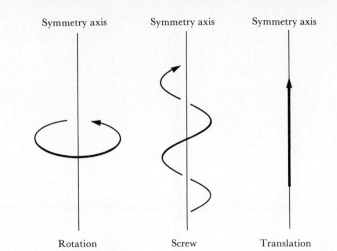

Figure 5.3
Three related symmetry operations.

contacts are situated such that they can both be satisfied in a single interaction, the resulting dimer will possess a 2-fold axis (Figure 5.4a). Such an association is termed **isologous,** because the surfaces engaged in holding the pair together are identical (A plus A′ on each protomer). If all complementary contacts are satisfied only by multiple interactions, the aggregate will possess greater than 2-fold symmetry (Figure 5.4b). Such associations are termed **heterologous** because the surfaces linking any pair are different (A on one protomer, A′ on the other).

C. Aggregates that possess more than a single axis of rotational symmetry belong to higher-order point groups, called **dihedral** or **cubic** (Table 5.1). Both these classes of symmetry require more than one pair of complementary contacts (B and B′ in addition to A and A′). Aggregates with dihedral (D) symmetry can be considered as back-to-back (isologous) associations of two identical multimers that each possess simple cyclic symmetry (Figure 5.5). These aggregates exhibit n 2-fold axes that lie in a plane perpendicular to the one n-fold axis.

Aggregates in the cubic point group can possess **tetrahedral** (T), **octahedral** (O), or **icosahedral** (I) symmetry (Table 5.1, Figure 5.5). These aggregates exhibit the four

Table 5.1
Biological Point Group Symmetries

Point group symmetry	Number of protomers	Minimum contacts (type)[a]	Rotation axes	Example
Cyclic				
C2	2	1 (i)	1 2-fold	Hemoglobin
C3	3	1 (h)	1 3-fold	Aldolase from *Pseudomonas putida*
Cn	n	1 (h)	1 n-fold	
Dihedral				
D2	4	2 (ii)	3 2-fold	*Lac* repressor
D3	6	2 (hi)	1 3-fold	Aspartate transcarbamylase
			3 2-fold	
Dn	$2n$	2 (hi)	1 n-fold	
			n 2-fold	
Cubic				
T	12	2	3 2-fold	Aspartate-β-decarboxylase
			4 3-fold	
O	24	2	6 2-fold	Dihydrolipoyl transacetylase
			4 3-fold	
			3 4-fold	
I	60	2	15 2-fold	Spherical viruses
			10 3-fold	
			6 5-fold	

[a]The symbol i represents isologous association; h, heterologous.

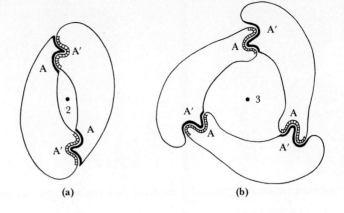

Figure 5.4
Examples of aggregates with 2-fold **(a)** and 3-fold **(b)** rotational symmetry.

3-fold axes of a cube, which are the lines connecting the opposite corners. Molecular aggregates with icosahedral symmetry form shells that can enclose space. Such aggregates encase the genetic material of many viruses.

5.5 Molecular flexibility can lead to nonequivalence of protomers.

If identical protomers become nonidentical as a result of aggregation, they are termed **quasi-equivalent.** Because all molecules are somewhat flexible, associations between them often introduce small distortions into each (Figure 5.6). If mutual distortion of interacting protomers is not symmetric, the protomers will not be identical in the aggregate. Many common aggregates are not perfectly symmetric when examined at a fine enough level. For example, careful spectroscopic examination of the heme groups in hemoglobin (C2 symmetry) indicates that the two protomers are not identical. This general concept of quasi-equivalence initially was introduced to explain the observation that many icosahedral viruses contain more than 60 protomers, which is the maximum number that can be accommodated in strictly equivalent configurations in an icosahedral shell.

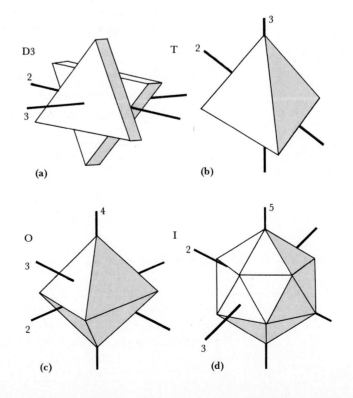

Figure 5.5
Higher-order point group symmetries. **(a)** Dihedral, D3. **(b)** Tetrahedral T. **(c)** Octahedral, O. **(d)** Icosahedral, I. A representative symmetry axis of each kind is shown (see Table 5.1).

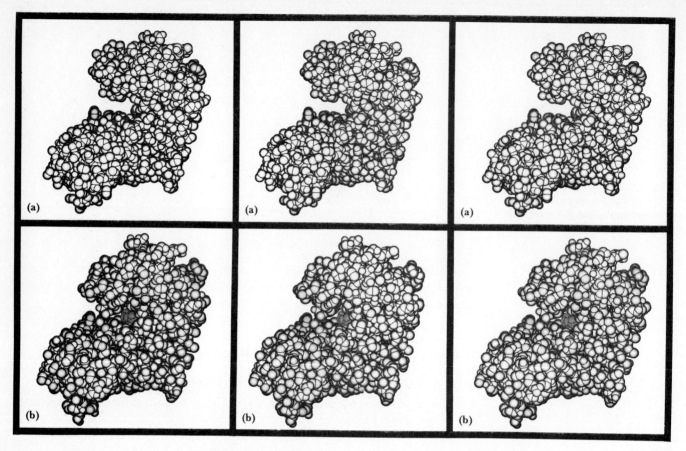

Figure 5.6
Stereo triptychs illustrating distortion of the enzyme hexokinase **(a)** on binding of its substrate, ATP **(b).** The atoms of ATP are shown in black. For stereo viewing, see instructions in the Appendix to Chapter 4. [Adapted from C. M. Anderson, F. H. Zucker, and T. A. Steitz, *Science,* **204,** 375 (1979).]

5.6 Molecular aggregates possessing translational or screw symmetry are open-ended chains.

Molecular aggregates with translational or screw symmetry are formed by heterologous associations in such a way that all complementary contacts cannot be occupied, thereby forming open-ended chains. In biological systems helical structures with screw symmetry are the usual form for such chains. Screw symmetries are described by the number of protomers per turn, which need not be integral, the distance along the symmetry axis per turn (pitch), and handedness (Figure 5.7). The tobacco mosaic virus, one of the first helical structures described, has 16.3 protomers per turn and a pitch of 2.3 nm; it is right-handed. With an additional set of complementary contacts (B and B′), chains with translational or screw symmetry can dimerize (by isologous association) or form multistranded aggregates (by heterologous association).

5.7 Helical fibers make up the cytoarchitectural elements of eucaryotic cells.

A. A few proteins form long helical fibers that account for most of the extracellular and intracellular structural supports for eucaryotic cells. Extracellular helices are exported as subunits that assemble externally and then are cross-linked covalently for added

Figure 5.7
Examples of left- and right-handed helices. If a strand on the front surface of a vertically oriented helix points upward to the left, the helix is left-handed; if it points upward to the right, the helix is right-handed. Each of these helices has four protomers (hands) per turn.

Left-handed helix

Right-handed helix

strength. These helices include collagen, a three-stranded helix that forms a tough, degradation-resistant supporting structure for many cells; elastin, an extensible polymer of connective tissue; and fibrin, the circulating precursor form of which is cleaved by thrombin to produce a fibrous network that can plug holes.

Table 5.2
Cytoarchitectural
Components of Eucaryotic
Cells

Fiber	Fiber diameter (nm)	Number of major subunits	Used in
Microtubules	25	2 (α, β tubulin)	Cytoskeletal elements, spindle fibers, flagella, cilia
Actin	6	1	Cellular microfilaments, muscle myofibrils
Myosin	15	2	Cellular thick filaments, muscle myofibrils
Intermediate filaments			
Keratin filaments	8	Very heterogeneous (100–250 genes)	Fibrous networks in epithelial cells, tonofilaments
Desmin filaments; vimentin filaments	10	1	Cross-linking and registration of myofibrils in muscle cells; lattice surrounding the nucleus in mesenchymal cells
Neurofilaments	10	2–3	Structural lattice for axons of neurones
Glial filaments	8–10	1	Glial cells; function unknown

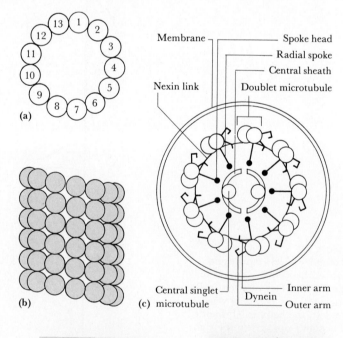

(a)

(b)

(c) microtubule

Membrane — Spoke head
Radial spoke
Central sheath
Nexin link — Doublet microtubule
Central singlet — Inner arm
Dynein
microtubule — Outer arm

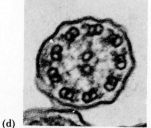

(d)

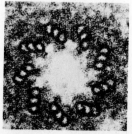

(e)

Figure 5.8
The variety of microtubule structures. **(a)** End-on view and **(b)** side view of cytoplasmic 25-nm microtubules, which are constructed from a protomer that is a dimer of α and β tubulin. **(c)/(d)** Drawing and electron micrograph of the 9 + 2 arrangement of microtubules characteristic of cilia and flagella. **(e)** Electron micrograph of a cross section through a basal body showing the nine triplets with no central microtubule. [Parts **(a)** and **(b)** from J. A. Snyder and J. R. McIntosh, *Annual Review of Biochemistry,* **45,** 706 (1976); part **(c)** adapted from J. D. Watson; electron micrographs courtesy of B. R. Brinkly, Baylor College of Medicine.]

B. Several different intracellular helices organize cellular space by providing skeletal elements for support and contractile elements for movement (Table 5.2). For example, 25-nm microtubules are universal cytoskeletal components. At cell division they form the spindle fibers that mediate chromosome segregation (Figures 5.8, 5.9). Microtubules with a more complex structure serve as the flexible backbones of cilia and flagella. Microtubules polymerize and depolymerize rapidly from regulated nucleation sites such as centrioles, basal bodies, and kinetochores, which can be activated or deactivated according to the cell's needs.

Actin and myosin are universal cytomuscular components of eucaryotic cells. Actin and myosin polymerize separately into long cables. The ATP-dependent, rachetlike movement of these cables relative to one another produces contraction and movement in both muscle and nonmuscle cells (Figure 5.10).

Intermediate filaments that are chemically and immunologically distinct perform a variety of specialized functions, most of which are not yet clearly understood, in different cell types (Table 5.2).

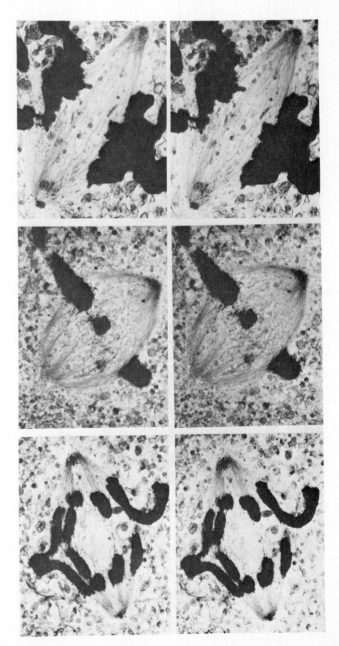

Figure 5.9
Stereo-pair electron micrographs of mitotic spindles at three successive stages of mitosis. Dark staining bodies are chromosomes. These pictures may be viewed with either proximal or distal convergence. For stereo viewing, see the Appendix to Chapter 4. (Pictures taken with the high-voltage electron microscope, Department of Molecular, Cellular, and Developmental Biology, University of Colorado, Boulder, Colo., by J. Richard McIntosh.)

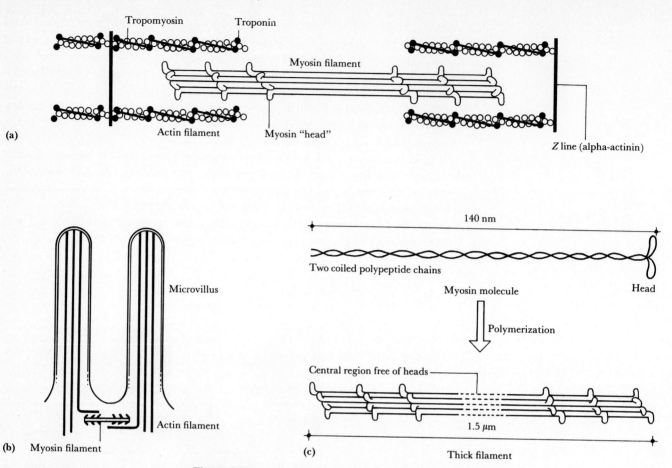

Figure 5.10
Interaction of actin and myosin in muscle and nonmuscle cells. **(a)** Schematic representation of a sarcomere from striated muscle showing interdigitating actin and myosin filaments. Note the accessory proteins associated with the actin helix. **(b)** Interaction of actin and myosin in an epithelial cell. Microvilli, which protrude from the epithelial cells lining the small intestine, contract much like muscle cells. **(c)** The polymerization of dimers of myosin molecules into thick filaments. [Parts **(a)** and **(b)** adapted from E. Lazarides and J. P. Revel, *Scientific American,* May 1979, p. 104; part **(c)** adapted from J. D. Watson, *Molecular Biology of the Gene,* Benjamin/Cummings, Menlo Park, Calif., 1975, p. 465.]

5.8   **Additional concepts and techniques are presented in the Problems section.**

A. Advantages of subassembly construction for quality control. Problems 5.4 and 5.5.

B. Symmetry of inversion and reflection. Problems 5.11 and 5.12.

C. Cross-linking to investigate subunit structure of proteins. Problems 5.18 and 5.19.

D. Pseudosymmetry in aggregates of similar units. Problems 5.24 and 5.25.

References   COMPREHENSIVE TEXTS

Lehninger: Chapter 36

Metzler: Chapter 4

Stryer: Chapters 30, 34

White et al.: Chapter 6

OTHER REFERENCES

D. Eisenberg and D. Crothers, *Physical Chemistry with Applications to the Life Sciences,* Benjamin/ Cummings, Menlo Park, Calif., 1979. Chapter 16.

E. Lazarides, "Intermediate Filaments as Mechanical Integrators of Cellular Space," *Nature,* **283,** 249 (1980).

E. Lazarides and J. P. Revel, "The Molecular Basis of Cell Movement," *Scientific American,* May 1979, p. 100.

J. Monod, J. Wyman, and J. Changeux, "On the Nature of Allosteric Transitions: A Plausible Model," *Journal of Molecular Biology,* **12,** 88–118 (1965).

J. A. Snyder and J. R. McIntosh, "Biochemistry and Physiology of Microtubules," *Annual Review of Biochemistry,* **45,** 699 (1980).

H. Weyl, *Symmetry,* Princeton University Press, Princeton, N.J., 1952.

W. B. Wood, "Bacteriophage T4 Assembly and the Morphogenesis of Subcellular Structure," The Harvey Lectures, Series 73, Academic Press, New York, 1979. P. 203.

Problems

5.1   Answer the following with true or false. If false, explain why.

a. One advantage of subassembly construction is that mistakes can be rejected with minimum waste of material.

b. Self-assembly requires structural information from preexisting templates.

c. Assembly at the supramolecular level is driven primarily by formation of H-bonds and ionic bonds.

d. An asymmetric object does not superimpose on itself at all in a 360° rotation about an axis.

e. A symmetry axis passes through the center of mass of any symmetric molecular aggregate.

f. All molecular aggregates that contain protomers linked in a head-to-tail ring of interactions possess cyclic point group symmetry.

g. All aggregates with dihedral symmetry, except for those with D2 symmetry, have one *n*-fold axis perpendicular to a plane containing *n* 2-fold axes.

h. Point group symmetries with more than one axis of rotational symmetry necessarily require more than one pair of complementary contacts.

i. Many common enzymes are dimers of identical subunits, which usually are held together by heterologous associations.

j. A tetramer is the largest closed structure (no binding surfaces unoccupied) that can be built with isologous associations only.

k. The helical spiral in Figure 5.3 is right-handed.

l. A left-handed helix can be constructed only from left-handed protomers.

5.2   a. The associative behavior of biological molecules is the principal concern of the field called _____.

b. The region of association defined by the interaction of complementary surfaces constitutes the _____ between subunits.

c. Symmetric biological structures are built from repeats of a fundamental asymmetric unit called a _____.

d. The symmetry of biological structures can be described by three related spatial manipulations: _____, a circular motion around an axis; _____, a spiral motion around an axis; and _____, a uniform motion along an axis.

e. If protomers become nonidentical as a result of their interaction with one another, they are called _____.

f. _____, _____, and _____ are structural helices that are present in nearly all eucaryotic cells.

g. Molecular aggregates with _____ symmetry encase the genetic material of many viruses.

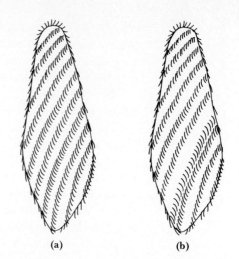

(a)   (b)

Figure 5.11
A generalized ciliated protozoan with **(a)** normal and **(b)** abnormal surface elements (Problem 5.3).

5.3   In many common ciliated protozoa, the surface elements are arranged in rows with each cilium pointing toward the rear of the animal (Figure 5.11a). By microsurgery it is possible to produce individuals in which a single row of elements is reversed (Figure 5.11b). When these individuals divide, each daughter cell exhibits the reversed row of elements, and this abnormality continues to be propagated through subsequent generations.

     a. If you somehow could dissociate the cell surface of an aberrant animal into its individual elements by mild denaturation and then allow reassociation under natural conditions, would you expect the surface structure to re-form correctly? Explain.

     b. What kind of assembly process is involved in laying down the surface structure of a new cell? Where does the information to direct this process reside?

5.4   The frequencies with which defective structures arise during assembly can be calculated as follows: In a building process involving n operations with a frequency of m mistakes per operation, the average number of mistakes will be mn. The probability that a structure will be built without a mistake is given by the zero term of the Poisson distribution, e^{-mn}. Therefore, the probability of a defective structure with at least one mistake is $1 - e^{-mn}$. At the low values of m encountered in biological systems, mn usually is $\ll 1$, so that the approximation $1 - e^{-mn} \simeq mn$ is valid. Therefore, the frequency with which a defective structure will occur is approximately equal to the average frequency of mistakes in the building process.

     Consider a situation in which each bacterium of a certain species contains one molecule of an essential 500-residue polypeptide. If the probability of inserting an incorrect amino acid during synthesis is 10^{-10} per residue, what will be the average number of defective bacteria resulting from such mistakes in a population of 10^9 cells?

5.5   By solving this problem you can prove to yourself that a multistage subassembly process allows better quality control than a one-stage process. Consider the synthesis of a multimeric enzyme complex containing six copies each of two polypeptides, A and B, which are 300 and 700 amino acid residues in length, respectively. Assume that the mistake frequency is 10^{-8} for each operation in the building process, from insertion of individual amino acids into a polypeptide chain to insertion of finished subunits into the multimer. Assume that polypeptide folding is always correct if the amino acid sequence is correct, and that rejection of defective substructures at each assembly stage is 100% efficient. Compare the frequencies of defective complexes when the following occur:

     a. The complex is synthesized in one stage as a continuous polypeptide chain 6000 amino acids long, containing six A sequences and six B sequences.

     b. The complex is constructed in three stages: (1) synthesis of A and B polypeptides, (2) formation of AB dimers, and (3) assembly of six AB dimers to form the complex.

5.6   Consider an equilibrium between a dimeric protein and its two hydrophobic subunits,

$$2 \text{ monomers} \rightleftarrows \text{dimer}$$

The free-energy change (ΔG) of the association reaction is given by $\Delta G = \Delta H - T \Delta S$ (equation 4.1). The entropy change, ΔS, for association varies with temperature as follows:

Temperature (°C)	ΔS (kcal/mol deg)
0	−0.014
25	−0.001
40	+0.026

The enthalpy change (ΔH) for association varies slightly over this temperature range as well, but it is small relative to the $T \Delta S$ term except near 25°C. What will be the effect on the state of association of this protein if the temperature is lowered from 40 to 0°C?

5.7   An increase in the stability of a multimeric protein with increasing temperature indicates that the association of its subunits is driven by a concomitant entropy increase (Problem 5.6), but it does not indicate necessarily that the interacting groups are hydrophobic. They also may be polar. Water molecules form H-bonds with polar groups in aqueous solution, thereby decreasing solvent entropy. Therefore, formation of an H-bond between two polar groups with release of the previously associated H_2O molecules has a positive (favorable) ΔS, resulting from the entropy increase of the solvent.

Suppose you observe that decreasing the temperature of a multimeric protein in aqueous solution shifts the equilibrium toward dissociation, and that addition of organic solvents such as ethanol to the solution shifts the equilibrium toward association. Would you conclude that the subunit interactions in the multimer are primarily hydrophobic or polar? Explain your answer.

5.8   A section of a drawing by M. C. Escher is pictured in Figure 5.12. Assume that the pattern repeats infinitely in the plane of the page. Describe its rotational and translational axes of symmetry.

5.9   List the rotational symmetry axes of a cube. Do these axes intersect? Which point group symmetry has the same list of rotation axes as a cube? Are the two sets of rotation axes actually identical? That is, could they be superimposed on one another?

5.10   Examine the icosahedron and the dodecahedron in Figure 5.13. An icosahedron has 20 faces, 12 vertices, and 30 edges. A dodecahedron has 12 faces, 20 vertices, and 30 edges. Compare their symmetries.

Figure 5.12
A symmetric drawing by M. C. Escher. (Angels and Devils © is reproduced with permission, Beeldrecht, Amsterdam/ VAGA, New York, 1980. Collection Haags Gemeentemuseum.)

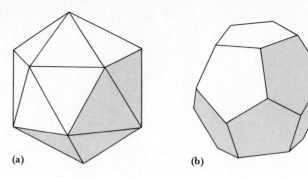

Figure 5.13
An icosahedron **(a)** and a dodecahedron **(b)** (Problem 5.10).

(a)   (b)

5.11   Any symmetry operation relates to a fundamental geometric entity: a point, a line, or a plane. For descriptions of biological symmetry we need consider only symmetry operations relative to a line. However, there are two other classes of symmetry operations, **inversion** and **reflection**, that are useful in more general discussions of symmetry. Inversion through a point and reflection through a plane are illustrated in Figure 5.14 along with rotation about a line. Why is it that biological molecules in association are rarely, if ever, related by symmetries of inversion or reflection?

5.12   Symmetry is a well-developed branch of mathematics. Consider the following relationships:

   I. Reflection   = inversion × 180° rotation
  II. Reflection   = 180° rotation × inversion
 III. Inversion   = reflection × 180° rotation
 IV. Inversion   = 180° rotation × reflection
  V. 180° rotation = reflection × inversion
 VI. 180° rotation = inversion × reflection

The first relationship should be read as follows: Any instance of reflection through a plane can be thought of equally well as an inversion through a point followed by a 180° rotation about a line. (Follow the same formula in reading the other relationships.)

a. Which of these statements is true?
b. For the statements that are valid, depict the relationship between the point, line, and plane involved in the symmetry operations.

5.13   There are three related spatial manipulations relative to a line. Consider the following relationships:

   I. Screw   = rotation × translation
  II. Screw   = translation × rotation
 III. Rotation   = screw × translation
 IV. Rotation   = translation × screw
  V. Translation = rotation × screw
 VI. Translation = screw × rotation

Figure 5.14
Three symmetry operations
(Problem 5.11).

Inversion   Rotation   Reflection

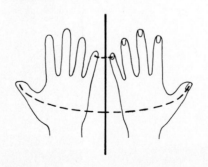
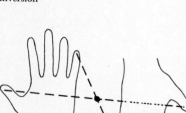
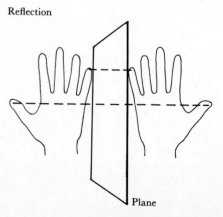

Point   Line   Plane

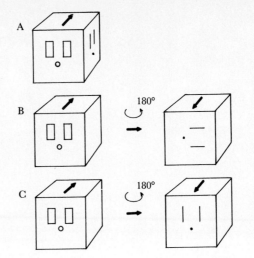

Figure 5.15
Cubic protomers (Problem 5.14).

The first relationship should be read as follows: Any instance of screw about a line can be thought of equally well as rotation about the line followed by translation along the line. (Follow the same formula in reading the other relationships.)

a. Which of these statements is true?

b. For the statements that are valid, depict the relationships among the three movements relative to a line.

5.14 Consider the different cubic protomers in Figure 5.15. Complementary binding surfaces are indicated by a three-prong plug (to the right) and its socket (to the left). Describe the symmetry of aggregates composed entirely of protomer A, entirely of protomer B, or entirely of protomer C.

5.15 Consider the pairs of identical cubic protomers shown in Figure 5.16. Complementary binding surfaces are indicated by a three-prong plug and its socket.

a. Which of the pairs can bind together to form a dimer with a 2-fold axis of rotational symmetry?

b. This problem illustrates a fundamental rule governing associations across isologous surfaces. Can you formulate the rule?

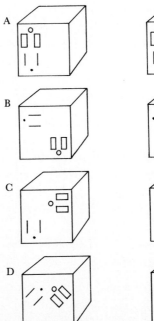

Figure 5.16
Cubic protomers (Problem 5.15).

Figure 5.17
Stereo triptych of a model of yeast fatty acid synthetase (Problem 5.16). For stereo viewing, see the Appendix to Chapter 4. (Model courtesy of S. J. Wakil, Baylor College of Medicine.)

5.16 Fatty acid synthetase from yeast is a molecular aggregate containing six copies each of two different polypeptide chains. A molecular model consistent with electron microscopic observations and chemical cross-linking data is shown in Figure 5.17. Identify the protomer, describe all symmetry axes, determine its point group symmetry, and classify the associations between protomers.

5.17 An exploded schematic diagram of an important metabolic enzyme is shown in Figure 5.18. This molecular aggregate is composed of six molecules each of two different polypeptide chains. Three catalytic chains are shown above and three below a central region made up of the six regulatory chains. Identify the protomer, describe all symmetry axes, determine its point group symmetry, and classify the associations between protomers.

5.18 Electrophoresis on polyacrylamide gels in the presence of the detergent sodium dodecyl sulfate (SDS), a powerful denaturing agent for proteins, is a convenient method for separating polypeptides solely on the basis of size. After a run, the protein bands can be made visible by staining. Small polypeptides travel faster than large ones; rate of migration through the gel is inversely proportional to the logarithm of molecular weight (MW).

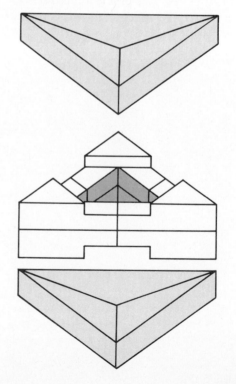

Figure 5.18
An exploded view of an important metabolic enzyme (Problem 5.17). [Adapted from Evans et al., *Science*, **179**, 683–685 (1973). © 1973 by the American Association for the Advancement of Science.]

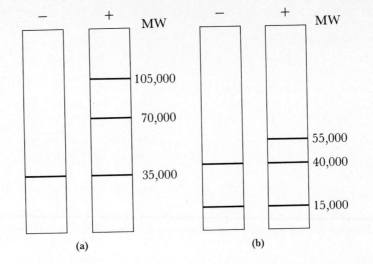

Figure 5.19
SDS–polyacrylamide gel electrophoresis of two proteins **(a)** with and **(b)** without cross-linking (Problem 5.18). A plus indicates treatment with the cross-linking reagent before electrophoresis; a minus indicates no treatment.

The subunit (quaternary) structure of a multimeric protein often can be deduced using this technique in conjunction with a protein cross-linking agent. These bifunctional reagents react with amino acid residues of two polypeptides that are in contact, thereby linking them by covalent bonds. After limited treatment with the reagent, so that some but not all subunits become cross-linked to their neighbors, the protein is subjected to SDS–gel electrophoresis and the molecular weights of the resulting bands are estimated. The results of such experiments on two proteins are shown in Figure 5.19. What is the most likely subunit structure and symmetry of each protein?

5.19   You and a friend, whose work you respect, have been characterizing the same regulatory enzyme independently. By sedimentation analysis your friend has demonstrated that the active enzyme is an aggregate of two identical subunits. However, you have made an equally convincing determination that there are exactly three equivalent binding sites for substrate on each active enzyme aggregate. You and your friend have

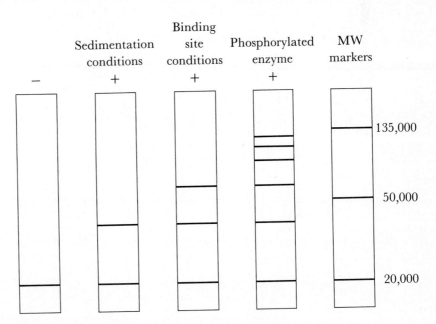

Figure 5.20
SDS–polyacrylamide gel electrophoresis of your enzyme under a variety of conditions (Problem 5.19). A plus indicates treatment with the cross-linking reagent before electrophoresis; a minus indicates no treatment. The lane on the far right displays three polypeptides of known molecular weight for comparison.

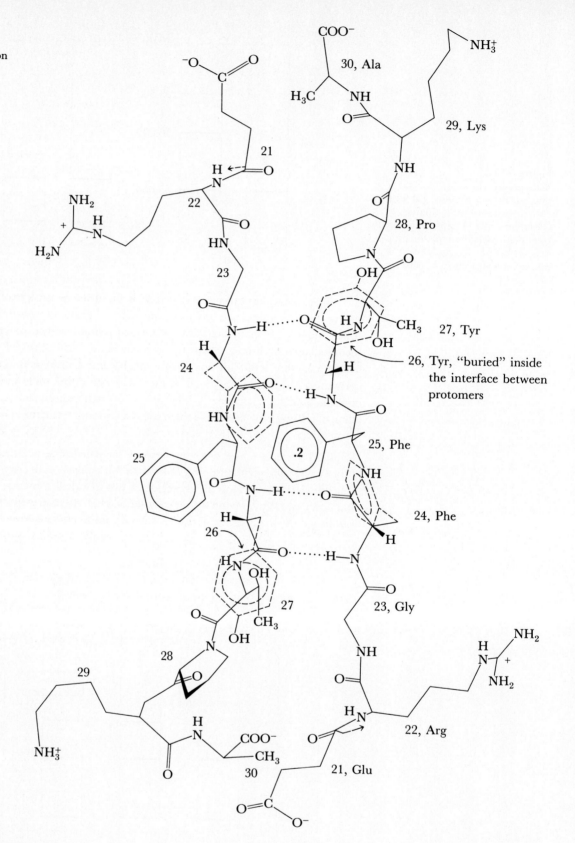

Figure 5.21
View along the 2-fold axis of an
insulin dimer (Problem 5.20).
(From D. E. Metzler, *Biochemistry,* Academic Press, New York,
1977, p. 219.)

had long discussions on how to interpret this apparent symmetry paradox. As your friend puts it, "How can three identical sites exist on an isologous dimer?"

Today your friend phones you with a startling new result. Phosphorylation of the subunits of the enzyme by a protein kinase leads to a 10-fold increase in activity. This increase in activity appears to be associated with a change in the state of aggregation. Upon hanging up the phone, you design and carry out a series of protein cross-linking experiments, the results of which are shown in Figure 5.20.

By applying symmetry concepts, you deduce the structure of the enzyme under all conditions and resolve the symmetry paradox with an explanation that satisfies all experimental observations. How will you explain it to your friend?

5.20   A portion of an insulin dimer is shown in Figure 5.21. This view is along the 2-fold axis and shows a close-up of the interacting surfaces. The two protomers involved in this dimer have become quasi-equivalent as a result of their association. Describe the nonsymmetric distortions (differences) between the two protomers.

5.21   Molecular chains, which usually form by heterologous associations, can dimerize by isologous associations. If both molecular chains point in the same direction, they are said to be parallel. If the molecular chains point in opposite directions, they are said to be antiparallel.
   a. Which of the drawings in Figure 5.22 shows parallel chains, and which shows antiparallel chains?
   b. Simple aggregates composed of two protomers possess an axis of 2-fold rotational symmetry. Do either of the dimers of chains in Figure 5.22 possess a 2-fold axis? If so, show its position.
   c. Compare the two edges, the two sides, and the two ends of aggregate A in Figure 5.22. In each case decide whether they are the same or different. Analyze aggregate B in the same way.
   d. If the two aggregates in Figure 5.22 possessed screw symmetry instead of translational symmetry, would any of your conclusions be altered? Which ones?

5.22   a. Examine the actin helices in Figure 5.10. Decide whether the two actin chains in each helix are parallel or antiparallel and give reasons for your answer.
   b. What is the protomer for a complete actin filament as illustrated in Figure 5.10?
   c. Describe the symmetry of an actin filament.

5.23   A section of a cytoplasmic 25-nm microtubule has been opened up and laid out as a sheet in Figure 5.23. The protomer of microtubules is a dimer of α and β tubulin. However, it is unknown how these protomers associate into complete microtubules. Because microtubules are multistranded aggregates, two sets of complementary contacts must be involved in their assembly (Concept 5.4). One set of contact surfaces (A,

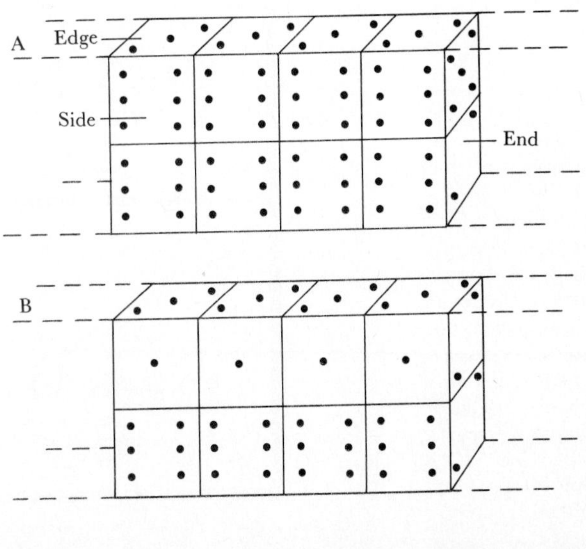

Figure 5.22
Parallel and antiparallel chains (Problem 5.21). In this drawing each protomer is represented by a die. Dice are convenient for demonstrating symmetry principles because each surface is numbered and opposite surfaces sum to seven. In these examples each molecular chain was formed by heterologous association between surface 2 and surface 5. In each case the chains have dimerized by isologous association across surface 4.

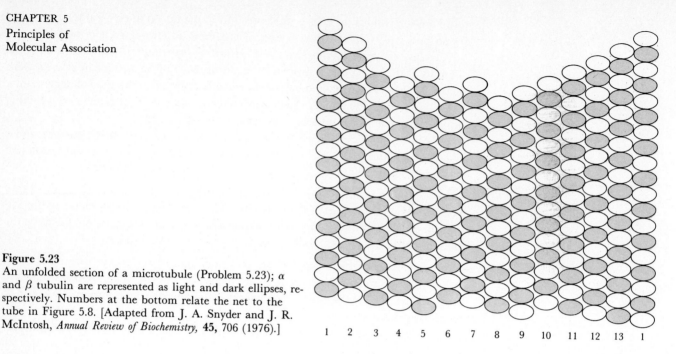

Figure 5.23
An unfolded section of a microtubule (Problem 5.23); α and β tubulin are represented as light and dark ellipses, respectively. Numbers at the bottom relate the net to the tube in Figure 5.8. [Adapted from J. A. Snyder and J. R. McIntosh, *Annual Review of Biochemistry,* **45,** 706 (1976).]

A') links the protomers into molecular chains. The second set of contacts (B, B') links multiple chains together into the complete microtubule.

a. By examining the net of protomers shown in Figure 5.23, find all the different possible chains of tubulin dimers. Describe these by their handedness and the number of protomers per turn in a microtubule.

b. For each molecular chain you find, determine how many copies of the chain would need to be linked together to form the complete microtubule.

5.24   Hemoglobin is an aggregate of two α and two β globin chains (Figure 5.2). The α and β subunits of hemoglobin are shown from the same viewpoint in Figure 5.24. You will

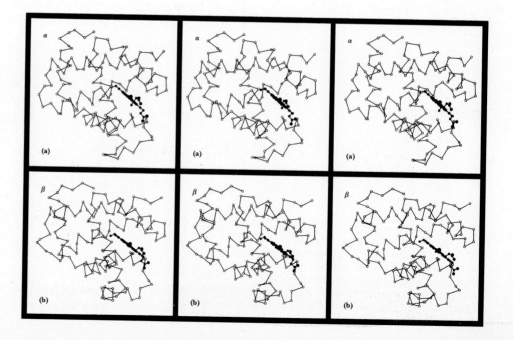

Figure 5.24
Stereo triptychs of the α and β chains of hemoglobin (Problem 5.24). Only the C_α-atoms of the protein are shown. The atoms of the heme group are shown in black. For stereo viewing, see instructions in the Appendix to Chapter 4. (Stereo figures courtesy of Richard J. Feldmann, NIH.)

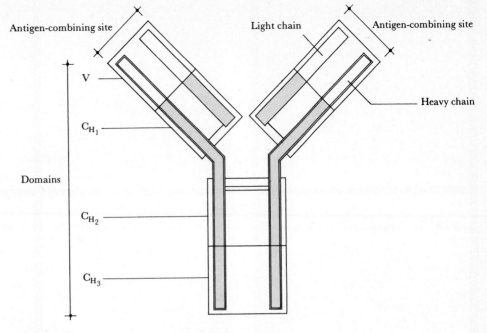

Figure 5.25
A schematic representation of an IgG antibody molecule
(Problem 5.25). (Adapted from L. E. Hood, I. Weissman,
and W. B. Wood, *Immunology,* Benjamin/Cummings, Menlo
Park, Calif., 1978, p. 214.)

notice several differences, but the similarities are striking. If the different parts are
ignored, one can ask whether the identical portions in the aggregate are related symmetrically. If they are, the aggregate is said to possess approximate symmetry or, more
commonly, pseudosymmetry.

a. Does hemoglobin possess pseudosymmetry? If so, describe its pseudosymmetry axes.
b. What would be the point group symmetry of hemoglobin if the axes of pseudosymmetry were included?

5.25 a. Antibodies are a vertebrate's first line of defense against foreign invaders of the body.
The structure of the circulating immunoglobin IgG is well known. An IgG molecule is
an aggregate of two identical heavy (H) chains and two identical light (L) chains
(Figure 5.25). The chains are linked covalently by disulfide bonds after they have
associated. Identify the protomer, describe all symmetry axes, determine the point
group symmetry, and classify the associations between protomers of IgG.

b. Details of antibody structure have revealed repeated domains of similar structure in
the IgG heavy and light chains (Figure 5.26). These observations have fostered the
speculation that the genes for each chain arose by duplication and modification of a
more primitive gene for the original domain. The light and heavy chain variable (V)
domains are shown separately and in combination in Figure 5.26. Describe the
pseudosymmetry of this section of an IgG molecule.

☆ 5.26   The quaternary structure of a multimeric protein in a dilute aqueous buffer solution is
thought to be stabilized almost exclusively by hydrophobic associations between its
subunits. Which of the following observations would *not* support this conclusion? The
protein is dissociated into subunits under the following conditions:

a. In salt solutions of high ionic strength
b. At 4°C
c. When a water-miscible nonpolar solvent is added to the solution
d. At high concentrations of urea

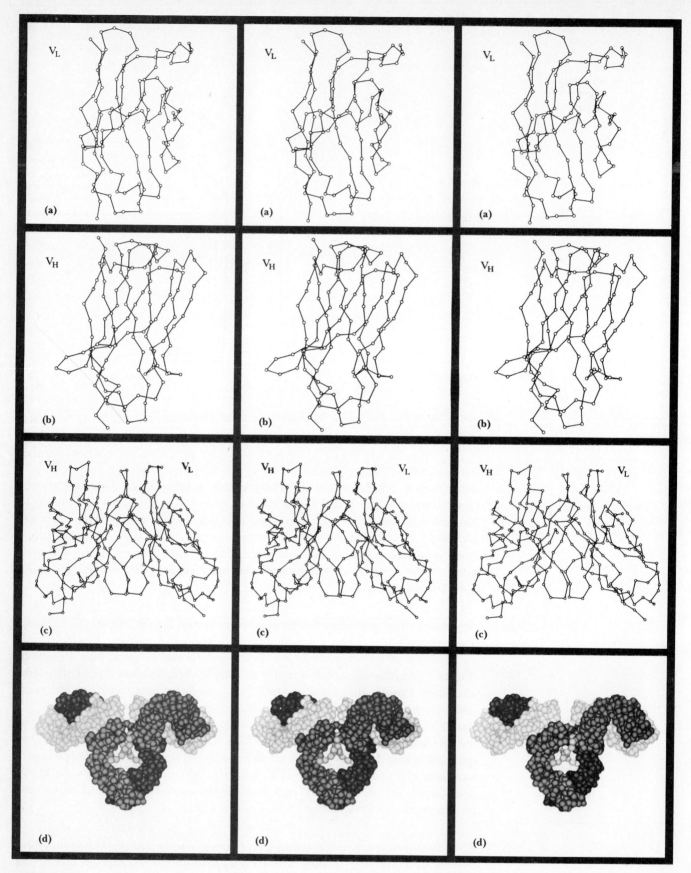

Figure 5.26

Stereo triptychs of an antibody variable domain (Problem 5.25). The variable domains of a light chain **(a)** and a heavy chain **(b)** are combined in **(c)**. Skeletal models show only the C_α-atoms. A complete IgG molecule is shown in **(d)**. Light chains are light and heavy chains are dark. For stereo viewing, see instructions in the Appendix to Chapter 4. (Stereo figures courtesy of Richard J. Feldmann, NIH.) [Adapted from L. M. Amzel and R. J. Poljak, *Annual Review of Biochemistry*, **48**, 968, 972 (1979).]

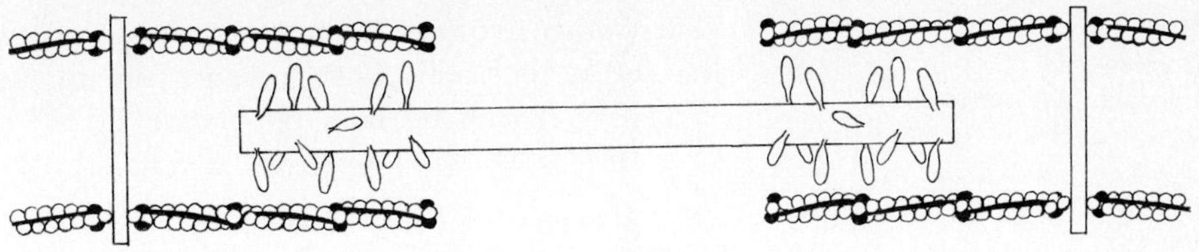

Figure 5.27
Schematic representation of interacting actin and myosin filaments. (E. Lazarides and J. P. Revel, *Scientific American*, May 1979, p. 100.)

☆ 5.27 When the protein in Problem 5.26 is subjected to electrophoresis on a polyacrylamide gel in the presence of the anionic detergent SDS, two bands are observed corresponding to molecular weights of 14,000 and 38,000, in approximately equimolar amounts. When the native protein first is treated with a bifunctional protein–cross-linking reagent and then is subjected to electrophoresis as described, six bands are seen, corresponding to molecular weights of 14,000, 38,000, 52,000, 76,000, 90,000, and 104,000. The reagent is known to cross-link only subunits that are in contact in the native structure. Briefly describe or diagram the quaternary structure of the native protein.

☆ 5.28 What principle of biological structure is violated in Figure 5.27?

Answers

5.1 a. True
b. False. Template-directed assembly requires structural information from preexisting templates.
c. False. Supramolecular assembly is driven primarily by hydrophobic interactions and van der Waals bonds; H-bonds and ionic bonds provide the specificity.
d. False. An asymmetric object superimposes on itself once in a 360° rotation about any axis.
e. True
f. False. Molecular aggregates with dihedral point group symmetry also contain protomers linked in a head-to-tail ring.
g. False. All aggregates with dihedral symmetry, including those with D2 symmetry, have one *n*-fold axis perpendicular to a plane containing *n* 2-fold axes.
h. True
i. False. Dimers of identical subunits are held together by isologous associations.
j. True
k. True
l. False. The handedness of the helix is independent of the handedness of the protomer.

5.2 a. molecular biology
b. domain of binding
c. protomer
d. rotation; screw; translation
e. quasi-equivalent
f. Microtubules, actin, myosin
g. icosahedral

5.3 a. Correct re-formation would be a self-assembly process, requiring that the elements themselves carry the specificity to determine the structure uniquely. Because artificial reversal of a row is propagated, there are at least two surface patterns, normal and one-row reversed, that are compatible with the structure of the elements. Hence one would not expect the correct structure to re-form.
b. Propagation of a reversed row shows that preexisting structure determines the pattern of newly associating elements. Therefore, surface pattern formation is a template-directed assembly process. At least some of the information that directs assembly comes from the preexisting pattern; information in the elements themselves, derived from the genes of the organism, is not sufficient to determine its surface structure.

5.4   The average frequency of mistakes per polypeptide, and therefore per bacterium, will be $500 \times 10^{-10} = 5 \times 10^{-8}$; hence the frequency of defective bacteria will be 5×10^{-8}. Therefore, in a population of 10^9 cells, on the average, there will be $5 \times 10^{-8} \times 10^9 = 50$ defective bacteria.

5.5   a. The average frequency of mistakes per structure will be $6000 \times 10^{-8} = 6 \times 10^{-5}$, and this value will equal approximately the frequency of defective structures.

b. Because defective dimers are rejected, the average frequency of mistakes per structure will be only the number of operations in the final stage (five operations to assemble six subunits) times the error frequency, or 5×10^{-8}. This value approximately equals the frequency of defective structures, which is therefore about 1000 times less than the frequency resulting from a one-stage process.

5.6   Because the ΔH term is small relative to the $T\,\Delta S$ term at 40°C and at 0°C, it can be neglected. At 40°C, the ΔS for association is positive; consequently, the ΔG for association will be negative, favoring association. At 0°C, the ΔS for association is negative; consequently, the ΔG for association will be positive, favoring dissociation. Hence as the temperature is lowered from 40 to 0°C, the dimeric form of the protein, which predominates at high temperature, will tend to dissociate into free monomers.

5.7   The addition of an organic (nonpolar) solvent will decrease the polarity of the medium. A more nonpolar medium will tend to stabilize free hydrophobic groups, thereby favoring dissociation of hydrophobically interacting surfaces. Conversely, it will tend to destabilize free polar groups by decreasing the H-bonding of water to them and thereby will tend to promote H-bonding between polar groups. Consequently, a less polar medium will favor association of subunits whose interactions are primarily polar. Because in this problem addition of organic solvent favors association of the multimer, its bonding must be primarily polar.

5.8   This drawing has 2-fold rotational symmetry axes at the angels' feet and 4-fold rotational axes where the angels' wing tips meet. The translational symmetry axes run vertically, horizontally, and at 45° angles.

5.9   A cube possesses 13 axes of rotational symmetry. All symmetry axes intersect at the center of the cube. There are six 2-fold axes connecting the midpoints of opposite edges; four 3-fold axes connecting opposite corners; and three 4-fold axes connecting the centers of opposite faces. These axes are identical to those for octahedral point group symmetry. The two sets of axes would superimpose on one another.

5.10 The symmetries of an icosahedron and a dodecahedron are identical. Each has fifteen 2-fold axes that pass through the midpoints of opposite edges; each has ten 3-fold axes, passing through opposite vertices in a dodecahedron and centers of opposite faces in an icosahedron; and each has six 5-fold axes, passing through opposite vertices in an icosahedron and centers of opposite faces in a dodecahedron.

5.11 Inversion and reflection each produce a change in handedness. At the molecular level handedness refers to D and L configurations about asymmetric carbon atoms (Figure 5.28). Most biological molecules possess handedness, and one member of the mirror pair is considerably enriched relative to its opposite. For example, cells contain L-

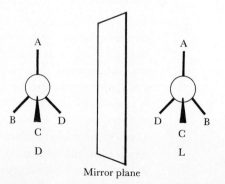

Figure 5.28
Two possible configurations
about asymmetric carbon atoms
(Answer 5.11).

Mirror plane

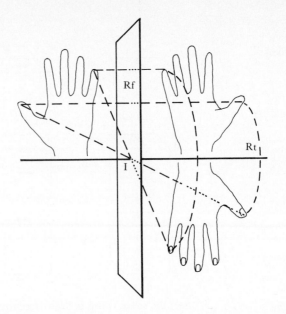

Figure 5.29
Relationship between inversion
(I), 180° rotation (Rt), and re-
flection (Rf) (Answer 5.12).

amino acids primarily, and almost all proteins are composed entirely of L-amino
acids. Thus protein aggregates do not display symmetry of reflection or inversion,
because those symmetries would require a complementary set of proteins constructed
from D-amino acids. Biological enrichment for one member of a mirror pair may be a
consequence of interaction across complementary surfaces.

5.12 a. All six statements are true.
      b. The point is the intersection of the line with the plane, as indicated for a particular
         case in Figure 5.29. This is not a unique solution. However, in all solutions the line is
         perpendicular to the plane. Note that the plane and the line form a coordinate system
         that can be used to describe symmetry operations algebraically.

5.13 a. All six statements are true.
      b. See Figure 5.30.

5.14 See Figure 5.31. Aggregates composed entirely of protomer A will have C4 symmetry.
      Aggregates composed entirely of protomer B will have screw symmetry, with four
      protomers per left-handed turn. Aggregates composed entirely of protomer C will
      have translational symmetry.

5.15 a. Pairs A, B, and D each can form a dimer with a 2-fold axis of symmetry.
      b. Pairs of complementary binding components make up interacting surfaces. To form a
         dimer with a 2-fold axis of symmetry, complementary members of each pair must be
         equidistant from a common line drawn between them (Figure 5.32). Another way to

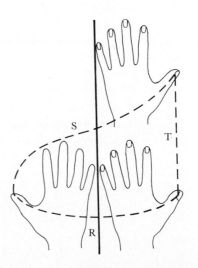

Figure 5.30
Relationship between rotation
(R), translation (T), and screw
(S) (Answer 5.13).

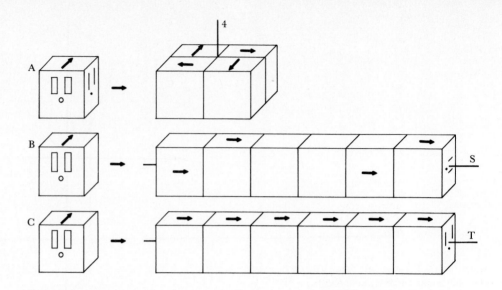

Figure 5.31
Assembly of protomers A, B, and
C (Answer 5.14).

say the same thing is that there must exist a line about which one binding surface can
be rotated 180° so that it will stick exactly onto its complementary partner. The line
about which a successful rotation can be performed is identical to the 2-fold axis of the
dimer.

5.16 This model of fatty acid synthetase has C3 point group symmetry. Its one axis of
rotational symmetry runs vertically through the center of the hexagonal ring. The
protomer consists of two adjacent subunits of the hexagonal ring and two arches, one
above and one below the ring. Because the model possesses C3 point group symmetry,
the contacts between protomers must be heterologous.

5.17 The aspartate transcarbamylase protomer consists of one catalytic (C) subunit joined
to one regulatory (R) subunit. These protomers associate heterologously into two rings
with 3-fold symmetry. The two rings associate back-to-back by isologous interactions
between R subunits, so that the point group symmetry of aspartate transcarbamylase
is D3. Its rotation axes are indicated in Figure 5.33.

5.18 a. From the one band found with untreated protein, you can conclude that there is only
a single kind of subunit of MW = 35,000. Cross-linking produces polypeptides of
twice and three times this molecular weight, but nothing larger. Therefore, the native
protein must be a trimer of identical subunits with C3 point group symmetry.

b. The untreated protein denatures to give a large and a small subunit. Cross-linking
produces only one more band, whose molecular weight equals the sum of the subunit
molecular weights. Therefore, the original structure must be a dimer that contains one
of each subunit and consequently must be asymmetric.

5.19 You show your friend the picture in Figure 5.34 and suggest that there is no symmetry
paradox, because each of you has been studying a different form of the enzyme. The
fully assembled enzyme (with phosphorylated subunits) has D3 point group symmetry. Your friend has been studying the enzyme under conditions where the heterologous B–B′ interactions are unstable. Thus the enzyme appears to be an isologous
dimer. You have been studying the enzyme under conditions where the isologous
A–A′ interactions are unstable. Thus for you the enzyme behaves as a trimer with
three identical binding sites. Phosphorylation of the subunits apparently stabilizes
both interactions and causes an increase in the catalytic activity of the enzyme.

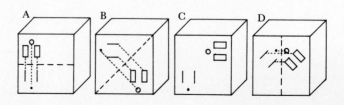

Figure 5.32
Isologous binding surfaces (Answer 5.15).

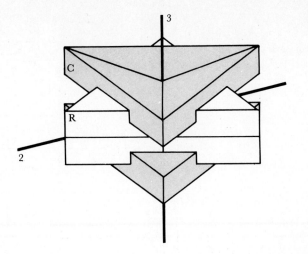

Figure 5.33
Symmetry of aspartate transcarbamylase (Answer 5.17). One of each kind of rotation axis is shown.

5.20 A close examination reveals several differences. The most notable difference is the folding of Phe 25. There is not enough room between the protomers to accommodate both Phe residues, and one must fold out of the way.

5.21 a. Aggregate A in Figure 5.22 is antiparallel and aggregate B is parallel.
b. Both aggregates possess one 2-fold axis of symmetry. See Figure 5.35.
c. For aggregate A, the two edges and the two ends are identical; the two sides are different. For aggregate B, the two edges and the two sides are identical; the two ends are different.
d. None of the foregoing conclusions would be altered if the aggregates possessed screw symmetry instead of translational symmetry.

5.22 a. The two actin chains in an actin helix have a parallel orientation. This fact can be deduced from two observations: The two ends are different (one is attached and one is free), and the two sides are the same (troponin and tropomyosin bind to each side). As derived in Problem 5.21, these two properties characterize parallel chains.
b. The protomer of the actin filament shown in Figure 5.10 consists of one troponin molecule, one tropomyosin molecule, and seven actin molecules. Dimers of these protomers are linked end to end in the filament.
c. The actin filament possesses 2-fold rotational symmetry about its long axis and translational symmetry along that axis with a dimer of protomers as the repeat unit. Instead of translational symmetry it could be regarded as having right-handed (or left-handed) screw symmetry along the long axis with two protomer dimers per turn.

5.23 a. There are four possible chains of tubulin dimers (Figure 5.36). Chain I has 13 protomers per right-handed turn; chain II has translational symmetry instead of screw

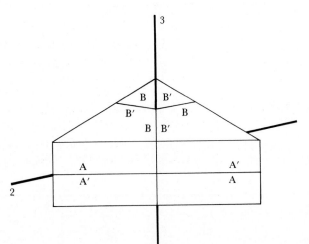

Figure 5.34
Fully assembled enzyme (Answer 5.19).

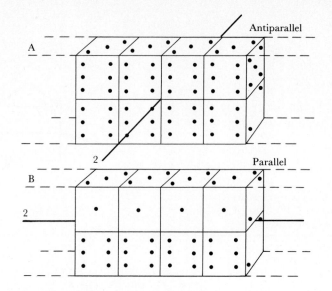

Figure 5.35
Symmetry of parallel and antiparallel chains (Answer 5.21).

symmetry; chain III has 13 protomers per left-handed turn; and chain IV has 6.5 protomers per left-handed turn.

b. Chain I requires 5 copies per microtubule; chain II, 13 copies; chain III, 8 copies; and chain IV, 3 copies. Under certain in vitro conditions the ends of microtubules splay out into 13 protofilaments (chain II), which may represent the true molecular chains from which microtubules are constructed.

5.24 a. Hemoglobin possesses two 2-fold axes of pseudosymmetry. The pseudosymmetry axes are at right angles to each other and to the true 2-fold rotation axis shown in Figure 5.2.

b. If pseudosymmetry axes were included, the point group symmetry of hemoglobin would be D2.

5.25 a. The protomer of an IgG molecule consists of one heavy and one light chain. Two protomers are linked by isologous associations into a dimer with C2 point group symmetry. The axis of 2-fold rotational symmetry runs vertically between the two protomers.

b. This portion of an IgG molecule has 2-fold rotational pseudosymmetry about an axis that runs between the light and heavy chains.

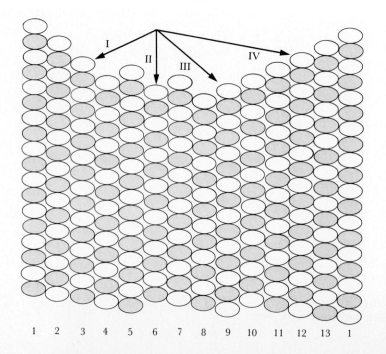

Figure 5.36
Possible chains of tubulin dimers
(Answer 5.23).

6 Biological Membranes

All cells possess at their periphery a membrane, which provides the essential barrier that separates "inside" from "outside." Procaryotic cells have only a single external membrane system. Eucaryotic cells, however, make extensive use of internal membrane compartments. This chapter considers membrane structure and biogenesis, and describes the relationships between the intracellular compartments of eucaryotic cells. Transport across membranes is considered in Chapter 14.

Concepts

6.1 Membrane biogenesis involves assembly of phospholipids and proteins.

A. Phospholipids are the major class of lipids in membranes. They are small molecules relative to proteins. Phospholipids are characterized by two hydrophobic fatty acid side chains ("tails") attached to a strongly hydrophilic phosphorylated polar group ("head"). The structure of a common phospholipid, phosphatidylcholine, is shown in Figure 6.1. The polar head group can vary in size and charge. The fatty acid tails can vary in length and degree of saturation (percentage of C—C single bonds).

B. In aqueous surroundings, hydrophobic interactions cause membrane lipids to form bilayers, with their tails to the inside and only their polar groups in contact with the solvent, as illustrated in Figure 6.2. Consequently, membranes, like protein molecules, have hydrophilic surfaces and hydrophobic interiors, and the thermodynamic principles discussed in Concept 4.3 apply to membrane structure and biogenesis. Although phospholipid bilayers can be formed readily in vitro, they apparently are not created de novo by cells. Rather, the basic bilayer structure is passed on from cell to cell. New cell membranes are formed by adding components to existing membranes and then pinching off a new membrane. Thus membrane formation in vivo appears to be a template-directed process.

Figure 6.1
Phosphatidylcholine, a common phospholipid.

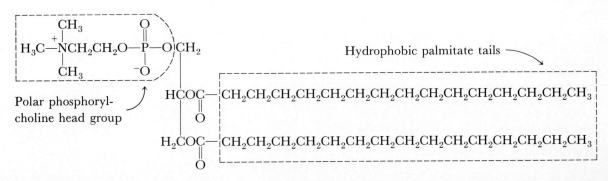

Polar phosphoryl-choline head group

Hydrophobic palmitate tails

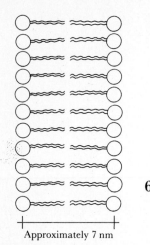

Approximately 7 nm

Figure 6.2
A phospholipid bilayer. Individual phospholipid molecules are represented schematically by an open circle and two wavy lines, indicating the charged head group and the hydrophobic tails, respectively.

C. Most membranes consist of 40–70% protein by weight. Membrane proteins generally are insoluble in water. Their hydrophobic portions are embedded in the interior of the membrane and their hydrophilic portions are exposed to the aqueous environment at the surfaces. Membrane proteins are classed as peripheral or integral, depending on their degree of immersion in the bilayer. **Peripheral proteins** are confined to the membrane surface and can be removed easily without disrupting the basic membrane structure. **Integral proteins** may extend partly or completely through the membrane and usually cannot be removed without disrupting the membrane.

6.2   A fluid mosaic is the most satisfactory model for membrane structure.

A. Because membrane components are held together entirely by noncovalent bonds, it is difficult to determine the structure of membranes by direct chemical means. Of the general models proposed for membrane structure, the fluid-mosaic model is the most satisfactory in explaining the known properties of membranes. According to this model, the membrane proteins "float" in the lipid bilayer (Figure 6.3). Both proteins and lipids can diffuse rapidly in the plane of the membrane and can rotate about an axis perpendicular to this plane (**lateral diffusion**), but neither can flip readily from one side of the membrane to the other (**transverse diffusion**). Free lateral diffusion allows individual proteins and protein aggregates to distribute randomly in the membrane. Any protein that maintains a nonrandom distribution must be anchored in place by intracellular (or extracellular) supports.

B. The fluidity of the internal phase of a membrane depends on the packing of the fatty acid side chains. Long, straight-chain, saturated fatty acids pack most densely and give the lowest fluidity. The presence of shorter fatty acids, or unsaturated fatty acids in the *cis* configuration (kinked side chain), increases fluidity. Cholesterol, a steroid found in certain eucaryotic membranes, decreases fluidity.

   Membrane fluidity increases with increasing temperature. At some temperature characteristic of its fatty acid composition, every membrane undergoes a sharp increase in fluidity, or "melting," corresponding to a transition of the internal phase from a solid to a liquid state.

   Cells maintain the internal phases of membranes at a viscosity (about that of olive oil at room temperature) that is optimal for the lateral diffusion of membrane proteins. For example, in response to a decrease in temperature, which increases inter-

Figure 6.3
The fluid-mosaic model of plasma membrane structure, showing integral proteins immersed in the phospholipid bilayer. (Adapted from H. F. Lodish and J. E. Rothman, *Scientific American*, January 1979, p. 52.)

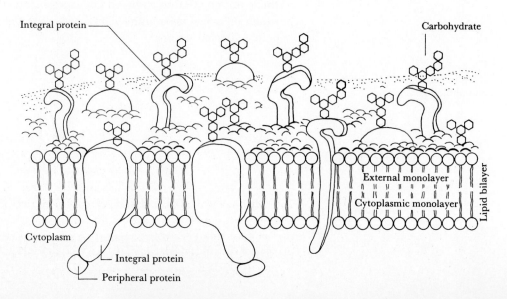

nal phase viscosity, most cells will synthesize new lipids with appropriate side chains and incorporate them into membranes, thereby maintaining optimal fluidity.

6.3   Proteins are oriented asymmetrically in the membrane.

A.   Because membranes enclose space, they possess two distinct surfaces: one in contact with the inside environment and the other in contact with the outside environment. The hydrophilic portions of membrane proteins extend into these environments. Identical molecules of membrane proteins all are oriented in the same direction relative to the two sides of the membrane. Therefore, the two surfaces of a membrane display different proteins and different enzyme activities. This membrane asymmetry derives from three phenomena: the restriction on transverse diffusion discussed earlier (Concept 6.2), the asymmetry of protein insertion into membranes (Concept 20.6), and the conservation of asymmetry during exchange of material between compartments (Concept 6.7).

B.   Phospholipids also are distributed unevenly between the two surfaces of a membrane. However, different phospholipid species do not display the same all-or-none asymmetry as proteins. For example, in one bacterial species 70% of phosphatidylethanolamine molecules are in the external monolayer of the plasma membrane and 30% are in the cytoplasmic monolayer. This distribution is fundamentally different from that of proteins. It has been suggested that certain membrane proteins catalyze the transverse diffusion (flipping) of lipids to allow them to reach thermodynamic equilibrium. If this is true, then the uneven distribution of lipid species simply reflects differences in the environments on the two sides of a membrane.

6.4   Procaryotic cells have a single membrane-enclosed compartment.

The cells of **procaryotes** (bacteria) have a single intracellular compartment, separated from the environment by the cytoplasmic membrane. This compartment is differentiated functionally into a central nucleoid region containing the DNA, and a surrounding cytoplasmic region containing ribosomes and cytoplasmic proteins, but there is no nuclear membrane. Most procaryotes have a cell wall external to the protoplasmic membrane. Between the wall and the membrane is the periplasmic space, which is freely accessible to small molecules in the environment but not to macromolecules.

6.5   Eucaryotic cells have several functionally specialized internal compartments.

A.   The nucleus in a **eucaryotic cell** distinguishes it from a procaryotic cell. The **nuclear membrane** is continuous with the membrane of the **endoplasmic reticulum,** and the nucleus can be pictured as an inpocketing of the endoplasmic reticulum (Figure 6.4). Strictly speaking, the nuclear compartment, which contains the cell's chromosomes, is not membrane bounded. Although most of the nucleus is surrounded by a double membrane, up to 30% of its surface is occupied by specialized holes, termed **nuclear pores,** each about 50–100 nm in diameter (Figure 6.5). At a nuclear pore the cytoplasm and nucleoplasm are in direct contact. Free exchange of materials between nucleoplasm and cytoplasm is restricted somewhat by nuclear pores. However, most

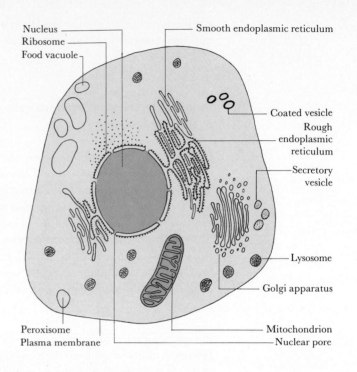

Figure 6.4
Typical membrane-bounded
compartments of eucaryotic cells.

metabolites and small proteins have ready access to the nucleus. Notably, chromosomes are retained within the nucleus and ribosomes are excluded from it. Indeed a principal function of the nuclear membrane may be to separate transcription from translation (Concept 20.8).

B. A variety of compartments in addition to the cell itself are bounded by single bilayer membranes. These compartments include the endoplasmic reticulum, the **Golgi apparatus,** and an assortment of specialized smaller vesicles such as **lysosomes, coated vesicles,** and **secretory vesicles** (Figure 6.4). There appears to be a carefully regulated flow of membrane material between compartments bounded by single membranes (Concept 6.7).

C. **Mitochondria** and **chloroplasts** are complex compartments that are bounded by double bilayer membranes (Figure 6.4). This double membrane may reflect a symbiosis of ancient origin that arose when a procaryotic cell was engulfed by a precursor of

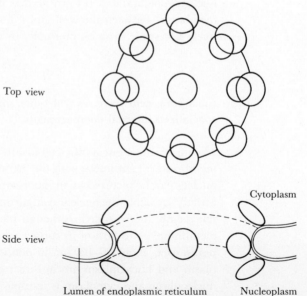

Figure 6.5
A nuclear pore viewed end-on
and in cross section. (Adapted
from J. D. Watson, *Molecular Biology of the Gene,* Benjamin/
Cummings, Menlo Park, Calif.,
1975, p. 487.)

eucaryotic cells. Mitochrondria, which are found in all eucaryotes that use oxygen (Concept 12.1), and chloroplasts, which are found in plants (Concept 13.3), are the major sites of cellular energy production. The outer mitochondrial membrane is freely permeable to many metabolites. The inner mitochondrial and chloroplast membranes, which form the major permeability barriers, contain nearly crystalline arrays of proteins involved in energy production.

6.6 Transport proteins increase the permeability of membranes to specific molecules.

Lipid bilayers are permeable to water and neutral nonpolar molecules, much less permeable to neutral polar molecules, and almost impermeable to charged molecules. However, biological membranes contain proteins that combine specifically with certain polar molecules and ions and facilitate their transport across the membrane (Chapter 14). By locating different specific transport proteins in different membranes, eucaryotic cells can maintain functionally distinct internal compartments that differ markedly in molecular composition from each other and from the external environment.

6.7 Almost any two membranes can fuse.

A. The universality of membrane structure and the nonspecific nature of the hydrophobic interactions maintaining it permit almost any two membranes to fuse into one continuous membrane. This property has been exploited to achieve fusion of eucaryotic cells from different species. The viability of the resulting hybrid cells indicates that function as well as structure is maintained when plasma membranes of different origin are fused.

B. Transport of macromolecules and larger particles between the various compartments bounded by single bilayer membranes occurs by cycles of vesicle formation and fusion. Typical cycles for exchanges of material with the extracellular environment are shown in Figures 6.6 and 6.7. The existence of ordered pathways for such processes suggests precise cellular control of these cycles. There is increasing evidence that coated vesicles may facilitate exchange of material between compartments bounded

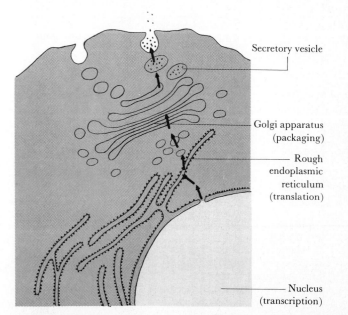

Secretory vesicle

Golgi apparatus (packaging)

Rough endoplasmic reticulum (translation)

Nucleus (transcription)

Figure 6.6
Export of a secretory protein. The mRNA made in the nucleus moves through a nuclear pore into the cytoplasm, where it is translated on ribosomes bound to the endoplasmic reticulum. The protein, which is inserted through the membrane during translation, is carried by cycles of vesicle formation and fusion first to the Golgi apparatus and then to the outside of the cell. (Adapted from R. D. Dyson, *Cell Biology: A Molecular Approach,* Allyn & Bacon, Boston, 1978, p. 473.)

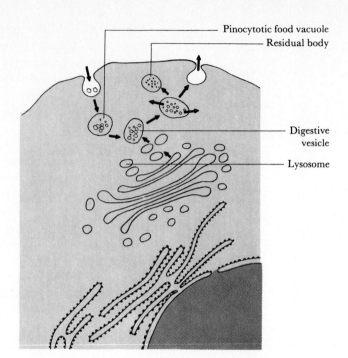

Figure 6.7
Import of extracellular material. Endocytosis results in a
pinocytotic food vacuole, which then fuses with a lysosome.
Lysosomes, which are derived from the Golgi apparatus,
provide digestive enzymes to break down vesicle contents.
Indigestible material is either expelled or condensed into a
residual body. (Adapted from R. D. Dyson, *Cell Biology: A
Molecular Approach,* Allyn & Bacon, Boston, 1978, p. 453.)

by single membranes. These vesicles, which are encased in a shell formed by a specific
protein, clathrin, bud from one membrane and rapidly fuse with another, thereby
shuttling material from compartment to compartment (see Figures 6.16 and 6.17,
Problems 6.13 and 6.15).

C. The flow of membrane material between compartments bounded by single membranes occurs with conservation of membrane asymmetry. In describing this asymmetry, *inside* and *outside* become confusing terms for compartments within compartments. It is more convenient to designate the two surfaces of the membranes that
bound compartments as **cytoplasmic** (in contact with cytoplasm) and **external** (not in
contact with cytoplasm). In terms of this definition, conservation of asymmetry means
that a membrane surface in contact with the cytoplasm is always in contact with the
cytoplasm regardless of the compartment with which it is associated (Figure 6.8).
Conversely, membrane surfaces in contact with an external environment are always in
contact with an external environment. (Note that the interior of an intracellular
compartment, such as the lumen of the endoplasmic reticulum, is topologically outside the cytoplasm.)

It is not clear whether membrane flow also occurs between simple compartments

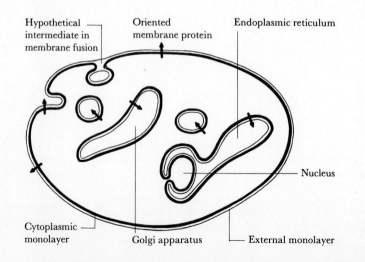

Figure 6.8
A schematic diagram of a eucaryotic cell. Cytoplasmic and
external halves of membrane
bilayers are indicated by heavy
and light lines, respectively.

and the complex mitochondrial and chloroplast compartments, where the distinction between cytoplasmic and external membrane surfaces becomes less useful.

6.8   Specialized intercellular junctions link cells in a tissue.

Membrane structures that link cells in many tissues either fasten the cells together or provide intercellular communication channels. **Desmosomes** are like spot welds that fasten cells together in a tissue. **Tight junctions** extend around the cell circumference to seal the spaces between cells in a sheet. Tight junctions link intestinal cells, for example, to ensure that liquid flows through the cells and not between them. **Gap junctions** provided channels about 2 nm across through which cells in a tissue can exchange metabolites of molecular weight less than 1000 (Figure 6.9).

6.9   Additional concepts and techniques are presented in the Problems section.

A.   Use of nonpenetrating reagents to follow protein and lipid asymmetries. Problems 6.10 and 6.12.

B.   Membrane budding. Problem 6.13.

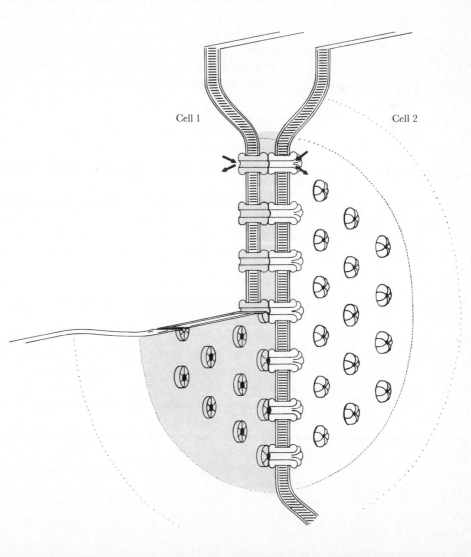

Figure 6.9
Model of a gap junction. (Redrawn from L. A. Staehelin and B. E. Hull, *Scientific American,* May 1978, p. 150.)

C. Symmetry of aggregates of membrane proteins. Problems 6.14 and 6.15.

D. Membrane corrals. Problems 6.16 and 6.17.

References

COMPREHENSIVE TEXTS

Lehninger: Chapter 11   Stryer: Chapter 10
Metzler: Chapter 5   White et al.: Chapters 3 and 11

OTHER REFERENCES

H. F. Lodish and J. E. Rothman, "The Assembly of Cell Membranes," *Scientific American*, January 1979, p. 48.

J. E. Rothman and J. Lenard, "Membrane Asymmetry," *Science*, **195**, 743 (1977).

L. A. Staehelin and B. E. Hull, "Junctions between Living Cells," *Scientific American*, May 1978, p. 140.

Problems

6.1 Answer the following with true or false. If false, explain why.

a. The basic membrane bilayer structure is passed on from cell to cell with heritable characteristics that are independent of genetic (DNA) information.

b. The polar head groups of phospholipids are similar to the side chains of amino acids in that both can vary in charge and polar character.

c. Membranes, like proteins, have hydrophilic surfaces and hydrophobic interiors.

d. Biological membranes most probably are formed by a template-directed assembly process.

e. Most individual proteins and protein aggregates maintain a nonrandom distribution in the membrane.

f. Membrane integral proteins generally are more hydrophobic than peripheral proteins.

g. Any change in fatty acid structure that interferes with close packing in the membrane interior decreases membrane fluidity.

h. The two surfaces of a membrane display different proteins and different enzyme activities.

i. The nuclear membrane is continuous with the membrane of the endoplasmic reticulum.

j. The finding that cell membranes of different species can fuse suggests that all cell membranes are constructed from identical components.

k. The cytoplasmic and external surfaces of a membrane switch with each cycle of vesicle formation and fusion.

6.2 a. Membranes consist primarily of two kinds of molecules: _____ and _____.

b. _____ the chain length of phospholipid fatty acid tails increases the fluidity of a membrane.

c. The fluid-mosaic model of membrane structure states that most proteins and lipids have free and rapid _____, but do not readily _____ from one membrane surface to the other.

d. Eucaryotic cells contain three distinct types of internal compartments, which are bounded, respectively, by _____, _____, or _____ sheets of membrane.

e. Holes in nuclear membranes that permit communication between the nucleus and the cytoplasm are called _____.

f. The universality of general membrane structure is demonstrated by _____ experiments.

g. _____ and _____ glue cells of a tissue together, whereas _____ provide intercellular channels for exchange of small metabolites.

6.3   Suppose that you are a
traveling salesman with a
predeliction for Avis rental cars.

You have just been
*hired by an employer
in Los Angeles County.*
In order to enter
a neighboring county
and *earn a commission*
you must
put down a deposit on a rental car

at a total cost to you of 50 *dollars.*
In *San Bernardino County*
there are *Avis rental car agencies*

that will *refund your deposit.*

In *Orange County*
there are only
Hertz rental car agencies.

At your *rank of promotion*
the net *profit you can make*

when you enter either
county and sell your product

is 48 *dollars.*

a. Taking into account the
small *mileage charge*

is it *economically* feasible for
you to go into *Orange County?*
How many *dollars* will you gain
by doing so?

b. How many *dollars*
will you gain by going into
San Bernardino County instead?

c. Convert this problem to one
in membrane biosynthesis by substituting the expressions at the
right for the italicized phrases
in the scenario.

d. Which would you prefer to
be, a traveling salesman in San
Bernardino County or a hydrophobic protein in the mitochondrial membrane? Explain your
answer.

---

hydrophobic protein
certain configuration of 10
   surface polar groups

synthesized
the cell cytoplasm

a membrane
attain a lower free-energy state

give up the water molecules H-bonded
   to your surface polar groups
kcal/mol
the mitochondrial membrane
hydrophobic structural protein
   surfaces with complementary
   configurations of polar groups
allow your surface polar
   group to re-form H-bonds
the endoplasmic reticulum

hydrophobic proteins with
   noncomplementary con-
   figurations of polar groups
temperature
negative free-energy change
   you can bring about

membrane and increase the
   entropy of the aqueous
   phase by removing your
   hydrophobic surface from it
kcal/mol

positive ΔH of transferring your
   hydrophobic groups from
   the aqueous to the lipid phase
energetically
the endoplasmic reticulum
kcal/mol

kcal/mol

the mitochondrial membrane

6.4 Suppose that you are a bacterium growing happily at 25°C. Suddenly a scientist moves you into a 37°C environment, thereby increasing the fluidity of your cell membrane. What can you do to regain your original optimal membrane fluidity?

6.5 Species-specific marker antigens can be located on the plasma membranes of mouse white blood cells and chicken red blood cells by reacting them with fluorescent antibodies that allow the two kinds of antigens to be distinguished through the use of a microscope. These two cell types can be induced to fuse and form living hybrid cells. After fusion, the marker membrane antigens have the distributions with time shown in Figure 6.10. How would you explain these observations, and what would you conclude from them about the membrane structure?

6.6 Lipid bilayers are stable structures when surrounded by a polar solvent. Bilayers can be formed artificially by placing a droplet of phospholipid into a small aperture surrounded by an aqueous solution. Such artificial bilayers are useful as models for studying membrane properties.

Elegant experiments on the dynamics of lipid bilayer structures were carried out by Roger Kornberg and Harden McConnell, using so-called spin-labeled lipids. These are chemically synthesized phospholipid analogues whose polar head groups contain a paramagnetic nitroxide radical. The radical can be detected by electron spin resonance (ESR) spectroscopy. Treatment with a mild reducing agent such as ascorbic acid destroys the nitroxide radical and abolishes its ESR signal. In the experiments, very small vesicles (20–30 nm in diameter) were produced by ultrasound treatment (sonication) of spin-labeled lipid bilayers. The vesicles were shown to be impermeable to ascorbic acid. They then were placed in an ESR spectrometer and exposed to ascorbic acid. The plot of kinetic data in Figure 6.11 was obtained for decay of the ESR signal.

a. Give a detailed interpretation of this result in terms of the bilayer structure shown in Figure 6.2.

b. How do you think the curve would change if the experiment were carried out at higher temperature?

c. Can you suggest a reason why the initial decay is to about 40%?

6.7 In which of the following does the inner surface of a closed membrane or vesicle become the outer surface of a closed membrane or vesicle?

a. Fusion of two intracellular vesicles

b. Exocytosis of a secretory vesicle

c. Transfer of endoplasmic reticular membrane into the Golgi membrane via vesicle formation and fusion as in transport of pancreatic digestive enzymes

d. Endocytosis of a bacterium by a white blood cell

e. Division of a bacterial cell

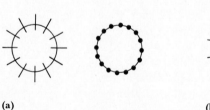
(a)

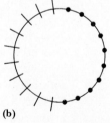
(b)

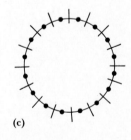
(c)

Figure 6.10
Distribution of species-specific marker antigens as a function of time after cell fusion (Problem 6.5). Chicken marker antigens are indicated as spikes and mouse antigens as solid circles. (a) Chicken and mouse cells before fusion. (b) Chicken–mouse hybrid cell 5 min after fusion. (c) Chicken–mouse hybrid cell 40 min after fusion.

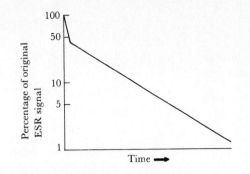

Figure 6.11
Decay of ESR signal as a function of time after exposure to ascorbic acid (Problem 6.6).

6.8   Tell how many boundary membranes of distinct topological compartments must be crossed in going from—

a. The periplasmic space of a procaryotic cell to its DNA

b. The inner matrix of a plant mitochondrion to the inner matrix of a chloroplast in a neighboring cell

c. The interior of the nucleus to the exterior of the cell

d. The interior of the endoplasmic reticulum through the Golgi apparatus to the cell exterior

6.9   In tissue T, protein P is secreted by C cells. It has been shown that P is synthesized as free molecules in compartment A, then passes through compartment B and finally is released as free protein molecules into the extracellular space (Figure 6.12). One famous electron microscopist has claimed that the ultrastructure of C cells is as shown in Figure 6.12a. A second famous electron microscopist argues that the first is seeing artifacts, and that the structure is that shown in Figure 6.12b. Which electron microscopist is more likely to be right?

6.10   The major glycoprotein (protein with carbohydrate attached) of the human red blood cell (RBC) membrane is glycophorin. This glycoprotein has the following properties:

1. Its molecular weight is 50,000 (60% carbohydrate, 40% protein).

2. It is an integral protein.

3. Five fragments are produced by CNBr treatment (Concept 3.5). Three of these fragments have carbohydrates attached as indicated in Figure 6.13.

4. Twenty-five percent of the carbohydrate is sialic acid. It can be removed completely from intact RBC with an enzyme, neuraminidase.

5. Lactoperoxidase is an enzyme that can label exposed Tyr groups with iodine. When intact RBCs are treated with lactoperoxidase, CNBr fragments 1, 2, and 3 are labeled. When RBC ghosts (ruptured, empty membranes) are treated with lactoperoxidase, CNBr fragments 1, 2, 3, and 5 are labeled.

a. Why is fragment CB-5 labeled with iodine by lactoperoxidase treatment of RBC ghosts only?

b. Why does fragment CB-4 fail to be labeled with iodine by lactoperoxidase treatment of intact or ruptured RBCs? (Assume that it has Tyr residues.)

c. What would you predict about the amino acid composition of fragment CB-4?

d. Draw a diagram showing the orientation of glycophorin in the RBC membrane.

6.11   Consider a membrane vesicle containing a protein oriented with its head in the outside monolayer (Figure 6.14). Suppose that such a vesicle could be microinjected into

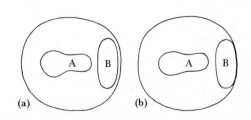

Figure 6.12
Alternative claims for ultrastructure of C cells (Problem 6.9).

(a)   (b)

Figure 6.13
A schematic representation of glycophorin showing attached carbohydrates (CHO) and CNBr cleavage points (arrows) (Problem 6.10).

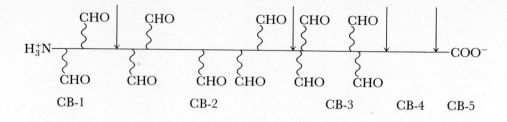

CB-1   CB-2   CB-3   CB-4   CB-5

various compartments within a cell. If the vesicle were to fuse with the nearest membrane, what would be the resulting orientation of the vesicle protein? For the locations listed, decide whether the head (arrow) of the vesicle protein would be associated with the cytoplasmic monolayer or with the external monolayer of the membrane with which the vesicle fuses. Assume that all fusions occur with conservation of membrane asymmetry.

a. Inside the nucleus
b. Into the lumen of the endoplasmic reticulum
c. Outside the cell
d. Into the cytoplasm
e. Into the interior of a secretory vesicle

6.12   Membranes grow by expansion as new protein and phospholipid components are inserted. Most proteins are inserted as they are synthesized (Concept 20.6). Phospholipids are synthesized within the membrane by synthetic enzymes that are integral membrane proteins. In procaryotes these synthetic enzymes are in the plasma membrane, and in eucaryotes they are in the endoplasmic reticulum. To determine whether new phospholipids are synthesized in one or both monolayers of the membrane, James Rothman and Eugene Kennedy made use of trinitrobenzenesulfonic acid (TNBS), which reacts specifically with the head group of phosphatidylethanolamine (PE). Because this reagent does not penetrate the membrane, it tags external PE exclusively. In the bacterium *Bacillus megaterium,* TNBS labeling of intact cells has shown that 30% of membrane PE is in the external monolayer and 70% is in the cytoplasmic monolayer (Figure 6.15a). Using this method Rothman and Kennedy examined the distribution of PE synthesized during a 1-min pulse of ^{32}P-labeled inorganic phosphate, which is incorporated into phospholipid heads. TNBS was added either immediately after the pulse or 30 min later. The results are shown in Figure 6.15b.

a. Is new PE synthesized in one or both monolayers of the membrane? If it is synthesized only in one monolayer, indicate which one.
b. Given the negligible rate of spontaneous phospholipid flipping on this time scale, how could you explain the different distributions of newly synthesized PE immediately after synthesis and 30 min later?

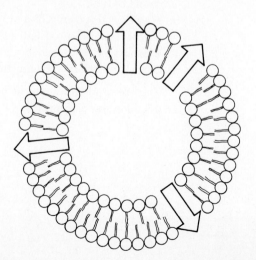

Figure 6.14
Vesicle with oriented protein (Problem 6.11).

Figure 6.15
Chromatographic separation of
PE and TNBS-tagged PE (Problem 6.12). **(a)** Total PE isolated
from intact cells after reaction
with excess TNBS. **(b)** Pulse-
labeled PE reacted immediately
with TNBS or after a delay of
30 min.

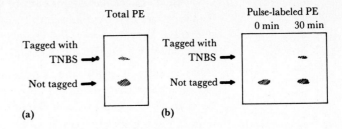

c. Phosphatidylserine in red blood cells is different from most phospholipids in that it
appears to reside exclusively in the cytoplasmic monolayer. How might you explain
this observation?

6.13 Protein shells and membrane vesicles are the two basic biological containers. Protein
shells with icosahedral symmetry encase the genetic material of many viruses, and
membranes enclose all cells. These two methods for enclosing space are involved
together in a number of processes. Consider the schematic diagrams of a coated vesicle
and an RNA-containing animal virus in Figure 6.16a. In both cases the formation of
the protein shell occurs simultaneously with formation of the vesicle by budding from
the membrane (Figure 6.16b). Coated vesicles bud into the cytoplasm, whereas the
animal viruses bud into the external environment.

a. For both structures in Figure 6.16, decide which monolayer of the membrane, cytoplasmic or external, is in contact with the protein shell, and sketch a likely budding
process for the animal virus.

b. An intermediate in the assembly of the bacterial virus PM2 appears similar in structure to the animal virus in Figure 6.16a except that it exists in the cytoplasm. Could a
budding process like the one described account for such an observation? If so, how?

c. Classify each of the three structures encountered in this problem (coated vesicle, animal virus, PM2 virus) according to which surface of the protein shell (inside or outside) is in contact with which monolayer of the vesicle membrane (cytoplasmic or
external). By this classification each of the structures is different and a fourth is possible. Describe how the fourth structure might bud from the membrane and whether
you would expect it to bud into the cytoplasm or into the external environment.

6.14 Protomers in the cytoplasm can aggregate with rotational, translational, and screw
symmetry. However, unlike cytoplasmic proteins, membrane proteins are confined to
the plane of the membrane. Because each species of membrane protein maintains a
unique orientation relative to the surfaces, membrane-bound aggregates have somewhat restricted symmetries.

a. Consider the classes of biological symmetry listed in Table 5.1. Which of these symmetries are permitted for aggregates that span a single planar membrane? Does your
analysis suggest a function for such aggregates?

(a) Coated vesicle   Animal virus

Figure 6.16
(a) Two protein shells in association with membrane vesicles.
(b) Coated vesicles form by budding from the membrane (Problem 6.13). The hexagon represents the protein shell and the
circles represent the membrane
bilayer. To distinguish the two
sides of the bilayer, one is indicated as a dashed line.

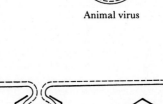

(b) Coated pit   Coated vesicle

b. Open-ended molecular chains can form with either translational or screw symmetry (Concept 5.6). In the cytoplasm the usual form of molecular chain is a helix with screw symmetry. Do you expect that chains of membrane proteins will show a bias toward either screw or translational symmetry?

6.15 The symmetry of membrane aggregates is less restricted if multiple membranes and membrane flexibility are taken into account. Describe the symmetry of an intercellular channel in a gap junction (Figure 6.9) and of the coated vesicle in Figure 6.17.

6.16 If an open-ended molecular chain is flexible, the two ends can find one another and complete a ring of interactions. In a membrane, such a ring of interactions would form a fence that would divide the surface of the membrane into two distinct areas, as illustrated in Figure 6.18a. A view from membrane level of such a hypothetical chain is shown in Figure 6.18b.

a. A scientist in Texas has suggested that such a molecular fence could function as a corral to restrict free diffusion of membrane components between the two areas of the membrane. What are some implications of this idea, assuming that the fence is static and has no gates?

b. Decide whether a tight junction fulfills the requirements for a molecular fence.

c. Electron microscope pictures of the endoplasmic reticulum occasionally show a continuous membrane, of which one portion is studded with ribosomes and an adjacent portion is free of ribosomes (Figure 6.4). Could such a division between rough and smooth endoplasmic reticulum be accomplished by a corral?

6.17 A nuclear pore viewed along its 8-fold axis of rotational symmetry is diagrammed in Figure 6.19. At each of the many nuclear pores the cytoplasm and nucleoplasm are in direct contact, and exchange material. Also at each of the pores the inner nuclear membrane flows into the outer nuclear membrane, which is continuous with the rest of the endoplasmic reticulum (Figure 6.4). Given this arrangement, decide whether the nuclear pore proteins corral an area of membrane. If so, specify the area and explain your answer.

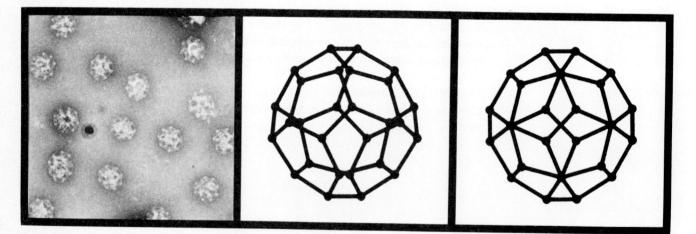

Figure 6.17
An electron micrograph of coated vesicles and a stereo-pair diagram illustrating a possible structure for the shell (Problem 6.15). Coated vesicles apparently can form with a variety of related shells made up of pentagons and hexagons. For stereo viewing see instructions in the Appendix to Chapter 4. [Electron micrograph from B. M. F. Pearse, *Proceedings of the National Academy of Sciences (U.S.)*, **73**, 1256 (1976); stereo diagram from R. A. Crowther, J. T. Finch, and B. M. F. Pearse, *Journal of Molecular Biology*, **103**, 789 (1976).]

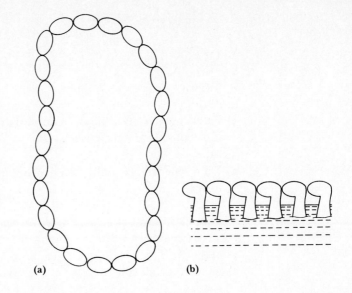

Figure 6.18
Closed molecular chains in membranes (Problem 6.16). **(a)** View perpendicular to membrane.
(b) View parallel to membrane.

(a)   (b)

☆ 6.18   A certain integral protein exists as an isologous dimer in the membrane, with several polar groups on the interacting protomer surfaces. Is dimerization most likely to occur during or after insertion of the protomers into the membrane? Explain your answer.

☆ 6.19   The bacterium *E. coli* has both saturated and unsaturated fatty acid side chains in its membrane phospholipids. A particular mutant of *E. coli* has lost the ability to synthesize its own unsaturated fatty acids; it can synthesize palmitic acid (saturated $C_{16:0}$) but requires an unsaturated fatty acid supplement to grow. This requirement can be satisfied by adding any one of four unsaturated fatty acids to the growth medium:

a. *cis*-Δ^9-$C_{14:1}$ (a cis unsaturated 14-carbon fatty acid with one double bond between C-9 and C-10)

b. *cis*-Δ^9-$C_{18:1}$

c. *cis*-Δ^9-$C_{16:1}$

d. *cis, cis*-$\Delta^{9,12}$-$C_{14:2}$

Cultures of the mutant are grown on each of the four unsaturated fatty acids at 30°C, and then the ratio of palmitate to unsaturated fatty acid in membrane phospholipid is determined. The four results, in random order, are 53:47, 79:21, 46:54, and 70:30.

Match each of the four unsaturated fatty acids in a–d with its most likely result. Give reasons for your answer.

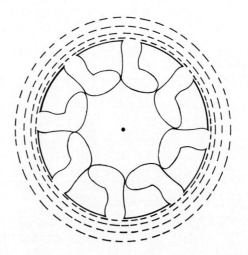

Figure 6.19
Schematic representation of a nuclear pore (Problem 6.17).

Answers

6.1 a. True

b. True

c. True

d. True

e. False. Free lateral diffusion ensures that most membrane components are randomly distributed in the membrane.

f. True

g. False. Interference with close packing increases membrane fluidity.

h. True

i. True

j. False. Cell membranes of different species fuse because of the universality of general membrane structure and the nonspecific nature of the hydrophobic interactions that maintain it, not because all membranes contain identical components.

k. False. Membrane asymmetry is conserved during cycles of vesicle formation and fusion.

6.2 a. phospholipids, proteins

b. Decreasing (or shortening)

c. lateral diffusion, flip

d. 0, 1, 2

e. nuclear pores

f. fusion

g. Desmosomes, tight junctions, gap junctions

6.3 a. No. You will lose $2 (or about 2 kcal/mol; that is, your net ΔG will be about $+2$ kcal/mol).

b. You will gain $48 (or about 48 kcal/mol; that is, $\Delta G \simeq -48$ kcal/mol. The answer is exactly -48 kcal/mol if the H-bonds re-formed in the membrane are isoenergetic with the H-bonds broken upon entry—that is, if the refund exactly equals the deposit).

c. *Moral*: Neither traveling by rental car nor entering a membrane costs much if you get your deposit back.

d. This is a ridiculous question.

6.4 You can return your membrane to its former state by incorporating phospholipid with longer-chain fatty acids or more fully saturated fatty acids. Synthesis and incorporation of some compound analogous to cholesterol also will do the job. Because you are a procaryote, you cannot synthesize cholesterol itself.

6.5 These results indicate that antigenic groups can migrate from one membrane into the other. The antigens (presumably proteins) are not fixed relative to each other and have freedom of lateral movement.

6.6 a. The rapid decay of the signal to 40% of its original intensity must be due to reduction of the spin-label of lipids whose heads are on the outer membrane surfaces of the vesicles. Because the vesicles are impermeable to ascorbic acid, the continuing slow, first-order decay must mean that spin-labeled lipids are flipping through the membrane. In other words, their polar heads, initially inside a vesicle, are migrating to the outside, where they immediately become reduced.

b. Increasing the temperature will increase the kinetic energy of the lipids and make the membrane more fluid; hence flipping will be faster and the slope of the second portion will be significantly steeper. The first half of the curve should be affected less significantly.

c. The initial decay to 40% reflects the difference in area of the inside and outside surfaces of the vesicle membranes; 60% of the lipids are on the outside and 40% are on the inside.

6.7   Refer to Figure 6.8. Reversal will occur only in the situations described in parts b and d.

6.8   a. One: the protoplasmic membrane.

b. Six: the inner and then the outer mitochondrial membrane; then the cytoplasmic membrane of the first cell followed by the cytoplasmic membrane of the second cell; then the outer and then the inner chloroplast membrane.

c. Only the cytoplasmic membrane has to be crossed. The nucleus, because of its pores, is not a distinct topological compartment bounded by membrane.

d. Four: the membrane of the endoplasmic reticulum; the Golgi membrane twice (first in and then out); and finally the cytoplasmic membrane.

6.9   When a protein is transported, its passage into successive compartments involves alternate packaging of the free protein into a vesicle, and then vesicle–membrane fusion, with release of the free protein again. To go by this mechanism from free protein in one compartment to free protein in another requires traversing an even number of membranes. Therefore, the first electron microscopist is more likely to be correct.

6.10   a. CB-5 is not labeled in intact RBCs because it is on the inside surface of the membrane, and lactoperoxidase cannot penetrate the membrane. CB-5 can be labeled in RBC ghosts because there are holes in the membrane through which lactoperoxidase can enter.

b. CB-4 is in the interior of the membrane, and its Tyr residues are sequestered from the lactoperoxidase under either set of conditions.

c. Because CB-4 lies in a hydrophobic environment, it must contain a high proportion of hydrophobic amino acid residues.

d. See Figure 6.20.

6.11   In all cases the head of the vesicle protein associates with the adjacent monolayer of the membrane with which the vesicle fuses (Figure 6.21). Thus when the vesicle is topologically inside the cell cytoplasm, as in parts a and d, the head of the vesicle protein associates with the cytoplasmic monolayer. When the vesicle is topologically outside the cell, as in parts b, c, and e, the head of the vesicle protein associates with the external monolayer.

6.12   a. None of the PE synthesized during the pulse is tagged with TNBS when the reagent is added immediately after the pulse. Therefore newly synthesized PE is present only in the cytoplasmic monolayer—the monolayer inaccessible to TNBS.

b. Newly synthesized PE is rapidly distributed between the two membrane monolayers, so that within 30 min it attains the distribution characteristic of the total membrane PE. This process is faster, by several orders of magnitude, than would be expected from the spontaneous rate of phospholipid flipping. The rapid observed distribution suggests the existence of membrane proteins that catalyze flipping of phospholipids.

c. The observation that one particular phospholipid, phosphatidylserine, is confined to the cytoplasmic monolayer of red blood cells might be explained by the absence of an enzyme to catalyze its flipping.

6.13   a. A likely budding process is illustrated in Figure 6.22. Both kinds of containers are formed by protein shells that are in contact with the cytoplasmic monolayer. Their cytoplasmic or extracellular destinations are determined by whether the shells bind membrane on their inside or their outside surfaces.

b. The PM2 intermediate could bud as indicated in Figure 6.22. This budding process would require that the protein shell form in the external monolayer and bind mem-

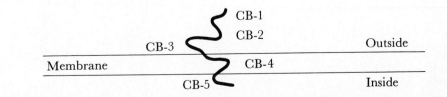

Figure 6.20
Orientation of glycophorin in the RBC membrane (Answer 6.10).

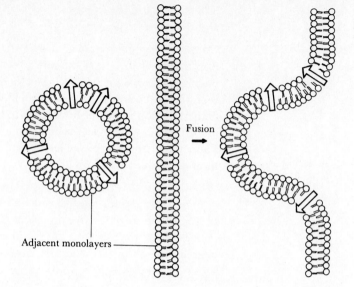

Figure 6.21
Conservation of asymmetry during membrane fusion (Answer 6.11).

brane on its outside surface. Such a budding process could be accomplished by an integral membrane protein whose assembly determinants are on the external side of the membrane.

c. The three structures encountered so far can be classified as inside surface bound to the cytoplasmic monolayer (coated vesicle), outside surface bound to the cytoplasmic monolayer (animal virus), and outside surface bound to the external monolayer (PM2 virus). The fourth possible structure would be a protein shell whose inside surface binds the external monolayer. Such a structure would be expected to bud into the external environment (Figure 6.22).

6.14 a. Because membrane proteins are oriented uniquely, membrane-bound aggregates can have rotational symmetry only about an axis perpendicular to the plane of the membrane. This restriction limits their rotational symmetry to cyclic point groups. Mem-

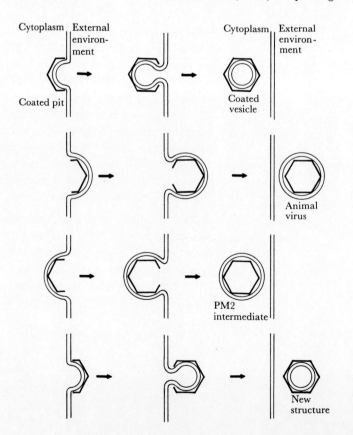

Figure 6.22
A variety of budded structures (Answer 6.13).

brane aggregates with cyclic symmetry can form a hole or channel that passes through the membrane along the axis of symmetry. Transport proteins, which selectively pass specific molecules through the membrane, may well function as cyclic aggregates (Chapter 14).

b. Open-ended aggregates of membrane proteins will be biased toward translational symmetry. Screw symmetry relative to a planar membrane is highly unlikely because it would require that protomers possess more than one orientation relative to the membrane. In the special case where the membrane itself forms a cylinder, a membrane aggregate could show screw symmetry by spiraling around the cytoplasmic or external surface of the membrane cylinder.

6.15 An intercellular channel in a gap junction has dihedral (D6) point group symmetry with a 6-fold axis running down the center of the channel and six 2-fold axes in the plane between the two membranes. The coated vesicle has tetrahedral point group symmetry with the four hexagons at the vertices of the tetrahedron.

6.16 a. A molecular chain in the membrane, such as that illustrated in Figure 6.18b, would affect the free lateral diffusion of membrane components. Lipids, because of their small size, would be affected only if the holes in the fence were extremely small. However, the diffusion of proteins might be affected more severely. Small proteins or specially shaped proteins could diffuse through the holes in the fence and thus would be represented on both sides of the fence. However, large proteins could not pass through the fence and thus should be distributed unequally on the two sides of the fence. Whether or not such a molecular fence would function as a corral depends additionally on how new membrane components are added to the membrane. If they are added only on one side of the fence, then the fence would function as a corral. If membrane components are added to both sides of the fence, then there would be no qualitative difference in the kinds of proteins on the two sides of the fence.

b. Tight junctions result from interactions between molecular chains in different cells. In order to form a tight junction the interactions between chains must pass entirely around the linked cells so that the spaces between the cells are sealed. This requirement means that the molecular chains, which interact to form tight junctions, must form closed structures on the surfaces of the linked cells. Thus tight junctions are a kind of molecular fence. Whether they affect the distribution of membrane components is unknown.

c. The division between rough and smooth endoplasmic reticulum could be accomplished by a molecular chain that encircles the fingerlike projection of the endoplasmic reticulum referred to in Figure 6.4. The membrane component, presumably protein, to which ribosomes attach would have to be fenced out by the corral. If corrals with different exclusion characteristics existed in the endoplasmic reticulum, they could serve as a first step in parceling out the variety of newly synthesized membrane proteins to their final cellular destinations.

6.17 Nuclear pore proteins separate the inner nuclear membrane from the outer nuclear membrane and the rest of the endoplasmic reticulum. Any protein that floats in the endoplasmic reticulum would have to pass through a nuclear pore complex in order to reach the inner nuclear membrane. Thus the nuclear pore proteins do form a corral in the sense developed in Problem 6.16. The principal difference is that instead of one large fence a large number of small fences make up the corral.

7 Proteins in Solution and Enzyme Mechanisms

The interaction of proteins with other molecules is determined by amino acid residues exposed to the surrounding medium. This chapter considers protein surface properties that influence aqueous-solution behavior and enzyme catalysis.

Concepts

7.1 Surface groups on proteins are responsible for their acid–base and solubility properties.

A. The acid–base behavior of proteins determines many of their properties in solution. Proteins with ionizable surface groups behave as zwitterions (Concept 2.1). These groups can be titrated, unless involved in ionic or H-bonding with cofactors or other surface groups. The pH at which a protein has no net charge is designated its **isoelectric point, pI**. The isoelectric points of several proteins are listed in Table 7.1.

Table 7.1
Isoelectric Points of Some Proteins

Protein	pI	Protein	pI
Pepsin	<1.0	Hemoglobin	6.8
Egg albumin	4.6	Myoglobin	7.0
Serum albumin	4.9	Chymotrypsinogen	9.5
Urease	5.0	Cytochrome c	10.7
β-Lactoglobulin	5.2	Lysozyme	11.0
γ_1-Globulin	6.6		

B. The solubility of a protein varies with the solvent pH, temperature, ionic strength, and dielectric constant (a measure of solvent polarity; see Concept 1.3, part A). The protein–protein interactions that lead to aggregation and precipitation are promoted by solvent conditions that minimize net surface charge, decrease interaction of surface polar groups with water molecules, or cause unfolding of internal hydrophobic groups. Thus, solubility is decreased by titrating proteins to their pI (eliminating charge repulsion between molecules) or by adding organic solvents to lower the dielectric constant of the solution (decreasing hydrophobic interactions as well as H-bonding to water, and thereby promoting both unfolding and H-bonding between surface polar groups). At temperatures above 40–50°C H-bonds and ionic bonds begin to break, and most proteins denature, allowing their exposed hydrophobic interiors to interact. Low concentrations of neutral salts increase the solubility of proteins in water (**salting in**) by stabilizing surface charged groups. At higher concentrations, salt ions compete with proteins for water molecules. As a result, H-bonding of protein surface polar groups to each other becomes more important, and precipitation is favored (**salting out**).

126

7.2 Several common techniques for separating proteins rely on their acid–base and solubility properties.

A. **Ion-exchange chromatography** is the most widely used technique for separating proteins. **Ion-exchange resins** consist of a neutral matrix to which ionizable groups have been attached chemically. Two commonly used resins are the anion exchanger diethylaminoethylcellulose (DEAE-cellulose), which carries a positive charge on the DEAE group at pH values below about 10, and the cation exchanger carboxymethylcellulose (CM-cellulose), which carries a negative charge on the CM group at pH values above about 4. Proteins generally are applied in a low ionic strength buffer to a column containing the resin, and are eluted with buffers of different pH, higher ionic strength, or both. The affinity of a protein for the charged resin is lowered by pH changes that decrease the ionization of oppositely charged protein groups, and by ions in the buffer, which compete with the protein for the charged resin. Different proteins, with different distributions of charged surface groups, elute under different conditions.

B. Proteins, like amino acids, can be separated by **electrophoresis** at pH values favoring zwitterionic forms. Electrophoresis of proteins generally is carried out on a solid support gel composed of starch, agarose, or polyacrylamide.

C. Proteins may be **precipitated selectively** by manipulating the pH, ionic strength, and dielectric constant of the solvent. Precipitation either at the isoelectric pH or at high salt concentration is preferred, because both methods involve the least danger of denaturing proteins.

7.3 Enzyme catalysis and specificity depend on surface groups in the enzyme active site.

A. Enzymes increase the rate at which a reaction reaches equilibrium by lowering the activation energy, that is, the free energy of one or more unstable reaction intermediates. Enzymes do not alter the equilibrium positions of the reactions they catalyze. The energetics of catalyzed and uncatalyzed reactions are compared schematically in Figure 7.1.

B. The catalytic properties and specificity of an enzyme are determined by the chemical groups in a region of the protein surface called the **active site.** The active site of a protein usually constitutes less than 5% of its surface area. Enzymes must be larger than their active sites so that the side chains responsible for binding and for catalytic reactions can be juxtaposed appropriately in three dimensions. The active site always

Figure 7.1
Energetics of catalyzed (solid line) and uncatalyzed (dashed line) conversion of substrate (S) to product (P), showing the ability of the enzyme (E) to lower the activation energy of the reaction by stabilizing the transition state. ES and EP represent complexes of enzyme-bound substrate and product, respectively. The ΔG of activation determines the rate of the forward reaction, and the ΔG of reaction determines the equilibrium position (see Concept 9.2).

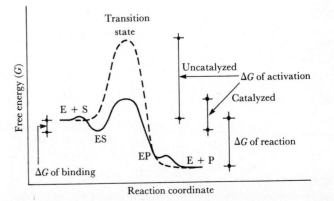

is found in a cleft or crevice and has two distinct functions: binding of substrate(s) and catalysis. Generally, different amino acid side chains are involved in each function.

1.   Enzymes exhibit remarkable specificity because of the precise fit between their binding sites and their substrates. Substrate binding can involve ionic bonds, H-bonds, and van der Waals bonds. Van der Waals bonds contribute significantly to the binding energy only when several are formed; that is, when there is considerable molecular complementarity between enzyme and substrate. Typical substrate binding energies are in the range of $\Delta G = -3$ to -12 kcal/mol.

Enzymes bind substrates so that the atoms participating in the bond to be made or broken are oriented properly with respect to catalytic groups on the enzyme. Degradative enzymes may bind a substrate in such a way that its conformation is distorted, thereby increasing the lability of the bond to be broken and facilitating cleavage. Molecules other than substrate that bind to an enzyme active site act as competitive inhibitors of catalysis.

2.   Only a few of the 20 amino acid side chains participate directly in catalysis. In general, these are the polar side chains; known participants are Cys, His, Ser, Asp, Glu, and Lys. The amino and carboxyl termini of an enzyme also sometimes are involved. Most enzymes exhibit a characteristic pH dependence of activity, because of the titration of one or more charged groups that participate in catalysis (Figure 7.2).

C.   Amino acid side chains cannot catalyze all the chemical reactions required by biological systems. For example, no side chains are good electron acceptors. Therefore, small molecules or metal ions (cofactors or coenzymes) with additional chemical potentialities are required in addition to enzymes for catalysis of some reactions. Some cofactors bind transiently to the enzyme during the reaction; others, called **prosthetic groups,** are permanently bound to an amino acid side chain in the enzyme active site. The most important small-molecule cofactors are described in Chapter 11.

7.4   Most enzymes operate by general acid–base or covalent catalysis.

A.   General acid–base catalysis involves groups that donate or accept protons (H^+ ions) during the course of a reaction, such as the side chains of Glu, Asp, and His. General acid–base catalysis does not involve covalent-bond formation between substrate and enzyme.

Catalysis by lysozyme is one of the best understood enzyme mechanisms employing general acid–base catalysis. Lysozyme is a single polypeptide chain of 129 amino acid residues, folded into an egg-shaped configuration with a cleft in one side (Figure 4.9). This enzyme catalyzes hydrolysis of a bacterial cell-wall polysaccharide made up of N-acetylglucosamine (NAG) and N-acetylmuramic acid (NAM) in alternating sequence (Figure 7.3). A competitive inhibitor, tri-NAG or $(NAG)_3$, binds at the active site, filling half the cleft. Model building with $(NAG-NAM)_3$ suggests the enzyme–substrate H-bonds shown in Figure 7.3. A large number of van der Waals contacts are suggested as well.

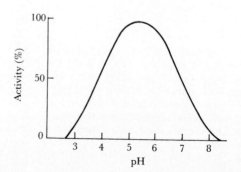

Figure 7.2
The pH–activity profile of lysozyme.

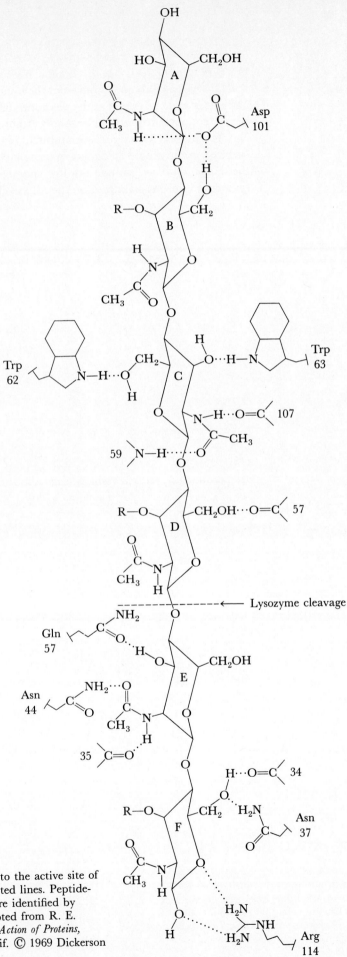

Figure 7.3
Binding of the substrate (NAG-NAM)$_3$ to the active site of
lysozyme. H-bonds are indicated by dotted lines. Peptide-
bond atoms that H-bond to substrate are identified by
amino acid residue number only. (Adapted from R. E.
Dickerson and I. Geis, *The Structure and Action of Proteins,*
Benjamin/Cummings, Menlo Park, Calif. © 1969 Dickerson
and Geis.)

Lysozyme cleaves the bond between the C-1 carbon atom of residue D and the oxygen atom of the glycosidic linkage to residue E (Figure 7.3). Only two amino acid side chains in the region of this bond can serve as proton donors or acceptors: Asp 52 and Glu 35, each about 0.3 nm from the bond. Asp 52 is in a polar environment and almost certainly is ionized at the pH optimum of lysozyme (pH = 5), whereas Glu 35 is in a nonpolar region and probably is not ionzied.

The proposed catalytic mechanism of lysozyme is diagrammed in Figure 7.4. The carboxyl group of Glu 35 donates a proton, cleaving the C-1—O bond, and releasing the dimer EF. The resulting positive charge on the C-1 carbon atom of the D ring (carbonium ion) is stabilized by the negatively charged Asp 52. The carbonium ion

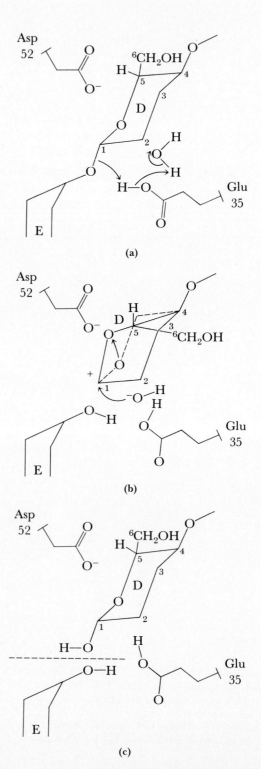

Figure 7.4
Probable mechanism of bond cleavage by lysozyme. Arrows indicate displacement of electron pairs during the reaction. Each arrow originates at a bond or free electron pair and terminates at the nucleus to which the electrons transfer. (Adapted from R. E. Dickerson and I. Geis, *The Structure and Action of Proteins,* Benjamin/Cummings, Menlo Park, Calif. © 1969 Dickerson and Geis.)

intermediate reacts with hydroxyl ion from the solvent to release the tetramer ABCD. Glu 35 becomes reprotonated and the enzyme is ready for another round of catalysis.

Two aspects of this scheme are probably common to many enzyme mechanisms. First, binding of the substrate distorts the chair conformation of sugar residue D to a higher-energy, half-chair conformation, thereby providing part of the activation energy needed for subsequent cleavage. Second, the cleft of the active site creates a hydrophobic environment, which shields certain active-site side chains from the solvent, thereby altering their pK's and nucleophilicities. When the substrate is sequestered in the active-site cleft, this environment permits strong charge interactions that would be impossible in aqueous surroundings because of shielding by water molecules.

B. Covalent catalysis differs from general acid–base catalysis in that transient covalent bonds are formed between the substrate and the enzyme or coenzyme. Amino acid side chains that participate in such reactions are Ser, Cys, His, Lys, Asp, and Glu. All these side chains react by donating a pair of electrons to a center of partial positive charge on a substrate molecule (**nucleophilic attack**) to form the bonds shown in Table 7.2. The resulting highly reactive enzyme–substrate complexes are attacked by water or a second substrate molecule to yield the characteristic products of the enzyme reaction. Coenzymes react with substrates either by nucleophilic attack or electrophilic attack (accepting a pair of electrons). Examples of coenzyme-dependent covalent catalysis are given in Problem 7.18 and Chapter 11.

Table 7.2
Enzyme–Substrate Bonds
Formed in Covalent
Catalysis

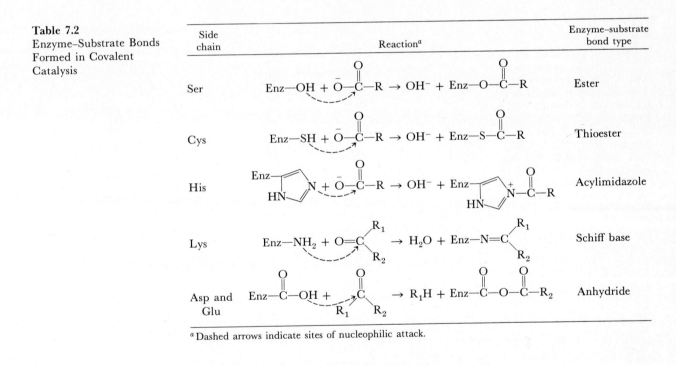

Side chain	Reaction[a]	Enzyme–substrate bond type
Ser	Enz—OH + ⁻O—C(=O)—R → OH⁻ + Enz—O—C(=O)—R	Ester
Cys	Enz—SH + ⁻O—C(=O)—R → OH⁻ + Enz—S—C(=O)—R	Thioester
His	Enz-imidazole + ⁻O—C(=O)—R → OH⁻ + Enz-imidazolium—N—C(=O)—R	Acylimidazole
Lys	Enz—NH₂ + O=C(R₁)(R₂) → H₂O + Enz—N=C(R₁)(R₂)	Schiff base
Asp and Glu	Enz—C(=O)—OH + C(=O)(R₁)(R₂) → R₁H + Enz—C(=O)—O—C(=O)—R₂	Anhydride

[a] Dashed arrows indicate sites of nucleophilic attack.

Cleavage of polypeptides by carboxypeptidase A (Concept 3.4) is an example of covalent catalysis. The structure of the enzyme is shown in Figure 4.10. Its probable mechanism, inferred from x-ray analysis and chemical experiments, is diagrammed in Figure 7.5 for the cleavage of a C-terminal Tyr residue from a polypeptide substrate. The substrate binds to Arg 145, the Zn atom, and a hydrophobic pocket in the enzyme active site (a). Nucleophilic attack of Glu 270 on the peptide carbonyl group is accompanied by uptake of a proton from Tyr 248 (b), resulting in cleavage of the peptide bond allowing the C-terminal residue to diffuse away as a free amino acid (c). The covalently bound polypeptide is released to regenerate free enzyme by nucleophilic attack of a water molecule on the anhydride bond to Glu 270 (c) and reprotonation of Tyr 248 (d).

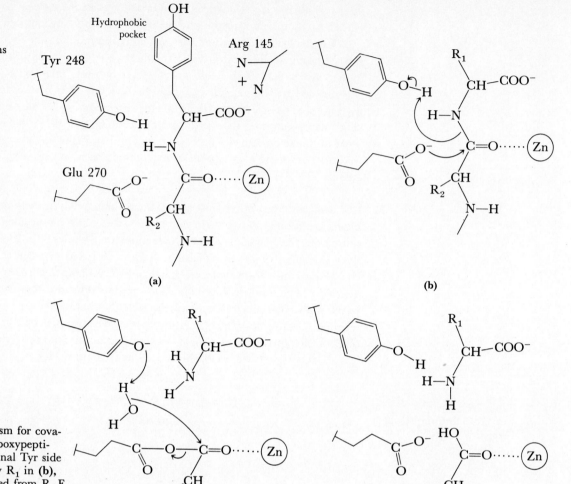

Figure 7.5
A probable mechanism for covalent catalysis by carboxypeptidase A. The C-terminal Tyr side chain is indicated by R_1 in **(b)**, **(c)**, and **(d)**. (Adapted from R. E. Dickerson and I. Geis, *The Structure and Action of Proteins*, Benjamin/Cummings, Menlo Park, Calif. © 1969 Dickerson and Geis.)

7.5 Additional concepts and techniques are presented in the Problems section.

A. Relationship of reaction rate constants to equilibrium constants. Problem 7.5.

B. Titration of protein surface groups. Problem 7.9.

C. Gel filtration and disc electrophoresis of proteins. Problem 7.10.

D. Mechanism of the enzyme trypsin. Problem 7.17.

E. Mechanism of the coenzyme thiamine pyrophosphate. Problem 7.18.

References

COMPREHENSIVE TEXTS

Lehninger: Chapters 7 and 9
Metzler: Chapters 6 and 7

Stryer: Chapters 6 and 7
White et al.: Chapters 5 and 9

OTHER REFERENCES

R. E. Dickerson and I. Geis, *The Structure and Action of Proteins,* Benjamin/Cummings, Menlo Park, Calif., 1969. Chapter 4.

D. E. Koshland, "Protein Shape and Biological Control," *Scientific American*, October 1973, p. 52.

R. M. Stroud, "A Family of Protein-Cutting Proteins," *Scientific American*, July 1974, p. 74.

Problems

7.1   Answer the following with true or false. If false, explain why.

a. The N-terminal amino group and C-terminal carboxyl group constitute a large percentage of the charged groups on most proteins.

b. The pH at which a protein is least soluble in aqueous solution is usually its pI.

c. Cytochrome c will migrate toward the cathode ($-$) upon electrophoresis at pH = 7.

d. Only charged amino acid residues in the active site are known to participate directly in enzyme catalysis.

e. Enzymes are not useful for biological reactions with a $K_{eq} \simeq 1$ (equal concentrations of reactants and products at equilibrium), because such reactions cannot be driven toward product formation.

f. Enzyme catalysis can be explained by a lock-and-key concept of substrate fit at the active site.

g. Van der Waals bonds are not useful in enzyme–substrate binding, because they are only slightly stronger than the kinetic energy of gas molecules at room temperature (0.6 kcal/mol).

h. In a dimeric enzyme with an active site that involves amino acid residues from both polypeptide chains, each subunit, inactive by itself, is called a coenzyme.

7.2   a. Solubilizing a protein by increasing the ionic strength of a solution is termed _____. Precipitating a protein at high ionic strength is termed _____.

b. DEAE-cellulose is a(n) _____ exchanger. CM-cellulose is a(n) _____ exchanger.

c. _____, _____, and _____ bonds are important in substrate binding.

d. Two general classes of enzymatic catalysis are _____ and _____.

e. A nucleophile is an electron-pair _____. An electrophile is an electron-pair _____.

f. A protein with a net negative charge will bind strongly to an anion-exchange resin. A buffer with a _____ pH or _____ ionic strength than the original buffer will be needed to elute such a protein.

g. The pK_a of a carboxyl group is _____ and that of an amino group is _____ when the group is sequestered in a hydrophobic crevice on an enzyme.

7.3   In what order would the indicated proteins be eluted from the following ion exchange columns by an increasing salt gradient (see Table 7.1)? Explain your answers.

a. Cytochrome c, lysozyme, egg albumin, and myoglobin, from an anion exchanger

b. Cytochrome c, pepsin, urease, and hemoglobin, from a cation exchanger

7.4   Briefly explain why most globular proteins in solution do the following:

a. Precipitate at low pH

b. Increase in solubility, then decrease in solubility, and finally precipitate as the ionic strength is increased from zero to a high value

c. Show minimum solubility of a given ionic strength at their isoelectric pH

d. Precipitate upon heating

e. Decrease in solubility as the dielectric constant of the medium is decreased by addition of a water-miscible, nonpolar solvent

f. Denature if the dielectric constant is decreased substantially to give a predominantly nonpolar solvent

7.5   Consider the reaction

$$A \underset{k_r}{\overset{k_f}{\rightleftharpoons}} B$$

The rates or velocities, v, of the forward and reverse reactions will be proportional to the concentrations of A and B, respectively. The proportionality constants are the so-called rate constants k_f and k_r, whose units are inverse time (in this case, sec^{-1}). Thus

$$v_f = k_f[A] \quad \text{and} \quad v_r = k_r[B]$$

The overall reaction rate is

$$v = k_f[A] - k_r[B]$$

Assume $k_f = 10^{-4}$ sec^{-1}, $k_r = 10^{-7}$ sec^{-1}, $[A]_0 = 10^{-4}M$, and $[B]_0 = 0$. $[A]_0$ and $[B]_0$ are the initial concentrations of A and B, respectively.

a. The equilibrium constant of a reaction is defined as the ratio of product concentration to reactant concentration when equilibrium has been reached:

$$K_{eq} = \frac{[B]}{[A]}$$

Calculate the value of K_{eq} for this reaction.

b. Suppose you add an enzyme that increases k_f by a factor of 10^9. What would K_{eq} be then? What would k_r be?

c. Neglecting the reverse reaction, estimate the time it would take to reach equilibrium with and without enzyme. Note that the concentration of A will change as the reaction proceeds, so that the equation $v = k_f[A]$ must be integrated to obtain an expression for [A] as a function of time. This expression, called the **rate equation** for the reaction, is $[A]/[A]_0 = e^{-k_f t}$. It indicates that the fraction of A remaining at any particular time t will be independent of $[A]_0$, the initial concentration.

d. Derive the rate equation in part c.

7.6   Suppose you want to purify by ion-exchange chromatography an enzyme of DNA metabolism whose substrate is DNA. Would you select an anion- or cation-exchange resin? Why? (See Concept 17.2 for the structure of DNA.)

7.7   An enzyme has the pH–activity profile shown in Figure 7.6.
a. How might you explain this behavior? (See Tables 2.1 and 2.2.)
b. How would you test your hypothesis?
c. Suppose you were told that an Asp residue is responsible for a portion of this pH curve. Explain how this might be so.

7.8   Many enzymes show pH–activity profiles similar to the curve in Figure 7.6, but with different activity maxima. What side chains could be involved in the active sites of enzymes with activity maxima at
a. pH = 4
b. pH = 11
Neglect the possibility of ionization suppression by a hydrophobic environment.

7.9   The titration curve for a protein consisting of a single polypeptide chain with unblocked termini is shown in Figure 7.7.
a. Using the data in Tables 2.1 and 2.2, list all possible titratable groups in proteins and their approximate pK_a values.

Figure 7.6
The pH–activity profile of a hypothetical enzyme (Problem 7.7).

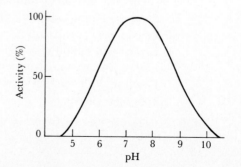

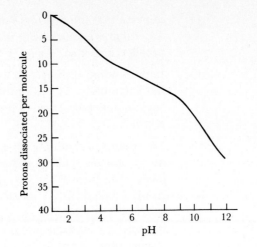

Figure 7.7
Dissociation of protons as a function of pH in the titration of a protein to pH = 12 (Problem 7.9).

b. Estimate how many of each titratable group are present in the protein of Figure 7.7 (assume that there are 36 titratable groups per molecule, and that all Cys residues are involved in disulfide bonds).

c. Estimate the molecular weight of the protein, stating any assumptions that you make to do so.

7.10 **Gel filtration** or **molecular-sieve chromatography** is a method for separating proteins on the basis of their sizes (or, more precisely, their effective radii in solution; radius is proportional to the $\frac{1}{3}$ power of molecular weight for a spherical protein). A solution of protein is placed on a column packed with tiny beads of a highly hydrated cross-linked polymeric material (e.g., Sephadex). Proteins of differing size vary in their ability to penetrate the hydrated pores of the beads. Smaller proteins penetrate these pores more readily and accordingly pass down the column more slowly than larger proteins.

A second technique for separating proteins, **disc electrophoresis,** subjects proteins to an electric field in a polyacrylamide gel support. When electrophoresis is carried out in the presence of a denaturing reagent, sodium dodecyl sulfate [SDS: $CH_3(CH_2)_{11}SO_4Na_2$], protein molecules are separated by size, with the smaller molecules migrating most rapidly. (SDS denatures proteins and binds to them nonspecifically, giving them a constant charge-to-mass ratio.)

Both procedures fractionate proteins on the basis of size, and both employ cross-linked polymers as a supporting medium. How is it possible that in gel filtration small molecules are retarded relative to larger ones, whereas the reverse is true in SDS–polyacrylamide gel electrophoresis?

7.11 Why does the pH–activity profile of lysozyme drop sharply on either side of the optimum at pH = 5?

7.12 a. Calculate the binding energy of lysozyme and its substrate as depicted in Figure 7.3, assuming that the average strength of H-bonds is 5 kcal/mol. (Neglect van der Waals bonds.)

b. This binding energy is larger than that of most substrate–enzyme interactions. Can you offer an explanation?

7.13 Given the information in Table 7.3, what can you conclude about the nature of the binding between lysozyme and its substrate?

Table 7.3
Relative Rates of Lysozyme-Catalyzed Hydrolysis for Various Oligosaccharide Substrates (Problem 7.13)

Substrate	Relative rate of hydrolysis	Substrate	Relative rate of hydrolysis
(NAG)$_2$	0	(NAG)$_5$	4,000
(NAG)$_3$	1	(NAG)$_6$	30,000
(NAG)$_4$	8	(NAG)$_8$	30,000

7.14 Suppose that the hydrolysis of $(NAG)_6$ by lysozyme is carried out in the presence of water that is enriched with the ^{18}O isotope. Will ^{18}O be incorporated into a cleavage product, and if so, where?

7.15 In the binding of $(NAG)_6$ to lysozyme all the sugar residues except D contribute to the binding affinity. The ΔG of binding residue D is about $+3$ kcal/mol. How can you explain this observation? What bearing does it have on the proposed enzymatic mechanism?

7.16 The technique of affinity labeling is employed to identify residues in or near the active site of proteins. This procedure relies on treatment of enzyme with a substrate analogue of the form substrate—X, in which X is a reactive group that can attach covalently to one or a few specific amino acid side chains. Because the analogue binds specifically at the active site, X will react only with nearby amino acids, which can be identified by subsequent hydrolysis and fingerprinting analysis. Explain the following results from affinity-label experiments in which labeled residues are indicated by asterisks:

a. No labeled side chain is recovered.

b. Two labeled sequences are obtained:

$$\text{Met-Gly-Asp-}\overset{*}{\text{Ser}}\text{-Gly-Gly-Pro}$$

$$\text{Arg-Lys-Val-}\overset{*}{\text{Ser}}\text{-Glu-Asp-Gly}$$

c. Two labeled sequences are obtained:

$$\text{Met-Gly-Asp-}\overset{*}{\text{Ser}}\text{-Gly-Gly-Pro}$$

$$\text{Val-Gly-Asp-}\overset{*}{\text{Ser}}\text{-Gly-Gly-Pro}$$

7.17 Three intermediate stages in the proposed mechanism whereby trypsin catalyzes cleavage of polypeptides are shown in Figure 7.8.

a. Fill in the most likely missing intermediate stages, II and IV, including arrows to show shifts of electrons at each stage.

b. The catalytic mechanism for trypsin appears to be identical to that of chymotrypsin. How do you explain the difference in substrate specificity? (See Concept 3.5, part A.)

7.18 Thiamine pyrophosphate (TPP) is a cofactor for several enzyme-catalyzed reactions that involve decarboxylation of α-keto acids (Concept 11.1). The relevant portion of the structure of TPP is its thiazolium ring, shown in Figure 7.9.

TPP forms a relatively stable carbanion (a carbon atom that carries a negative charge) and consequently is a strong nucleophile. Diagram a plausible mechanism whereby enzyme-associated TPP catalyzes the decarboxylation of pyruvate:

$$CH_3-\overset{\overset{\textstyle O}{\|}}{C}-CO_2H \xrightarrow{E \cdot TPP} CH_3-\overset{\overset{\textstyle O}{\|}}{C}-H + CO_2$$

☆ 7.19 The amino acid His is present in the active sites of many enzymes. Can you explain this observation in terms of the chemical properties of His?

☆ 7.20 An enzyme catalyzing the reaction $A \rightarrow B$ is isolated from three different sources and found to give approximately the same pH-versus-activity curve in each case (Figure 7.10). Each enzyme is affinity-labeled with a substrate analogue carrying a reactive group that labels Tyr residues. After tryptic digestion, one peptide from each enzyme is found to be labeled. These peptides are sequenced with the following results:

Chicken liver enzyme:	Tyr-Asn-Cys-Gly-His-Thr-Lys
Bat pancreas enzyme:	Tyr-Ser-Gln-Cys-Gly-Asn-Arg
Ostrich brain enzyme:	Tyr-Gln-Cys-Gly-His-Ser-Lys

What is the simplest interpretation of the pH-versus-activity curve? Explain your answer.

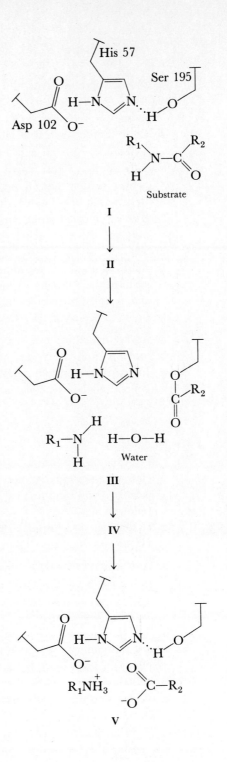

Figure 7.8
Intermediate stages in the proposed mechanism of trypsin catalysis (Problem 7.17).

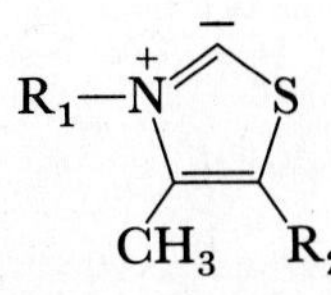

Figure 7.9
The thiazolium ring of thiamine pyrophosphate (Problem 7.18).

Figure 7.10
The pH–activity curve for a hypothetical enzyme (Problem 7.20).

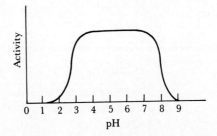

Answers

7.1 a. False. There are generally many more charged side groups.
   b. True
   c. True
   d. False. Some neutral polar residues such as Ser and Cys also are known to participate.
   e. False. Because most reactions in living organisms take place at substrate and product concentrations that are far from equilibrium, an enzyme will be useful for any reaction that approaches equilibrium slowly, regardless of the equilibrium position. It is true, of course, that enzymes cannot drive a reaction toward the products; they can only speed the approach to equilibrium.
   f. False. This concept can explain substrate binding, but not catalysis.
   g. False. Molecular complementarity juxtaposes many atoms from the enzyme and substrate at their van der Waals' radii; consequently, van der Waals bonds can contribute significantly to the binding energy.
   h. False. A coenzyme is a low-molecular-weight, nonprotein molecule.

7.2 a. salting in, salting out
   b. anion, cation
   c. Ionic, hydrogen, van der Waals
   d. general acid–base, covalent
   e. donor, acceptor
   f. lower, higher
   g. increased, decreased

7.3 Ion-exchange columns separate on the basis of net charge. The more negatively charged a protein, the more strongly it will bind to an anion exchanger and the more weakly it will bind to a cation exchanger. Therefore, the elution sequences will be as follows:
   a. Lysozyme, cytochrome c, myoglobin, and egg albumin, from the anion exchanger
   b. Pepsin, urease, hemoglobin, and cytochrome c, from the cation exchanger

7.4 a. At low pH, carboxyl groups become protonated, leaving the protein with a large net positive charge. The resulting intramolecular charge repulsion causes many proteins to denature and become insoluble as their hydrophobic interiors are exposed to the aqueous environment.
   b. The increase in salt concentration initially stabilizes charged groups, but as the concentration increases further the salt ions compete for water molecules, thereby decreasing protein solvation, which in turn promotes both polar and hydrophobic interaction between protein molecules and leads to precipitation.
   c. There is minimum electrostatic repulsion between the molecules of a protein at its pI.
   d. Heating denatures proteins, thereby exposing their hydrophobic interiors and decreasing their solubility.
   e. The nonpolar solvent decreases solvation of surface polar groups, thereby promoting H-bond formation between proteins in place of H-bonds to water.
   f. A decreased dielectric constant stabilizes nonpolar groups exposed to the solvent, thereby promoting protein unfolding.

7.5 a. At equilibrium, the overall reaction rate is 0; hence $k_f[A] = k_r[B]$. Therefore,

$$K_{eq} = \frac{[B]}{[A]} = \frac{k_f}{k_r} = \frac{10^{-4}\,\text{sec}^{-1}}{10^{-7}\,\text{sec}^{-1}} = 1000$$

   b. Enzyme catalysis cannot change the equilibrium position of a reaction. Enzymes simply speed the approach to equilibrium from either direction. Thus, if an enzyme increases k_f by a factor of 10^9, k_r must be increased by the same factor, and K_{eq} will not change.

$$K_{eq} = 1000 = \frac{k_f}{k_r} = \frac{10^5 \text{ sec}^{-1}}{k_r}$$

$$k_r = 10^2 \text{ sec}^{-1}$$

c. To simplify the calculation, rewrite the rate law in its logarithmic form:

$$\ln \frac{[A]}{[A]_0} = k_f t \quad \text{or} \quad 2.3 \log \frac{[A]}{[A]_0} = -k_f t$$

Rearrangement yields

$$t = \frac{-2.3}{k_f} \log \frac{[A]}{[A]_0}$$

At equilibrium, 99.9% of the A initially present will be converted to B, hence $[A]/[A]_0 = 0.1/100$, so that

$$\log \frac{[A]}{[A]_0} = -3$$

and

$$t = \frac{6.9}{k_f}$$

Without enzyme, $k_f = 10^{-4} \text{ sec}^{-1}$, hence $t = 6.9 \times 10^4$ sec (about 19 hr). With enzyme, $k_f = 10^5 \text{ sec}^{-1}$, hence $t = 6.9 \times 10^{-5}$ sec or 69 microseconds (μsec).

d. When the reverse reaction is neglected, the overall rate of reaction is equal to the disappearance of A as a function of time:

$$v = \frac{-d[A]}{dt} = k_f[A]$$

or

$$\frac{d[A]}{[A]} = -k_f \, dt$$

This differential equation can be integrated:

$$\int_{[A]_0}^{[A]} \frac{d[A]}{[A]} = -k_f \int_0^t dt$$

to yield

$$\ln [A] - \ln [A]_0 = -k_f t$$

or

$$\ln \frac{[A]}{[A]_0} = -k_f t$$

Conversion to exponential form gives the rate law:

$$\frac{[A]}{[A]_0} = e^{-k_f t}$$

7.6   DNA is a polyanion by virtue of negative charges on its sugar–phosphate backbone. It is reasonable to guess that an enzyme that normally binds to a polyanion substrate also would stick to a negatively charged resin (cation exchanger). In practice most but not all such enzymes behave in this manner.

7.7   a. An unprotonated His residue ($pK_a \simeq 6$) and a protonated N-terminal α-amino group ($pK_a \simeq 8$) or sulfhydryl group ($pK_a \simeq 8$) necessary for enzymatic activity might give rise to the ascending and descending portions of the curve, respectively. As suggested in part c, certain other groups also could be involved.

b. X-ray crystallographic studies could determine whether these residues were juxtaposed in the active site, particularly if the structure of the enzyme could be determined with a stable substrate analogue bound in place for catalysis. One also could attempt to modify chemically the residues involved and determine how these modifications influence enzyme activity. (For one approach to specific modification of active-site groups, called **affinity labeling,** see Problem 7.16.)

c. A nonpolar environment suppresses the ionization of charged groups. Such an effect could raise the pK_a of the Asp carboxyl group to $pH \simeq 6$. See the discussion on the mechanism of lysozyme, Concept 7.4.

7.8 a. For an activity maximum at $pH = 4$, the ascending portion of the curve could represent ionization of an Asp β-carboxyl or C-terminal α-carboxyl group; the descending portion could represent deprotonation of His or ionization of Glu.

b. For an activity maximum at $pH = 11$, the ascending portion of the curve could represent deprotonation of the N-terminal α-amino group or a Lys ϵ-amino group; the descending portion could represent deprotonation of Arg.

7.9 a. There are eight titratable groups, as shown in Table 7.4.

Table 7.4
Approximate pK_a Values of the Titratable Groups in Proteins (Answer 7.9)

Titratable group	Approximate pK_a	Titratable group	Approximate pK_a
C-terminal α-carboxyl	3	β-Sulfhydryl	8
γ- and β-carboxyl	4–5	Phenolic hydroxyl	9–10
Imidazole	6–7	ϵ-Amino	10–11
N-terminal α-amino	8	Guanidino	12–13

b. The protein has one C-terminal α-carboxyl group and one N-terminal α-amino group. The side-chain carboxyl groups are likely to titrate below $pH = pK_a + 1$, or below about $pH = 5.5$. From the curve, there are about 11 titratable groups in the range of $pH = 2$–5.5; because one is the C-terminal α-carboxyl group, there are 10 side-chain carboxyl groups.

Imidazole groups and the N-terminal α-amino group should titrate in the range of $pH = 5.5$–8.5. There are five groups (16 − 11) titrating in this region; hence, there are four imidazole groups.

If you assume that all phenolic hydroxyl groups titrate below $pH = 10$, then there must be six (22 − 16) phenolic hydroxyl groups.

The 14 remaining dissociable protons must come from ϵ-amino groups and guanidino groups. Because most ϵ-amino groups should titrate below $pH = 12$ and most guanidino groups above $pH = 12$, it is reasonable to guess that there are eight and six of these groups present, respectively, although the steepness of the curve around $pH = 12$ shows that the two cannot be distinguished clearly. The titration data shown in Figure 7.7 were obtained with bovine pancreatic ribonuclease. The actual numbers of titratable groups in this protein are listed in Table 7.5.

Table 7.5
Titratable Groups in Ribonuclease (Answer 7.9)

Titratable group	Number present	Titratable group	Number present
C-terminal α-carboxyl	1	Phenolic hydroxyl	6
γ- and β-carboxyl	10	ϵ-Amino	10
Imidazole	4	Guanidino	4
N-terminal α-amino	1		

c. Six amino acids are present 34 times. Assuming that the mean frequency of these six is representative, the number of amino acids in the protein can be estimated as

$$\tfrac{34}{6} \times 20 = 113 \text{ amino acids}$$

The average molecular weight of an amino acid is about 120. Therefore, the molecular weight of the protein can be estimated as

$$113 \times 120 = 13,600$$

This value is fortuituously close to the actual molecular weight of bovine pancreatic ribonuclease (MW = 13,700). Generally, however, the assumption of representative mean frequency of titratable amino acids is incorrect, and such calculations of molecular weight are greatly in error.

7.10   The cross-linked matrix of each Sephadex bead excludes large proteins but admits small proteins. Therefore, large proteins must pass between the beads, that is, through the column volume minus the bead volume (this difference is called the **void volume**). Small proteins pass through the total column volume. The larger the protein is, the less time it spends in the beads and, consequently, the more rapidly it elutes. The polyacrylamide gel support for electrophoresis is equivalent to one large bead; there are no interbead spaces and all proteins must navigate through the cross-linked matrix. The smaller the protein, the more readily it can pass through the matrix and the more rapidly it migrates.

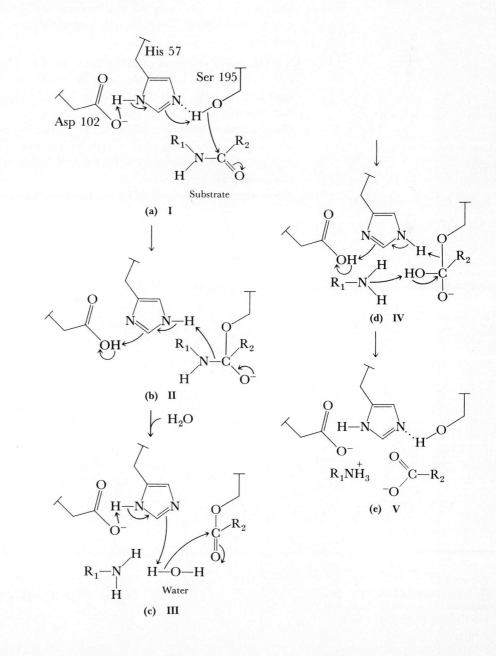

Figure 7.11
The proposed mechanism of
trypsin catalysis (Answer 7.17).

7.11 The pH–activity profile drops on the acid side because the Asp 52 carboxyl group becomes protonated. The profile drops on the basic side because the Glu 35 carboxyl group becomes ionized.

7.12 a. Fourteen H-bonds are formed between the enzyme and its substrate. Consequently, the binding energy is $14 \times 5 = 70$ kcal/mol.

b. Higher binding energy may be required to hold the long polysaccharide chain in position at the active site. In addition, some of the binding energy is used to distort sugar ring D as the first step in catalysis.

7.13 The active-site cleft can accommodate six sugar residues. Binding any fewer causes a significant decrease in catalytic rate. This decrease could occur because binding of the fifth and sixth residues normally promotes binding of the first four by perturbing the active-site conformation, or because the binding energy of the fifth and sixth residues is necessary to effectively distort ring D for catalysis.

7.14 The cleavage products will be ABCD—C-1—^{18}OH + HO—C-4—EF (see Figure 7.4). This method actually was used to determine the side of the oxygen on which cleavage occurred.

7.15 Residue D becomes distorted to the energetically unfavorable half-chair conformation during binding. The half-chair conformation stabilizes the carbonium ion intermediate.

7.16 a. X is positioned so that it cannot react with appropriate side chains, or there are no side chains reactive with X in or near the active site. (Most affinity-label reagents can react with one or at most a few residues—usually those with polar side chains such as Tyr, His, and Ser.)

b. These sequences are quite different. They could represent two different regions of the same polypeptide folded so that both Ser residues are in or near the active site, two separate polypeptides present in the same molecule, or two independent enzyme molecules with similar activities.

c. These sequences are identical except for a single amino acid substitution. This varia-

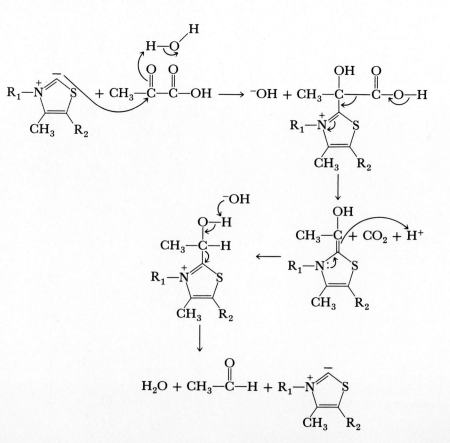

Figure 7.12
The mechanism of thiamine pyrophosphate action in the decarboxylation of pyruvate (Answer 7.18).

tion might indicate that two molecular species of the enzyme are present in the mixture, perhaps the products of two nearly identical genes.

7.17 a. See Figure 7.11.

b. The binding site for trypsin has a pocket for positively charged side groups (with a carboxyl group for neutralization), whereas chymotrypsin has a hydrophobic pocket for nonpolar side chains.

7.18 The mechanism is shown in Figure 7.12. The thiazolium ring, by virtue of its quaternary nitrogen atom, temporarily accommodates the electron pair that otherwise would be left on the α carbon of pyruvate by the leaving carboxyl group.

8 Enzyme Kinetics

The kinetics of enzyme-catalyzed reactions are affected by enzyme and substrate concentrations, pH, temperature, cofactors, inhibitors, and activators. Analysis of these effects has contributed to our understanding of the nature of enzyme catalysis, the mechanisms of specific enzymes, and the regulation of enzyme activity under physiological conditions. This chapter considers the kinetics of both classical and regulatory (allosteric) enzymes, and some factors that promote and inhibit enzyme catalysis.

Concepts

8.1 Classical enzyme-catalyzed reactions show a hyperbolic relationship of rate to concentration of substrate.

A. The initial rate, v (velocity), of an enzyme-catalyzed reaction is usually directly proportional to the concentration of the enzyme. At any given enzyme concentration, v will depend on the level of substrate [S]. For the majority of enzymes, v is related to [S] by the hyperbolic curve shown in Figure 8.1. At very low [S], v increases almost linearly as a function of [S]. As [S] increases further, however, v increases less rapidly. Eventually v reaches a limiting value called V_{max} at saturating [S]. When the rate of an enzyme-catalyzed reaction depends on substrate concentration in this manner and is independent of sterically unrelated ligands, the reaction is said to obey classical or **Michaelis–Menten kinetics**. The [S] at which v equals $V_{max}/2$ is called K_M, the **Michaelis constant**.

B. A simple enzyme-catalyzed reaction (sometimes called a **Uni–Uni reaction**) in which one substrate, S, is converted to one product, P, can be written as follows:

$$S + E \underset{k_2}{\overset{k_1}{\rightleftharpoons}} ES \underset{k_4}{\overset{k_3}{\rightleftharpoons}} E + P \tag{8.1}$$

Here E represents free enzyme, ES represents the **central complex** (enzyme with substrate bound at the active site), and k_1, k_2, k_3, and k_4 are rate constants. These con-

Figure 8.1
Initial rate (v) as a function of substrate concentration, [S], for an enzyme-catalyzed reaction obeying Michaelis–Menten kinetics (solid line). The units of v are usually micromoles of substrate converted per minute (μmol/min), and the units of [S] are moles per liter (mol/L).

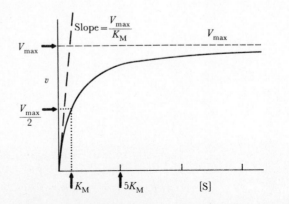

stants are proportional to the corresponding ΔG's of activation diagrammed previously for a similar reaction in Figure 7.1.

C. Equation 8.1 can be related intuitively to the relationship between v and [S] shown in Figure 8.1: At low [S] ([S] $\ll K_M$), most of the enzyme is in the free form, E; hence added S is bound immediately to E and converted to P, so that the initial rate is proportional to [S]. At higher [S], v rises less rapidly as the enzyme begins to saturate. At high [S]([S] $\gg K_M$), the enzyme is saturated, that is, entirely in the ES form. In this situation $v(= V_{max})$ is determined by the catalytic capacity or **turnover number** of the enzyme (k_3 in equation 8.1), and cannot be increased by further increases in [S].

8.2 The Michaelis–Menten equation quantitatively describes the kinetics of most enzyme-catalyzed reactions.

A. A simple quantitative relationship between v and [S] called the **Michaelis–Menten equation** can be derived for equation 8.1 if $k_3 \gg k_4$, so that the reaction is essentially irreversible. First, $[E]_0$ is defined as the total enzyme concentration, that is, the sum of the free enzyme [E] and the central complex [ES]:

$$[E]_0 = [E] + [ES] \tag{8.2}$$

For almost all enzyme-catalyzed reactions [S] $\gg [E]_0$, even at rate-limiting [S], so that $[S] - [ES] \simeq [S]$.

The derivation of the Michaelis–Menten equation depends on the so-called Briggs–Haldane steady-state assumption, that [ES] remains constant during any rate measurement; that is, ES re-forms from E and S as fast as it breaks down to either E + S or E + P. This steady-state assumption is written as

$$\frac{d[ES]}{dt} = 0 \tag{8.3}$$

in which $t =$ time in minutes. The expression $d[ES]/dt$ also can be written, in terms of rate constants and concentrations for equation 8.1, as the rate of ES formation, $k_1[E][S]$, minus the rate of ES disappearance, $k_2[E][S] + k_3[ES]$. Making the steady-state assumption,

$$\frac{d[ES]}{dt} = k_1[E][S] - k_2[ES] - k_3[ES] = 0 \tag{8.4}$$

Substituting for [E] (which cannot be measured directly) from equation 8.2 gives

$$k_1[S]([E]_0 - [ES]) - k_2[ES] - k_3[ES] = 0$$

Collection of terms gives

$$k_1[S][E]_0 - [ES](k_1[S] + k_2 + k_3) = 0$$

or

$$[ES] = \frac{k_1[S][E]_0}{k_1[S] + k_2 + k_3}$$

Division by $k_1[S]$ gives

$$[ES] = \frac{[E]_0}{1 + \left(\dfrac{k_2 + k_3}{k_1}\right)\dfrac{1}{[S]}} \tag{8.5}$$

The ratio of rate constants, $(k_2 + k_3)/k_1$, is equal to the Michaelis constant, K_M. For many enzymes, k_3 is small relative to k_2, so that K_M is approximately equal to k_2/k_1, which is the dissociation constant (K_S) for the enzyme–substrate complex. Thus, for many enzymes K_M is a measure of the affinity of the enzyme for the substrate. Note, however, that it is incorrect to assume $K_M \simeq K_S$ without knowing that $k_3 \ll k_2$.

The rate of reaction, v, is the increase in [P] as a function of time or $d[P]/dt$, which in turn is equal to $k_3[ES]$ from equation 8.1:

$$v = \frac{d[P]}{dt} = k_3[ES] \tag{8.6}$$

Substituting for [ES] from equation 8.5 gives

$$v = \frac{k_3[E]_0}{1 + K_M/[S]}$$

Because $k_3[E]_0$ equals V_{max} (the value of v when all the enzyme is in the ES form),

$$v = \frac{V_{max}}{1 + K_M/[S]} \tag{8.7}$$

Equation 8.7 is the Michaelis–Menten equation. Verify for yourself that variation of [S] from $\ll K_M$ to $\gg K_M$ affects v qualitatively as shown by the curve in Figure 8.1, and that at very low [S], $v \simeq [S](V_{max}/K_M)$.

V_{max} is often expressed as $k_{cat}[E]_0$, in which k_{cat} is the overall catalytic constant for the reaction, k_3/k_4. For the simple irreversible reaction we have been considering, $k_{cat} \simeq k_3$.

B. The **stoichiometry** of equation 8.1 is S → P (Uni–Uni). Many enzyme-catalyzed reactions involve more complex stoichiometries, such as S → P_1 + P_2 (Uni–Bi), S_1 + S_2 → P (Bi–Uni), S_1 + S_2 → P_1 + P_2 (Bi–Bi), and so on. Fortunately the simple Michaelis–Menten equation (8.7) is approximately valid for these more complex reactions despite the differences in mechanism. Rigorous mathematical treatment of more complex reactions can be found in sources listed in the References section.

8.3 Graphical methods often are used to determine K_M and V_{max} from experimental data.

A. The Michaelis–Menten equation (8.7) can be arranged into various forms that give a straight line when one variable is plotted against the other. These forms have several advantages: V_{max} and K_M can be determined more accurately; departures from Michaelis–Menten kinetics are easily observed as departures from linearity; and the effects of inhibitors can be analyzed more readily.

The three most common straight-line forms of the Michaelis–Menten equation are the double-reciprocal or **Lineweaver–Burk equation,**

$$\frac{1}{v} = \frac{K_M}{V_{max}} \frac{1}{[S]} + \frac{1}{V_{max}} \tag{8.8}$$

the v against $v/[S]$ or **Eadie–Hofstee equation,**

$$v = -K_M \frac{v}{[S]} + V_{max} \tag{8.9}$$

and the [S]/v against [S] or **Hanes–Woolf equation,**

$$\frac{[S]}{v} = \frac{K_M}{V_{max}} + \frac{[S]}{V_{max}} \tag{8.10}$$

Experimentally, the initial rate, v, is measured at each of several substrate concentrations, [S], and the variables are plotted as shown in Figure 8.2. The double-reciprocal or Lineweaver–Burk plot is the most widely used; however, it is statistically the least satisfactory and its use should be discouraged. The plot is [S]/v against [S] is statisti-

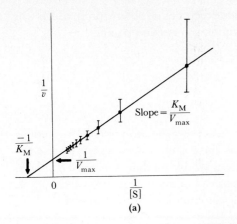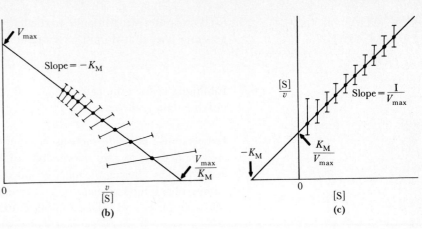

(a)   **(b)**   **(c)**

Figure 8.2
Graphical determinations of K_M and V_{max} using straight-line forms of the Michaelis–Menten equation: **(a)** the double-reciprocal or Lineweaver–Burk plot; **(b)** the v against $v/[S]$ or Eadie–Hofstee plot; and **(c)** the $[S]/v$ against $[S]$ or Hanes–Woolf plot. The error bars represent ± 0.05 V_{max} and illustrate the dramatic effect of small errors, particularly in low v determinations, on the Lineweaver–Burk plot.

cally the most satisfactory of the three, but it is still inferior to the method described in the following section.

B.   A new graphical method, the direct linear plot of Eisenthal and Cornish-Bowden, is strongly preferred for experimental determinations of K_M and V_{max}. For this method, the Michaelis–Menten equation (8.7) is rearranged to relate V_{max} to K_M:

$$V_{max} = v + \frac{v}{[S]} K_M \qquad (8.11)$$

For each pair of experimentally determined $[S]$ and v values, a straight line is drawn with intercept $[S]$ on the K_M axis and v on the V_{max} axis, as shown in Figure 8.3. K_M and V_{max} are indicated by the point at which these lines meet.

   The direct linear plot has three major advantages: (1) No calculations are required; (2) it is based on nonparametric statistics, that is, it yields a median rather than a mean value, and therefore is almost unaffected by a few very bad values; and

Figure 8.3
Graphical determination of K_M and V_{max} using the direct linear plot of Eisenthal and Cornish-Bowden.

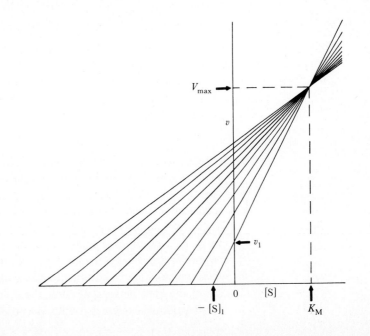

(3) it facilitates recognition of particularly poor experimental observations, which will generate lines that do not pass near the common intersection point.

8.4 Inhibitors reduce the rates of enzyme-catalyzed reactions.

Irreversible inhibitors such as heavy-metal ions are catalytic poisons that reduce enzyme activity to zero. **Reversible inhibitors** form central complexes with the enzyme, thereby altering the reaction kinetics. **Competitive inhibitors** increase K_M; **non-competitive inhibitors** reduce V_{max}; **uncompetitive inhibitors** reduce K_M and V_{max} in the same ratio; and **mixed inhibitors** exhibit combinations of these effects.

1.   A competitive inhibitor, I, competes with the substrate, S, for binding to the active site of the enzyme. The simple (Uni–Uni) reaction sequence of equation 8.1 is thereby altered to

$$I + E + S \underset{k_2}{\overset{k_1}{\rightleftharpoons}} ES \underset{k_4}{\overset{k_3}{\rightleftharpoons}} E + P \tag{8.12}$$
$$k_6 \Big\Uparrow k_5$$
$$EI$$

To derive the Michaelis–Menten equation in the presence of a competitive inhibitor, the expression for the total enzyme concentration $[E]_0$ in equation 8.2 is replaced by

$$[E]_0 = [ES] + [EI] + [E] \tag{8.13}$$

Substituting this expression in the derivation outlined earlier gives, in place of equation 8.7,

$$v = \frac{V_{max}}{1 + \dfrac{K_M}{[S]}\left(1 + \dfrac{[I]}{K_I}\right)} \tag{8.14}$$

where

$$K_I = \frac{k_6}{k_5} = \frac{[E][I]}{[EI]} \tag{8.15}$$

The apparent K_M is thus increased by the factor $(1 + [I]/K_I)$. The effect of competitive inhibition on the graphical determination of K_M and V_{max} is shown in Figure 8.4.

2.   A noncompetitive inhibitor, I, binds to the enzyme in a manner that is independent of [S]. The ESI complex formed when both S and I are bound is inactive. When I is present, some of the enzyme will be complexed as ESI even at saturating [S]. Therefore, V_{max} under these conditions will be lowered, and will be equal to $k_{cat}([E]_0 - [ESI])$.

8.5 Regulatory enzymes change their kinetic properties in response to specific ligands.

A. Regulatory enzymes are always multimeric proteins that usually do not obey classical Michaelis–Menten kinetics. Their kinetic properties, K_M and k_{cat}, can be altered by the specific binding of small molecules called **effectors**. Regulatory enzymes carry specific binding sites of two different kinds: catalytic, where S binds, and regulatory, where effectors bind. Binding of an effector at a regulatory site changes the conformation of the enzyme so as to alter the kinetic properties of the catalytic site.

Regulatory enzymes usually are found at key branch points in metabolic path-

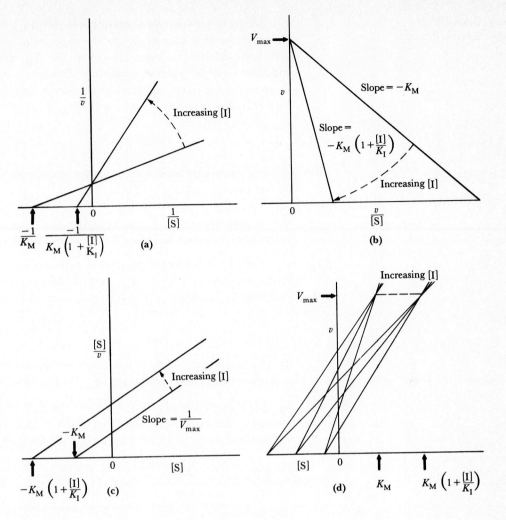

Figure 8.4
Effects of competitive inhibition on **(a)** the Lineweaver–Burk plot; **(b)** the Eadie–Hofstee plot; **(c)** the Hanes–Woolf plot; and **(d)** the direct linear plot.

ways; they allow the cell to regulate the rates of key reactions in response to changes in the concentration of related metabolites. If the substrate of a regulatory enzyme acts as an effector, its effects on rate are called **homotropic.** If another small molecule acts as an effector, its effects are called **heterotropic** or **allosteric,** because the effector may bear no steric resemblance to the substrate.

1. Homotropic effects result in cooperative substrate binding; that is, binding of the first substrate molecules enhances the binding of subsequent substrate molecules. Cooperative binding produces a sigmoidal dependence of v on [S], as shown in Figure 8.5. V_{max} and K_M for such enzymes can be determined empirically, but they are *not* related by the Michaelis–Menten equation (8.7).

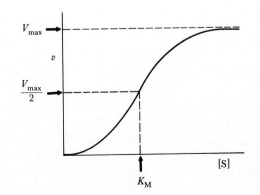

Figure 8.5
The homotropic effect: v is shown as a function of [S] for a reaction catalyzed by a regulatory enzyme that shows homotropic substrate dependence.

2.   Heterotropic effectors alter the curve relating v and [S], as shown in Figure 8.6. In the most common class of regulatory enzymes (Figure 8.6a), activating effectors increase the affinity for substrate (lower the K_M) and decrease the cooperativity of substrate binding, whereas inhibitory effectors do the opposite. V_{max} is not affected. However, there is another class of regulatory enzymes (Figure 8.6b), in which substrate binding is noncooperative and effectors alter k_{cat}, thereby changing V_{max} while K_M remains unchanged.

8.6   A simple two-state model accounts for the kinetics of regulatory enzymes.

A.   The behavior of most regulatory enzymes can be approximated by a simple two-state model (diagrammed in Figure 8.7), which has the following properties:

1.   The enzyme can exist in either of two conformational states, designated T (nonfunctional: high K_M or low k_{cat}) and R (functional: low K_M or high k_{cat}). The two states are in equilibrium at some ratio of concentrations, defined by

$$K_{eq} = \frac{[R]}{[T]} \qquad (8.16)$$

2.   A change in conformational state alters the properties of the binding sites, so that a given effector binds preferentially to one or the other form of the enzyme.

3.   Effectors that bind preferentially to the R form (e_A in Figure 8.7) shift the equilibrium to the right, increasing the fraction of functional molecules and thereby activating the enzyme. Effectors that bind preferentially to the T form shift the equilib-

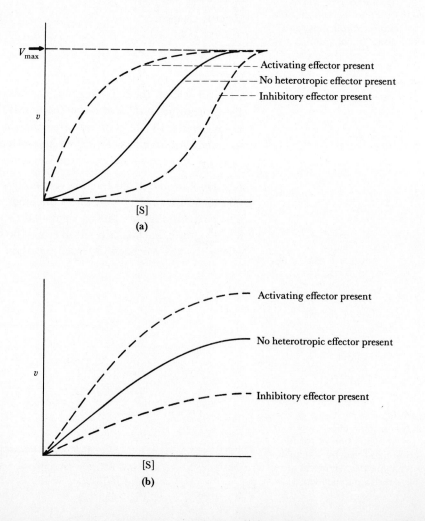

Figure 8.6
Heterotropic effects: v is shown as a function of [S] alone and in the presence of heterotropic activating and inhibiting effectors for **(a)** a K_M-type regulatory enzyme and **(b)** a k_{cat}-type regulatory enzyme.

Figure 8.7
The two-state model for behavior of a regulatory enzyme. The enzyme is represented as a tetramer of identical subunits that can exist in either of two conformational states: T (circles) or R (squares); e_A and e_I represent activating and inhibiting effectors, respectively.

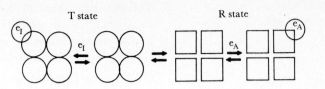

rium to the left, increasing the fraction of nonfunctional molecules and thereby inhibiting the enzyme.

B. Such regulatory effects are not limited to enzymes. The cooperative binding of O_2 to hemoglobin and the effects of H^+ ion on this binding are common examples, respectively, of homotropic and heterotropic regulatory effects on an oxygen-carrier protein.

8.7 Additional concepts and techniques are presented in the Problems section.

A. Integrated forms of the Michaelis–Menten equation. Problems 8.13 and 8.14.

B. Relationship of specific activity to purity of an enzyme preparation. Problem 8.17.

C. Analysis of ligand binding by equilibrium dialysis. Problem 8.20.

References

COMPREHENSIVE TEXTS

Lehninger: Chapter 8
Metzler: Chapter 6

Stryer: Chapter 6
White et al.: Chapter 8

OTHER REFERENCES
A. Cornish-Bowden, *Fundamentals of Enzyme Kinetics,* Butterworths, London, 1979.

Problems

8.1 Answer the following with true or false. If false, explain why.
a. The initial rate of an enzyme-catalyzed reaction is independent of substrate concentration.
b. At saturating levels of substrate, the rate of an enzyme-catalyzed reaction is proportional to the enzyme concentration.
c. The Michaelis constant K_M equals the substrate concentration at which $v = V_{max}/2$.
d. The K_M for a regulatory enzyme varies with enzyme concentration.
e. If enough substrate is added, the normal V_{max} of an enzyme-catalyzed reaction can be attained even in the presence of a noncompetitive inhibitor.
f. The K_M of some enzymes may be altered by the presence of metabolites structurally unrelated to the substrate.
g. The rate of an enzyme-catalyzed reaction in the presence of a rate-limiting concentration of substrate decreases with time.
h. The sigmoidal shape of the v-versus-[S] curve for some regulatory enzymes indicates that the affinity of the enzyme for substrate decreases as the substrate concentration is increased.

8.2 a. The _____ of a reaction is the numerical relationship between substrates and products.
b. The rate constant _____ of an enzyme-catalyzed reaction is a measure of the catalytic efficiency at saturating levels of substrate.
c. _____ inhibitors do not alter the V_{max} of an enzyme-catalyzed reaction.

d. The sigmoidal shape of the v-versus-[S] curve for some regulatory enzymes results from a _____ effect of substrate on the substrate binding sites.

e. For an enzyme whose K_M can be regulated, the presence of an _____ effector increases the level of substrate required to attain a given reaction rate.

8.3 Consider the following reaction:

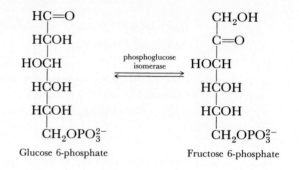

a. What is its stoichiometry?
b. What is the simplest representation of this reaction in terms of S, E, and P?
c. What are S, E, and P in this reaction?

8.4 Concept 8.1, part A, indicates that the K_M of an enzyme can be found empirically by determining the substrate concentration at which half the maximal rate is attained. Using the Michaelis–Menten equation (equation 8.7), show that $v = V_{max}/2$ when $[S] = K_M$.

8.5 A more general form of equation 8.1 is

$$E + S \underset{k_2}{\overset{k_1}{\rightleftharpoons}} ES \underset{k_4}{\overset{k_3}{\rightleftharpoons}} EP \underset{k_6}{\overset{k_5}{\rightleftharpoons}} E + P \qquad (8.17)$$

Consider the essentially irreversible reaction represented by the free-energy diagram in Figure 8.8.

a. Using the letters indicated in the diagram, relate each of the rate constants in equation 8.17 to the energy-level difference that determines it.
b. Which rate constant limits the rate of formation of product?
c. Can k_4, k_5, and k_6 be neglected in the quantitative treatment of the kinetics of this reaction? (See Concept 8.2, part A.)
d. Does $K_M \simeq K_S$ for this enzyme?

8.6 To study the dependence of the rate of an enzyme-catalyzed reaction on the substrate concentration, a constant amount of enzyme is added to a series of reaction mixtures containing different concentrations of substrate (usually expressed in moles per liter). The initial reaction rates are determined by measuring the number of moles, or micromoles, of substrate consumed (or product produced) per minute. Consider such

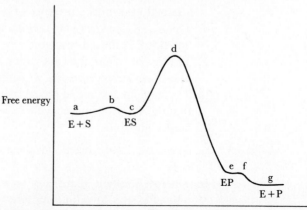

Figure 8.8
Energy diagram for an irreversible, enzyme-catalyzed reaction (Problem 8.5).

an experiment in which the initial rates in Table 8.1 were obtained at the indicated substrate concentrations.

    a. What is V_{max} for this reaction?

    b. Why is v constant above substrate concentrations of $2.0 \times 10^{-3} M$?

    c. What is the concentration of free enzyme at $2.0 \times 10^{-2} M$ substrate concentration?

Table 8.1
Initial Rates at Various Substrate Concentrations for a Hypothetical Enzyme-Catalyzed Reaction (Problem 8.6)

[S](mol/L)	v(μmol/min)	[S](mol/L)	v(μmol/min)
2.0×10^{-1}	60	2.0×10^{-4}	48
2.0×10^{-2}	60	1.5×10^{-4}	45
2.0×10^{-3}	60	1.3×10^{-5}	12

8.7   By means of the experimental procedure described in Problem 8.6, the data in Table 8.2 were obtained for an enzyme in 10 mL reaction mixtures. Use numerical (not graphical) calculations in answering the following questions.

Table 8.2
Initial Rates at Various Substrate Concentrations for a Hypothetical Enzyme-Catalyzed Reaction (Problem 8.7)

[S](mol/L)	v(μmol/min)	[S](mol/L)	v(μmol/min)
5.0×10^{-2}	0.25	5.0×10^{-5}	0.20
5.0×10^{-3}	0.25	5.0×10^{-6}	0.071
5.0×10^{-4}	0.25	5.0×10^{-7}	0.0096

    a. What is V_{max} for this concentration of enzyme?

    b. What is the K_M of this enzyme?

    c. Show that this reaction does or does not follow simple Michaelis–Menten kinetics.

    d. What are the initial rates at $[S] = 1.0 \times 10^{-6} M$ and at $[S] = 1.0 \times 10^{-1} M$?

    e. Calculate the total amount of product made during the first 5 min at $[S] = 2.0 \times 10^{-3} M$. Could you make the same calculation at $[S] = 2.0 \times 10^{-6} M$?

    f. Suppose that the enzyme concentration in each reaction mixture were increased by a factor of 4. What would be the value of K_M? Of V_{max}? What would be the value of v at $[S] = 5.0 \times 10^{-6} M$?

8.8   The K_M of a certain enzyme is $1.0 \times 10^{-5} M$ in a reaction that is described by Michaelis–Menten kinetics. At a substrate concentration of $0.10 M$, the initial rate of the reaction is 37 μmol/min for a certain concentration of enzyme. However, you observe that at a lower substrate concentration of $0.010 M$ the initial reaction rate remains 37 μmol/min.

    a. Using numerical calculations, show why this 10-fold reduction in substrate concentration does not alter the initial reaction rate.

    b. Calculate v as a fraction of V_{max} for $[S] = 0.20 K_M$, $0.50 K_M$, $1.0 K_M$, $2.0 K_M$, $4.0 K_M$, and $10 K_M$.

    c. From the results in part b, sketch the curve relating v/V_{max} to $[S]/K_M$. What is the best range of [S] to use in determining K_M or investigating the dependence of v on [S]?

8.9   Ten reaction mixtures, each containing the same concentration of enzyme, were made up to various substrate concentrations and the initial velocities were determined as shown in Table 8.3. Using the Lineweaver–Burk equation, graphically determine K_M and V_{max}. One of the critical factors in the accuracy of this determination is the proper selection of scales for the ordinate and the abscissa. What range of substrate concentrations is most useful for these determinations? Plot the same data using the direct linear plot. What are the advantages of this plot over the Lineweaver–Burk plot?

Table 8.3
Initial Rates at Various Substrate Concentrations for a Hypothetical Enzyme-Catalyzed Reaction (Problem 8.9)

[S](mol/L)	v(μmol/min)	[S](mol/L)	v(μmol/min)
1.0×10^{-3}	65	2.0×10^{-5}	27
5.0×10^{-4}	63	1.0×10^{-5}	17
1.0×10^{-4}	51	5.0×10^{-6}	9.5
5.0×10^{-5}	42	1.0×10^{-6}	2.2
3.0×10^{-5}	33	5.0×10^{-7}	1.1

8.10 Several reaction mixtures containing equal concentrations of an enzyme were made up to the substrate concentrations shown in Table 8.4 and the initial reaction rates were observed. Using the Eadie–Hofstee equation, graphically determine K_M and V_{max}. What is the advantage of this type of plot over the Lineweaver–Burk plot? Plot the same data using the direct linear plot. What are the advantages of this plot over the Eadie–Hofstee plot?

Table 8.4
Initial Rates at Various Substrate Concentrations for a Hypothetical Enzyme-Catalyzed Reaction (Problem 8.10)

[S](mol/L)	$v(\mu mol/min)$		[S](mol/L)	$v(\mu mol/min)$
4.0×10^{-4}	130		4.0×10^{-5}	53
2.0×10^{-4}	110		2.5×10^{-5}	38
1.0×10^{-4}	89		2.0×10^{-5}	32
5.0×10^{-5}	62			

8.11 Professor Thomas Charles wants to find out if the nucleotide sequences are the same at both ends of some DNA molecules. He plans to determine this by treating his DNA with an enzyme called nibblase, which catalyzes stepwise hydrolysis of nucleotides from opposite strands of a DNA duplex as shown in reaction 1 of Figure 8.9. Then he plans to determine whether the resulting single-stranded ends will base-pair with each other to form circles (reaction 2).

To carry out reaction 1 without destroying all his DNA, he needs to know the precise kinetics of nibbling by the enzyme. Therefore, he sets up and incubates a series of reaction mixtures, each containing the same amount of enzyme and a different concentration of DNA. At various times he takes a sample of each mixture, precipitates the DNA with trichloroacetic acid, and determines the number of picomoles (moles $\times 10^{-12}$, pmol) of free nucleotides that have been released into solution. His data are shown in Table 8.5.

Table 8.5
Nibblase-Catalyzed DNA Degradation as a Function of Time and DNA Concentration (Problem 8.11)

[DNA] (mol total nucleotides/L)	Free nucleotides in solution (pmol) at			
	0 min	10 min	20 min	60 min
1.0×10^{-5}	0.05	5.1	9.8	30
1.0×10^{-6}	0.04	5.0	9.6	28
1.0×10^{-7}	0.06	4.1	8.1	25
1.0×10^{-8}	0.04	1.4	2.9	8.5
1.0×10^{-9}	0.04	0.23	0.42	1.2

a. What is the V_{max} of the reaction in picomoles per minute?
b. Does the reaction obey Michaelis–Menten kinetics?
c. What is the K_M of the enzyme for DNA?
d. If the reaction volume is 1 mL and the average chain length of the DNA strands is 6.0×10^3 nucleotides, how many nucleotides will be nibbled off each strand (average) per minute when the concentration of DNA is 10^{-6} mol nucleotides/L?

8.12 a. From the data in Table 8.6a for a hypothetical enzyme-catalyzed reaction, determine K_M and V_{max} by inspection. Then plot the data using a direct linear plot and determine these constants graphically. Check your results with a calculation. Can you explain the discrepancy in your two determinations?

b. From the data in Table 8.6b for a hypothetical enzyme-catalyzed reaction, determine K_M and V_{max} by the method of Lineweaver and Burk and by the direct linear plot. If there is a discrepancy between the values obtained by the two methods, can you explain it?

Figure 8.9
Degradation of DNA by nibblase and intramolecular base pairing to form circles (Problem 8.11).

Table 8.6
Initial Rates at Various
Substrate Concentrations
for Two Hypothetical
Enzyme-Catalyzed
Reactions (Problem 8.12)

	[S](mol/L)	$v(\mu\text{mol/min})$		[S](mol/L)	$v(\mu\text{mol/min})$
a.	5.0×10^{-4}	125	b.	1×10^{-4}	6
	2.0×10^{-4}	125		2×10^{-4}	11.5
	6.0×10^{-5}	121		5×10^{-4}	38
	4.0×10^{-5}	111		8×10^{-4}	52
	3.0×10^{-5}	96.5		10×10^{-4}	59
	2.0×10^{-5}	62.5		15×10^{-4}	72
	1.6×10^{-5}	42.7		18×10^{-4}	78
	1.0×10^{-5}	13.9		25×10^{-4}	88
	8.0×10^{-6}	7.50			

8.13 Consider a reaction that proceeds via Michaelis–Menten kinetics. Equation 8.7, which relates the initial rate of the reaction to the substrate concentration, can be written in the form

$$v = \frac{V_{max}[S]}{K_M + [S]} \tag{8.18}$$

By definition, $v = -d[S]/dt$.

a. Solve this differential equation by integrating from t_0 to t and obtaining a rate equation that relates t to $[S]_t$ at any time t. The integrations can be looked up in a table of integrals. If you are not familiar with elementary calculus, take the answer on faith, and use it to answer parts b and c.

b. What is the limit of the rate equation from part a when $[S]_0$, the initial value of [S], is very large compared to K_M?

c. What is the limit of the rate equation from part a when $[S]_0$ is very small compared to K_M?

8.14 a. Rearrange the rate equation obtained in Problem 8.13a (equation 8.18) into a form analogous to the Lineweaver–Burk equation that will allow graphical determination of K_M and V_{max}. (Remember from Problem 8.13 that the log term and the difference term behave as dependent variables, and that the best graphical method is one that results in a straight line.) This rearranged expression is valuable experimentally because it allows K_M and V_{max} to be determined from the course of one reaction in which [S] is measured as a function of t, rather than numerous reactions with various initial substrate concentrations.

b. How can the expression obtained in part a be used to determine V_{max} and K_M from the time course of appearance of product?

8.15 a. Five reaction mixtures containing equal concentrations of an enzyme are made up to the substrate concentrations indicated in Table 8.7 and the initial rates of reaction are measured. The experiment then is repeated with an enzyme inhibitor present at a concentration of $2.2 \times 10^{-4}M$ in each reaction mixture. Using Lineweaver–Burk plots of these data, graphically determine K_M for the substrate, K_I for the inhibitor, and V_{max} in the absence and presence of inhibitor (See Figure 8.4). Is this a competitive or noncompetitive inhibitor?

Table 8.7
Initial Rates at Various
Substrate Concentrations
in the Presence and
Absence of an Inhibitor for
an Enzyme-Catalyzed
Reaction (Problem 8.15)

[S](mol/L)	Inhibitor absent $v(\mu\text{mol/min})$	Inhibitor present $(2.2 \times 10^{-4}M)$ $v(\mu\text{mol/min})$
1.0×10^{-4}	28	17
1.5×10^{-4}	36	23
2.0×10^{-4}	43	29
5.0×10^{-4}	65	50
7.5×10^{-4}	74	61

b. Now determine K_M, K_I, and V_{max} using a direct linear plot. What are the relative advantages of the two methods?

8.16   Make a direct linear plot from the data in Table 8.8, which were obtained from an
        experiment similar to that of Problem 8.15.
        a. Is the inhibitor competitive or noncompetitive?
        b. What additional information would you need to determine K_I from your plot?
        c. Outline how you would use your plot to determine K_I (no calculations).

Table 8.8
Initial Rates at Various
Substrate Concentrations
in the Presence and
Absence of an Inhibitor for
an Enzyme-Catalyzed
Reaction (Problem 8.16)

[S](mol/L)	Inhibitor absent $v(\mu mol/min)$	Inhibitor present $v(\mu mol/min)$
0.50×10^{-4}	0.42	0.17
0.67×10^{-4}	0.50	0.20
1.0×10^{-4}	0.60	0.24
1.3×10^{-4}	0.66	0.27
2.7×10^{-4}	0.80	0.32
5.3×10^{-4}	0.88	0.36

8.17   The specific activity (Q) of an enzyme preparation is defined as its catalytic activity,
        in arbitrary units, per milligram of protein. A unit usually is defined as the amount of
        enzyme catalyzing the formation of 1 μmol of product per minute at 25°C under
        optimal assay conditions in the presence of excess substrate. As an enzyme is purified,
        its specific activity obviously increases. Therefore, Q commonly is used as an index of
        relative purity. Q can be used to calculate absolute purity (P), in milligrams of enzyme
        per milligram of total protein, if the molecular weight (M) and the turnover number
        (k_{cat} = molecules of product produced per minute per molecule of enzyme) of the
        enzyme are known. Write an expression for P in terms of Q, M, and k_{cat}.

8.18   An ATPase from Australian dodo liver has been purified to homogeneity and found to
        have a molecular weight of 5×10^4, a K_M for ATP of $1 \times 10^{-4}M$, and a turnover
        number (k_{cat}) of 1×10^4 molecules of ATP hydrolyzed to ADP and inorganic phos-
        phate (P_i) per minute per molecule of enzyme at 37°C. However, at this temperature
        the enzyme is unstable, having a half-life of 6.9 min. (Assume first-order inactivation
        kinetics; at time t, $[E] = [E]_0 e^{-kt}$, in which $[E]_0$ is the initial enzyme concentration
        and k is the first-order inactivation rate constant.) In an experiment with a partially
        pure enzyme preparation obtained during the purification procedure, 10 μg of total
        protein are added to a 1 mL reaction mixture containing 0.02M ATP and incubated
        at 37°C. After 12 hr no further reaction can be detected, and the P_i concentration is
        found to have increased from 0.000M to 0.002M. Calculate what fraction of the
        protein added was represented by the enzyme—that is, how pure the preparation was.

8.19   A competitive inhibitor for the enzyme in Problem 8.18 exhibits a K_I of $1 \times 10^{-3}M$. If
        1 μmol of this substance is present in the 1 mL reaction mixture, by what fraction will
        the initial rate of hydrolysis be decreased relative to the initial rate in the absence of
        inhibitor?

8.20   A ligand is a small molecule such as a substrate or effector that binds to a protein
        molecule. Ligand binding to a protein can be measured by equilibrium dialysis, as
        follows: A solution of the protein is sealed into a dialysis sack (impermeable to the
        protein but permeable to small molecules), which then is suspended in a large volume
        of solution containing the ligand. When the system has reached equilibrium, the sack
        is opened and the concentrations of ligand inside and outside of the sack are deter-
        mined. The difference is a measure of the bound ligand inside the sack.
            Give the concentration in moles per liter of a protein, P, that possesses one bind-
        ing site per molecule for a ligand, L, if analysis by equilibrium dialysis gives the
        following data:

        Concentration of free ligand (L) $= 10^{-5}M$
        Concentration of bound ligand (PL) $= 5 \times 10^{-6}M$
        K_{assoc} for the reaction P + L $\rightleftarrows$ PL $= 10^5$

8.21 For the enzyme aspartate transcarbamylase, succinate acts as a competitive inhibitor of one of the two substrates, aspartate. The dependence of v on [aspartate] is shown in Figure 8.10a. (Assume that the second substrate is present in excess in these experiments and can be ignored.) In the experiment in Figure 8.10b, [aspartate] is held constant at a low level (indicated by the arrow in Figure 8.10a), and increasing amounts of succinate are added. Succinate cannot participate as a substrate in the reaction. Explain these results.

8.22 In response to effector metabolites, some regulatory enzymes alter their k_{cat}, whereas others change their apparent K_M for substrate. Describe general metabolic situations in terms of substrate levels for which (a) the first type of regulatory enzyme clearly would be better suited than the second and (b) the second clearly would be better than the first.

8.23 Consider the following reaction sequence:

$$E + S \underset{k_2}{\overset{k_1}{\rightleftarrows}} ES \underset{k_4}{\overset{k_3}{\rightleftarrows}} E + P$$

At any time t let

[E] = the free-enzyme concentration
[S] = the free-substrate concentration
[ES] = the enzyme–substrate complex concentration
[P] = the product concentration
$[E]_0$ = the total concentration of enzyme present

Assume that the initial substrate concentration $[S]_0 \gg [E]_0$.

a. Set up the differential equations describing the rate of change of [E], [S], [ES], and [P] and the equation expressing the conservation of enzyme.
b. Solve these simultaneous equations for $d[P]/dt$ in terms of k_1, k_2, k_3, k_4, [S], [P], and $[E]_0$. Make the required steady-state assumptions.
c. Under what conditions can this solution be transformed into the standard Michaelis–Menten form? What are K_M and V_{max} in terms of $[E]_0$, k_1, k_2, k_3, and k_4?
d. Because the second step of the reaction is reversible, the product is an inhibitor of the reaction. What kind of inhibition is this? If product is present initially, what is the expression representing K_I for P?
e. By symmetry, what would be the expression representing K_I for S in the reverse reaction (reading the reaction sequence from right to left)?
f. Data from an experiment with the enzyme alkaline phosphatase, which obeys these kinetics, are

$[E]_0 = 6.6 \times 10^{-9} M$ (assume one active site per molecule)
$K_M = 3.7 \times 10^{-5} M$ for the substrate p-nitrophenylphosphate (NPP)
$V_{max} = 1.8 \times 10^{-5}$ mol/min
$K_I = 1.8 \times 10^{-5} M$ for the product inorganic phosphate (P_i)

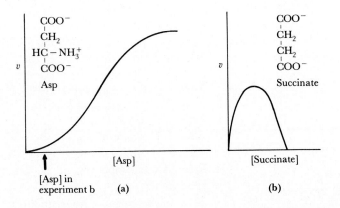

Figure 8.10
Effects of aspartate and succinate concentrations on the rate of catalysis by aspartate transcarbamylase (Problem 8.21).

Calculate k_1, k_2, k_3, and k_4, given that the reaction sequence is

$$\text{NPP} + \text{E} \underset{k_2}{\overset{k_1}{\rightleftharpoons}} \text{ES} \underset{k_4}{\overset{k_3}{\rightleftharpoons}} \text{P}_i + \text{NP} \ (p\text{-nitrophenol}) + \text{E}$$

and that k_2/k_1 or $K_S = 1.0 \times 10^{-6}M$.

g. What empirical data could be obtained to determine the rate constants without knowing the value of K_S?

☆ 8.24   For an enzyme obeying classical kinetics, in the presence of a substrate at concentration $[S] = K_M$ and a competitive inhibitor at concentration $[I] = K_I$, the initial reaction rate (v) will be

   a. $\frac{2}{3}V_{max}$
   b. $\frac{1}{3}V_{max}$
   c. $\frac{1}{2}V_{max}$
   d. $\frac{1}{4}V_{max}$

☆ 8.25   a. For an enzyme that obeys simple Michaelis–Menten kinetics, what is the V_{max} in micromoles per minute if $v = 35 \ \mu mol/min$ when $[S] = K_M$?
   b. What is the K_M of this enzyme if $v = 40 \ \mu mol/min$ when $[S] = 2 \times 10^{-5}M$?
   c. If I is a competitive inhibitor of the enzyme with a K_I of $4 \times 10^{-5}M$, what will be the value of v when $[S] = 3 \times 10^{-2}M$ and $[I] = 3 \times 10^{-5}M$?
   d. If I is a noncompetitive inhibitor, what will be the value of v if K_I, $[S]$, and $[I]$ are the same as in part c?
   e. Roughly sketch the curves relating v to $[S]$ for this enzyme (1) in the absence of inhibitor, (2) in the presence of the competitive inhibitor (as in part c), and (3) in the presence of the noncompetitive inhibitor (as in part d). Indicate V_{max}, K_M, and the approximate value of $[S]$ at which the rate will be half-maximal for each curve.

☆ 8.26   A biochemist studying the properties of a newly isolated metabolic enzyme obtains the following rate data during kinetic experiments in the absence and presence of two different inhibitors, A and B, one a substrate analogue and the other an alkylating agent:

$[S](mol/L)$	$v(\mu mol/min)$	$v(\mu mol/min)$ with A present	$v(\mu mol/min)$ with B present
5.0×10^{-4}	1.25	0.74	0.48
2.5×10^{-4}	0.87	0.45	0.33
1.7×10^{-4}	0.67	0.32	0.25
1.2×10^{-4}	0.54	0.25	0.20
1.0×10^{-4}	0.45	0.21	0.17

The concentration of inhibitor A is $5 \times 10^{-4}M$; that of inhibitor B is $3.2 \times 10^{-6}M$.
   a. Determine the K_M and V_{max} for this enzyme.
   b. Which inhibitor is which?
   c. What are the inhibition constants for A and B?

Answers

8.1   a. False. The rate, v, is independent of $[S]$ only at levels of $S \gg K_M$.
   b. True. Here $v = V_{max} = k_{cat}[E]_0$.
   c. True
   d. False. The value of K_M is independent of enzyme concentration for almost all enzymes.
   e. False. A noncompetitive inhibition cannot be overcome by increasing substrate concentration.
   f. True. These enzymes are regulatory.

g. True. As substrate is used up, the rate decreases.

h. False. The initial increasing slope of the curve shows that binding of the first substrate molecules *increases* the affinity of the enzyme for subsequent substrate molecules.

8.2 a. stoichiometry

b. k_3 (or k_{cat})

c. Competitive

d. homotropic

e. inhibitory

8.3 a. 1 glucose 6-phosphate $\rightleftarrows$ 1 fructose 6-phosphate or $S \rightleftarrows P$

b. $E + S \underset{k_2}{\overset{k_1}{\rightleftarrows}} ES \underset{k_4}{\overset{k_3}{\rightleftarrows}} E + P$

Notice that k_4 must be included.

c. S = glucose 6-phosphate

E = phosphoglucose isomerase

P = fructose 6-phosphate

8.4 The Michaelis–Menten equation is

$$v = \frac{V_{max}}{1 + K_M/[S]} \tag{8.7}$$

When $[S] = K_M$, the equation becomes

$$v = \frac{V_{max}}{1 + (K_M/K_M)}$$

or

$$v = \frac{V_{max}}{2}$$

8.5 a. The rate constant for each step is inversely related to the difference between the energy level of the reactants and the highest energy barrier between the reactants and the products of that step. In terms of the letters in Figure 8.8,

k_1 is determined by b − a

k_2 is determined by b − c

k_3 is determined by d − c

k_4 is determined by d − e

k_5 is determined by f − e

k_6 is determined by f − g

b. Rate constant k_3 corresponds to a much higher energy barrier than the other forward rate constants, and therefore must limit the rate of product formation.

c. Because k_4 is very small relative to k_3, this reaction is essentially irreversible and k_4 can be neglected. Since k_5 is greater than k_6 and much, much greater than k_3, EP is broken down to E + P as fast as it forms. The ratio k_1/k_2 (the association constant for ES) is much larger than k_6/k_5 (the association constant for EP). Therefore, P does not compete significantly with S for the enzyme, and k_5 and k_6 can be neglected. For most enzymes the more general equation 8.17 reduces to equation 8.1 and can be treated quantitatively as described in Concept 8.2, part A.

d. Because k_3 is small relative to k_2, $K_M \simeq K_S$ for this enzyme. Therefore, K_M is a measure of affinity for substrate.

8.6 a. $V_{max} = 60$ μmol/min.

b. The rate v is constant because it has reached V_{max}; the enzyme is saturated with substrate.

c. The concentration of free enzyme is negligible because all the enzyme is in the ES form.

8.7 a. $V_{max} = 0.25$ μmol/min.

b. For a reaction obeying Michaelis–Menten kinetics, V_{max} and K_M are simply constants relating v to [S] according to equation 8.7. K_M can be calculated by substituting V_{max} and any pair of v and [S] values at $v < V_{max}$ from Table 8.2 into equation 8.7. For example, at $[S] = 5.0 \times 10^{-5}M$ and $v = 0.20$ μmol/min the equation becomes

$$0.20 = \frac{0.25}{1 + (K_M/5.0 \times 10^{-5})}$$

$$1 + \frac{K_M}{5.0 \times 10^{-5}} = \frac{0.25}{0.20} = 1.25$$

$$K_M = (0.25)(5.0 \times 10^{-5}) = 1.25 \times 10^{-5}M$$

c. If the reaction follows simple Michaelis–Menten kinetics, then equation 8.7 should relate v to [S] over a wide range of [S]. This can be tested by determining whether the equation yields the same value of K_M at several different values of [S] and $v < V_{max}$. Under the conditions of this problem, the same value, $K_M = 1.3 \times 10^{-5}M$, is obtained at $[S] = 5.0 \times 10^{-6}M$, $v = 0.071$ μmol/min and at $[S] = 5.0 \times 10^{-7}M$, $v = 0.0096$ μmol/min. Therefore, Michaelis–Menten kinetics are obeyed.

d. At $[S] = 1.0 \times 10^{-6}M$,

$$v = \frac{0.25}{1 + \dfrac{1.3 \times 10^{-5}}{1.0 \times 10^{-6}}} = \frac{0.25}{1 + 13} = 0.018 \ \mu\text{mol/min}$$

At $[S] = 1.0 \times 10^{-1}M$, $v = V_{max} = 0.25$ μmol/min.

e. At $[S] = 2.0 \times 10^{-3}M$, $v = V_{max} = 0.25$ μmol/min. Because 0.25 μmol is much less than the amount of substrate present $(2.0 \times 10^{-3} \text{ mol/L} \times 10^{-2} \text{ L} \times 10^6 \ \mu\text{mol/mol} = 20 \ \mu\text{mol})$, the reaction can proceed for 5 min without significantly changing the substrate concentration. Thus,

$$0.25 \ \mu\text{mol/min} \times 5 \ \text{min} = 1.25 \ \mu\text{mol}$$

At $[S] = 2.0 \times 10^{-6}M$,

$$v = \frac{0.25}{1 + \dfrac{1.3 \times 10^{-5}}{2.0 \times 10^{-6}}} = \frac{0.25}{1 + 6.5} = \frac{0.25}{7.5} = 0.033 \ \mu\text{mol/min}$$

During 5 min at this rate, 0.033 μmol/min $\times$ 5 min $= 0.17$ μmol of product would be produced. However, this value exceeds the total amount of substrate present $(2.0 \times 10^{-6} \text{ mol/L} \times 10^{-2} \text{ L} \times 10^6 \ \mu\text{mol/mol} = 0.020 \ \mu\text{mol})$. Clearly, during the 5 min reaction, [S] and therefore v would decrease significantly. Calculation of the exact amount of product made would require integration of a differential equation; this amount obviously cannot exceed 0.020 μmol.

f. K_M is independent of enzyme concentration, because a change in [E] does not affect the three rate constants, k_1, k_2, and k_3. Hence K_M would remain equal to $1.25 \times 10^{-5}M$.*

Because $V_{max} = k_{cat}[E]_0$, increasing the enzyme concentration by a factor of 4 increases V_{max} by a factor of 4. Therefore, $V_{max} = 1.0$ μmol/min.
At $[S] = 5.0 \times 10^{-6}M$,

$$v = \frac{1.0}{1 + \dfrac{1.3 \times 10^{-5}}{5.0 \times 10^{-6}}} = \frac{1}{1 + 2.6} = \frac{1}{3.6} = 0.28 \ \mu\text{mol/min}$$

8.8 a. Because both substrate concentrations are well above K_M, you can assume that $V_{max} = 37$ μmol/min. Then

$$v = \frac{37}{1 + \dfrac{1.0 \times 10^{-5}}{1.0 \times 10^{-2}}} = \frac{37}{1 + 1.0 \times 10^{-3}} \simeq 37 \ \mu\text{mol/min}$$

Therefore, at $[S] = 1.0 \times 10^{-2}M$, v still is equal to V_{max}.

b. From equation 8.7, the following relationships can be calculated:

[S]	v		[S]	v
$0.20\ K_M$	$0.17\ V_{max}$		$2.0\ K_M$	$0.67\ V_{max}$
$0.50\ K_M$	$0.33\ V_{max}$		$4.0\ K_M$	$0.80\ V_{max}$
$1.0\ \ K_M$	$0.50\ V_{max}$		$10\ \ \ K_M$	$0.91\ V_{max}$

From the plot of these values shown in Figure 8.11, you can see that the best range of [S] for studying the dependence of v on [S] is in the neighborhood of K_M or below it, because changes in [S] below K_M cause greater changes in v than do changes in [S] above K_M. Therefore, when using graphical methods to determine K_M and V_{max}, several measurements should be made at [S] well below K_M.

8.9   The variables in the Lineweaver–Burk equation are the reciprocals 1/[S] and 1/v. These can be calculated from the values in Table 8.3 for [S] and v. The Lineweaver–Burk plot of these figures, shown in Figure 8.12a, gives

$$V_{max} = \frac{1}{0.015} = 67\ \mu mol/min \text{ (the reciprocal of the y-intercept)}$$

$$K_M = \frac{-1}{-3.3 \times 10^{-4}} = 3.0 \times 10^{-5} M \text{ (the negative reciprocal of the x-intercept)}$$

The most useful substrate concentrations are those in the neighborhood of K_M (from $5K_M$ to $0.1K_M$).

The direct linear plot is shown in Figure 8.12b. Notice that the data in Table 8.3 can be used directly, that it is easier to select the scales for the ordinate and abscissa, and that the K_M and V_{max} can be read directly from the plot without further calculation. On the basis of convenience alone, the direct plot is preferable to the Lineweaver–Burk plot.

8.10   To construct an Eadie–Hofstee plot it is necessary to calculate v/[S] values from the data in Table 8.4. The units can be left as they are, because you wish to obtain K_M in moles per liter and V_{max} in micromoles per minute. Analysis of an Eadie–Hofstee plot of these data (Figure 8.13a) gives

$$V_{max} = 160\ \mu mol/min$$

$$\frac{V_{max}}{K_M} = 20 \times 10^5$$

$$K_M = 8.0 \times 10^{-5} M$$

The Eadie–Hofstee plot can display data over a greater range of substrate concentrations. Thus data that appear linear in a Lineweaver–Burk plot sometimes show significant departures from linearity with the Eadie–Hofstee plot.

The direct linear plot is shown in Figure 8.13b. The advantages of the direct

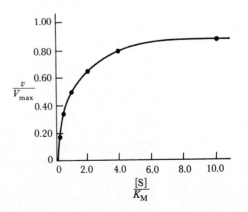

Figure 8.11
The relationship between v as a fraction of V_{max} and [S] as a multiple of K_M (Answer 8.8).

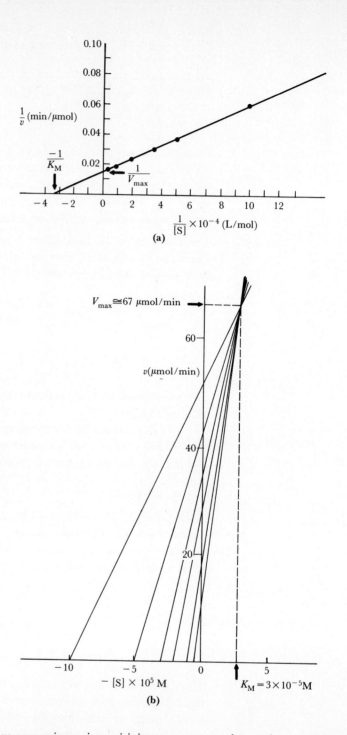

Figure 8.12
Plots from the data of Table 8.3 (Answer 8.9): **(a)** Lineweaver–Burk plot; **(b)** direct linear plot.

linear plot are convenience, insensitivity to erroneous data points, and direct readout of K_M and V_{max}. The Eadie–Hofstee plot has the advantages of greater range as well as indicating whether Michaelis–Menten kinetics are obeyed (see Problem 8.11).

8.11   First you must calculate the rates of degradation corresponding to the various DNA concentrations. From inspection of the data in Table 8.5 you can see that digestion is linear with time to 60 min in each reaction. (Note that the 0 min background level of free nucleotides must be subtracted from the values for later times.) Therefore, each rate can be calculated as the mean number of picomoles released per minute for three time points, as shown in Table 8.9. Because of the range of [S], the best method of analysis is probably an Eadie–Hofstee plot as explained in Answer 8.10, although a direct linear plot also could be used. Values of $v/[DNA]$ for the Eadie–Hofstee plot are given in Table 8.9. From this plot (Figure 8.14a) you should find the following:

a. $V_{max} = 0.50$ pmol/min.

Table 8.9
Analysis of DNA
Degradation Data
(Answer 8.11)

[DNA] (μM)	v (pmol/min)	$\dfrac{v}{[DNA]}$
10	$\left(\dfrac{5.1-0.05}{10}+\dfrac{9.8-0.05}{20}+\dfrac{30-0.05}{60}\right)\dfrac{1}{3}=0.50$	0.050
1.0	$\left(\dfrac{5.0-0.04}{10}+\dfrac{9.6-0.04}{20}+\dfrac{28-0.04}{60}\right)\dfrac{1}{3}=0.48$	0.48
0.10	$\left(\dfrac{4.1-0.06}{10}+\dfrac{8.1-0.06}{20}+\dfrac{25-0.06}{60}\right)\dfrac{1}{3}=0.41$	4.1
0.010	$\left(\dfrac{1.4-0.04}{10}+\dfrac{2.9-0.04}{20}+\dfrac{8.5-0.04}{60}\right)\dfrac{1}{3}=0.14$	14
0.0010	$\left(\dfrac{0.23-0.04}{10}+\dfrac{0.42-0.04}{20}+\dfrac{1.2-0.04}{60}\right)\dfrac{1}{3}=0.019$	19

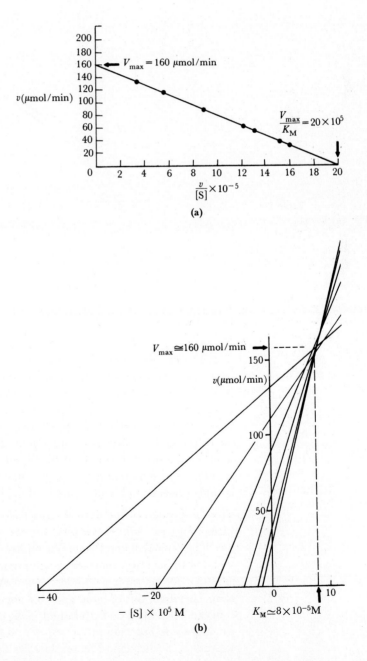

Figure 8.13
Plots from the data of Table 8.4
(Answer 8.10): **(a)** Eadie–
Hofstee plot; **(b)** direct linear
plot.

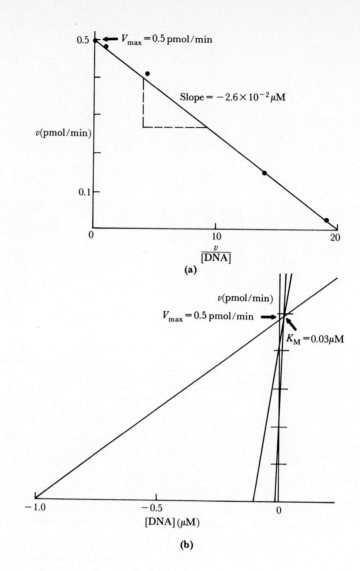

Figure 8.14
Plots from the data of Table 8.9
(Answer 8.11): **(a)** Eadie–
Hofstee plot; **(b)** direct linear
plot.

b. The reaction obeys Michaelis–Menten kinetics, because the points fall on a straight line.

c. $K_M = 2.6 \times 10^{-8}M$.

The same values are obtained from the direct linear plot (Figure 8.14b). The scales are less accurate, but the K_M is easier to estimate by inspection.

d. A DNA concentration of 10^{-6} mol nucleotides/L corresponds to 6×10^{17} nucleotides/L [6×10^{23} nucleotides/mol (Avogadro's number) $\times 10^{-6}M$], 6×10^{14} nucleotides/mL, or 10^{11} strands of 6×10^3 nucleotides/strand in the 1 mL reaction mixture. From Table 8.9 the rate of nibbling at this DNA concentration is about 0.5 pmol/min. This value corresponds to 5×10^{-13} mol nucleotides/min or 3×10^{11} nucleotides/min (5×10^{-13} mol/min $\times 6 \times 10^{23}$ nucleotides/mol). Because there are 10^{11} DNA strands present, each will be nibbled at the average rate of 3 nucleotides/min.

8.12 a. From inspection of the data, $V_{max} = 125$ μmol/min. Regardless of reaction mechanism, K_M is defined empirically as the substrate concentration at which $v = V_{max}/2 = 62.5$ μmol/min. Therefore, $K_M = 2 \times 10^{-5}M$ from the data given.

The direct linear plot is shown in Figure 8.15. Obviously the lines obtained at low substrate concentrations do not intersect those obtained at high substrate concentration. Therefore, this enzyme does not obey Michaelis–Menten kinetics. This conclusion can be checked by calculations using equation 8.7 and the value of K_M obtained by inspection. For example, at $[S] = 1 \times 10^{-5}M$, v should be given by the following expression if Michaelis–Menten kinetics apply:

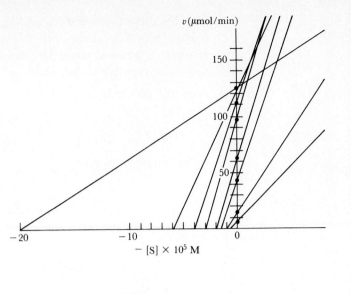

Figure 8.15
Direct linear plot of the data in Table 8.6a (Answer 8.12).

$$v = \frac{125}{1 + \dfrac{2 \times 10^{-5}}{1 \times 10^{-5}}} = 41.7 \ \mu\text{mol/min}$$

However, the observed value is 13.9 μmol/min, confirming the conclusion that Michaelis–Menten kinetics do not apply to this reaction. If you plot v against [S], you will see why. The same conclusion also could be drawn from an Eadie–Hofstee plot, in which v would not be linearly related to v/[S]. However this plot involves more calculations and therefore is less convenient.

b. Calculate 1/[S] and 1/v from the data in Table 8.6b, and graph the data. The correct Lineweaver–Burk plot and a very common error are shown in Figure 8.16a. The error arises because low values of [S] are the most heavily weighted, yet they are the most likely to contain experimental errors. The data given in Table 8.6b are imprecise for [S] values of 1×10^{-4} and $2 \times 10^{-4}M$. The expected values for v would be 9 (instead of 6) and 18.5 (instead of 11) μmol/min. Similar errors at low substrate concentrations are common and can lead to gross errors in K_M and V_{max}: In this case, 40 and 250 instead of 12 and 130, respectively.

A direct linear plot of the same data is shown in Figure 8.16b. The two imprecise data points clearly stand out and would alert the experimenters. It is also apparent by inspection that v has not reached saturating values.

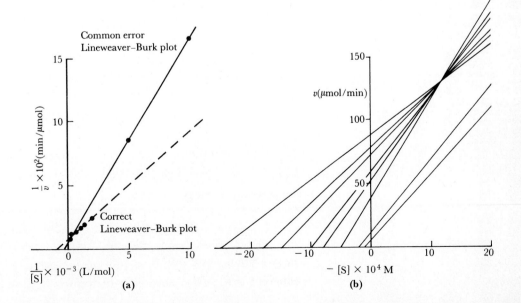

Figure 8.16
Plots from the data of Table 8.6b (Answer 8.12): **(a)** Lineweaver–Burk plot; **(b)** direct linear plot.

The correct values of K_M and V_{max} are $12 \times 10^{-4} M$ and $130 \ \mu mol/min$, respectively. There is no discrepancy between the two methods if each is used correctly. However, it is easy to abuse the Lineweaver–Burk method; the direct linear plot is not only more convenient, but easier to understand intuitively.

8.13 a. From the problem,

$$-\frac{d[S]}{dt} = \frac{V_{max}[S]}{K_M + [S]}$$

Collection of terms gives

$$V_{max} \, dt = -\frac{K_M + [S]}{[S]} d[S] = -\frac{K_M}{[S]} d[S] - d[S]$$

Integration yields

$$V_{max} \int_{t_0}^{t} dt = -K_M \int_{[S]_0}^{[S]} \frac{d[S]}{[S]} - \int_{[S]_0}^{[S]} d[S]$$

$$V_{max} t \Big|_{t=0}^{t=t} = -K_M \ln [S] \Big|_{[S]_0}^{[S]_t} - [S] \Big|_{[S]_0}^{[S]_t}$$

$$V_{max} t = -K_M \ln \frac{[S]_t}{[S]_0} - ([S]_t - [S]_0)$$

Rearrangement gives

$$V_{max} t = K_M \ln \frac{[S]_0}{[S]_t} + ([S]_0 - [S]_t)$$

or

$$V_{max} t = 2.3 K_M \log \frac{[S]_0}{[S]_t} + ([S]_0 - [S]_t) \tag{8.19}$$

b. When $[S]_0 \gg K_M$, the second term of equation 8.19 will be large relative to the first. Consequently,

$$V_{max} t \simeq [S]_0 - [S]_t$$

Thus the amount of substrate consumed (or product produced) under conditions of substrate excess is approximated by $V_{max} t$.

c. When $[S]_0 \ll K_M$, then the first term of equation 8.19 will be large relative to the second; consequently,

$$V_{max} t \simeq 2.3 K_M \log \frac{[S]_0}{[S]_t}$$

Converting this to exponential form gives an expression for the fraction of substrate remaining at time t:

$$\frac{[S]_t}{[S]_0} \simeq e^{-V_{max} t / K_M}$$

Under these conditions, the fraction of substrate remaining after a given time t is independent of the initial substrate concentration.

8.14 The best expression is

$$\frac{2.3}{t} \log \frac{[S]_0}{[S]_t} = -\frac{1}{K_M} \left(\frac{[S]_0 - [S]_t}{t} \right) + \frac{V_{max}}{K_M} \tag{8.20}$$

a. When $(2.3/t) \log ([S]_0/[S]_t)$ is plotted against $([S]_0 - [S]_t)/t$ the slope is $-(1/K_M)$; the y-intercept is V_{max}/K_M; and the x-intercept is V_{max}, as shown in Figure 8.17.

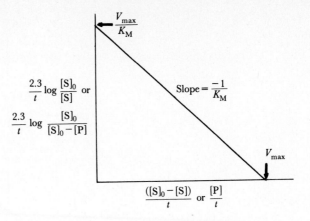

Figure 8.17
Plot of the integrated Michaelis–Menten equation (Answer 8.14).

b. Because $[P]_t = [S]_0 - [S]_t$, equation 8.20 can be rewritten in the form

$$\frac{2.3}{t} \log \frac{[S]_0}{[S]_0 - [P]_t} = -\frac{1}{K_M} \frac{[P]_t}{t} + \frac{V_{max}}{K_M}$$

and used to determine K_M and V_{max} from the time course of product appearance (Figure 8.17).

8.15 a. For the Lineweaver–Burk plot, compute values for $1/[S]$, $1/v$ without inhibitor, and $1/v$ with inhibitor for each substrate concentration. Then plot $1/v$ versus $1/[S]$. You should obtain the results shown in Figure 8.18a. From these results you can calculate

$$K_M = \frac{-1}{-3.7 \times 10^3 \text{ L/mol}} = 2.7 \times 10^{-4} M$$

$$-1/K_M \left(1 + \frac{[I]}{K_I}\right) = -2.0 \times 10^3 \text{ L/mol}$$

$$K_I = \frac{2.0 \times 10^3 K_M [I]}{1 - 2.0 \times 10^3 K_M} M$$

$$K_I = \frac{(2.0 \times 10^3)(2.7 \times 10^{-4})(2.2 \times 10^{-4})}{1 - (2.0 \times 10^3)(2.7 \times 10^{-4})}$$

$$K_I = 2.6 \times 10^{-4} M$$

$$V_{max} = \frac{1}{0.01 \text{ min/}\mu\text{mol}} = 100 \text{ }\mu\text{mol/min}$$

Because V_{max} is the same in the presence or absence of this inhibitor, it must be a competitive inhibitor.

b. To determine kinetic parameters by the direct linear method, graph the data in Table 8.7 as shown in Figure 8.18b. By inspection, K_M is $2.7 \times 10^{-4} M$. V_{max} in the presence or absence of the inhibitor is the same (100 μmol/min); this result is diagnostic for a competitive inhibitor. The K_M apparent in the presence of the inhibitor is $5 \times 10^{-4} M$, from equation 8.20:

$$K_M^{apparent} = K_M \left(1 + \frac{[I]}{K_I}\right)$$

Substituting,

$$(5 \times 10^{-4}) = 2.7 \times 10^{-4} \left(1 + \frac{2.2 \times 10^{-4}}{K_I}\right)$$

$$K_I = 2.6 \times 10^{-4} M$$

The direct linear plot is far easier to use, involving no calculations. The values of K_M and V_{max} can be read directly and K_I can be easily calculated. The only advantage of the Lineweaver–Burk plot is its familiarity to enzymologists through common use.

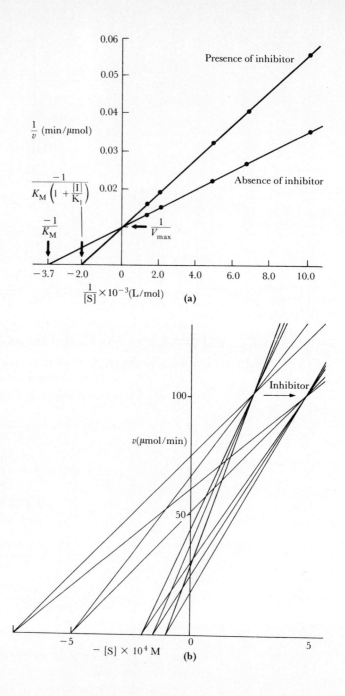

Figure 8.18
Plots from the data of Table 8.7
(Answer 8.15): **(a)** Lineweaver–
Burk plot; **(b)** direct linear plot.

8.16   A direct linear plot of the data in Table 8.8 is shown in Figure 8.19.

a. By inspection V_{max} is reduced by the inhibitor, whereas K_{M} is not. Therefore, the inhibitor is noncompetitive.

b. You would need to know the concentration of inhibitor [I] at which the rates in the third column were measured.

c. The apparent V_{max} ($V_{\text{max}}^{\text{apparent}}$) in the presence of a noncompetitive inhibitor is given by

$$V_{\text{max}}^{\text{apparent}} = \frac{V_{\text{max}}}{1 + \dfrac{[I]}{K_{\text{I}}}}$$

which can be derived from the information given in Concept 8.4. [Compare this equation to equation 8.14. A competitive inhibitor reduces K_{M} by the factor $(1 + [I]/K_{\text{I}})$, whereas a noncompetitive inhibitor reduces V_{max} by the same factor.] This expression can be rearranged to give

$$K_I = \frac{[I]}{(V_{max}/V_{max}^{apparent}) - 1}$$

from which K_I can be computed if $[I]$ is known. V_{max} and $V_{max}^{apparent}$ are obtained from the direct linear plot.

8.17

$$P\left(\frac{\text{mg enzyme}}{\text{mg protein}}\right) = \frac{Q\left(\dfrac{\mu\text{mol product}}{\min \times \text{mg protein}}\right) \times M\left(\dfrac{\mu\text{g enzyme}}{\mu\text{mol enzyme}}\right)}{1000\left(\dfrac{\mu\text{g enzyme}}{\text{mg enzyme}}\right) \times k_{cat}\left(\dfrac{\mu\text{mol product}}{\min \times \mu\text{mol enzyme}}\right)}$$

or

$$P = \frac{QM}{1000\ k_{cat}}\ \text{mg enzyme/mg protein}$$

8.18   First determine the inactivation rate constant, k, from the half-life of the enzyme:

$$[E]_{6.9\,min} = \tfrac{1}{2}[E]_0 = [E]_0 e^{-6.9k}$$

$$e^{-6.9k} = 0.5$$

Conversion to logarithmic form gives

$$-6.9k = \ln 0.5 = -0.69$$

$$k = 0.1\ \text{min}^{-1}$$

The substrate, ATP, is present at a concentration well above the K_M of $1 \times 10^{-4} M$ and therefore is in excess. Thus the rate of appearance of product, $d[P]/dt$, during the incubation is given by

$$\frac{d[P]}{dt} = V_{max} = k_{cat}\,[E]$$

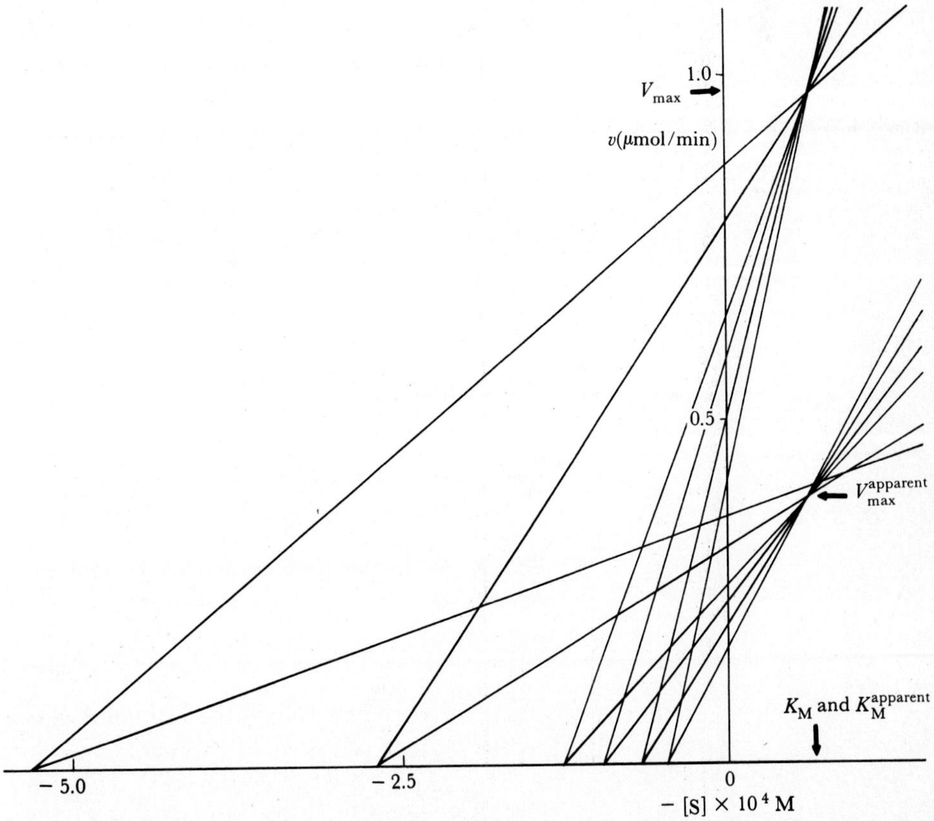

Figure 8.19
Direct linear plot of the data in Table 8.8 (Answer 8.16).

in which k_{cat} is the turnover number and $[E] = [E]_0 e^{-kt}$. Hence

$$\frac{d[P]}{dt} = k_{cat}[E]_0 e^{-kt}$$

To determine the amount of product produced over a period of t min, this expression must be integrated from 0 to t:

$$[P] = k_{cat}[E]_0 \int_0^t e^{-kt}\, dt$$

From a table of integrals:

$$[P] = k_{cat}[E]_0 \frac{-(e^{-kt} - 1)}{k}$$

or

$$[P] = \frac{k_{cat}[E]_0}{k}(1 - e^{-kt})$$

Note that in the limit as t becomes large, e^{-kt} becomes $\ll 1$, so that

$$[P] \simeq \frac{k_{cat}[E]_0}{k}$$

This approximation is clearly valid for the long incubation time of 12 hr ($t = 720$ min) in the problem. From the data given,

$$[E]_0 = \frac{k[P]}{k_{cat}}$$

$$= \frac{(0.1\ \text{min}^{-1})\,(2\ \mu\text{mol product/mL})}{1 \times 10^4\ \mu\text{mol product/min per }\mu\text{mol enzyme}}$$

$$= 2 \times 10^{-5}\ \mu\text{mol enzyme/mL present in the 1 mL reaction mixture}$$

The molecular weight of the enzyme is $5 \times 10^4\ \mu\text{g}/\mu\text{mol}$, therefore, the weight of enzyme added to the reaction was 1 μg. Because 10 μg total protein was added, the enzyme preparation is 10% pure.

8.19   The initial rates in the absence and presence of inhibitor can be calculated using equations 8.7 and 8.14, respectively.
Without inhibitor:

$$v = \frac{V_{max}}{1 + \dfrac{K_M}{[S]}} = \frac{V_{max}}{1 + \dfrac{1 \times 10^{-4}}{2 \times 10^{-2}}} = \frac{V_{max}}{1.005}$$

With inhibitor:

$$v = \frac{V_{max}}{1 + \dfrac{K_M}{[S]}\left(1 + \dfrac{[I]}{K_I}\right)} \tag{8.14}$$

Because $[I]$ in the problem equals 1 μmol/mL $= 1 \times 10^{-3}M = K_I$, equation 8.14 reduces to

$$v = \frac{V_{max}}{1 + 2\dfrac{K_M}{[S]}}$$

$$= \frac{V_{max}}{1.01}$$

Thus the fractional decrease in v is negligible:

$$v = \frac{V_{max}}{1.01} \times \frac{1.005}{V_{max}} = \frac{1.005}{1.01} = 0.995$$

8.20   The binding reaction can be written as

$$P + L \underset{k_2}{\overset{k_1}{\rightleftarrows}} PL$$

in which

$$K_{assoc} = \frac{k_1}{k_2} = 10^5 \text{ L/mol}$$

At $d[P]/dt = 0$ (i.e., at equilibrium)

$$\frac{d[P]}{dt} = -[P][L]k_1 + [PL]k_2 = 0$$

$$[P][L]k_1 = [PL]k_2$$

$$[P] = \frac{[PL]k_2}{[L]k_1} = \frac{[PL]}{[L]K_{assoc}}$$

$$[P] = \frac{5 \times 10^{-6}}{(1 \times 10^{-5})(10^5)}$$

$$[P] = 5 \times 10^{-6} M$$

8.21   The sigmoidal shape of the curve in the experiment in Figure 8.10a shows that the enzyme is regulatory, and that aspartate has a homotropic effect on its own binding. The result in the experiment in Figure 8.10b occurs because succinate, as an analogue of aspartate, has a similar effect on the enzyme; succinate binding at catalytic sites shifts more enzyme molecules into the R state, thereby increasing the affinity of the remaining catalytic sites on these molecules for aspartate and increasing the rate of reaction. However, because succinate competitively inhibits the binding of aspartate, the reaction rate ceases to increase and then drops sharply as the succinate concentration is raised.

8.22   A change in the k_{cat} of an enzyme alters its catalytic rate at all substrate concentrations, but the effect is most profound at saturating levels of substrate, where rate is independent of K_M. (Note that an increase in k_{cat} *increases* K_M, the value of [S] at which the enzyme operates at half-maximal efficiency.) A change in K_M alone affects the rate only at substrate concentrations in the range of K_M, and not at all at saturating substrate levels. Thus k_{cat}-type regulatory enzymes are clearly best suited for reactions in which the level of substrate is usually saturating, and K_M-type regulatory enzymes are useful only for reactions in which the level of substrate is rate-limiting.

8.23 a.
$$\frac{d[E]}{dt} = -k_1[E][S] + (k_2 + k_3)[ES] - k_4[E][P] \tag{8.21}$$

$$\frac{d[S]}{dt} = -k_1[E][S] + k_2[ES] \tag{8.22}$$

$$\frac{d[ES]}{dt} = k_1[E][S] - (k_2 + k_3)[ES] + k_4[E][P] \tag{8.23}$$

$$\frac{d[P]}{dt} = k_3[ES] - k_4[E][P] \tag{8.24}$$

$$[E] + [ES] = [E]_0 \tag{8.25}$$

b. The steady-state assumptions are $d[ES]/dt \simeq d[E]/dt \simeq 0$. Therefore, from either equation 8.21 or equation 8.23,

$$(k_2 + k_3)[ES] = [E](k_1[S] + k_4[P]) \tag{8.26}$$

Substituting for [E] from equation 8.25, expanding, collecting terms, and rearranging gives

$$(k_2 + k_3)[ES] = ([E]_0 - [ES])(k_1[S] + k_4[P])$$

$$[ES](k_2 + k_3 + k_1[S] + k_4[P]) = [E]_0(k_1[S] + k_4[P])$$

$$[ES] = \frac{[E]_0(k_1[S] + k_4[P])}{(k_2 + k_3 + k_1[S] + k_4[P])} \tag{8.27}$$

Substituting for [ES] from equation 8.25 into equation 8.26 and rearranging gives

$$(k_2 + k_3)([E]_0 - [E]) = [E](k_1[S] + k_4[P])$$

$$[E] = \frac{[E]_0(k_2 + k_3)}{(k_2 + k_3 + k_1[S] + k_4[P])} \tag{8.28}$$

Let α equal the expression $k_2 + k_3 + k_1[S] + k_4[P]$ in equations 8.27 and 8.28. Substituting from these equations into equation 8.24 and rearranging yields the desired solution:

$$\frac{d[P]}{dt} = k_3\left[\frac{[E]_0(k_1[S] + k_4[P])}{\alpha}\right] - k_4[P]\left[\frac{[E]_0(k_2 + k_3)}{\alpha}\right]$$

$$= \frac{[E]_0(k_1 k_3[S] + k_3 k_4[P] - k_4 k_2[P] - k_4 k_3[P])}{\alpha}$$

$$= \frac{[E]_0(k_1 k_3[S] - k_4 k_2[P])}{k_2 + k_3 + k_1[S] + k_4[P]} \tag{8.29}$$

c. Remember that $d[P]/dt = v$, the rate of the reaction. Equation 8.29 becomes the Michaelis–Menten equation (8.7) if $k_4 = 0$. Substituting $V_{max} = k_3[E]_0$ and $K_M = (k_2 + k_3)/k_1$, and rearranging gives

$$v = \frac{k_3[E]_0}{1 + K_M/[S]}$$

d. The inhibition is competitive (see Concept 8.4). The expression representing K_I for P is

$$K_I = \frac{[E][P]}{[ES]} = \frac{k_3}{k_4}$$

e. For S as a competitive inhibitor of the reverse reaction,

$$K_I = \frac{[E][S]}{[ES]} = \frac{k_2}{k_1}$$

f.
$$k_3 = V_{max}/[E]_0 = 2700 \text{ min}^{-1}$$

$$k_1 = \frac{k_2 + k_3}{K_M} = \frac{k_3}{K_M - K_S} = 7.5 \times 10^7 \text{ L/mol min}$$

$$k_2 = k_1 K_S = 75 \text{ min}^{-1}$$

$$k_4 = \frac{k_2 + k_3}{K_I} = 1.5 \times 10^8 \text{ L/mol min}$$

g. You could calculate the rate constants without knowing K_s by determining V_{max} and K_M for both the forward and reverse reactions [V_{max} for reverse reaction $= k_2[E]_0$; K_M for reverse reaction $= (k_2 + k_3)/k_4$].

Bioenergetics and Metabolism

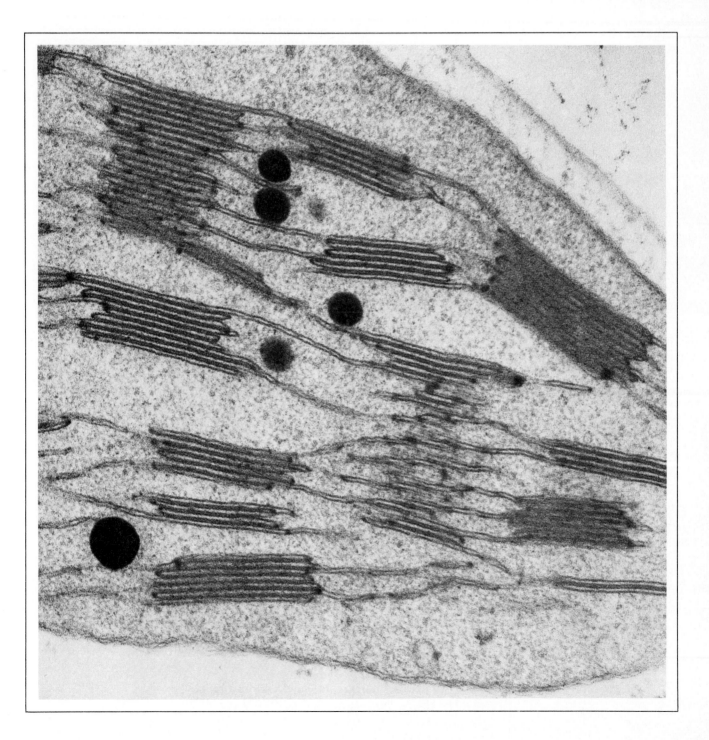

9 Bioenergetics and the Strategy of Metabolism

To carry out the energy-requiring processes of life, organisms must extract energy from their surroundings and convert it to chemically useful forms. This chapter considers the general nature of biological energy transformations, the thermodynamics of biochemical reactions, and the functions of the universal carrier molecules, ATP, NADH, and NADPH.

Concepts

9.1 Organisms convert raw materials into living matter at the expense of energy from their environment.

Organisms can be divided into two classes, depending on the kind of energy source they utilize. **Chemotrophs** require fuel molecules that can be oxidized to produce chemically useful energy. **Phototrophs** convert the radiant energy of sunlight into a chemically useful form. Each class of organisms is dependent on the other, as shown in Figure 9.1.

9.2 Biological energy transformations obey the laws of thermodynamics.

A. Energy transformations in biological systems are governed by equation 9.1, which is derived from the first and second laws of thermodynamics:

$$\Delta G = \Delta H - T \Delta S \tag{9.1}$$

This expression relates the change in **free energy** (ΔG) of a system and its surround-

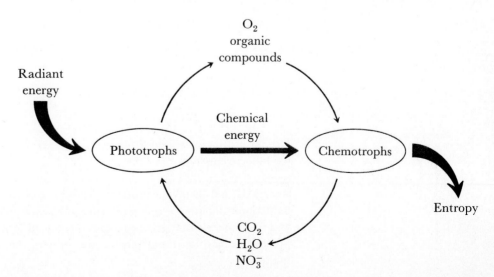

Figure 9.1
The flow of energy and matter through the biosphere.

175

ings to the change in its **enthalpy** or heat content (ΔH), the change in its **entropy** or degree of disorder (ΔS), and the absolute temperature (T). Almost all biological processes occur at constant (usually atmospheric) pressure, essentially constant volume, and constant temperature. Free energy can be defined as the component of the total energy that is available for useful work under these conditions.

B. All systems tend toward thermodynamic equilibrium, the point at which the free energy of the system is a minimum. Consequently, any reversible process proceeds in the direction that leads to a decrease in free energy, so that ΔG is negative. Therefore, the value of ΔG for a biochemical reaction indicates its tendency to proceed, and the free energy it will release.

To make this concept quantitatively useful, the **standard free-energy change** for a reaction (ΔG_0) is defined as the value of ΔG (in kilocalories per mole) under standard conditions of temperature ($25\,°C$ or 298 K), pressure (1 atm), and concentration (all reactants and products at 1 molal concentration). Because most biological reactions occur in aqueous solution near pH = 7, biochemists adopt two additional conventions in determining standard free energies: The pH of the solution is specified as 7, and the concentration of water is assumed to be constant. By convention, both H^+ ion concentration and water concentration are left out of the equilibrium expression (equation 9.4) and are included in the value of K'_{eq} for any reaction in which they appear. The standard free-energy change under these conditions is symbolized by $\Delta G'_0$.

C. For the general chemical reaction

$$a\text{A} + b\text{B} \rightleftharpoons c\text{C} + d\text{D} \tag{9.2}$$

in which a, b, c, and d are the number of molecules of A, B, C, and D, respectively, participating in the reaction, the free-energy change at pH = 7 under *nonstandard* conditions ($\Delta G'$) is given by

$$\Delta G' = \Delta G'_0 + RT \ln \frac{[\text{C}]^c[\text{D}]^d}{[\text{A}]^a[\text{B}]^b} \tag{9.3}$$

in which R is the gas constant (1.98×10^{-3} kcal/deg mol), and [A], [B], [C], and [D] are the molar concentrations of A, B, C, and D. (Actually [A], [B], [C], and [D] in this expression represent activities, but these are approximately equal to molarities at the low concentrations generally encountered in biological reactions.)

D. At equilibrium there is no longer any tendency for the reaction to proceed; that is, $\Delta G' = 0$. The concentrations of reactants and products at equilibrium define K'_{eq}, the **equilibrium constant** at pH = 7:

$$\frac{[\text{C}]^c[\text{D}]^d}{[\text{A}]^a[\text{B}]^b} = K'_{eq} \tag{9.4}$$

Substituting these values into equation 9.3 gives the relationship between $\Delta G'_0$ and K'_{eq}:

$$\Delta G'_0 = -RT \ln K'_{eq} \tag{9.5}$$

9.3 Organisms obtain energy from oxidation–reduction reactions.

A. Reactions that involve transfer of electrons from one molecule to another are called **oxidation-reduction** or **redox** reactions. The molecule that loses electrons is **oxidized,** and the molecule that gains electrons is **reduced.** The tendency for redox reactions to proceed depends on the difference in energy of the transferable electrons in the two molecules.

1. Consider the pair of electrons that is transferred to a molecule A_{ox} to produce A_{red} in the half-reaction

$$A_{ox} + 2e^- \rightarrow A_{red}$$

The oxidized and reduced forms of A are called a **redox couple** or **half-cell,** written as

$$A_{ox} + 2e^-/A_{red}, \text{ or, more simply, } A_{ox}/A_{red}$$

By convention, the reduced form is written to the right. The energy of the transferred electrons under standard biological conditions (Concept 9.2, part B) is expressed as a **standard half-cell potential, E_0',** in volts.

2. In a complete redox reaction, the electrons accepted by A_{ox} in the formation of A_{red} must be donated by another molecule, B_{red}, which concomitantly undergoes oxidation to B_{ox}. The tendency of the electrons to be transferred, in the overall reaction

$$A_{ox} + B_{red} \rightleftarrows A_{red} + B_{ox}$$

is given by $\Delta E_0'$, which is computed by subtracting E_0' for the half-cell undergoing oxidation from E_0' for the half-cell undergoing reduction:

$$\Delta E_0' = E_{0(A_{ox}/A_{red})}' - E_{0(B_{ox}/B_{red})}'$$

$\Delta E_0'$ can be measured as a voltage if the two half-cells are connected by a conductor to make an **electrochemical cell.**

3. To make the parameter $\Delta E_0'$ quantitatively useful, values of E_0' are expressed relative to an arbitrary standard, the hydrogen half-cell under standard conditions (pH $= 0$):

$$2H^+ + 2e^-/H_2 \qquad E_0 = 0.00 \text{ V}$$

The E_0' values for half-cells involving electrons with **higher** energy than those in the standard half-cell are assigned a **negative** sign, whereas those involving electrons with **lower** energy than those in the standard half-cell are assigned a **positive** sign.

4. Several biologically important half-cell potentials are listed in Table 9.1, with the highest-energy electrons at the top. Spontaneous electron transfer occurs only in the downward direction, from the reduced member of a given couple to the oxidized member of a couple lower on the list. [Note that under standard biological conditions (pH $= 7$), E_0' for the hydrogen half-cell is -0.42 V.]

B. $\Delta E_0'$, like $\Delta G_0'$, indicates the tendency of a reaction to proceed under standard conditions. The two are related by the equation

$$\Delta G_0' = -n\mathscr{F} \, \Delta E_0' \qquad (9.6)$$

in which n is the number of electrons transferred and $\mathscr{F}$ is the Faraday constant, 23 kcal/V mol.

When a redox reaction takes place under **nonstandard** conditions of temperature and concentration, the potential difference $\Delta E'$ is related to $\Delta E_0'$ by the Nernst equation,

$$\Delta E' = \Delta E_0' - \frac{RT}{n\mathscr{F}} \ln \frac{[A_{red}][B_{ox}]}{[A_{ox}][B_{red}]}$$

which is analogous to equation 9.3. Likewise, the potential of a half-cell under nonstandard conditions is given by

$$E' = E_0' - \frac{RT}{n\mathscr{F}} \ln \frac{[A_{red}]}{[A_{ox}]}$$

Table 9.1
Some Standard Half-cell
Potentials of Biological
Interest

Half-cell	n^a	$E_0'(V)^{b,c}$
Acetate + CO_2 + $2H^+$/pyruvate + H_2O	2	-0.70
Succinate + CO_2 + $2H^+$/α-ketoglutarate + H_2O	2	-0.67
Acetate + $2H^+$/acetaldehyde + H_2O	2	-0.60
Chlorophyll: P_I^+/P_I^{*d}	1	-0.6
3-P-glycerate + $2H^+$/glyceraldehyde-3-P + H_2O	2	-0.55
Ferredoxin ox/red	1	-0.43
$2H^+/H_2$	2	-0.42
H^+ + CO_2/formate	2	-0.42
Acetyl CoA + $2H^+$/acetaldehyde + HSCoA	2	-0.41
CO_2 + pyruvate + $2H^+$/malate + H_2O	2	-0.33
$NAD(P)^+$ + $2H^+$/$NAD(P)H$ + H^+	2	-0.32
Lipoate$_{ox}$ + $2H^+$/lipoate$_{red}$	2	-0.29
1,3-diP-glycerate + $2H^+$/glyceraldehyde-3-P + P_i^e	2	-0.29
Acetoacetate + $2H^+$/β-hydroxybutyrate	2	-0.27
S + $2H^+$/H_2S	2	-0.23
Chlorophyll: P_{II}^+/P_{II}^{*f}	1	-0.2
Acetaldehyde + $2H^+$/ethanol	2	-0.20
Pyruvate + $2H^+$/lactate	2	-0.19
FAD (flavin adenine dinucleotide) + $2H^+$/$FADH_2$(free)	2	-0.18^g
Oxaloacetate + $2H^+$/malate	2	-0.17
α-Ketoglutarate + NH_4^+ + $2H^+$/glutamate + H_2O	2	-0.14
Pyruvate + NH_4^+ + $2H^+$/alanine + H_2O	2	-0.13
Standard hydrogen half-cell ($2H^+/H_2$)	2	$E_0 = 0.00$
Methylene blue ox/red	2	0.01
Fumarate + $2H^+$/succinate	2	0.03
Cytochrome b (Fe^{3+}/Fe^{2+})	1	0.06
Ubiquinone ox/red	2	0.10
Cu^{2+}/Cu^+	1	0.15
Hemoglobin (Fe^{3+}/Fe^{2+})	1	0.17
Cytochrome c (Fe^{3+}/Fe^{2+})	1	0.22
Cytochrome a (Fe^{3+}/Fe^{2+})	1	0.29
$2H^+$ + O_2/H_2O_2	2	0.30
Chlorophyll: $P_I^+/P_I^{\circ d}$	1	0.4
NO_3^- + $2H^+$/NO_2^- + H_2O	2	0.42
SO_4^{2-} + $2H^+$/SO_3^{2-} + H_2O	2	0.48
Fe^{3+}/Fe^{2+}	1	0.77
$2H^+$ + $\frac{1}{2}O_2$/H_2O	2	0.82
Chlorophyll: $P_{II}^+/P_{II}^{\circ f}$	1	0.9

[a] n is the number of transferred electrons.
[b] For a $2e^-$ reaction, $\Delta E_0'$ of 0.10 V corresponds to $\Delta G_0'$ of -4.6 kcal/mol.
[c] Determined at pH = 7 and 25°C, relative to the standard hydrogen half-cell (pH = 0).
[d] Chlorophyll at the photoreactive center of photosystem I in photosynthesis. P_I^*, P_I^+, and P_I° represent the excited, the electron-deficient, and the ground-state forms, respectively, of the pigment molecule. See Chapter 13.
[e] P_i represents inorganic phosphate, HPO_4^{2-}.
[f] Chlorophyll at the photoreactive center of photosystem II in eucaryotic photosynthesis. P_{II}^*, P_{II}^+, and P_{II}° represent the excited, the electron-deficient, and the ground-state forms, respectively, of the pigment molecule. See Chapter 13.
[g] This value is for the free coenzyme. Different flavoproteins, carrying bound FAD (Chapter 11), vary in E_0' from approximately 0.0 to 0.3 V.

Note that the signs of $\Delta G'$ and $\Delta E'$ are opposite. A spontaneously occurring redox reaction has a positive $\Delta E'$ and a negative $\Delta G'$.

C. Both chemotrophs and phototrophs obtain energy from redox reactions. Chemotrophs require an environmental source of high-energy electrons (e.g., an organic molecule) and an acceptor to which the electrons can be transferred (e.g., oxygen) with release of free energy. Phototrophs use the energy of light to raise electrons from low to high energy, and then transfer them to an internal acceptor with release of free energy.

9.4 ATP is the universal carrier of free energy.

A. In all organisms the free energy released in redox reactions is conserved in the energy-carrier molecule **adenosine triphosphate (ATP)**. ATP functions as an energy carrier by virtue of its two "high-energy" phosphate anhydride bonds. The structure of ATP is shown in Figure 9.2, and the two anhydride linkages are indicated by the symbol $\sim$. The term *high energy* refers not to bond energy, but to the free energy released when either of these two bonds is hydrolyzed in reactions such as

$$\text{ATP} + \text{H}_2\text{O} \rightleftarrows \text{ADP} + \text{P}_i + \text{H}^+ \qquad \Delta G_0' = -7.3 \text{ kcal/mol}$$

$$\text{ADP} + \text{H}_2\text{O} \rightleftarrows \text{AMP} + \text{P}_i + \text{H}^+ \qquad \Delta G_0' = -7.3 \text{ kcal/mol}$$

ADP and **AMP** represent **adenosine diphosphate** and **adenosine monophosphate,** respectively, and **P_i** represents **inorganic phosphate, HPO_4^{2-}**. The high, negative $\Delta G_0'$ values indicate that hydrolysis of the two bonds is strongly favored thermodynamically.

There is nothing unique about the two bonds themselves; their high negative $\Delta G_0'$ of hydrolysis is due to the nature of the neighboring groups in the molecule. Hydrolysis of either bond relieves the localized concentration of negative charge, and provides greater opportunity for delocalization of electrons associated with the phosphate groups. Hence the products of ATP hydrolysis have considerably lower free energy than ATP.

B. ATP formation from ADP and P_i is driven by the energy generated when fuel molecules are oxidized in chemotrophs, or light is trapped in phototrophs. The energy in ATP is utilized, via breakdown to ADP + P_i, to drive thermodynamically unfavorable processes such as biosynthesis, active transport, and motility. Organisms do not contain sufficient ATP to use it for storage of large amounts of energy. Rather, ATP serves as the carrier of energy in a readily accessible form. Thus ATP and ADP cycle between energy-requiring and energy-generating reactions, as shown for chemotrophs in Figure 9.3. In a typical cell the steady-state ratio of ATP to ADP is usually around 10.

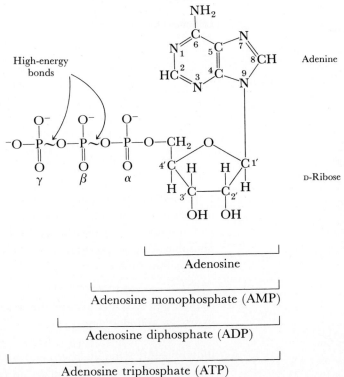

Figure 9.2
The structure of ATP, showing the ionized form that predominates at pH = 7.0.

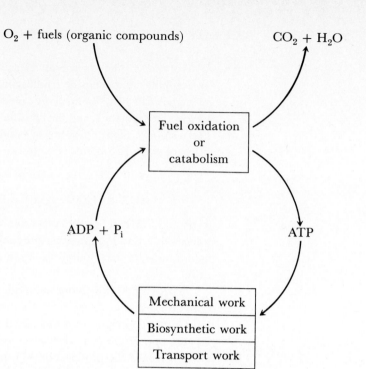

Figure 9.3
The ATP–ADP cycle in
chemotrophs. Catabolism is a
collective term for the metabolic
reactions that degrade fuel molecules to produce energy.

C. Energy transfer via ATP is accomplished by transfer of phosphate groups. In the breakdown of fuel molecules (catabolism), energetically favorable redox reactions produce either ATP or high-energy phosphorylated compounds whose negative $\Delta G_0'$ values for hydrolysis are even greater than that of ATP. Such compounds can spontaneously transfer phosphate groups to ADP, producing ATP, with a net negative $\Delta G_0'$. A few examples of such compounds are listed above ATP in Table 9.2. Their mechanisms of formation in catabolism are discussed in Chapters 10 and 11. In biosynthesis, ATP is used to phosphorylate intermediates, thereby producing activated derivatives that can react spontaneously. A few such derivatives are listed below ATP in Table 9.2. Their mechanisms of formation and reaction are discussed in Chapters 15 and 16.

Table 9.2
$\Delta G_0'$ Values for Hydrolysis
of Some Phosphorylated
Metabolic Intermediates[a]

Compound	$\Delta G_0'$ of hydrolysis (kcal/mol)
P-enol pyruvate	−14.8
1,3-diP-glycerate	−11.8
P-creatine	−10.3
P-arginine	−7.7
ATP	−7.3
Glucose 1-P	−5.0
Glucose 6-P	−3.3
Glycerol 1-P	−2.2

[a] The general reaction is R—P + H_2O → RH + P_i, in which P represents the phosphoryl group, —PO_3^{2-}, and P_i represents inorganic phosphate, HPO_4^{2-}.

The high-energy phosphorylated intermediates produced in catabolism are said to have a high phosphate-transfer potential, whereas the phosphorylated intermediates in biosynthesis generally have a low phosphate-transfer potential. Note that the phosphate-transfer potential of ATP is intermediate, suiting it ideally to be a carrier of energy from catabolic to synthetic reactions.

9.5 NADH and NADPH are the universal carriers of hydrogen and electrons.

A. Biosynthesis requires hydrogen and electrons, or **reducing power,** in addition to ATP. When fuel molecules are oxidized in catabolism, they lose hydrogen and electrons.

Most of these hydrogens and electrons are transferred to an environmental acceptor such as oxygen, with concomitant ATP production. However, some of them must be conserved and reutilized in the synthesis of cellular components—generally large reduced molecules—from the small oxidized precursors produced in catabolism.

All organisms use the same pair of **pyridine nucleotides** as carrier molecules for hydrogen and electrons: **nicotinamide adenine dinucleotide (NAD$^+$),** and **nicotinamide adenine dinucleotide phosphate (NADP$^+$)** (Figure 9.4). Both molecules accept hydrogen and electrons in the oxidation reactions of catabolism, and become reduced as shown in Figure 9.5.

The oxidative half-reactions of catabolism generally produce two H$^+$ ions and two electrons. For example,

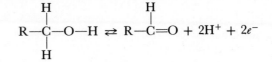

Figure 9.4
The oxidized form of nicotinamide adenine dinucleotide (NAD$^+$). In nicotinamide adenine dinucleotide phosphate (NADP$^+$) a phosphate group is esterified to the hydroxyl group indicated by the arrow.

Figure 9.5
Reduction of NAD(P)$^+$ to NAD(P)H. Only the nicotinamide ring is shown; the rest of the molecule is represented by R.

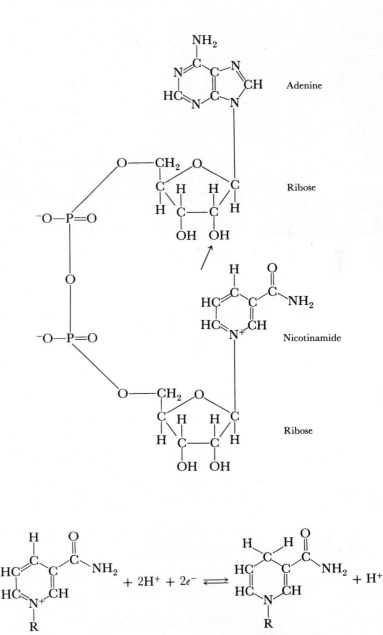

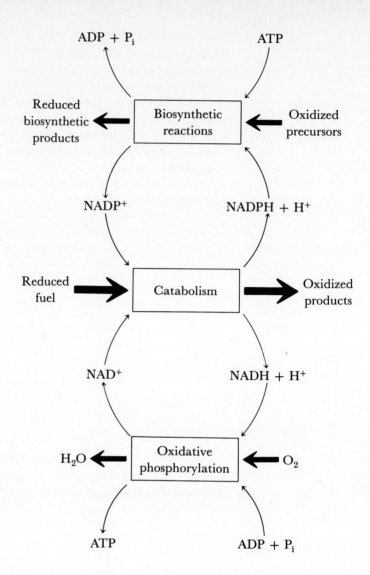

Figure 9.6
The roles of NADH and
NADPH in the overall strategy
of metabolism.

The nicotinamide ring of a pyridine nucleotide can accept two electrons and one H^+ ion, as shown in Figure 9.5. Because the second H^+ is released into solution, most redox reactions in biological systems take the form

$$AH_2 + NAD(P)^+ \rightleftarrows A + NAD(P)H + H^+$$

B. NADH and NADPH have different metabolic functions. NADH generally transfers H^+ and $2e^-$ to oxygen with concomitant ATP production (Chapter 12). However, NADPH transfers H^+ and $2e^-$ to oxidized precursors in the reduction reactions of biosynthesis. Therefore, NADPH cycles between catabolic and biosynthetic reactions and serves as the carrier of reducing power in the same way that ATP serves as the carrier of energy. The roles of NADH and NADPH in the overall strategy of metabolism are shown in Figure 9.6.

References

COMPREHENSIVE TEXTS

Lehninger: Chapters 13, 14, and 15

Stryer: Chapters 11 and 14

Metzler: Chapters 3 and 7

White et al.: Chapters 10 and 12

OTHER REFERENCES

R. E. Dickerson, *Molecular Thermodynamics*, Benjamin/Cummings, Menlo Park, Calif., 1969. Chapter 7.

A. L. Lehninger, *Bioenergetics,* Benjamin/Cummings, Menlo Park, Calif., 1971, 2nd ed. Chapters 1, 2, and 3.

J. D. Watson, *Molecular Biology of the Gene,* Benjamin/Cummings, Menlo Park, Calif., 1976, 3rd ed. Chapter 2.

Problems

Unless stated otherwise, assume pH = 7 and $T = 298$ K (25 °C) in all problems.

9.1 Answer the following with true or false. If false, explain why.

a. Energy flows through the community of living organisms, from phototrophs to chemotrophs, whereas matter cycles between the two classes of organisms.

b. Work can be performed in living organisms by transferring heat energy from hotter to cooler parts of the organism.

c. A system is in thermodynamic equilibrium when its entropy has decreased to a minimum.

d. A $\Delta G'_0$ value of 0.0 indicates that a reaction is at equilibrium.

e. Electrons from the reduced member of a redox couple can transfer spontaneously to the oxidized member of a couple with a more negative standard half-cell potential.

f. E' is approximately equal to

$$E'_0 - 0.03 \log [\text{reduced form}]/[\text{oxidized form}]$$

for a redox couple with $n = 2$ when the concentrations of the reduced and oxidized forms are unequal.

g. $\Delta G'_0$ is approximately equal to ΔG_0 for the reaction of ATP hydrolysis to ADP.

h. High-energy phosphate compounds are produced in some redox reactions of metabolism.

i. NADH carries reducing power in a cycle between catabolic and synthetic reactions in much the same way that ATP carries energy.

9.2 a. In a redox reaction the molecule that loses electrons becomes _____, and the molecule that gains electrons becomes _____.

b. _____ require fuel molecules that can be oxidized to produce chemically useful energy, whereas _____ convert the radiant energy of sunlight into a chemically useful form.

c. For half-cells involving electrons with higher energy than those in the standard hydrogen half-cell, the E'_0 values are assigned a _____ sign.

d. The "high energy" of the two _____ bonds in ATP refers to the free energy released when these bonds are _____.

e. _____ transfers H^+ and $2e^-$ to oxygen for ATP production, whereas _____ transfers H^+ and $2e^-$ to oxidized precursors in biosynthesis.

9.3 Construct a table showing $\Delta G'_0$ values for reactions whose K'_{eq} values are 10^{-3}, 10^{-2}, 10^{-1}, 10^0, 10^1, 10^2, and 10^3.

9.4 The $\Delta G'_0$ for hydrolysis of ATP to ADP + P_i is -7.3 kcal/mol.

a. Calculate the equilibrium constant for this reaction.

b. Is this reaction at equilibrium in the cell?

9.5 Do you expect that $\Delta G'$ for ATP hydrolysis within a cell is usually more or less negative than $\Delta G'_0$? Why?

9.6 The $\Delta G'$ for hydrolysis of a sugar phosphate (sugar-P)

$$\underset{\text{Sugar-P}}{R-OPO_3^{2-}} + H_2O \rightarrow \underset{\text{Sugar}}{R-OH} + P_i$$

is -6.2 kcal/mol in a hypothetical, homogeneous cell in which the steady-state concentrations of sugar phosphate, free sugar, and inorganic phosphate (P_i) are $10^{-3}M$, $2 \times 10^{-4}M$, and $5 \times 10^{-2}M$, respectively. What is $\Delta G'_0$ for the reaction? (*Note:*

"Steady state" refers to a *nonequilibrium* situation that prevails because of a balance between reactions that supply and remove these substances.)

9.7   Assume that you have a solution of $0.1 M$ glucose 6-P. To this solution you add the enzyme phosphoglucomutase, which catalyzes the reaction:

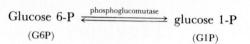

$$\text{Glucose 6-P} \xrightleftharpoons{\text{phosphoglucomutase}} \text{glucose 1-P}$$
$$\text{(G6P)} \hspace{5cm} \text{(G1P)}$$

The $\Delta G_0'$ of this reaction is $+1.8\,\text{kcal/mol}$.

a. Does this reaction proceed at all as written, and if so what are the final concentrations of G6P and G1P?

b. Under what cellular conditions, if any, would this reaction continuously produce G1P at a high rate?

9.8   The high-energy phosphate compounds P-creatine and P-arginine (Table 9.2) are used as energy reservoirs when the intracellular concentration of ATP becomes very high. Estimate the $\Delta G_0'$ values of the reactions in which these compounds are formed by transfer of phosphate from ATP to creatine and arginine, respectively.

9.9 a. Using the Henderson–Hasselbalch equation (equation 2.2), calculate the total negative charge on the phosphate groups of ATP at pH $= 7.0$, given that for three of the ionizable —OH groups, $pK_a = 2.5$, and for the fourth, $pK_a = 6.5$.

b. Make the same calculation for ADP, given that for two of the groups $pK_a = 2.5$ and for the third, $pK_a = 7.2$.

c. What significance does this difference in charge have for the $\Delta G_0'$ of ATP hydrolysis?

9.10   The complete combustion of glucose to $CO_2 + H_2O$ proceeds with an overall $\Delta G_0'$ of $-686\,\text{kcal/mol}$. When this process occurs in a typical cell, 36 mol ATP are produced concomitantly from ADP $+ P_i$.

a. Assuming that $\Delta G'$ for ATP $\rightarrow$ ADP hydrolysis is $-10\,\text{kcal/mol}$ and that $\Delta G' \simeq \Delta G_0'$ for glucose oxidation under intracellular conditions, what fraction of the potential energy of glucose is conserved in the form of ATP?

b. What happens to the energy that is not conserved in ATP?

9.11   The second law of thermodynamics states that any system and its surroundings must increase continually in entropy. However, living organisms constantly create highly ordered structures from less-ordered raw materials. Do living organisms violate the second law?

9.12   Which of the following redox reactions will proceed as written if the initial concentrations of reactants and products are equal? (Assume that an appropriate enzyme is present to catalyze each reaction.) Indicate the basis for your conclusions.

a. Acetaldehyde $+ H_2O + FAD \rightarrow$ acetate $+ FADH_2$

b. $FADH_2 + NAD^+ \rightarrow FAD + NADH + H^+$

c. Succinate $+ NAD^+ \rightarrow$ fumarate $+ NADH + H^+$

d. β-Hydroxybutyrate $+ NAD^+ \rightarrow$ acetoacetate $+ NADH + H^+$

e. Acetate $+ NADPH + H^+ \rightarrow$ acetaldehyde $+ NADP^+ + H_2O$

9.13 a. List the following underlined substances in order of decreasing reducing power:

Succinate $\rightarrow$ fumarate $+ 2H^+ + 2e^-$

Glyceraldehyde 3-P $+ P_i \rightarrow$ 1,3-diP-glycerate $+ 2H^+ + 2e^-$

Lactate $\rightarrow$ pyruvate $+ 2H^+ + 2e^-$

Chlorophyll: P_I^* (excited state) $\rightarrow$
 chlorophyll: P_I^+ (electron-deficient free radical) $+ e^-$

NADH $+ H^+ \rightarrow NAD^+ + 2H^+ + 2e^-$

b. List the following underlined substances in order of increasing tendency to accept electrons:

Chlorophyll: P_{II}^+ (electron-deficient free radical) $+ e^- \rightarrow$
    chlorophyll: P_{II}^o (ground state)

$\underline{FAD} + 2H^+ + 2e^- \rightarrow FADH_2$

$\underline{Oxaloacetate} + 2H^+ + 2e^- \rightarrow malate$

$2H^+ + \frac{1}{2}O_2 + 2e^- \rightarrow H_2O$

$\underline{Cytochrome\ c_{ox}} + e^- \rightarrow cytochrome\ c_{red}$

9.14   From the data in Table 9.1, calculate $\Delta G_0'$ for the reaction catalyzed by the enzyme alcohol dehydrogenase:

$$\underset{\text{Acetaldehyde}}{CH_3\overset{\overset{\displaystyle H}{|}}{C}\!\!=\!\!O} + NADH + H^+ \rightarrow \underset{\text{Ethanol}}{CH_3CH_2OH} + NAD^+$$

9.15   Give the equilibrium constant of the cytochrome oxidase reaction,

$$2\ cytochrome\ a_{red}(Fe^{2+}) + \tfrac{1}{2}O_2 + 2H^+ \rightarrow 2\ cytochrome\ a_{ox}(Fe^{3+}) + H_2O$$

9.16   For a phosphorylation-coupled, two-electron redox reaction to produce an ATP molecule from $ADP + P_i$, what must be its minimum $\Delta E'$? Assume that the $\Delta G'$ for $ATP \rightarrow ADP$ hydrolysis is -10 kcal/mol under intracellular conditions.

9.17   Would it be *energetically* possible for bacteria to survive on X as sole carbon and hydrogen source, and Y as sole environmental electron acceptor, if
   a. X is β-hydroxybutyrate and Y is elemental sulfur?
   b. X is acetaldehyde and Y is acetaldehyde?
   c. X is ethanol and Y is SO_4^{2-}?
   d. X is ethanol and Y is elemental sulfur?
   Give the reasons for your answer in each case. Assume that the concentrations of reactants and products are such that $\Delta E' = \Delta E_0'$.

9.18   Which of the following 14 environments theoretically can support cellular life, as you understand it, and which cannot? Assume that all environments offer hospitable temperature and pH, and supply inorganic phosphate, inorganic sulfate (SO_4^{2-}), inorganic nitrate (NO_3^-), essential metal ions, and water. No carbon compounds, no oxygen, and no light are present unless specified. The additional components of each environment are given. Indicate for each whether it can support life. If not, state in one sentence what general requirement for life is missing.
   a. Formate, O_2
   b. Light, CO_2
   c. CO_2, NO_2^-, O_2
   d. CO_2, H_2S
   e. H_2S, NO_2^-, O_2
   f. SO_3^{2-}, CO_2
   g. Light, CO_2, O_2
   h. Light, CO_2, formate
   i. Formate
   j. Formate, CO_2
   k. DNA, O_2
   l. O_2, CO_2
   m. Formate, NO_2^-
   n. NO_2^-, CO_2

9.19   Consider the following reactions and their standard free-energy changes:

		$\Delta G_0'$ (kcal/mol)
1.	Fumarate + $H_2O \rightleftarrows$ malate	-0.9
2.	Malate + $\frac{1}{2}O_2 \rightleftarrows$ oxaloacetate + H_2O	-45.3
3.	$NAD^+ + H_2O \rightleftarrows NADH + H^+ + \frac{1}{2}O_2$	$+52.4$

a. If the partial pressure of O_2 is 1.0 atm, what is the ratio of [oxaloacetate]/[malate] at equilibrium for reaction 2 ($RT = 0.60$ kcal/mol)?

b. In a common metabolic pathway, reaction 2 is coupled to the reduction of NAD^+. If NAD^+ and NADH are present in equimolar amounts, and if $P_{O_2} = 1$ atm, what ratio of [oxaloacetate]/[malate] would result in no free-energy change for the coupled reaction?

c. What concentration of malate yields the greatest free-energy change going from fumarate to oxaloacetate via reactions 1 and 2?

☆ 9.20   Proceeding from greatest to least, the relative free-energy yields per mole from the complete combustion of

1.   ribose ($C_5H_{10}O_5$)
2.   valeric acid ($C_5H_{10}O_2$)
3.   pentane (C_5H_{12})
4.   glutamic acid ($C_5H_9NO_4$)

may be represented in one of the following orders. Which one is correct?
a. 1, 2, 3, 4
b. 4, 2, 1, 3
c. 3, 2, 4, 1
d. 4, 3, 2, 1
e. 3, 4, 2, 1

☆ 9.21   In a hypothetical cell the steady-state concentrations of a phosphorylated intermediate, R—O—P, and its hydrolysis products, R—OH and P_i, are $2 \times 10^{-2} M$, $4 \times 10^{-5} M$, and $5 \times 10^{-2} M$, respectively. The $\Delta G'$ of the hydrolysis reaction

$$R—O—P + H_2O \rightarrow R—OH + P_i$$

in this cell is -8.22 kcal/mol.

a. Calculate the equilibrium constant, K'_{eq}, for the hydrolysis reaction.

b. Would you classify R—O—P as a high-energy phosphate compound? Give $\Delta G'_0$ for the following reaction:

$$R—O—P + ADP \rightarrow ROH + ATP$$

Answers

9.1   a. True. (See Figure 9.1.)

b. False. Because organisms are essentially isothermal systems, no useful work can be performed within an organism by transfer of heat energy.

c. False. At equilibrium the free energy is at a minimum, and the entropy is generally at a maximum.

d. False. $\Delta G'_0$ is a constant for any given reaction, related to K'_{eq} by equation 9.5. At equilibrium, $\Delta G' = 0$.

e. False. Electrons from the reduced member of a redox couple can transfer spontaneously only to the oxidized member of a couple with a more *positive* standard potential.

f. True

g. False. Because the reaction produces H^+, the standard free-energy change will be quite different at H^+ concentrations of $1M$ (ΔG_0) and $10^{-7}M$ ($\Delta G'_0$).

h. True

i. False. NADPH is the carrier of reducing power for biosynthesis.

9.2   a. oxidized, reduced

b. Chemotrophs, phototrophs

c. negative

d. phosphate anhydride, hydrolyzed

e. NADH, NADPH

9.3

K'_{eq}	$\Delta G'_0$
10^{-3}	4.1
10^{-2}	2.7
10^{-1}	1.4
10^0	0.0
10^1	-1.4
10^2	-2.7
10^3	-4.1

9.4 a. This problem can be solved using equation 9.5,

$$\Delta G'_0 = -RT \ln K'_{eq}$$

$$-7.3 \text{ kcal/mol} = -(1.98 \times 10^{-3} \text{ kcal/deg mol})(298 \text{ deg})(2.3 \log K'_{eq})$$

$$\log K'_{eq} = 5.35$$

$$K'_{eq} = 2.2 \times 10^5$$

b. No. If the reaction were at equilibrium, (1) the concentration of ATP would be vanishingly small, and (2) the $\Delta G'$ of ATP hydrolysis would be zero, thereby making it impossible for ATP to perform useful work. The usefulness of ATP depends on maintaining this reaction far from equilibrium, using energy from catabolism.

9.5 From equation 9.3,

$$\Delta G' = \Delta G'_0 + RT \ln \frac{[\text{ADP}][\text{P}_i]}{[\text{ATP}]}$$

Because the concentration of ATP in the cell is greater than that of ADP, the second term is negative. Thus $\Delta G'$ is more negative than $\Delta G'_0$ ($\Delta G' \simeq -10 \text{ kcal/mol}$).

9.6 From equation 9.3,

$$\Delta G' = \Delta G'_0 + RT \ln \frac{[\text{sugar}][\text{P}_i]}{[\text{sugar-P}]}$$

Substituting the values given in the problem yields

$$-6.2 \text{ kcal/mol} = \Delta G'_0 + (1.98 \times 10^{-3} \text{ kcal/deg mol}) \times$$

$$(298 \text{ deg})(2.3) \log \frac{(2 \times 10^{-4})(5 \times 10^{-2})}{(1 \times 10^{-3})}$$

$$\Delta G'_0 = (-6.2 + 2.7) \text{ kcal/mol}$$
$$\Delta G'_0 = -3.5 \text{ kcal/mol}$$

9.7 a. Because the initial conditions are not equilibrium conditions, the reaction will proceed until it reaches equilibrium. At equilibrium

$$\Delta G'_0 = -RT \ln K'_{eq}$$

$$+1.8 = -(1.98 \times 10^{-3} \text{ kcal/deg mol}) \times (298 \text{ deg})(2.3) \log \frac{[\text{G1P}]}{[\text{G6P}]}$$

$$-\frac{1.8}{1.36} = \log \frac{[\text{G1P}]}{[\text{G6P}]} = -1.32$$

$$1.32 = \log \frac{[\text{G6P}]}{[\text{G1P}]}$$

$$2.1 \times 10^1 = {K'_{eq}}^{-1}$$

$$K'_{eq} = 4.8 \times 10^{-2}$$

Because [G6P]/[G1P] = 21, there is 1 G1P molecule for every 21 G6P molecules.

Thus

$$[G1P] = \frac{1}{22}(0.1M) \simeq 0.0045M$$

$$[G6P] = \frac{21}{22}(0.1M) \simeq 0.096M$$

b. If G6P is supplied constantly and G1P is removed constantly by other reactions, so that a high G6P/G1P ratio is maintained, then G1P production will continue at an appreciable rate.

9.8 The reactions are

1. ATP + creatine $\rightleftarrows$ ADP + P-creatine
2. ATP + arginine $\rightleftarrows$ ADP + P-arginine

The $\Delta G_0'$ values of these reactions can be estimated by summing the $\Delta G_0'$ values for the individual hydrolysis reactions in the direction written (Table 9.2).

$$\Delta G_0' \simeq -7.3 + 10.3 = +3.0 \text{ kcal/mol for reaction 1 as written}$$
$$\Delta G_0' \simeq -7.3 + 7.7 = +0.40 \text{ kcal/mol for reaction 2 as written}$$

9.9 a. The Henderson–Hasselbalch equation is

$$\text{pH} = \text{p}K_a + \log\frac{[A^-]}{[HA]}$$

At pH = 7, the three groups with $\text{p}K_a = 2.5$ are essentially completely in the ionized state. For the fourth group, the $\text{p}K_a = 6.5$. From the Henderson–Hasselbalch equation,

$$7 = 6.5 + \log\frac{[-O^-]}{[-OH]}$$

$$\log\frac{[-O^-]}{[-OH]} = 0.5$$

$$\frac{[-OH]}{[-O^-]} = 1.6$$

Thus 3.2/4.2 = 76% of the groups with $\text{p}K_a = 6.5$ are ionized, and the total number of negative charges on the ATP molecule is 3 + 0.76 or 3.8.

b. At pH = 7 the two groups with $\text{p}K_a = 2.5$ are essentially completely in the ionized state. For the third group the $\text{p}K_a = 7.2$. From the Henderson–Hasselbalch equation,

$$7 = 7.2 + \log\frac{[-O^-]}{[-OH]}$$

$$\log\frac{[-O^-]}{[-OH]} = -0.2$$

$$\log\frac{[-OH]}{[-O^-]} = 0.2$$

$$\frac{[-OH]}{[-O^-]} = 1.6$$

Thus 1/2.6 = 38% of the groups with $\text{p}K_a = 7.2$ are ionized, and the total number of negative charges on the ADP molecule is 2 + 0.38 or 2.4.

c. The high localized concentration of negative charge on the ATP molecule is relieved by hydrolysis to form the less negatively charged ADP.

9.10 a. Energy released = −686 kcal/mol glucose

Energy conserved $= -10$ kcal/mol ATP $\times$ 36 mol ATP/mol glucose

$$= -360 \text{ kcal/mol glucose}$$

Fraction conserved $= -360/-686 = 52\%$

b. Most of the energy not conserved in ATP is dissipated primarily as heat. This energy drives the combustion to completion, ensuring that the 36 mol of ATP are produced per mole of glucose degraded.

9.11 Living organisms do not violate the second law of thermodynamics. An organism is constantly decreasing the entropy of the matter taken from its environment, but it can do so only at the expense of enough free energy from its surroundings so that the overall entropy of the organism and its surroundings increases. (Surroundings include the sun, which is the ultimate source of free energy for all living systems.)

9.12 Try answering these questions qualitatively before computing any $\Delta E_0'$ values. Ask where the transferred electrons originate in the reaction as written and where they end up. Then find the two redox couples in Table 9.1, and note whether the electrons are being transferred to a state of lower or higher energy than their original state. If lower, the reaction will proceed and $\Delta E_0'$ is positive. If higher, the reaction will not proceed and $\Delta E_0'$ is negative. In this way you can avoid confusion with sign conventions, because you will know the sign of $\Delta E_0'$ before computing it. The computations for the five reactions are

a. Acetate $+ 2H^+$/acetaldehyde $+ H_2O$ $E_0' = -0.60$ V

   FAD $+ 2H^+$/FADH$_2$ $E_0' = -0.18$ V

   $\Delta E_0' = -0.18 - (-0.60) = +0.42$ V. Will proceed as written.

b. NAD$^+ + 2H^+$/NADH $+ H^+$ $E_0' = -0.32$ V

   FAD $+ 2H^+$/FADH$_2$ $E_0' = -0.18$ V

   $\Delta E_0' = -0.32 - (-0.18) = -0.14$ V. Will not proceed as written.

c. Fumarate $+ 2H^+$/succinate $E_0' = +0.03$ V

   NAD$^+ + 2H^+$/NADH $+ H^+$ $E_0' = -0.32$ V

   $\Delta E_0' = -0.32 - 0.03 = -0.35$ V. Will not proceed as written.

d. Acetoacetate $+ 2H^+$/β-hydroxybutyrate $E_0' = -0.27$ V

   NAD$^+ + 2H^+$/NADH $+ H^+$ $E_0' = -0.32$ V

   $\Delta E_0' = -0.32 - (-0.27) = -0.05$ V. Will not proceed as written.

e. Acetate $+ 2H^+$/acetaldehyde $+ H_2O$ $E_0' = -0.60$ V

   NADP$^+ + 2H^+$/NADPH $+ H^+$ $E_0' = -0.32$ V

   $\Delta E_0' = -0.60 - (-0.32) = -0.28$ V. Will not proceed as written.

9.13 a. Chlorophyll: P_I^*

   NADH

   Glyceraldehyde 3-P

   Lactate

   Succinate

b. FAD

   Oxaloacetate

   Cytochrome c_{ox}

   $\frac{1}{2}O_2$

   Chlorophyll: P_{II}^+

9.14 In this reaction two electrons are transferred from NADH to acetaldehyde, thereby producing ethanol and NAD$^+$. Hence the two redox couples involved are

$$\text{NAD}^+ + 2H^+/\text{NADH} + H^+ \qquad E_0' = -0.32 \text{ V}$$

$$\text{Acetaldehyde} + 2H^+/\text{ethanol} \qquad E_0' = -0.20 \text{ V}$$

Because the electrons are transferred from a higher to a lower energy level, the reaction is favored thermodynamically. Thus $\Delta E_0'$ will be positive and $\Delta G_0'$ will be negative. The value of $\Delta E_0'$ is the difference in the two half-cell potentials, or $+0.12$ V.

From equation 9.6,

$$\Delta G_0' = -n\mathscr{F}\,\Delta E_0' = -(2)(23\ \text{kcal/V mol})(0.12\ \text{V})$$
$$\Delta G_0' = -5.5\ \text{kcal/mol}$$

9.15   Because the transfer of electrons is in a favorable direction, $\Delta E_0'$ is positive and $\Delta G_0'$ is negative.

$$\Delta E_0' = 0.82\ \text{V} - 0.29\ \text{V} = 0.53\ \text{V}$$

From equations 9.5 and 9.6

$$\Delta G_0' = -n\mathscr{F}\,\Delta E_0' = -RT \ln K_{\text{eq}}'$$

Hence

$$\Delta E_0' = \frac{RT}{n\mathscr{F}} \ln K_{\text{eq}}'$$

For the reaction as written, $n = 2$, hence

$$0.53 = 0.03 \log K_{\text{eq}}'$$

$$\log K_{\text{eq}}' = 18$$

$$K_{\text{eq}}' = 10^{18}$$

9.16   If the $\Delta G'$ for ATP hydrolysis is -10 kcal/mol, then 10 kcal/mol must be supplied to drive ATP formation from ADP $+$ P$_\text{i}$. Thus $\Delta G'$ for the redox reaction must be equal to or more negative than -10 kcal/mol.

$$-n\mathscr{F}\,\Delta E' \geq -10\ \text{kcal/mol}$$
$$\Delta E' \geq \frac{10\ \text{kcal/mol}}{2(23\ \text{kcal/V mol})}$$
$$\Delta E' \geq 0.22\ \text{V}$$

9.17   To provide energy for the bacterium, the transfer of electrons from X to Y must provide at least enough free energy to drive ATP production. From Problem 9.16, this $\Delta G'$ corresponds to a $\Delta E'$ of about 0.2 V. In this problem $\Delta E' = \Delta E_0'$, so a comparison of the E_0' values for the appropriate redox couples in Table 9.1 is sufficient to answer the question.

a. Acetoacetate $+$ 2H$^+$/β-hydroxybutyrate $E_0' = -0.27$ V
   S $+$ 2H$^+$/H$_2$S $E_0' = -0.23$ V
   $\Delta E_0' = -0.23 - (-0.27) = +0.04$ V; not sufficient

b. Acetate $+$ 2H$^+$/acetaldehyde $+$ H$_2$O $E_0' = -0.60$ V
   Acetaldehyde $+$ 2H$^+$/ethanol $E_0' = -0.20$ V
   $\Delta E_0' = -0.20 - (-0.60) = +0.40$ V; possible

c. Acetaldehyde $+$ 2H$^+$/ethanol $E_0' = -0.20$ V
   SO$_4^{2-}$ $+$ 2H$^+$/SO$_3^{2-}$ $+$ H$_2$O $E_0' = +0.48$ V
   $\Delta E_0' = +0.48 - (-0.20) = +0.68$ V; possible

d. Acetaldehyde $+$ 2H$^+$/ethanol $E_0' = -0.20$ V
   S $+$ 2H$^+$/H$_2$S $E_0' = -0.23$ V
   $\Delta E_0' = -0.23 - (-0.20) = -0.03$ V; impossible

9.18   Each of the environments contains sources of all the required elements but carbon. Therefore, life support requires a carbon source, and a means of obtaining sufficient free energy to drive ATP production (see Problems 9.16 and 9.17). The latter can be obtained from light by phototrophs or from a suitable redox reaction by chemotrophs. Remember that inorganic sulfate and nitrate ions can serve as electron acceptors (see Table 9.1).

a. Yes
b. Yes
c. Yes
d. Yes

e. No; there is no carbon source.

f. No; there is no electron acceptor of more positive E'_0.

g. Yes

h. Yes

i. Yes

j. Yes

k. Yes

l. No; there is no electron donor.

m. Yes

n. No; the potential span from NO_3^-/NO_2^- to SO_4^{2-}/SO_3^{2-} is insufficient unless the concentration ratio $[NO_2^-][SO_4^{2-}]/[NO_3^-][SO_3^{2-}]$ is $\geq 10^5$, which would give a $\Delta E'$ of $\geq +0.21$ V.

9.19 a. At equilibrium, [oxaloacetate]/[malate] $= K'_{eq}$

$$\Delta G'_0 = -2.3\, RT \log K'_{eq}$$

$$\log K'_{eq} = \frac{-45.3}{-1.38} = 32.8$$

$$[\text{Oxaloacetate}]/[\text{malate}] \simeq 10^{33}$$

b. The sum of reactions 2 and 3 is

$$\text{Malate} + NAD^+ \rightleftarrows \text{oxaloacetate} + NADH + H^+$$

$$\Delta G'_0 = 7.1 \text{ kcal/mol}$$

Again, when $\Delta G' = 0$, the reaction is at equilibrium; thus

$$\Delta G'_0 = 2.3\, RT \log K'_{eq} = -1.38 \log [\text{oxaloacetate}]/[\text{malate}]$$

if $[NAD^+] = [NADH]$. Hence

$$\log [\text{Oxaloacetate}]/[\text{malate}] = \frac{+7.1}{-1.38} = -5.1$$

$$[\text{Oxaloacetate}]/[\text{malate}] \simeq 10^{-5}$$

c. In any two-step process, $A \rightarrow B \rightarrow C$, the ΔG can be expressed as follows:

$$\Delta G_{(A \to B)} = \Delta G_{0(A \to B)} + RT \ln [B]/[A]$$

$$\Delta G_{(B \to C)} = \Delta G_{0(B \to C)} + RT \ln [C]/[B]$$

$$\overline{\Delta G_{(A \to C)} = \Delta G_{0(A \to B)} + \Delta G_{0(B \to C)} + RT \ln \frac{[\cancel{B}][C]}{[A][\cancel{B}]}}$$

Therefore ΔG will be independent of [B] in the general example, and independent of malate concentration in this problem.

10 Catabolic Principles and the Breakdown of Carbohydrates

Catabolism includes all the metabolic reactions by which organisms degrade fuel molecules to obtain energy and starting materials for biosynthesis. This chapter considers the overall strategy of catabolism and describes the most important pathways for initial breakdown of sugars and polysaccharides: glycolysis, glycogenolysis, and the phosphogluconate pathway.

Concepts

10.1 All organisms employ a common strategy for catabolism.

A. Chemotrophs depend on the breakdown of fuel molecules from their surroundings to provide energy and precursors for biosynthesis. Phototrophs degrade stored fuel reserves to obtain energy when light is not available. The principal fuel molecules for all organisms are carbohydrates, lipids (fats), and proteins.

B. The catabolic pathways for energy production in chemotrophs can be considered in four stages, as diagrammed in Figure 10.1.

1. In stage I, lipids, polysaccharides, and proteins are broken down to their precursor components: fatty acids, sugars, and amino acids, respectively. These pathways are short, each consisting of only one or a few degradative steps.

2. Stage II includes many distinct pathways, corresponding to the variety of small molecules that organisms can use for fuel. The stage II pathways degrade these molecules to a small number of common intermediates, primarily pyruvate and acetyl-CoA (Concept 11.1, part A). Only a small fraction of the energy available from fuel molecules is released in stages I and II.

3. Stage III consists of a single pathway, called the **Krebs cycle, citric acid cycle,** or **tricarboxylic acid (TCA) cycle** (Chapter 11). In this sequence of reactions the intermediates derived from the pathways of stages I and II are oxidized completely to CO_2. The resulting electrons are transferred to NAD^+ with little release of energy. The TCA cycle also serves as a source of intermediates for biosynthesis.

4. Stage IV includes the reactions of electron transport and oxidative phosphorylation (Chapter 12). In electron transport, the electrons trapped in NADH during stages II and III are transferred to oxygen, thereby releasing the bulk of the energy available from the original fuel molecules. This energy is used to drive ATP formation by the process of oxidative phosphorylation.

C. Production of reducing power occurs by a separate process of carbohydrate degradation called the **pentose phosphate pathway, hexose monophosphate pathway,** or **phosphogluconate pathway.** This pathway oxidizes sugars to CO_2 and traps the re-

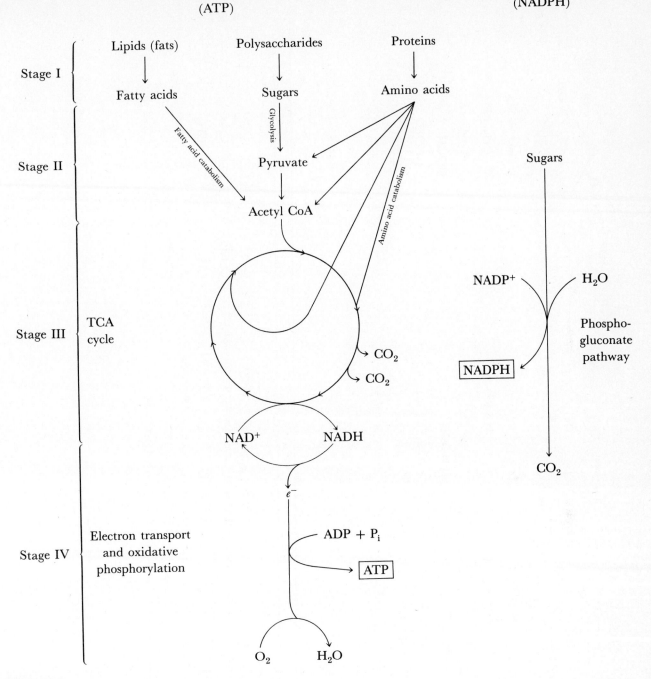

Energy
(ATP)

Reducing power
(NADPH)

Figure 10.1
Outline of catabolic pathways
for generating energy and reducing power in chemotrophic cells.

leased electrons in NADPH (Figure 10.1). The phosphogluconate pathway also produces intermediates for synthesis of amino acids and nucleotides.

**10.2 Glycolysis is the central pathway in the initial
breakdown of carbohydrates.**

A. The Embden–Meyerhof or glycolytic pathway is shown in Figure 10.2 as it operates in
muscle cells to degrade glucose. The $\Delta G_0'$ values and the enzymes that catalyze the
various steps are listed in Table 10.1. Glycolysis can operate to produce ATP in the
absence of oxygen, and therefore is designated a **fermentation**. It involves no external
electron acceptor, and no net oxidation.

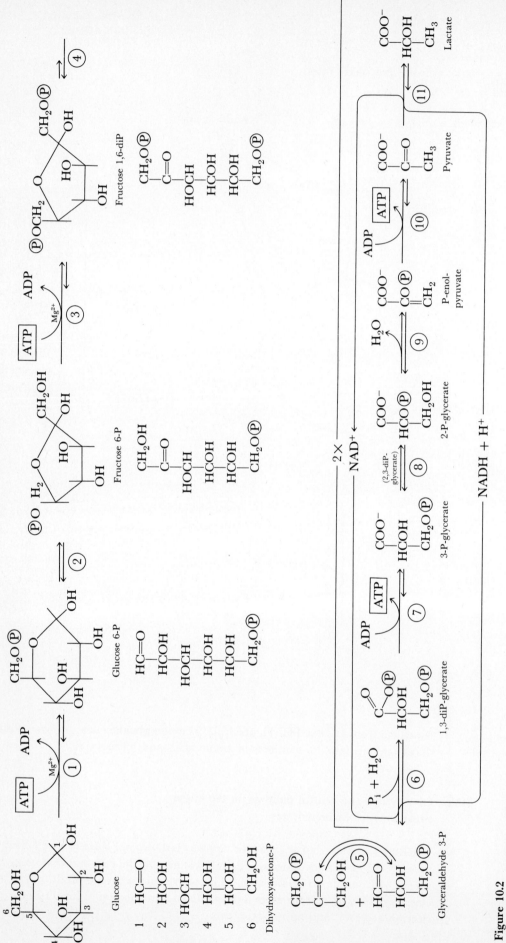

Figure 10.2
Degradation of glucose via the glycolytic pathway in muscle cells. The ring forms of the sugars shown in the top line predominate; open-chain structures are shown below each for clarity. The symbol Ⓟ represents the phosphoryl group, —PO$_3^{2-}$.

Table 10.1
Standard Free Energies of
the Enzymatic Steps in
Muscle Glycolysis

Step[a]	Enzyme	$\Delta G_0'$ (kcal/mol)	
1	Hexokinase	-4	
2	Phosphohexose isomerase	$\simeq 0$	
3	Phosphofructokinase	-3	
4	Aldolase	$+5$	
5	Triose phosphate isomerase	$\simeq 0$	
6	Triose phosphate dehydrogenase	$\simeq 0$	
7	Phosphoglycerate kinase	-7	
8	Phosphoglyceromutase	$\simeq 0$	$2\times$
9	Enolase	$\simeq 0$	
10	Pyruvate kinase	-6	
11	Lactate dehydrogenase	-6	
	Theoretical total	-38^b	

[a] Numbers correspond to the circled numbers in Figure 10.2.
[b] The theoretical total of -38 kcal/mol does not represent the sum of the figures shown, because the values indicated as $\simeq 0$ are not equal to zero.

The strategy of glycolysis can be understood by considering the pathway in four parts, as follows:

1.   Phosphorylation and isomerization of glucose to a sugar that can be cleaved into two interconvertible triose phosphates (reactions 1 through 5)

2.   Oxidation of the aldehyde group of glyceraldehyde 3-P to a carboxyl group by NAD^+, with concomitant uptake of P_i (reaction 6). This reaction forms the phosphate anhydride 1,3-diP-glycerate, which has sufficient energy to spontaneously transfer phosphate to ADP and form ATP (reaction 7).

3.   Transfer of phosphate from the 3-position to the 2-position of glycerate so that dehydration will produce the α-carboxyenol phosphate, P-enolpyruvate, which has sufficient energy to transfer phosphate to ADP (reactions 8 through 10)

4.   Utilization of the carbonyl group of pyruvate as an electron acceptor to oxidize the NADH produced in reaction 6, thereby regenerating NAD^+ (reaction 11) for another cycle of reactions 6 through 10

B. Regulation of the glycolytic pathway is accomplished by feedback control of phosphofructokinase (reaction 3), a regulatory enzyme that is inhibited by ATP and is activated by ADP or AMP. This control ensures entry of sugar molecules into the pathway when the ATP supply is low, and retards entry when ATP is plentiful. The phosphofructokinase reaction is the step in glycolysis at which sugars are irreversibly committed to breakdown; the preceding steps also can be used for interconversion of hexoses (see Figure 10.5). Regulation of the first enzyme unique to a pathway is a general feature of metabolic control.

10.3   Glycogenolysis mobilizes glucose reserves for ATP production.

A. Glycogen, the storage polymer of glucose in animals, is an important source of sugar for the glycolytic pathway. It is a highly branched polymer, consisting of chains of glucose monomers connected by α-1,4 linkages, with α-1,6 linkages forming branch points about every 10 residues (Figure 10.3). In the stage I breakdown of glycogen (glycogenolysis), the α-1,4 linkages are cleaved by stepwise phosphorolysis from the nonreducing ends of outer chains to yield glucose 1-P monomers. The phosphorylyzing enzyme, glycogen phosphorylase, stops four residues from a branch point. The actions of a glucotransferase, which transfers three residues from the branch to the main chain, and α-1,6-glucosidase, which hydrolyzes the α-1,6 linkage, are required to permit phosphorolysis to continue.

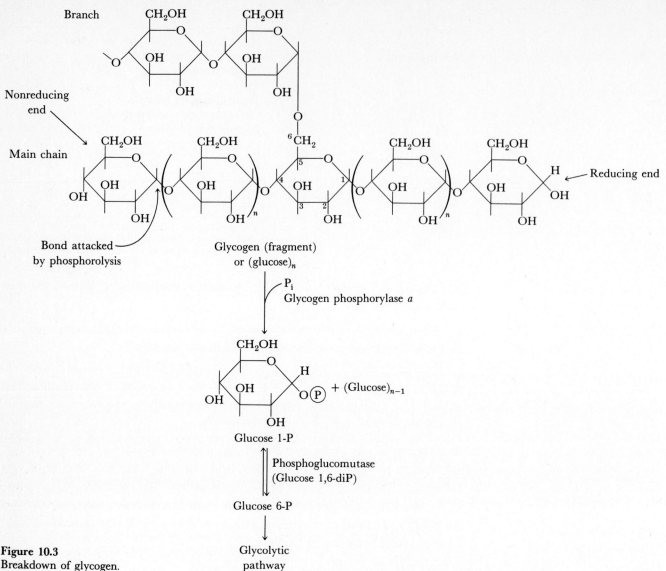

Figure 10.3
Breakdown of glycogen.

The glucose 1-P produced by phosphorolysis enters the glycolytic pathway as shown in Figure 10.3. The reaction catalyzed by phosphoglucomutase proceeds in two steps (equations 10.1 to 10.3); the regenerated intermediate, glucose 1,6-diP, must be synthesized in catalytic amount (by phosphorylation of glucose 6-P) before the phosphoglucomutase reaction can proceed.

$$\text{Glucose 1,6-diP} + \text{enzyme} \rightleftarrows \text{P-enzyme} + \text{glucose 6-P} \tag{10.1}$$

$$\underline{\text{Glucose 1-P} + \text{P-enzyme} \rightleftarrows \text{enzyme} + \text{glucose 1,6-diP}} \tag{10.2}$$

Net: $\qquad\qquad \text{Glucose 1-P} \rightleftarrows \text{glucose 6-P} \tag{10.3}$

B. Glycogen phosphorylase is under a complex set of controls that prevent glycogen breakdown except when ATP is needed. The chain of events leading to glycogenolysis is initiated by cyclic AMP (cAMP) as diagrammed in Figure 10.4. The cAMP is synthesized from ATP by the adenyl cyclase reaction in response to hormones such as epinephrine and glucagon, and is an important intermediate in many biological control processes.

10.4   Other hexoses also are broken down by glycolysis.

Although glucose is the principal source of sugar for glycolysis, other sugars such as mannose, fructose, and galactose also can enter the pathway, as shown in Figure 10.5.

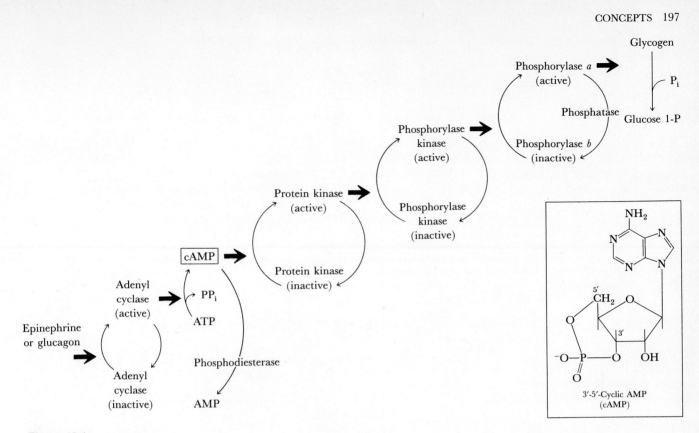

Figure 10.4
Control of glycogen phosphorylase activity via cyclic AMP (structure shown in inset).

Mannose is phosphorylated at the 6-position by hexokinase, an enzyme with a rather broad specificity for hexoses, and then is converted to fructose 6-P by phosphomannose isomerase. Although fructose also can be phosphorylated by hexokinase, in the liver most is phosphorylated at the 1-position by a fructokinase. A specific aldolase catalyzes cleavage of fructose 1-P to dihydroxyacetone P and glyceraldehyde, which then is phosphorylated at the 3-position by a specific kinase.

Galactose utilization requires the nucleoside diphosphate sugar, uridine diP-glucose (UDP-glucose), which is formed by reaction of UTP with glucose 1-P,

$$\text{Glucose 1-P} + \text{UTP} \underset{\text{Mg}^{2+}}{\overset{\substack{\text{UDP-glucose} \\ \text{pyrophosphorylase}}}{\rightleftharpoons}}$$

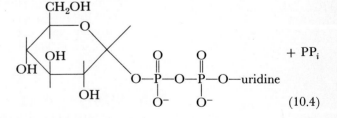

$$+ \text{PP}_i \tag{10.4}$$

in which PP_i represents inorganic pyrophosphate, $\text{P}_2\text{O}_7^{4-}$. Conversion of galactose to glucose 1-P proceeds in three steps (equations 10.5 to 10.8):

$$\text{Galactose} + \text{ATP} \underset{\text{Mg}^{2+}}{\overset{\text{galactokinase}}{\rightleftharpoons}} \text{galactose 1-P} + \text{ADP} \tag{10.5}$$

$$\text{Galactose 1-P} + \text{UDP-glucose} \overset{\substack{\text{phosphogalactose} \\ \text{uridyl transferase}}}{\rightleftharpoons} \text{UDP-galactose} + \text{glucose 1-P} \tag{10.6}$$

$$\text{UDP-galactose} \overset{\text{UDP-glucose epimerase}}{\rightleftharpoons} \text{UDP-glucose} \tag{10.7}$$

Net: $$\text{Galactose} + \text{ATP} \rightarrow \text{glucose 1-P} + \text{ADP} \tag{10.8}$$

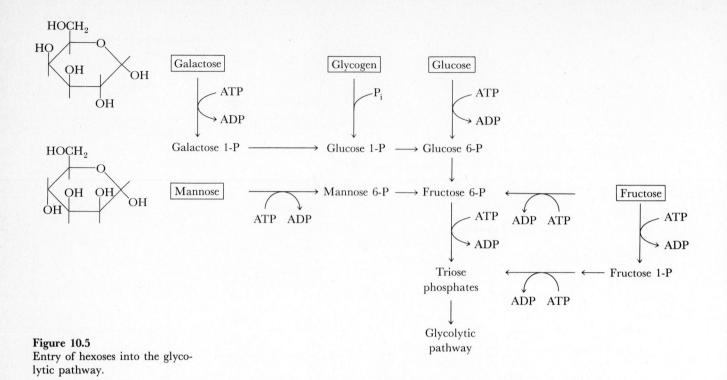

Figure 10.5
Entry of hexoses into the glycolytic pathway.

10.5 The phosphogluconate pathway is the principal source of reducing power in chemotrophs.

The phosphogluconate pathway oxidizes glucose completely to CO_2 with trapping of electrons and hydrogen in NADPH. The pathway is complex, and includes four reactions in common with glycolysis. A simplified outline of the pathway is shown in Figure 10.6.

    The phosphogluconate pathway can be considered conveniently as a two-stage process. In the first stage (reactions 1 through 3), glucose is phosphorylated and oxidatively decarboxylated to CO_2 and a pentose. In the second stage (reactions 4 through 11), the pentose molecules are combined and rearranged to regenerate phosphorylated glucose. Reactions 1, 2, 3, and 10 are essentially irreversible. However, the remainder are readily reversible and are important in sugar interconversions for biosynthesis as well as in production of reducing power. Transketolase (reaction 6) requires thiamine pyrophosphate as a cofactor (see Concept 11.1). The structures of the four-, five-, and seven-carbon intermediates and the interconversion of the pentoses are shown in Figure 10.7.

10.6 Additional concepts and techniques are presented in the Problems section.

A. Alcoholic fermentation of glucose in microorganisms. Problems 10.8, 10.12, and 10.16.

B. The Entner–Doudoroff pathway of glucose fermentation. Problems 10.9 and 10.16.

C. The phosphoketolase pathway of glucose fermentation. Problem 10.11.

D. Entry of disaccharides into glycolysis. Problem 10.12.

E. Adenylate control of carbohydrate metabolism. Problems 10.14 and 10.15.

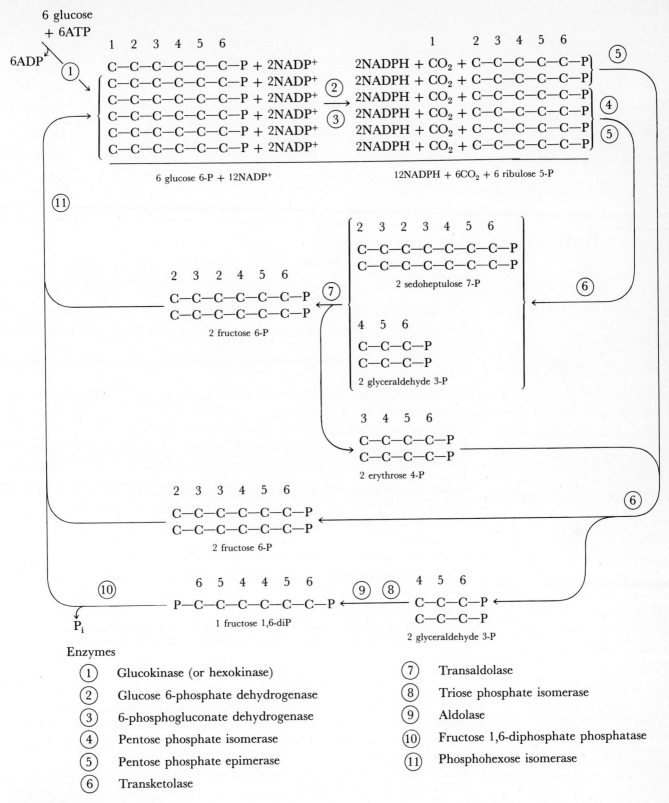

Figure 10.6
The phosphogluconate pathway.
This simplified scheme shows
only carbon and phosphorus
atoms, with numbering to indicate how the input carbon atoms
become distributed among the
intermediates. Glucokinase is a
glucose-specific hexokinase found
in liver.

Figure 10.7
Structures of five intermediates
and interconversion of pentoses
in the phosphogluconate pathway. Circled numbers correspond
to steps in Figure 10.6.

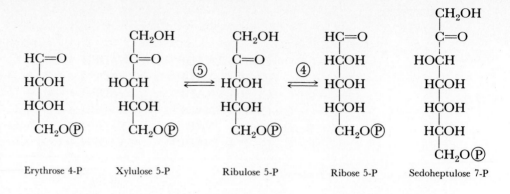

Erythrose 4-P   Xylulose 5-P   Ribulose 5-P   Ribose 5-P   Sedoheptulose 7-P

References

COMPREHENSIVE TEXTS

Lehninger: Chapters 14, 16, and 17   Stryer: Chapters 12, 15, and 16
Metzler: Chapter 9   White et al.: Chapters 14 and 15

OTHER REFERENCES

A. L. Lehninger, *Bioenergetics,* Benjamin/Cummings, Menlo Park, Calif., 1971, 2nd ed. Chapter 4.

H. L. Segal, "Enzymatic Interconversion of Active and Inactive Forms of Enzymes," *Science,*
180, 25 (1973).

J. D. Watson, *Molecular Biology of the Gene,* Benjamin/Cummings, Menlo Park, Calif., 1976, 3rd
ed. Chapter 2.

Problems

10.1   Answer the following with true or false. If false, explain why.
a. Nucleic acids are not among the principal fuel molecules of most cells.
b. In stage I of catabolism, complex fuel molecules are broken down to their precursor
components.
c. Most of the available energy of fuel molecules is released in their stage II degradation
to TCA-cycle intermediates.
d. The phosphogluconate pathway yields ATP and reducing power at the expense of
glucose degradation.
e. Five steps in glycolytic fermentation proceed with a high negative $\Delta G'_0$.
f. Only one of the two series of steps in glycolysis that lead to ATP formation involves a
true redox reaction.
g. The last step of the glycolytic pathway in muscle cells (lactate dehydrogenase) does
not function if there is sufficient oxygen present to allow aerobic oxidation of NADH.
h. Cyclic AMP functions as a cofactor in the glycogen phosphorylase reaction.
i. Degradation of glycogen by hydrolysis to glucose would be more efficient than phosphorolysis to glucose 1-P in terms of the total amount of ATP produced upon breakdown to pyruvate.
j. All the reducing power derived from the phosphogluconate pathway is produced in
the first three steps of each cycle.
k. Transketolase is a key enzyme in the nonoxidative portion of the phosphogluconate
pathway.

10.2 a. Carbohydrates, lipids, and _____ are the principal fuel molecules for chemotrophic
cells.
b. In stage _____ of catabolism the electrons transferred to _____ in stages _____
and _____ are transferred to O_2 with concomitant _____ production.
c. _____ is the carrier of reducing power for biosynthesis. In chemotrophs it is produced primarily in the _____ pathway.

d. Feedback control of the regulatory enzyme _____ inhibits the entry of glucose into the glycolytic pathway if the level of _____ is high.

e. In the first part of the glycolytic pathway, glucose is _____ and _____ to produce a molecule that can be cleaved into two _____ triose phosphates.

f. The first energy payoff in glycolysis results from transfer of a phosphate group from the phosphate anhydride _____ to ADP to form _____ .

g. The complex control of _____ activity ensures that glycogen will be broken down only when _____ is needed.

h. Interconversion of galactose and glucose occurs via their activated nucleoside _____ derivatives, _____ and _____ .

i. In the first stage of the phosphogluconate pathway, _____ is oxidized by _____ and decarboxylated to yield _____ , _____ , and _____ .

10.3 a. What are the three principal commodities provided to a cell by catabolic pathways?

b. Which of these commodities are the principal products of each of the following pathways? (Assume that all NADH is oxidized by O_2 with concomitant ATP production.)

1. Fatty acid oxidation to CO_2
2. The Krebs or TCA cycle
3. Breakdown of glycogen to lactate
4. The phosphogluconate pathway

10.4 A muscle extract is dialyzed exhaustively against dilute phosphate buffer. Assume this procedure quantitatively removes all small molecules not bound tightly to protein, and that the extract contains no ATPase activity. If ATP now is added back, what other cofactors must be added for the extract to convert glucose to (a) glucose 6-P; (b) glucose 1-P; (c) galactose 1-P; (d) ribulose 5-P; (e) lactate?

10.5 In a cell operating anaerobically, what is the energy yield in molecules of ATP per glucose monomer converted to lactate from the following?

a. Free glucose, via the glycolytic pathway
b. Glycogen, via the Embden–Meyerhof pathway

10.6 The enzyme phosphofructokinase in the Embden–Meyerhof pathway is feedback-inhibited by ATP, which is also a substrate for the phosphofructokinase reaction. Why doesn't this situation render the enzyme useless?

10.7 A fermentation pathway is said to be balanced if there is no net oxidation or reduction of the substrate. Such pathways produce energy by splitting the substrate into two fragments such that electrons can be transferred from one to the other with a negative $\Delta G'$ sufficient to drive ATP formation. What is the electron donor and what is the electron acceptor when the glycolytic pathway operates anaerobically as a balanced fermentation (Figure 10.2)?

10.8 Fermentations often are named for their end products. In yeast the glycolytic pathway is termed an **alcoholic** fermentation because its end product is ethanol rather than lactate. The final step of Figure 10.2 is replaced by two others: decarboxylation of pyruvate to acetaldehyde [catalyzed by pyruvate decarboxylase, which requires the coenzyme thiamine pyrophosphate (TPP), Concept 11.1], and reduction of the acetaldehyde by NADH to yield ethanol and NAD^+ (catalyzed by alcohol dehydrogenase), as shown in Figure 10.8. Thus in such a pathway an aldehyde serves as both the electron donor and the electron acceptor.

a. Explain how such a process can yield energy.

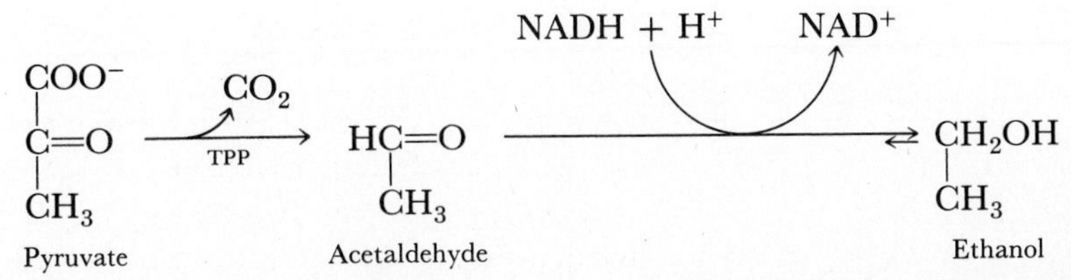

Figure 10.8
The terminal two steps of glycolysis in yeast (Problem 10.8).

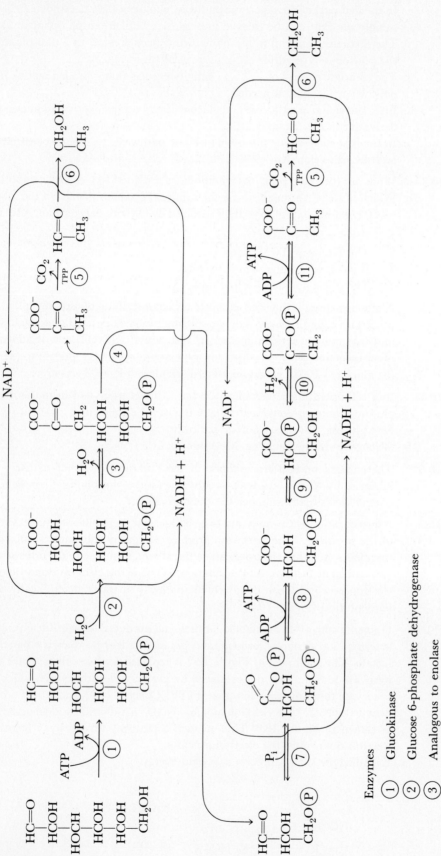

Figure 10.9
Alcoholic fermentation in *Pseudomonas lindneri* (Problem 10.9).

Enzymes

① Glucokinase

② Glucose 6-phosphate dehydrogenase

③ Analogous to enolase

④ Analogous to fructose 1,6-diphosphate aldolase

⑤ through ⑪ Same as yeast glycolysis

b. Calculate the $\Delta G'_0$ values for transfer of electrons from glyceraldehyde 3-P to NAD$^+$, and from NADH to acetaldehyde (Concept 9.3).

10.9 Although most organisms use the glycolytic pathway for anaerobic production of ATP from glucose, a few use other pathways. Figure 10.9 shows the fermentation employed by an anaerobic bacterium of the genus *Pseudomonas*. This scheme is called the **Entner–Doudoroff pathway** after its discoverers. If this bacterium were competing in an anaerobic environment for a limited supply of glucose with another bacterial species employing the glycolytic fermentation to ethanol (see Problem 10.8), which do you predict would predominate? Why?

10.10 Drinking methanol can be fatal. The methanol itself is not harmful, but it is converted rapidly via the alcohol dehydrogenase reaction into formaldehyde, which is toxic (Figure 10.10). Surprisingly, one treatment for methanol poisoning is to get the patient drunk. Can you suggest an explanation for why this treatment is effective?

10.11 An obligate anaerobic bacterium is found to carry out an "unbalanced" oxidation (a pathway that provides both ATP and reducing power) of glucose 3-^{14}C with net formation of two molecules of ATP, two molecules of reduced pyridine nucleotide, and one molecule each of CH$_3$^{14}COOH, unlabeled CO$_2$, and unlabeled lactate, per equivalent of glucose degraded. Extracts of the organism contain an enzyme that catalyzes the reaction shown in Figure 10.11.

a. Discuss the following proposition with regard to this evidence: The new enzyme is irrelevant to the fermentation, which is simply a variant of the glycolytic pathway in which half the pyruvate serves as substrate for lactic dehydrogenase, and the other half is acted upon by pyruvate decarboxylase followed by an acetaldehyde dehydrogenase.

b. Assuming that the new enzyme *is* involved in the fermentation, write the pathway you think most likely on the basis of the evidence given. For each step, either give the name of the enzyme or cite an analogous enzyme reaction from the glycolytic or phosphogluconate pathways.

c. Would you expect to find both NAD$^+$ and NADP$^+$ in an obligate anaerobe such as this one? Explain your answer.

d. In terms of ATP yield per glucose, the pathway in this organism is as efficient a fermentation as the glycolytic pathway, yet the former is restricted to a few species of anaerobic bacteria. Can you propose an explanation for why glycolysis, rather than this pathway, was selected by evolution as the major route of glucose breakdown in most cells?

10.12 A professor of molecular enology at Napa Valley State turns out an unusually fine batch of champagne, and is able to trace the cause to contamination of one of her vats by a strange microorganism. She isolates the organism, and begins to investigate its carbohydrate metabolism by studying its growth on a synthetic medium containing various sugars at a growth-limiting concentration of 1 g/L. She obtains the results shown in Table 10.2 (under Parent).

Figure 10.10
Alcohol dehydrogenase–catalyzed oxidation of methanol by NAD$^+$ (Problem 10.10).

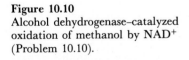

Figure 10.11
Reaction catalyzed by an enzyme from an anaerobic bacterium (Problem 10.11).

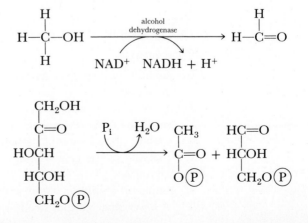

Table 10.2
Data from a Paper in *J. Mol. Enol.* (Problem 10.12)

Sugar	Cell doublings per hour		Final yield of cells per liter (mg of cell nitrogen)	
	Parent	Mutant	Parent	Mutant
Glucose	2.1	2.1	65.0	64.8
Fructose	2.0	2.0	65.1	65.0
Galactose	1.9	No growth	64.6	No growth
Sucrose	1.9	1.9	63.9	32.8
Lactose	1.9	2.0	64.1	32.4

On further investigation, she finds that cells grown on galactose, sucrose, or lactose, but not on glucose or fructose, accumulate an intracellular polysaccharide during the early phase of the growth period. When the sugar in the medium has disappeared, the amount of polysaccharide decreases until it is depleted, at which point growth stops. Experiments with extracts of the organism show that the polysaccharide is glycogen, and that it is synthesized by a reaction involving transfer of glucose residues from UDP-glucose to the growing chain:

$$\text{UDP-glucose} + (\text{glucose})_n \rightarrow \text{UDP} + (\text{glucose})_{n+1}$$

In the course of this work, the professor comes across a mutant of the organism that is unable to grow on galactose, although she shows that it can take up galactose from the medium. By genetic tests, she demonstrates that the mutant differs from the parent strain by a single mutation (i.e., loss of only one enzyme activity). Results of growth experiments with the mutant also are shown in Table 10.2. When grown on sucrose or lactose the mutant accumulates polysaccharide as before, but growth ceases as soon as the sugar in the medium is depleted. Sucrose and lactose are disaccharides. Sucrose is glucosyl fructose and lactose is galactosyl glucose. Assume that the first step in metabolism of each is as follows:

Sucrose: phosphorolysis to fructose + glucose 1-P
Lactose: hydrolysis to glucose + galactose

a. Write the sequence of reactions by which sucrose and lactose give rise to polysaccharide and enter the glycolytic pathway in the parent strain.
b. What enzyme is defective in the mutant strain?

10.13 Following is a list of hereditary metabolic defects involving loss of single enzymes of catabolism, and a second list of possible consequences of such defects. Match each enzyme with its most likely consequence (only one) from the second list.

Defects:

a. Lack of phosphoglucomutase
b. Lack of UDP-glucose pyrophosphorylase
c. Lack of triose phosphate isomerase
d. Lack of phosphofructokinase
e. Lack of glycogen phosphorylase kinase
f. Lack of α-1,6-glucosidase
g. Lack of phosphorylase *a* phosphatase

Consequences:

1. Inability to use glycogen as an energy source, with no effect on ability to use galactose
2. Lower than normal production of glucose 1-P in response to a sudden, large increase in cAMP level
3. Lethal; prevents use of carbohydrates for ATP production
4. Inability to use galactose as an energy source, with no effect on ability to use glycogen
5. Impaired ability to obtain energy from carbohydrates
6. A lower than normal steady-state level of glycogen

7. Inability to use either glycogen or galactose as an energy source
8. Inability to use sucrose as an energy source (see Answer 10.12)

10.14 The feedback effects that ATP, ADP, and AMP exert on regulatory enzymes of carbohydrate metabolism sometimes are referred to collectively as the **adenylate control system.** This control operates on at least one enzyme of the phosphogluconate pathway; fructose 1,6-diphosphate phosphatase (Figure 10.6, reaction 10) is activated by ATP and inhibited by ADP. It seems likely that other enzymes of the pathway are under adenylate control as well. Would you predict that the enzymes aldolase and phosphohexose isomerase might be under such control? Explain your answer. Which other enzymes might be under adenylate control?

10.15 Defend or demolish the following assertions: In the phosphogluconate pathway, glucose 6-phosphate dehydrogenase and transketolase, in addition to fructose 1,6-diphosphate phosphatase, should be under adenylate control. When ATP levels are high, glucose 6-phosphate dehydrogenase should be activated and transketolase inhibited. When ATP levels are low, glucose 6-phosphate dehydrogenase should be inhibited and transketolase activated.

10.16 It has been postulated for some time that the basis for biologic clocks may be some controlled periodic process at the metabolic level. Searching for such a process, Pye and Chance found that a yeast extract given a constant, slow influx of glucose showed a sustained oscillation of the NADH/NAD$^+$ ratio with a period of about 7 min over an interval of several hours. From your knowledge of adenylate control in carbohydrate metabolism, explain qualitatively the sequence of events that might produce this phenomenon.

10.17 You have isolated three strains of bacteria, each of which ferments glucose by a different pathway. By painstaking analysis you determine that the pathways used in these microorganisms are the glycolytic pathway, the phosphogluconate pathway, and the Entner–Douderoff pathway (see Problem 10.9). But alas, you forgot to label the strains. To clarify the situation you grow each of the strains anaerobically with radioactively labeled glucose as the sole carbon source and analyze for the appearance of the ^{14}C label in ethanol (see Problem 10.8). The results are shown in Table 10.3. Which organism ferments glucose by which pathway?

Table 10.3
Appearance of Glucose Carbons in Ethanol ($\overset{2}{C}H_3\overset{1}{C}H_2OH$) during Fermentation by Three Bacterial Strains (Problem 10.17)

Carbon source	Position of ^{14}C label in ethanol		
	Strain A	Strain B	Strain C
Glucose 1-^{14}C	None	C-2	None
Glucose 2-^{14}C	C-2	C-1	C-1
Glucose 3-^{14}C	C-1	None	C-2
Glucose 4-^{14}C	None	None	None
Glucose 5-^{14}C	C-1	C-1	C-1
Glucose 6-^{14}C	C-2	C-2	C-2

10.18 Fluhardy Pharmaceuticals has just sent you a sample of mythomycin, a newly discovered antibiotic that inactivates one enzyme involved in carbohydrate metabolism. Included with the sample is the information in Table 10.4. Unfortunately, Fluhardy Pharmaceuticals neglected to list which enzyme is inactivated by mythomycin.

a. Deduce the identity of the affected enzyme from the information in Table 10.4.
b. Write the balanced equation for the metabolism of glucose to pyruvate in the (1) absence and (2) presence of mythomycin.

☆ 10.19 An infant is admitted to the hospital with suspected glycogen-storage disease, which is confirmed by finding markedly elevated levels of glycogen in a liver biopsy. A series of tests gives the following results:

1. Blood glucose is abnormally low.
2. Feeding of glucose results in a rapid elevation of blood glucose; there is no increase in blood glucose upon feeding of fructose or galactose.

Table 10.4
Analysis of Mythomycin
Action (Problem 10.18)[a]

Yeast grown anaerobically with glucose as the sole carbon source		Without mythomycin	With mythomycin
	ATP/glucose	2.00	1.67

		Position of ^{14}C label in pyruvate	
		Without mythomycin	With mythomycin
Yeast grown anaerobically with ^{14}C-labeled glucose	Glucose 1-^{14}C	C-3	None
	Glucose 2-^{14}C	C-2	C-1, C-3
	Glucose 3-^{14}C	C-1	C-1, C-2
	Glucose 4-^{14}C	C-1	C-1
	Glucose 5-^{14}C	C-2	C-2
	Glucose 6-^{14}C	C-3	C-3

[a] The carbons of pyruvate are numbered starting with the carboxyl group.

3. No hyperglycemic effect (release of glucose into the bloodstream) is observed upon administration of epinephrine or glucagon.
4. Examination of liver glycogen shows an essentially normal structure.
5. Examination of the activities of enzymes of glycogen synthesis and breakdown shows them all to be within normal limits.

In view of these findings, which *one* of the following enzymes is most likely to be defective in this patient?

a. Glucokinase
b. Fructose 1,6-diphosphate phosphatase
c. Glucose 6-phosphate phosphatase
d. Hexose 1-P-uridyl transferase (catalyzes galactose 1-P + UDP-glucose $\rightleftarrows$ UDP-galactose + glucose 1-P)
e. None of those listed.

☆ 10.20   What would be the *predominant* consequences to individuals who are unable to synthesize each of the following enzymes?

a. Liver fructokinase

1. Inability to metabolize fructose
2. Lowered yield of ATP production per mole of glucose metabolized
3. Failure to split fructose diphosphate into triose phosphates
4. Failure to resynthesize glucose from lactic acid produced during exercise

b. Liver phosphorylase *a* phosphatase

1. A very low steady-state level of liver glycogen
2. Production of unbranched glycogen
3. Inability to make liver glycogen
4. Production of phosphorylated glycogen

c. Muscle α-1,6-glucosidase

1. Production of unbranched glycogen in muscle
2. Failure of epinephrine to produce the usual increase in blood glucose
3. Inability of the liver to metabolize sucrose
4. Production of glycogen having a greater ratio of outer glucose residues to outer branch points

d. Liver pyruvate kinase

1. Inability to fix CO_2 into organic linkage
2. Inability to make GTP
3. Markedly reduced capacity for glycolysis
4. Inability to make Asp from oxaloacetate

☆ 10.21   Picture a cell that normally employs both the Embden–Meyerhof glycolytic pathway
and the phosphogluconate pathway but is carrying a genetic defect rendering the
enzyme phosphoglucose isomerase (glucose 6-P $\rightleftarrows$ fructose 6-P) inactive.

a. Can you write a series of known enzymatic reactions that the cell might use nevertheless to convert glucose 6-P to fructose 6-P?

b. How do you think glucose breakdown in this cell would be affected by a lowering of
the ATP/ADP ratio? Would this mutation seriously affect the cell's ability to meet its
metabolic needs when growing on glucose as substrate? Explain.

Answers

10.1   a. True
b. True
c. False. Most of the available energy of fuel molecules is released in stage IV.
d. False. No ATP is produced by the reactions of the phosphogluconate pathway alone
(Figure 10.6).
e. True
f. True
g. True
h. False. Cyclic AMP is required in the first of the steps leading to glycogen phosphorylase activation, but it is not involved in the phosphorolysis reaction itself.
i. False. Phosphorolysis conserves the energy of the glycogen glycosidic linkages in glucose 1-P, thereby eliminating the need for a phosphorylation of the glucose monomers
at ATP expense prior to entry into the glycolytic pathway.
j. True
k. True

10.2   a. proteins
b. IV, NAD^+, II, III, ATP
c. NADPH, phosphogluconate
d. phosphofructokinase, ATP
e. phosphorylated, isomerized, interconvertible
f. 1,3-diP-glycerate, ATP
g. glycogen phosphorylase, ATP
h. diphosphate, UDP-galactose, UDP-glucose
i. glucose 6-P, $NADP^+$, NADPH, CO_2, ribulose 5-P

10.3   a. The three commodities are energy (ATP), reducing power (NADPH), and starting
materials for biosynthesis (intermediates).
b. 1.   ATP, intermediates
2.   ATP, intermediates
3.   ATP, intermediates
4.   NADPH, intermediates

10.4   a. Mg^{2+}, which is required for the hexokinase reaction.
b. Mg^{2+}. (The cofactor glucose 1,6-diP for the phosphoglucomutase reaction can be
synthesized from glucose 6-P and ATP.)
c. Mg^{2+} and UTP. Galactose 1-P is made from glucose 1-P by the reaction shown in
equations 10.4 to make UDP-glucose, followed by equations 10.7 and 10.6 in reverse.
d. Mg^{2+} and $NADP^+$. Conversion of glucose to ribulose 5-P requires reactions 1, 2, and 3
of the phosphogluconate pathway.
e. Mg^{2+}, ADP, P_i, and NAD^+. Conversion of glucose to lactate + CO_2 requires the
entire glycolytic pathway.

10.5   a. From Figure 10.2, the yield will be 2 ATP per glucose.
b. Because glycogen phosphorolysis ultimately yields glucose 6-P without expenditure of
ATP, the yield is increased to 3 ATP per glucose.

10.6   The two binding sites for ATP, regulatory and catalytic, must have appropriately different ATP affinities. The catalytic site has a high affinity, whereas the regulatory site has a relatively low affinity. Thus when [ATP] is high, binding will occur at both the catalytic and regulatory sites, and the latter binding will inhibit the enzyme; when [ATP] is low, binding will occur only at the catalytic site and the enzyme will function.

10.7   The electron donor is glyceraldehyde 3-P. Specifically, electrons are given up by the aldehyde group at the 1-position, which becomes oxidized to the carboxyl group of 1,3-diP-glycerate. The electron acceptor is the carbonyl group of pyruvate, which becomes reduced to the secondary hydroxyl group in lactate.

10.8   a. The paradox is only apparent. Energy is released because two quite different redox couples are involved (Table 9.1). The pair of electrons given up when glyceraldehyde 3-P is oxidized to 3-P-glycerate has a relatively high energy:

$$\text{3-P-glycerate} + 2H^+/\text{glyceraldehyde 3-P} + H_2O \qquad E_0' \simeq -0.55 \text{ V}$$

The pair of electrons accepted by acetaldehyde ends up in ethanol, and has much lower energy:

$$\text{Acetaldehyde} + 2H^+/\text{ethanol} \qquad E_0' = -0.20 \text{ V}$$

   b. NAD^+ is suited ideally for transferring electrons from one carbonyl group to another, because the reduction potential of the couple $NAD^+ + 2H^+/NADH + H^+$ ($E_0' = -0.32$ V) is between the two potentials in part a. (This property may explain the selection of NAD^+ as the primary electron carrier in early anaerobic organisms.) Hence the two $\Delta E_0'$ values are $+0.23$ and $+0.12$ V, respectively, and the corresponding $\Delta G_0'$ values (from equation 9.6) are $\simeq -11$ kcal/mol and $\simeq -6$ kcal/mol. The energy released in the first of these reactions is sufficient to drive ATP formation from $ADP + P_i$ (Figure 10.2), reactions 6 and 7).

10.9   The strategy of the *Pseudomonas* pathway does not appear to be as effective as that of glycolysis. As a consequence of the early oxidation step (reaction 2), only one of the 2 three-carbon fragments obtained in reaction 4 can be utilized for ATP production. Consequently, the yield of ATP per glucose degraded is 1 in the *Pseudomonas* pathway compared to 2 for glycolysis, so that the organism employing glycolysis would undoubtedly predominate. This conclusion is consistent with the observation that some version of the glycolytic pathway is found today in almost all cells, procaryotic as well as eucaryotic, whereas pathways such as those of *Pseudomonas lindneri* are restricted to a few species of bacteria.

10.10   The K_M of alcohol dehydrogenase for ethanol is lower than the K_M for methanol. Thus flooding the system with ethanol can competitively inhibit oxidation of methanol until it is excreted.

10.11   a. The label introduced as glucose-3-^{14}C into the glycolytic pathway yields pyruvate labeled in the carboxyl group. Therefore, the two last steps proposed would yield labeled lactate, labeled CO_2, and unlabeled acetate, contrary to the results found. The proposition is therefore false.
   b. See Figure 10.12.
   c. In aerobic organisms, NADH and NADPH are produced in different pathways and serve different functions (Concept 9.5, part B). In an anaerobe such as this one, in which all the reduced pyridine nucleotide is used for biosynthesis, there is no need for two carriers of reducing power.
   d. Glycolysis degrades glucose completely to 1 three-carbon product (pyruvate). This molecule retains sufficient energy to be converted without further ATP expenditure to the activated two-carbon substrate acetyl CoA for complete oxidation (Concepts 11.1, part A, and 11.4). The phosphoketolase pathway, in yielding 2 ATP per glucose, produces free acetate, which would have to be activated at the expense of an ATP to undergo further metabolism. Thus if coupled with the TCA cycle in an aerobic organ-

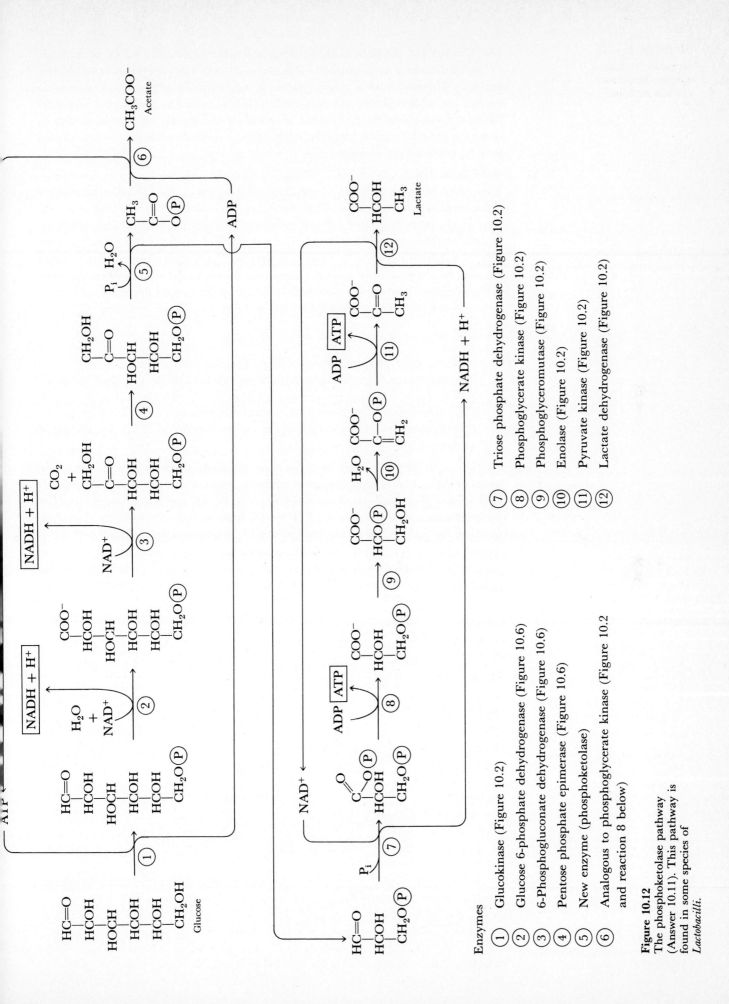

Figure 10.12
The phosphoketolase pathway
(Answer 10.11). This pathway is
found in some species of
Lactobacilli.

Enzymes

① Glucokinase (Figure 10.2)
② Glucose 6-phosphate dehydrogenase (Figure 10.6)
③ 6-Phosphogluconate dehydrogenase (Figure 10.6)
④ Pentose phosphate epimerase (Figure 10.6)
⑤ New enzyme (phosphoketolase)
⑥ Analogous to phosphoglycerate kinase (Figure 10.2 and reaction 8 below)

⑦ Triose phosphate dehydrogenase (Figure 10.2)
⑧ Phosphoglycerate kinase (Figure 10.2)
⑨ Phosphoglyceromutase (Figure 10.2)
⑩ Enolase (Figure 10.2)
⑪ Pyruvate kinase (Figure 10.2)
⑫ Lactate dehydrogenase (Figure 10.2)

ism (Chapter 11), the phosphoketolase pathway would yield only 1 ATP per glucose.

This difference might explain the selection of glycolysis over the phosphoketolase pathway. However, such a rationalization is very tentative at best. For example, an equally plausible explanation would be that early in evolution some completely independent feature strongly favored an organism employing glycolysis over organisms using the phosphoketolase pathway, so that glycolysis became the predominant pathway by evolutionary accident.

10.12 a. See Figure 10.13.

b. To account for polysaccharide accumulation the K_M of enzyme 2 (UDP-glucose pyrophosphorylase) must be lower than the K_M of enzyme 1 (phosphoglucomutase), so that sugars yielding glucose 1-P are converted partially to polysaccharide until the external carbon source is exhausted. The properties of the mutant can be explained best by a defect in enzyme 1. A defect in enzyme 3 (glycogen phosphorylase) cannot account for the mutant properties because the parent strain must have enzyme 1 to grow on galactose and utilize polysaccharide, and if the mutant has enzyme 1, then a defect in enzyme 3 could not explain the inability to grow on galactose.

10.13 a. 7.

b. 4.

c. 5.   Half the triose produced in the aldolase reaction will be wasted.

d. 3.   This step is essential for all carbohydrate metabolized by the glycolytic pathway.

e. 1.

f. 2.   Only the outermost glycogen chains can be broken down by phosphorylase.

g. 6.   Phosphorylase *a* will remain active, even in the absence of cAMP stimulation of glycogenolysis.

10.14   The glycolytic pathway functions to produce ATP, and therefore is activated at low levels of ATP. The phosphogluconate pathway functions to produce NADPH and biosynthetic precursors, which are needed by the cell only under conditions favorable for biosynthesis, that is, when the ATP level is high. Because the two pathways must compete for glucose, adenylate control would be expected to operate on them in *opposite* ways, activating one while deactivating the other. Control of enzymes common to both, such as aldolase and phosphohexose isomerase, would activate and deactivate the two pathways in parallel; hence such control would not be expected.

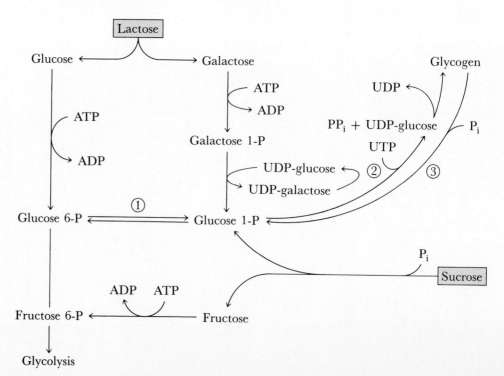

Figure 10.13
Entry of lactose and sucrose into glycolysis (Answer 10.12).

More likely would be control of the first enzyme unique to the phosphogluconate pathway, glucose 6-phosphate dehydrogenase. One would expect this enzyme to be activated by ATP and inhibited by ADP, AMP, or both.

10.15 These assertions are reasonable. The reasons for expecting the proposed control of glucose 6-phosphate dehydrogenase were explained in answer 10.14. At high ATP levels, the proposed opposite control of transketolase would not affect NADPH production, but would ensure a supply of pentose phosphate precursors for nucleic acid synthesis by inhibiting the conversion of these intermediates back to hexose phosphates. At low ATP levels, activation of transketolase would promote conversion of pentose phosphates derived from catabolism to hexose phosphates, which could feed into the glycolytic pathway for ATP production.

10.16 The key control element is the regulatory enzyme phosphofructokinase in the glycolytic pathway. A low ATP/ADP ratio activates the enzyme, thereby allowing degradation of glucose via glycolysis and the TCA cycle with production of NADH; hence the NADH/NAD$^+$ ratio increases. As NADH transfers electrons into the mitochondrial electron-transport chain, ATP is produced, thereby raising the ATP/ADP ratio. When this ratio becomes high enough, phosphofructokinase is inhibited, but transfer of electrons from NADH to O$_2$ continues, maintaining a high ATP/ADP ratio until the NADH is depleted. The ATP/ADP ratio then starts to fall as more glucose is converted to glucose 6-phosphate, until it reaches a low enough value to activate phosphofructokinase, and the cycle starts over again.

10.17 Strain A employs the phosphogluconate pathway (Figure 10.6). Strain B employs the glycolytic pathway (Figure 10.2 and Problem 10.8). Strain C employs the Entner–Doudoroff pathway (Figure 10.9).

10.18 In the absence of mythomycin, both the labeling and the ATP/glucose ratio are consistent with metabolism via the glycolytic pathway. In the presence of the drug, the data are consistent with conversion of glucose 6-P to fructose 6-P and fructose 1,6-diP by one turn of the phosphogluconate pathway, and then production of ATP from fructose 1,6-diP via the glycolytic pathway as usual.

a. The enzyme blocked is phosphohexose isomerase.

b. 1. Glucose + 2ADP + 2P$_i$ + 2NAD$^+$ →
2 pyruvate + 2ATP + 2NADH + 2H$^+$

2. 3 glucose + 5ADP + 5P$_i$ + 6NADP$^+$ + 5NAD$^+$ →
3CO$_2$ + 5 pyruvate + 5ATP + 6NADPH + 5NADH + 11H$^+$

11 Breakdown of Lipids and Proteins

A large portion of the energy available to chemotrophs is derived from lipid and protein catabolism. This chapter considers the breakdown of lipids and proteins, and the oxidation of the resulting common intermediates to CO_2 via the tricarboxylic acid (TCA) cycle. The roles of coenzymes in these pathways and some nutritional implications of TCA-cycle function also are discussed.

Concepts

11.1 Coenzymes assist in the catalysis of many catabolic reactions.

A. **Coenzyme A or CoA,** also abbreviated **HSCoA,** is the universal carrier of activated acyl $(R-\overset{\overset{\textstyle O}{\|}}{C}-)$ groups (Figure 11.1a). Acyl groups are linked to CoA through thioester bonds, which are high-energy linkages ($\Delta G_0'$ of hydrolysis $\simeq -9$ kcal/mol). CoA is derived from the vitamin pantothenic acid.

B. **Thiamine pyrophosphate (TPP),** derived from the vitamin thiamine (B_1), is required for decarboxylation of α-keto acids (Figure 11.1b). It also is involved in some transfer reactions of aldehyde derivatives, such as the transketolase reaction of the phosphogluconate pathway (Concept 10.5). All these reactions include a step in which the

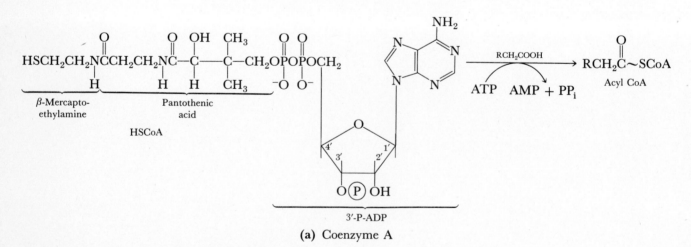

(a) Coenzyme A

Figure 11.1
Structures and reactions of five coenzymes in catabolism. Coenzymes are specialized organic molecules that help to catalyze reactions for which amino acid chemistry alone is inadequate (see Concept 7.3, part C). A sixth coenzyme, pyridoxal phosphate, is discussed in detail in Concept 11.3, part C.

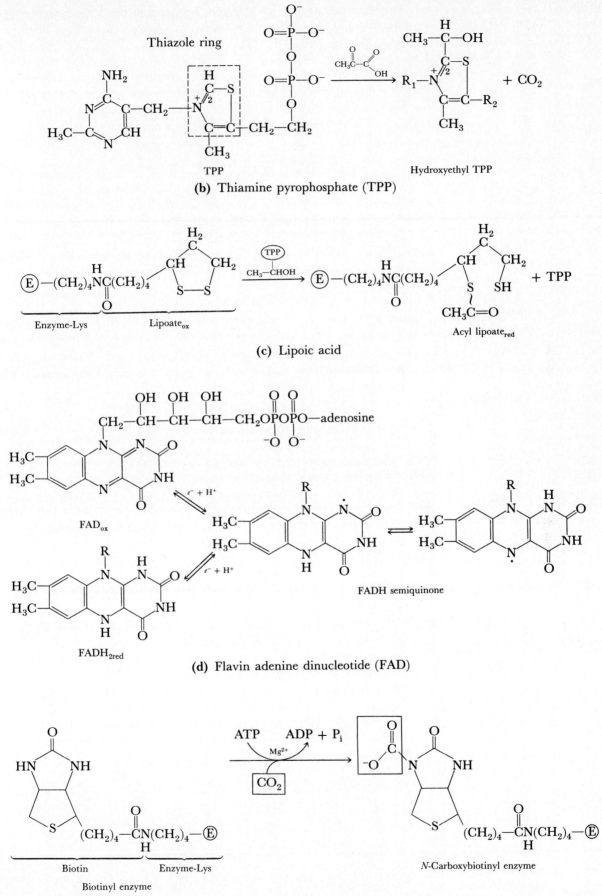

(b) Thiamine pyrophosphate (TPP)

(c) Lipoic acid

(d) Flavin adenine dinucleotide (FAD)

(e) Biotin

Figure 11.1 (*Continued*)

intermediate is covalently bound to the 2-position of the TPP thiazole ring, which transiently can accommodate an extra pair of electrons by virtue of its quaternary nitrogen atom (see Problem 7.18).

C. **Lipoic acid** functions as the oxidant and acyl-group carrier in the oxidative decarboxylation of α-keto acids (Figure 11.1c). In this process lipoate accepts an aldehyde intermediate from TPP and oxidizes it to an acyl group. Lipoate always is covalently bound to the ϵ-amino group of a Lys residue as a prosthetic group in the active site of an enzyme.

D. **Flavin adenine dinucleotide (FAD)** is derived from the vitamin riboflavin (B_2). FAD (Figure 11.1d) is an electron-carrier coenzyme like NAD^+. However, unlike NAD^+ it always occurs as a prosthetic group, never as a free carrier. The protein to which it is bound is termed a **flavoprotein (FP)**. Also unlike NAD^+, FAD accepts two electrons and *both* hydrogen ions in a typical oxidation reaction. Conversion of FAD to the reduced form ($FADH_2$) can occur in two steps, because the intermediate semiquinone form is fairly stable. Thus FAD can participate in either one- or two-electron transfer reactions.

E. **Biotin,** itself a vitamin, is required for all carboxylation reactions involving CO_2 fixation in animal cells (Figure 11.1e). Biotin functions as a prosthetic group bound to the ϵ-amino group of a Lys residue, and participates in ATP-dependent CO_2 activation. All biotin-dependent reactions are inhibited by **avidin,** a biotin-binding protein found in egg white.

11.2 Fatty acids are degraded to acetyl CoA by successive cycles of β oxidation.

A. The predominant lipids used for fuel molecules by chemotrophs are neutral fats or triglycerides (Figure 11.2) and phospholipids (Figure 6.1). In stage I breakdown of these lipids, the glycerol ester bonds are hydrolyzed to produce free fatty acids and glycerol. The enzymes that catalyze these hydrolyses are called **lipases.**

B. In stage II catabolism, glycerol is phosphorylated to glycerol 3-P at the expense of ATP and then is oxidized to dihydroxyacetone-P, which is degraded to pyruvate via the glycolytic pathway. The free fatty acids are activated to their CoA derivatives and then degraded to acetyl CoA by successive β oxidation and removal of two-carbon fragments, as diagrammed in Figure 11.3. All the enzymes that catalyze these reactions are located in the mitochondrial matrix in eucaryotes.

The most common fatty acids contain an even number of carbon atoms and are converted completely to acetyl CoA by the reactions shown in Figure 11.3. The terminal step of odd-chain fatty acid breakdown produces the three-carbon derivative propionyl CoA, which subsequently undergoes a biotin-dependent carboxylation, followed by rearrangement to succinyl CoA in a reaction requiring a vitamin B_{12} derivative as a coenzyme. Both acetyl CoA and succinyl CoA are metabolized via the TCA cycle (Concept 11.4).

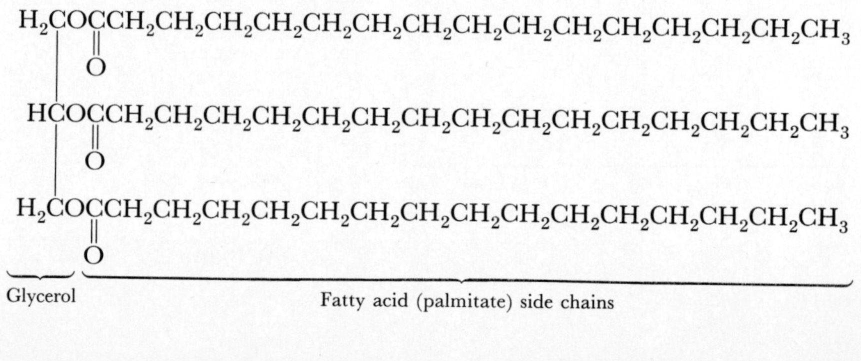

$$H_2COCCH_2CH_2CH_2CH_2CH_2CH_2CH_2CH_2CH_2CH_2CH_2CH_2CH_2CH_3$$
$$\underset{O}{\overset{\|}{|}}$$

$$HCOCCH_2CH_2CH_2CH_2CH_2CH_2CH_2CH_2CH_2CH_2CH_2CH_2CH_2CH_3$$
$$\underset{O}{\overset{\|}{|}}$$

$$H_2COCCH_2CH_2CH_2CH_2CH_2CH_2CH_2CH_2CH_2CH_2CH_2CH_2CH_2CH_3$$
$$\underset{O}{\overset{\|}{|}}$$

Figure 11.2
Tripalmitin, a typical triglyceride.

Glycerol   Fatty acid (palmitate) side chains

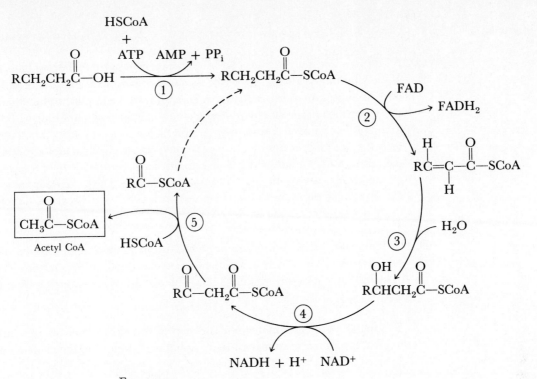

Figure 11.3
Activation and β oxidation of fatty acids to acetyl CoA. Activation is accomplished by reaction 1. Each cycle of β oxidation (reactions 2 through 5) removes a two-carbon fragment and primes the remainder of the molecule for the next cycle.

Enzymes

1. Fatty acid thiokinase
2. Acyl dehydrogenase
3. Enoyl hydratase
4. β-Hydroxyacyl dehydrogenase
5. β-Ketothiolase

11.3 Amino acids are degraded to pyruvate, acetyl CoA, and TCA-cycle intermediates.

A. In stage I catabolism, proteins are hydrolyzed to free amino acids by proteolytic enzymes such as those described in Chapter 3. In stage II, each of the resulting 20 amino acids is degraded via a specific pathway. The following discussion is limited to a few general aspects of amino acid catabolism.

B. The first step in stage II degradation of almost all amino acids is a **transamination** reaction, in which the α-amino group is transferred to the acceptor α-ketoglutarate, with production of the α-keto derivative of the amino acid (equation 11.1). In the process, α-ketoglutarate is converted to Glu, which then is oxidatively deaminated in the glutamate dehydrogenase reaction to produce free ammonia and to regenerate α-ketoglutarate (equation 11.2). Under appropriate conditions, these two reactions can function in reverse to fix free ammonia for amino acid synthesis.

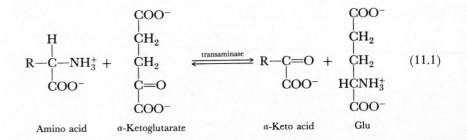

$$\text{(11.1)}$$

$$\text{Glu} + \text{NAD}^+ + \text{H}_2\text{O} \xrightleftharpoons[\text{dehydrogenase}]{\text{glutamate}} \text{NADH} + \text{H}^+ + \text{NH}_4^+ + \alpha\text{-ketoglutarate} \quad (11.2)$$

C. All transamination reactions require the coenzyme **pyridoxal phosphate,** a derivative of the vitamin pyridoxine (B_6). The structure of pyridoxal phosphate and the mechanism of transamination are shown in Figure 11.4. The important functional groups of the coenzyme are the aldehyde group, which can form a Schiff base with the α-amino group of an amino acid, and the pyridine ring, which temporarily can accommodate an extra pair of electrons by virtue of its quaternary nitrogen atom. In the first part of the reaction an amino acid is converted to an α-keto acid. In the second part, the amino group carried on the coenzyme is transferred to α-ketoglutarate to produce Glu. Pyridoxal phosphate also is involved in racemization, decarboxylation, and a few other reactions of amino acids.

D. In mammals, excess ammonia produced by deamination is excreted after conversion to urea in a pathway called the **urea cycle,** which utilizes mitochondrial as well as cytoplasmic enzymes (Figure 11.5). The overall process starting from free NH_3 is

$$2NH_4^+ + CO_2 + 3ATP + 3H_2O \rightarrow \text{urea} + 2ADP + AMP + 4P_i$$

Two high-energy phosphate bonds are expended per molecule of ammonia converted to urea, for a total of four high-energy phophate bonds per molecule of urea formed.

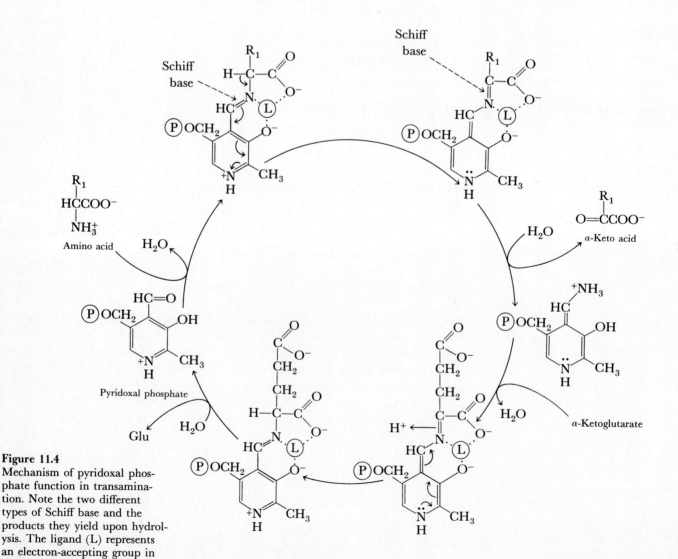

Figure 11.4
Mechanism of pyridoxal phosphate function in transamination. Note the two different types of Schiff base and the products they yield upon hydrolysis. The ligand (L) represents an electron-accepting group in the active site of the enzyme.

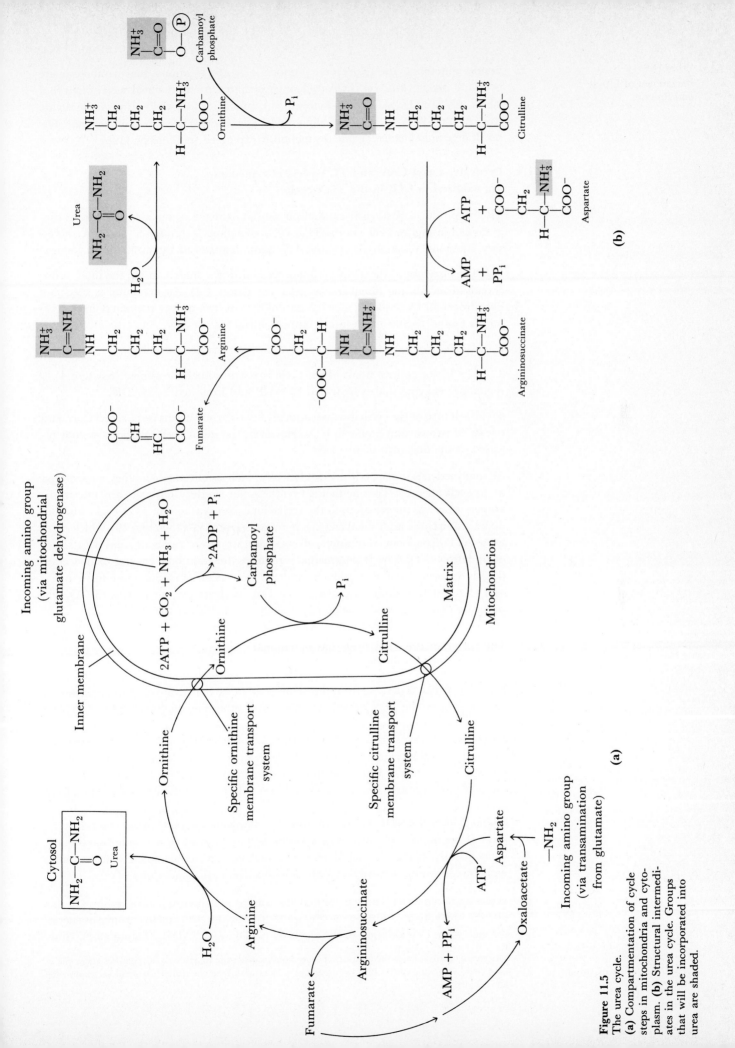

Figure 11.5
The urea cycle.
(a) Compartmentation of cycle steps in mitochondria and cytoplasm. (b) Structural intermediates in the urea cycle. Groups that will be incorporated into urea are shaded.

E. Besides ammonia, the major end products of stage II amino acid catabolism are pyruvate, acetyl CoA, and TCA-cycle intermediates. An amino acid such as Leu that yields only acetyl CoA is called **ketogenic.** Amino acids that yield primarily pyruvate (e.g., Ala) or TCA-cycle intermediates (e.g., Glu or Asp) are called **glucogenic.** The nutritional significance of this distinction is explained in Concept 11.5.

11.4 Pyruvate, acetyl CoA, and TCA-cycle intermediates are oxidized to CO_2 in the TCA cycle.

A. All end products of stage II catabolism can be oxidized completely to CO_2, as diagrammed in Figure 11.6, via the TCA cycle (reactions 2 through 9) and three accessory reactions (reactions 1, 10, and 11). Some features of the cycle are as follows:

1. The enzymes of the TCA cycle are located in the matrix inside the inner mitochondrial membrane in eucaryotic cells (see Figure 6.4). An exception is succinate dehydrogenase (reaction 7), which is part of the electron-transport chain (Chapter 12) and is bound tightly to the inner mitochondrial membrane.

2. All TCA-cycle reactions, except 2 and 5, are readily reversible.

3. The major control point of the cycle is isocitrate dehydrogenase (reaction 4), a regulatory enzyme that is activated by ADP and inhibited by NADH.

4. Each turn of the cycle involves uptake of two carbon atoms from acetyl CoA, and release of two carbon atoms as CO_2. However, the input acetyl carbons are not released in the first turn of the cycle.

B. All intermediates in the cycle act catalytically; each is consumed and then regenerated as the cycle operates. Thus neither net synthesis nor net degradation of any intermediate can occur via the reactions of the cycle alone. Net synthesis of TCA-cycle intermediates requires the additional enzyme pyruvate carboxylase (reaction 10), which catalyzes ATP-dependent formation of oxaloacetate from pyruvate and CO_2. Net degradation of TCA-cycle intermediates requires the additional enzyme oxaloacetate decarboxylase (reaction 11), which catalyzes conversion of oxaloacetate to pyruvate and CO_2.* The resulting pyruvate then can be degraded completely to CO_2 via pyruvate dehydrogenase (reaction 1) and the remainder of the cycle.

11.5 The design of the TCA cycle has nutritional consequences in animals.

A. Pyruvate, which is derived from the breakdown of carbohydrate or glucogenic amino acids, can enter the TCA cycle in the absence of other metabolites (Figure 11.6). The bulk of the pyruvate is oxidized to acetyl CoA (reaction 1), but a small amount is converted to oxaloacetate (reaction 10), thereby allowing acetyl CoA to enter the cycle (reaction 2) and be oxidized to CO_2. By contrast, acetyl CoA derived from the breakdown of fatty acids or ketogenic amino acids cannot enter the cycle unless oxaloacetate is already present, because mammals are unable to synthesize oxaloacetate from acetyl CoA. Because TCA-cycle intermediates serve as starting materials for sugar and amino acid synthesis (Chapters 15 and 16), they must be replenished constantly by stage II breakdown of glucogenic substances for the cycle to continue functioning. Consequently, ketogenic fuel molecules cannot be oxidized completely in mammals without concomitant breakdown of some glucogenic fuel molecules.

B. When lipids alone are fed to an animal, the condition known as **ketosis** results. On this diet the breakdown of fatty acids (Figure 11.3) provides the principal source of energy through stage IV oxidation of the resulting NADH and $FADH_2$ (Figure 10.1). How-

---

*Although this reaction is the most direct route from oxaloacetate to pyruvate, it is not the major one in most cells, which also utilize PEP carboxykinase (Concept 15.2) or the malic enzyme to accomplish the same conversion.

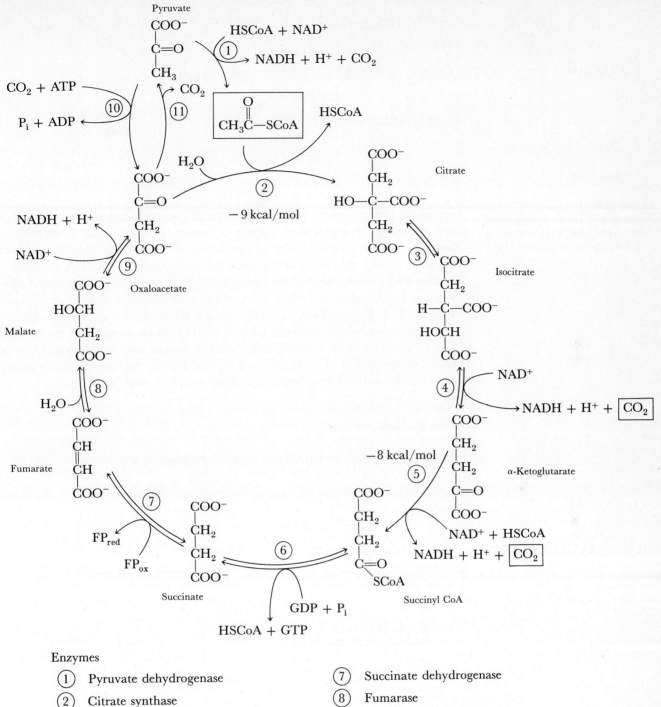

Enzymes

1. Pyruvate dehydrogenase
2. Citrate synthase
3. Aconitase
4. Isocitrate dehydrogenase
5. α-Ketoglutarate dehydrogenase
6. Succinate thiokinase

7. Succinate dehydrogenase
8. Fumarase
9. Malate dehydrogenase
10. Pyruvate carboxylase
11. Oxaloacetate decarboxylase

Figure 11.6
The TCA cycle and accessory reactions. Pyruvate dehydrogenase and α-ketoglutarate dehydrogenase require TPP and lipoate as coenzymes. GTP, formed in reaction 6, is isoenergetic with ATP and phosphorylates ADP to yield ATP and GDP.

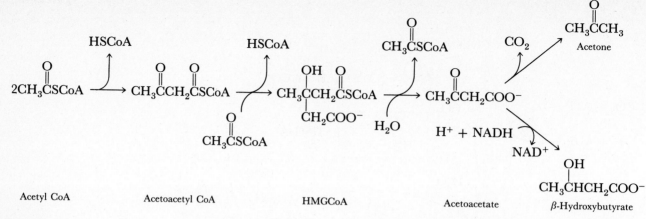

Figure 11.7
Formation of ketone bodies from acetyl CoA. HMGCoA stands for 3-hydroxy-3-methylglutaryl CoA.

ever, in the liver the acetyl CoA produced by β oxidation does not enter the TCA cycle efficiently, because gluconeogenesis (Chapter 15) drains cycle intermediates. Accumulation of acetyl CoA limits the amount of free HSCoA available for continued fatty acid breakdown, which is necessary for energy production. This problem is circumvented by conversion of the excess acetyl CoA to the so-called **ketone bodies** (acetoacetate, β-hydroxybutyrate, and acetone), with liberation of HSCoA as shown in Figure 11.7. Ketone bodies are exported by the liver and are used as fuel by peripheral tissues, which reconvert them to acetyl CoA for metabolism through the TCA cycle. Some of the acetone, being volatile, escapes into the lungs and can be smelled on the breath of an animal in advanced ketosis. Because the principal fuel reserves in animals are fats, fasting and starvation also result in ketosis.

11.6   Additional concepts and techniques are presented in the Problems section.

A.   Three-point substrate attachment to enzyme. Problem 11.6.

B.   Synthesis and degradation of γ-amino butyrate, an inhibitory synaptic transmitter. Problem 11.10.

References

COMPREHENSIVE TEXTS
Lehninger: Chapters 17, 20, and 21   Stryer: Chapters 13, 17, and 18
Metzler: Chapters 8, 9, and 14   White et al.: Chapters 17, 20, 21, 22, and 23

OTHER REFERENCES
A. L. Lehninger, *Bioenergetics,* Benjamin/Cummings, Menlo Park, Calif., 1971, 2nd ed. Chapter 5.
J. D. Watson, *Molecular Biology of the Gene,* Benjamin/Cummings, Menlo Park, Calif., 1976, 3rd ed. Chapter 2.

Problems

11.1   Answer the following with true or false. If false, explain why.
a. All carboxylation reactions involving CO_2 fixation in animal cells require the coenzyme thiamine pyrophosphate.
b. Because FAD must acquire two hydrogen atoms to become reduced, it can participate only in two-electron transfer reactions.
c. Oxidative degradation of a fatty acid begins at the carboxyl end of the molecule.
d. Only fatty acids with an even number of carbon atoms produce acetyl CoA upon oxidative degradation.
e. All transamination reactions of amino acids require the coenzyme pyridoxal phosphate.

f. Conversion of the α-amino nitrogen of an amino acid to NH_3 is an oxidative process that uses one molecule of NAD^+ as the oxidizing agent.

g. Of all the TCA-cycle intermediates, only oxaloacetate can be degraded in net amounts solely by the enzymes of the cycle.

h. The TCA cycle itself produces reduced pyridine and flavin nucleotides but no high-energy phosphate compounds.

i. Amino acids that yield exclusively pyruvate and acetyl CoA in stage II degradation are ketogenic.

j. Ketosis is beneficial to an animal in that it allows continued oxidation of fatty acids in the absence of TCA-cycle function.

11.2 a. TPP is required as a cofactor in the _____ reaction of the phosphogluconate pathway (Concept 10.5).

b. The major carrier of activated acyl compounds in all cells is _____.

c. Neutral fats, the principal lipid storage form in animals, consist of three _____ molecules esterified to _____.

d. Activation of free fatty acids for stage II degradation requires reaction with _____ and _____.

e. Fixation of ammonia for amino acid synthesis can occur in animals via reductive amination of _____ to produce _____ in a reaction using NADH as the reducing agent.

f. Most amino acid breakdown products feed into the mainstream of catabolism as pyruvate, TCA-cycle intermediates, or _____.

g. Animal cells cannot carry out net synthesis of TCA-cycle intermediates from acetyl CoA alone; however, they can synthesize these intermediates by combining pyruvate with _____ in a reaction requiring the coenzyme _____.

h. Ala, Asp, and Glu are glucogenic because transamination of these amino acids yields _____, _____, and _____, respectively.

11.3 Erythrocytes (mature red blood cells) can convert added glucose to CO_2 via the phosphogluconate pathway (Figure 10.6), but lack the complete glycolytic pathway. If you were to compare erythrocytes from a normal and a thiamine-deficient animal, what differences, if any, would you expect to find in the rates of $^{14}CO_2$ release from glucose-1-^{14}C? From glucose-2-^{14}C? Explain your answer.

11.4 One micromole of a fully tritiated, 12-carbon, straight-chain, saturated fatty acid $C^3H_3 (C^3H_3)_{10}COO^3H$ is added to a preparation of disrupted mitochondria, which degrades it completely to acetyl CoA. If the 6 μmol of product are re-isolated from the reaction mixture, hydrolyzed to free acetate, and assayed for radioactivity, what will be their overall tritium-to-carbon ratio?

11.5 Pyridoxal phosphate is required in several enzymatic reactions of amino acid metabolism, including transamination, racemization, and decarboxylation. Its mechanism is well understood, primarily because free pyridoxal in the presence of a trivalent metal ion will catalyze these reactions in the absence of enzymes (at $\simeq 10^{-6}$ of the enzymatic rate). Consequently, the effects of changes in the coenzyme structure on rate of catalysis can be studied without regard for interaction with the active site of an enzyme. Pyridoxal and four analogues are shown in Figure 11.8. Using your knowledge of the mechanism of pyridoxal phosphate action, tell which of these analogues you would expect to be active, and which inactive, in the nonenzymatic reactions. Write a sentence or two explaining your opinion for each.

11.6 In accordance with the original Krebs hypothesis, the symmetrical molecule of citric acid is an intermediate in the TCA cycle. During the 1940s this idea was questioned on the basis of two experimental findings.

1. *E. coli* grows on most intermediates in the cycle, but *not* on citrate as the sole carbon source.

2. When actively respiring tissue preparations are incubated very briefly with

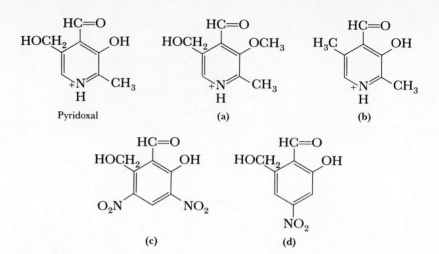

      (a)   (b)

(c)   (d)

Figure 11.8
Pyridoxal and four analogues
(Problem 11.5).

$CH_3{}^{14}COOH$ and then analyzed, the α-ketoglutarate formed is found to be labeled in one of the two carboxyl groups, but not the other:

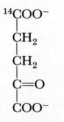

$$
\begin{array}{c}
{}^{14}COO^- \\
| \\
CH_2 \\
| \\
CH_2 \\
| \\
C{=}O \\
| \\
COO^-
\end{array}
$$

Discuss very briefly the significance of these findings and how they can be reconciled with the presence of citrate as an intermediate in the pathway.

11.7   Write a sequence of known enzymatic reactions that results in the conversion of malate to four molecules of CO_2 without the *net* uptake or production of any other metabolites besides H_2O, P_i, ADP, NAD^+, and FAD.

11.8   Write a sequence of known enzymatic reactions that will lead to the *net* synthesis of α-ketoglutarate from pyruvate, without the *net* utilization of other TCA-cycle intermediates.

11.9   Pyruvate carboxylase (Figure 11.6, reaction 10) is a regulatory enzyme that is activated by the allosteric effector acetyl CoA. Explain why this control is advantageous to the organism.

11.10   Tissues of the mammalian central nervous system contain a pyridoxal phosphate-dependent glutamate decarboxylase that catalyzes conversion of Glu to γ-amino butyrate (γ-ABA), an inhibitory synaptic transmitter, as shown in equation 11.3:

$$^-OOCCH_2CH_2\underset{\underset{COO^-}{|}}{CH}NH_3^+ + H^+ \rightarrow {}^-OOCCH_2CH_2CH_2NH_3^+ + CO_2 \quad (11.3)$$

Glu γ-ABA

γ-ABA is degraded by transamination with α-ketoglutarate as the acceptor (equation 11.4) to yield succinic semialdehyde (SSA), which then is oxidized to succinate (equation 11.5) by an NAD-linked dehydrogenase.

$$\gamma\text{-ABA} + {}^-OOCCH_2CH_2\overset{\overset{\textstyle O}{\|}}{C}COO^- \rightarrow \text{Glu} + {}^-OOCCH_2CH_2CH{=}O \quad (11.4)$$

α-Ketoglutarate   SSA

$$\text{SSA} + NAD^+ + H_2O \rightarrow {}^-OOCCH_2CH_2COO^- + NADH + 2H^+ \quad (11.5)$$

Succinate

a. Show how these reactions can operate as a shunt pathway that allows the TCA cycle to function without the enzymes α-ketoglutarate dehydrogenase and succinate thiokinase (Figure 11.6, reactions 5 and 6).

b. Is the shunt more or less efficient than the normal cycle from the standpoint of energy recovery? Explain.

11.11   Glucose added to a culture of aerobically respiring yeast cells is broken down quantitatively to CO_2 and acetyl CoA, which then is oxidized completely to CO_2 and H_2O.

a. If the glucose is labeled with ^{14}C at the 2-position, how many turns of the TCA cycle must each two-carbon fragment go through before all the isotope is released as CO_2?

b. If the glucose label is in the 1-position, what fraction of the isotope will *not* have been released after each two-carbon fragment has gone through four complete turns of the cycle?

c. If the glucose label is in the 6-position, what fraction of the original isotope will be found in each of the carbon atoms of oxaloacetate after each two-carbon fragment has gone through two complete turns of the cycle?

11.12   Following is a list of hereditary metabolic defects involving loss of single enzymes of catabolism, and a second list of possible consequences of such defects. Match each enzyme defect with its *most likely* consequence (only one) from the second list.

Defects:

a. Lack of pyridoxal kinase (catalyzes conversion of pyridoxal to pyridoxal phosphate)
b. Lack of propionyl CoA carboxylase (conversion of propionyl CoA to succinyl CoA)
c. Lack of isocitrate dehydrogenase
d. Lack of oxaloacetate decarboxylase
e. Lack of pyruvate dehydrogenase

Consequences:

1. Impaired ability to obtain energy from short-chain fatty acids of odd carbon number, with little if any effect on ability to obtain energy from proteins
2. Impaired ability to obtain energy from all fatty acids
3. Impaired ability to obtain energy from proteins, with little if any effect on ability to obtain energy from carbohydrate
4. Inability to synthesize or degrade almost all amino acids
5. Impaired ability to obtain energy from proteins, and inability to obtain energy from carbohydrate
6. Impaired ability to excrete amino acid nitrogen
7. Lethal; prevents complete oxidation of all fuel molecules

11.13   Explain why an Eskimo with inadequate carbohydrate intake would be nutritionally better off eating fats with fatty acids of odd-numbered chain length rather than even-numbered chain length.

11.14   A farmer's young daughter, living on a normal balanced diet, nevertheless shows occasional mild ketosis. As her pediatrician, you are about to conclude that she suffers from some congenital enzymatic defect of carbohydrate metabolism when you discover that she also metabolizes odd-chain fatty acids less well than even-chain fatty acids, and that she secretly sneaks off to the chicken coop each morning and eats raw eggs. Propose another explanation for her symptoms.

11.15   Estimate the amount of energy a mammal can obtain from oxidation of palmitate, $CH_3(CH_2)_{14}COO^-$, in the liver under conditions of ketosis, relative to the amount obtainable under conditions of a balanced diet providing glucogenic fuel molecules.

11.16   A once popular but controversial diet for losing weight rapidly is high in protein and lipid but lacks carbohydrates almost entirely. Its proponents claim that on this diet you can eat as much protein- and lipid-rich food as you wish and nevertheless lose weight. Patients on the diet often complain of bad breath.

a. Give a plausible metabolic explanation for why this diet is effective.

b. Discuss the claim that there is no limit to the amount of protein and lipid you can eat and still lose weight.

11.17 Look up the pathway for Trp degradation in a comprehensive biochemistry text. Although the end products of Trp degradation are acetyl CoA and acetoacetyl CoA, Trp behaves as a *glucogenic* amino acid in animals; that is, it can serve as a substrate for net synthesis of glucose. Outline or describe the reactions that make this possible.

☆ 11.18 Which of the choices listed *best* completes the following statement: In transamination reactions, the coenzyme pyridoxal phosphate—
a. Forms Schiff bases with amino acids
b. Stabilizes reactive anions on the α carbons of amino acids
c. Interacts through its phosphate group with the α-amino nitrogen and an α-carboxyl oxygen of bound amino acids to form planar three-ring complexes.
d. a and b
e. a, b, and c

☆ 11.19 Write a sequence of known enzymatic reactions that will result in the net conversion of oxaloacetate to four molecules of CO_2 without net uptake or production of other TCA-cycle intermediates.

☆ 11.20 Write a sequence of known enzymatic reactions that will result in the net synthesis of citrate from two molecules of pyruvate, without net uptake or production of other TCA-cycle intermediates.

Answers

11.1 a. False. All carboxylases require biotin. TPP is required by enzymes that catalyze decarboxylation of α-keto carboxylic acids.
b. False. FAD can accept two electrons and two hydrogens in two steps to form $FADH_2$. The intermediate semiquinone is sufficiently stable that FAD can participate in both one- and two-electron transfer reactions.
c. True
d. False. All fatty acids are degraded primarily to acetyl CoA. Odd-chain acids are not converted completely to acetyl CoA, because the terminal three-carbon fragment, propionyl CoA, is converted to succinyl CoA by carboxylation and rearrangement.
e. True
f. True
g. False. None of the TCA-cycle intermediates can be degraded in net amounts solely by enzymes of the cycle. All require the oxaloacetate decarboxylase bypass reaction, which converts oxaloacetate to pyruvate + CO_2 (Figure 11.6, reaction 11).
h. False. The succinate thiokinase reaction (Figure 11.6, reaction 6) produces one GTP per turn of the cycle.
i. False. Ketogenic amino acids yield exclusively acetyl CoA upon stage II breakdown.
j. True

11.2 a. transketolase
b. coenzyme A
c. fatty acid, glycerol
d. ATP, HSCoA
e. α-ketoglutarate, Glu
f. acetyl CoA
g. CO_2, biotin
h. pyruvate, oxaloacetate, α-ketoglutarate

11.3 A lack of thiamine and consequently of TPP will inhibit the transketolase reaction. This deficiency will have little effect on $^{14}CO_2$ release from the C-1 position of glucose, which occurs in the first step. However, it will significantly decrease the rate of release from the C-2 position, which occurs only in the second turn of the phosphogluconate cycle, because completion of the first turn depends upon transketolase.

11.4 As shown in Figure 11.3, oxidation of each successive two-carbon segment of the chain involves a dehydrogenation step that removes one of the two hydrogens from the penultimate carbon, which ultimately becomes the CH_3 group of the next acetyl CoA removed. Thus each resulting acetate fragment will carry only one ^3H atom (the ratio of ^3H to C is 1:2) except the last, which never undergoes oxidation and therefore will retain all three ^3H atoms (a $^3H/C$ ratio of 3:2). Because the reaction produces 5 μmol acetate with the lower ratio and 1 with the higher ratio, the overall $^3H/C$ ratio is 8:12 or 2:3.

11.5 Pyridoxal phosphate function depends primarily on two properties of the molecule:
 1. The presence of an electron-accepting group at the *para* position of the ring (opposite the aldehyde) allows the molecule to accommodate an extra electron pair in the conversion of one Schiff base to another (Figure 11.4).
 2. The presence of a hydroxyl group at the *ortho* position allows formation of a three-ring, planar, Schiff-base intermediate by coordination with a ligand in the active site of the enzyme or a trivalent metal ion in free solution.

 a. Inactive. The blocked *ortho* hydroxyl group prevents coordination with the ligand.
 b. Active. The *ortho* hydroxymethyl group of pyridoxal must be phosphorylated for interaction with the transaminase enzyme to occur, but this group plays no direct role in the catalysis.
 c. Inactive. The aromatic ring is unable to accommodate an electron pair without an electron-accepting group at the *para* position.
 d. Active. The *para* NO_2 group can accommodate electrons in place of the quaternary nitrogen of the pyridine ring. The structure of the resulting intermediate is shown in Figure 11.9.

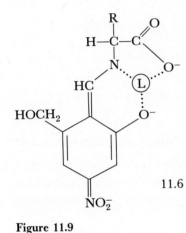

Figure 11.9
An intermediate structure in nonenzymatic catalysis by pyridoxal analogue (Figure 11.8d; Answer 11.5).

11.6 Both findings can be reconciled with citrate as an intermediate.
 1. Citrate is a highly charged molecule and therefore does not pass readily through a membrane (Concept 6.5). *E. coli* fails to grow on citrate only because this molecule cannot enter the cell; extracts of *E. coli* metabolize citrate as rapidly as any other TCA-cycle intermediate.
 2. Early biochemists assumed that the two ends of the citrate molecule were indistinguishable, and argued that if it were an intermediate the label would be randomized and appear in both carboxyl groups of α-ketoglutarate. In fact, the two ends of citrate are distinguishable if the molecule is bound to the enzyme aconitase at three points. For example, an enzyme surface with binding sites as shown in Figure 11.10 always will interact with the same carboxyl group.

11.7
$$\text{Malate} + NAD^+ \xrightarrow[\text{dehydrogenase}]{\text{malate}} \text{oxaloacetate} + NADH + H^+$$

$$\text{Oxaloacetate} \xrightarrow[\text{decarboxylase}]{\text{oxaloacetate}} \text{pyruvate} + CO_2$$

$$\text{Pyruvate} + NAD^+ + HSCoA \xrightarrow[\text{dehydrogenase}]{\text{pyruvate}} NADH + H^+ + \text{acetyl CoA} + CO_2$$

$$\text{Acetyl CoA} + 3NAD^+ + FAD + P_i + ADP + 2H_2O \xrightarrow[\text{cycle}]{\text{TCA}}$$
$$2CO_2 + HSCoA + 3NADH + 3H^+ + FADH_2 + ATP$$

Net: $\text{Malate} + 5NAD^+ + FAD + P_i + ADP + 2H_2O \longrightarrow$
$$4CO_2 + 5NADH + 5H^+ + FADH_2 + ATP$$

11.8
$$\text{Pyruvate} + HSCoA + NAD^+ \xrightarrow[\text{dehydrogenase}]{\text{pyruvate}} \text{acetyl CoA} + NADH + H^+ + CO_2$$

$$\text{Pyruvate} + CO_2 + ATP \xrightarrow[\text{carboxylase}]{\text{pyruvate}} \text{oxaloacetate} + ADP + P_i$$

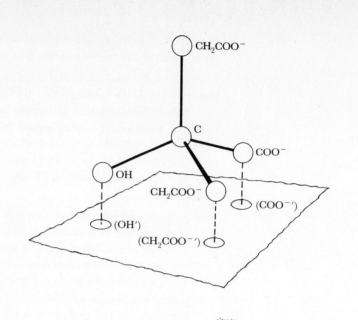

Figure 11.10
Asymmetric recognition of a
symmetric molecule by three-
point attachment to enzyme
(Answer 11.6).

$$H_2O + \text{oxaloacetate} + \text{acetyl CoA} \xrightarrow[\text{synthase}]{\text{citrate}} \text{citrate} + HSCoA$$

$$\text{Citrate} \xrightarrow{\text{aconitase}} \text{isocitrate}$$

$$\text{Isocitrate} + NAD^+ \xrightarrow[\text{dehydrogenase}]{\text{isocitrate}} \alpha\text{-ketoglutarate} + NADH + H^+ + CO_2$$

Net: $2 \text{ pyruvate} + ATP + 2NAD^+ + H_2O \longrightarrow$
$\alpha\text{-ketoglutarate} + CO_2 + ADP + P_i + 2NADH + 2H^+$

11.9   Acetyl CoA accumulates when it is being produced faster than it can enter the TCA
cycle. Through the regulatory enzyme pyruvate carboxylase, accumulated acetyl CoA
can stimulate the conversion of pyruvate to oxaloacetate and thereby increase its own
rate of entry into the cycle (Figure 11.6, reaction 2).

11.10 a. The net effect of the three reactions is oxidation of α-ketoglutarate by NAD^+ to
succinate plus CO_2:

$$\text{Glu} + H^+ \rightarrow \gamma\text{-ABA} + CO_2 \tag{11.3}$$

$$\alpha\text{-Ketoglutarate} + \gamma\text{-ABA} \rightarrow \text{Glu} + \text{SSA} \tag{11.4}$$

$$\text{SSA} + NAD^+ + H_2O \rightarrow \text{succinate} + NADH + 2H^+ \tag{11.5}$$

Net: $\alpha\text{-Ketoglutarate} + NAD^+ + H_2O \rightarrow \text{succinate} + CO_2 + NADH + H^+$

Hence these three steps carry out the same overall oxidation as reactions 5 and 6 of
the TCA cycle.
   b. The shunt is less efficient, because the equivalent TCA-cycle steps yield a molecule of
GTP as well as NADH.

11.11   Use the pathway in Figure 11.5 to follow the fate of incoming carbon atoms.
   a. Glucose labeled (*) in the 2-position will produce carbonyl-labeled acetyl CoA:

$$\overset{\quad\overset{\displaystyle O}{\|}}{CH_3 \overset{*}{C}}\text{—SCoA}.$$ Two turns of the cycle will release all of this label as CO_2.

   b. Glucose labeled in the 1-position will produce $\overset{\quad\overset{\displaystyle O}{\|}}{*CH_3 C}\text{—SCoA}$. After four complete
turns, one-fourth of the input-labeled carbon still will be present in oxaloacetate.
   c. Label at the 6-position is equivalent to label at the 1-position; it will produce

$$\overset{\quad\overset{\displaystyle O}{\|}}{*CH_3 C}\text{—SCoA}.$$ After two turns, none of this label will have been released as CO_2. It

will be distributed equally among the four carbon atoms of oxaloacetate. Note that label at one end of an intermediate will be distributed equally between both ends after passage through the symmetrical intermediate succinate, whose two ends cannot be distinguished by succinate dehydrogenase (Figure 11.6, reaction 7). Thus, for example,

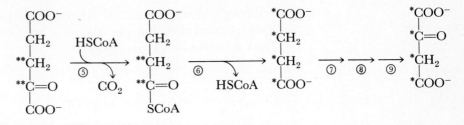

11.12 a. 4.

b. 1.

c. 7.   The isocitrate dehydrogenase reaction is an essential step for TCA-cycle operation.

d. 3.   Net oxidation of TCA-cycle intermediates resulting from glucogenic amino acid breakdown cannot occur without this step (Concept 11.4), but carbohydrate catabolism does not require it.

e. 5.   Net oxidation of TCA-cycle intermediates and pyruvate resulting from breakdown of glucogenic amino acids cannot occur without this step, which is also essential for entry of all carbohydrate into the TCA cycle.

11.13   She would be better off because the final cleavage in stage II degradation of an odd-chain fatty acid yields propionyl CoA. This compound is further metabolized to succinyl CoA, which will help to alleviate the Eskimo's carbohydrate deficiency and the accompanying ketosis by increasing the level of TCA-cycle intermediates (Concept 11.2, part B).

11.14   Raw egg white contains a protein, avidin, which binds the vitamin biotin and prevents its uptake during digestion. Biotin is required as a coenzyme in all ATP-linked carboxylation reactions (Concept 11.1, part E). Therefore, the girl's passion for raw eggs may have led to a biotin deficiency, which results in low activity of her ATP-linked carboxylase enzymes. One of these, pyruvate carboxylase, is required for producing TCA-cycle intermediates from carbohydrates; its low activity therefore causes mild ketosis. Another is propionyl CoA carboxylase, which is required for metabolism of the terminal three-carbon fragment of odd-chain fatty acids.

11.15   An estimate of the relative amounts of obtainable energy can be made without precise knowledge of caloric values by comparing the number of electron pairs transferred to carrier molecules for subsequent stage IV oxidation. Conversion of palmitate to 8 acetyl CoA via the reactions in Figure 11.3 releases two electron pairs (1 to FAD and 1 to NAD$^+$) for each two-carbon fragment but the last; hence 14 electron pairs per palmitate. Oxidation of each acetyl CoA to CO_2 via the TCA cycle releases 4 electron pairs (1 to FAD and 3 to NAD$^+$), yielding 32 additional electron pairs per palmitate. In ketosis, only the first 14 pairs can be released, whereas on a balanced diet, all 46 are utilized. Hence only about 30% of the energy normally available from palmitate can be obtained under conditions of ketosis. A more precise estimate could be made by calculating the number of ATP molecules produced by palmitate oxidation under the two conditions, using the P/O ratios for $FADH_2$ and NADH in stage IV oxidative phosphorylation, as explained in Chapter 12.

11.16 a. Because there is almost no carbohydrate intake, TCA-cycle intermediates must be produced almost entirely from glucogenic amino acids in the dietary protein. The bad breath symptom (odor of acetone) suggests that this source is insufficient to fill the patient's biosynthetic needs and maintain adequate TCA-cycle operation, so that ketosis results (Concept 11.5). Under these conditions, dietary and body lipids become the patient's principal energy source. As explained in Answer 11.15, fatty acids are oxidized inefficiently during ketosis and therefore must be expended rapidly to supply the patient's caloric needs.

b. This claim seems unlikely, because increased lipid and protein intake means that less of the body lipid must be degraded to supply energy, and consequently weight loss should occur more slowly.

11.17   Although the end products for Trp degradation are acetyl CoA and acetoacetyl CoA, Ala is formed along the way. Ala can be transaminated to pyruvate, which can serve as a substrate for gluconeogenesis.

12 Electron Transport and Oxidative Phosphorylation

In the first three stages of energy metabolism, electrons from fuel molecules are transferred to the carriers NAD^+ and FAD with little loss of free energy. This chapter considers the final stage, in which these electrons are transferred through a chain of carriers to an external acceptor, releasing a substantial amount of energy. This process is coupled to ion transport and ATP formation to produce most of the phosphate-bond energy in chemotrophic cells.

Concepts

12.1 **In respiration, electrons are transferred from donor molecules to an external acceptor.**

A. Transfer of electrons from donor molecules (NADH and substrates) to an external acceptor is called **electron transport** or **respiration.** The equation for electron transport from NADH is

$$NADH + H^+ + A \rightarrow NAD^+ + H_2A \qquad (12.1)$$

in which A is a general electron acceptor. In all organisms, with the exception of a few genera of bacteria, the acceptor is oxygen, the product is water, and the potential span $\Delta E_0' = 1.1$ V (Table 9.1). Therefore, the standard free-energy change ($\Delta G_0'$) is -52 kcal/mol electron pairs transferred. Some bacteria can utilize other electron acceptors, such as the inorganic ions NO_3^-, SO_4^{2-}, and Fe^{3+}.

B. Respiration occurs in eucaryotic cells on the inner mitochondrial membrane (Figure 12.1) and in procaryotic cells on the plasma membrane.

C. During respiration, electrons are transferred through an assembly of membrane proteins called the **electron-transport chain.** These proteins are classified according to

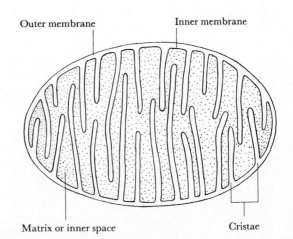

Outer membrane   Inner membrane

Matrix or inner space   Cristae

Figure 12.1
Structure of a mitochondrion. The cristae are infoldings of the inner membrane that increase its surface area. Note that the space within the cristae is topologically outside of the inner membrane.

their electron-transferring prosthetic group; **flavoproteins** carry FAD (Figure 11.1), and **cytochrome proteins** carry heme-bound iron (Figure 4.6).

In mitochondria the electron-transport chain consists of the carriers shown in Figure 12.2. In addition to flavoproteins (FP) and cytochromes, the chain includes iron–sulfur proteins and coenzyme Q (CoQ), a lipid-soluble quinone (Figure 12.3). The various oxidizable metabolites from stages II and III of catabolism (Chapters 10 and 11) feed electrons into the chain at different points. The differences in half-cell potential between adjacent carriers are small, so that energy is released in small steps as electrons are transported down the chain.

NADH is a two-electron carrier, whereas the cytochromes carry only one transferable electron in their reduced (Fe^{2+}) forms. The links between these two carriers include FAD and CoQ, both of which carry two transferable electrons in their reduced states, but can transfer them one at a time (Concept 11.1, part D).

In the steady-state condition, when electrons are flowing from substrates to O_2, the average oxidation states of the carriers vary from more reduced near the substrate

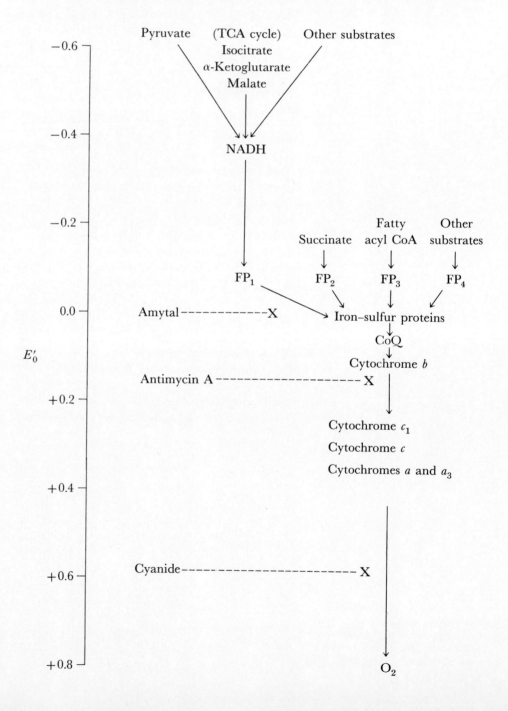

Figure 12.2
The electron-transport chain in mitochondria. Carriers designated FP are flavoproteins, carrying FAD as a prosthetic group. The points at which three inhibitors block electron transport are indicated by X.

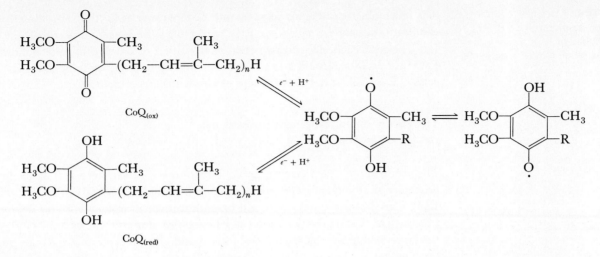

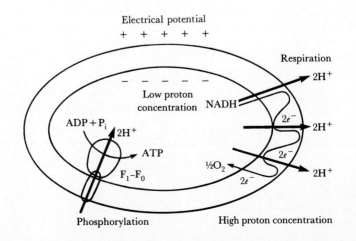

Figure 12.3
Structure of coenzyme Q, showing quinone (oxidized) semiquinone, and hydroquinone (reduced) forms.

end to more oxidized near the O_2 end of the chain. Inhibitors of electron transport (Figure 12.2 and Concept 12.4, part A) block the chain at specific points, thereby causing all preceding carriers to become fully reduced and all subsequent carriers to become fully oxidized.

12.2 Oxidative phosphorylation of ADP to ATP is coupled to electron transport by a chemiosmotic mechanism.

A. In intact mitochondria and bacteria, electron transport cannot occur without concomitant formation of ATP from ADP + P_i. This coupling depends on properties of the membrane that contains the electron-transport chain. The chemiosmotic coupling mechanism, first proposed by Peter Mitchell in the early 1960s, can be considered in two distinct parts (Figure 12.4).

1. The energy derived from electron transport is used to translocate protons across the membrane, from inside to outside, thereby forming a pH differential and an electrochemical (charge) differential between the inside and the outside compartments.

2. The energy stored in the proton gradient then is used to drive ATP formation, as hydrogen ions flow back across the membrane from outside to inside with loss of free energy. Some of the energy from the gradient also is used to drive the translocation of other small molecules across the membrane by coupled transport mechanisms (Chapter 14). For example, ADP and P_i are imported by this mechanism into the inner mitochondrial matrix for ATP synthesis.

Figure 12.4
The topology of mitochondrial respiration and oxidative phosphorylation. F_1-F_0 is the membrane-bound enzyme complex responsible for ATP formation (see text).

B. The stoichiometry of P_i ions taken up into ATP per pair of electrons traveling through the transport chain is called the $P/2e^-$ ratio, or, with oxygen as acceptor, the P/O ratio, because each electron pair reduces one atom of oxygen. In mitochondria the P/O ratio is 3 for NADH and substrates that transfer electrons to NADH. The P/O ratio is 2 for substrates that transfer electrons to flavoproteins.

12.3 The chemiosmotic coupling process is not completely understood.

A. The carriers in the electron-transport chain appear to be arranged so that an electron pair traverses the membrane several times in passing from NADH to oxygen (Figure 12.4). Carriers whose reduction and oxidation involve protonation and deprotonation, such as NADH, $FADH_2$ and $CoQH_2$, acquire protons from water or substrate at the inner membrane surface upon reduction and give up protons at the outer surface upon oxidation (Figure 12.5). This mechanism can account for the translocation of 6 protons per electron pair transported from NADH to oxygen. However, measurements indicate that up to 12 protons per electron pair may be translocated in mitochondria. Probably the large increment in free energy gained in transferring electrons from cytochrome *a* to oxygen (Figure 12.2) is used to pump protons from inside to outside by an unknown mechanism.

B. ATP formation driven by the proton gradient is mediated by a membrane-bound enzyme complex, which includes an integral membrane protein called F_0, and a peripheral globular complex called F_1 (Figure 12.4). In electron micrographs, F_1 complexes can be seen as characteristic knobs on the mitochondrial inner membrane surface. If the proton gradient is dissipated, or if the complex is dissociated from the membrane, F_1 acts as an ATPase, catalyzing ATP hydrolysis. However, in its normal state with a proton gradient across the membrane, F_1 catalyzes the reverse reaction to form ATP and water from ADP, P_i, and incoming protons. The molecular mechanism by which influx of protons through F_0 drives ATP hydrolysis in reverse at the active site of F_1 is not understood.

12.4 Three classes of inhibitors block oxidative phosphorylation.

A. Inhibitors of electron transport, such as amytal, antimycin A, and cyanide, block the actual flow of electrons down the chain (Figure 12.2), thereby preventing ATP formation.

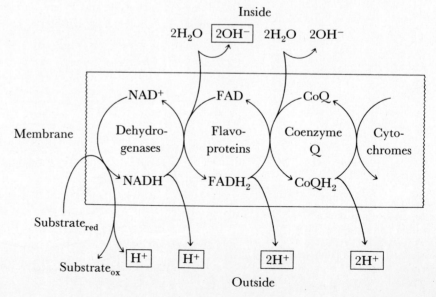

Figure 12.5
Proton translocation during electron transport in the inner mitochondrial membrane.

B. Inhibitors of phosphorylation prevent the formation of ATP more directly. Oligomycin, for example, blocks the function of the F_1 ATPase complex. Because electron transport is coupled to phosphorylation, such inhibitors also block electron transport.

C. Uncoupling agents dissipate the proton gradient across the membrane, thereby allowing electron transport without oxidative phosphorylation. At least two kinds of molecules can produce this effect. Lipid-soluble weak acids such as dinitrophenol shuttle protons rapidly through the lipid bilayer. Cyclic polypeptide antibiotics such as gramicidin associate within the bilayer to form hydrophilic channels through which protons can flow from outside to inside. Uncoupling agents prevent ATP formation without inhibiting electron transport.

12.5 Additional concepts and techniques are presented in the Problems section.

A. Deduction of electron-carrier sequences using inhibitors of electron transport. Problems 12.12 and 12.13.

B. Reverse electron transport. Problems 12.14 and 12.15.

C. Experimental evidence on the mechanism of coupling in oxidative phosphorylation. Problem 12.16.

D. Functional separation of the two components of the proton gradient. Problem 12.17.

References

COMPREHENSIVE TEXTS

Lehninger: Chapters 18 and 19

Metzler: Chapter 10

Stryer: Chapter 14

White et al.: Chapters 12 and 13

OTHER REFERENCES

P. C. Hinkle and R. E. McCarty, "How Cells Make ATP," *Scientific American,* March 1978, p. 104.

P. Mitchell, "Keilin's Respiratory Chain Concept and Its Chemiosmotic Consequences" (Nobel lecture), *Science,* **206,** 1148–1159 (1979).

Problems

12.1 Answer the following with true or false. If false, explain why.
a. Respiration can occur only in the presence of oxygen.
b. The molecular apparatus for respiration is found only in eucaryotic cells.
c. Electron-transport proteins carrying FAD as a prosthetic group are called cytochromes.
d. On a molar basis the electron-transport system contains more FAD than cytochrome *c*.
e. The P/O ratio for $FADH_2$ in mitochondria is 3.
f. The barbiturate amytal blocks ATP formation from isocitrate oxidation but not from succinate oxidation.
g. In the presence of an uncoupling agent, the energy derived from electron transport is dissipated as heat.
h. If the intramitochondrial concentration of ADP is low, addition of an uncoupling agent will retard electron transport.

12.2 a. The transfer of electrons from a substrate molecule to an electron acceptor in the environment is called _____.

b. In addition to flavoproteins and _____ proteins, the respiratory chain of mitochondria includes the small molecule _____.

c. The potential span between _____ and _____ represents the largest step in the mitochondrial electron-transport chain.

d. Two H^+ ions must be released for each pair of electrons transferred from _____ to _____ within the mitochondrial membrane.

e. In the process of electron transport, H^+ ions are released to the _____ of the mitochondrial membrane.

f. The antibiotic _____ blocks electron transport indirectly by inhibiting ATP formation.

12.3 a. Write a balanced equation for the respiratory oxidation of NADH in a bacterium that uses SO_4^{2-} as an electron acceptor.

b. What is the potential span ($\Delta E_0'$) of the electron-transport chain in this organism?

c. Assume that 15 kcal of free energy are required to efficiently drive the formation of 1 mol ATP under intracellular conditions. If $\Delta E' \simeq \Delta E_0'$, what is the maximum number of ATP molecules that theoretically can be produced per pair of electrons transferred from NADH to SO_4^{2-} in this bacterium?

d. What is the theoretical maximum number of ATP molecules that can be produced in a bacterium that uses O_2 as electron acceptor?

12.4 The heme prosthetic groups of the mitochondrial cytochromes are essentially identical in their structure. Can you explain in general terms how it is possible that their half-cell potentials (Table 9.1) differ by more than 0.2 V?

12.5 In a preparation of mitochondria, oxidation of fatty acids is being carried out in the presence of coenzyme A, O_2, ADP, and P_i.

a. How many molecules of ATP will be produced per two-carbon fragment converted to $2CO_2$?

b. What will this number be if amytal is added to the preparation?

c. What will it be if dinitrophenol is added?

12.6 a. The $\Delta G_0'$ for complete combustion of glucose to $CO_2 + H_2O$ is -686 kcal/mol. When this process occurs in a cell via the glycolytic pathway, the TCA cycle, and mitochondrial electron transport, how many molecules of ATP are produced per molecule of glucose degraded? (*Note:* Electrons in the cytoplasmic NADH produced by glycolysis are transferred across the mitochondrial membrane to a flavoprotein, without concomitant ATP formation, before entering the electron-transport chain.)

b. Assuming $\Delta G' = -10$ kcal/mol for ATP hydrolysis under intracellular conditions, what fraction of the energy liberated by glucose oxidation is conserved in the form of ATP?

c. What happens to the rest of the energy?

12.7 All oxidation steps in the pathway from glucose to CO_2 result in the production of NADH, except the succinate dehydrogenase reaction, which yields $FADH_2$. How can you explain this exception, considering that an NAD-linked reaction here would allow recovery of two additional ATP molecules per molecule of glucose degraded?

12.8 Assume that the following catabolic reactions are carried out aerobically via the most common routes. Briefly outline the pathway of degradation and indicate the maximum energy yield in molecules of ATP generated per molecule of substrate utilized (Concepts 11.3 and 11.4).

a. Ala → NH_4^+, CO_2, and H_2O

b. Glu → NH_4^+, CO_2, and H_2O

c. Asp → urea, CO_2, and H_2O

d. Which one of the following enzymes is *not* involved in the degradative pathway in part c?

1. Glutamate dehydrogenase
2. Pyruvate carboxylase

    3.   Succinate dehydrogenase
    4.   Oxaloacetate decarboxylase
    5.   Citrate synthase

12.9   Injection of dinitrophenol into a rat causes an immediate increase in its body temperature. Can you explain why?

12.10   Tell which of the following phrases is most likely to complete the following statement correctly: Tissues that actively carry out electron transport from NADH to O_2 *without* coupled oxidative phosphorylation are
  a. Found in the frog but not in the water rat
  b. Found in neither rabbits nor tortoises
  c. Found in the otter but not in the crocodile
  d. Found in both whales and sharks
    Explain your choice.

12.11   Fluhardy Pharmaceuticals has sent you samples of two new metabolic inhibitors to characterize as possible antibiotics. Using a preparation of isolated liver mitochondria incubated with pyruvate, O_2, ADP, and P_i, you find that addition of inhibitor A blocks both electron transport and oxidative phosphorylation. When you add inhibitor B in addition to A, you find to your surprise that electron transport is restored, but not oxidative phosphorylation.
  a. How would you classify these inhibitors in regard to their mode of action in electron transport and oxidative phosphorylation?
  b. Name a pair of known inhibitors that would give the same results.

12.12   Four carriers, a, b, c, and d, whose reduced and oxidized forms can be distinguished spectrophotometrically, are required for respiration in a bacterial electron-transport system. In the presence of substrates and oxygen, three different inhibitors block respiration, yielding the patterns of oxidation states shown in Table 12.1. What is the order of carriers in the chain from substrates to O_2?

Table 12.1
Effects of Inhibitors on Carrier Oxidation Levels in a Hypothetical Electron-Transport Pathway (Problem 12.12)[a]

Inhibitor	a	b	c	d
1	+	+	−	+
2	−	−	−	+
3	+	−	−	+

[a] The symbols + and − indicate fully oxidized and fully reduced, respectively.

12.13   During the investigation of energy production in a thermophilic bacterium isolated from Old Faithful, a new coenzyme, QED, is discovered. Careful experiments reveal that this bacterium produces $QEDH_2$, NADH, and $FADH_2$ in substrate oxidations and regenerates the oxidized coenzymes in the presence of O_2 via the electron-transport system. In addition to the three coenzymes, five cytochromes appear to be involved in electron transport. The oxidized and reduced states of all eight components of the system can be distinguished spectrophotometrically. In an effort to elucidate the position of QED within the pathway, the following are determined: (1) the steady-state level of oxidation of each component in the presence of substrates and oxygen, and (2) the degree of oxidation in the presence of substrate, O_2, and inhibitors of electron transport. The results are reported in Table 12.2. Diagram the most likely pathway for electron transport in this organism.

12.14   Because electron transport is coupled to ADP phosphorylation, it is theoretically possible to drive electrons backward up the chain, against the potential gradient, at the expense of ATP. This mechanism has been observed in some organisms. Consider a bacterium at 25°C that can transfer electrons from succinate to NAD^+ by means of reverse electron transport:

$$\text{Succinate} + NAD^+ \rightarrow \text{fumarate} + NADH + H^+.$$

Table 12.2
Oxidation Levels of
Carriers in an Imaginary
Electron-Transport
Pathway (Problem 12.13)^a

	NAD	FAD	QED	Cytochromes 1	2	3	4	5
Steady-state degree of oxidation	+	+	+	+ +	+ + +	+ +	+ +	+ +
Electron-transport inhibitors								
A	−	−	−	−	−	−	−	−
B	−	−	+	−	+ + +	+ +	+ +	+ +
C	−	−	−	−	+ + +	−	−	+ + +
D	+	+	−	+ +	+ + +	−	+ +	+ +

^{a} The symbols + + + and − indicate fully oxidized and fully reduced, respectively.

If the intracellular concentration of P_i is constant at $0.01 M$, calculate the [ATP]/[ADP] ratio that would be required to maintain the steady-state ratio of [NADH]/[succinate] at 0.01. Assume that the intracellular concentrations of fumarate and NAD^+ are equal.

12.15 A species of *Nitrobacter* can live and grow happily in the presence of NO_2^-, with CO_2 as sole carbon source, but it requires O_2 to do so. Biochemical studies show that under these conditions the organism phosphorylates ADP, reduces NAD^+, and uses the resulting ATP and NADH to drive biosynthesis of cellular components from CO_2. The data in Table 9.1 may suggest to you that this is impossible, but the creature exists! Outline the processes by which such an organism might produce NADH and ATP.

12.16 Until recently an alternative hypothesis, quite different from the chemiosmotic theory, was entertained by many biochemists. This chemical-coupling hypothesis proposed that oxidative phosphorylation occurs by mechanisms analogous to the substrate-level phosphorylation in stage II and stage III pathways, in which oxidation of an intermediate converts it to a high-energy phosphate donor. Two proposed types of mechanisms are shown in equations 12.2 and 12.3, in which C is an electron carrier protein and X is a cofactor analogous to coenzyme A:

$$C_{red} + X \rightarrow C_{red}-X \xrightarrow{-2e^-} C_{ox}{\sim}X \xrightarrow{P_i}$$

$$\begin{array}{c} C_{ox}{\sim}\textcircled{P} \quad ADP \\ \text{or} \qquad\qquad \xrightarrow{} \boxed{ATP} + X + C_{ox} \quad (12.2)\\ X{\sim}\textcircled{P} \end{array}$$

$$+2e^-$$

$$C_{red} \xrightarrow{P_i} C_{red}-\textcircled{P} \xrightarrow{-2e^-} C_{ox}{\sim}\textcircled{P} \xrightarrow{ADP} \boxed{ATP} + C_{ox} \quad (12.3)$$

$$+2e^-$$

Three experimental findings are cited in defense of one of the two opposing theories. Interpret each of them briefly in terms of the hypothesis it supports, and explain whether it is compatible with the alternative hypothesis.

a. When concentrated mitochondria supplied with substrate in an anaerobic environment are given a short pulse of O_2, the pH of the external solution transiently decreases.

b. Spectrophotometric evidence suggests that in normal intact mitochondria inhibition of phosphorylation by oligomycin blocks electron transport at three specific sites preceding NADH-dehydrogenase (FP_1), cytochrome c, and O_2 (see Figure 12.2).

c. When mitochondrial membranes are disintegrated physically by ultrasound treatment to progressively smaller and smaller fragments, oxidative phosphorylation becomes uncoupled from electron transport long before electron transport itself is affected.

12.17 The proton gradient created across the mitochondrial membrane by respiration can be considered as having two components: a pH differential resulting from the excess of H^+ ions outside, and an electrochemical membrane potential resulting from the excess of positive ions outside and negative ions inside. These two components are utilized differently in driving different energy-requiring mitochondrial processes. ATP synthesis from ADP and P_i can be driven by either component. Pumping of Na^+ ions out of the mitochondrion is driven by the pH gradient; Na^+ efflux is coupled specifically to H^+ influx. Uptake of Ca^{2+} ions into the mitochondrion is driven by the electrochemical potential; the ions are pulled through a specific Ca^{2+} channel from the positively charged outer surface to the negatively charged inner surface of the membrane. Explain the effects on ATP synthesis, Na^+ export, and Ca^{2+} uptake that will result from treatment of actively respiring mitochondria with the following antibiotics. Assume that the medium contains K^+ ions such that the starting $[K^+_{inside}] = [K^+_{outside}]$.

    a. Valinomycin, an ionophore (membrane-soluble ion carrier) that allows K^+ ions to leak rapidly across the mitochondrial membrane

    b. Nigericin, another ionophore that allows an equal (electrically neutral) exchange of K^+ for H^+ ions across the membrane

    c. Both valinomycin and nigericin

☆ 12.18   Caltequinone (CTQ), a recently discovered respiratory coenzyme, is a suspected component of the electron-transport chain in armadillo kidney mitochondria, which show tight coupling between electron transport and oxidative phosphorylation. If the standard half-cell potential E'_0 of the couple $CTQ/CTQH_2$ is $+0.32$ V, what is the theoretical maximum number of ATP molecules that could be produced per pair of electrons transferred from NADH to CTQ under standard conditions?

    a. 0

    b. 1

    c. 2

    d. 3

    e. 4

☆ 12.19   Dinitrophenol and oligomycin inhibit mitochondrial oxidative phosphorylation. Dinitrophenol is an uncoupling agent. Oligomycin blocks the phosphorylation process per se. Therefore dinitrophenol will do the following in the presence of oligomycin:

    a. Block electron transport

    b. Allow electron transport

    c. Block oxidative phosphorylation

    d. Allow oxidative phosphorylation

    e. None of the above

☆ 12.20   An antibiotic has been discovered that blocks electron transport between NADH and the flavoprotein NADH dehydrogenase (FP_1). Indicate whether the following statements are true or false for mitochondria in the presence of the inhibitor and O_2. (Consider electron transport from the indicated substrates only.)

    a. Malate still can be oxidized with a P/O ratio of 2.

    b. Succinate still can be oxidized with a P/O ratio of 2.

    c. In the presence of pyruvate, all carriers will be in their fully oxidized forms except NAD-linked dehydrogenases and the flavoprotein NADH-dehydrogenase.

Answers

12.1   a. False. Respiration can occur only in environments that furnish an electron acceptor with a more positive E'_0 value than that of the available electron donors, but this acceptor need not be O_2.

    b. False. Mitochondria are found only in eucaryotic cells, but many procaryotes have an analogous respiratory apparatus associated with their plasma membrane.

    c. False. These proteins are called flavoproteins. The cytochromes carry heme prosthetic groups.

d. True

e. False. The P/O ratio is 2 because the electrons feed into coenzyme Q and generate fewer protons (Figure 12.5).

f. True

g. True

h. False. Because electron transport and oxidative phosphorylation are coupled, the rate of electron transport is limited by low availability of ADP for phosphorylation. An uncoupling agent removes this restriction and consequently increases the rate of electron transport.

12.2   a. electron transport (or respiration)

b. cytochrome (or heme), coenzyme Q

c. cytochrome a_3, O_2

d. $FADH_2$, cytochromes

e. outside

f. oligomycin

12.3   a. $NADH + H^+ + SO_4^{2-} \rightarrow NAD^+ + SO_3^{2-} + H_2O$

b. From Table 9.1:
E_0' for $NAD^+ + 2H^+/NADH + H^+ = -0.32$ V
E_0' for $2H^+ + SO_4^{2-}/SO_3^{2-} + H_2O = +0.48$ V
Hence $\Delta E_0' = +0.80$ V.

c. Because a $\Delta E_0'$ of 0.1 V is equivalent to a $\Delta G_0'$ of 4.6 kcal/mol for a two-electron reaction (equation 9.6), the $\Delta G_0'$ of this electron-transport process will be $8 \times (-4.6) \simeq -37$ kcal/mol electron pairs. The production of three ATP/$2e^-$ would require -45 kcal; therefore, only two can be produced per electron pair.

d. With O_2 as acceptor, the potential span is 1.14 V. The corresponding $\Delta G_0'$ is $11.4 \times (-4.6) \simeq -52$ kcal/mol electron pairs. Hence a maximum of three ATP can be produced per electron pair.

12.4   Differences in half-cell potentials result from the influence of amino acid side chains adjacent to the heme structure in the protein interiors of the various cytochromes. The half-cell potential of free iron ions, Fe^{3+}/Fe^{2+}, is 0.77 V (Table 9.1). The four heme nitrogen atoms, as well as the side chains of neighboring amino acids in the protein, coordinate with the iron ion to varying extents, thereby decreasing the electron affinity of the Fe^{3+} form and making the reduction potential of the Fe^{3+}/Fe^{2+} couple less positive.

12.5   a. Conversion of each two-carbon fragment to acetyl CoA results in the formation of one molecule of $FADH_2$ and one molecule of NADH (Concept 11.2). Complete oxidation of each acetyl CoA to $2CO_2$ via the TCA cycle yields one molecule of $FADH_2$, three molecules of NADH, and one molecule of ATP (Concept 11.4). The P/O ratios for $FADH_2$ and NADH in oxidative phosphorylation are 2 and 3, respectively; hence a total of 17 ATP molecules will be produced.

b. Amytal blocks the transport of electrons from NADH via FP_1 to oxygen, but not the transport from the flavoproteins succinate dehydrogenase (FP_2) and acyl CoA dehydrogenase (FP_3) to oxygen (Figure 12.2). Therefore, five molecules of ATP will be produced in the presence of the inhibitor (one by substrate-level phosphorylation).

c. One ATP will be produced (by substrate-level phosphorylation). Dinitrophenol completely uncouples electron transport from phosphorylation.

12.6   a. The net yields of ATP and reduced carrier molecules per molecule of glucose oxidized are as follows:

From glycolysis, two ATP and two $FADH_2$ (after transfer of the electrons from NADH across the mitochondrial membrane to a flavoprotein); from pyruvate oxidation, one NADH for each of two pyruvate molecules; from the TCA cycle, one ATP, one $FADH_2$, and three NADH from each of two molecules of acetyl CoA. Therefore, these reactions produce a total of four ATP, four $FADH_2$, and eight NADH per glucose oxidized. Because $FADH_2$ has a P/O ratio of 2 and NADH a P/O ratio of 3, the total ATP production is 36 molecules per molecule of glucose oxidized.

b. The fraction of the energy conserved is

$$\frac{-10 \times 36}{-686} = \frac{360}{686} = 52\%$$

c. The rest of the energy is released as heat.

12.7 The standard potential of the fumarate $+ 2H^+$/succinate couple is $+0.03$ V, whereas that of $NAD^+ + 2H^+$/NADH $+ H^+$ is -0.32 V. Therefore, transfer of electrons from succinate to NAD^+ would have a $\Delta E'_0$ of -0.35 V, a $\Delta G'_0$ of approximately $+16$ kcal/mol, and a K'_{eq} of less than 10^{-11}. Clearly, this reaction will not proceed spontaneously.

12.8 a. Ala $+ \alpha$-ketoglutarate $\rightarrow$ pyruvate $+$ Glu

Glu $+ NAD^+ \rightarrow NH_4^+ + NADH + \alpha$-ketoglutarate

NADH $\rightarrow NAD^+$, via electron transport, yields 3 ATP

Pyruvate $\rightarrow 3CO_2$, via pyruvate dehydrogenase, the TCA cycle, and electron transport, yields 15 ATP

Hence the total is 18 ATP.

b. Glu $+ NAD^+ \rightarrow NH_4^+ + NADH + \alpha$-ketoglutarate

NADH $\rightarrow NAD^+$, via electron transport, yields 3 ATP

α-Ketoglutarate $\rightarrow$ oxaloacetate, via the TCA cycle, yields 9 ATP

Oxaloacetate $\rightarrow$ pyruvate $+ CO_2$

Pyruvate $\rightarrow 3CO_2$, as in part a, yields 15 ATP

Hence the total is 27 ATP.

c. Asp $+ \alpha$-ketoglutarate $\rightarrow$ oxaloacetate $+$ Glu

Glu $+ NAD^+ \rightarrow \alpha$-ketoglutarate $+ NADH + NH_4^+$

NADH $\rightarrow NAD^+$, yields 3 ATP

Oxaloacetate $\rightarrow$ pyruvate $+ CO_2 \rightarrow 3CO_2$, as in part a, yields 15 ATP

Because incorporation of NH_4^+ into urea requires the expenditure of four high-energy phosphate bonds (Concept 11.3, part D), the net gain will be 14 ATP.

d. Pyruvate carboxylase

12.9 Dinitrophenol uncouples electron transport from oxidative phosphorylation. Therefore, the energy released by electron transport no longer can be conserved in ATP, and is released as heat instead.

12.10 To maintain a constant body temperature higher than that of their environment, warm-blooded animals must use some of the energy derived from respiration to produce heat. Therefore, warm-blooded animals, but not cold-blooded animals, contain tissues (brown fat) in which the degree of coupling between electron transport and oxidative phosphorylation is either very low or can be regulated. Thus the most likely answer is c.

12.11 a. The results can be explained only if inhibitor A blocks the phosphorylation process, and inhibitor B is an uncoupler of electron transport from phosphorylation. When A alone is added, the two processes are coupled and therefore both are blocked. Addition of B uncouples the system and allows electron transport to proceed even though oxidative phosphorylation is inhibited.

b. The same results would be obtained with oligomycin as inhibitor A and dinitrophenol or gramicidin as inhibitor B.

12.12 The order of carriers is substrates, c, b, a, d, O_2.

12.13 From the steady-state levels of oxidation of the carriers, NAD, FAD, and QED are closer to the reducing end of the chain than any of the cytochromes, and cytochrome 2 is at the oxidizing end.

Inhibitor A must block transfer from cytochrome 2 to O_2. The finding that all carriers are reduced indicates that all are part of transport chains terminating with cytochrome 2.

Inhibitor C blocks oxidation of all but cytochromes 5 and 2, thereby establishing the sequence of the two terminal carriers.

Inhibitor B blocks oxidation of NAD, FAD, and one cytochrome, but not QED and the other cytochromes, suggesting a branched pathway with $QED \rightarrow (3,4) \rightarrow 5 \rightarrow 2 \rightarrow O_2$ as one branch.

Inhibitor D confirms this notion by inhibiting the QED but not the $NAD \rightarrow FAD \rightarrow 1$ branch; D also establishes the order of cytochromes 3 and 4. Therefore, the pathway is as shown in Figure 12.6.

12.14   From Table 9.1 the relevant potentials are $E_0' = +0.03$ V for fumarate $+ 2H^+$/succinate and $E_0' = -0.32$ V for $NAD^+ + 2H^+$/$NADH + H^+$. Thus $\Delta E_0'$ for the reaction equals -0.35 V, and $\Delta G_0' = 16.1$ kcal/mol. If $[NAD^+] = $ [fumarate] and [NADH]/[succinate] = 0.01, from equation 9.3,

$$\Delta G' = \Delta G_0' + 2.30RT \log \frac{[NADH][fumarate]}{[succinate][NAD^+]}$$

$$= +16.1 + 1.37 \log 10^{-2}$$

$$= 16.1 - 2.7 = 13.4 \text{ kcal/mol}$$

To balance this reaction, ATP hydrolysis must yield 13.4 kcal/mol. Therefore, applying equation 9.3 to ATP hydrolysis at $[P_i] = 0.01M$,

$$\Delta G' = \Delta G_0' + 2.30RT \log \frac{[ADP][10^{-2}]}{[ATP]}$$

$$-13.4 = -7.3 + 1.37(-2) + 1.37 \log \frac{[ADP]}{[ATP]}$$

$$\log \frac{[ADP]}{[ATP]} = \frac{-3.4}{1.37} = -2.5$$

$$\frac{[ADP]}{[ATP]} \simeq \frac{1}{300}$$

The [ATP]/[ADP] ratio must be maintained at 300.

12.15   The remarkable feature of this organism is that it must transfer the electrons it obtains from NO_2^-, its sole source of reducing power $(2H^+ + NO_3^-/NO_2^- + H_2O$; $E_0' = +0.42$ V), to NAD^+ $(NAD^+ + 2H^+/NADH + H^+$; $E_0' = -0.32$ V), which is thermodynamically a most unfavorable reaction $(\Delta E_0' = -0.74$ V, $\Delta G_0' = +34$ kcal/mol).

The organism accomplishes this feat by means of two separate electron-transport pathways. In the first, electrons are transferred from NO_2^- to O_2 $(\Delta E_0' = +0.40$ V; $\Delta G_0' \simeq -18$ kcal/mol) with production of ATP via coupled oxidative phosphorylation. Some of this ATP is used to drive the second coupled electron-transport system in reverse, with transfer of electrons up the chain from NO_2^- to NAD^+.

12.16   a. This observation supports the chemiosmotic hypothesis, which predicts that hydrogen

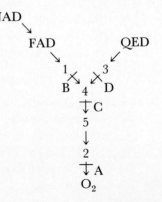

Figure 12.6
Sequence of carriers in an imaginary electron-transport pathway (Answer 12.13).

ions will be translocated from the inside to the outside of the mitochondrion by electron transport. The chemical hypothesis does not predict such a shift.

b. This observation supports the chemical hypothesis, because it suggests that the ADP phosphorylation reactions can be localized at three specific sites. The chemical hypothesis predicts such sites, whereas the chemiosmotic hypothesis postulates no relation of phosphorylation to specific carriers in the electron-transport chain.

c. This observation supports the chemiosmotic hypothesis, which predicts that membrane fragments large enough to form closed vesicles will be required for coupled oxidative phosphorylation. According to the chemical hypothesis, oxidative phosphorylation would be expected to persist until the structural units for electron transport are disintegrated.

12.17 The two antibiotics each specifically affect different components of the proton gradient.

a. Valinomycin will allow K^+ ions to flow in as H^+ ions are pumped out by respiration, thereby neutralizing the electrochemical gradient without altering the pH gradient. Valinomycin therefore will prevent Ca^{2+} uptake, but will not prevent Na^+ export or ATP synthesis.

b. Nigericin will allow external H^+ ions to exchange with internal K^+ ions, thereby dissipating the pH gradient without altering the electrochemical gradient. Nigericin therefore will prevent Na^+ export but will not prevent Ca^{2+} uptake or ATP synthesis.

c. A combination of the two antibiotics will eliminate both components of the proton gradient, thereby preventing all three energy-requiring processes.

13 Photosynthesis

Phototrophic organisms trap light energy and convert it into chemical energy in the process called **photosynthesis**. This chapter considers the light-induced formation of ATP (**photophosphorylation**) and NADPH (**photoreduction**). The reactions by which phototrophs use ATP and NADPH in the biosynthesis of glucose from CO_2 are described in Chapter 15.

Concepts

13.1 Phototrophic organisms use the energy of visible light.

Visible light is electromagnetic radiation of wavelength 400 to 700 nm (Figure 13.1). Each quantum or photon of light has an energy of $h\nu$, in which h is Planck's constant (1.58×10^{-37} kcal sec/photon), and ν is the frequency of radiation in sec^{-1}. Therefore, the energy, $\mathscr{E}$, of 1 mol (einstein) of photons is

$$\mathscr{E} = Nh\nu = Nh\frac{c}{\lambda} = \frac{2.86 \times 10^4}{\lambda} \text{ kcal/einstein} \tag{13.1}$$

in which N is Avogadro's number (6.02×10^{23} photons/einstein), c is the velocity of light (3.0×10^{17} nm/sec), and λ is the wavelength in nanometers. Note that $\mathscr{E}$ is inversely proportional to wavelength. Therefore, photons at the violet end of the spectrum have the highest energy.

13.2 Phototrophic organisms contain pigments that absorb the energy of photons.

One or more of the pigments called **chlorophylls** are common to almost all phototrophic organisms. The structures of all chlorophylls are closely related; chlorophylls *a* and *b* are shown in Figure 13.2. Photosynthetic cells may contain pigments of two other classes: carotenoids (yellow) and phycobilins (red and blue). These pigments serve as supplementary light receptors for portions of the visible spectrum not covered

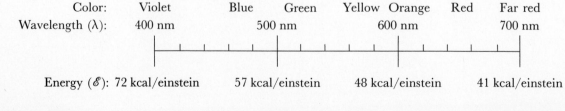

Color:	Violet		Blue	Green	Yellow	Orange	Red		Far red
Wavelength (λ):	400 nm			500 nm		600 nm			700 nm

Energy ($\mathscr{E}$): 72 kcal/einstein   57 kcal/einstein   48 kcal/einstein   41 kcal/einstein

Figure 13.1
The visible spectrum, showing the energy of light at different wavelengths.

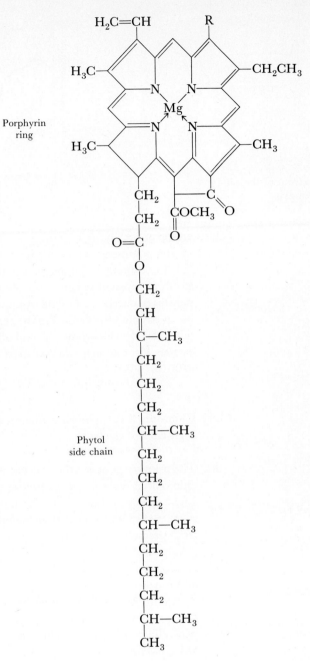

Figure 13.2
The structure of chlorophyll.
The group designated —R is
—CH₃ in chlorophyll *a* and
—CH=O in chlorophyll *b*.

by chlorophyll. The absorption spectrum of the pigments in a green alga is shown in
Figure 13.3.

**13.3   Photosensitive pigments are organized into
specialized light-trapping structures.**

The pigment molecules of the light-trapping apparatus are assembled into arrays that
funnel absorbed energy into photoreactive centers. These arrays are called **photosystems.**

In phototrophic bacteria the photosystems are located on specialized portions of
the plasma membrane. In eucaryotic phototrophs the light-trapping apparatus is
located on the inner membranes of organelles called **chloroplasts.** A schematic diagram of chloroplast ultrastructure is shown in Figure 13.4. The inner membranes of
the chloroplast are organized into flattened vesicles (thylakoid disks) that are stacked

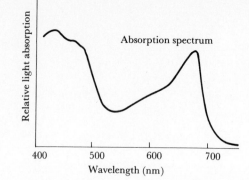

Figure 13.3
Absorption spectrum of the pigments in a green alga.

on top of each other to form **grana** and **stroma.** The grana and stroma contain nearly all the photosensitive pigment in a chloroplast.

In addition to pigments, the light-sensitive membranes of phototrophs contain electron-transport systems with components analogous to those of the respiratory apparatus (Concept 12.1). The components in phototrophs include **plastoquinone,** similar in structure to CoQ (Figure 12.3), two *b*-type cytochromes, a *c*-type cytochrome (also called cytochrome *f*), and **plastocyanin,** a copper-containing protein. These carriers form an electron-transport chain that covers the potential span from about -0.1 to $+0.4$ V.

13.4 Chlorophyll can absorb a photon and give up a high-energy electron.

A. The primary photosynthetic event is light-induced excitation of electrons in a special chlorophyll molecule (P in Figure 13.5), which is located in a photoreactive center. Light energy transferred to the photoreactive center by surrounding accessory pigment molecules raises P from its ground state (P^0) to an excited state (P^*). P^* is a strong reducing agent, that is, a good electron donor. P^* gives up an electron to a suitable acceptor near the top of the electron-transport chain, thereby becoming an electron-deficient free radical (P^+). P^+ is a strong oxidizing agent, that is, a good electron acceptor. To return to the ground state, P^+ accepts an electron of lower energy from a suitable donor, as described in Concept 13.5. The potential span between the excited couple P^+/P^* and the ground-state couple P^+/P^0 varies somewhat depending on the photosystem and the energy of the incident light, but, in general, absorption of one photon raises the energy of one electron by about 1 V.

B. Chloroplasts contain two photosystems, designated **photosystem I** and **photosystem II.** Photosystem I, located in the membranes of grana and stroma, raises the energy of

Figure 13.4
Structure of a chloroplast. Stroma are thought to contain only photosystem I, whereas grana contain photosystems I and II.

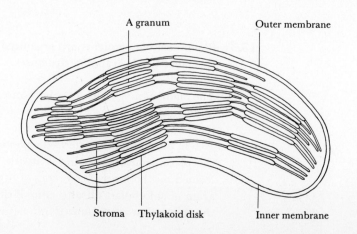

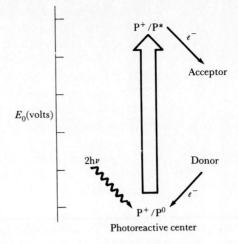

Figure 13.5
Excitation of an electron in chlorophyll by light absorption.

electrons from about $E_0' = +0.4$ to $E_0' = -0.6$ V. A similar photosystem is found in the membranes of all photosynthetic bacteria. Photosystem II, found only in the membranes of grana in chloroplasts and oxygen-evolving photosynthetic bacteria, raises the energy of electrons from about $E_0' = +0.9$ V to $E_0' = -0.2$ V. The two photosystems work together in chloroplasts but have different functions, as described in Concepts 13.6 and 13.7.

13.5 Photosystems drive ATP synthesis by a chemiosmotic mechanism.

Transport of electrons from excited chlorophyll molecules down the chain of electron carriers in the thylakoid membranes of grana and stroma yields energy, which is used to translocate protons from one side of the membrane to the other. The mechanism of this chemiosmotic process, still poorly understood, appears similar to the process in mitochondrial membranes (Concept 12.2), except that the topology is reversed (compare Figures 12.4 and 13.6). In chloroplasts, protons are translocated from the outside to the inside of the grana and stroma (Figure 13.6). In photosynthetic bacteria, vesicles formed from invaginations of the plasma membrane function similarly to the grana and stroma in chloroplasts. The flow of protons from the inside of these com-

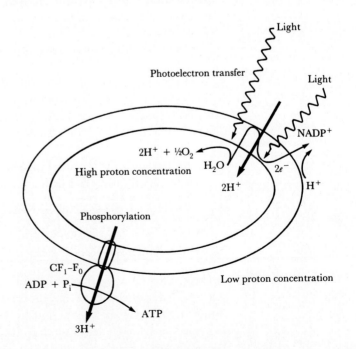

Figure 13.6
Topology of photosynthetic electron transport and phosphorylation in the thylakoid membrane of a chloroplast. (Adapted from *Scientific American,* March 1978, p. 106.)

partments back to the outside drives ATP synthesis. The membrane-bound ATPase that catalyzes this reaction is similar to the analogous enzyme complex in mitochondria, except that it is located on the outside of the thylakoid membrane. The stoichiometry of the reaction is also different; three protons must flow through the ATPase per ATP synthesized, as compared to $2H^+$ per ATP in mitochondria.

The apparently opposite topologies in mitochondria and chloroplasts lead to the same result: production of ATP in the internal lumen of the organelle. In photosynthetic bacteria, similarly arranged photosystems produce ATP inside the cell.

13.6 Photosystem I can operate in either a cyclic or a noncyclic mode.

A. When photosystem I operates in the **cyclic mode,** an electron given up by P_I^* is passed from ferredoxin (a small nonheme protein containing iron and labile sulfur) through cytochrome b_6 and the electron-transport chain, and ultimately back to P_I^+, regenerating P_I^0 (Figure 13.7). This process drives proton translocation coupled to ATP formation, as described in Concept 13.5. The stoichiometry for cyclic photophosphorylation is probably

$$2h\nu + ADP + P_i \rightarrow ATP \qquad (13.2)$$

that is, the $P/2e^-$ ratio of this process is 1.

B. When photosystem I operates in the **noncyclic mode,** two electrons from successive oxidation of P_I^* are transferred through ferredoxin to $NADP^+$ with uptake of an H^+ ion, to yield reducing power for biosynthesis in the form of NADPH. The electrons for returning P_I^+ to the ground state and two H^+ ions are obtained from an external donor of the general form H_2D (D = donor), as shown in Figure 13.7.

C. By switching between the cyclic and noncyclic modes, phototrophic organisms can regulate their relative outputs of ATP and reducing power according to changing physiological needs.

13.7 Non–oxygen-evolving and oxygen-evolving phototrophs utilize different electron donors for noncyclic electron transport.

A. The non–oxygen-evolving photosynthetic bacteria contain only photosystem I. Therefore, they require donors with reduction potentials (E_0' for the couple $2H^+ + D/H_2D$) less positive than $+0.3$ V, the reduction potential of P_I^+/P_I^0. Different bacterial species have become adapted to utilize a variety of donors, such as H_2, H_2S, $H_2S_2O_3$, lactate, succinate, and so on. Electrons from the donor flow into the system at a point that depends on the reduction potential of H_2D, and are transferred along the electron-transport chain to P_I^+ with concomitant proton translocation coupled to ATP production when the potential span permits (Figure 13.7). The stoichiometry for bacterial noncyclic electron flow is

$$2h\nu + H_2D + nADP + nP_i + NADP^+ \rightarrow nATP + NADPH + H^+ + D \qquad (13.3)$$

in which n probably can range from 0 to 2 depending on the reduction potential of the electron donor.

B. The oxygen-evolving photosynthetic bacteria (**cyanobacteria,** formerly called blue-green algae), as well as all the eucaryotic phototrophs (plants and algae), use H_2O, a more widely available compound, as the electron donor. However, H_2O cannot transfer electrons directly to the electron-transport chain, because its reduction potential is

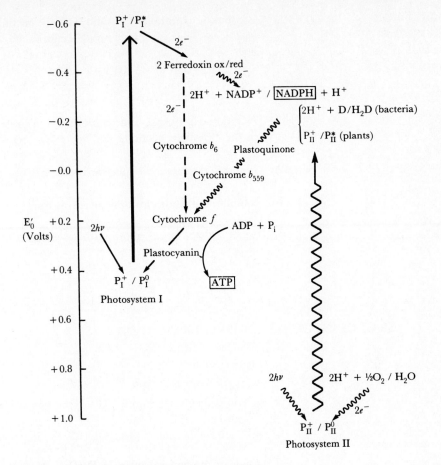

Figure 13.7
Cyclic and noncyclic pathways of photosynthetic electron transport. Dashed and wavy arrows indicate reactions unique to cyclic and noncyclic pathways, respectively; the remainder of the reactions are common to both pathways. Because two electrons are required to reduce a molecule of $NADP^+$, electrons and photons are indicated in pairs, although the excited pigments P_I^* and P_{II}^* can give up only one electron at a time.

+0.8 V. To permit utilization of H_2O, these organisms have evolved the second pigment system, photosystem II, for raising the energy of electrons from H_2O to a level from which they can flow into the electron-transport chain. Light absorption by photosystem II generates P_{II}^*, which can give up an electron to plastoquinone. This electron passes down the electron-transport chain, with concomitant proton translocation and coupled ATP production, to P_I^+, thereby regenerating P_I^0. The electron-deficient free radical, P_{II}^+, is a strong enough acceptor to extract electrons spontaneously from H_2O, thereby regenerating P_{II}^0 and producing oxygen. Because two photons must be absorbed by each photosystem to transfer a pair of electrons from H_2O to $NADP^+$, the overall stoichiometry for noncyclic electron flow in eucaryotes is probably

$$4h\nu + H_2O + 2ADP + 2P_i + NADP^+ \rightarrow 2ATP + NADPH + H^+ + \tfrac{1}{2}O_2 \quad (13.4)$$

13.8   Glucose is the primary product of photosynthesis.

The ATP and NADPH generated by photosynthetic electron transport are used primarily for biosynthesis of glucose from CO_2 (Concept 15.4). The stoichiometry for this process is

$$6CO_2 + 12NADPH + 12H^+ + 18ATP \rightarrow$$
$$C_6H_{12}O_6 + 12NADP^+ + 18ADP + 18P_i + 6H_2O \quad (13.5)$$

Combining equations 13.4 and 13.5 (neglecting the excess ATP) yields the familiar, and deceptively simple, overall equation for eucaryotic photosynthesis of glucose:

$$6H_2O + 6CO_2 \xrightarrow{\text{light}} C_6H_{12}O_6 + 6O_2 \qquad (13.6)$$

13.9 Additional concepts and techniques are presented in the Problems section.

A. Photosynthetic action spectra. Problem 13.7.

B. Inhibitors of photosynthetic electron transport. Problems 13.11 and 13.12.

C. Genetic dissection of photosynthetic electron transport using mutant algae. Problem 13.14.

References

COMPREHENSIVE TEXTS

Lehninger: Chapter 22   Stryer: Chapter 19
Metzler: Chapter 13   White et al.: Chapter 16

OTHER REFERENCES

Govindjee and R. Govindjee, "The Absorption of Light in Photosynthesis," *Scientific American*, December 1974, p. 68.

P. C. Hinkle and R. E. McCarty, "How Cells Make ATP," *Scientific American*, March 1978, p. 104.

R. P. Levine, "The Mechanism of Photosynthesis," *Scientific American*, December 1969, p. 58.

Problems

13.1   Answer the following with true or false. If false, explain why.
a. Blue light is more energetic than yellow light.
b. Plants are green because their chlorophylls absorb and utilize green light most efficiently.
c. In most phototrophic organisms the ultimate electron acceptor is CO_2.
d. All oxygen-evolving phototrophic organisms contain photosystem I and photosystem II, whereas other phototrophic organisms have only photosystem II.
e. All phototrophs carry out photosynthesis in a specialized organelle, the chloroplast.
f. The principal photosynthetic event is photoreduction.
g. In the overall reaction for photosynthesis, the oxygen from H_2O is incorporated into glucose.
h. In noncyclic electron flow in plants, electrons taken from O_2 are used ultimately to reduce $NADP^+$ to NADPH.
i. Two einsteins of photons must be absorbed by photosystem I to produce 1 mol of NADPH.
j. The equation for noncyclic reduction of $NADP^+$ in a phototrophic bacterium that uses H_2 as an electron donor is

$$H_2 + 2ADP + 2P_i + 2NADP^+ \rightarrow 2ATP + 2NADPH$$

k. The energy, $\mathscr{E}$, of 1 quantum of light of wavelength 400 nm is 72 kcal.
l. Although a second photosystem and extra light absorption are required to extract electrons from water, phototrophs that can utilize water have a substantial ecological advantage because water is almost ubiquitous in the biosphere.

13.2 a. _____ and _____ are the two light-induced processes that produce chemical energy and reducing power for fixation of CO_2.

   b. No NADPH is generated during _____ electron flow.

   c. P_I^* is a strong electron _____ and P_{II}^+ is a strong electron _____.

   d. Photosensitive pigments are _____ electron producers, whereas biosynthetic reductions are _____ electron consumers. The "gear wheel" between these two processes is _____.

   e. The class of pigments known as the _____ is represented in all photosynthetic organisms. The two classes of accessory pigments, _____ and _____, are used less universally.

13.3 a. Assuming a $\Delta G'$ of $+10$ kcal/mol for ATP formation from ADP and P_i under intracellular conditions, calculate the theoretical maximum number of ATP molecules that could be formed upon absorption of 1 quantum of violet light (420 nm), of green light (520 nm), and of red light (650 nm).

   b. What is the efficiency of conversion of light energy to chemical energy at each of these wavelengths, assuming cyclic photophosphorylation and an ATP/$2e^-$ ratio of 1?

13.4 When light of 700 nm is absorbed by photosystem I under standard conditions, what fraction of its total energy is trapped as free energy of transferable electrons?

13.5 You are studying two new species of photosynthetic bacteria. To fix CO_2 into organic material the first species requires H_2S as an external electron donor, and the second requires NO_2^- ion. Estimate the minimum number of light quanta at 700 nm that a bacterium of each species will have to absorb to produce two molecules of ATP and one molecule of NADPH. Briefly explain how you arrive at your answer and any assumptions you make. The relevant half-cell potentials are

$$S + 2H^+/H_2S \qquad\qquad E_0' = -0.23 \text{ V}$$

$$NO_3^- + 2H^+/NO_2^- + H_2O \qquad E_0' = +0.42 \text{ V}$$

13.6 A pigmented unicellular organism will carry out photosynthesis of glucose when illuminated in the presence of CO_2 and H_2O, but only if butyrate ($CH_3CH_2CH_2COO^-$) also is present in the medium. In the course of the reaction butyrate is converted to crotonate ($CH_3CH=CHCOO^-$; $E_{0(crotonate + 2H^+/butyrate)}' = +0.25$ V). Answer the following with true or false. If false, explain why.

   a. The light-trapping apparatus of the organism *must* include both photosystem I and photosystem II.

   b. CO_2 assimilation is accompanied by evolution of molecular oxygen.

   c. In the course of photosynthesis with $C^{18}O_2$, some ^{18}O is incorporated into glucose.

   d. In the course of photosynthesis with $C^{18}O_2$, some ^{18}O is incorporated into water.

   e. Most of the ATP generated by this organism in photosynthetic reactions is produced by a noncyclic photophosphorylation process.

13.7 To make up additional units so you can graduate with your classmates, you have been working on a special research project to compare photosynthesis in an avocado plant, a cyanobacterium, and a purple sulfur bacterium. The goal of your project was to obtain a photochemical action spectrum for each of the organisms. Your general technique was to measure O_2 evolution in avocado and the cyanobacterium, or S production in the purple sulfur bacterium as a function of the wavelength of incident light. Just yesterday you completed the project. Last night the biology building and your notes were destroyed in a campus fire. In searching through the ashes you come across the charred remains of your laboratory notebook. The three action spectra you so carefully determined are intact; however, the labels no longer are legible. When you tell your advisor of your misfortune, he offers to give you credit if you can deduce which spectrum corresponds to which organism. The three action spectra are reproduced in Figure 13.8. Will you graduate?

13.8 a. It often is suggested that if life exists on Mars it must include photosynthetic organisms. Do you agree? Why or why not?

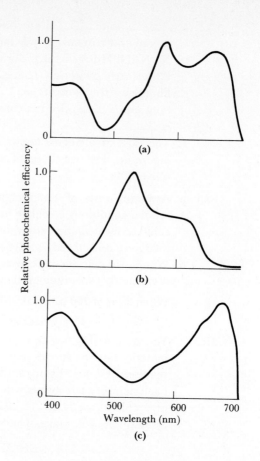

Figure 13.8
Photosynthetic action spectra for
three different organisms (Problem 13.7).

b. Although Mars should have sufficient mass to retain O_2 in its atmosphere, the available evidence indicates that there is little or none present. Does this argue against the
widespread occurrence of actively photosynthesizing organisms?

c. It has been pointed out that because Mars apparently has very little hydrogen, the
nature of the reducing agent for photosynthesis poses a problem. Given that the only
available source of hydrogen is water, but that no O_2 is produced by photosynthesis,
can you diagram a plausible *noncyclic* photophosphorylation system capable of producing ATP and reducing $NADP^+$ to NADPH, using SO_3^{2-} as the electron donor (see
Table 9.1)? Assume an electron-transport chain and photosensitive pigments similar
to those found in known organisms.

d. Explain briefly any major differences between your system and those of non-oxygen-
evolving bacteria on earth.

13.9 What, if anything, is wrong with each of the schematic representations shown in
Figure 13.9 for photosynthesis in hypothetical organisms?

13.10 The actual $ATP/2e^-$ ratio for noncyclic electron flow in terrestrial eucaryotic phototrophs is uncertain. Calculate the theoretical maximum $ATP/2e^-$ ratio for the flow of
electrons from photosystem II to photosystem I (Figure 13.7). Assume the $\Delta G'$ for ATP
formation is $+10$ kcal/mol under intracellular conditions. Assume $\Delta E' \simeq \Delta E_0'$.

13.11 Write the overall stoichiometry for photoreduction and photophosphorylation in
plants in the presence of the following compounds.

a. DCMU, a herbicide that prevents the oxidation of H_2O to O_2

b. Methylviologen (MV), a dye that accepts electrons from P_I^* (E_0' for $MV_{ox}/MV_{red} =
-0.55$ V; $n = 2$)

c. Desaspidin, an uncoupler of photophosphorylation

d. Ferricyanide (FC_{ox}), which accepts electrons from the electron-transport chain and
becomes reduced to ferrocyanide (FC_{red}) (E_0' for $FC_{ox}/FC_{red} \simeq 0.4$ V; $n = 1$)

e. Phenazine methosulfate, a dye that accepts electrons from ferredoxin and donates

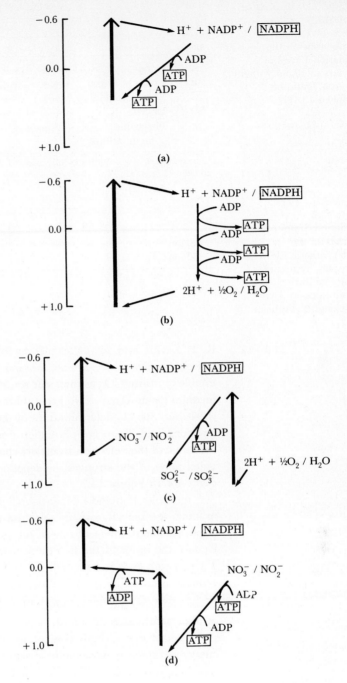

Figure 13.9
Electron flow in four hypothetical photosynthetic systems (Problem 13.9).

them directly to the electron-transport chain, thereby producing a cyclic electron flow in photosystem I that bypasses cytochrome b_6

13.12 Several components of the electron-transport chain in eucaryotic phototrophs have been identified. Their positions in the scheme of cyclic and noncyclic electron flow are shown in Figure 13.7. Assume that you can follow spectrophotometrically the oxidation levels of ferredoxin, $NADP^+$, and each of the other five electron carriers during photosynthetic electron transport in the presence of various inhibitors and electron acceptors. From the data in Table 13.1 deduce which numbered column corresponds to each of the seven carriers in the electron-transport chain.

13.13 Photosystems I and II absorb light at different wavelengths. At 720 nm one system absorbs and the other does not; at 650 nm the converse is true. From the data in Table 13.2 deduce which photosystem absorbs at each wavelength.

Table 13.1

Effects of Various Compounds on the Oxidation Levels of Carriers in Photosynthetic Electron Transport (Problem 13.12)[a]

Experi-ment	Compound added	\multicolumn{7}{c}{Oxidation levels of seven electron carriers}
		1	2	3	4	5	6	7
A	None	+++	++	++	++	+	++	++
B	Methylviologen	+++	++	++++	++	+	++++	++++
C	Ferricyanide	+++	++	++++	++	+	++++	++++
D	DCMU	+++	++++	++	++	++++	++	++++
E	Phenazine methosulfate	+++	++++	++	++	++++	++++	++++

[a] The symbol $+++$ indicates fully oxidized. See Problem 13.11 for the specific effects of the compounds added.

Table 13.2

Oxidation States of Four Carriers in the Photosynthetic Electron-Transport System of a Eucaryote during Illumination at Two Wavelengths (Problem 13.13)

Wavelength	Plastoquinone	Cytochrome b_{559}	Cytochrome f	Plastocyanin
720 nm	ox	ox	ox	ox
650 nm	red	red	red	red

13.14 R. P. Levine and his colleagues have isolated a large number of mutants of the unicellular alga *Chlamydomonas reinhardi* that are defective in photosynthesis. They are unable to utilize CO_2 as their sole source of carbon and require acetate in the growth medium (*ac* mutants). Two general kinds of experiments have been carried out with these mutants: (1) determinations of their ability to carry out partial photosynthetic reactions, and (2) spectrophotometric measurements of light-induced oxidation and reduction of their electron-transport-chain components. Such investigations have provided some of the strongest evidence in favor of the scheme of photosynthesis diagrammed in Figure 13.7.

In Tables 13.3 and 13.4, data on five of these mutants are reproduced. Four of the mutants are defective in the electron-transport chain and the fifth is lacking the photoreactive pigment of one of the photosystems.

a. Deduce the order of the five mutational blocks along the electron-transport chain.

b. Try to assign each mutationally identified component to a known component of the system. Assume that each mutant carries only a single gene defect.

13.15 If you can solve the following problem, you indeed have learned what the energetics of photosynthesis is all about.

Photosynthetic organisms presumably evolved from forms whose sole method of energy metabolism was anaerobic degradation of organic substrates by means of "soluble" enzyme systems. This development seems like a large evolutionary step, inas-

Table 13.3

Ability of *Chlamydomonas* Wild Type and Mutant Strains to Carry Out Partial Reactions of Photosynthesis (Problem 13.14)

	Experiment	Wild type	\multicolumn{5}{c}{Strain}
			ac-21	ac-80	ac-115	ac-206	ac-208
A	Measure photoreduction of $NADP^+$ by illuminated chloroplast fragments	+	−	−	−	−	−
B	Same as A, but add plastocyanin purified from wild-type cells	+	−	−	−	−	+
C	Same as A, but add ascorbate, an artificial electron donor	+	+	−	+	+	−
D	Measure O_2 evolution in chloroplast fragments in presence of ferricyanide, an artificial electron acceptor	+	+	+	−	+	+

Table 13.4
Light-Induced Oxidation and Reduction of Three Mutationally Identified Electron-Transport-Chain Components in *Chlamydomonas* Wild Type and Mutant Strains (Problem 13.14). Missing components are indicated by 0.

Component	Wild type	Strain				
		ac-21	*ac-80*	*ac-115*	*ac-206*	*ac-208*
Experiment A: Illumination at 720 nm						
Component defective in *ac-80* (C_{80})	ox	ox	0	ox	ox	ox
Component defective in *ac-115* (C_{115})	ox	red	red	0	red	red
Component defective in *ac-206* (C_{206})	ox	ox	red	ox	0	red
Experiment B: Illumination at 650 nm						
C_{80}	red	red	0	red	red	red
C_{115}	red	red	red	0	red	red
C_{206}	red	ox	red	ox	0	red

much as present-day photophosphorylation requires both a light-trapping apparatus and a membrane-associated electron-transport system. See if you can design a hypothetical, primitive, cyclic photophosphorylation system consisting of a soluble (or enzyme-bound) photosensitive pigment, soluble enzymes, and cofactors. Use phosphoglycerate kinase (Figure 10.2, reaction 7) for the actual ATP-generating step, and, as far as possible, other enzymes known to exist in anaerobic cells. Draw a schematic diagram or reaction sequence to indicate the path of electron flow and the mechanism of ATP generation in your system. How would you expect its efficiency to compare with that of present-day photosynthetic systems?

☆ 13.16 a. Consider a photosynthetic bacterium that utilizes H_2S as its electron donor. Which *one* of the following statements about this organism is true?

1. ATP production always is accompanied by H_2S oxidation.
2. In the absence of H_2S, H_2O can serve as the electron donor provided that light of the proper wavelength is available.
3. Production of ATP by noncyclic photosynthetic electron transport will be more efficient (higher $P/2e^-$ ratio) in this bacterium than in one that uses succinate as its electron donor.
4. NADPH can be produced by either cyclic or noncyclic photosynthetic electron transport.
5. Conversion of CO_2 to glucose requires ATP and NADPH and results in evolution of oxygen.

b. Which *one* of the following is false? In the course of photosynthesis by a suspension of green algae, ^{18}O added as

1. $C^{18}O_2$ will appear rapidly in carbohydrate.
2. $C^{18}O_2$ will appear rapidly in H_2O.
3. $C^{18}O_2$ will appear rapidly in O_2.
4. $H_2^{18}O$ will appear rapidly in O_2.
5. $H_2^{18}O$ will not appear rapidly in carbohydrate.

☆ 13.17 Calculate the equilibrium constant for the transfer of an electron from excited photosystem II to electron-deficient photosystem I in a green plant ($P_{II}^* + P_I^+ \rightarrow P_{II}^+ + P_I^0$).

☆ 13.18 Algal mutants that no longer can utilize CO_2 as sole carbon source because of defects in photosynthetic electron transport can be grown in a medium containing acetate and studied to determine the nature of the mutational defect, as described in Problem 13.14.

a. Explain very briefly why the mutants require acetate, whereas the normal strain does not, and how the mutants manage to grow in the presence of acetate.

b–e. Table 13.5 gives the results of experiments carried out with isolated chloroplasts from four different strains. From these results, determine which component of the photosynthetic electron-transport system is most likely to be defective in each mutant. Remember that photosystem I does not respond to light of 650 nm, and photosystem II does not respond to light of 720 nm. None of the mutants can carry out photoreduction of NADP$^+$ using H_2O as the electron donor.

Table 13.5
Experiments with Isolated
Mutant Chloroplasts
(Problem 13.18)

Measurement	Mutant strains			
	b	c	d	e
Cyclic photophosphorylation when irradiated with 720 nm light	+	+	−	+
Hill reaction ($H_2O + A \rightarrow H_2A + O_2$) when irradiated with 650 nm light in the presence of an oxidant that can accept electrons from plastoquinone	+	+	+	−
Photoreduction of $NADP^+$ when irradiated with 720 nm light in the presence of a reductant that can donate electrons to plastocyanin	+	−	+	+
Oxidation state upon irradiation with 650 nm light:				
Plastoquinone	red	red	red	ox
Plastocyanin	ox	red	red	ox

Answers

13.1 a. True

b. False. The color of an object is due to reflected light; that is, light that is not absorbed. Plants are green because they absorb green light least efficiently.

c. True

d. False. Phototrophs that do not evolve oxygen have photosystem I only.

e. False. In phototrophic bacteria the light-trapping apparatus is associated with the plasma membrane.

f. True

g. False. The oxygen from H_2O is evolved as O_2.

h. False. Electrons taken from H_2O are used to reduce $NADP^+$ to NADPH.

i. True

j. False. A molecule of H_2 has only two electrons. Therefore, the equation is

$$H_2 + 2ADP + 2P_i + NADP^+ \rightarrow 2ATP + NADPH + H^+$$

k. False. 72 kcal is the energy of 1 *einstein* of light at 400 nm.

l. True

13.2 a. Photophosphorylation, photoreduction

b. cyclic

c. donor, acceptor

d. one-, two-, ferredoxin

e. chlorophylls, carotenoids, phycobilins

13.3 a. The energy, $\mathscr{E}$, of light with a wavelength of 420 nm is 28,600/420 or 68 kcal/einstein. Therefore, 1 quantum of violet light could yield a theoretical maximum of six ATP molecules. Similarly, green light, at 55 kcal/einstein, could produce five ATP molecules, and red light, at 44 kcal/einstein, could produce four ATP molecules.

b. Because cyclic photophosphorylation probably produces only one ATP per $2e^-$, that is, one ATP per 2 quanta, the efficiency of conversion of violet-light energy is $\frac{10}{140}$ or about 7%. The efficiency of green light is 9% and that of red light is 11%.

13.4 $\mathscr{E}$ for 700 nm light is 41 kcal/einstein. Absorption of light by photosystem I raises the energy of its transferable electrons from $E'_0 = +0.4$ V to -0.6 V, a $\Delta E'_0$ of -1.0 V. Under standard conditions the corresponding free-energy change is given by

$$\Delta G'_0 = -n\mathscr{F} \, \Delta E'_0$$

$$= -(1)(23 \text{ kcal/V mol})(-1.0 \text{ V})$$

$$= 23 \text{ kcal/mol electrons}$$

Because 1 mol of absorbed photons produces 1 mol of excited electrons, the fraction of energy trapped is $\frac{23}{41} = 56\%$.

13.5 Photosynthetic bacteria have only photosystem I. To produce a molecule of NADPH, this system must absorb 2 quanta and accept $2e^-$ from the external donor. If the donor is H_2S, the $2e^-$ enter the electron-transport chain near the top, and probably generate two ATP molecules in the course of their transport back to P_I^+. If the donor is NO_2^-, the $2e^-$ must transfer directly to P_I^+ without traversing the electron-transport chain, and no ATP is produced. The second bacterium must absorb an additional 4 quanta to produce two ATP molecules by cyclic photophosphorylation. Therefore, the minimum numbers are 2 quanta for the first bacterium and 6 for the second.

13.6 a. False. The electrons in butyrate (at $+0.25$ V) are sufficiently energetic to transfer directly into the electron-transport chain without an additional boost from a second photosystem.
   b. False. Because butyrate is the electron donor, there will be no oxidation of water and no O_2 production.
   c. True
   d. True
   e. False (probably). Electrons transferred from butyrate ($+0.25$ V) to P_I^+ ($+0.40$ V) in noncyclic electron flow will not generate sufficient energy to produce ATP under conditions where $\Delta G' \simeq \Delta G_0'$. ($\Delta E_0' = +0.15$ V; hence for $2e^-$, $\Delta G_0' = 46$ kcal/V mol $\times 0.15$ V $= -6.9$ kcal/mol electron pairs.) At some concentrations of reactant and products the $\Delta G'$ value will be sufficient to produce ATP. However, it seems likely that the organism produces most of its ATP by *cyclic* photophosphorylation.

13.7 Action spectra generally parallel absorption spectra, because the photochemical efficiency is directly dependent on absorption. Light that is not absorbed is reflected. Because the color of an object is due to reflected light, you can guess the color of the organism by examining the efficiency minima on the action spectra. Spectrum a has an efficiency minimum at a wavelength of 500 nm, midway between blue and green. Thus spectrum a most likely represents the action spectrum of the cyanobacterium. Similarly, spectrum b has minima in the blue and red wavelengths and thus is most likely the purple sulfur bacterium. Spectrum c is probably the avocado, because its minimum is at the green wavelength.

13.8 a. Because the chemical energy sources in any ecosystem are limited, the long-term existence of life requires photosynthetic organisms that can use external energy from the sun to regenerate organic material. If life exists on Mars it must include such organisms, unless it is in a very early stage of evolution and has not yet exhausted the available chemical energy sources.
   b. Not necessarily. Photosynthetic organisms that use electron donors other than water do not produce oxygen.
   c. To carry out noncyclic photoreduction and photophosphorylation, the Martian organism must have a second photosystem; electrons cannot flow spontaneously from SO_3^{2-} ($E_0' = +0.48$ V) to P_I^+ ($E_0' = +0.40$ V) unless energy is supplied from an additional light reaction. A possible scheme for noncyclic electron flow in this organism is shown in Figure 13.10.
   d. The major difference is that non-oxygen-evolving bacterial systems on earth never employ a second photosystem.

13.9 All photosynthetic organisms must be able to produce net amounts of both ATP and NADPH. Net production of NADPH requires an external electron donor.
   a. This scheme is impossible. There is no external electron donor; no net NADPH production can occur.
   b. This scheme is logically possible but unlikely, because it would require a pigment that could generate a potential difference of 1.6 V between its ground and excited states.

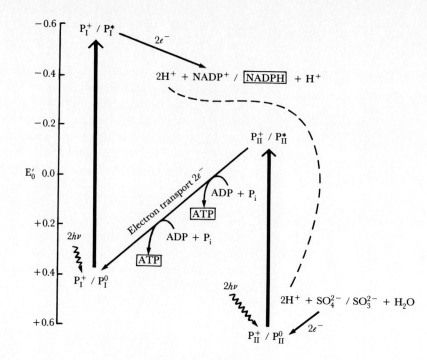

Figure 13.10
Noncyclic photoreduction of
$NADP^+$ by $SO_3^{2-} + H_2O$ in a
hypothetical Martian organism
(Answer 13.8).

c. This scheme is possible. (The second photosystem would be unnecessary if the organism could carry out cyclic photophosphorylation with the first photosystem.)

d. This scheme is possible.

13.10   The free energy available to drive ATP formation can be calculated from E_0' values for the relevant pigment half-cells:

$$P_I^+/P_I^0: \quad E_0' = +0.4 \text{ V}$$

$$P_{II}^+/P_{II}^*: \quad E_0' = -0.2 \text{ V}$$

$$\Delta G_0' = -n\mathscr{F}\,\Delta E_0'$$

$$= -(2)(23\text{ kcal/V mol})(+0.6 \text{ V})$$

$$= 28 \text{ kcal/mol electron pairs}$$

Thus the maximum $ATP/2e^-$ ratio is 28/10 or 2.8.

13.11 a. DCMU prevents photosystem II from operating; consequently, only cyclic electron flow occurs and the stoichiometry is

$$2h\nu + ADP + P_i \rightarrow ATP$$

b. $8h\nu + 2H_2O + 4ADP + 4P_i + 2MV_{ox} \rightarrow 2MV_{red} + 4ATP + 4H^+ + O_2$

c. $8h\nu + 2H_2O + 2NADP^+ \rightarrow 2NADPH + 2H^+ + O_2$

d. Ferricyanide prevents photosystem I from operating. Therefore, the stoichiometry is

$$4h\nu + 2H_2O + 4ADP + 4P_i + 4FC_{ox} \rightarrow 4FC_{red} + 4ATP + 4H^+ + O_2$$

e. When photosystem I is operating in the cyclic mode, photosystem II cannot operate, because there is no acceptor for its electrons. Therefore, the stoichiometry is

$$2h\nu + ADP + P_i \rightarrow ATP$$

13.12   Experiment A indicates the normal steady-state oxidation level of each component. The low oxidation level of 5 suggests that it is near a source of electrons and therefore is probably plastoquinone or ferredoxin. The high oxidation level of 1 suggests that it is near an electron acceptor and therefore is probably plastocyanin or NADPH (the electron acceptors for NADPH are oxidized biosynthetic precursor molecules).

    In experiments B and C the carriers unique to photosystem I will be bypassed, but photosystem II will operate normally. Because carriers 3, 6, and 7 are fully oxidized, they must be components only of photosystem I. Thus 3, 6, and 7 are cytochrome b_6, ferredoxin, and NADPH. These results, taken together with those of experiment A, indicate that carriers 1 and 5 are plastocyanin and plastoquinone, respectively.

In experiment D photosystem II will be blocked, so that only cyclic electron flow will be possible. Consequently, plastoquinone, cytochrome b_{559}, and NADPH will be fully oxidized. Thus, 2, 5, and 7 are plastoquinone, cytochrome b_{559}, and NADPH. These results, taken together with those of experiments A, B, and C, indicate that carrier 2 is cytochrome b_{559}, carrier 7 is NADPH, and carrier 4 is cytochrome f.

Experiment E distinguishes between cytochrome b_6 and ferredoxin, because phenazine methosulfate causes a cyclic electron flow in photosystem I that bypasses cytochrome b_6. Therefore,

$$1 = \text{plastocyanin}$$
$$2 = \text{cytochrome } b_{559}$$
$$3 = \text{ferredoxin}$$
$$4 = \text{cytochrome } f$$
$$5 = \text{plastoquinone}$$
$$6 = \text{cytochrome } b_6$$
$$7 = \text{NADPH}$$

13.13   These data can be explained in the following manner: Photosystem I absorbs light at 720 nm and transfers electrons out of the system. Because photosystem II does not absorb light at 720 nm, the normal flow of electrons from photosystem II to photosystem I is cut off. Under these conditions, photosystem I bleeds the electron carriers of all available electrons, thereby causing their oxidation.

At 650 nm, photosystem II absorbs but photosystem I does not. In the absence of the electron acceptor, P_I^+, the electron carriers "fill" with the electrons produced by photosystem II, thereby becoming reduced.

13.14 a. The scheme of photosynthetic electron transport is as shown in Figure 13.7. Photoreduction of $NADP^+$ requires transfer of electrons from water through P_{II}, along the main electron-transport chain, and through P_I to ferredoxin. As shown in Table 13.3, experiment A, none of the mutants can carry out this transfer. Experiment B identifies the component defective in mutant ac-208 as plastocyanin. Experiments C and D establish some order in the sequence of mutationally identified components. The mutational defects in ac-80 and ac-208 must be beyond (on the P_I side of) the point at which ascorbate feeds electrons into the chain, whereas the defects in the other three mutants must be on the P_{II} side of this point. By the same kind of reasoning, because ac-115 cannot transfer electrons from water through P_{II} to ferricyanide, the defect in ac-115 must be on the P_{II} side of the point at which ferricyanide can accept electrons, whereas all the other defects are beyond this point. Therefore, the data in Table 13.3 establish a partial order of mutationally identified components (C_{mutant}) to be:

$$\text{ascorbate}$$
$$P_I \leftarrow (C_{80}, C_{208}) \overset{\swarrow}{\leftarrow} (C_{21}, C_{206}) \leftarrow C_{115} \leftarrow P_{II}$$
$$\underset{\text{ferricyanide}}{\swarrow}$$

The data in Table 13.4 support this scheme, and also allow a unique order to be deduced. Remember from Answer 13.13 that 720 nm illumination drives only photosystem I, causing all carriers in the wild-type chain to become oxidized, whereas 650 nm illumination drives only photosystem II, causing all carriers in wild type to become reduced. In the mutant ac-208, 720 nm illumination oxidizes C_{80} (but not C_{115} and C_{206}); hence C_{80} must be on the P_I side of C_{208}. In ac-21, 720 nm illumination oxidizes C_{206} and 650 nm illumination does not reduce C_{206}; hence C_{206} must be on the P_I side of C_{21}, and the complete order is

$$C_{80} \leftarrow C_{208} \leftarrow C_{206} \leftarrow C_{21} \leftarrow C_{115}$$

b. Because one of the five mutants is known to carry a photosystem defect, either C_{80}

must be P_I or C_{115} must be P_{II}. A choice between these alternatives can be made with the knowledge that a photopigment will give up an electron and become oxidized only when excited by light of the proper wavelength. Thus if C_{115} were P_{II}, it should remain reduced in wild type illuminated at 720 nm. Because it becomes oxidized (Table 13.4, experiment A), C_{115} must be a carrier in the electron-transport chain and C_{80} must be P_I. This conclusion is supported by the observation that in mutants *ac-21* and *ac-115* at 650 nm, C_{206} is oxidized but C_{80} is not (Table 13.4, experiment B). Thus the most likely assignments for the five components, based on the scheme in Figure 13.5 and the information given, is

$$C_{80} = P_I$$
$$C_{208} = \text{plastocyanin}$$
$$C_{206} = \text{cytochrome } f \text{ (also called cytochrome } c_{553})$$
$$C_{21} = \text{cytochrome } b_{559}$$
$$C_{115} = \text{plastoquinone}$$

13.15 The basic mechanism must be the same as in present-day cyclic photophosphorylation; that is, the primary event must be excitation of the pigment with release of electrons to an acceptor, and the terminal event must be transfer of electrons back to the pigment. Because the ATP-generating step is the phosphoglycerate kinase reaction from the glycolytic pathway (Figure 10.2, reaction 7), the energy-generating redox step should be the triose phosphate dehydrogenase reaction (Figure 10.2, reaction 6).

Hence electrons will be transferred from P* to 3-phosphoglycerate (R—C(=O)—O$^-$), to NAD$^+$, and back to P$^+$ as shown in Figure 13.11. The enzymes are

1. "Photosynthetic 3-phosphoglycerate reductase" (hypothetical) carrying a photosensitive pigment molecule P
2. Triose phosphate dehydrogenase
3. Phosphoglycerate kinase

In the final step, NADH presumably could interact directly with the electron-deficient form of enzyme 1. The system should be considerably slower than present-day photosystems, where the electron carriers are juxtaposed in a membrane, rather than free in solution.

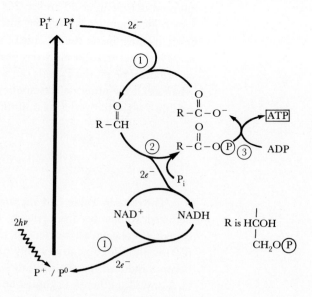

Figure 13.11
A hypothetical soluble system for cyclic photophosphorylation (Answer 13.15).

14 Transport Across Membranes

Phospholipid membranes provide barriers that regulate the exchange of materials and information between a cell's internal compartments and the external environment. These membranes are permeable to nonpolar molecules and water, less permeable to neutral polar molecules, and virtually impermeable to charged molecules and ions. However, most membranes include specific proteins that selectively mediate the transport of certain polar solutes. These transport systems concentrate nutrients from the environment, excrete toxic waste products, and maintain transmembrane ionic gradients. In addition, many cellular membranes contain proteins that sense the presence of certain molecules in the external environment and communicate that information to the cytoplasm. Such transmembrane signaling is an important component of communication between cells. This chapter considers the transport of materials and informational signals across membranes.

Concepts

14.1 **Proteins regulate most communication across membranes.**

A. Small polar molecules (and ions) that cells need for physiological processes, such as energy production and biosynthesis, generally are carried across membranes by specific transport proteins. These protein-mediated transport processes are the principal concern of this chapter.

B. In eucaryotic cells a variety of **endocytotic** (engulfing) mechanisms provide for bulk transport of components from the external environment. **Phagocytosis** is a specialized process carried out by **macrophages,** specialized cells that remove cellular and noncellular debris from the body. Two other mechanisms of endocytosis, **pinocytosis** and **coated vesicle formation,** are more universally employed for uptake of soluble material from extracellular fluid. Pinocytosis involves relatively large gulps of the external environment and can be observed with the light microscope (Figure 6.7). By contrast, coated vesicles are 50–100 nm in diameter, and their formation can be observed only with the electron microscope. Evidence suggests that all animal cells continually form specialized regions of membrane, termed **coated pits,** that pinch off to form small coated vesicles inside the cell (Figure 14.1). The coat consists of a specific protein, clathrin, which forms a spherical shell surrounding the membranous vesicle. Pinocytotic vesicles and coated vesicles arising from the plasma membrane usually fuse with lysosomes, which contain digestive enzymes. Hydrolysis of the macromolecular contents of the fused vesicles permits the smaller constituents to be carried across the vesicle membrane by normal transport mechanisms. The function of coated pits and vesicles is not well understood, but they may provide for turnover of membrane proteins and any attached ligands, or for delivery of extracellular macromolecules to defined intracellular compartments.

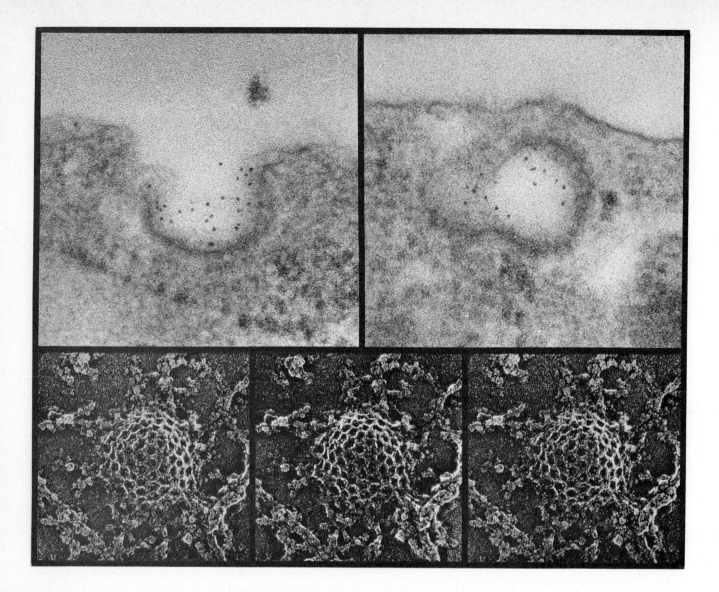

Figure 14.1
Electron micrographs showing coated pits and a coated vesicle. In the upper micrographs the black spots above the surface of the pit and inside the vesicle show the location of ferritin-labeled low-density lipoprotein (see Problem 14.16). (Electron micrographs by Richard Anderson, Joseph Goldstein, and Michael Brown.) The lower micrographs show a stereo triptych of a coated pit as viewed from the cytoplasm. For stereo viewing, see the Appendix to Chapter 4. (Electron micrographs courtesy of John Heuser.)

C. Some molecules in the external environment bind to cells and thereby effect a change within the cell, but are themselves not transported across the membrane. In such cases an **informational signal** is transported. For example, the polypeptide hormone glucagon, when bound to a receptor on the surface of a cell, activates an integral membrane protein, adenyl cyclase, which then increases the intracellular concentration of cyclic AMP (cAMP). This second, intracellular messenger triggers a sequence of events that leads to the activation of glycogen phosphorylase (Concept 10.3). Transmembrane signaling (information transport) is probably an essential, though poorly understood, feature in the mechanism of action of peptide hormones and neurotransmitters, in bacterial chemotaxis, and in cell–cell recognition and development.

14.2 Transport proteins catalyze the diffusion of solutes across membranes.

A. The general reaction for diffusion of a solute, A, between the inside and outside of a membrane-bounded compartment is

$$A_{out} \rightleftarrows A_{in} \tag{14.1}$$

The equilibrium constant for any such reaction is

$$K'_{eq} = \frac{[A]_{in}}{[A]_{out}} = 1 \tag{14.2}$$

because at equilibrium the solute concentrations on the two sides of the membrane must be equal. **Transport proteins** are membrane-bound enzymes that catalyze such diffusion reactions.

B. Like soluble enzymes, transport proteins become saturated at high solute concentrations. As the concentration of solute, [A], increases, the initial rate of mediated transport increases only up to the point of saturation (Figure 14.2). By contrast, nonmediated diffusion does not saturate; its initial rate continues to increase as [A] increases. The K_M of a transport protein can be defined as the value of [A] at which the initial rate of transport is half-maximal.

C. Transport proteins catalyze diffusion of one or a few structurally related solute molecules. This specificity is due to a precise fit between the solute and a binding site on the protein. The transport of a solute often can be inhibited competitively by compounds that are related structurally to the normally transported solute.

D. Transport proteins catalyze diffusion by binding solute molecules so as to shield their polar groups from the nonpolar membrane interior. As expected, transport proteins are integral components of the membranes in which they function. However, the mechanism by which solute molecules are translocated through the 7 nm thickness of the membrane is not yet known for any transport protein. It is unlikely that an integral membrane protein could rotate through a membrane. Instead transport proteins probably form hydrophilic channels through which specific solutes can pass from one side of the membrane to the other (Figure 14.3).

14.3 Mediated transport can be passive, active, or coupled.

The simple facilitated diffusion described in Concept 14.2, part A, is called **passive transport**. Net transport by this process can occur only from a region of higher solute concentration to one of lower solute concentration. Transport against a concentration gradient is called **active transport**. This process must be driven by some energy-yielding reaction, as described in Concepts 14.4 and 14.5. Cotransport of two different

Figure 14.2
Initial rates of mediated and nonmediated transport with increasing solute concentration on the outside of a membrane-bounded compartment in which the initial value of $[A]_{in} = 0$.

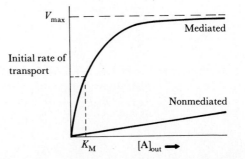

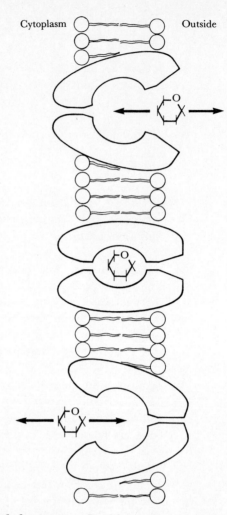

Figure 14.3
A model for protein-mediated
transport. From top to bottom,
the figures represent successive
stages in the transport of a polar
molecule from outside the cell
into the cytoplasm.

solutes is called **coupled transport.** In this process, passage of one solute molecule across the membrane must occur concomitantly with passage of the other, either in the same direction (**symport**), as in equation 14.3, or in opposite directions (**antiport**), as in equation 14.4.

$$(A_{out} + B_{out}) \rightleftarrows (A_{in} + B_{in}) \tag{14.3}$$

$$(A_{out} + B_{in}) \rightleftarrows (A_{in} + B_{out}) \tag{14.4}$$

In such a coupled system, passive transport of one solute can drive active transport of the other. For example, in the system represented by equation 14.3, at equilibrium,

$$\frac{[A]_{in}[B]_{in}}{[A]_{out}[B]_{out}} = 1 \tag{14.5}$$

or

$$\frac{[A]_{out}}{[A]_{in}} = \frac{[B]_{in}}{[B]_{out}} \tag{14.6}$$

Thus in the nonequilibrium situation where $[A]_{out}/[A]_{in} > [B]_{in}/[B]_{out}$, the tendency toward equilibrium results in net passive transport of $A_{out} \rightarrow A_{in}$ with accompanying active transport of $B_{out} \rightarrow B_{in}$ (see Figure 14.4).

14.4 Active transport requires energy.

The amount of energy required to drive an active-transport process can be determined by applying equation 9.3 to the general diffusion reaction in equation 14.1:

$$\Delta G' = \Delta G'_0 + RT \ln \frac{[A]_{in}}{[A]_{out}} \tag{14.7}$$

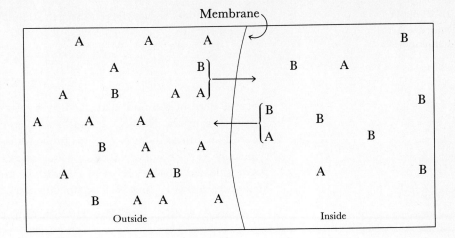

Figure 14.4
Conditions leading to coupled active and passive transport of two solutes. The system can reach equilibrium by net transport of two AB pairs to the inside.

At equilibrium, $[A]_{in}/[A]_{out} = K'_{eq} = 1$ for any diffusion reaction (equation 14.2). From equation 9.5,

$$\Delta G'_0 = -RT \ln K'_{eq} = 0$$

Therefore, under nonequilibrium conditions,

$$\Delta G' = RT \ln \frac{[A]_{in}}{[A]_{out}} \tag{14.8}$$

The expression for free-energy change during transport of a charged solute contains an additional term to account for the gradient of charge. However, because of the compensating movement of other ions, the electrical component is usually small enough to be neglected.

14.5 All active-transport processes are coupled to energy-yielding reactions.

A. In mitochondria and chloroplasts, active transport of H^+ ions is coupled to electron transport as described in Chapters 12 and 13. In a few species of bacteria, H^+ ion transport appears to be driven directly by light. This process is mediated by a membrane protein, bacteriorhodopsin, whose similarity to the rhodopsin of animal visual receptors suggests that a similar light-driven transport process may be important in the eye as well.

B. Most active-transport processes are coupled to the breakdown of high-energy phosphate bonds. In some systems, the phosphate-bond energy is used to drive the transport process itself, as shown in Figure 14.5a. In other systems, the energy is used to change the direction of the gradient by modifying entering solute molecules, as shown in Figure 14.5b.

Active transport of many ions, particularly Na^+, K^+, and Ca^{2+}, is directly coupled to ATP hydrolysis, but the coupling mechanism is not well understood. The linked Na^+–K^+ transport system found in animal cells is one of the best studied ion

Figure 14.5
Two general mechanisms for transport of solute against a concentration gradient using phosphate-bond energy.

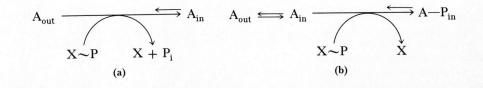

pumps. In animal tissues the relative extracellular and intracellular concentrations of Na^+ and K^+ are

$$[Na^+]_{out} > [Na^+]_{in}$$

$$[K^+]_{out} < [K^+]_{in}$$

About a third of the ATP expended by a resting animal is used to maintain these gradients using the Na^+-K^+ pump. The operation of the pump is diagrammed in Figure 14.6. Intracellular Na^+ binds to the transport protein, which then is phosphorylated by ATP. Phosphorylation somehow causes the bound Na^+ to be translocated to the outside and released. K^+ then binds to the protein, which becomes dephosphorylated and releases K^+ inside. The stoichiometry of the pump reaction is

$$3Na^+_{in} + 2K^+_{out} + ATP + H_2O \rightarrow 3Na^+_{out} + 2K^+_{in} + ADP + P_i + H^+ \quad (14.9)$$

C. In animal cells, the active uptake of organic solutes such as sugars and amino acids is driven by the energy stored in the Na^+ gradient. The coupling is accomplished by transport proteins that specifically bind and cotransport one solute molecule and one Na^+ ion, as in equation 14.3. Thus passive transport of Na^+ back into the cell is accompanied by active symport of the solute (equation 14.10):

$$(Na^+_{out} + A_{out}) \rightleftharpoons (Na^+_{in} + A_{in}) \quad (14.10)$$

Ultimately, of course, such solute uptake is driven by the ATP-linked Na^+-K^+ pump, which maintains the Na^+ gradient.

D. In bacterial cells, the active uptake of many organic solutes is driven by phosphorylation of incoming molecules to change gradient direction, according to the general scheme shown in Figure 14.5b. The bacterial sugar-transport system is the best understood such process. It involves three protein components: a membrane-associated transport protein (E_{II}) that is specific for one or a few sugars, and two less specific cytoplasmic proteins (E_I and HPr). The source of energy for this transport system is phosphoenolpyruvate instead of ATP. The action of these components in the transport of glucose is shown in equations 14.11 through 14.15. Protein-bound glucose is indicated in parentheses.

$$\text{P-enolpyruvate} + HPr \xrightarrow{E_I} \text{pyruvate} + P \sim HPr \quad (14.11)$$

$$\text{Glucose}_{out} + E_{II} \rightleftharpoons E_{II}(\text{glucose})_{out} \quad (14.12)$$

$$E_{II}(\text{glucose})_{out} \rightleftharpoons E_{II}(\text{glucose})_{in} \quad (14.13)$$

$$\underline{E_{II}(\text{glucose})_{in} + P \sim HPr \rightarrow HPr + \text{glucose 6-}P_{in} + E_{II}} \quad (14.14)$$

Net: $\text{P-enolpyruvate} + \text{glucose}_{out} \rightarrow \text{pyruvate} + \text{glucose 6-}P_{in}$ $\quad (14.15)$

The actual transport in this system (equation 14.12) is passive, because conversion of

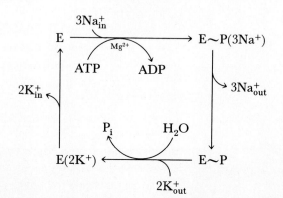

Figure 14.6
Operation of the Na^+-K^+ pump in animal cells. E represents the transport protein, and parentheses indicate protein-bound ions.

the incoming glucose to glucose 6-P maintains the intracellular concentration of free glucose at a level lower than the external concentration.

E. The basic difference in the method of energy coupling in animal cells and bacterial cells probably reflects the difference in their environments. Because of the constant high level of external Na^+, animal cells can rely on depleting their internal Na^+ concentration and coupling all other transport to the resulting Na^+ gradient. In the frequently changing environment of most bacteria, such a mechanism is impossible, and active transport must be coupled directly to the breakdown of high-energy phosphate bonds.

14.6 Active transport is directional.

A. Directional transport requires that at least one component of the transport system be oriented asymmetrically with respect to the two sides of the membrane. Asymmetrically oriented membrane proteins maintain such asymmetry; that is, they do not flip from one side of the membrane to the other (Chapter 6). However, transport proteins must be accessible to solutes on both sides of the membrane, and therefore cannot possess the asymmetry required for directional transport.

B. Directionality in active transport is provided by the energy-coupling system. The coupling proteins either are located on the cytoplasmic side of the membrane or are positioned asymmetrically within the membrane. As expected, when energy production or coupling is inhibited, most active-transport systems lose their directionality and promote simple facilitated diffusion.

14.7 Additional concepts and techniques are presented in the Problems section.

A. Structures and mechanisms of antibiotics that promote ion transport. Problems 14.5 and 14.6.

B. Transport against an electrochemical gradient. Problem 14.12.

C. Coated pit and vesicle formation in cholesterol metabolism. Problem 14.16.

References

COMPREHENSIVE TEXTS

Lehninger: Chapter 28   Stryer: Chapter 36
Metzler: Chapter 5   White et al.: Chapters 11 and 12

OTHER REFERENCES

M. S. Brown and J. L. Goldstein, "Receptor-Mediated Endocytosis: Insights from the Lipoprotein Receptor System," *Proceedings of the National Academy of Sciences*, **76**, 3330 (1979).

D. B. Wilson, "Cellular Transport Mechanisms," *Annual Review of Biochemistry*, **47**, 933 (1978).

Problems

14.1   Answer the following with true or false. If false, explain why.
  a. Pinocytosis and coated vesicle formation are the two primary mechanisms used by eucaryotic cells for bulk sampling of the external environment.
  b. Because membranes are essentially impermeable to charged metabolites, the K'_{eq} for diffusion of charged metabolites out of the cell is much less than 1.

c. The source of energy for all active transport is the breakdown of high-energy phosphate bonds.

d. $\Delta G_0' = 0$ for all transmembrane diffusion reactions.

e. With increasing solute concentration, both mediated and nonmediated transport reach a maximum initial rate of transport. However, the maximum initial rate is different for each and occurs at a different solute concentration.

f. Facilitated diffusion occurs only from a region of lower solute concentration to a region of higher solute concentration.

g. Active transport has two distinguishing features: It occurs against a concentration gradient and it requires metabolic energy.

h. Directionality of active transport is provided by the asymmetric orientation of the transport proteins in the membrane.

14.2 a. Some molecules bind to membrane receptors and transmit _____ across the membranes to initiate a chain of intracellular events, but do not cross the membrane themselves.

b. Phospholipid-bilayer membranes are almost impermeable to _____.

c. When the cotransport of two different solutes is _____, _____ transport of one can drive _____ transport of the other.

d. In bacteria most active-transport processes are coupled _____ to the breakdown of high-energy phosphate bonds, whereas in animal cells the coupling usually is

_____.

e. In the absence of an energy source most active-transport systems promote _____.

f. Obligatory cotransport of two solutes in the same direction is called _____; obligatory contransport in the opposite direction is called _____.

14.3 Arrange the following compounds in increasing order of spontaneous diffusion rate through a typical biological membrane, from a higher concentration on one side to a lower one on the other, at pH = 7. Assume that the membrane contains no specific transport proteins.

a. $HOCH_2CH_2CH_2OH$

b. $^+H_3NCHCOO^-$
    |
    OH

c. $^+H_3NCHC\!\!\begin{array}{c}=O\\ \diagdown NH_2\end{array}$
    |
    OH

d. $CH_3CH_2CH_2CH_2OH$

e. $^+H_3NCHCOO^-$
    |
    OPO_3^{2-}

f. $CH_3C\!\!\begin{array}{c}=O\\ \diagdown NH_2\end{array}$

14.4 Suppose that you can measure the rates of transport of glucose and ethylene glycol from the exterior to the interior of red blood cells from an imaginary creature. You find that the initial rates vary with initial external concentration as shown in Figure 14.7. Propose an explanation for the difference between the two curves.

14.5 The lipid-soluble ion carrier valinomycin is a powerful antibiotic and nervous-system poison. The composition of valinomycin is (D-Val-D-α-hydroxyvalerate-L-Val-L-lactate)$_3$ in a cyclic structure with polar groups inside and nonpolar groups outside. Valinomycin folds in the form of three sine waves, so that the carbonyl oxygen of each of the six valine residues coordinates with the naked (unsolvated) ion carried in the center of the cyclic molecule. Valinomycin will mediate selective transport of K^+ across a membrane from a solution containing both K^+ and Na^+; it will not transport Na^+. Na^+ (0.098 nm radius) is a smaller ion than K^+ (0.13 nm radius); thus Na^+ binds water more tightly (has a greater solvation energy) than K^+. Can you explain why K^+ is transported but Na^+ is not?

14.6 Two classes of peptide antibiotics promote ion transport. Members of the first class, exemplified by valinomycin (Problem 14.5), are lipid-soluble, cyclic molecules that bind ions and diffuse with them across the membrane. Members of the second class, exemplified by the antibiotic gramicidin, are lipid-soluble, open-chain peptides.

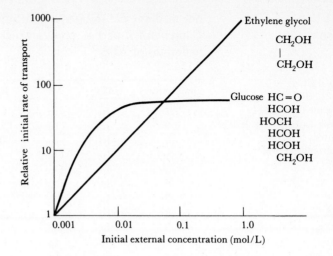

Figure 14.7
Transport of two solutes across red blood cell membranes (Problem 14.4).

These molecules somehow associate within the membrane to form cylindrical aggregates with hydrophobic exteriors and hydrophilic interiors that provide channels for ion flow through the membrane.

Fluhardy Pharmaceuticals has just isolated two new peptide antibiotics that promote cation transport and has sent them to you for testing. To investigate their mode of action, you prepare two artificial phospholipid-bilayer membranes, each containing one of the two antibiotics, and measure the initial rate of K^+ transport as a function of temperature. The data you obtain are shown in Figure 14.8. Which of the antibiotics is analogous in its mechanism to valinomycin, and which to gramicidin? Explain the reasoning behind your answer.

14.7 Gastric juice in man has a pH of $\simeq 1$. However, the cells of the gastric mucosa that secrete the gastric juice have an internal pH of $\simeq 7$. Calculate the ΔG for transport of H^+ ions against this gradient at $37°C$.

14.8 What is the maximum number of Na^+ ions that can be transported out of a cell per ATP hydrolyzed by a simple Na^+ pump that operates independently of K^+, assuming external $[Na^+] = 140mM$; internal $[Na^+] = 10mM$; $\Delta G' = -10$ kcal/mol for ATP hydrolysis under intracellular conditions; and $T = 37°C$?

14.9 When erythrocytes are exposed to a hypotonic medium (a medium of lower osmotic pressure than cell cytoplasm), they swell, and their cytoplasm leaks out, leaving an empty membrane or ghost. If these ghosts subsequently are placed in an isotonic solution (same osmotic pressure as cell cytoplasm), they shrink to their normal size and regain their usual impermeability. In the process, a sample of the isotonic solution becomes trapped inside. The directionality of the linked Na^+–K^+ pump has been demonstrated elegantly by analyzing for ATP hydrolysis after "resealing" ghosts in

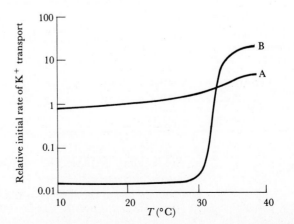

Figure 14.8
Temperature dependence of K^+ transport across artificial phospholipid-bilayer membranes containing antibiotic A or antibiotic B (Problem 14.6).

one medium and transferring them to another. From the description of the pump in Concept 14.5, part B, predict which of the experiments in Table 14.1 will lead to hydrolysis of ATP.

Table 14.1
Conditions for Experiments on ATP Hydrolysis by "Resealed" Erythrocyte Ghost Membranes (Problem 14.9)[a]

Experiment	ATP	Na$^+$	K$^+$	Experiment	ATP	Na$^+$	K$^+$
1	In	In	In	12	Out	In	0
2	In	In	Out	13	Out	Out	In
3	In	In	0	14	Out	Out	Out
4	In	Out	In	15	Out	Out	0
5	In	Out	Out	16	Out	0	In
6	In	Out	0	17	Out	0	Out
7	In	0	In	18	Out	0	0
8	In	0	Out				
9	In	0	0				
10	Out	In	In				
11	Out	In	Out				

[a] The ghosts have been resealed in one medium and then placed in another so that ATP, Na$^+$, and K$^+$ each are present inside, present outside, or absent (0) as indicated.

14.10   In animal cells the active uptake of many different solutes is coupled to the passive transport of Na$^+$ ions. Consider the situation in which the transport of 10 solutes is driven by a gradient of Na$^+$ ions, each catalyzed by a specific transport protein. If the internal Na$^+$ ion concentration is *maintained* at 0.01 of the external concentration, what ratio of internal to external concentration will be maintained for each of the 10 solutes?

14.11   Ouabain is a specific inhibitor of Na$^+$ transport out of the cell. How will it affect the following transport processes?
   a. Nonmediated transport of glucose in cow erythrocytes
   b. Active transport of Leu in man

14.12   In resting nerve cells the internal and external concentrations of K$^+$ and Na$^+$ are such that there is a slight excess negative charge on the inside of the cell membrane. Such a gradient of both concentration and charge is called an electrochemical gradient. The expression for $\Delta G'$ of transport in the presence of an electrochemical gradient is

$$\Delta G' = RT \ln \frac{[A]_{in}}{[A]_{out}} + Z\mathscr{F}\,\Delta\psi \qquad (14.16)$$

in which Z is the number of charges on the solute molecule, $\mathscr{F}$ is Faraday's constant (23 kcal/V mol), and $\Delta\psi$ is the electrical potential difference across the membrane in volts. Calculate $\Delta G'$ for the transport of K$^+$ ions into a nerve cell, assuming external $[K^+] = 7mM$, internal $[K^+] = 140mM$, $\Delta\psi = -60mV$, and $T = 37°C$.

14.13   From wild-type *E. coli* you have isolated a large number of mutants that are defective in the ability to transport one or more sugars as the result of single-gene mutations. These mutants fall into the five functional classes listed in Table 14.2.

Table 14.2
Uptake of Sugars by Wild Type and Five Classes of *E. coli* Mutant Strains (Problem 14.13)

Strain	Glucose	Galactose	Fructose	Mannose	Mannitol
Wild type	+	+	+	+	+
Class 1	+	−	+	+	+
Class 2	−	+	+	+	+
Class 3	−	−	−	−	−
Class 4	+	+	+	+	−
Class 5	+	+	+	−	+

(Header: Sugar spans Glucose, Galactose, Fructose, Mannose, Mannitol)

   a. Are the data in Table 14.2 consistent with your understanding of active transport of sugars in bacteria?
   b. Can you assign the defects in the five mutant classes to particular components of the transport system?

c. Do you expect that all the mutants in any one class are defective in the same protein?

14.14 To a number of identical cell suspensions you add different amounts of ^{3}H-labeled Leu and determine the initial rates of Leu uptake as shown in Table 14.3. What is the K_M of the leucine transport protein in these cells (see Concept 14.2, part B)?

Table 14.3
Initial Rates of ^{3}H-Leu Uptake by Cells in Various Concentrations of Leu (Problem 14.14)

[Leu] (M)	Rate $(cpm/min)^a$		[Leu] (M)	Rate $(cpm/min)^a$
1.0×10^{-3}	3200		1.0×10^{-5}	830
5.0×10^{-4}	3100		5.0×10^{-6}	480
1.0×10^{-4}	2600		1.0×10^{-6}	110
5.0×10^{-5}	2100		5.0×10^{-7}	55
3.0×10^{-5}	1700			
2.0×10^{-5}	1300			

^{a}cpm = counts per minute, the usual measure of radioactivity.

14.15 The β-galactoside transport protein from *E. coli* has a molecular weight of 31,000 daltons. When *E. coli* is induced for galactoside transport it contains about 10^4 molecules of this transport protein per cell. What fraction of the total membrane protein does this protein represent when the cell is induced? Assume the following parameters: *E. coli* is a cylinder 1 μm in diameter and 2 μm in length; its membrane is 7.5 nm thick and is 50% protein ($\rho = 1.30$ g/cm^3) and 50% lipid ($\rho = 1.00$ g/cm^3) on a weight basis.

14.16 Michael Brown and Joseph Goldstein have investigated coated pit and vesicle formation using the membrane receptor for low-density lipoprotein (LDL) particles, which are the primary intercellular carriers of cholesterol. Cholesterol is an essential component of the plasma membranes of all animal cells, yet the body cannot tolerate excessive cholesterol because the insoluble sterol deposits in artery walls, causing atherosclerosis. In humans intercellular cholesterol is packaged into LDL that circulates in the blood. LDL has a core of cholesterol in the form of cholesterol esters, surrounded by a polar coat consisting principally of phospholipid and a protein called apoprotein B. The apoprotein B component of LDL binds to specific receptors that are on the surface of virtually all human cells. The LDL receptors are localized in coated pits. Upon binding of LDL to the receptor, coated vesicles pinch off and rapidly fuse with lysosomes. The protein of LDL is hydrolyzed to amino acids and the cholesterol esters are hydrolyzed to free cholesterol. The free cholesterol crosses the lysosomal membrane and enters the cytoplasm, where it fulfills its cellular functions (Figure 14.9).

a. Coated pits are transient structures (5 min life span) that continually form and pinch off from the membrane as coated vesicles. The formation and internalization of coated pits are *not* influenced by the presence of either LDL or LDL receptors. Indeed each coated pit contains receptors for many different macromolecules. It is curious that LDL receptors when synthesized apparently are added randomly to the membrane and yet are found almost exclusively in coated pits. Speculate on how LDL receptors might become localized in coated pits.

b. Familial hypercholesterolemia is a genetic disease caused by defects in the LDL receptor. Biochemical experiments with cultured fibroblasts from two affected individuals are illustrated in Figure 14.10. Other experiments demonstrate that the rate of coated pit and vesicle formation is normal in the mutant fibroblasts. Deduce the defects in the LDL receptors in the mutant fibroblasts.

c. Ferritin, which is electron opaque, permits visualization of LDL in the electron microscope. Predict the cell-surface distribution of ferritin "spots" in electron micrographs prepared from the three cell types in Figure 14.10 after incubation with ferritin-labeled LDL.

☆ 14.17 How many moles of ATP (assume $\Delta G'$ of hydrolysis = -10 kcal/mol under intracellular conditions) must be expended by a culture of thermophilic bacteria at 57°C to take up 1 mol of Ala from the medium, if the steady-state internal Ala concentration is 100 times the external concentration? Indicate which answer is correct.

a. 0.13 mol

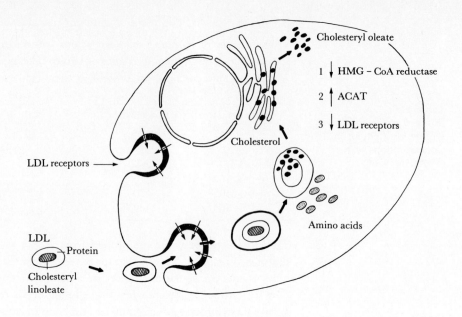

1 ↓ HMG – CoA reductase

2 ↑ ACAT

3 ↓ LDL receptors

LDL binding ➡ Internalization ➡ Lysosomal ➡ Regulatory actions
hydrolysis

Figure 14.9
Sequential steps in the LDL pathway in cultured mammalian cells (Problem 14.16). HMG-CoA reductase is 3-
hydroxy-3-methylglutaryl-coenzyme A reductase, which controls the first committed step in intracellular cholesterol synthesis; ACAT denotes acyl CoA:cholesterol acyl transferase.
Vertical arrows indicate regulatory effects of cholesterol.
[Adapted from M. S. Brown and J. L. Goldstein, *Proceedings
of the National Academy of Sciences*, **76**, 3332 (1979).]

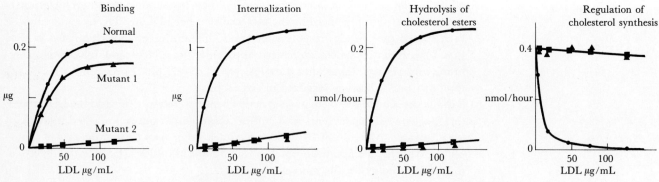

Figure 14.10
LDL receptors in normal and mutant fibroblasts (Problem
14.16). The units for each assay are as follows: Binding, micrograms of ^{125}I-LDL bound to cell surface; internalization,
micrograms of ^{125}I-LDL contained within the cell; hydrolysis of cholesterol esters, nanomoles of [^{3}H]-cholesterol
formed per hour from [^{3}H]-cholesteryl linoleate–labeled
LDL; regulation, nanomoles of [^{14}C]-acetate incorporated
into [^{14}C]-cholesterol per hour by intact cells. [Adapted
from M. S. Brown and J. L. Goldstein, *Proceedings of the
National Academy of Sciences*, **76**, 3333 (1979).]

    b. 0.30 mol

    c. 13 mol

    d. 30 mol

    e. 300 mol

☆ 14.18   A single gene mutation renders wild-type *E. coli* incapable of using glucose as a carbon and energy source. However, the mutant grows as well as wild type on maltose (a disaccharide consisting of two glucose residues in α-1,4 linkage). What is the probable nature of the defect in the mutant? Describe a simple experiment to test your hypothesis.

☆ 14.19   A polypeptide with the following amino acid sequence has been isolated:

$$1 \quad 2 \quad 3 \quad 4 \quad 5 \quad 6 \quad 7 \quad 8 \quad 9 \quad 10 \quad 11$$
Pro-Asp-Val-Leu-Ala-Glu-Ilu-Leu-Glu-Ilu-Ala

The following set of observations has been collected:

1.   It contains no free amino groups.
2.   It contains three free carboxyl groups.
3.   All peptide bonds are α linkages.
4.   The polypeptide can transport alkali-metal cations across artificial membranes.
5.   The polypeptide shows nonlinear cooperative behavior that indicates six or more molecules are involved together in ion transport.
6.   The ion-transport capability of the peptide is sharply decreased at pH values below 3.

a. Propose a peptide structure and a mechanism to explain observation 4.

b. Propose an explanation for observation 5.

c. Would you expect this peptide to show any discrimination among the various alkali-metal cations? Explain the reasoning behind your answer.

d. Explain the pH dependence of the ion-transport capability of the peptide in observation 6.

Answers

14.1   a. True

    b. False. $K'_{eq} = 1$ for all membrane-diffusion reactions. The impermeability of the membrane to charged metabolites makes their approach to equilibrium very slow.

    c. False. Some active-transport processes are driven directly by light or electron transport.

    d. True

    e. False. Only mediated transport is saturated with increasing solute concentration.

    f. False. Facilitated diffusion occurs only from a region of higher concentration to one of lower solute concentration.

    g. True

    h. False. Directionality is provided by the asymmetric orientation of the energy-coupling system.

14.2   a. information (an informational signal)

    b. charged molecules (or ions, or both)

    c. coupled, passive, active

    d. directly, indirect

    e. facilitated diffusion

    f. symport, antiport

14.3   The molecules with the most charged groups will diffuse most slowly. Neutral molecules will diffuse faster with decreasing polar character and increasing nonpolar character. Hence the order of rates will be

$$\text{Slowest—(e)—(b)—(c)—(f)—(a)—(d)—fastest}$$

14.4   Glucose has more polar character than ethylene glycol; therefore, spontaneous diffusion of glucose across a membrane should be slower. The higher initial slope and the subsequent plateau of the glucose curve suggest that the membranes contain a specific glucose carrier, which increases the rate of transport but becomes saturated at high glucose concentration. By contrast, the rate of ethylene glycol transport is linear up to very high external concentrations, suggesting that this transport is not mediated by a specific carrier.

14.5   The K^+ ion fits perfectly into the interior of valinomycin, forming with the six carbonyl groups a coordination complex whose free energy is approximately equal to that of the solvated K^+ ion in water. The smaller Na^+ ion fits less well into valinomycin and has a higher solvation energy; consequently, the free energy of Na^+ ion in water is considerably lower than that of the valinomycin-bound form. As a result, the antibiotic will combine preferentially with K^+ in a mixture of the two ions, and only K^+ will be transported.

14.6   Ion-carrying antibiotics of the valinomycin class must be able to diffuse across the membrane to promote transport, whereas channel-forming antibiotics of the gramicidin class remain stationary during transport. Therefore, the transport rate of ion carriers is influenced strongly by the fluidity of the membrane, whereas that of the channel formers is not. The fluidity of this artificial phospholipid bilayer increases sharply at around 30°C, as the internal phase of the membrane goes from a solid to a liquid state. Therefore, antibiotic A, whose action is relatively temperature independent, is analogous in mechanism to gramicidin, and antibiotic B is analogous to valinomycin.

14.7   Because this reaction involves a pH gradient, the free-energy change must be calculated as ΔG, rather than $\Delta G'$.

$$\Delta G = RT \ln \frac{[H^+]_{out}}{[H^+]_{in}}$$

$$= RT \ln \frac{10^{-1}}{10^{-7}}$$

$$= 1.98 \times 10^{-3} \, \text{kcal/deg mol} \times 310 \, \text{deg} \times 2.3 \log 10^6$$

$$= 8.47 \, \text{kcal/mol}$$

14.8

$$\Delta G' = RT \ln \frac{[Na^+]_{out}}{[Na^+]_{in}}$$

$$= RT \ln \frac{140}{10}$$

$$= 1.98 \times 10^{-3} \, \text{kcal/deg mol} \times 310 \, \text{deg} \times 2.3 \log 14$$

$$= 1.62 \, \text{kcal/mol} \, Na^+ \, \text{ion transported}$$

Because hydrolysis of ATP provides 10 kcal of free energy per mole, the maximum number of Na^+ ions transported per ATP molecule hydrolyzed will be $10/1.62 \simeq 6$.

14.9   In the linked Na^+–K^+ pump internal ATP is used to pump Na^+ out and K^+ in. Only experiment 2 has all three components in the proper relationship to the membrane for transport and concomitant ATP hydrolysis to occur.

14.10   Because the transport of each solute is independent of the others, the final ratio for each solute depends only on the magnitude of the Na^+ gradient. Therefore, the ratio of internal to external concentration for each of the 10 solutes is maintained at 100 to 1.

14.11   Active uptake of sugars and amino acids is linked to transport of Na^+ out of the cell in animals, but not in bacteria. Therefore, the effects of ouabain on the processes listed will be as follows:

a. No effect
b. Inhibition
c. No effect
d. Inhibition

14.12

$$\Delta G' = RT \ln \frac{[K^+]_{in}}{[K^+]_{out}} + Z\mathscr{F}\,\Delta\psi$$

$$= RT \ln \frac{140}{7} + Z\mathscr{F}(-0.06\,\text{V})$$

$$= 1.98 \times 10^{-3}\,\text{kcal/deg mol} \times 310\,\text{deg} \times 2.3 \log 20$$
$$\quad - 1 \times 23\,\text{kcal/V mol} \times 0.06\,\text{V}$$

$$= 1.84\,\text{kcal/mol} - 1.38\,\text{kcal/mol}$$

$$= 0.46\,\text{kcal/mol K}^+\,\text{ions}$$

14.13 a. The data in Table 14.2 are consistent with the system of active sugar transport in bacteria.

b. Mutant classes 1, 2, 4, and 5 are defective in the specific transport proteins (E_{II}) for galactose, glucose, mannitol, and mannose, respectively. Mutant class 3 could contain mutants that are defective in E_I or HPr.

c. Further genetic analysis (a complementation test) or biochemical characterization would be needed to decide whether the mutants in class 3 fall into one or two sub-classes.

14.14 K_M equals the substrate concentration at which the initial rate of transport is half the maximum rate. By inspection, the K_M is close to $3 \times 10^{-5}M$, because at that concentration of Leu the rate of uptake is approximately half the rate observed at $1 \times 10^{-3}M$, which appears to be saturating. A more precise determination using a graphical solution shows that $K_M = 2.9 \times 10^{-5}M$.

14.15 To answer this problem it is necessary to calculate the total number of grams of protein in the membrane of a single cell and then compare to that figure the number of grams of galactoside transport protein in a single cell.

$$\text{Total membrane protein in grams} = \text{volume of membrane} \times \text{average } \rho \times \% \text{ protein}$$

$$\text{Volume of membrane} = \text{surface area} \times \text{thickness}$$

$$= (2\pi rh + 2\pi r^2) \times \text{thickness}$$

$$= 7.85\,\mu\text{m}^2 \times 7.5 \times 10^{-3}\mu\text{m}$$

$$= 5.9 \times 10^{-2}\,\mu\text{m}^3$$

$$= 5.9 \times 10^{-14}\,\text{cm}^3$$

$$\text{Average } \rho = 0.5 \times 1.30\,\text{g/cm}^3 + 0.5 \times 1.00\,\text{g/cm}^3$$

$$= 1.15\,\text{g/cm}^3$$

$$\text{Total membrane protein} = 5.9 \times 10^{-14}\,\text{cm}^3 \times 1.15\,\text{g/cm}^3 \times 0.50$$

$$= 3.39 \times 10^{-14}\,\text{g}$$

$$\begin{aligned} \text{Total galactoside} \\ \text{transport protein} \end{aligned} = \frac{31{,}000\,\text{g}}{\text{mol}} \times \frac{1\,\text{mol}}{6.02 \times 10^{23}\,\text{molecules}} \times 10^4\,\text{molecules}$$

$$= 5.16 \times 10^{-16}\,\text{g}$$

$$\begin{aligned} \text{Percentage galactoside} \\ \text{transport protein} \end{aligned} = (5.16 \times 10^{-16}\,\text{g}/3.39 \times 10^{-14}\,\text{g}) \times 100$$

$$= 1.5\%$$

14.16   a. The localization of LDL receptors in coated pits could be explained by random insertion into the plasma membrane, rapid diffusion in the plane of the membrane, and
specific binding to a component of coated pits, perhaps clathrin itself.

b. Mutant fibroblasts from patient 2 do not bind LDL at all. Therefore the LDL receptors must be absent or defective to the extent that they do not bind LDL. Mutant
fibroblasts from patient 1 bind LDL but do not internalize it. Because coated pit and
vesicle formation is normal in these cells, the lack of internalization suggests that the
LDL receptors in these cells bind LDL but are defective in that part of their structure
that permits them to localize in coated pits.

c. Normal cells show ferritin spots exclusively in coated pits (see Figure 14.1). Fibroblasts
from mutant 2, which do not bind LDL, show no ferritin spots. Fibroblasts from
mutant 1 show ferritin spots on the surface of the cell outside of coated pits.

15 Biosynthetic Principles and the Synthesis of Carbohydrates

Organisms use the energy, reducing power, and precursors produced by catabolism to synthesize the molecular components they require for growth and reproduction. This chapter considers some general principles of biosynthetic reactions, and describes the major pathways of carbohydrate synthesis in chemotrophs and phototrophs.

Concepts

15.1 **All biosynthetic pathways share common features.**

A. **Biosynthesis** is a thermodynamically unfavorable process that requires energy in the form of nucleoside triphosphates, generally ATP. This energy is utilized by chemical coupling through an activated intermediate, formed by transfer of a phosphate, a pyrophosphate, or an adenylate group from ATP to one of the reactants. The mechanisms of coupling are illustrated by the general reactions shown in equations 15.1 through 15.8.

Equation 15.1 represents a typical energy-requiring biosynthetic step, involving elimination of water to form a new bond.

$$X{-}OH + H{-}Y \rightleftarrows X{-}Y + H_2O \qquad \Delta G_0' = +4\,\text{kcal/mol} \qquad (15.1)$$

X—Y synthesis can be coupled to ATP → ADP hydrolysis via the activated intermediate X—O ⓟ, with a favorable overall $\Delta G_0'$ as shown in equations 15.2 through 15.4.

$$X{-}OH + ATP \rightleftarrows ADP + X{-}O\,ⓟ \qquad \Delta G_0' = -2\,\text{kcal/mol} \qquad (15.2)$$

$$X{-}O\,ⓟ + H{-}Y \rightleftarrows X{-}Y + P_i \qquad \Delta G_0' = -1\,\text{kcal/mol} \qquad (15.3)$$

Net:
$$X{-}OH + H{-}Y + ATP \rightleftarrows X{-}Y + ADP + P_i \qquad \Delta G_0' = -3\,\text{kcal/mol} \qquad (15.4)$$

Alternatively, X—Y synthesis can be coupled to ATP → AMP hydrolysis via the activated intermediates X—O ⓟⓟ or X—AMP, with a more favorable overall $\Delta G_0'$. The steps in activation by adenylate transfer are shown in equations 15.5 through 15.8.

$$X{-}OH + ATP \rightleftarrows X{-}AMP + PP_i \qquad \Delta G_0' = -2\,\text{kcal/mol} \qquad (15.5)$$

$$X{-}AMP + H{-}Y \rightleftarrows X{-}Y + AMP \qquad \Delta G_0' = -1\,\text{kcal/mol} \qquad (15.6)$$

$$PP_i + H_2O \rightleftarrows 2P_i \qquad \Delta G_0' = -6\,\text{kcal/mol} \qquad (15.7)$$

Net:
$$X{-}OH + H{-}Y + ATP + H_2O \rightleftarrows X{-}Y + AMP + 2P_i$$
$$\Delta G_0' = -9\,\text{kcal/mol} \qquad (15.8)$$

The extra energy in the second example is provided by hydrolysis of pyrophosphate (PP_i) to $2P_i$ (equation 15.7). Either pyrophosphate or adenylate coupling is used when the biosynthetic reaction is very unfavorable, or when complete irreversibility is essential, as in nucleic acid and protein synthesis.

B. Biosynthesis also requires reducing power in the form of NADPH to convert oxidized precursors to the more reduced state characteristic of cellular components. A typical NADPH-linked reduction reaction is shown in equation 15.9.

$$RCHO + NADPH + H^+ \rightarrow RCH_2OH + NADP^+ \qquad (15.9)$$

C. Pathways for breakdown and synthesis of a particular metabolite are always distinct, utilizing unique enzymes in one or more reactions. Distinct pathways are necessary to allow either degradation or synthesis to proceed with a net negative $\Delta G'_0$. Moreover, separate enzymatic steps permit independent control of degradation and synthesis in response to the cell's physiological needs.

D. The first enzyme unique to a biosynthetic pathway is a regulatory enzyme. In pathways leading to synthesis of energy-storage molecules (carbohydrates and fats) the regulatory enzyme is directly or indirectly responsive to the level of ATP. In pathways for synthesis of protein and nucleic acid precursors, the product amino acid or nucleotide generally inhibits the regulatory enzyme. This control mechanism is referred to as **feedback inhibition**.

15.2 **Carbohydrate synthesis in chemotrophs resembles glycolysis in reverse.**

A. The synthesis of glucose (**gluconeogenesis**) in chemotrophic cells includes several glycolytic reactions operating in reverse (see Figure 10.2). However, the pathway of gluconeogenesis is characterized by unique initial and terminal steps that make the process thermodynamically feasible (Figure 15.1). At the beginning of the pathway, pyruvate carboxylase and phosphoenol pyruvate carboxykinase (reactions 2 and 3) bypass the essentially irreversible pyruvate kinase reaction of glycolysis. At the end of the pathway, two phosphatases (reactions 10 and 12) bypass the ATP-driven phosphofructokinase and glucokinase reactions of glycolysis.

B. Glycogen is synthesized from the activated glucose monomer UDP-glucose, which is formed by reaction of glucose 1-P with UTP (equation 10.4 and Figure 15.1, reaction 14). Glycogen synthase (Figure 15.1, reaction 15) catalyzes addition of activated monomers in α-1,4 linkage to the growing (nonreducing) ends of glycogen outer chains (Figure 10.3). The α-1,6 branch points are created by the action of amylo-(1,4 → 1,6)-transglycosylase, which catalyzes transfer of short, terminal, outer-chain segments from α-1,4 into α-1,6 linkage.

Activated nucleoside diphosphate sugars, analogous to UDP-glucose, are precursors for synthesis of many sugar oligomers and polymers. In most plants, ADP-glucose is the precursor for starch and GDP-glucose is the precursor for cellulose.

C. Regulatory enzymes catalyze the reactions at the three major control points in carbohydrate synthesis (Figure 15.1). Pyruvate carboxylase (reaction 2) is activated by acetyl CoA. Fructose 1,6-diphosphate phosphatase (reaction 10) is activated by ATP and inhibited by AMP, the opposite response to that of phosphofructokinase (Concept 10.2, part B). Glycogen synthase (reaction 15) is inhibited indirectly by cAMP, which initiates a cascade of protein phosphorylation reactions. Phosphorylation of glycogen synthase and glycogen phosphorylase inhibits glycogen synthesis and stimulates glycogen breakdown. (See Figure 10.4.) The pattern of regulation of these enzymes and the additional glycolytic enzymes indicated in Figure 15.1 ensure that glucose and glycogen synthesis will proceed only when the cell has sufficient ATP.

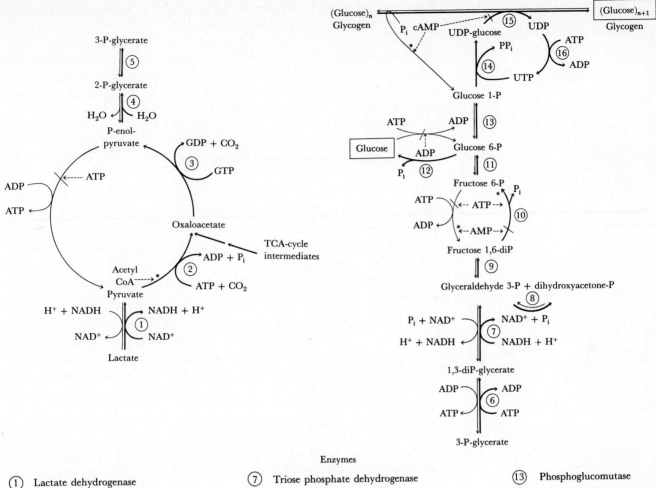

Enzymes

①	Lactate dehydrogenase	⑦	Triose phosphate dehydrogenase
②	*Pyruvate carboxylase (requires biotin)*	⑧	Triose phosphate isomerase
③	*Phosphoenol pyruvate carboxykinase*	⑨	Aldolase
④	Enolase	⑩	*Fructose 1,6-diphosphate phosphatase*
⑤	Phosphoglyceromutase	⑪	Phosphohexose isomerase
⑥	Phosphoglycerate kinase	⑫	*Glucose 6-phosphate phosphatase*

⑬	Phosphoglucomutase
⑭	*UDP-glucose pyrophosphorylase*
⑮	*Glycogen synthase*
⑯	*Nucleoside diphosphate kinase*

Figure 15.1
Gluconeogenesis in liver cells. Heavy and light arrows indicate the reactions of gluconeogenesis and glycolysis, respectively. Enzymes in italics are unique to gluconeogenesis; the remainder also are employed in glycolysis. Regulating metabolites (effectors) and their target enzyme reactions are connected by dashed arrows: / indicates inhibition; * indicates activation.

15.3 Most animals cannot synthesize carbohydrates from acetyl CoA.

A. In most animal cells, the precursors for gluconeogenesis are pyruvate, TCA-cycle intermediates, or any glucogenic molecule that breaks down to these metabolites. Acetyl CoA *cannot* serve as a precursor, because animal cells are unable to carry out its net conversion to either pyruvate or TCA-cycle intermediates (Concept 11.5). Consequently, animals are unable to convert stored fat into sugars or amino acids that are synthesized from glucogenic precursors (Chapter 16).

B. Synthesis of carbohydrate from acetyl CoA is possible only in microorganisms and plants that possess the **glyoxylate-cycle** enzymes. The glyoxylate cycle (Figure 15.2) short-circuits the TCA cycle prior to CO_2 release, thereby permitting net synthesis of a molecule of succinate from two molecules of acetyl CoA.

15.4 Phototrophs synthesize glucose from CO_2 via the Calvin cycle.

A. Carbohydrate synthesis in phototrophic cells occurs via a complex pathway known as the **Calvin cycle** (Figure 15.3). This pathway can be visualized as a two-stage process:

1. In the first stage, 6 CO_2 molecules and 6 pentose acceptors combine to produce 12 trioses, 2 of which are converted to the product, glucose 6-P.
2. In the second stage, the remaining 10 trioses are rearranged to regenerate the 6 pentose acceptors.

The Calvin cycle resembles the phosphogluconate pathway operating in reverse (Figure 10.6). Several enzymes are common to both pathways, and it is likely that the Calvin cycle evolved from the phosphogluconate pathway in primitive phototrophs.

Reactions 1, 6, 9, and 12 are essentially irreversible. The remaining reactions are reversible and are also important in the interconversions of sugars for biosynthesis.

B. Three enzymes in the Calvin cycle are regulated. The K_M of ribulose diphosphate carboxylase is lowered by a factor of 10 in the presence of light. Fructose 1,6-diphosphate phosphatase and phosphoribulose kinase are activated by ATP and inhibited by AMP. This pattern of regulation ensures that a cell will synthesize glucose only when light and sufficient ATP are present.

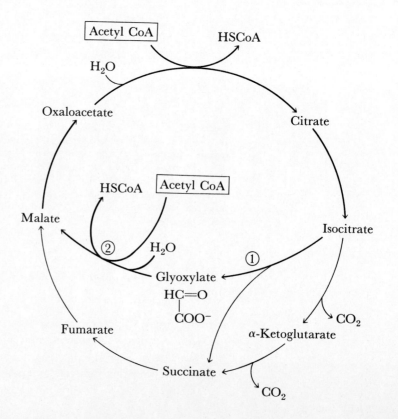

Figure 15.2
The glyoxylate cycle. Heavy arrows represent the reactions of the glyoxylate cycle. Light arrows represent the remaining TCA-cycle reactions. Two enzymes are unique to the glyoxylate cycle: ① isocitratase, and ② malate synthase.

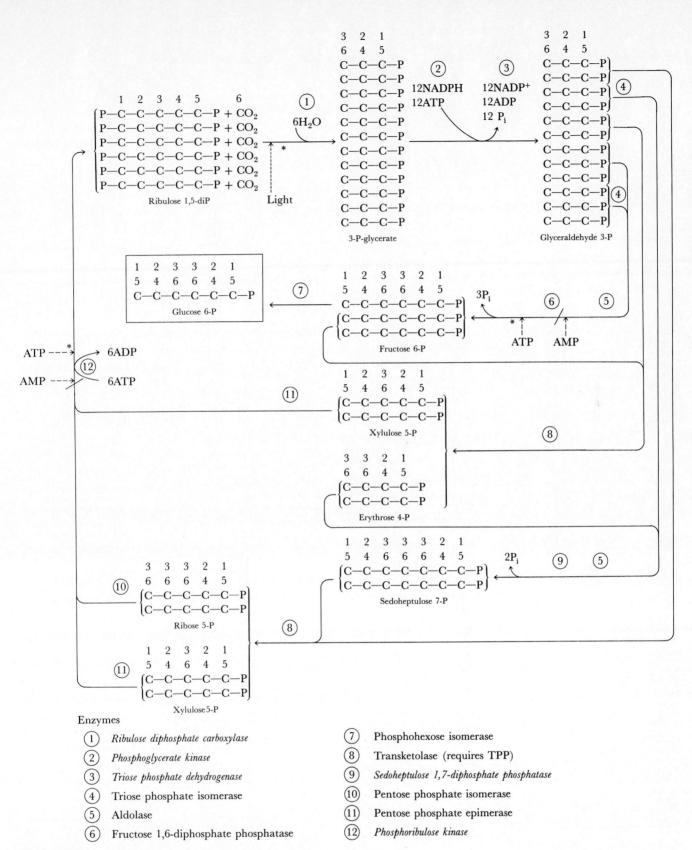

Figure 15.3
The pathway of carbon through the Calvin cycle. This simplified diagram shows only carbon and phosphorus atoms, with numbering to indicate how the input carbon atoms become distributed among the intermediates. Structures for these compounds are shown in Figures 10.2 and 10.6. Enzymes in italics are unique to the Calvin cycle; the remainder also are used in the phosphogluconate pathway (Figure 10.6). Regulating effectors and their target enzyme reactions are connected by dashed arrows: / indicates inhibition; * indicates activation.

15.5 **Additional concepts and techniques are presented in the Problems section.**

A. Analysis of early experiments on CO_2 fixation. Problem 15.12.

B. Analysis of reaction mechanisms by measurement of enzyme-catalyzed, substrate-dependent exchange. Problems 15.15, 15.16, and 15.17.

References

COMPREHENSIVE TEXTS

Lehninger: Chapter 23   Stryer: Chapters 15 and 16

Metzler: Chapter 11   White et al.: Chapters 14 and 15

OTHER REFERENCES

J. A. Bassham, "The Path of Carbon in Photosynthesis," *Scientific American*, June 1962, p. 88. Also reprinted in *Bio-Organic Chemistry, Readings from Scientific American*, W. H. Freeman, San Francisco, 1968.

O. Björkman and J. Berry, "High-Efficiency Photosynthesis," *Scientific American*, October 1973, p. 80.

J. D. Watson, *Molecular Biology of the Gene*, Benjamin/Cummings, Menlo Park, Calif., 1976, 3rd ed. Chapter 5.

Problems

15.1   Answer the following true or false. If false, explain why.
  a. Biosynthesis produces ATP and NADPH.
  b. In some ATP-coupled reactions both high-energy phosphate bonds of ATP are expended.
  c. When PP_i is produced in a synthetic reaction in the cell, it is hydrolyzed to $2P_i$, thereby yielding an additional 6 kcal/mol.
  d. The pathways for breakdown and synthesis of some metabolites are identical. The direction of flow in these pathways is controlled simply by supply and demand at either end.
  e. In many biosynthetic pathways the terminal step is catalyzed by a regulatory enzyme that is inhibited by its own product, the end product of the pathway.
  f. The regulatory effector cAMP has opposite effects on glycogen breakdown and synthesis.
  g. The precursors for net synthesis of carbohydrate in animal cells may be pyruvate, acetyl CoA, or any TCA-cycle intermediate.
  h. Net synthesis of oxaloacetate from acetyl CoA can occur via the glyoxylate cycle.
  i. In the first reaction of the Calvin cycle, CO_2 combines with a pentose acceptor to produce glucose 6-P.
  j. Labeled $^{14}CO_2$ fixed by the Calvin cycle is incorporated into the 1-position of the first glucose produced.

15.2   a. ATP energy in biosynthesis generally is used to drive _____ reactions in reverse.
  b. Pathways leading to the synthesis of energy-storage molecules (primarily _____ and _____) are regulated by the level of _____.
  c. In gluconeogenesis the regulatory enzyme fructose 1,6-diphosphate phosphatase is inhibited by _____ and stimulated by _____.
  d. The Calvin cycle resembles the _____ pathway operating in reverse.
  e. Most of the triose produced in the first steps of the Calvin cycle is converted to _____ in the first cycle.

15.3   How many high-energy phosphate bonds are consumed in the conversion of each of the following to a glucosyl monomer in glycogen?

   a. Glucose 1-P
   b. Fructose 1,6-diP
   c. Free glucose
   d. Two molecules of oxaloacetate

15.4 a. How many high-energy phosphate bonds are consumed in the conversion of two molecules of pyruvate to one molecule of glucose?
   b. How many NADPH-equivalents of reducing power are consumed in the same process?

15.5 Which of the following conversions in gluconeogenesis will not occur in a rat-liver extract treated with avidin (a potent inhibitor of all enzymatic reactions that require the coenzyme biotin; Concept 11.1)?
   a. Glyceraldehyde 3-P $\rightarrow$ glucose 6-P
   b. Glucose 6-P $\rightarrow$ glycogen
   c. Lactate $\rightarrow$ oxaloacetate
   d. Malate $\rightarrow$ oxaloacetate
   e. Fumarate $\rightarrow$ P-enolpyruvate
   f. Pyruvate $\rightarrow$ P-enolpyruvate
   g. P-enolpyruvate $\rightarrow$ glycogen

15.6 If a rat-liver preparation carrying out active gluconeogenesis from pyruvate is exposed to $^{14}CO_2$, which carbon(s) in the newly synthesized glucose molecules will become radioactively labeled?

15.7 As a part of her science project, a high-school student has been measuring the net synthesis of glucose in rats when they are fed individual amino acids as the sole carbon source. As expected the rats cannot survive on a diet of any one amino acid, but over a period of a few days their livers show an increase in glycogen content when the rat has been fed any amino acid except Leu. The student decides to investigate the "Leu anomaly" further and repeats her experiments using uniformly ^{14}C-labeled amino acids. She finds that all rats, including those fed Leu, produce $^{14}CO_2$ at approximately the same rate. In addition, much to her surprise, she finds that some ^{14}C label from Leu appears in glucose even though no net glucose has been synthesized. Puzzled by these apparently contradictory results she seeks your advice on the problem. How do you explain her results?

15.8 Write a balanced equation for the net synthesis of glucose from acetyl CoA in a bacterial cell possessing the glyoxylate-cycle enzymes. (See Figure 11.6 for details of TCA-cycle reactions.)

15.9 Following is a list of hereditary metabolic defects involving loss of function of single enzymes of carbohydrate metabolism, and a second list of possible consequences of such defects. Match each enzyme defect with its most likely consequence (only one) from the second list.

Defects:
   a. Lack of fructose 1,6-diphosphate phosphatase
   b. Lack of amylo-(1,4 $\rightarrow$ 1,6)-transglycosylase
   c. Lack of UDP-glucose pyrophosphorylase
   d. Lack of ability to synthesize glucose 1,6-diP (see Concept 10.3, part A)
   e. Lack of glucose 6-phosphate phosphatase
   f. Lack of UDP-glucose epimerase (see equation 10.7)

Consequences:
   1. Inability to make glycogen from any sugar or to utilize galactose as an energy source
   2. Inability to convert either glycogen or lactate to free glucose, with no effect on ability to use galactose as an energy source
   3. Inability to use galactose as an energy source, with no effect on ability to utilize glycogen

4. Inability to use either galactose or glycogen as an energy source
5. Inability to use lactose (see Answer 10.12) as an energy source
6. Production of unbranched glycogen
7. Inability to convert TCA-cycle intermediates to fructose 1,6-diP
8. Inability to resynthesize glucose 6-P from lactic acid

15.10 When an actively photosynthesizing plant is exposed to $^{14}CO_2$, which two carbon atoms in the resulting radioactive glucose will be labeled first?

15.11 Consider one turn of the Calvin cycle, in which 6 μmol $^{14}CO_2$ and 6 μmol unlabeled ribulose 1,5-diP react to produce 1 μmol glucose 6-P, and 6 μmol ribulose 1,5-diP are regenerated.
   a. Which two carbon atoms of the regenerated ribulose 1,5-diP will be unlabeled?
   b. What fraction of the input label will be found in each of the other three carbon atoms of regenerated ribulose 1,5-diP?

15.12 In Bassham and Calvin's early experiments on glucose photosynthesis, green plants were exposed to light and $^{14}CO_2$ in various combinations for various times, and then extracted quickly with hot methanol. Labeled intermediates in glucose synthesis were separated by two-dimensional chromatography, and their levels of radioactivity determined by subjecting the chromatogram to autoradiography (pressing the dried chromatogram against x-ray film so that radioactive spots expose the area that they touch). From your knowledge of the Calvin cycle, predict the kinetics of labeling or loss of label for the intermediates ribulose 1,5-diP and 3-P-glycerate in the following experiments. Indicate your answers as rough plots of radioactivity in the intermediate (ordinate) versus time (abscissa). Remember that the light reactions of photosynthesis produce ATP and NADPH, which are depleted quickly in the absence of light.
   a. After prolonged light exposure in the presence of unlabeled CO_2, the light is turned off, $^{14}CO_2$ is added, and samples are extracted for analysis at subsequent times.
   b. After prolonged exposure to light and $^{14}CO_2$, the light is turned off, $^{14}CO_2$ is flushed out with unlabeled CO_2, and samples are extracted as in experiment a.
   c. After prolonged exposure to $^{14}CO_2$ in the dark, all CO_2 is removed, the light is turned on, and samples are extracted as in experiment a.

15.13 Six micromoles of ribulose 1,5-diP and 12 μmol $^{14}CO_2$ are added to a preparation of chloroplasts containing all the enzymes and cofactors necessary for carbohydrate synthesis. Assume that the CO_2 is quantitatively converted to hexose, and the 6 μmol ribulose 1,5-diP are regenerated. In the 2 μmol hexose produced, what will be the ratio of label in C-3 to that in C-5?

15.14 The Calvin cycle is essentially the phosphogluconate pathway operating in reverse (Concept 10.5). This observation suggests that the phosphogluconate pathway was adapted for glucose synthesis in the evolution of the first photosynthetic organisms.
   a. Explain the energetic features of the two present-day pathways that allow one to be used for synthesis of glucose from CO_2 and the other for degradation of glucose to CO_2.
   b. What are the remaining differences between the two pathways?

15.15 In most ATP-coupled synthetic reactions the two bond-forming steps (equations 15.2 and 15.3 or 15.5 and 15.6) are catalyzed by the same enzyme, and the activated intermediate is formed only transiently on the enzyme surface. The nature of the intermediate often can be deduced from the substrate-dependent radioactive exchange reactions catalyzed by the enzyme. For example, consider a crude enzyme preparation from a soil bacterium that catalyzes the formation of an acetyl thioester:

$$CH_3COOH + RSH + ATP \rightarrow CH_3\overset{O}{\underset{\parallel}{C}}\sim S\text{---}R + AMP + PP_i$$

Suppose that you carry out several exchange experiments as indicated in Table 15.1. The reaction components are incubated with enzyme, after which the ATP is isolated

Table 15.1
Exchange Experiments
with a Hypothetical
Enzyme (Problem 15.15)

Components present with enzyme	Exchange into ATP
$CH_3COOH + ATP + {}^{32}PP_i$	−
$CH_3COOH + ATP + {}^{14}C\text{-}AMP$	+
$ATP + {}^{14}C\text{-}AMP$	−
$RSH + ATP + {}^{32}PP_i$	−
$RSH + ATP + {}^{14}C\text{-}AMP$	−

and assayed for radioactivity. Exchange is scored as positive when radioactive label is incorporated into ATP during the incubation. Deduce the structure of the activated intermediate and write a two-step mechanism for the reaction.

15.16 You have found and purified to homogeneity three enzymes from horseshoe crab ovaries that catalyze, for no obvious reason, the three reactions of compound X and ethanol shown in Figure 15.4. You obtain the data in Table 15.2 from experiments in

Table 15.2
Exchange Experiments
with Three Hypothetical
Enzymes (Problem 15.16)

Enzyme	Components present in reaction mixture								Exchange observed
	ATP	X	CH_3CH_2OH	${}^{14}C\text{-}AMP$	${}^{14}C\text{-}ADP$	${}^{32}PP_i$	${}^{32}P_i$		
I	+	+		+					No
	+	+				+			Yes
	+		+	+					No
	+	+				+			No
II	+	+		+					Yes
	+	+				+			No
	+		+	+					No
	+	+				+			No
III	+	+			+				No
	+	+			+		+		No
	+		+		+				Yes
	+	+					+		No

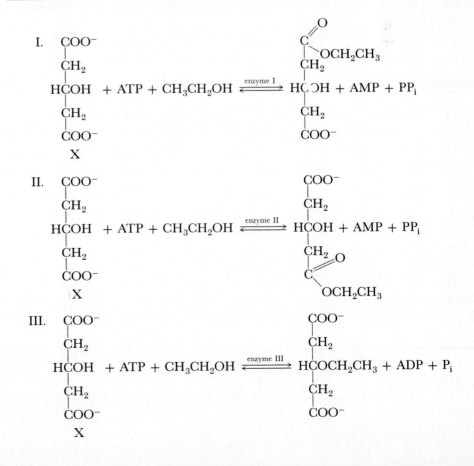

Figure 15.4
Reactions of compound X and ethanol (Problem 15.16).

which the reaction mixture is incubated and fractionated by chromatography, and the ATP is isolated and assayed for radioactivity. Exchange is scored as positive when radioactive label is incorporated into ATP during the incubation.

a. Write a two-step mechanism for each of the three reactions.

b. Explain how enzymes I and II distinguish between the two carboxyl groups of compound X.

15.17   Glutamine synthase, which catalyzes formation of an amide bond in the reaction

$$NH_4^+ + Glu + ATP \rightarrow Gln + ADP + P_i + H^+$$

will not catalyze exchange of either ^{14}C-ADP or $^{32}P_i$ into ATP in the presence of ATP and either NH_4^+ or Glu alone.

a. Write a plausible two-step mechanism for the reaction and propose an explanation for why no exchange is observed.

b. Propose another kind of experiment to test your mechanism.

☆ 15.18   When a liver preparation carrying out gluconeogenesis from pyruvate is exposed to $^{14}CO_2$, the label will be incorporated into glucose at

a. C-1

b. C-4

c. C-1 and C-6

d. C-3 and C-4

e. None of the above

☆ 15.19   You would be justifiably skeptical if you were told that a cell extract carrying out gluconeogenesis from acetyl CoA—

a. Required ATP

b. Came from a South African clawed toad liver

c. Was not inhibited by avidin

d. Required GTP

e. Did not contain active acetyl CoA carboxylase

☆ 15.20   The human liver cannot produce—

a. Ketone bodies from fatty acids

b. Glucose from fatty acids

c. Glucose from amino acids

d. Amino acids from glucose + NH_3

e. Fatty acids from glucose

☆ 15.21   An ATP-linked synthetic reaction proceeds in two steps as shown. (The bracketed intermediate exists only as an enzyme-bound species not released into the solvent.)

1. $X—OH + ATP \rightleftarrows [X—O\,\textcircled{P}\,] + ADP + H^+$
2. $[X—O\,\textcircled{P}\,] + Y—H \rightleftarrows X—Y + P_i$

Exchange of radioactive isotope into ATP may occur in the presence of—

a. Enzyme, ATP, X—OH, and $^{32}P_i$

b. Enzyme, ATP, Y—H, and $^{32}P_i$

c. Enzyme, ATP, X—OH, and ^{14}C-ADP

d. Enzyme, ATP, Y—H, and ^{14}C-ADP

e. Enzyme, ATP, X—Y, and ^{14}C-ADP

☆ 15.22   When an actively photosynthesizing plant is exposed to $^{14}CO_2$,

a. Which carbons of glucose *will not* become labeled during the first turn of the Calvin cycle?

b. What will be the relative levels of radioactivity in these carbons after a second turn of the cycle?

Answers

15.1 a. False. Biosynthesis consumes these compounds.
   b. True
   c. True
   d. False. The pathways for breakdown and synthesis are always distinct.
   e. False. The first enzyme unique to the pathway generally is inhibited by the end product.
   f. True
   g. False. Acetyl CoA can serve as a precursor for net synthesis of carbohydrate only in cells of plants and microorganisms that possess the glyoxylate-cycle enzymes.
   h. True
   i. False. The product of the reaction is 3-P-glycerate.
   j. False. The label is incorporated into C-3 and C-4 of the first glucose produced.

15.2 a. hydrolysis (or hydrolytic)
   b. carbohydrates, fats, ATP
   c. AMP, ATP
   d. phosphogluconate
   e. the pentose acceptor, ribulose 1,5-diP

15.3 a. Write balanced equations for each intermediate step and add them to the net reaction:

$$\text{Glucose 1-P} + \text{UTP} \rightarrow \text{UDP-glucose} + \text{PP}_i \qquad (15.10)$$

$$\text{UDP-glucose} + (\text{glucose})_n \rightarrow \text{UDP} + (\text{glucose})_{n+1} \qquad (15.11)$$

$$\underline{\text{PP}_i + \text{H}_2\text{O} \rightarrow 2\text{P}_i \qquad\qquad\qquad\qquad\qquad (15.12)}$$

Net: $\text{Glucose 1-P} + \text{UTP} + (\text{glucose})_n \rightarrow (\text{glucose})_{n+1} + \text{UDP} + 2\text{P}_i$ (15.13)

There is no net expenditure of high-energy phosphate bonds in equation 15.10. One is expended in equation 15.12. PP_i hydrolysis must be included when considering the energetics of any process that produces PP_i. Therefore the answer is one.
   b. One. Another reasonable answer is two. However, the hemiacetal phosphate at the 1-position of fructose 1,6-diP has a $\Delta G_0'$ of hydrolysis of only -5 kcal/mol, and therefore is not classed as a high-energy phosphate bond. This term generally is reserved for phosphate–anhydride linkages such as those in ATP, PP_i, 1.3-diP-glycerate, and so on, which have $\Delta G_0'$ values for hydrolysis ranging from -6 to -15 kcal/mol.
   c. Two
   d. Five

15.4 a. Six
   b. Two

15.5 c. and f. Biotin is required specifically in most ATP-linked CO_2-fixation reactions. The only such reaction in gluconeogenesis is the first step, which is catalyzed by pyruvate carboxylase.

15.6 None. The CO_2 incorporated in the pyruvate-carboxylase reaction is released again in the conversion of oxaloacetate to P-enolpyruvate.

15.7 Of all the amino acids, only Leu yields acetyl CoA exclusively upon stage II breakdown. All others yield some pyruvate or other precursor for gluconeogenesis. Animals cannot carry out net conversion of acetyl CoA to carbohydrate. However, some label will appear in carbohydrate because, although net synthesis of sugars from acetyl CoA is impossible, ^{14}C-acetyl CoA will enter the TCA cycle and contribute ^{14}C to the pool of precursors for gluconeogenesis.

15.8 The equation for synthesis of glucose from acetyl CoA via the glyoxylate cycle is the sum of the following four steps. Step 1 is the sum of the glyoxylate-cycle reactions; step

2 is the sum of three TCA-cycle steps: succinate → fumarate → malate → oxaloacetate; and steps 3 and 4 represent gluconeogenesis from oxaloacetate.

1. 4 acetyl CoA + 2NAD⁺ + 4H₂O → 2 succinate + 4HSCoA + 2NADH + 2H⁺

2. 2 succinate + 2FAD + 2NAD⁺ + 2H₂O →
    2 oxaloacetate + 2FADH₂ + 2NADH + 2H⁺

3. 2 oxaloacetate + 2GTP → 2 P-enolpyruvate + 2GDP + 2CO₂

4. 2 P-enolpyruvate + 2ATP + 2NADH + 2H⁺ →
    glucose + 2ADP + 4Pᵢ + 2NAD⁺

Net: 4 acetyl CoA + 2NAD⁺ + 2FAD + 2ATP + 2GTP + 6H₂O →
glucose + 4HSCoA + 2NADH + 2H⁺ + 2FADH₂ +
2ADP + 2GDP + 4Pᵢ + 2CO₂

15.9 a. 8
      b. 6
      c. 1
      d. 4
      e. 2
      f. 3

15.10 C-3 and C-4 of glucose will be labeled first, because they are derived from the carboxyl groups of 3-P-glycerate.

15.11 a. C-4 and C-5 of the regenerated ribulose 1,5-diP will be unlabeled.
       b. One-sixth of the input label will be in C-1, one-sixth in C-2, and one-half in C-3. (The remaining one-sixth of the input ¹⁴C will be distributed equally between C-3 and C-4 of glucose 6-P.)

15.12 a. In the absence of light, ATP and NADPH are depleted quickly. Under these conditions ribulose 1,5-diP can be converted to 3-P-glycerate, but 3-P-glycerate cannot be processed further. Thus the added ¹⁴CO₂ accumulates in 3-P-glycerate and does not appear in ribulose 1,5-diP (Figure 15.5a).
       b. As in part a, ribulose 1,5-diP can be converted to 3-P-glycerate, but 3-P-glycerate cannot be processed further. Thus labeled ribulose 1,5-diP decreases and labeled 3-P-glycerate increases by the amount contributed by ribulose 1,5-diP (Figure 15.5b).
       c. The initial distribution of label in this experiment is similar to the final distribution of label in part b; a very small amount is present in ribulose 1,5-diP and a large amount

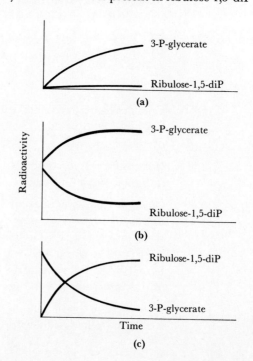

Figure 15.5
Labeling experiments on glucose
photosynthesis (Answer 15.12).

in 3-P-glycerate. When the light is turned on, ATP and NADPH are produced and 3-P-glycerate is converted to ribulose 1,5-diP. However, in the absence of CO_2, ribulose 1,5-diP is not converted to 3-P-glycerate. Therefore, labeled 3-P-glycerate will decrease and labeled ribulose 1,5-diP will increase (Figure 15.5c).

15.13   Use Figure 15.3 to follow the path of the labeled carbon. Two turns of the Calvin cycle are necessary, because the molar ratio of CO_2 to ribulose 1,5-diP is 2. After the first turn the 1 μmol of hexose produced will contain $\frac{1}{24}$ of the label at C-3, $\frac{1}{24}$ at C-4, and none in the other carbons. The $^{14}CO_2$ in the second turn of the cycle will add an additional $\frac{1}{24}$ of the label at C-3 and C-4 of the hexose. The 6 μmol of acceptor produced in the first round will carry $\frac{1}{12}$ of the label in C-1, $\frac{1}{12}$ in C-2, $\frac{3}{12}$ in C-3. The 1 μmol of hexose produced in the second turn will carry some of this label distributed as follows: $\frac{1}{144}$ at C-1, C-2, C-5, and C-6; $\frac{3}{144}$ at C-3 and C-4. Therefore, the label at C-3 and C-5 for the first and second turn hexoses is $\frac{15}{144}$ and $\frac{1}{144}$ of the total label, respectively, and the ratio is 15:1.

15.14 a. Most of the sugar interconversion reactions in both pathways are nearly isoenergetic. The Calvin cycle is "pushed" toward glucose synthesis by the initial energy-yielding step of CO_2 fixation catalyzed by ribulose diphosphate carboxylase and "pulled" additionally by the three phosphatase steps and the phosphoribulokinase reaction. The phosphogluconate pathway is "pushed" in the direction of glucose degradation by the two initial energy-yielding oxidation steps.

      b. The principal difference in the sugar interconversions is that transaldolase is not used in the Calvin cycle; an aldolase is used instead. This substitution makes the strategies of the two pathways somewhat different, as shown in Figure 15.6. You can see the detailed differences in the enzymes employed by the two pathways by comparing the lists in Figures 10.6 and 15.3.

15.15   From Table 15.1, you can see that only labeled AMP exchanges into ATP, and that this occurs only when CH_3COOH is present. To understand this result, refer to equations 15.5 and 15.6, in which the activated intermediate is X—AMP. If H—Y is not present to allow the reaction in equation 15.6, the enzyme will catalyze the forward and reverse reaction of equation 15.5, alternately releasing PP_i with formation of X—AMP, and taking it up again to re-form X—OH and ATP. $^{32}PP_i$ added to this mixture will become incorporated into ATP as a result of the reverse reaction, whereas ^{14}C-AMP will not. The situation in the problem is the opposite. Verify for yourself that the following two-step reaction sequence is the only one that is consistent with the experimental results in Table 15.1. (The enzyme-bound intermediate is enclosed in brackets.)

$$CH_3COOH + ATP \rightleftarrows [CH_3COO\textcircled{PP}] + AMP$$

$$[CH_3COO\textcircled{PP}] + RSH \rightleftarrows CH_3CO—SR + PP_i$$

Net: $CH_3COOH + RSH + ATP \rightleftarrows CH_3CO—SR + AMP + PP_i$

15.16 a. Use the same approach as in Problem 15.15. The two-step mechanisms for each reaction are shown in Figure 15.7.

      b. Enzymes I and II distinguish between the two carboxyl groups of compound X in the same way that aconitase in the TCA cycle distinguishes between the two ends of the citrate molecule (Answer 11.6).

Phosphogluconate pathway	Calvin cycle
6[(6) → (5) + (1)]	6[(5) + (1) → 2(3)]
2[(5) + (5) → (7) + (3) → (6) + (4)]	3[(3) + (3) → (6)]
2[(5) + (4) → (6) + (3)]	2[(6) + (3) → (5) + (4)]
(3) + (3) → (6)	2[(4) + (3) → (7)]
	2[(7) + (3) → (5) + (5)]
Net: (6) → 6(1)	Net: 6(1) → (6)

Figure 15.6
A comparison of the strategies of the phosphogluconate pathway and the Calvin cycle (Answer 15.14). The symbol (1) represents CO_2, (3) represents a triose, (5) a pentose, and so on.

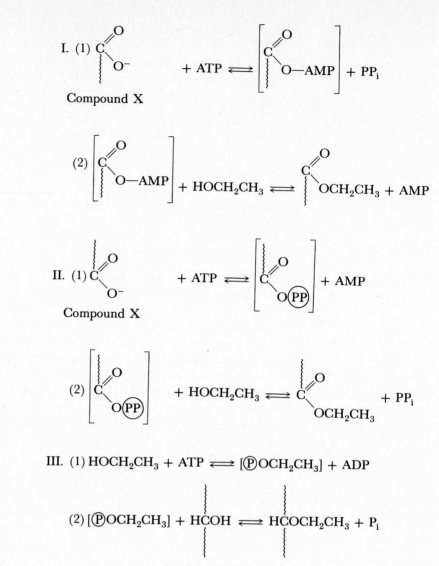

Figure 15.7
Two-step mechanisms for the three reactions of Figure 15.4 (Answer 15.16). Enzyme-bound intermediates are enclosed in brackets.

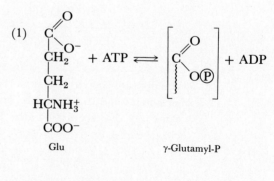

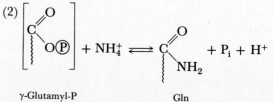

Figure 15.8
Mechanism of the glutamine synthase reaction (Answer 15.17). The enzyme-bound intermediate is enclosed in brackets.

15.17 a. The mechanism of the glutamine synthase reaction is shown in Figure 15.8. The reason for the lack of exchange in this and a number of related C—N bond-forming reactions appears to be that substrate binding affects the conformation of the enzyme in a way such that the active configuration of the catalytic site is attained only when all three substrates are present. The result here is that although step 1 takes place in the absence of NH_3, the ADP formed is not released from the enzyme surface. Therefore, exchange with free labeled ADP is impossible.

b. The best experiment for establishing the mechanisms of such enzymes is to incubate ATP and one of the other substrates with a large amount of the protein, roughly equivalent to the molar concentration of substrate. Then any enzyme-bound intermediate that forms is present in sufficient quantity to be extracted and characterized chemically.

16 Biosynthesis of Lipids, Amino Acids, and Nucleotides

Lipids include neutral fats, the predominant energy-storage molecules in animals, and phospholipids, the building blocks of membranes. Amino acids and nucleotides are the monomer units of proteins and nucleic acids, respectively. This chapter considers the most important aspects of lipid, amino acid, and nucleotide biosynthesis and discusses some nutritional implications of human biosynthetic capabilities.

Concepts

16.1 **Fats and phospholipids are synthesized from acetyl CoA and glycerol.**

A. All fatty acids, the most common of which is palmitate, $CH_3(CH_2)_{14}COO^-$, are synthesized from acetyl CoA in two stages via the sequence of reactions diagrammed in Figure 16.1. In the first stage, acetyl CoA is activated by carboxylation to yield malonyl CoA in a reaction that requires biotin as cofactor (reaction 1). The enzyme that catalyzes this reaction, acetyl CoA carboxylase, is activated by the TCA-cycle intermediate citrate. Because citrate accumulates only when acetyl CoA is plentiful and the ATP/ADP ratio is high, this regulation ensures that fatty acid synthesis will proceed only when the cell has an adequate supply of energy.

In eucaryotes citrate serves the additional function of carrying acetyl groups from the mitochondrial matrix where they are formed to the cytoplasm where they are used in biosynthesis. The enzyme citrate lyase catalyzes cleavage of citrate to produce oxaloacetate and acetyl CoA. The oxaloacetate can be used in gluconeogenesis or converted to malate and shuttled back into the mitochondria for oxidation.

In the second stage of fatty acid synthesis, one molecule of acetyl CoA and seven molecules of malonyl CoA react to form palmitate. Acetyl CoA and malonyl CoA are transferred to sulfhydryl groups of acyl carrier proteins, ACP (reactions 2 and 3, respectively). The ACP-bound acetyl group first is transferred to a sulfhydryl group on the condensing enzyme (reaction 4) and then is coupled to the ACP-bound malonyl group (reaction 5), which releases CO_2 in the process. The ACP-bound intermediate then is reduced (reaction 6), dehydrated (reaction 7), reduced again (reaction 8), and finally transferred back to the condensing enzyme (reaction 9), thereby freeing ACP to pick up another malonyl group and repeat the cycle. The growing acyl group remains protein bound until seven turns of the cycle are completed, at which point a hydrolytic step (reaction 10) releases free palmitate. Reactions 2 and 4 occur only at the start of the first cycle; reaction 10 occurs only at the end of the last cycle.

Seven turns of the cycle result in the net reaction

Acetyl CoA + 7 malonyl CoA + 14NADPH + 14H$^+$ →

$$\text{palmitate} + 7CO_2 + 8HSCoA + 14NADP^+ + 6H_2O \quad (16.1)$$

In most eucaryotes all the reactions in the second stage (reactions 2 through 10) are catalyzed by an enzyme complex, fatty acid synthetase, that contains all the required

290

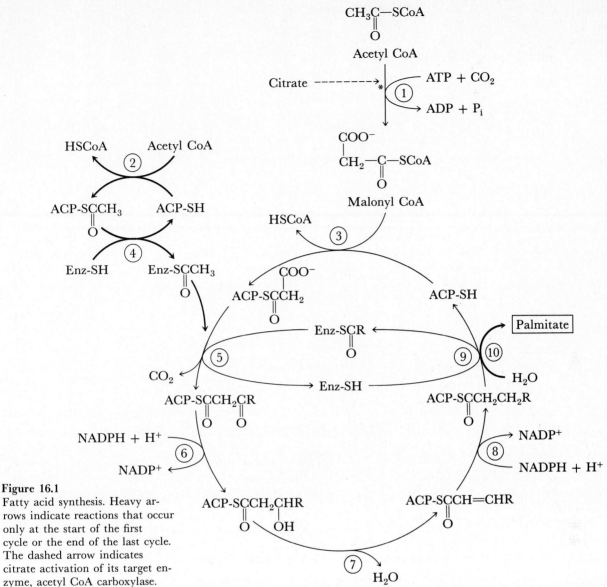

Figure 16.1
Fatty acid synthesis. Heavy arrows indicate reactions that occur only at the start of the first cycle or the end of the last cycle. The dashed arrow indicates citrate activation of its target enzyme, acetyl CoA carboxylase.

enzymatic activities, including the carrier function of ACP, on a 250,000 MW polypeptide.

B. Synthesis of neutral fats (Figure 11.2) and phospholipids (Figure 6.1) is initiated by transfer of two activated fatty acyl residues from thioester linkage with CoA into ester linkage with the 1- and 2-hydroxyl groups of glycerol 3-P to form a phosphatidic acid (Figure 16.2). A neutral fat or triglyceride can be formed from this intermediate by hydrolysis of the phosphate group, followed by esterification of the resulting hydroxyl group with a third fatty acyl residue.

Synthesis of phospholipids from diacylglycerols can occur by more than one route. The most common pathway for phospholipid synthesis is illustrated in Figure 16.3. Initially, a phosphatidic acid reacts with cytidine triphosphate (CTP) to yield PP_i and an activated CDP-diacylglycerol, analogous to the activated nucleoside diphosphate sugars involved in polysaccharide synthesis. The CDP-diacylglycerol then reacts with a polar compound such as Ser to yield CMP and the corresponding phosphatidyl derivative. Phosphatidylserine can be converted by decarboxylation to phosphatidylethanolamine. This compound in turn can be converted to phosphatidylcholine by three successive methylations in which the activated methionine derivative *S*-adenosylmethionine is the methyl group donor.

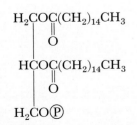

Figure 16.2
Structure of the phosphatidic acid dipalmityl glycerol-P.

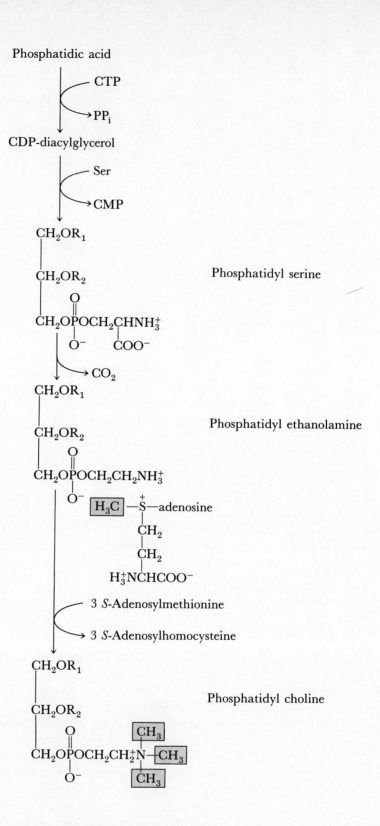

Figure 16.3
Synthesis of a phosphatidylcholine. R_1 and R_2 represent fatty acyl groups. The transferred methyl group of S-adenosylmethionine is indicated by the gray screen.

16.2 Amino acids are synthesized from intermediates of carbohydrate metabolism.

A. The metabolic origins of the 20 amino acids are indicated in Figure 16.4. Several are synthesized as their corresponding α-keto derivatives, and then transaminated to yield α-amino acids as described in Concept 11.3, part B. The amino group donor, Glu, is replenished by fixation of free ammonia in the glutamate dehydrogenase reaction (Concept 11.3, part B).

The synthesis of Thr and three other related amino acids is outlined in Figure

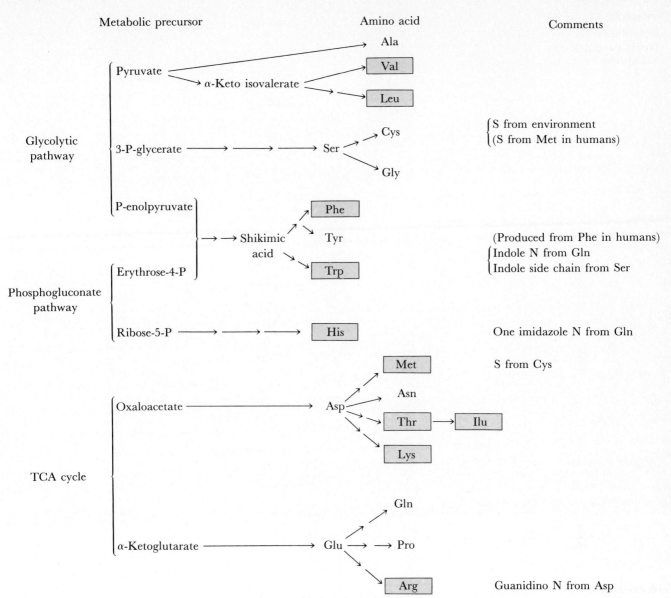

Figure 16.4
Metabolic origins of the 20 amino acids in bacteria. Amino acids indicated by gray screens cannot be synthesized in humans and are required in the diet.

16.5 as a representative example to show the complex controls in a branched pathway. Generally, in amino acid biosynthesis the first enzyme unique to a pathway is inhibited by the end product of the pathway.

B. Many chemotrophs lack the more complex pathways of amino acid synthesis, and therefore must acquire certain amino acids from their environment. An adult human can synthesize 10 amino acids in amounts sufficient for good health, and requires a dietary source of the remaining 10. The required (essential) amino acids for humans are indicated by gray screens in Figure 16.4. The remaining 10 (nonessential) amino acids can be synthesized as shown in the figure with two exceptions: Tyr is synthesized by hydroxylation of Phe; and S for Cys synthesis is obtained from Met. Nutritional implications of amino acid requirements in humans are discussed in Concept 16.4.

C. Unlike animals, plants and many microorganisms can synthesize all 20 amino acids, starting with ammonia, nitrite, or nitrate as a source of nitrogen. Nitrate most generally is used, because almost all ammonia reaching the soil becomes oxidized to NO_3^- by nitrifying bacteria. The amino acids produced by plants are utilized by animals, which excrete the excess nitrogen primarily as ammonia or urea. Therefore, on a large

CHAPTER 16
Biosynthesis:
Lipids, Amino Acids,
Nucleotides

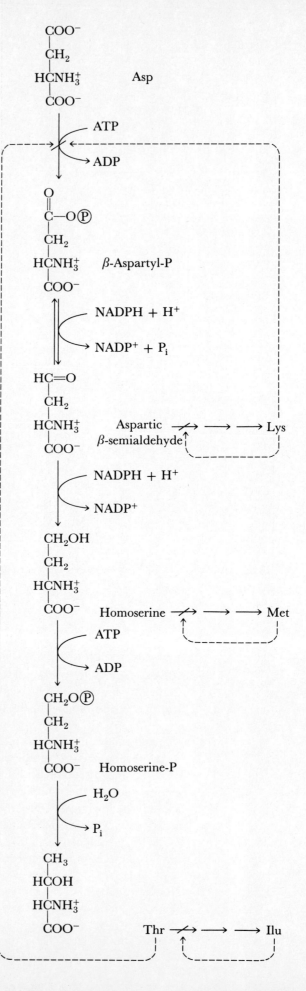

Figure 16.5
Regulation of the branched
pathway for Thr, Lys, Met, and
Ilu biosynthesis in *E. coli*. Regulating metabolites and their target enzyme reactions are connected by dashed arrows: / indicates inhibition.

scale, nitrogen cycles through microorganisms, plants, and animals as diagrammed in Figure 16.6.

Atmospheric nitrogen enters the cycle by reduction of N_2 to NH_3 through the action of a few species of nitrogen-fixing bacteria and cyanobacteria, some free-living and others existing as symbionts in the root nodules of leguminous plants. The overall reaction (equation 16.2) is catalyzed by nitrogenase, a soluble complex of two iron-containing proteins, in conjunction with a hydrogenase (if H_2 is the electron donor) and ferredoxin (Concept 13.6). Four molecules of ATP are expended for each pair of electrons transferred from H_2 or other donors to N_2. The mechanism is not understood.

$$N_2 + 3H_2 + 12ATP \rightarrow 2NH_3 + 12ADP + 12P_i \qquad (16.2)$$

16.3 Nucleotides are synthesized via two major pathways.

A. Purine and pyrimidine ribonucleotides are synthesized de novo as shown in Figures 16.7 and 16.8, respectively. The two pathways differ in strategy in that the purines are built as nucleotides via phosphoribosyl intermediates, whereas the pyrimidine ring is completed to the stage of orotate before coupling to ribose.

The feedback controls in ribonucleotide synthesis are diagrammed in Figure 16.9. An additional control that coordinates the two branches of purine nucleotide synthesis operates upon the conversion of IMP and XMP to AMP and GMP, respectively. GTP is required for AMP formation, and ATP is required for GMP formation, thereby ensuring that at high concentration of ATP, GTP formation will be promoted and vice versa.

B. Ribonucleotides also can be synthesized by so-called **salvage pathways.** In these pathways, free purines and pyrimidines derived from nucleic acid catabolism react with P-ribosyl-PP to liberate PP_i and form the corresponding ribonucleotides (cf. orotate $\rightarrow$ orotidine 5'-P, Figure 16.8).

C. Deoxyribonucleotides are produced by reduction of the corresponding ribonucleoside diphosphates at the 2-position of the ribose ring, using NADPH as the reducing agent. The pathways and regulatory controls for deoxyribonucleotide synthesis are outlined

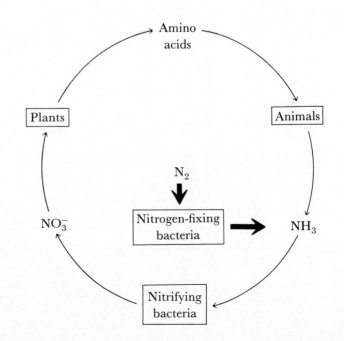

Figure 16.6
A simplified diagram of the nitrogen cycle. The heavy arrows indicate fixation of atmospheric nitrogen.

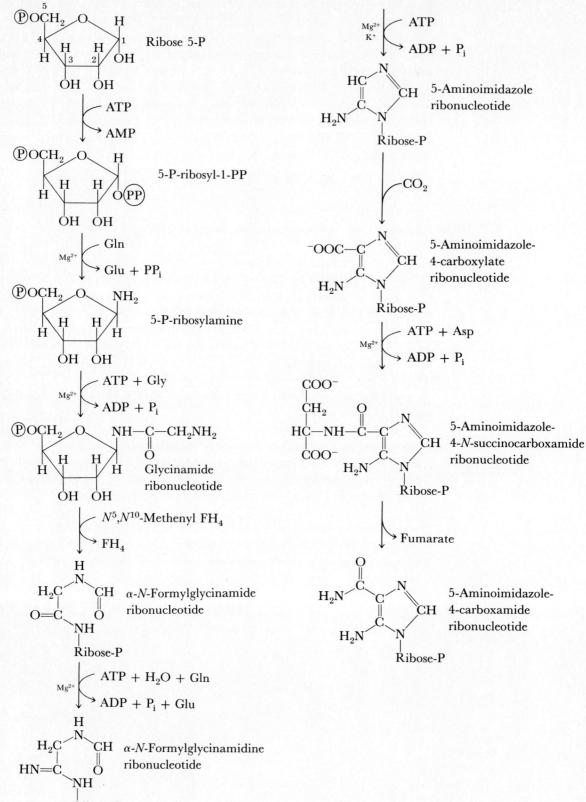

Figure 16.7
Synthesis of purine nucleotides.
For further details of nucleotide
structure and nomenclature, see
Chapter 17.

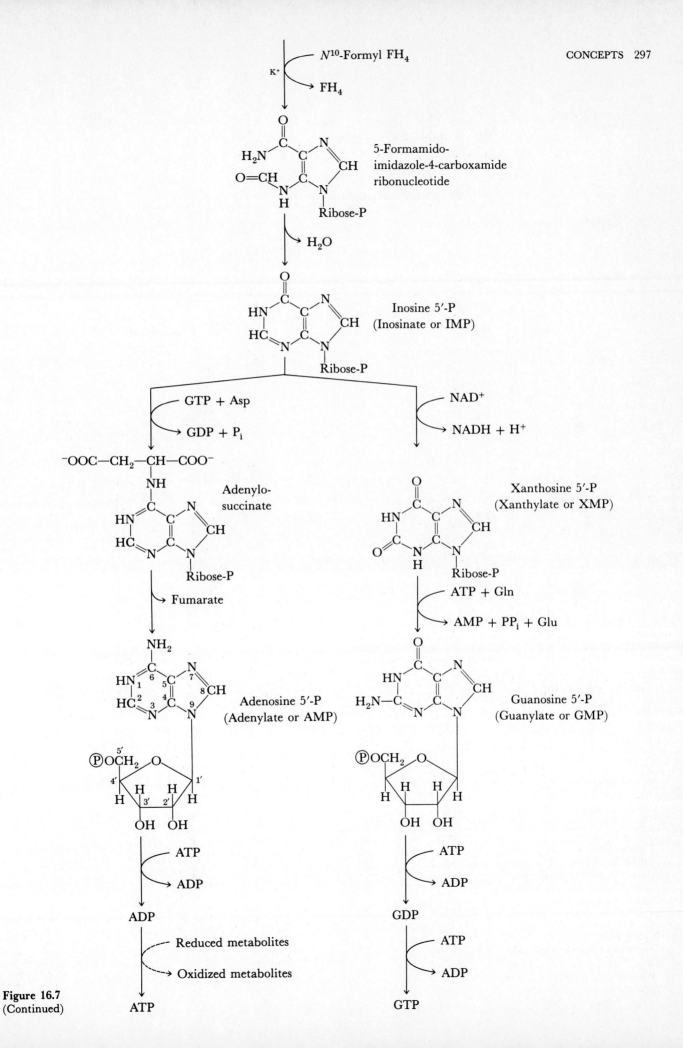

Figure 16.7
(Continued)

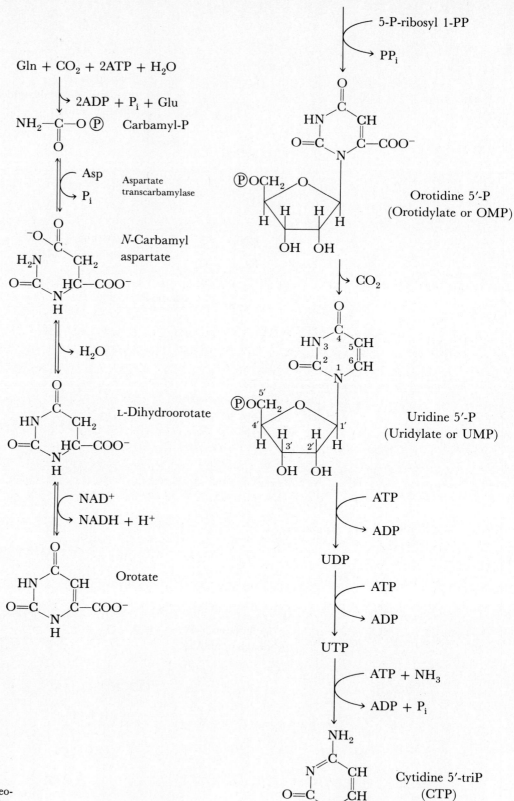

Figure 16.8
Synthesis of pyrimidine nucleotides. For further details on nucleotide structure and nomenclature, see Chapter 17.

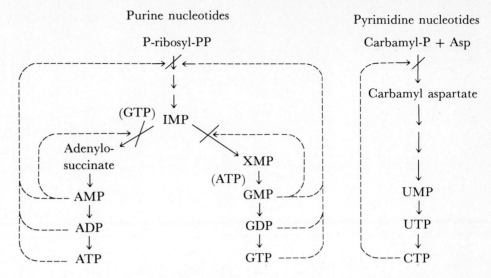

Purine nucleotides

Pyrimidine nucleotides

Figure 16.9
Feedback controls in ribonucleotide biosynthesis. Regulatory metabolites and their target enzymes are connected by dashed arrows; / indicates inhibition. GTP and ATP are reactants in the formation of AMP and GMP, respectively (see Figure 16.7). In animals the principal regulatory site for pyrimidine nucleotide synthesis is the formation of carbamyl-P by carbamyl phosphate synthetase.

in Figure 16.10. Deoxythymidylate (dTMP) is formed from deoxyuridylate (dUMP) in the thymidylate synthetase reaction.

D. The coenzyme tetrahydrofolate (FH_4) is required for two steps in purine synthesis as well as for the thymidylate synthetase reaction in pyrimidine synthesis. This coenzyme, which is derived by a two-step reduction from the vitamin folate, functions as an acceptor, carrier, and donor of one-carbon units at the formyl, hydroxymethyl, or methyl oxidation level (Figure 16.11). FH_4-bound one-carbon fragments can be oxidized, reduced, or otherwise modified before transfer to a substrate. The thymidylate synthetase reaction involves the coenzyme in a unique role; FH_4 simultaneously transfers and reduces a hydroxymethyl group to provide the 5-methyl group of the thymine ring (Figure 1.3). In the process, FH_4 becomes oxidized to dihydrofolate (FH_2) and must be reduced again to FH_4 by the enzyme dihydrofolate reductase. FH_4 also is required for several reactions in the breakdown and synthesis of amino acids.

16.4 The limitations of biosynthesis in humans have important nutritional consequences.

The bulk of the available stored fuel in humans is fat, as shown in Table 16.1. However, many peripheral tissues obtain their energy from breakdown of glucose. Most

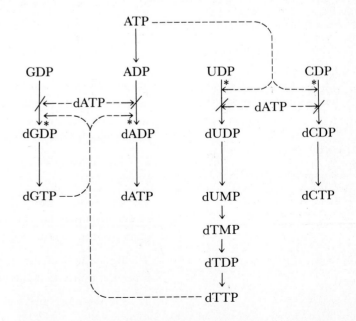

Figure 16.10
Outline of deoxyribonucleotide biosynthesis and control. All phosphorylations involve ATP → ADP (not shown) and are catalyzed by various nucleotide kinases. Regulatory metabolites and their target enzymes are connected by dashed arrows; * indicates activation; / indicates inhibition. For details of structure and nomenclature, see Chapter 17.

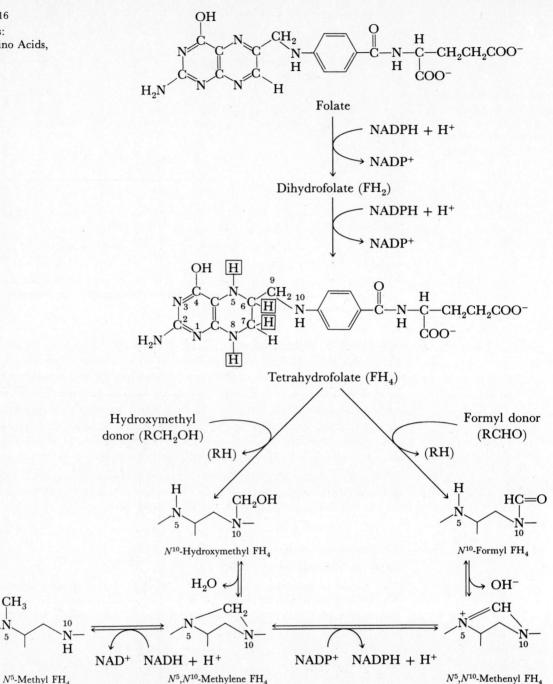

Figure 16.11
Origin of the coenzyme tetrahydrofolate and its conversion to various one-carbon-carrying derivatives.

notable is the brain, which requires 100–150 g of glucose per day. Humans cannot convert stored fat to either glucose or glucogenic amino acids, as explained in Concept 15.3. Moreover, humans can synthesize only 10 of the 20 amino acids de novo from glucogenic precursors. These metabolic limitations have several consequences.

1. The human diet must include glucogenic fuel to supply peripheral tissues with glucose.

2. During even the normal overnight fast, some muscle protein is broken down to supply precursors for gluconeogenesis. Glycogen reserves, which would be barely adequate to meet the need for glucose, are not utilized under these conditions.

3. Resynthesis of the degraded protein, which normally occurs when the fast is broken, requires that the diet contain the 10 essential amino acids.

4. During more prolonged fasting, the daily demand (about 75 g) on protein re-

Table 16.1
Fuel Reserves in an
Average Man[a]

Fuel	Grams	Caloric equivalent (kcal)
Fat (in adipose tissue)	15,000	141
Protein (primarily in muscle)	6,000[b]	24[b]
Glycogen (in muscle)	150	0.6
Glycogen (in liver)	75	0.3

[a] From G. F. Cahill, Jr., *New England Journal of Medicine,* **282,** 668 (1970).
[b] The bulk of this protein obviously cannot be consumed without impairment of muscle function.

serves for gluconeogenesis quickly becomes intolerable. Under these conditions the brain switches to utilization of ketone bodies as its principal energy source, thereby sparing muscle protein.

5.   Whereas adults can tolerate prolonged fasting resulting in loss of up to one-quarter of normal body weight without harm, children cannot, because normal growth requires continued protein synthesis. Protein deficiency in children leads to stunted growth and the pathological condition known as *kwashiorkor.* This disease, characterized by apathy, edema, and low levels of many key enzymes, is one of the most widespread childhood afflictions in the world today.

16.5   **Additional concepts and techniques are presented in the Problems section.**

A.   Mechanism of fatty acid length determination. Problem 16.6.

B.   Use of mutants in determining biochemical pathways. Problems 16.9, 16.10, 16.11, and 16.12.

References

COMPREHENSIVE TEXTS

Lehninger: Chapters 24, 25, and 26

Metzler: Chapter 11

Stryer: Chapters 20, 21, and 22

White et al.: Chapters 17, 20, 22, 23, and 24

OTHER REFERENCES

G. F. Cahill, Jr., "Starvation in Man," *New England Journal of Medicine,* **282,** 668 (1970).

V. R. Young and N. S. Scrimshaw, "The Physiology of Starvation," *Scientific American,* October 1971, p. 14.

Problems

16.1   Answer the following with true or false. If false, explain why.
   a. In the synthesis of a molecule of palmitate from acetyl CoA, eight ATP must be expended.
   b. In the course of fatty acid synthesis, the growing acyl group is transferred between an acyl carrier protein and the condensing enzyme.
   c. Phosphatidic acids are intermediates in the synthesis of both neutral fats and phospholipids.
   d. The precursors for biosynthesis of the aromatic amino acids are intermediates of the glycolytic pathway and the TCA cycle.
   e. Although Phe is a required amino acid in man, Tyr is not, because man can synthesize Tyr from Phe.
   f. NO_3^- is the principal nitrogen source for plants, because they are unable to utilize soil ammonia.
   g. Nitrogen-fixing bacteria can produce ammonia from N_2, H^+, and an inorganic electron donor, as well as from N_2 and H_2.

h. The pathways for purine and pyrimidine nucleotide biosynthesis are similar in that both proceed by formation of the basic ring structure followed by attachment of a phosphorylated ribose.

i. The methyl donor in conversion of dUMP to dTMP is FH_4 carrying a methyl group.

j. ATP is a reactant in GMP synthesis, and GTP is a reactant in AMP synthesis. A shortage of either triphosphate therefore tends to curtail synthesis of the other.

k. In the stored fuel supply of an average human there is about 10 times by weight as much fat and protein as there is glycogen.

l. During a short fast, glycogen reserves of liver and muscle are utilized to provide glucose for peripheral tissues, particularly the brain.

m. During prolonged fasting, the brain's 150 g/day demand for glucose is met by gluconeogenesis from amino acids derived from muscle protein breakdown.

16.2 a. The reducing power for biosynthesis is supplied in the form of _____.

b. Formation of _____ from acetyl CoA and CO_2 requires expenditure of _____ high-energy phosphate bond(s) and participation of the coenzyme _____.

c. A phosphatidic acid is formed by sequential reaction of two molecules of _____ with one molecule of _____.

d. _____, an activated intermediate for _____ synthesis, is functionally analogous to the nucleoside diphosphate sugar intermediates in polysaccharide synthesis.

e. The methyl group donor in the conversion of phosphatidylethanolamine to phosphatidylcholine is an activated derivative of _____ called _____.

f. The first enzyme unique to pyrimidine synthesis in bacteria, _____, is inhibited by _____, the end product of the pathway.

g. The coenzyme _____, derived from the vitamin _____, is a metabolic carrier of one-carbon fragments at all levels of oxidation.

h. Protein deficiency in children leads to the widespread disease of malnutrition known as _____.

16.3 Draw the structure of CDP-dipalmitylglycerol.

16.4 A dialyzed pigeon-liver extract will catalyze the conversion of acetyl CoA to palmitate and HSCoA if supplied with Mg^{2+}, NADPH, ATP, HCO_3^-, and citrate. Consider only this reaction when answering the following questions.

a. If $H^{14}CO_3^-$ is supplied, what other compound(s) will become labeled during the course of the reaction? In what compounds will ^{14}C accumulate as a result of the reaction?

b. How does citrate participate in the reaction? Explain its role.

c. What conclusions can you draw from the finding that the reaction is inhibited by avidin?

d. Purification reveals that two enzyme fractions are required for activity. If the enzyme I–catalyzed reaction utilizes ATP, write this reaction as well as the reaction catalyzed by enzyme II.

16.5 The following experiments are carried out using a pure preparation of the enzyme that catalyzes palmitate synthesis from acetyl CoA and malonyl CoA in the presence of all the cofactors required for reaction.

a. If acetyl CoA is supplied in the form $C^3H_3COSCoA$, and malonyl CoA is unlabeled, how many tritium atoms will be incorporated into each molecule of palmitate formed?

b. If malonyl CoA is supplied in the form of $^-OOC^3H_2COSCoA$, and acetyl CoA is unlabeled, how many tritium atoms will be incorporated into each molecule of palmitate formed?

16.6 Purified fatty acid synthetase from liver cytoplasm normally catalyzes the synthesis of palmitate (C_{16}) from acetyl CoA, malonyl CoA, and NADPH. The enzyme also will function, although at considerably reduced rates, if the acetyl CoA is replaced by (1) propionyl CoA or (2) butyryl CoA.

a. What do you predict will be the major product of the reaction in each of the latter cases?

b. Briefly explain your predictions and the kind of information these experiments provide regarding the mechanism of palmitate synthesis by the synthetase complex.

16.7 A normal, well-fed animal is given an intravenous injection of radioactive acetate labeled with ^{14}C in the methyl group. Several hours later the animal is sacrificed, glycogen and triglycerides (neutral fats) are isolated from the liver, and the distribution of radioactivity is determined.

a. Explain briefly why you would or would not expect the levels of radioactivity in the two isolated materials to be roughly the same.

b. Using structural formulas indicate the carbon atoms that will be labeled most heavily in triglycerides.

16.8 a. Which of the 20 amino acids can be synthesized directly from glycolytic and TCA-cycle intermediates in a single step?

b. Write out these reactions, using Glu as the donor for transamination.

16.9 Analysis of mutant organisms with single enzymatic defects is a powerful tool for elucidating biochemical processes. Several of the pathways for amino acid and nucleotide synthesis were worked out originally using mutant fungi or bacteria. As an illustration of the method, consider an amino acid, D, synthesized by the pathway in Figure 16.12, in which A, B, and C represent intermediates and ①, ②, and ③ are enzymes. Mutants defective in any one of the three enzymes will not grow unless supplied with D or an intermediate that they can convert to it. In the absence of D, such mutants accumulate large amounts of the intermediate preceding the blocked step, because enzyme 1 is not inhibited.

Complete Table 16.2 by filling in the blank entries. Note that if you did not know the order of either the enzymatic steps or the intermediates, you could deduce them by determining experimentally the results in the last column, and assuming that a mutant will not grow on an intermediate that precedes the mutational block, but will grow on any intermediate beyond the block.

Table 16.2
Metabolic Consequences of Mutational Defects in the Hypothetical Pathway in Figure 16.12 (Problem 16.9)

Mutant	Defective enzyme	Accumulates intermediate	Grows on intermediates	Cross-feeding properties
1	①	(a) _____	(b) _____	Will grow on intermediate accumulated by mutants (c) _____ or (d) _____.
2	②	(e) _____	(f) _____	Will grow on intermediate accumulated by mutant (g) _____, but not (h) _____.
3	③	(i) _____	(j) _____	Will not grow on intermediates accumulated by mutants (k) _____ or (l) _____.

16.10 A mutant microorganism (1) requires two amino acids, B and C, for growth. A second mutant (2) requires only B. Two other mutants (3 and 4) require only C. Mutant 3 accumulates a metabolite, D, that will support the growth of mutant 4 but not the growth of 1 or 2. Mutant 4 accumulates a metabolite, A, that alone will support the growth of mutant 1.

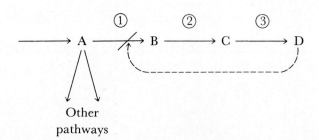

Figure 16.12
A hypothetical amino acid biosynthetic pathway (Problem 16.9).

a. Diagram the biosynthetic pathway relating A, B, C, and D, indicating the step at which each mutant is blocked.

b. Which step is most likely to be inhibited by C?

16.11 You have isolated three bacterial mutants, each of which carries a single mutation. Mutants 1 and 2 each require the presence of three different amino acids, A, B, and C, for growth. Mutant 3 requires A and B but not C. You find that in the absence of A, B, and C,

1. A metabolite X from your biochemistry set will support the growth of 1 and 2, but not of 3.

2. A second metabolite, Y, which is accumulated and released into the medium by mutant 1, will support the growth of 2 but not of 3.

3. A third metabolite, Z, isolated from mung bean extracts, will support the growth of 3 but not of 1 or 2.

Outline the biosynthetic pathways relating A, B, C, X, Y, and Z, indicating the stage at which each of the three mutants is blocked. Also indicate the likely points of feedback control by A, B, and C.

16.12 A soil sample brought back from the moon yields spores of an unusual microorganism. When cultured and analyzed, its proteins are found to contain, in addition to the 20 amino acids common to terrestrial organisms, a new one, named lunine (Lun), which has the structure shown in Figure 16.13.

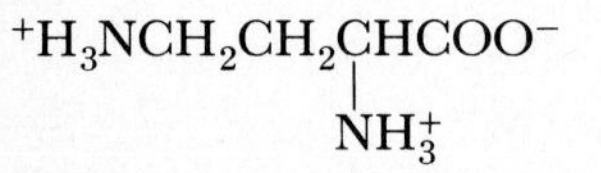

To investigate its biosynthesis, scientists isolate a number of amino acid–requiring mutants (the original strain will grow on an unsupplemented glucose-salts medium) and find five that appear to be relevant. Genetic tests show that each mutant carries a single mutation in a different gene. Growth experiments with the mutants yield the following results:

1. Mutant I requires Thr for growth, and in its absence accumulates an unidentified amino acid that supports the growth of mutant IV.

2. Mutant II requires both Thr and Lun; it will not grow if either is omitted from the medium.

3. Mutant III shows a single requirement for Lun.

4. Mutant IV shows a single requirement for Thr and in its absence synthesizes small amounts of Lun.

5. Mutant V shows a single requirement for Asp and in its absence synthesizes no Lun.

a. What is the amino acid accumulated by mutant I?

b. Write the most likely pathway for Lun biosynthesis, indicating the metabolic relationships between Lun, Asp, and Thr, and the step at which each of the five mutants is blocked.

c. Lun is found to inhibit one enzymatic step in the pathway. Indicate which you would expect it to be, and explain very briefly the reason for your choice.

16.13 The reduction of N_2 by H_2 to form NH_3 in the nitrogenase reaction requires four ATP per pair of electrons transferred (equation 16.2).

a. Is the requirement for ATP in this reaction expected? (E_0' for the half-cell $\frac{1}{2}N_2 + 3H^+/NH_3 = -0.34$ V.)

b. Speculate on how the energy might be used, and how it might be coupled into the system.

c. Briefly outline how one might try to elucidate the role of ATP in nitrogen fixation.

16.14 What intermediate in purine biosynthesis will accumulate in mutant bacteria unable to synthesize the following?

a. N^5,N^{10}-Methenyl FH_4

b. Gly

c. Asp

d. Gln

$$^+H_3NCH_2CH_2\underset{\underset{NH_3^+}{|}}{C}HCOO^-$$

Figure 16.13
Structure of lunine (Problem 16.12).

16.15 Indicate the principal position(s) in the purine ring that will become isotopically labeled during synthesis in cells exposed to the following:
a. ^{15}N-Asp
b. ^{14}C-Gly (carboxyl group labeled)
c. ^{14}C-Ser (hydroxymethyl group labeled)

16.16 Indicate the principal position(s) in the pyrimidine ring of UMP that will become isotopically labeled during synthesis in cells exposed to the following:
a. ^{14}C-succinate (uniformly labeled)
b. ^{15}N-Asp
c. ^{3}H-oxaloacetate (uniformly labeled)

16.17 Explain how synthesis of each of the four deoxynucleoside triphosphates will be affected by inhibition of the enzyme dihydrofolate reductase.

16.18 How many molecules of glucose must be fermented by an anaerobically growing *E. coli* cell to provide the high-energy phosphate bonds required to synthesize two molecules of CTP from CO_2, NH_3, Asp, and ribose 5-P?

16.19 a. Specify the oxidation state (as formyl, hydroxymethyl, or methyl) of the transferable or transferred C_1 unit in each of the following:

1. N^5,N^{10}-Methylene FH$_4$
2. Choline
3. N^5,N^{10}-Methenyl FH$_4$
4. S-Adenosylmethionine
5. Ser
6. Deoxythymidylate

b. What is the primary reducing agent in the FH$_4$-mediated conversion of dUMP to dTMP?

c. If aminopterin, a potent inhibitor of dihydrofolate reductase, is added to a culture of growing cells, which of the following major biosynthetic processes will be inhibited first? Why and how?

1. Carbohydrate synthesis
2. Lipid synthesis
3. DNA synthesis
4. RNA synthesis
5. Protein synthesis

16.20 In addition to the inability to synthesize adequate protein, what would be the metabolic consequence of a diet that is deficient in the essential amino acid Met?

16.21 Dr. F. Olding Munney, a recent graduate of the Franklin Stein Institute of Genetic Engineering, reports that he has perfected a safe and effective new approach to weight control for the chronically obese. Dr. Munney has succeeded in transferring genes for the enzymes isocitratase and malate synthetase from a pink bread mold into cultured human liver cells, which he then reimplants into the patient. Following this treatment, he claims, the patient can simply stop eating with no loss of vitality or threat to health, and can continue to fast until the desired weight loss is achieved.
a. What specific effect do you think Dr. Munney expects his treatment to have on liver intermediary metabolism?
b. When a person begins fasting, the brain must continue to be supplied with over 100 g of glucose per day for the first week or so. Outline the metabolic events that make this possible in a normal person. How might these events differ in one of Dr. Munney's patients? Can you see any particular advantage or disadvantage of undergoing Dr. Munney's treatment before beginning a fast if you want to lose a lot of weight?

16.22 Humans can survive longer by total fasting than on a diet consisting entirely of carbohydrate. Can you explain this apparent paradox?

☆ 16.23 Activation of acetate to acetyl CoA in the reaction catalyzed by thiokinase,

$$CH_3COO^- + ATP + HSCoA \rightarrow CH_3COSCoA + AMP + PP_i$$

proceeds via the enzyme-bound intermediate acetyl adenylate. Which of the following combinations of substrates and products, when incubated with the enzyme, will lead to exchange of radioactive label into ATP?

   a. ATP, AMP, $^{32}PP_i$

   b. ATP, HSCoA, $^{32}PP_i$

   c. ATP, HSCoA, ^{32}P-AMP

   d. ATP, acetate, $^{32}PP_i$

   e. ATP, acetate, ^{32}P-AMP

☆ 16.24   A purified preparation of liver fatty acid synthetase complex is incubated with acetyl CoA and ^{14}C-carboxyl-labeled malonyl CoA,

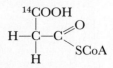

acyl carrier protein, and NADPH. The palmitic acid synthesized,

$$\overset{16}{C}H_3\overset{15}{C}H_2 \dots \overset{3}{C}H_2\overset{2}{C}H_2\overset{1}{C}OOH$$

is isolated and the distribution of ^{14}C is determined. Which one of the following results would you expect?

   a. All the odd-numbered C atoms are labeled.

   b. All the odd-numbered C atoms except C-1 are labeled.

   c. All the even-numbered C atoms are labeled.

   d. All the even-numbered C atoms except C-16 are labeled.

   e. None of the C atoms is labeled.

☆ 16.25   Three bacterial mutants are unable to synthesize amino acid A. In the absence of A, one of them accumulates an intermediate, B, that will support the growth of the other two. A second mutant accumulates an intermediate, C, that will not support the growth of any one of the three. The third accumulates another intermediate, D, that will support the growth of the second mutant. Which of the following is the order of intermediates in normal A biosynthesis?

   a. C → D → B → A

   b. D → C → B → A

   c. B → D → C → A

   d. B → C → D → A

   e. D → B → C → A

☆ 16.26   Consider the following branched biosynthetic pathway:

$$A \xrightarrow{1} B \xrightarrow{2} C \xrightarrow{3} D \overset{\overset{\textstyle 4}{\nearrow}}{\underset{\underset{\textstyle 7}{\searrow}}{}} \quad \begin{array}{l} E \xrightarrow{5} F \xrightarrow{6} P_1 \\ \\ G \xrightarrow{8} H \xrightarrow{9} I \xrightarrow{10} P_2 \end{array}$$

The products are P_1 and P_2, the intermediates are A through I, and the enzymes are numbered. Both products P_1 and P_2 are necessary for the growth of the organism containing this pathway. For efficient regulation of these pathways in an environment that often contains P_1, P_2, or P_1 and P_2, what enzymes would you expect to be inhibited by what compounds in the pathway?

☆ 16.27   Early biochemists were surprised to discover that CO_2 fixation, originally thought to be unique to plants, is involved in two major biosynthetic pathways in animals: gluconeogensis from pyruvate and fatty acid synthesis from acetyl CoA.

   a. Indicate how CO_2 participates in each of these processes by writing the relevant reactions.

   b. What is the function of CO_2 in each of these processes? Explain its role in as much detail as you can.

Answers

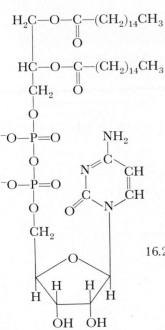

Figure 16.14
Structure of
CDP-dipalmityl-
glycerol (Answer 16.3).

16.1 a. False. Only seven ATP are expended—one for each acetyl CoA converted to malonyl CoA.

b. True

c. True

d. False. They are derived from the phosphogluconate pathway and the glycolytic pathway.

e. True

f. False. NO_3^- is the principal source because the abundant nitrifying bacteria in most soils oxidize any available ammonia to nitrate.

g. True

h. False. Attachment of the initial purine nitrogen to P-ribosyl-PP is the first step in assembly of the ring.

i. False. The FH_4 carries a methylene group at the hydroxymethyl level of oxidation. In the reaction, it is reduced to a methyl group at the expense of the cofactor, which becomes oxidized to FH_2.

j. True

k. False. The weight ratio of fat plus protein to glycogen is about 100.

l. False. Muscle protein is broken down to provide precursors for gluconeogenesis.

m. False. The demand for glucose is reduced to a fraction of this amount by a metabolic switch that allows ketone bodies to be used for fuel in place of glucose.

16.2 a. NADPH

b. malonyl CoA, one, biotin

c. fatty acyl CoA, glycerol 3-P

d. CDP-diacylglycerol, phospholipid

e. Met, S-adenosylmethionine

f. aspartate transcarbamylase, CTP

g. FH_4, folate

h. kwashiorkor

16.3 See Figure 16.14.

16.4 a. Malonyl CoA will become labeled in the acetyl CoA carboxylase reaction. However, ^{14}C will not *accumulate* in any compound, because the label will be released again as CO_2 when the malonyl CoA is converted to palmitate.

b. Citrate participates only as an allosteric effector required to activate the regulatory enzyme acetyl CoA carboxylase. The rationale is that increase in the level of citrate (the first TCA-cycle intermediate) is a signal that acetyl CoA should be diverted into fatty acid synthesis for storage rather than fed into the TCA cycle.

c. The reaction must involve a biotin-requiring enzyme. Avidin is a protein from egg white that specifically inhibits biotin-requiring enzymes. These enzymes always catalyze ATP-coupled fixation of CO_2 as a carboxyl group.

d. Enzyme I is acetyl CoA carboxylase:

$$\text{Acetyl CoA} + \text{ATP} + CO_2 \xrightarrow[\text{Mg}^{2+}]{\text{citrate}} \text{malonyl CoA} + \text{ADP} + P_i$$

Enzyme II is fatty acid synthetase:

$$\text{Acetyl CoA} + 7 \text{ malonyl CoA} + 14\text{NADPH} + 14\text{H}^+ \rightarrow$$
$$\text{palmitate} + 8\text{HSCoA} + 14\text{NADP}^+$$

16.5 a. The acetyl CoA contributes the terminal two-carbon fragment for condensation in the second reaction of Problem 16.4d. Because the terminal methyl carbon is not involved in a dehydration step, all the tritium is retained. Therefore, the answer is three.

b. There will be one ^3H retained in each malonate incorporated. The second is lost in the dehydration step that occurs with each two-carbon unit added (Figure 16.1, reaction 6). Thus the answer is seven.

16.6 a. The most reasonable predictions are

1. C_{15} or C_{17}
2. C_{16} or C_{18}, depending on the mechanism of fatty acid synthetase

b. If chain length of product is determined by "measuring" the growing chain and releasing at the preferred length, then (2) will give C_{16}; if chain length is determined by "counting" the number of two-carbon units added from malonyl CoA, then (2) will give C_{18}. It has been reported in the literature that the results are (1) C_{17} and (2), remarkably enough, C_{18}.

16.7 a. Animals cannot carry out net conversion of acetate to carbohydrate, but they can convert acetate directly to fatty acids, which will be incorporated into storage triglycerides. Thus lipids will be labeled more heavily than carbohydrates. However, some label will appear in carbohydrate because, although net synthesis of sugars from acetate is impossible, some ^{14}C-acetate will enter the TCA cycle and contribute ^{14}C to the pool of precursors for gluconeogenesis.

b. In triglycerides the label will be primarily in alternate positions on the fatty acid side chains, as follows:

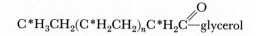

16.8 a. Ala, Asp, and Glu
b. Ala, Asp, and Glu are synthesized from the corresponding α-keto acids by transamination, as shown in Figure 16.15.

16.9 a. A   g. 3
b. B, C, or D   h. 1
c. 2   i. C
d. 3   j. D
e. B   k. 1
f. C or D   l. 2

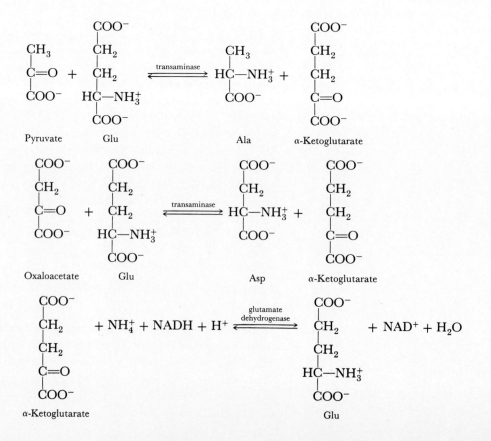

Figure 16.15
Conversion of three α-keto acids to the corresponding α-amino acids (Answer 16.8).

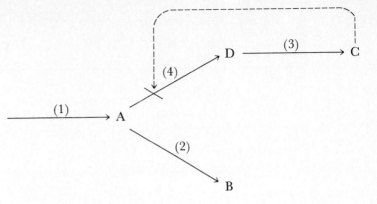

Figure 16.16
Biosynthetic pathway for amino acids B and C (Answer 16.10).

16.10 a. The finding that a single mutation results in a growth requirement for two amino acids means that the pathway for their synthesis must be branched, so that both are derived from a common intermediate lacking in mutant 1. Mutants 3 and 4 are blocked in the branch leading to C, and 2 in that leading to B. The step blocked in mutant 4 must precede that blocked in mutant 3, because 3 accumulates D, which will support the growth of 4. Finally, A, accumulated by 4, must be the common precursor of B and C, because it satisfies the dual growth requirement of mutant 1. Hence the pathway is as shown in Figure 16.16.

b. Amino acid C probably will inhibit the A → D conversion, because it is the first step unique to C synthesis. Inhibition of the first reaction by C alone is less likely, because the presence of C then would curtail production of B as well.

16.11 See Figure 16.17.

16.12 a. Homoserine
b. See Figure 16.18.
c. Lun probably inhibits only its own synthesis from aspartate β-semialdehyde (the reaction blocked in mutant III); inhibition of a previous step by Lun would interfere with Thr synthesis as well.

16.13 a. You can calculate from half-cell potentials whether the nitrogenase reaction requires energy, and if so, how much. Because E'_0 for the hydrogen half-cell is -0.42 V, reduction of N_2 by H_2 should not require energy; using the half-cell potential given for the

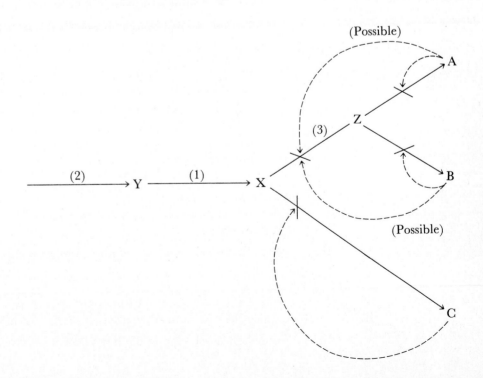

Figure 16.17
Biosynthetic pathway for amino acids A, B, and C (Answer 16.11). Secondary feedback effects are designated as "possible." Each solid arrow may represent several steps, only one of which is blocked by the indicated mutation.

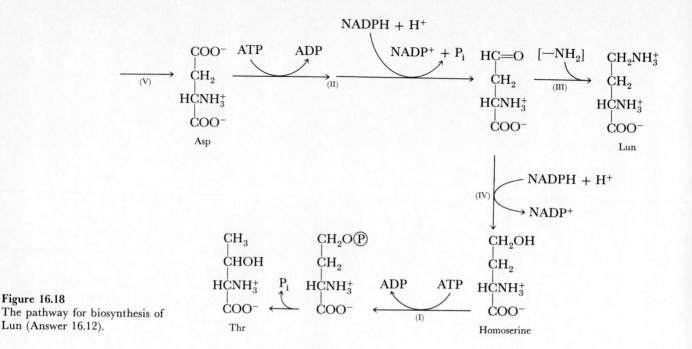

Figure 16.18
The pathway for biosynthesis of Lun (Answer 16.12).

nitrogen half-cell you can calculate that for this reaction $\Delta G'_0 = -11$ kcal/mol. Therefore, the ATP requirement is unexpected.

b. The mechanism of ATP coupling is also mysterious. ATP generally is used to drive hydrolytic reactions in reverse via high-energy intermediates (chemical coupling), to drive electrons up a potential gradient by increasing the pH differential across a membrane (chemiosmotic coupling), or to transport solutes across membranes against a concentration gradient (active transport). None of these can be involved here, because no reverse hydrolytic reaction occurs, and the enzyme is a large soluble protein that is active in the absence of a membrane system. Another possibility is that the enzyme cannot lower the activation energy sufficiently for an adequate rate of reaction, and that the ATP is utilized somehow to supply a portion of the activation energy.

c. Some possible approaches are as follows:

1. Use the purified enzyme to look for substrate-dependent exchange reactions (see Problem 15.15) that might provide evidence for high-energy intermediates derived from ATP.

2. Determine whether the ratio of ATP consumed to electron pairs transferred varies for donor and acceptor pairs with differing half-cell potentials, as would be expected if ATP energy is used for electron activation.

3. Look for ATP-dependent changes in the enzyme; perhaps energy is required to convert the protein to an unstable active form for each catalytic event.

4. Others?

16.14 a. Glycinamide ribonucleotide
   b. 5-P-ribosylamine
   c. 5-Aminoimidazole-4-carboxylate ribonucleotide
   d. 5-P-ribosyl-1-PP

16.15 Standard numbering for the ring positions is shown in Figure 16.7.
   a. N-1
   b. C-4
   c. C-2 and C-8. These two carbons are derived from the one-carbon pool via FH_4, to which the hydroxymethyl group of Ser is a common donor (Figure 16.11).

16.16 Standard numbering of the ring positions is shown in Figure 16.8.

a. C-4, C-5, and C-6. Succinate is converted to Asp, which becomes incorporated into orotate with subsequent loss of the α-carboxyl carbon.

b. N-1

c. H on C-5. Two atoms of ^{3}H will be present on the β carbon of Asp derived from oxaloacetate by transamination, and will be incorporated into the 5-position of dihydroorotate. However, one of the two will be lost upon dehydrogenation to orotate.

16.17 Inhibition of dihydrofolate reductase will block dTTP production specifically, because the formation of dTMP from dUMP oxidizes the C_1 donor FH_4 to FH_2, and this must be reduced back to FH_4 before it again can perform its C_1 donor function.

Because dTTP is an activator of the nucleoside diphosphate reductase enzymes converting ADP → dADP and GDP → dGDP, inhibition of FH_2 reductase will decrease dATP and dGTP production indirectly. This production may be decreased further as the shortage of FH_4 begins to prevent the C_1 transfers required in de novo purine synthesis. The inhibition of FH_2 reductase should have no marked effect on dCTP production.

16.18 The steps in CTP synthesis are

1. $CO_2 + NH_3 + 2ATP \rightarrow$ carbamyl-P $+ 2ADP + P_i$
2. Carbamyl-P $+$ Asp $\rightarrow \rightarrow \rightarrow$ orotate $+ P_i$
3. Ribose 5-P $+$ ATP $\rightarrow$ 5-P-ribosyl-1-PP $+$ AMP
4. Orotate $+$ PRPP $\rightarrow \rightarrow$ UMP $+ PP_i$
5. $PP_i + H_2O \rightarrow 2P_i$
6. UMP $+ 2ATP \rightarrow \rightarrow$ UTP $+ 2ADP$
7. UTP $+$ ATP $+ NH_3 \rightarrow$ CTP $+$ ADP $+ P_i$

Net: $CO_2 + 2NH_3 +$ Asp $+$ ribose 5-P $+ 6ATP \rightarrow$ CTP $+$ AMP $+ 5ADP + 5P_i$

Seven high-energy phosphate bonds are expended in this process, although two are conserved in each CTP produced. Because each molecule of glucose fermented yields two ATP, the cell must ferment seven glucose molecules to produce two CTP molecules.

16.19 a. 1. Hydroxymethyl   4. Methyl
        2. Methyl   5. Hydroxymethyl
        3. Formyl   6. Methyl

b. FH_4. It becomes oxidized to FH_2 during reduction of the transferred C_1 unit from the hydroxymethyl to the methyl oxidation level.

c. Because aminopterin blocks dihydrofolate reductase, its first effect will be to curtail dTMP production and therefore to inhibit DNA synthesis.

16.20 All reactions that require S-adenosylmethionine will be inhibited by the Met deficiency. Notable among the resulting defects will be inability to synthesize phosphatidylcholine from phosphatidylethanolamine.

16.21 a. Dr. Munney expects his treatment to make the glyoxylate-cycle reactions possible in human liver, thereby allowing it to carry out net synthesis of glucose from the acetyl CoA derived from fatty acid breakdown.

b. In a normal person, the glycogen supply of liver is sufficient to provide glucose for the brain for only a few hours. After this time, glucose is obtained primarily from gluconeogenesis in the liver, which requires as starting materials glucogenic amino acids derived from breakdown of muscle protein. After a week or two, the brain shifts its metabolism to use ketone bodies as its primary fuel, thus partially sparing muscle protein during a long fasting period. Dr. Munney's treatment, in theory, would be favorable in that muscle protein could be spared from the beginning by allowing direct conversion of fatty acids to glucose, a process impossible in normal animals. Therefore, fasting should lead only to loss of fat, without the normally accompanying impairment of muscle function. In practice, of course, many difficulties might arise. For example, the expression of the newly introduced genes might not be controlled properly, or antibodies might be made against the new proteins, leading to a patho-logical autoimmune reaction.

The explanation for this apparent paradox is probably that as long as carbohydrate from the diet is supplying glucose intermittently, the brain will continue as usual to use glucose as fuel. Therefore, during each overnight fast, protein still must be broken down to supply amino acids for gluconeogenesis. Consequently, protein reserves will be used up more quickly than in total fasting, where protein is maximally conserved by the brain's switch from glucose to circulating ketone bodies as its principal energy source.

Storage and Expression of
Genetic Information

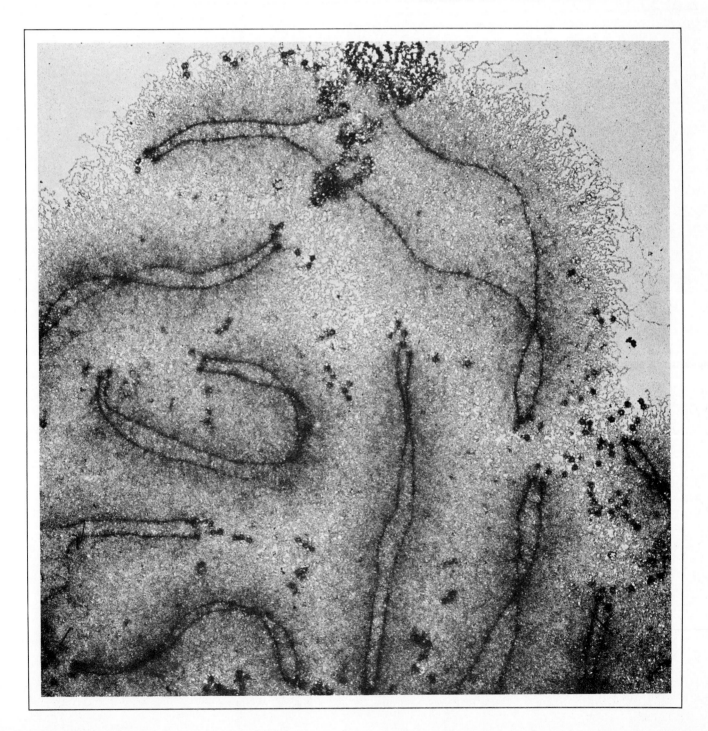

Part Three opener photograph: Silkworm chromosomes released from the nucleus during meiosis. Loops
of chromatin (threads in background) emanate from
chromosomes, which cross at *chiasmata*, putative sites of
genetic recombination. Transcriptionally active ribosomal precursor RNA genes are seen as darker loops on
the chromosome nearest the top of the photograph.
(Electron micrograph courtesy of B. Hamkalo and
J. B. Rattner, University of California, Irvine.)

17 Nucleic Acid Structure

Genetic information is stored and transmitted by the nucleic acids **DNA** (**deoxyribonucleic acid**) and **RNA** (**ribonucleic acid**). This chapter considers the structures and properties of DNA and RNA, the organization of DNA in chromosomes, and recombination of DNA to produce new combinations of genes.

Concepts

17.1 DNA and RNA are linear polymers of nucleotides.

A. **Nucleotides** are the monomer units of nucleic acids. Ribonucleotides and deoxyribonucleotides each consist of three components: an aromatic base, a pentose sugar, and one to three phosphate groups (Figure 17.1). **Ribonucleotides** contain the sugar **ribose** and a base, usually **adenine, guanine, cytosine, or uracil. Deoxyribonucleotides** contain the sugar **2′-deoxyribose** and a base, usually **adenine, guanine, cytosine, or thymine.** Figure 17.2 shows the structures of the common purine and pyrimidine bases. If the sugar is not phosphorylated, the structure is called a **nucleoside.** Phosphoryl groups may be attached to any hydroxyl group on the sugar moiety of a nucleoside to form the corresponding nucleotide. The nomenclature of nucleotides is summarized in Table 17.1.

Table 17.1
Nomenclature of Nucleic Acid Bases, Nucleosides, and Nucleotides

Base	(Deoxy)ribonucleoside[a]	5′-(Deoxy)ribonucleotide[a]
Adenine (A)	(Deoxy)adenosine	(Deoxy)adenylate, (d)AMP
Guanine (G)	(Deoxy)guanosine	(Deoxy)guanylate, (d)GMP
Cytosine (C)	(Deoxy)cytidine	(Deoxy)cytidylate, (d)CMP
Thymine (T)	(Thymidine)[b]	(Thymidylate)[b], (TMP)
	Ribothymidine	Ribothymidylate, rTMP
Uracil (U)	Uridine	Uridylate, UMP

[a]Nomenclature for deoxyribonucleosides and deoxyribonucleotides is indicated in parentheses.
[b]Thymine is found almost exclusively in DNA and uracil almost exclusively in RNA. For this reason, deoxythymidine and deoxythymidylate are written as thymidine and thymidylate, respectively. The much rarer ribosyl derivatives of thymine are indicated with the prefix *ribo-,* as shown.

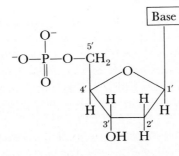 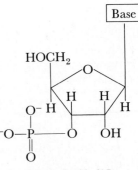

Deoxyribonucleoside 5′-P
or 5′-deoxyribonucleotide

Ribonucleoside 3′-P
or 3′-ribonucleotide

Figure 17.1
Structure of nucleotides. Positions in the pentose ring are indicated as 1′–5′ to distinguish them from positions in the purine or pyrimidine rings of the bases.

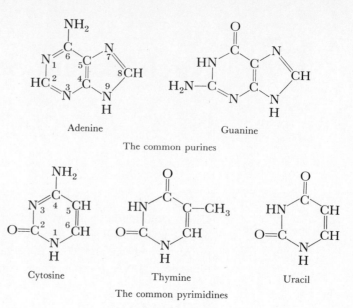

Figure 17.2
Structures of the five common bases in aqueous solution at pH = 7.

B. The mononucleotides in DNA and RNA are linked by 3′–5′-phosphodiester bonds, as shown for an oligoribonucleotide in Figure 17.3. Polynucleotides, like polypeptides, have polarity. The sugar at one end of the chain has a 3′-hydroxyl or phosphoryl group (3′ end), and the sugar at the other end has a 5′-hydroxyl or phosphoryl group (5′ end). By convention, the 5′ end of a polynucleotide is written to the left. The oligonucleotide in Figure 17.3 can be symbolized in abbreviated form as shown in Figure 17.4, or even more simply as pApGpCpUpC or AGCUC.

The presence of a 2′-hydroxyl group in ribose and its absence from deoxyribose cause differences in the chemical stabilities of RNA and DNA. The phosphodiester bonds in DNA are stable to alkali, whereas those in RNA are hydrolyzed rapidly by alkali to yield a mixture of 2′ and 3′ mononucleotides.

17.2 Nucleotide chains pair according to simple rules.

A. In 1953, James Watson and Francis Crick laid the foundations for an understanding of gene action by deducing the structure of DNA from its x-ray diffraction pattern. The DNA molecule is composed of two strands that are wound together into a right-handed helix. Bases on the two strands form H-bonded pairs that are stacked along the central axis of the molecule, with the sugar phosphate "backbones" on the outside (Figure 17.5a, b). Only two base pairs, A-T and G-C, can be accommodated in the double-helical (duplex) structure. As a consequence, the nucleotide sequence in one strand of the double helix dictates the nucleotide sequence in the other, and the two strands of a DNA duplex are said to be **complementary.** The A-T base pair has two H-bonds. The G-C base pair has three, and accordingly is more stable. The structures of the two H-bonded base pairs are shown in Figure 17.6. The average molecular weight of a nucleotide pair is about 650.

The two strands of the double helix are oriented with opposite (**antiparallel**) polarity. The helix has a diameter of about 2.0 nm and contains about 10 nucleotide pairs per turn with a pitch of 0.34 nm per nucleotide pair.

B. RNA molecules are generally single-stranded. However, they normally form irregular, partially helical structures with intrastrand H-bonding between complementary anti-parallel sequences, as shown schematically in Figure 17.7. The base pairs found in RNA are primarily A-U and G-C, although G-U also is acceptable. A perfectly paired

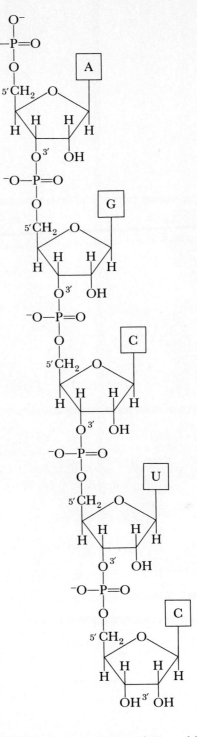

Figure 17.3
Structure of an oligoribonucleotide.

section of double-helical RNA is shown in Figure 17.8a and b. In many cases RNA secondary structure is important for the proper function of RNA molecules.

C. Forces that stabilize helical structure in DNA and RNA include hydrophobic interactions that maintain the predominantly nonpolar bases in the interior of the molecule, H-bonds between the bases of each pair, and the so-called stacking energy that results

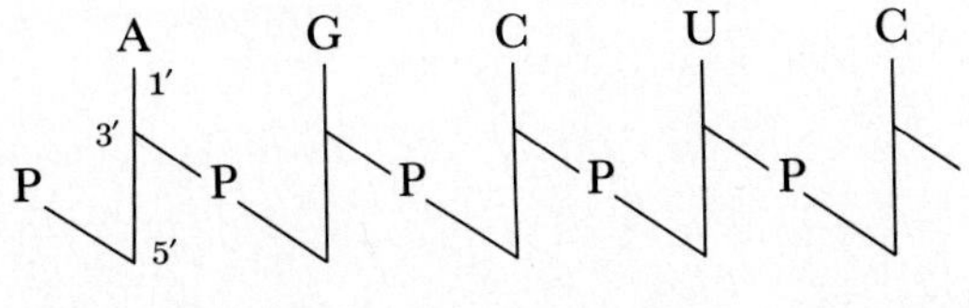

Figure 17.4
An abbreviated representation of an oligonucleotide. The vertical lines represent sugars.

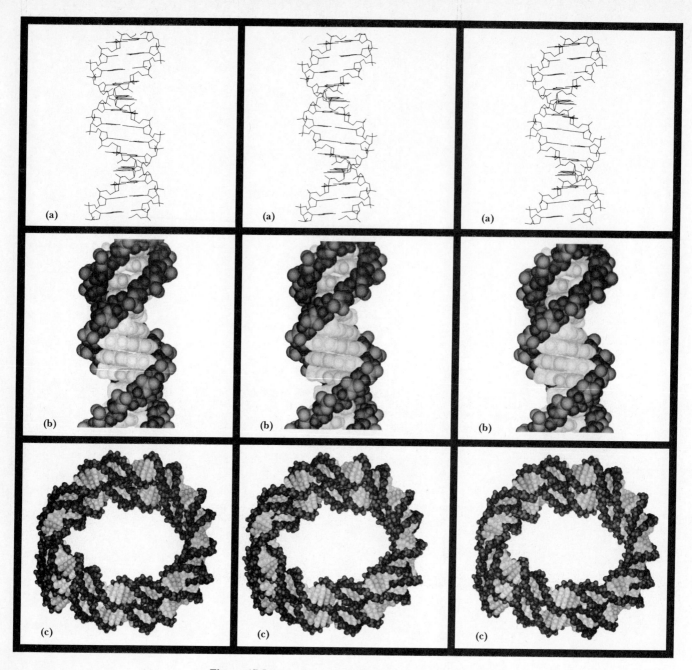

Figure 17.5
Stereo triptychs illustrating DNA structure. **(a)**, **(b)** Skeletal
and space-filling models, respectively, showing one turn of a
DNA helix. In the sugar-phosphate backbones, the phosphates are light and the deoxyriboses are dark; in the interior purines are light and pyrimidines are dark. **(c)** DNA as
it is coiled about a nucleosome. The bases are light and the
sugar-phosphate backbones are dark. For stereo viewing, see
instructions in the Appendix to Chapter 4. (Stereo figures
courtesy of Richard J. Feldmann, NIH.)

from a combination of van der Waals and dipole–dipole interactions between the
bases when they are aligned in parallel planes.

17.3 Nucleic acids denature and renature under appropriate conditions.

A. Nucleic acids unwind or **denature** into disordered single strands (**random coils**) when
subjected to high temperature, extremes of pH, or denaturing reagents such as formamide and urea. The "unstacking" of the bases that occurs upon denaturation causes

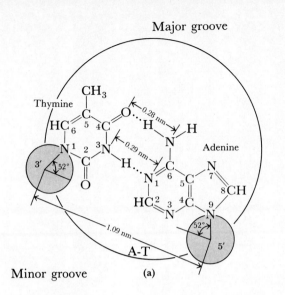

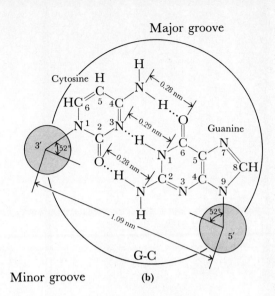

Figure 17.6
Schematic diagram of A-T (a) and G-C (b) base pairs as viewed along the duplex axis. H-bonds are indicated by dotted lines. Large circles represent the cylinders in which the duplexes spiral. Small shaded circles represent the sugar phosphate backbones with 5′ and 3′ ends pointing at the reader as indicated. The chemical groups that face the major and minor grooves in this drawing always face these grooves.

an increase in their absorption of ultraviolet light (**absorbance** or **optical density**) at wavelengths near 260 nm. This increase (**hyperchromic effect**) can be followed spectrophotometrically. Nucleic acids with highly ordered secondary structure, such as double-stranded DNA, exhibit cooperative denaturation that is characterized by a substantial sharp increase in absorbance over a narrow range of temperature or

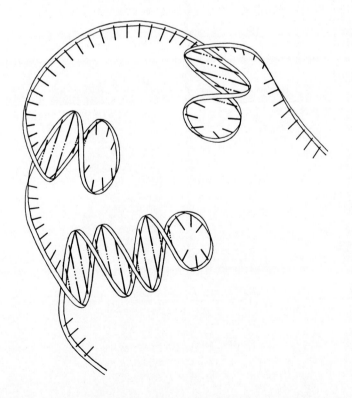

Figure 17.7
Conformation of a polyribonu-cleotide. (From James D. Watson, *Molecular Biology of the Gene*, 3rd ed. © 1976 by J. D. Watson, Benjamin/Cummings.)

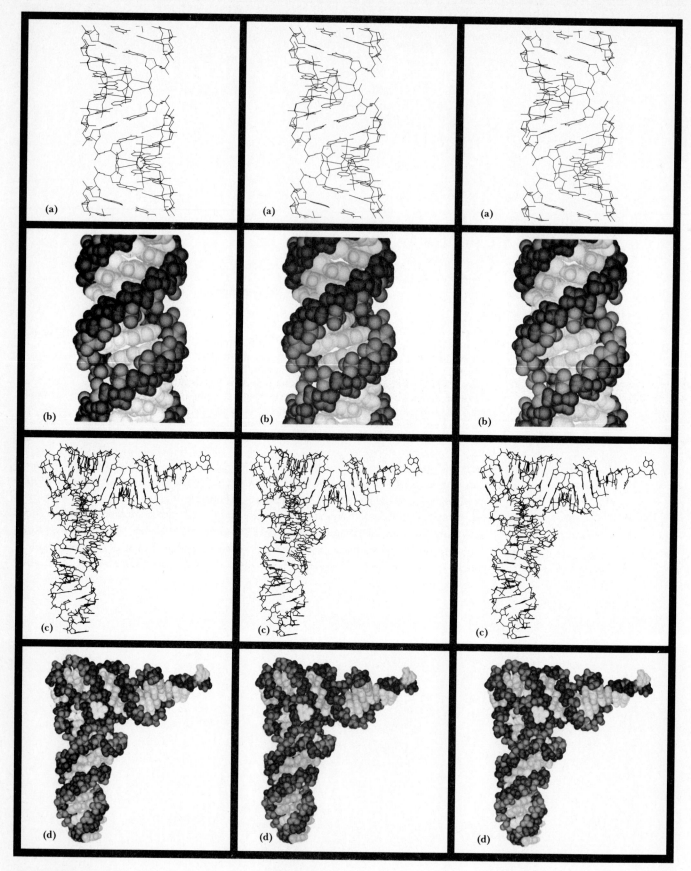

Figure 17.8
Stereo triptychs illustrating RNA structure. **(a), (b)** Skeletal and space-filling models showing one turn of an RNA duplex. **(c), (d)** Skeletal and space-filling models of a tRNA molecule. Color scheme is the same as in Figure 17.5b and c. For stereo viewing, see instructions in the Appendix to Chapter 4. (Stereo figures courtesy of Richard J. Feldmann, NIH.)

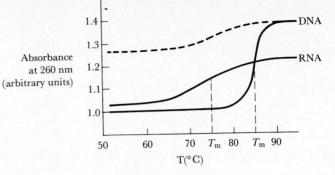

Figure 17.9
Absorbance–temperature profiles for DNA and RNA in solution. T_m varies with solvent conditions such as pH, ionic strength, and denaturant concentration. Solid curves are obtained by heating the solution; the dashed curve indicates the absorbance change observed when a solution of DNA above T_m is cooled rapidly.

denaturant concentration. Less ordered polynucleotides, such as single-stranded RNA, show a smaller increase over a broader range (Figure 17.9).

The **melting temperature** (T_m) of a nucleic acid is defined as the temperature corresponding to the midpoint of the optical-density increase caused by heat denaturation (Figure 17.9). Under fixed solvent conditions, the T_m of double-helical DNA increases linearly with increasing content of G-C base pairs. Thus the nucleotide composition of DNA can be estimated from measurement of T_m.

B. Complementary, single-stranded polynucleotides re-form double-stranded structures under **annealing** conditions. When a solution of DNA is heated past its T_m and then quickly cooled, the strands remain separated (Figure 17.9). However, if the solution is held at about 20°C below T_m, complementary strands ultimately associate into duplex structures. Under these conditions complementary RNA and DNA sequences form hybrid double helices. Thus the extent of annealing is a measure of the sequence complementarity in a mixture of single-stranded polynucleotides. (See the Appendix for further discussion of nucleic acid association.)

17.4   All cells store genetic information in double-stranded DNA.

Double-stranded DNA is the carrier of genetic information in all cells and most viruses. Viruses, which are essentially extracellular packages of genetic information, store genetic information in a wider variety of nucleic acids, including double-stranded and single-stranded RNA and single-stranded DNA. The sizes and conformations of several DNA molecules found in nature are listed in Table 17.2.

Table 17.2
Sizes and Conformations of a Few DNA Molecules

Source of DNA	Length (μm)	Nucleotide pairs (thousands)	Conformation
SV40, an animal virus	1.7	5.2	Circular
φX174, a bacterial virus	1.8	5.5	Circular (single-stranded)
Adenovirus, an animal virus	12	36	Linear
T4, a bacterial virus	58	170	Linear
Vaccinia, an animal virus	140	420	Linear
E. coli, a bacterium	1,300	4,000	Circular
Eucaryotic chromosomes	>3,500	>10,000	Linear

17.5 Cellular DNA duplexes are organized into chromosomes.

A. Procaryotic chromosomes contain a single circular DNA duplex. In addition many procaryotes possess small, autonomous, circular DNA duplexes, termed **plasmids.** The chromosomal DNA duplex is complexed with basic proteins and RNA molecules that fold it into a somewhat condensed state. The chromosome is organized into a nucleoid that is not separated from the cytoplasm by a membrane. Mitochondrial and chloroplast DNAs also are circular. This similarity is one of several that suggest a procaryotic origin for these eucaryotic organelles.

B. Eucaryotic genomes are composed of several linear DNA duplexes that are organized into separate chromosomes within the nucleus. Each eucaryotic chromosome appears to contain a single, very long, continuous DNA molecule. These long DNA molecules are stabilized structurally by interaction with a set of small basic proteins called **histones** (Table 17.3). Nucleosomal histones aggregate in a 2-fold symmetric octamer, which is composed of two molecules of each histone species. About 140 base pairs of DNA (called **core DNA**) are wrapped in approximately $1\frac{3}{4}$ turns around the surface of the octamer to form a nucleosome (Figure 17.5c).

Table 17.3 Nomenclature and Characteristics of Histones from Calf Thymus	Nomenclature	Description	Molecular weight
	Nucleosomal		
	H2A	Slightly Lys-rich	14,500
	H2B	Slightly Lys-rich	13,700
	H3	Arg-rich	15,300
	H4	Arg-rich	11,300
	Internucleosomal		
	H1	Lys-rich	21,000

The internucleosomal histone, H1, binds to the 10–60 base pairs of DNA (**linker DNA**) between nucleosomes. H1 is thought to be involved in higher states of DNA coiling. At present the intermediate states of coiling are not well defined in either structure or function. However, the most condensed state, which occurs at cell division, is contracted in length about 10,000-fold, making the chromosomes visible in the light microscope (Figure 17.10). This highly condensed state allowed early cytogeneticists to link chromosomes to heredity.

17.6 New combinations of genetic information are produced by recombination of DNA sequences.

A. Procaryotes are **haploid** (1N), which means that they have a single copy of their genetic information. DNA segments from one bacterium can be introduced into another bacterium (usually of the same species) by several mechanisms so that some genetic information is present in two copies. Such a partially diploid condition is unstable and the extra DNA is lost rather rapidly. However, the two homologous portions of the genome can recombine to produce new stable gene combinations that are passed on to daughter cells.

B. Most eucaryotes are **diploid** (2N), which means that they have two homologous sets of chromosomes, one set inherited from the female parent and the other set from the male parent. **Somatic** or body cells of eucaryotes divide by **mitosis,** a process in which each daughter cell receives the same diploid complement of chromosomes. **Germ line** cells additionally have the capacity to divide by **meiosis** to produce haploid sex **gametes,** that is, eggs or sperm. An egg and a sperm from different individuals combine to form a diploid **zygote,** which then develops into a new adult organism. During

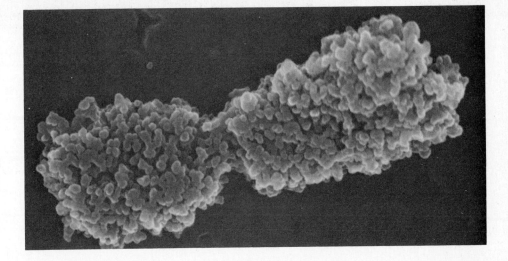

Figure 17.10
Scanning electron micrograph of an isolated metaphase chromosome from Chinese hamster at a magnification of 20,000. (Micrograph courtesy of Wayne Wray, Baylor College of Medicine.)

meiosis new combinations of genetic information arise by assortment of homologous chromosomes and by exchange of DNA segments between homologous chromosomes.

During meiosis homologous chromosomes pair and then segregate independently into different gametes. For humans, who have 46 chromosomes, there are 2^{23} different assortments of chromosomes that can be contributed to the gametes. In addition, when homologous chromosomes pair during meiosis, they can exchange DNA segments by breaking and rejoining at aligned points on the genetic map so that no genetic information is lost (Figure 17.11). This process is known as **general, homologous,** or **legitimate recombination.** It is exceedingly accurate and only rarely introduces mistakes.

C. One plausible mechanism for general recombination, which is based on analogous recombination processes in procaryotes, is illustrated in Figure 17.12. The overall accuracy of general recombination is due to the **heteroduplex joint,** which is formed by one DNA strand from each parent, and which holds the parental DNA segments together. Because proper base pairing in the heteroduplex region is only possible in regions of extensive homology, recombination occurs predominantly at corresponding points on homologous chromosomes.

17.7 Genetic information in DNA is transcribed into several classes of RNA.

A. **Messenger RNA (mRNA)** molecules are the copies of DNA nucleotide sequences that direct the synthesis of proteins (Chapter 20). They vary in length from a few hundred

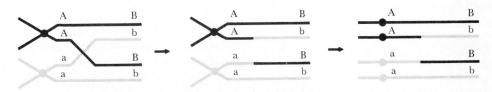

Figure 17.11
Schematic diagram illustrating general recombination at the chromosome level. Paired homologous chromosomes, which here have recombined, separate at the first meiotic division. Sister chromatids, which are linked at the centromere (small circle), separate at the second meiotic division, producing four haploid gametes. *A* and *a* represent different forms of one gene, and *B* and *b* represent different forms of a second gene.

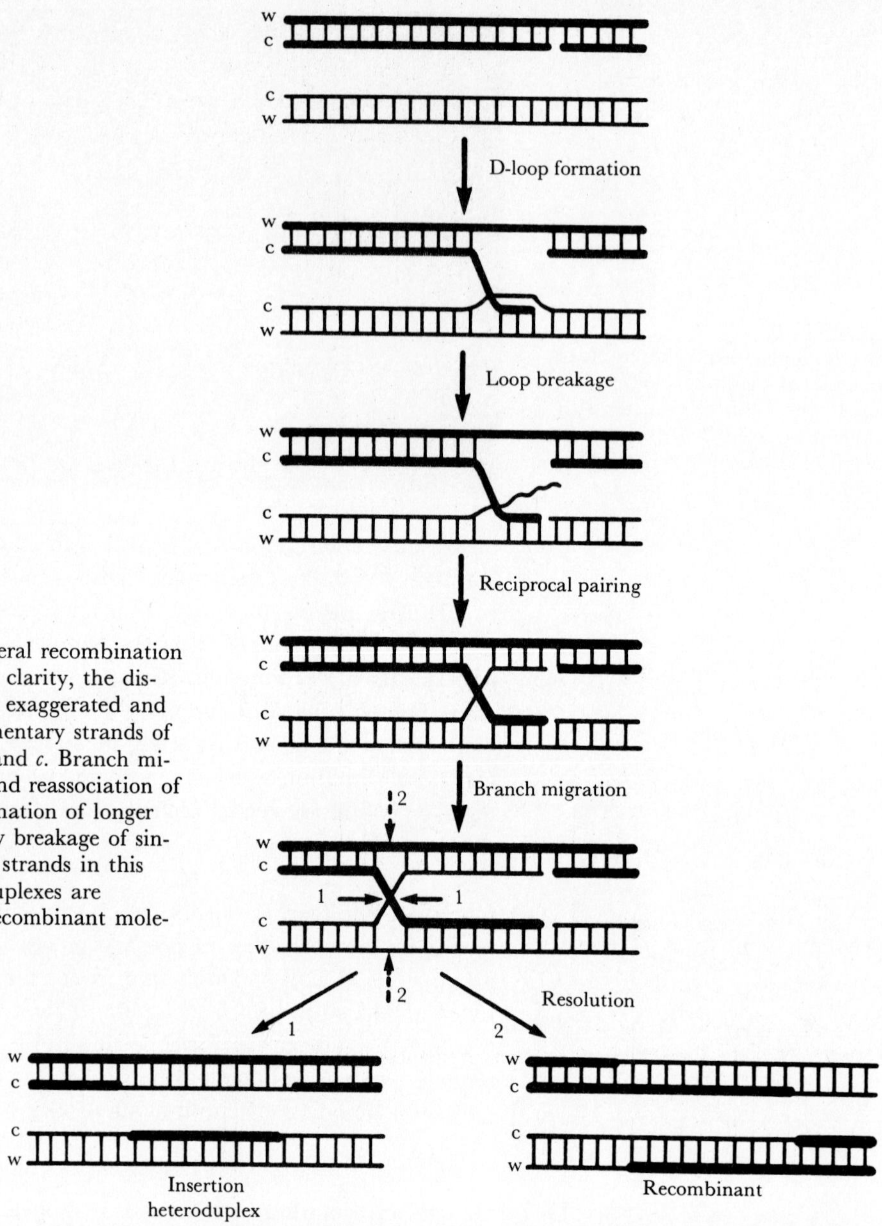

Figure 17.12
A plausible molecular mechanism for general recombination between homologous DNA molecules. For clarity, the distance between the two duplexes is greatly exaggerated and helical coiling is not shown. The complementary strands of each duplex are arbitrarily designated *w* and *c*. Branch migration occurs by concerted dissociation and reassociation of complementary strands and results in formation of longer heteroduplex regions. Resolution occurs by breakage of single strands at the crossover point. If the *c* strands in this diagram are broken (1), insertion heteroduplexes are formed; if the *w* strands are broken (2), recombinant molecules are formed.

to several thousand nucleotides. The genetic material of the RNA-containing viruses represents a special class of mRNA, which must serve as a template for its own replication as well as for protein synthesis.

B. **Ribosomal RNA (rRNA)** molecules are structural components of ribosomes (Concept 20.5). There are several discrete size classes of rRNA, usually referred to by their sedimentation coefficients as 5S, 16S, and 23S in procaryotic cells, and 5S, 5.8S, 18S, and 28S in eucaryotic cells. (*S* stands for **Svedberg unit,** a measure of the rate at which a molecule sediments through a solution when subjected to a centrifugal force.) The 5S, 16S, and 23S procaryotic molecules have lengths of approximately 120, 1700, and 4000 nucleotides, respectively.

C. **Transfer RNA (tRNA)** molecules are the carriers of activated amino acid monomers for protein synthesis (Concept 20.4). A number of tRNA species have been sequenced completely. All have the characteristic cloverleaf secondary structure diagrammed in

Figure 17.13. All tRNA molecules also have similar L-shaped three-dimensional structures, as shown in Figure 17.8c and d. All tRNA molecules terminate at the 5′ end with pG, and carry the 3′-terminal sequence pCpCpA. They contain rare nucleotides, such as pseudouridylate (ψ) and ribothymidylate, that are not found in other types of RNA.

D. Small nuclear RNA (**snRNA**) molecules of about 100–200 nucleotides in length are present in eucaryotic cells. Their function is uncertain, although recent evidence suggests that some may be involved in processing the larger transcripts that are precursors of the classes of RNA molecules already listed. RNA molecules with an analogous function are associated with some RNA-processing enzymes in procaryotes.

17.8 **Additional concepts and techniques are presented in the Problems section.**

A. Mutagenic action of base analogues. Problem 17.5.

B. Symmetry of DNA. Problems 17.9, 17.10, and 17.11.

C. Characterization of nucleic acids by equilibrium sedimentation. Problem 17.12.

D. Heteroduplex DNA analysis by electron microscopy. Problems 17.17, 17.18, and 17.19.

E. DNA supercoiling. Problems 17.21 and 17.22.

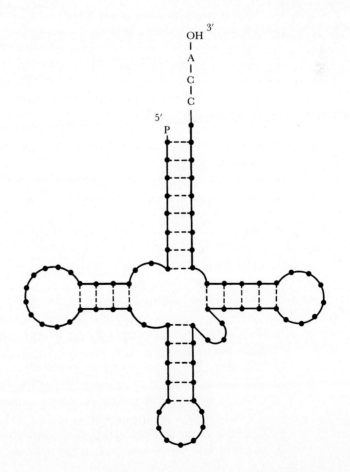

Figure 17.13
Cloverleaf structure of tRNA. Intramolecular H-bonding is shown by dotted lines. Transfer RNA molecules are about 80 nucleotides in length, with molecular weights of about 25,000.

References

COMPREHENSIVE TEXTS

Lehninger: Chapters 12 and 31   Stryer: Chapter 24

Metzler: Chapter 2   White et al.: Chapter 7

OTHER REFERENCES

W. R. Bauer, F. H. C. Crick, and J. H. White, "Supercoiled DNA," *Scientific American,* July 1980, p. 118.

C. M. Radding, "Genetic Recombination: Strand Transfer and Mismatch Repair," *Annual Review of Biochemistry,* **47,** 847 (1978).

J. D. Watson, *Molecular Biology of the Gene,* Benjamin/Cummings, Menlo Park, Calif., 1976, 3rd ed. Chapters 9 and 10.

Problems

17.1   Answer the following with true or false. If false, explain why.

   a. A nucleotide consists of three components: an aromatic base, a pentose sugar, and one or more phosphate groups.

   b. Adenine and guanine contain pyrimidine rings.

   c. A nucleotide without a phosphate group is called a nucleoside.

   d. Deoxyribonucleosides carry no hydroxyl group at the 3′-position of the sugar ring.

   e. The 3′-hydroxyl group of the nucleotide at the 5′ end of an RNA chain participates in the phosphodiester linkage to the 5′-hydroxyl group of the penultimate nucleotide.

   f. The DNA double helix makes a complete turn every 0.34 nm along its length.

   g. The A-T base pair could form three H-bonds like the G-C base pair if the O atom at C-2 of thymine were protonated to —OH.

   h. If the deoxynucleotide sequence in one strand of a short stretch of DNA double helix is pCpTpGpGpApC, then the complementary sequence in the opposite strand is pGpApCpCpTpG.

   i. Upon denaturation the two strands of the DNA double helix separate.

   j. If a sample of nucleic acid shows an increase of 30% or more in optical density (absorbance) at 260 nm over a temperature range of a few degrees, it was in a complementary base-paired, double-helical structure.

   k. If the T_m of DNA from species A is lower than that of DNA from species B, species A contains a higher proportion of A-T base pairs than species B.

   l. If the absorbance–temperature profile of a viral DNA with a G-C content of 40% and a length of 10^5 nucleotide pairs is compared with that of human liver DNA (G-C content 40%) that has been broken to fragments of the same length, the two curves should be identical.

   m. In procaryotes and eucaryotes chromosomal DNA is complexed with histones.

   n. The protomer of the histone octamer of a nucleosome consists of one molecule each of the nucleosomal histones.

   o. New combinations of genetic information in eucaryotes are produced during meiosis by independent assortment of chromosomes and by exchange of DNA segments between homologous chromosomes.

   p. All procaryotic cells are haploid and all eucaryotic cells are diploid.

17.2 a. The monomer units of nucleic acids are called _____.

   b. The bases commonly found in RNA are _____, _____, _____, and _____.

   c. The H-bonding properties of the pyrimidine bases _____ in DNA and _____ in RNA are similar.

   d. The deoxyribonucleoside of guanine is called _____.

   e. The sequences in the two strands of a DNA double helix are _____.

   f. Only _____ different base pairs can be accommodated in the DNA double helix. Thymine always occurs opposite _____, and cytosine opposite _____.

   g. Complementary single-stranded nucleotide sequences will associate to form double-stranded molecules under _____ conditions.

h. _____ RNA molecules direct the synthesis of proteins; _____ RNA molecules serve as carriers of activated amino acids for protein synthesis.

i. Two molecules each of histones H2A, H2B, H3, and H4 aggregate to form an octamer about which 140 base pairs of _____ DNA are wrapped. Histone H1 binds to the _____ DNA between such aggregates.

j. Recombination between chromosomes at aligned homologous points on the genetic map is termed _____ recombination.

17.3   Which of the following modified bases will have H-bonding properties different from the common base to which it is related?

    a. 2-Methyladenine
    b. 5-Methylcytosine
    c. 5-Hydroxymethylcytosine
    d. 1-Methylguanine

17.4   Draw and, if possible, build a model of the H-bonded dinucleotides from a double-

$$5'\text{-pCpT-}3'$$
$$3'\text{-GpAp-}5'$$

helical DNA molecule. Make the two dinucleotides antiparallel, and indicate the H-bonds joining each base pair.

17.5   Several artificial nitrogenous bases, called **base analogues,** can be taken up by cells, converted to nucleotides, and incorporated into nucleic acids. They are often potent mutagens (Concept 21.5), and some are used in cancer chemotherapy. Two such analogues are 5-bromouracil (5-BU), and 2-aminopurine (2-AP).

    a. Draw 5-BU and show its H-bonding to the base with which it is most likely to pair.
    b. Draw 2-AP and show its H-bonding to the base with which it is most likely to pair.
    c. The bases G, C, T, and U can exist in either **keto** or **enol** tautomeric forms. The keto forms of these bases predominate almost completely under physiological conditions. However, in 5-BU the bromine group shifts the equilibrium toward an enol form (Figure 17.14). By drawing the H-bonded bases, show how this shift might cause 5-BU to pair with the purine that you did not choose as most likely in part a.

17.6   The pK_a values for adenine (N-1) and guanine (N-7) are 4.2 and 3.2, respectively.
    a. Using the Henderson–Hasselbalch equation (equation 2.2), calculate the percentage of these groups in the protonated form at pH = 7.0.
    b. What significance do the predominant forms at pH = 7.0 have with regard to the formation of the DNA double helix?

17.7   Diagram the two most stable monomeric structures in solution for a polyribonucleotide with the sequence
    AUUACGUGGUGCACUCGGGGAACAUCCCGAGUGCACCACGUAAUGGA
    Which do you predict will predominate when the two are in equilibrium? Why?

17.8   Self-complementary antiparallel sequences in RNA can pair to form short duplex structures (Figure 17.7). Imagine that you have transcribed both complementary strands of a DNA segment into RNA. During transcription Watson–Crick base-pairing rules are followed so that each RNA molecule is complementary to the DNA strand from which it was copied. As a consequence, the two RNA molecules are complementary to each other and could pair to form a perfect RNA duplex.

    a. Would the individual RNA molecules form the same or different numbers of *intramolecular* H-bonded base pairs?

Figure 17.14
Keto and enol forms of 5-BU
(Problem 17.5).

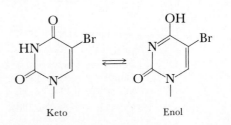

Keto   Enol

b. Imagine that the sequence of one of the RNA molecules was such that it could form several short intramolecular hairpins along its length. How would the hairpins in the complementary RNA molecule differ?

17.9   DNA is a dimeric aggregate of two molecules—the complementary single strands. The sugar phosphate backbones of the individual strands are identical and oriented in opposite directions, antiparallel. For these reasons one might expect the sugar phosphate backbones to be related by 2-fold rotational symmetry (see Problem 5.21). Such a relationship is difficult to discern in native DNA (Figure 17.5). However, it can be seen more clearly in an untwisted nonchemical representation that preserves the basic symmetry relationships (Figure 17.15).

a. There are two distinctly different axes of 2-fold rotational symmetry that relate the sugar phosphate backbones of the two DNA strands. Describe them.

b. Certain segments of DNA possess nucleotide sequences that show perfect 2-fold rotational symmetry. Write one and show the position of the axis of symmetry. Can sequences with *perfect* 2-fold symmetry be drawn about either of the 2-fold axes in part a?

c. Imagine that you are standing on the minor groove, facing one end. Note that the strand on your left side runs from 5′ in back of you to 3′ in front of you. Is this relationship the same if you turn around and face the other end? Why? Label the 5′–3′ orientation of strands in the native structure in Figure 17.5b.

17.10   Four phosphate–ester bonds hold each nucleotide pair in its position within the DNA double helix. Imagine that you could break these four bonds for one nucleotide pair and slide it out of the helix. Describe all the ways you could reinsert the nucleotide pair and still preserve the basic structure of the double helix.

17.11   Consider the set of dimeric proteins and DNA sequences in Figure 17.16. Each protein dimer consists of two identical subunits. The left protein subunit and the left six-base-pair DNA sequence are the same in all cases.

a. In which cases is there a matching symmetry between the protein dimer and its adjacent DNA sequence?

b. In several instances a dimeric protein is known to bind to a symmetric sequence in DNA and regulate expression of an adjacent gene. Which of the symmetry matches in part a is likely to be involved in such a regulation?

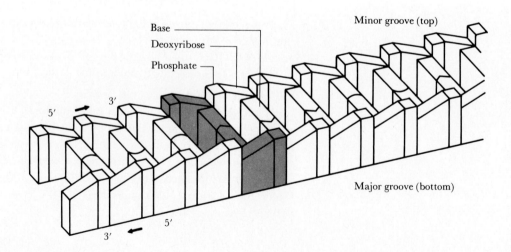

Figure 17.15
Schematic representation of untwisted DNA (Problem 17.9). The upper, jagged surface of this railroad track model corresponds to the minor groove of the helix; the lower, flat surface corresponds to the major groove of the helix. One nucleotide pair is shaded.

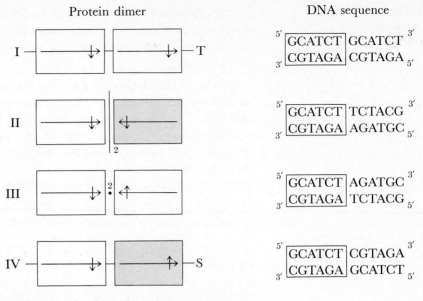

Protein dimer

DNA sequence

Figure 17.16
Symmetry match between protein and DNA (Problem
17.10). Arrows on the protein subunits are to assist you in
following their symmetry relationships. Light and dark
shading indicate front and back surfaces. Ignore the twist in
the protein dimer that would be necessary to align it precisely with the helical DNA sequence. In other words, view
the DNA sequence as unwound, like the railroad track
model in Figure 17.15.

17.12　Equilibrium sedimentation in density gradients is an important method for separating and characterizing nucleic acids. In this technique a concentrated solution of a
heavy-metal salt (usually CsCl) containing a sample of nucleic acid is centrifuged at
high speed. The salt forms a linear concentration gradient in the centrifugal field,
varying in density (for an $8M$ CsCl solution) from about 1.550 to 1.800 g/cm^3. The
nucleic acid accumulates as a narrow band at the point in the gradient corresponding
to its buoyant density, ρ. Measuring the density of the solution at this point gives a
value of ρ for the nucleic acid. The value of ρ for double-stranded DNA increases
linearly with increasing content of G-C base pairs, thereby providing another method,
in addition to T_m determination, for estimating DNA nucleotide compositions ($\rho \simeq$
1.700 for 50% G-C content). Single-stranded DNA is 0.015 g/cm^3 more dense than
double-stranded DNA of the same nucleotide composition. RNA is more dense than
DNA in CsCl solution, and generally goes to the bottom of a CsCl gradient without
forming a band. However, it can be banded in other heavy-metal salts, such as
(Cs)$_2$SO$_4$.

　　Suppose that you are presented with an unknown sample of nucleic acid, and are
asked to characterize it. You find the following:

a. It shows a sharp absorbance–temperature transition with 30% hyperchromicity. On
quick cooling there is little decrease in optical density.

b. The undenatured material bands as a single species in a CsCl density gradient at
1.770 g/cm^3.

c. Upon heat denaturing and quick cooling (as in part a) followed by recentrifugation,
the original band is gone, and one new band, containing only half the original
amount of UV-absorbing material, has appeared at $\rho = 1.720$. When the contents of
the centrifuge cell are mixed thoroughly, held at an intermediate temperature to
allow annealing, and recentrifuged, the new band is gone and almost all of the original UV-absorbing material is found again at $\rho = 1.770$.

d. The sequence of steps in part c is carried out except that denaturation is accomplished
prior to centrifugation by treating the sample for 1 hr at pH = 12 followed by rapid

re-neutralization to pH = 7. The result of the first centrifugation is as in part c, but this banding pattern is not changed by the annealing procedure.

Interpret each of the foregoing observations, and deduce the structure of the original nucleic acid.

17.13 A solution of double-stranded DNA is heated and then cooled to room temperature over a 2-min interval. How will the absorbance at 260 nm change during cooling under the following conditions?
a. The solution is heated to just below T_m.
b. The solution is heated to well above T_m.
c. Can you think of three kinds of double-stranded polydeoxyribonucleotide structures (natural or synthetic) that will give a fully reversible absorbance–temperature profile in aqueous solution?

17.14 What is the axial ratio (length:diameter) of a viral DNA molecule 20 μm long?

17.15 The genes of an *E. coli* bacterium (average dimensions: 1–5 μm long, about 1 μm diameter) are carried on a single, very large DNA molecule more than 1 mm long. This molecule must be highly folded inside the cell, raising perplexing problems about the logistics of DNA replication and DNA-directed RNA and protein synthesis (Chapters 18 and 20). To get an idea of the magnitude of these problems, calculate the percentage of the internal space occupied by DNA in a bacterial cell with a volume of π μm^3 and a chromosome 1 mm long.

17.16 By spreading DNA on a film of basic protein, picking it up on a support, and then shadowing it with platinum (the **Kleinschmidt procedure**), it is possible to see DNA strands in the electron microscope, and to measure their lengths accurately. From the parameters given in Concept 17.2, answer the following questions.
a. Predict the length of bacteriophage T7 DNA, a duplex of molecular weight 2.5×10^7.
b. What is the mass per micrometer of a viral DNA molecule of 130×10^6 daltons?
c. How long is the gene for a tRNA of 88 nucleotides? (One DNA nucleotide pair determines one RNA nucleotide.)
d. How long is the gene that codes for cytochrome *c* (104 amino acids—one amino acid is coded for by three nucleotides)?
e. Is "one gene, one neuron" a reasonable hypothesis to explain the organization of the human brain? Assume that there are 2×10^{12} neurons in the human brain and that each must be identified by a different protein of at least 100 amino acids.

17.17 When two nearly identical samples of DNA (such as DNA molecules from mutant and wild-type virus) are mixed, denatured, and reannealed, homoduplexes and heteroduplexes are formed, as shown in Figure 17.17. Homoduplexes contain two strands from the same sample of DNA; heteroduplexes contain one strand from each of two different samples of DNA.

Sequence differences between the two DNA samples lead to noncomplementary regions in heteroduplexes that cannot H-bond and therefore remain single-stranded. If these regions are longer than 50–100 nucleotides, they can be seen as loops when the DNA is spread under appropriate conditions and examined by electron microscopy. Two common noncomplementary heteroduplex structures are shown in Figure 17.18.

Examination of heteroduplex DNA is a powerful method for mapping the physical locations of gross mutational changes, such as large deletions, additions, and substitutions in DNA molecules. From the data shown in Figure 17.19, construct a map of the DNA from the wild-type organism, showing the positions of the segments that are deleted in the two mutants.

17.18 In a population of the bacteriophage ϕC, which you have isolated from the sewers of Flushing, New York, you have found three deletion mutants, ϕC8, ϕC23, and ϕC92. To map these deletions physically you mix various combinations of the phages, lyse the phage particles to release DNA, and denature and reanneal the mixture of DNA to generate heteroduplexes, which you examine by electron microscopy. The results are shown in Figure 17.20.

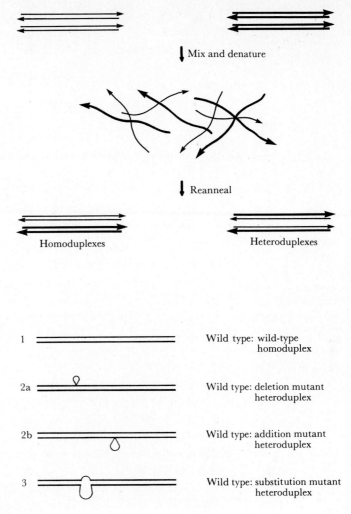

Figure 17.17
Formation of heteroduplex DNA
molecules (Problem 17.17).

Figure 17.18
Possible origins of deletion loops and substitution loops in
duplex structures (Problem 17.17). The complementary
strands of duplex DNA are represented as parallel lines,
with the wild-type strand uppermost in heteroduplex molecules. (In the electron microscope, double-stranded regions
appear thicker than the single-stranded loops.) In substitution mutants one sequence is replaced by another, often of
different length. Structures 2a and 2b are called **deletion
loops** (noncomplementarity in only one strand) and structure 3 is called a **substitution loop** (noncomplementarity in
both strands). A substitution loop does not necessarily indicate a substitution mutation.

Figure 17.19
The three heteroduplexes observed in pairwise mixtures of
wild-type and mutant DNAs
(Problem 17.17). Lengths of
DNA segments are indicated in
thousands of nucleotide pairs
(kilobases).

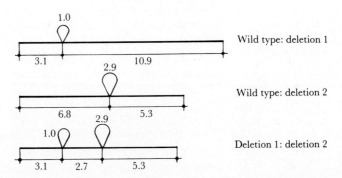

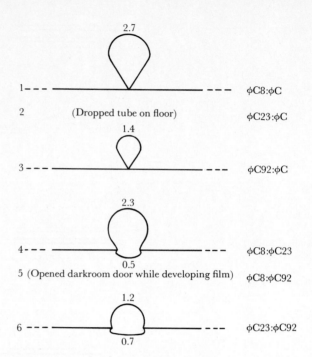

Figure 17.20
Heteroduplex analysis of DNA
from deletion mutants of bacteriophage φC (Problem 17.18).
Lengths of DNA segments are
indicated in kilobases.

a. Diagram as completely as possible the relative positions of the three deletions.

b. Draw the structure expected for the φC8:φC92 heteroduplex, whose picture was de-stroyed in the darkroom.

17.19   Heteroduplex analysis also can be used to determine sequence relationships between DNA molecules and to identify the origins of specific DNA substitutions, as in the following example.

Adenovirus type 2 (Ad2) normally will not infect African green monkey kidney (AGMK) cells in culture. However, if an AGMK cell is infected simultaneously with simian virus 40 (SV40) and Ad2, a large number of Ad2 progeny viruses are pro-duced. Evidently, Ad2 requires an additional function that can be supplied by SV40 for growth on AGMK cells.

Occasionally during a mixed infection of AGMK cells by Ad2 and SV40, SV40 DNA is inserted into an Ad2 DNA molecule. Usually, the resulting Ad2–SV40 hybrid viruses are defective in normal Ad2 growth; that is, they no longer infect human embryonic kidney (HEK) cells in culture. However, several nondefective Ad2–SV40 hybrid viruses have been isolated. The set of hybrid viruses described in this problem were isolated from *one* particular mixed infection. These nondefective (ND) hybrids infect both HEK and AGMK cells. Thus the nondefective hybrid viruses have ac-quired SV40 DNA without losing any *essential* Ad2 DNA.

To determine the size and position of the SV40 DNA that was inserted into Ad2, heteroduplex DNAs were prepared from pairwise mixtures of wild-type Ad2 and nondefective Ad2–SV40 hybrids and examined by electron microscopy.

a. From the data in Figure 17.21, calculate the amount of SV40 DNA that has been added and Ad2 DNA that has been deleted in each nondefective hybrid virus.

b. The formation of these nondefective hybrids involves three events: deletion of Ad2 DNA, deletion of SV40 DNA, and addition of SV40 DNA to Ad2 DNA. On the basis of the information in Figure 17.21, propose a sequence of reactions by which these hybrids were produced. (Remember that these nondefective hybrids all were isolated from *one* mixed infection.)

17.20   Explain why RNA is hydrolyzed by alkali, whereas DNA is not.

17.21   The two strands of duplex DNA cross one another a large number of times. If one could lay a stretch of DNA flat and count the number of times one strand crossed the other, one could determine directly the number of crossovers. For unnicked circular

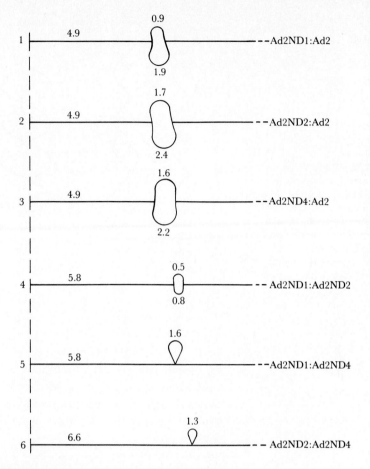

Figure 17.21
Heteroduplex analysis of DNA from nondefective Ad2–
SV40 hybrid virus (Problem 17.19). The left ends of all the
heteroduplexes are aligned at the position of the dashed
line. Lengths of DNA segments are indicated in kilobases.
Ad2 and SV40 are 36 kb and 5.2 kb in length, respectively.

DNA the number of crossovers equals the numbers of times the two strands are interlocked, which is a ˌpological quantity termed the **linking number**. For DNA in
solution the linkir. ˌumber is a combination of crossovers due to twisting of single
strands about the duplex axis (**primary coils**) and crossovers due to "writhing" of the
duplex about itself (**supercoils**). The relationship between primary coils and supercoils is not self-evident. This problem is designed to demonstrate that relationship
empirically.

The questions that follow can be examined best using a length of the kind of
twine that is helically wound from a number of smaller threads. By reference to Figure
17.22a decide whether your twine helix is wound right-handed or left-handed. Answer
the questions for your helix; the answers for a helix of opposite handedness will be the
opposite in every case.

a. Fix one end of your string and hold it away from you. Twist the end that is toward
   you clockwise as indicated in Figure 17.22b. Do the primary helices in your twine
   become wound more tightly (overwound) or more loosely (underwound)?
b. Twist your twine clockwise as in part a and then join the two ends to form a circle.
   Pull the twine tight to remove any tangles and then let it form interwound supercoils
   as shown in Figure 17.22c. Does your twine form right-handed or left-handed interwound supercoils? Carry out the same determination after twisting your twine counterclockwise. What is the relationship between overwinding or underwinding your
   primary helix and the handedness of the interwound supercoils?
c. A second class of supercoils, termed **toroidal supercoils,** is illustrated in Figure 17.22d.
   Hold a short section of twine between your fingers and overwind this section by

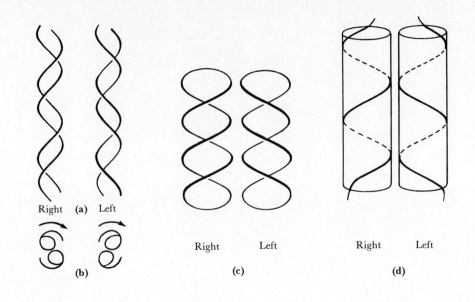

Figure 17.22
Primary coils and supercoils
(Problem 17.21). **(a), (b)** Vertical
and end-on views, respectively, of
right-handed and left-handed
helices. **(c)** Right-handed and
left-handed interwound
supercoils. **(d)** Right-handed and
left-handed toroidal supercoils.

twisting one end. If you hold just the right tension on the twine, it will form one or two toroidal supercoils before it flips into an interwound conformation. Does overwinding your twine produce right-handed or left-handed toroidal supercoils? Carry out the same determination after underwinding your twine. What is the relationship between overwinding or underwinding your primary helix and the handedness of the toroidal supercoils?

d. On the basis of your observations, deduce the relationship between overwinding and underwinding the primary DNA helix and the compensating interwound and toroidal supercoils.

17.22 a. DNA from the animal virus SV40 is a covalently closed, circular duplex. Under certain conditions it can be isolated from virus or infected cells in association with histones. In the electron microscope the DNA:histone aggregate appears as a circle of nucleosomes. However, when the histones are removed, the naked DNA forms right-handed supercoils (Figure 17.23a). From this information decide whether the primary helix in a native SV40 DNA molecule is underwound or overwound and deduce the handedness of the toroidal coiling of DNA around nucleosomes.

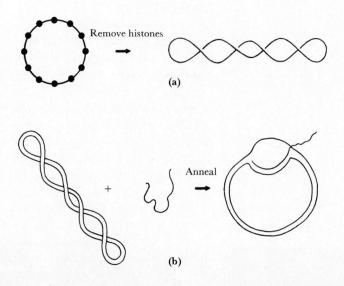

Figure 17.23
Supercoiled conformations of
SV40 DNA (Problem 17.22).
(a) Relationship between nucleosomal and naked DNA.
(b) D-loop formation.

b. If the naked, supercoiled DNA from SV40 is mixed with single-stranded SV40 DNA under reannealing conditions, displacement loops (D-loops) form (Figure 17.23b). That is because supercoiled DNA is in a higher energy state than nonsupercoiled DNA. The potential energy associated with supercoiling drives the uptake of exactly enough single-stranded DNA to remove all supercoils. Analyze the reaction indicated in Figure 17.23b and explain why uptake of single strands removes right-handed interwound supercoils.

c. D-loop formation illustrates the numerical relationship between primary coils and supercoils. It is possible to manipulate naked SV40 DNA in vitro to produce samples with various numbers of supercoils. Such DNAs take up different amounts of single-stranded DNA. From the data in Table 17.4, decide how many primary coils are equal to one supercoil.

Table 17.4
Uptake of Single Strands into D-loops (Problem 17.22)

DNA sample	Number of supercoils per molecule	Nucleotides of single-stranded DNA in D-loop
1	30	320
2	20	200
3	10	105

17.23   The nuclease DNase I hydrolyzes naked DNA in solution relatively nonspecifically to mononucleotides and dinucleotides. However, DNA that is wrapped around the surface of a nucleosome is much less susceptible to DNase I. If individual nucleosomes are incubated briefly with DNase I, the digested DNA forms a series of bands when it is denatured and subjected to gel electrophoresis. Each band in this "ladder" differs from adjacent bands by about 10 nucleotides. Offer an explanation for the difference in the digestion patterns between nucleosomal and naked DNA.

☆ 17.24   If one considers recombination by assortment only, how many different kinds of zygotes could one human couple potentially produce?

☆ 17.25   a. You are given two samples of DNA of equal molecular weight and equal percentage G-C. Analysis by sedimentation to equilibrium in a CsCl gradient reveals that one band is nearly twice as broad as the other. Propose an explanation.

b. Actinomycin preferentially binds to G-C rich regions, lowering their density in a CsCl gradient. How would actinomycin affect the density profiles of the two samples mentioned in part a?

☆ 17.26   It has been suggested that a DNA sequence bound by a tetrameric protein may be able to exist in a cloverleaf structure (Figure 17.24) that presents 4-fold symmetry to the protein. Assume such a structure, with strict 4-fold symmetry for five bases in every direction from the center of the cloverleaf and three random bases in the unpaired loops.

a. Write the base sequence of one strand of a region of DNA duplex that could form such a structure.

b. Draw the 4-fold symmetrical cloverleaf and an additional structure into which it could fold.

Figure 17.24
Potential cloverleaf structure for a DNA sequence (Problem 17.27).

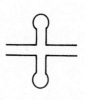

Answers

17.1 a. True

b. True. A purine base is composed of a six-membered pyrimidine ring fused to a five-membered imidazole ring.

c. True

d. False. There is no hydroxyl group at the 2'-position. The 3'-hydroxyl group is essential for formation of the 3'–5'-phosphodiester bonds in DNA.

e. True

f. False. The space occupied by one nucleotide pair along the axis of the helix is 0.34 nm. A complete turn of the helix occurs every 10 nucleotide pairs, or 3.4 nm.

g. False. There is no appropriate electronegative atom in adenine with which a thymine C-2 hydroxyl group could H-bond.

h. False. The complementary sequence must be pGpTpCpCpApG, because the two strands run in opposite directions.

i. True

j. True

k. True

l. False. Because all the viral DNA molecules are identical, they will have the same G-C content. Therefore, they will show a very sharp absorbance–temperature transition. Breaking the DNA of a human liver cell (total length about 5.5×10^9 nucleotide pairs) will yield many different fragments of 10^5 nucleotide pairs in length. These fragments are likely to be heterogeneous in G-C content and hence will give a broader absorbance–temperature transition.

m. False. Histones are present only in eucaryotic cells.

n. True

o. True

p. False. Procaryotic cells are occasionally partially diploid, and eucaryotic gametes are haploid.

17.2 a. nucleotides

b. adenine, guanine, cytosine, uracil

c. thymine, uracil

d. deoxyguanosine

e. complementary

f. two, adenine, guanine

g. annealing

h. Messenger (m), transfer (t)

i. core, linker

j. general (legitimate)

17.3 Only d; 1-methylguanine differs from guanine in its H-bonding properties.

17.4 See Figure 17.25.

17.5 See Figure 17.26.

17.6 a. The Henderson–Hasselbalch equation is

$$pH = pK_a + \log \frac{[A^-]}{[HA]}$$

For adenine,

$$7.0 = 4.2 + \log \frac{[\text{nonprotonated}]}{[\text{protonated}]}$$

$$2.8 = \log \frac{[\text{nonprotonated}]}{[\text{protonated}]}$$

$$\frac{[\text{nonprotonated}]}{[\text{protonated}]} = 6.3 \times 10^2$$

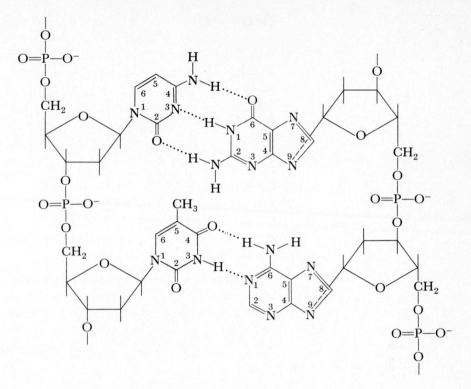

Figure 17.25
Structure of 5′-pCpT-3′

　　　⋮ ⋮

　　3′-GpAp–5′

(Answer 17.4).

that is, there are 6.3×10^2 molecules nonprotonated for every one protonated. Therefore, less than 0.2% of the adenine molecules will be protonated. For guanine, similar calculations indicate that less than 0.02% of the molecules will be protonated.

b. The predominance of the nonprotonated form is necessary for H-bonding of adenine. If the protonated form were predominant, then the plus charge and extra hydrogen at N-1 would make H-bond formation impossible. Protonation of guanine at N-7 has only minor effects on DNA helix formation, because N-7 is not involved in normal interstrand H-bonding.

17.7　See Figure 17.27. Structure a will predominate because more bases are H-bonded, thereby permitting more extensive stacking interactions.

17.8　a. In general the individual RNA molecules would not have the same potential for forming intramolecular H-bonds. This asymmetry is because the base pair G-U is permissible, whereas its complement A-C is not (Figure 17.28).

　　b. Except for the asymmetry due to G-U base pairing the two complementary RNAs would form identical hairpins. An array of such hairpins would be inverted in their $5' \rightarrow 3'$ order in the two RNA molecules (Figure 17.28).

17.9　a. The two 2-fold axes run vertically midway between the sugar phosphate backbones perpendicular to the long axis of the duplex. One passes through the center of one base pair; the second passes midway between adjacent base pairs.

　　b. A nucleotide sequence with perfect 2-fold symmetry is shown in Figure 17.29a. Nucleotide sequences with perfect 2-fold symmetry cannot be written for the other 2-fold axis in part a, because the center base pair cannot be made symmetric, as shown in Figure 17.29b. Note that the convention of placing the 5′ end of the top strand on the left means that we are looking at the minor groove surface of the sequence. Sequences with perfect and near-perfect (hyphenated) symmetry alike often are referred to as **palindromes,** by analogy to English phrases that read the same forward and backward, such as

ABLE WAS I ERE I SAW ELBA

2

　　c. The strand on your left always runs from 5′ in back of you to 3′ in front of you, regardless of which end you face. The 180° rotation makes no difference because it occurs about an axis parallel to the 2-fold axes of rotational symmetry. The orientation of strands in native DNA are shown in Figure 17.30.

17.10   The nucleotide pair can be reinserted in either of two ways: as it was originally, or rotated 180° about its axis of 2-fold rotational symmetry. Thus, for example, an ↑A-T↓ pair could be reinserted as a ↑T-A↓ pair.

17.11   a. There is matching symmetry between protein dimer and DNA sequence only in cases I and III. In cases II and IV the direction of the backbone spoils the symmetry match. For example, the DNA sequence that would be necessary to match the symmetry of II is

5′	3′	3′	5′
GCATCT		TCTACG	
CGTAGA		AGATGC	
3′	5′	5′	3′

b. The known examples of regulatory proteins that bind to symmetric DNA sequences all have an axis of 2-fold rotational symmetry as in III. This is most likely because stable protein dimers all have an axis of 2-fold rotational symmetry. Dimers with translational symmetry as shown in I are unlikely to form, because the open binding sites at both ends favor formation of long chains instead of discrete dimers.

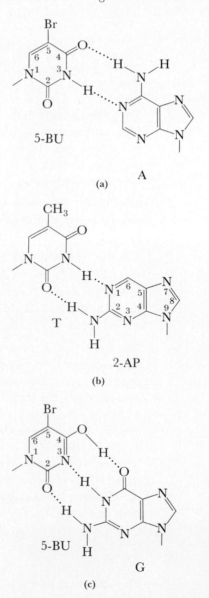

Figure 17.26
Structures of H-bonded base pairs. (a) 5-BU : A, (b) 2-AP : T, and (c) 5-BU : G (Answer 17.5).

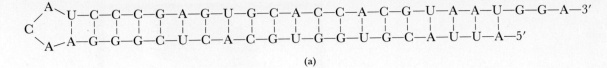

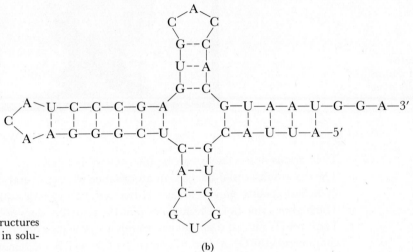

(a)

(b)

Figure 17.27
Alternative H-bonded structures for a polyribonucleotide in solution (Answer 17.7).

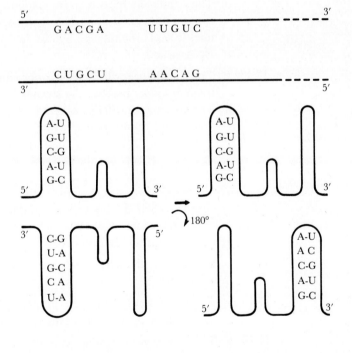

Figure 17.28
RNA secondary structure (Answer 17.8).

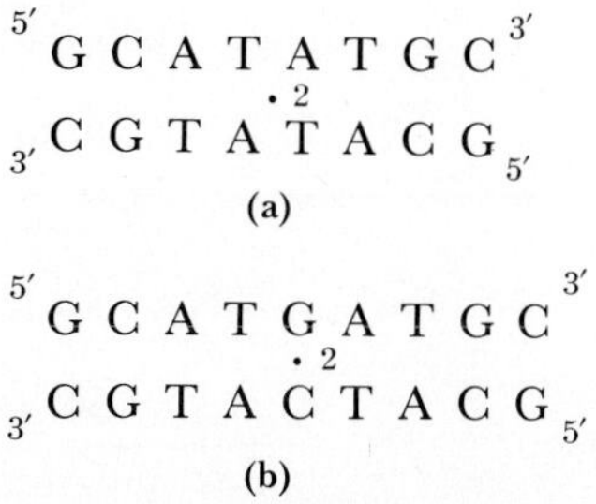

Figure 17.29
Sequences of nucleotide pairs with 2-fold symmetry (Answer 17.9). **(a)** A sequence with perfect 2-fold symmetry. **(b)** A sequence with partial 2-fold symmetry.

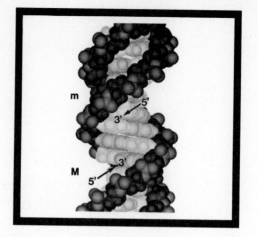

Figure 17.30
Strand orientation in native
DNA (Answer 17.9). M and m
denote the major and the minor
grooves, respectively.

17.12   The various observations can be interpreted as follows:
   a. The sharp substantial increase in absorbance with temperature and lack of decrease
      upon fast cooling suggest a fully H-bonded, two-stranded structure.
   b. The high ρ value in CsCl indicates that the structure does not consist of DNA alone.
   c. These results suggest that the two strands are of widely different ρ; one 1.720, which is
      characteristic of DNA, and the other >1.8, which is too dense to form a band in the
      gradient. The latter is still intact, however, and probably on the bottom of the cell in
      the first part of the experiment, because it can be recovered by annealing in the second
      part.
   d. The denser of the two strands apparently is destroyed by alkali. This observation
      confirms that it is not DNA, and suggests that it is RNA. Therefore, the original
      nucleic acid probably is a hybrid double helix, consisting of one RNA strand and one
      DNA strand.

17.13 a. The absorbance will decrease, approximately along the curve of increase, to near the
      original value, because the strands have not yet separated and are still in register.
   b. The absorbance will decrease only slightly, because complementary strands have sep-
      arated and cannot anneal again during the short period of cooling.
   c. A fully reversible melting curve requires either that the two strands do not separate
      above the T_m, or that the two strands are always in register, so that they can pair no
      matter how they come together. Three examples of such molecules would be a hair-
      pin-shaped (two strands joined at one end) or cross-linked double helix, a covalently
      closed circular double helix, or a double helix in which the two strands have very
      simple repeating sequences—for example, one strand poly dG, the other poly dC, or
      both strands alternating dAdT.

17.14   Because the diameter of DNA is 2.0 nm, and $1\ \mu m = 10^3$ nm, the axial ratio of this
      viral DNA is 1×10^4.

17.15   A DNA molecule 1 mm ($10^3\ \mu m$) long and 1.0 nm ($10^{-3}\ \mu m$) in radius will occupy a
      volume of $\pi \times 10^{-3}\ \mu m^3$. This represents 0.1% of a cell volume of $\pi\ \mu m^3$.

17.16 a. The length in nucleotide pairs is

$$\frac{2.5 \times 10^7 \text{ daltons}}{650 \text{ daltons/nucleotide pair}} = 3.8 \times 10^4 \text{ nucleotide pairs}$$

   Therefore, the contour length is

$$(3.8 \times 10^4 \text{ nucleotides})(0.34 \text{ nm/nucleotide}) = 1.3 \times 10^4 \text{ nm} = 13.0\ \mu m$$

   b. For any DNA, the mass per micrometer may be calculated as

$$\frac{650 \text{ daltons/nucleotide pair}}{0.34 \text{ nm/nucleotide pair} \times 10^{-3}\ \mu m/nm} = 1.9 \times 10^6 \text{ daltons}/\mu m$$

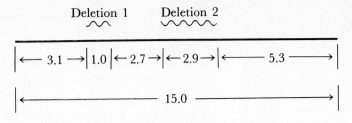

Deletion 1   Deletion 2

Figure 17.31
Map of a wild-type DNA (Answer 17.17). Segments that are deleted in the two mutants are indicated by wavy lines. Numbers indicate DNA lengths in kilobases.

c. 88 nucleotides $\times$ 0.34 nm/nucleotide = 30 nm or 0.03 μm

d. 312 nucleotides $\times$ 0.34 nm/nucleotide = 106 nm or 0.11 μm

e. Because each neuronal protein would require a gene $\simeq$ 0.1 μm in length, 2×10^{12} neuronal genes would require $\simeq 2 \times 10^{11}$ μm of DNA, which is 2×10^{5} m or 200 km of DNA. Needless to say, the hypothesis is not reasonable. (The total length of DNA in the human genome is about 2 m.)

17.17   See Figure 17.31.

17.18   a. Deletions that partially overlap lead to heteroduplexes with substitution loops, because each DNA strand carries nucleotide sequences that are not represented in the other. From heteroduplexes 1 and 3, the lengths of the deleted DNA segments in ϕC8 and ϕC92 are 2.7 kb and 1.4 kb, respectively. From heteroduplex 4, the length of the deleted DNA segment in ϕC23 is either 0.9 kb with a 0.4 kb overlap or 4.5 kb with a 2.2 kb overlap. Analysis of heteroduplex 6 indicates that ϕC23 must be 0.9 kb with a 0.2 kb overlap with ϕC92. Because of your somewhat sloppy technique there is an ambiguity in the relative positions of ϕC8 and ϕC92, as indicated in Figure 17.32a.

b. See Figure 17.32b.

17.19   a. In each of the substitution loops in heteroduplexes 1 through 3, one of the single strands is from the Ad2ND mutant and corresponds to the added SV40 DNA; the other single strand is from Ad2 and corresponds to the segment of Ad2 DNA that is deleted in the Ad2ND mutant. Analysis of heteroduplexes 4 through 6 shows which strand corresponds to which DNA.

Because SV40 DNA is inserted 4.9 kb from one end in each Ad2ND, the loops at 5.8 kb in heteroduplexes 4 and 5 indicate that there are 0.9 kb (5.8 kb − 4.9 kb) of paired SV40 DNA in each. From this observation it can be concluded that the SV40 added to Ad2ND1 is 0.9 kb in length and is complementary to the first 0.9 kb of the longer pieces of SV40 DNA in Ad2ND2 and Ad2ND4. The section of Ad2 DNA deleted in Ad2ND1 must be 1.9 kb.

Because all the SV40 DNA from Ad2ND1 is paired in heteroduplex 4, one of the single strands in the substitution loop of heteroduplex 4 corresponds to Ad2 DNA that is present in Ad2ND1 but deleted in Ad2ND2, and the other strand corresponds to the remaining portion of SV40 DNA in Ad2ND2. Therefore, Ad2ND2 contains 1.7 kb of SV40 DNA (1.7 kb − 0.9 kb = 0.8 kb) and is missing 2.4 kb of Ad2 DNA (2.4 kb − 1.9 kb = 0.5 kb).

Figure 17.32
Results of heteroduplex analysis of DNA from bacteriophage ϕC mutants (Answer 17.18). **(a)** Relative positions of the DNA segments deleted in three deletion mutants. **(b)** Possible ϕC8 : ϕC92 heteroduplexes. Numbers indicate lengths of DNA in kilobases.

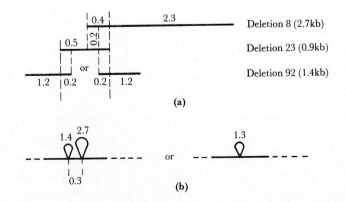

Because all the SV40 DNA from Ad2ND2 is paired in heteroduplex 6, the amount of SV40 DNA in Ad2ND4 must be equal to or greater than 1.7 kb. Thus 2.2 kb of SV40 DNA are in Ad2ND4 and 1.6 kb of Ad2 DNA are missing. The loop patterns in heteroduplexes 5 and 6 arise because Ad2ND4 contains more SV40 DNA and more Ad2 DNA than either Ad2ND1 or Ad2ND2. For example, in heteroduplex 6 the length of the single strand (1.3 kb) equals the extra SV40 DNA (2.2 kb − 1.7 kb) plus the excess Ad2 DNA (2.4 kb − 1.6 kb). These results are summarized in Table 17.5.

Table 17.5
Results of Heteroduplex
Analysis of DNA from
Nondefective Ad2–SV40
Hybrid Virus (Answer
17.19)

	SV40 added	Ad2 deleted
Ad2ND1	0.9 kb	1.9 kb
Ad2ND2	1.7 kb	2.4 kb
Ad2ND4	2.2 kb	1.6 kb

b. The information in Figure 17.21 provides three important pieces of data that are relevant to the formation of these nondefective hybrids.

  1. In all three hybrids SV40 DNA is inserted at the same point on the Ad2 DNA (4.9 kb from one end).
  2. In all three hybrids the insertion of SV40 DNA is at the same point on the SV40 DNA (because the inserted DNA in each is complementary).
  3. The Ad2 DNA deleted in all three hybrids extends from 4.9 kb (on the Ad2 DNA molecule) a variable distance toward the far end of the molecule.

A simple two-step mechanism can account for these three observations. Step 1 was common to the formation of all the hybrids and involved insertion of a complete SV40 molecule into Ad2 DNA (Figure 17.33). Step 2 was different for each hybrid and involved deletion of the contiguous segments of SV40 and Ad2 at the right-hand junction of SV40 and Ad2 DNA (Figure 17.33).

17.20 RNA is alkali labile because of the 2′-hydroxyl group of each ribonucleotide. This group is not present in deoxyribonucleotides. Alkaline hydrolysis of an RNA phosphodiester bond occurs by ionization of the 2′-hydroxyl group and attack by the resulting —O⁻ on the adjacent phosphoryl group. This reaction breaks the phosphate ester bond to the 5′-hydroxyl group of the next sugar, forming a 2′,3′-cyclic phosphodiester, which then is hydrolyzed to give either the 2′ or 3′ nucleotide.

17.21 See Table 17.6. The two kinds of DNA supercoils that can result from an underwound primary helix are termed negative supercoils. Similarly an overwound primary helix produces positive DNA supercoils.

Table 17.6
Relationship between
Primary Coils and
Supercoils (Answer 17.21)

Helix	Clockwise twisting	Counterclockwise twisting	Overwound primary helix		Underwound primary helix	
Left	Overwinds primary helix	Underwinds primary helix	Right interwound	Left toroid	Left interwound	Right toroid
Right (DNA)	Underwinds primary helix	Overwinds primary helix	Left interwound	Right toroid	Right interwound	Left toroid

17.22 a. This problem involves the relationship between primary coils and supercoils that was derived in Problem 17.21. The right-handed interwound supercoils that are formed when the histones are removed indicate that the primary helix is underwound and therefore that the toroidal coiling around nucleosomes must be left-handed.

  b. The only difference on the two sides of the arrow in Figure 17.23b is the absence of supercoils on the right. Note that the amounts of double-stranded DNA and single-stranded DNA on both sides of the arrow are identical. The formation of the bubble

Step 1: Insertion

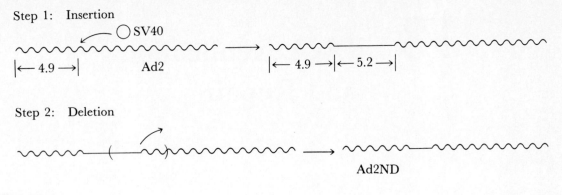

Step 2: Deletion

Figure 17.33
Proposed mechanism for generation of Ad2–SV40 nondefective hybrid virus (Answer 17.19). Distances are indicated in kilobases.

in the circular duplex essentially concentrates the underwinds in the primary helix into a single region of the molecule. Normally such a bubble does not form because the loss of base-pairing and stacking interactions makes it energetically less favorable than supercoiling. However, the pairing of single-stranded DNA with one strand in the bubble supplies the lost base-pairing and stacking interactions.

c. The average number of nucleotides of single-stranded DNA in D-loops per supercoil is 10.4. Because there are 10.4 nucleotides per primary coil of DNA in solution, these data indicate that one primary coil is equal to one supercoil.

17.23   The simplest explanation is that DNase I binds DNA in a specific orientation and that the histone octamer sterically restricts access of DNase I to the DNA. Evidently DNA on the surface of a nucleosome is accessible to DNase I cleavage only about once per turn of the helix. Support for this explanation comes from the observation that DNA bound to other surfaces gives a similar ladder pattern after digestion with DNase I.

18 DNA Replication and Repair

The genomes of all cells are composed of double-stranded DNA. Many viral genomes also consist of double-stranded DNA, but some are composed of single-stranded DNA or RNA. In all organisms genetic information is transmitted to subsequent generations by precise replication of nucleic acid genomes. These genomes are being damaged continually by radiation and chemicals in the environment, and must be repaired constantly to preserve their information. This chapter considers the basic steps and principal enzymes involved in DNA replication and DNA repair.

Concepts

18.1 Replication of cellular chromosomes follows a few simple rules.

    A. DNA replication begins at unique nucleotide sequences called **origins of replication** (Figure 18.1). The circular chromosomes of procaryotes generally have one origin of replication. The linear chromosomes of eucaryotes have many origins of replication usually spaced about 30–100 kilobase pairs (kb) apart. (One kilobase equals 1000 nucleotides of single-stranded DNA or 1000 nucleotide pairs of double-stranded DNA.)

    B. Each new strand of DNA is initiated by synthesis of an RNA primer (Figure 18.1). These primers are removed at a subsequent step and replaced with DNA.

    C. Nucleotides are added one at a time to the 3′ end of each growing nucleotide chain. The resulting 5′ → 3′ direction of chain growth is the same for both RNA and DNA (Figure 18.1).

    D. At each **replication fork** (Figure 18.1), synthesis of the **leading strand** is continuous and synthesis of the **lagging strand** is discontinuous (Figure 18.1). The short discontinuous segments, which later are joined, often are called **Okazaki fragments** after their discoverer. The leading strand is synthesized in the same direction as fork movement; the lagging strand is synthesized in the opposite direction.

    E. Replication forks move in both directions away from origins of replication (Figure 18.1). Bidirectional replication continues until adjacent forks fuse and replication of daughter strands is completed.

    F. Each daughter duplex consists of one parental strand and one newly synthesized strand (Figure 18.1). This mode of replication is called **semiconservative,** because the primary structures of the individual parental strands are conserved but the structure of the parental duplex is not.

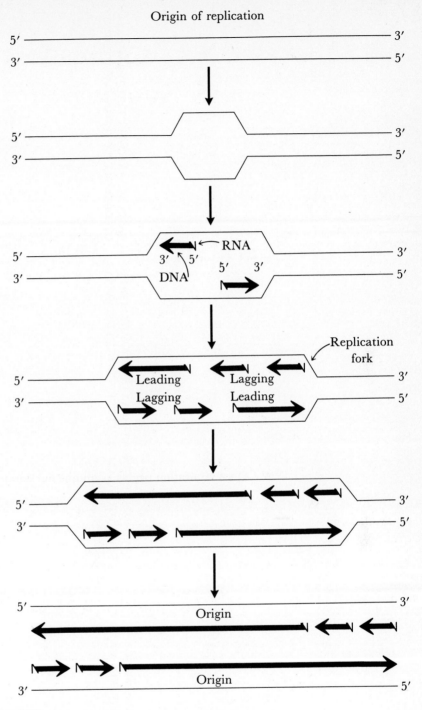

Figure 18.1
Overview of cellular DNA replication. Replication of a linear segment of a chromosome is shown here. In circular procaryotic genomes, the two replication forks eventually would fuse with one another. In linear eucaryotic chromosomes, these two replication forks would fuse with replication forks from adjacent origins.

18.2   DNA replication is regulated at initiation.

A.   DNA replication begins when special **initiation proteins** convert quiescent origins into active centers for replication. Neither initiation proteins nor origins are characterized sufficiently to define a molecular mechanism for initiation. An apparent characteristic of origins from which replication is bidirectional is the presence of palindromic regions with 2-fold symmetry. Such sequences can be arranged into secondary struc-

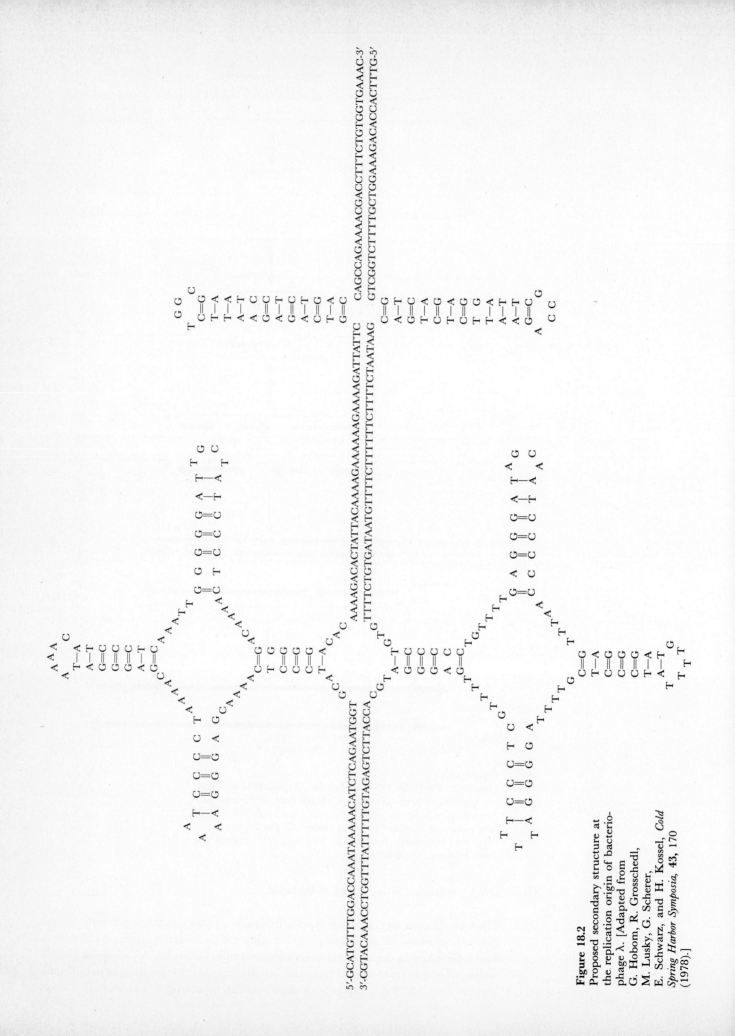

Figure 18.2
Proposed secondary structure at
the replication origin of bacterio-
phage λ. [Adapted from
G. Hobom, R. Grosschedl,
M. Lusky, G. Scherer,
E. Schwarz, and H. Kossel, *Cold
Spring Harbor Symposia*, **43**, 170
(1978).]

tures, as illustrated for the elaborate origin of bacteriophage λ in Figure 18.2. Because the mechanism of initiation is unclear, it is not known whether origin function depends on such secondary structures or simply on the symmetry present in the duplex.

B. Procaryotes grow and divide at rates that depend on cell culture conditions. However, the rate at which their chromosomes are replicated is relatively constant. Under fast growth conditions new rounds of replication are initiated before the first doubling is complete. Under slow growth conditions intervals without replication occur. The frequency of initiation of replication in procaryotes correlates well with cell mass, so that the cell mass per chromosome origin is relatively constant. The molecular mechanism underlying this constancy is unknown.

C. Eucaryotic cells replicate their DNA during a distinct portion of the cell cycle termed **S phase** (Figure 18.3). This DNA synthetic phase is separated from mitosis by two nonreplicative phases, G_1 and G_2. Actively growing cells progress around the cell cycle in a carefully regulated manner, becoming committed to replicate their DNA at a specific stage in G_1. Differentiated, nongrowing cells, which are the majority in an adult organism, are arrested earlier in G_1 in the G_0 offshoot.

18.3 **DNA replication is catalyzed in ordered steps by sequential enzyme action.**

A. The parental duplex in front of the moving replication fork is unwound and prepared for replication by several proteins (Figure 18.4). The process is best understood in procaryotes. In *E. coli* the product of the *rep* gene, DNA helicase, catalyzes energy-dependent unwinding of the duplex using two ATPs per nucleotide pair separated. Strand separation is stabilized by proteins that bind to single-stranded DNA. The twist generated ahead of the replication fork by unwinding is relieved by enzymes called **topoisomerases** that catalyze introduction and repair of transient "nicks" to provide swivels for rotation of one parental strand around the other. The coated single

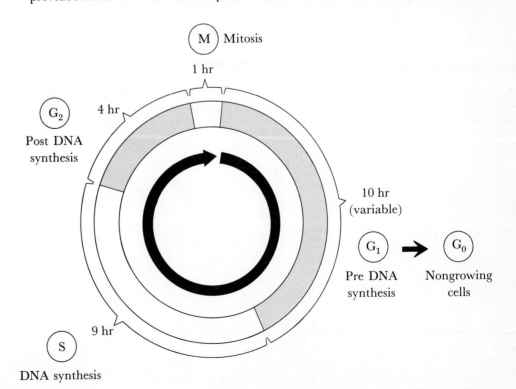

Figure 18.3
Sequence of stages in the eucaryotic cell cycle.

strands are bound by a collection of "prepriming" proteins, including the products of the *dnaB* and *dnaC* genes. These proteins in some manner prepare the way for nucleotide polymerization to begin.

B. An enzyme, termed **primase** in *E. coli*, binds to the preprimed strands and catalyzes synthesis of the RNA primers that begin each new strand of DNA (Figure 18.4). Primase, which is distinct from the RNA polymerase used in transcription (Concept 20.2), is encoded by the *dnaG* gene. Primase catalyzes polymerization of ribonucleoside 5'-triphosphates to form 3'—5'-phosphodiester bonds with release of PP_i. The sequence of monomer addition is dictated by complementary base pairing to a template strand of DNA. The direction of polymerization is always $5' \rightarrow 3'$; that is, incoming nucleoside triphosphates add to the 3' end of the growing chain. The chain lengths of primers typically are 10–50 nucleotides. The lagging, or discontinuous, strand at a replication fork is primed about once every 1000 nucleotides in procaryotes and about once every 200 nucleotides in eucaryotes.

C. The principal synthetic enzyme, DNA polymerase, extends the primers in the $5' \rightarrow 3'$ direction by catalyzing addition of deoxyribonucleoside 5'-triphosphates to the primer 3' ends (Figure 18.4). The details of DNA polymerization are analogous to those of RNA polymerization. However, DNA polymerases, unlike RNA polymerases, have an absolute requirement for a primer and cannot initiate DNA strands de novo. The identified DNA polymerases normally function preferentially in replicative or repair synthesis (Table 18.1; Concept 18.5). The replicative enzyme in *E. coli*, DNA polymerase III holoenzyme, is composed of several subunits, one of which is encoded by the *dnaE* gene. The $3' \rightarrow 5'$ exonuclease activity of DNA polymerase III permits the enzyme to "proofread" newly added nucleotides and catalyze removal of any that are base-paired incorrectly.

D. RNA primers are removed by stepwise degradation from the 5' end, and adjacent DNA fragments are elongated at the 3' end, thereby replacing RNA segments with DNA and juxtaposing the 3' and 5' ends of neighboring DNA fragments. In *E. coli*

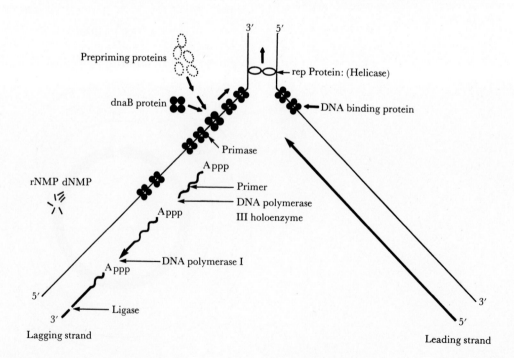

Figure 18.4
Diagram of a replication fork in *E. coli*. (Adapted from A. Kornberg, *DNA Replication*, W. H. Freeman, San Francisco, 1980, p. 411.)

these steps are catalyzed concomitantly by DNA polymerase I, which has $5' \rightarrow 3'$ exonuclease activity as well as polymerase activity (Figure 18.4; Table 18.1). Eucaryotic DNA polymerases do not possess this exonuclease activity (Table 18.1). Therefore, in eucaryotic cells RNA segments must be degraded by a separate enzyme. A probable candidate for this enzyme is ribonuclease H, which catalyzes hydrolysis of the RNA strand of a DNA:RNA hybrid duplex.

Table 18.1
Functions and Enzymatic Activities of Cellular DNA Polymerases

	E. coli			Eucaryotes	
	PolI	PolII	PolIII	Polα	Polβ
Function	Repair	Unknown	Replication	Replication	Repair
DNA polymerase ($5' \rightarrow 3'$)	+	+	+	+	+
Exonuclease ($3' \rightarrow 5'$)	+	+	+	−	−
Exonuclease ($5' \rightarrow 3'$)	+	−	+	−	−

E. Adjoining DNA segments are linked to form the growing daughter strands (Figure 18.4). DNA ligase catalyzes formation of a phosphodiester bond between the 3'-hydroxyl group and the 5'-phosphoryl group of adjacent nucleotides, as shown in Figure 18.5. The reaction is driven by coupling to breakdown of a high-energy phosphate bond. In *E. coli*, the source of phosphate-bond energy is NAD^+, which is cleaved to nicotinamide mononucleotide (NMN) and AMP. In eucaryotic cells ATP is cleaved to AMP and PP_i.

18.4 Organelles and viruses display a rich variety of replication mechanisms.

A. The circular duplex DNA genomes of mitochondria are replicated by **displacement-loop (D-loop)** synthesis (Figure 18.6). Synthesis of one daughter strand begins at a unique origin and proceeds unidirectionally around the circle. Synthesis of the other daughter strand begins from a second origin, which is activated when the displacement loop passes it. Each strand is initiated by an RNA primer and is completed by continuous synthesis.

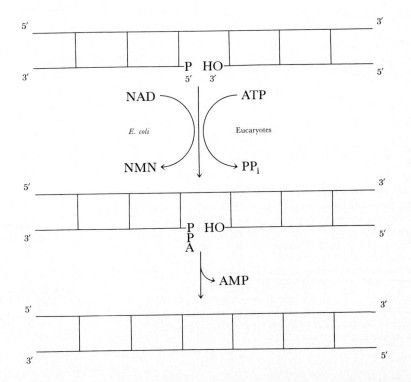

Figure 18.5
Closure of a nick by DNA ligase.

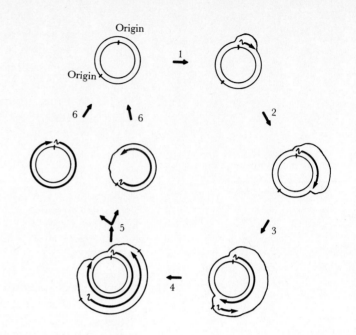

Figure 18.6
D-loop synthesis of mitochondrial DNA. (1) Synthesis of a single-stranded fragment of specific size (450 nucleotides in mouse cell mitochondria). (2) Expansion of D-loop. (3) Initiation of complementary strand synthesis. (4) Simultaneous unidirectional synthesis of both strands. (5) Resolution into nicked and gapped circular molecules. (6) Completion of the molecules and ligation.

B. Rolling-circle DNA replication is involved in amplification of ribosomal genes in some eucaryotes, in the late stage of bacteriophage λ DNA replication, and in the replication of small, single-stranded bacteriophages, such as ϕX174. Rolling-circle replication produces linear copies from a circular parental duplex. A specific single-strand nick in the parental duplex provides a 3'-hydroxyl group that is extended by continuous DNA synthesis. The displaced 5' end of the nicked strand serves as the template strand for discontinuous synthesis during gene amplification and λ replication, but remains single-stranded in ϕX174 viral-strand synthesis (Figure 18.7).

C. Replication of single-stranded RNA tumor-producing (**oncogenic**) viruses proceeds through a complementary DNA strand (Figure 18.8). Each virus brings into the in-

Figure 18.7
Rolling-circle replication of ϕX174 viral strands. Upon infection the single-stranded (+) DNA from the virus is replicated entirely by host-cell enzymes to form double-stranded (replicative form, RF1) DNA. RF1 is replicated to form several copies (not shown). The product of the phage A gene initiates viral-strand replication by nicking the viral strand at the origin of replication. Each time the A protein passes the origin after a round of replication, it nicks the regenerated origin and closes the ends of the single-stranded DNA to form a viral (+) circle. In the presence of the other products of the phage genes, this viral strand is packaged into a phage particle.

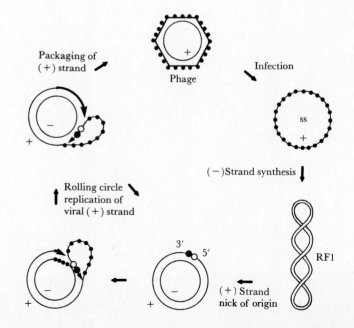

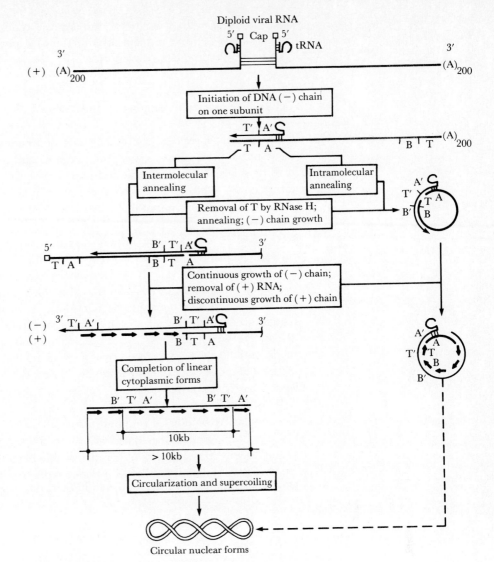

Figure 18.8
Replication of an RNA tumor virus. Avian sarcoma virus has a repeated sequence of about 80 nucleotides at each end, designated here as T for terminal redundancy. A and B stand for unique sequences bordering T. A tryptophan tRNA is H-bonded to the RNA adjacent to A. Letters with primes stand for complementary sequences. After infection, the tRNA primer is extended to the 5′ end of one genome. RNase H, which specifically hydrolyzes RNA in an RNA:DNA hybrid, removes the redundant sequence of RNA. After annealing of T′ to the same or the other genome, replication continues. (Adapted from A. Kornberg, *DNA Replication*, W. H. Freeman, San Francisco, 1980, p. 600.)

fected cell two copies of its RNA genome H-bonded together near their 5′ ends, two tryptophan tRNAs each H-bonded to one of the genomes about 100 nucleotides from the 5′ end, and several molecules of an RNA-dependent DNA polymerase, commonly called **reverse transcriptase**. The linear RNA template is copied into a circular DNA strand by reverse transcriptase, which uses the 3′-hydroxyl of the tRNA as primer. As synthesis of this DNA strand nears completion, the RNA chain is removed by the ribonuclease H activity of reverse transcriptase and replaced by DNA. The resulting circular DNA duplex can be incorporated into a host chromosome where it serves as a template for producing viral RNA.

18.5 Cells efficiently repair damage to their DNA.

A. Cellular DNA is exposed continually to radiation and chemicals from the environment and to highly reactive free radicals generated in metabolism. These agents can perturb the replication process and damage the DNA directly, leading to missing, incorrect, or altered bases, interstrand cross-links, and strand breaks. Unrepaired damage can produce mutations that reduce cell viability or cause cell death.

B. Normal cells possess a variety of pathways for removing damaged or unpaired nucleotides and replacing them with correct nucleotides. One major pathway is **excision repair** (Figure 18.9). The basic steps in excision repair are straightforward: The damage is recognized, an adjacent phosphodiester bond is broken, the damaged portion along with some neighboring nucleotides is excised, and the deleted stretch is resynthesized using the intact complementary strand as template. In some cases a glycosylase, which catalyzes hydrolysis of the bond holding the base to its adjacent sugar, initiates the repair process by removing an altered or incorrect base. The missing base also can be replaced directly by **"insertases,"** which catalyze transfer of the correct base from a free nucleotide to the vacant sugar residue in the DNA.

C. The repair of UV-induced radiation damage to DNA has been studied extensively. UV irradiation causes the dimerization of adjacent pyrimidine bases in the same strand, thereby forming a "kink" in the double helix (Figure 18.10). One process for repair of pyrimidine dimers, called **photoreactivation,** involves an enzyme that in the presence of visible light can reverse the damage by catalyzing hydrolysis of the dimers.

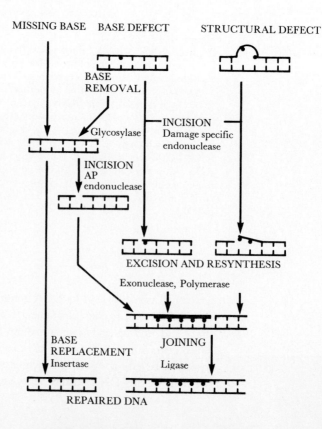

Figure 18.9
Overview of excision repair. AP stands for either apurinic or apyrimidinic. [Adapted from P. C. Hanawalt, P. K. Cooper, A. K. Ganesan, and C. A. Smith, *Annual Review of Biochemistry,* **48,** 783 (1979).]

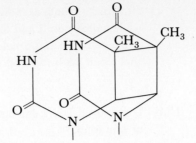

Figure 18.10
Structure of a UV-induced thymine dimer.

The mechanism of excision repair of pyrimidine dimers in *E. coli* is shown in Figure 18.11. Mutant *E. coli* defective in the *uvrA*, *uvrB*, or *uvrC* genes cannot carry out excision repair and consequently are abnormally sensitive to UV light.

If a replication fork passes a pyrimidine dimer before it has been repaired, the Okazaki fragment opposite the dimer cannot be synthesized. Excision repair cannot act opposite a single-stranded gap. In this case recombinational processes can furnish

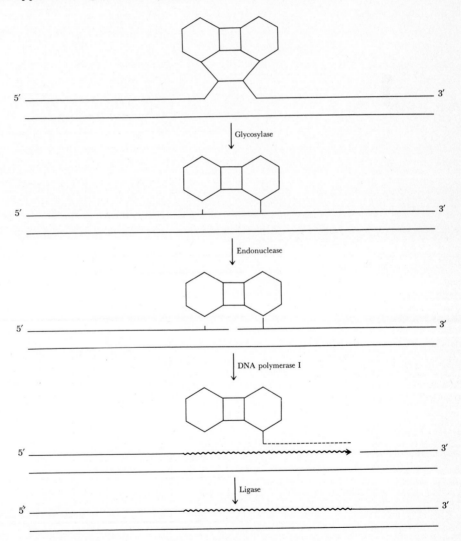

Figure 18.11
Excision repair of thymine dimers in *E. coli*. A glycosylase breaks the bond holding the 5′ member of the dimer to its deoxyribose. An endonuclease then breaks the phosphodiester bond between the two thymines. DNA polymerase I removes the damaged sections on either side of the nick and fills in the gap. Ligase seals the final nick to complete the repair process. (Wavy line indicates segment replaced by repair synthesis.)

a template strand, as shown in Figure 18.12. Both daughter duplexes then contain one undamaged strand and therefore can be restored by normal repair processes. Mutant *E. coli* defective in the *recA* or *recBC* genes cannot carry out the recombinational step in this repair pathway and thus are abnormally UV sensitive.

18.6 Unrepaired DNA damage is a potential source of mutation.

A. When a replication complex encounters DNA damage, it may copy the template strand incorrectly. Such mistakes alter the information content of the DNA, causing heritable mutations. If the damage is minor, the replication complex usually synthesizes an intact daughter strand in which any errors are confined to the site of the damage. If the damage is major, the replication complex may stall at the site. In *E. coli* such a stalled replication complex generates an undefined molecular signal, which induces a special set of survival enzymes, termed **SOS functions**. These functions

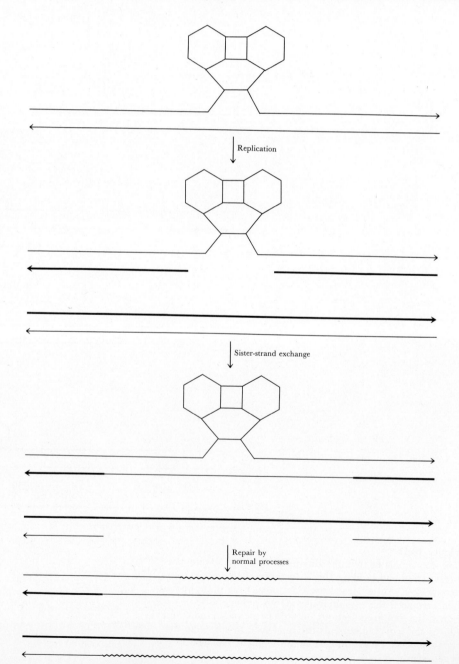

Figure 18.12
Recombinational repair of UV-induced DNA damage in *E. coli* utilizing sister-strand exchange. Heavy and wavy lines represent DNA synthesized by replication and repair, respectively.

apparently relax the fidelity of replication, permitting the replication complex to synthesize DNA opposite the damaged template strand. The result often is mutation not only at the site of the damage but elsewhere as well.

B. If mutations occur only at the site of the damage, the damaging agent is said to promote **direct mutagenesis.** Most mutagens used experimentally operate in this manner (see Table 21.1). If mutations occur at other sites as well because of the relaxed fidelity of replication, the damaging agent is said to promote **indirect mutagenesis.** Interestingly, most cancer-causing chemicals (**carcinogens**) in the environment apparently promote indirect mutagenesis.

18.7   Additional concepts and techniques are presented in the Problems section.

A. The Meselson–Stahl experiment. Problems 18.3 and 18.8.

B. A genetic approach to distinguishing unidirectional and bidirectional replication in bacteria. Problem 18.9.

C. Nearest-neighbor nucleotide analysis. Problems 18.14, 18.15, and 18.16.

D. Topoisomerases. Problem 18.17.

E. The mechanism of single-stranded viral RNA replication via complementary RNA. Problem 18.20.

F. Replication of chromosome ends. Problems 18.21 and 18.22.

G. Rolling-hairpin mechanism of parvovirus replication. Problem 18.22.

References

COMPREHENSIVE TEXTS

Lehninger: Chapter 32

Metzler: Chapter 15

Stryer: Chapter 24

White et al.: Chapter 25

OTHER REFERENCES

R. Devoret, "Bacterial Tests for Potential Carcinogens," *Scientific American,* August 1979, p. 40.

P. C. Hanawalt, P. K. Cooper, A. K. Ganesan, and C. A. Smith, "DNA Repair in Bacteria and Mammalian Cells," *Annual Review of Biochemistry,* **48,** 783 (1979).

A. Kornberg, *DNA Replication,* W. H. Freeman, San Francisco, 1980.

Problems

18.1   Answer the following with true or false. If false, explain why.

a. All nucleic acid replication is directed by complementary base pairing.

b. After one replication of a duplex DNA molecule, some of the daughter DNA molecules contain no parental material.

c. Each procaryotic chromosome has one origin of replication, whereas each eucaryotic chromosome has many.

d. In *E. coli* the rate of DNA chain elongation during chromosome replication varies with cell culture conditions.

e. Cells in the G_1 phase of the cell cycle are diploid, whereas cells in the G_2 phase are tetraploid.

f. Unidirectional replication of a closed circular DNA duplex requires introduction of swivel points to relieve twist. However, if replication is bidirectional, no swivels are needed because unwinding occurs in the opposite sense at the two replication forks, whose twists therefore cancel each other out.

g. Because all known DNA polymerases catalyze chain elongation in the $5' \rightarrow 3'$ direction, there must be an undiscovered enzyme for catalyzing $3' \rightarrow 5'$ elongation of the second strand at the replication fork.

h. All local chain growth at the replication fork proceeds in the $5' \rightarrow 3'$ direction, despite the occurrence of net elongation of one strand in the $3' \rightarrow 5'$ direction.

i. An inhibitor that blocked all RNA synthesis would not immediately affect DNA synthesis.

j. DNA polymerase I in *E. coli* and RNase H in eucaryotes both remove RNA primers.

k. In theory, a mutant defective in DNA ligase should be able to carry out neither chromosome replication nor excision repair.

l. The function of DNA polymerase III remains a mystery, because mutants lacking this enzyme appear normal in both chromosome replication and DNA repair synthesis.

m. Of all the known DNA polymerases, only the RNA-dependent DNA polymerase (reverse transcriptase) of RNA tumor viruses does not require a primer.

n. The DNA ligase reaction in *E. coli* requires NAD^+ as an oxidizing agent.

o. So far there is no evidence for RNA-directed DNA synthesis in either normal or virus-infected procaryotic cells.

p. During excision repair a damaged stretch of DNA is recognized, excised, and resynthesized using the intact complementary strand as template.

18.2 a. Each Okazaki fragment is synthesized with a short stretch of _____ linked to its _____ end.

b. Chain growth of all Okazaki fragments occurs in the _____ direction.

c. The $3' \rightarrow 5'$ exonuclease activity of DNA polymerase III serves a _____ function, which permits the enzyme to remove a newly added nucleotide that is incorrectly base-paired.

d. Synthesis of the _____ strand is _____ and in the same direction as the movement of the replication fork; synthesis of the _____ strand is _____ and opposite to the direction of fork movement.

e. Whereas bacterial chromosome replication occurs at only two sites at any time, _____ DNA synthesis may take place simultaneously at many sites on the bacterial chromosome.

f. The circular genomes of mitochondria are replicated by _____ synthesis.

g. _____ replication produces linear copies from a circular parental duplex.

h. In some cases damaged bases are removed by _____ and replaced directly by _____ .

i. Most mutagens used experimentally promote _____ mutagenesis, whereas most carcinogens promote _____ mutagenesis.

18.3 The semiconservative mode of replication was predicted by Watson and Crick from the base-pairing rules of the double helix. Subsequently, this prediction was proven correct by Meselson and Stahl, who showed that when cells of *E. coli* with isotopically labeled DNA were allowed to replicate their DNA from unlabeled precursors, the distribution of isotope in daughter DNA molecules after one, two, or three generations was in accordance with semiconservative replication (Concept 18.1, part F; Figure 18.1). Meselson and Stahl employed the heavy isotope ^{15}N as a density label for DNA. They used equilibrium sedimentation in CsCl solution (Problem 17.12) to separate fully substituted ^{15}N DNA from the half-substituted ($^{15}N-^{14}N$) and unsubstituted (^{14}N) DNA resulting from growth of ^{15}N-labeled cells in unlabeled ^{14}N medium.

If ^{15}N-labeled *E. coli* were grown for three generations (8-fold increase in population) in a ^{14}N medium, which of the following distributions of DNA among the three major density classes would you expect to find after DNA extraction, shearing to average molecular weight of 10^6, and density determination by equilibrium sedimentation?

	Pure ^{15}N	^{15}N–^{14}N hybrid	Pure ^{14}N
a.	1/8	1/8	6/8
b.	1/8	0	7/8
c.	0	1/8	7/8
d.	0	2/8	6/8
e.	0	4/8	4/8

18.4 The time required for two replication forks traveling in opposite directions to traverse the entire *E. coli* chromosome at 37°C is 40 min, regardless of the culture conditions. However, in a rich medium the cells divide every 20 min. Which of the following statements is true for cells growing in rich medium?

a. Half the daughter cells are nonviable.

b. One-fourth of the daughter cells are nonviable.

c. There is an average of four replication forks per chromosome.

d. There is an average of six replication forks per chromosome.

e. There must be an altered mechanism of chain growth so that four daughter duplexes are produced simultaneously at each replication fork.

18.5 John Cairns first managed to visualize radioactively labeled replicating chromosomes of *E. coli* by careful isolation and autoradiography. In his original model for chromosome replication, he proposed that there was one replication fork in the closed circular duplex and only one swivel, near the origin of replication, at which twist could be relieved. According to this model, if one round of chromosome replication takes 38 min, what would be the rate of rotation of the DNA helix at the swivel point, in revolutions per minute?

18.6 A line of mammalian cells in tissue culture has 1.2 m of duplex DNA per cell. The S phase in these cells is 5 hr long. If the rate of DNA strand growth in these cells is the same as that in *E. coli*, that is, about 16 μm/min, how many replication forks must be operating during chromosome replication?

18.7 Methotrexate, which is a commonly used anticancer drug, inhibits the important cellular enzyme dihydrofolate reductase. Methotrexate-resistant hamster cells synthesize large quantities of dihydrofolate reductase as the result of a many-fold replication amplification of the reductase gene. In some cell lines these amplified genes constitute nearly 50% of an enlarged chromosome number 2 and are readily identifiable as a homogeneously staining region in preparations of metaphase chromosomes.

To determine when during S phase the dihydrofolate reductase genes replicate, you pulse-label exponentially growing, asynchronous populations of cells for 10 min with radioactive thymidine. Subsequently you grow the cells in medium with excess unlabeled thymidine. At various times after the pulse you examine metaphase chromosomes of mitotic cells by autoradiography. (A thin photographic emulsion is layered over the slide containing the chromosomes. Radioactive decay of thymidine exposes nearby silver grains in the emulsion, leaving a visible black dot above the source when the slide is developed.) This technique allows you to determine whether radioactive thymidine was incorporated into the chromosomes during the pulse label and specifically enables you to determine whether radioactivity is present in the reductase genes. Your results are graphed in Figure 18.13.

a. Given that the cell cycle in these hamster cells is 13 hr long and that metaphase lasts 1 hr, what do your results tell you about the durations of the G_1, S, and G_2 phases?

b. When during S phase were the dihydrofolate reductase genes replicated?

18.8 It was a striking feature of the Meselson–Stahl experiment (Problem 18.3) that at all times only three discrete DNA densities were observed, corresponding to fully "heavy" ^{15}N, hybrid ^{14}N–^{15}N, and fully "light" ^{14}N-containing material. Even at fractional generation times, DNA of intermediate densities was not found. Describe the density distributions you would expect to find in such an experiment at 0.5, 1.0, and 1.5 generations after shift of ^{15}N-labeled *E. coli* cells into ^{14}N medium, assuming that the chromosome replicates and can be analyzed as a single structural unit. Explain and try to reconcile any discrepancies between your predictions and the results obtained by Meselson and Stahl, shown in Table 18.2.

Table 18.2
Results of a Meselson–Stahl Experiment
(Problem 18.8)

Generations after shift	Percentage of DNA found at		
	^{15}N density	^{14}N–^{15}N density	^{14}N density
0	100	0	0
0.5	33	67	0
1.0	0	100	0
1.5	0	67	33

18.9 For many years after Cairns first visualized the structure of a replicating *E. coli* chromosome, there was a controversy over whether replication is bidirectional or unidirectional. The two possibilities are distinguishable if the relative numbers of copies of several genes at known locations around the chromosome can be accurately measured. A growing population of cells, containing chromosomes at various stages of replication, should contain twice as many copies of genes at the origin as copies of genes at the terminus of replication, under conditions where a new round of replication does not initiate until the previous one is finished. Assume that you can accurately measure the relative numbers of copies of 12 genes, evenly spaced around the chromosome in numerical order (Figure 18.14) in a culture of cells under the foregoing conditions. If the origin of replication is just counterclockwise from gene 4, draw on the coordinates given in the figure the gene-frequency distributions you would expect to find under each of the following conditions.

a. Replication is bidirectional.

b. Replication is unidirectional in the clockwise direction.

18.10 Restriction endonucleases are bacterial enzymes that cleave duplex DNA at specific nucleotide sequences (Concept 19.1). The mode of replication of the animal virus SV40 has been investigated by using restriction endonucleases that cleave SV40 DNA into a number of unique segments. The map positions of the 11 fragments produced by a pair of restriction endonucleases are shown in Figure 18.15. Immediately following a 5 or 10 min pulse of radioactively labeled thymidine, labeled SV40 molecules that have completed replication during the pulse are isolated. These newly replicated DNA molecules are digested by the restriction endonucleases and the resulting fragments are analyzed for the relative amount of pulse label they contain. (Assume that at the time the label was added there was a random population of replicating SV40

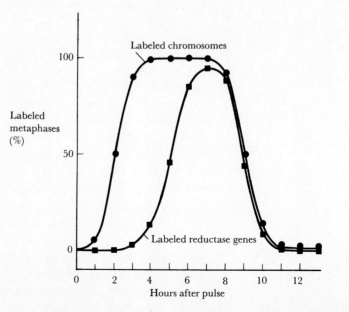

Figure 18.13
Replication of dihydrofolate reductase genes (Problem 18.7).

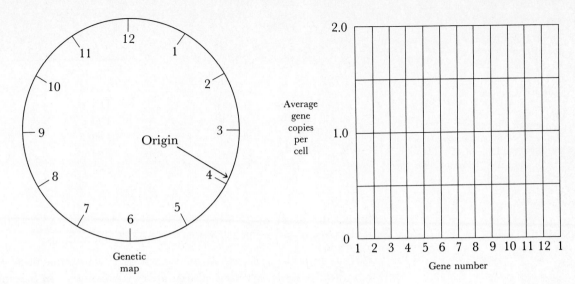

Figure 18.14
Distinction between unidirectional and bidirectional chromosome replication in *E. coli* by analysis of gene frequencies (Problem 18.9).

DNA molecules in all possible stages of synthesis.) From the information in Figure 18.15, decide whether SV40 replication is unidirectional or bidirectional and assign the origin and terminus to specific restriction fragments.

18.11   In the animal virus you are studying, DNA replication proceeds bidirectionally from a unique origin and terminates 180° around the circular genome (Figure 18.16). To investigate the terminus of replication, you create a series of large deletion mutants using recombinant DNA technology. For each mutant you determine where termination occurs (Figure 18.16). From these data, what can you conclude about the normal terminus of replication?

18.12   Kornberg's original experiments on DNA replication in vitro used uptake of radioactive nucleotides into DNA as a measure of enzymatic synthesis. The experiments were done with crude *E. coli* extracts in which the total amount of DNA actually decreased

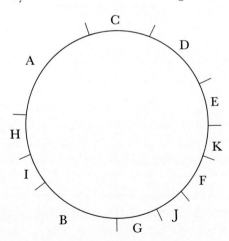

Map of SV40 genome fragments defined
by restriction endonuclease digestion

Relative amount of pulse label
(corrected for size and normalized
to 1.0 for fragment A)

Fragment	5 min	10 min
A	1.0	1.0
B	3.9	3.0
C	0	0.8
D	0.9	0.9
E	1.8	2.0
F	4.0	3.1
G	5.4	4.2
H	1.7	2.5
I	2.7	3.0
J	4.9	3.7
K	2.4	2.9

Figure 18.15
Analysis of SV40 DNA replication (Problem 18.10).

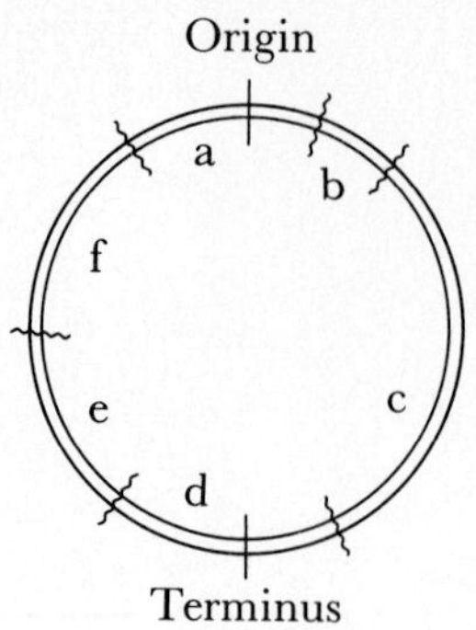

Origin

Terminus

Virus	Segment in which termination occurs
Wild type	d
Del a	(No replication)
Del b	d
Del c	e
Del d	c
Del e	c
Del f	c

Figure 18.16
Analysis of termination of replication (Problem 18.11). The deletion mutants are named for the deleted segment.

during the course of the reaction because of the presence of nucleases. How was it possible to measure DNA synthesis under these conditions?

18.13   IMP is present in *E. coli* as an intermediate in purine nucleotide biosynthesis. Kornberg's experiments showed that DNA polymerases will insert dIMP in place of dGMP if supplied with the triphosphate. Nevertheless, dIMP has never been found to occur naturally in DNA. Can you propose an explanation for how it is excluded?

18.14   The technique of nearest-neighbor (or dinucleotide-frequency) analysis allows determination of the frequency with which a given nucleotide is adjacent to each of the four nucleotides in enzymatically synthesized DNA. Synthesis is carried out with three of the deoxynucleoside triphosphates unlabeled and the fourth labeled with ^{32}P in the α position (Figure 9.2). The labeled synthetic DNA then is degraded using nucleases that cleave on the 5′ side of each phosphoryl group, thereby yielding 3′-mononucleotides. Thus an α-^{32}P that came in with dATP, for example, is left attached to the nucleotide that was adjacent to this A residue on the 5′ side, as follows (arrows indicate points of nuclease cleavage):

$$pX^*pApYpZ \rightarrow X^*p + Ap + Yp + \cdots$$

Therefore, the relative amounts of label recovered as Ap, Gp, Cp, and Tp indicate the relative frequencies of the dinucleotides ApA, GpA, CpA, and TpA, respectively. Using another labeled triphosphate in the synthetic reaction, for example, dTT^{32}P, the frequencies of ApT, GpT, CpT, and TpT can be obtained, and so on, for each of the 16 possible dinucleotides.

From your knowledge of DNA structure, predict which of the following pairs of dinucleotide frequencies will be equal in any double helical DNA, and which need not be:

a. ApA and TpT
b. ApG and TpC
c. CpA and TpG
d. CpG and ApT
e. CpT and ApG
f. GpT and CpA

18.15   The results of dinucleotide frequency analysis can be tabulated conveniently as shown in Table 18.3. The results in each half of the table were obtained using an artificial duplex DNA template containing only two of the four deoxyribonucleotides. Write the structure of the DNA double helix indicated by the nearest-neighbor analysis in each experiment.

18.16   Using a single-stranded, circular phage DNA as a template, it is possible to carry out synthesis of Okazaki fragments in *E. coli* extracts. The reaction produces DNA chains that are complementary to the circular template and carry a tail of RNA on one end. When synthesis is carried out with all four α-^{32}P-labeled deoxynucleoside triphosphates, and the product is degraded to 3′-deoxyribo- and ribonucleotides, the distri-

Table 18.3
Dinucleotide Frequencies in Two Synthetic DNAs
(Problem 18.15)

		a. Poly dAT: nucleotide composition = 50% A, 50% T				*b. Poly dGC: nucleotide composition = 50% G, 50% C*		
			Isolated 3′-mononucleotide				Isolated 3′-mononucleotide	
			Ap	Tp			Gp	Cp
Labeled substrate	dAT^{32}P		ApA <0.01	TpA 0.50	Labeled substrate	dGT^{32}P	GpG 0.50	CpG <0.01
	dTT^{32}P		ApT 0.50	TpT <0.01		dCT^{32}P	GpC <0.01	CpC 0.50

Table 18.4
Nearest-Neighbor Nucleotide Analysis of Okazaki Fragments in *E. coli* (Problem 18.16)

	3′-Ribonucleotide isolated			
Labeled substrate	Ap	Gp	Cp	Up
	^{32}P atoms per Okazaki fragment			
All four dNT^{32}P	0.99	<0.01	<0.01	<0.01
dAT^{32}P	0.20	—	—	—
dGT^{32}P	0.72	—	—	—
dCT^{32}P	<0.01	—	—	—
dTT^{32}P	0.08	—	—	—

bution of ^{32}P among the four *ribonucleotides* is as shown in the first line of Table 18.4. The next four lines show the results when only one of the four deoxynucleoside triphosphate substrates is labeled.

a. Is the RNA tail on the 3′ or the 5′ end of each new DNA strand?

b. What else can you conclude about the linkage of RNA to DNA?

c. What is the *minimum* number of different nucleotide sequences on the DNA template at which polydeoxynucleotide synthesis initiates?

d. If an Okazaki fragment is treated with alkali, will the 3′-terminal nucleotide of the RNA tail be released as a mononucleotide, or will it remain linked to the 5′ end of the DNA strand? Explain.

18.17 Topoisomerases are a class of enzymes that introduce and repair transient phosphodiester bond breaks in DNA. These enzymes are so named because they interconvert topological isomers of DNA. One example of such topological isomers is a pair of closed circular DNAs that differ only in the number of times one strand is wrapped around the other (**linking number**). Such a pair of isomers differs in the degree of supercoiling (Problem 17.21). Topoisomerases can be classified into two groups. Type I topoisomerases permit one single strand to pass through a second transiently broken single strand. This type provides swivels in advance of a moving replication fork (by transiently breaking a single strand to permit its swiveling around the intact strand opposite the disruption). Type II topoisomerases transiently break both strands of the double helix and permit passage of a duplex segment of DNA through the break.

Using this brief description of topoisomerases, predict the possible products that might result from incubation of the DNA substrates in Figure 18.17 with a

a. Type I topoisomerase

b. Type II topoisomerase

18.18 Suppose that you have two strains of a bacteriophage, whose double-stranded DNA can infect *E. coli* even when stripped of the phage protein coat. One strain of phage is normal. The other is a mutant that cannot produce progeny phage because of a nucleotide substitution in an essential gene. You have labeled the normal phage with ^{15}N. You now denature the DNA from the two phages, reanneal them, and isolate the DNA molecules of intermediate density containing one mutant and one normal strand. You then infect *E. coli* with the heteroduplex DNA under conditions where no cell is infected by more than one DNA molecule.

CHAPTER 18
DNA Replication
and Repair

Figure 18.17
DNA substrates (Problem
18.17). **(a)** Single-stranded circular DNA. **(b)** Double-stranded
circular DNA containing four
negative supercoils (see Answer
17.21). **(c)** Interlocked (catenated) circular DNA molecules.

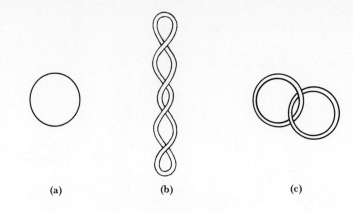

(a)   (b)   (c)

a. If the heteroduplex DNA, which contains one mismatched base pair, is replicated before it can be repaired, what fraction of the infected cells will produce progeny phage?

b. If the heteroduplex DNA is repaired before it is replicated, what fraction of the infected cells will produce progeny phage?

c. By examining the progeny phage from a single infected cell, how might you distinguish whether replication or repair occurred first?

18.19 A bacteriumlike microorganism is brought back from Mars and found to contain double-stranded DNA as its genetic material. To determine its mode of replication, a Meselson–Stahl experiment is performed. Cells are grown several generations in "heavy" medium containing ^{15}N, then transferred to "light" ^{14}N medium, and sampled for DNA extraction after 0, 1.0, and 2.0 generations. The three DNA samples are sheared to 10^6-dalton fragments and centrifuged to equilibrium in a CsCl gradient. The results shown in Figure 18.18 are obtained. In an attempt to understand this puzzling result, extracts of the organism are assayed for various enzyme activities related to nucleic acid synthesis, and only the following are found: (a) an RNA polymerase activity, (b) a DNA polymerase that functions only with single-stranded DNA as a template, and (c) a new enzyme that catalyzes the formation of a deoxyribonuclease-sensitive product when supplied with NADPH and a heat-stable deoxyribonuclease-insensitive, nondialyzable factor present in the extract. How does the organism replicate its DNA?

18.20 A single-stranded RNA phage called f2 replicates in *E. coli* with no DNA intermediates. In experiments designed to clarify its mode of replication the following results were obtained. When phage RNA was extracted from infected cells and sedimented on sucrose gradients, three fractions were observed. The first appeared homogeneous in size and was shown to be single-stranded. The second, also homogeneous, was shown to be double-stranded. The third, which appeared heterogeneous in size, was shown to consist of RNA structures 1 to 1.5 times the molecular weight of those in fraction 2. When an infected culture was labeled with a short pulse of ^3H-uridine and the RNA extracted and sedimented, most of the radioactivity was found in the heterogeneous fraction 3. When this fraction was treated with pancreatic ribonuclease, 50% of the radioactivity was released in acid-soluble form. When the ribonuclease-treated material was reanalyzed in a sucrose gradient, its sedimentation properties were found to be indistinguishable from those of fraction 2.

a. How does f2 replicate its RNA?

b. Is its mode of replication conservative or semiconservative?

c. How does the RNA of fractions 1, 2, and 3 fit into your replication scheme, and what is the nature of the heterogeneous RNA fraction?

18.21 Carefully examine the scheme proposed for replication in Figure 18.1. The daughter duplexes shown at the bottom of the figure *cannot* be completed by any mechanism yet

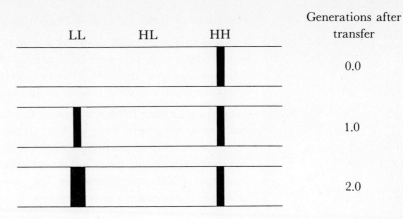

Figure 18.18
Results of a Meselson–Stahl experiment on an imaginary
Martian microorganism (Problem 18.19). HH, HL, and LL
indicate the expected band positions of fully heavy, half
heavy–half light, and fully light DNA, respectively, after centrifugation to equilibrium in a CsCl density gradient.

discussed in this chapter. What is the problem? Does it affect replication of linear and
circular chromosomes alike?

18.22   Parvoviruses are small animal viruses that contain single-stranded DNA genomes. At
each end these genomes have short, self-complementary sequences (palindromes) that
form hairpin-loop structures. Parvoviruses apparently replicate by a rolling-hairpin
mechanism in which these palindromes play a crucial role (Figure 18.19). Specific
endonucleases eventually cut viral genomes from multimeric intermediates. Propose a
mechanism involving terminal palindromes and specific endonucleases that would
solve the replication problem described in Problem 18.21.

☆ 18.23   If replication of the circular bacterial chromosome is bidirectional and starts at a
unique origin, if each replication fork moves at $16\,\mu m/min$, if the chromosome is
$1280\,\mu m$ long, and if the bacteria are growing with a doubling time of 20 min, what
does the chromosome look like 10 min before one round of replication is completed

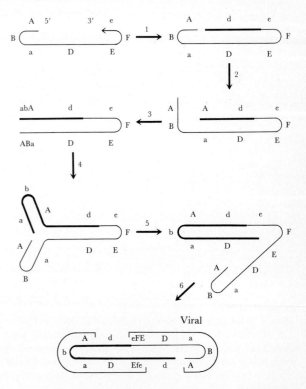

Figure 18.19
Rolling-hairpin model for parvovirus replication (Problem
18.22). (1) Gap filling, (2) displacement synthesis, (3) completion of synthesis to 5′ end, (4) rearrangement of terminal
palindromes, (5) displacement synthesis, and (6) gap filling.
Repetition of steps 2–6 would generate a tetramer from the
dimer. Complementary DNA sequences are represented by
corresponding letters. (Adapted from A. Kornberg, *DNA
Replication*, W. H. Freeman, San Francisco, 1980, p. 402.)

(i.e., midway in the cell cycle)? Draw a simple diagram of the replicating structure.

☆ 18.24 Imagine that you could examine a stretch of eucaryotic DNA containing several replication origins. If it were replicated in the absence of DNA ligase, which of the structures in Figure 18.20 would you expect to observe for aligned daughter duplexes? Show the positions of the origins on the appropriate diagram.

☆ 18.25 While investigating DNA synthesis in an unusual bacterium, you isolate a *ts* mutant carrying a defect analogous to those in the *dnaA* gene of *E. coli;* that is, when the temperature is raised to a nonpermissive level, DNA synthesis continues until each cell has completed the current round of replication and then stops. When the temperature is lowered, DNA synthesis resumes. The generation time of the mutant at the permissive (low) temperature is normal, that is, about 60 min. When supplied with 5-bromo-

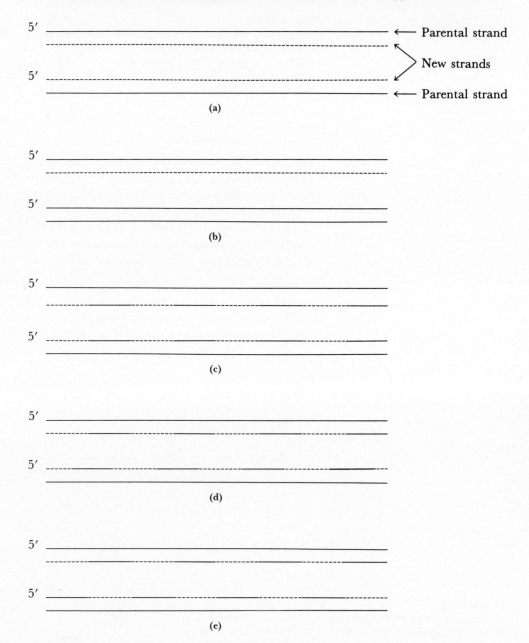

Figure 18.20
Possible structures for newly replicated duplexes (Problem 18.24). In each of the diagrams the outside strands are parental and the inside strands are newly synthesized. For the newly synthesized strands a solid line represents continuous synthesis and a dashed line represents discontinuous synthesis.

deoxyuridine (BrdU) in the medium, your bacterium will incorporate this nucleoside into DNA in place of thymidine throughout at least one replication cycle, giving DNA with one "heavy" and one "light" strand (HL) that has a higher buoyant density in CsCl solution than unsubstituted (LL) DNA. You realize that, using the mutant, you can answer the question of whether chromosome replication always begins at the same point or begins at a random point on the chromosome at the start of each replication cycle. To do so, you take the following steps:

1. Incubate a culture of cells at nonpermissive (high) temperature for about 1 hr.
2. Lower the temperature and expose the cells to highly radioactive ^{3}H-thymidine for 3 min.
3. Add a huge (>1000-fold) excess of unlabeled thymidine to the medium, and grow the cells at the permissive temperature for 3 hr.
4. Raise the temperature to the nonpermissive level and incubate the cells for 1 hr.
5. Lower the temperature and allow the cells to grow in medium containing BrdU.
6. Take samples at various times after growth resumes, extract DNA from the cells, fragment it into pieces no larger than 1% of the total chromosome size, and centrifuge it to equilibrium in CsCl solution.
7. Measure x, the fraction of total DNA in the HL-density band, and y, the fraction of total ^{3}H label in the HL-density band.

a. Make a plot of x as a function of time and sketch the curve you would expect to obtain.

b. Make a plot of y as a function of x, and predict the curve that you would obtain if the origin of chromosome replication is—

1. Fixed at a specific site from one generation to the next
2. Randomly selected at the start of each round of replication

Answers

18.1 a. True

b. False. After one round of replication, all progeny molecules contain 50% parental material.

c. True

d. False. The frequency of initiation of DNA replication varies with culture conditions. However, the rate of chain growth is constant.

e. True

f. False. Unwinding occurs in the same sense at the two replication forks, and the two twists add. Make a model and try it.

g. False. Discontinuous synthesis and joining of short fragments can produce net chain growth in the $3' \rightarrow 5'$ direction even though the fragments are made in the $5' \rightarrow 3'$ direction.

h. True

i. False. Because each Okazaki fragment apparently must be initiated by a short stretch of RNA, such an inhibitor would immediately block chromosome replication.

j. True

k. True

l. False. The statement would be true for DNA polymerase II. However, mutants lacking DNA polymerase III are unable to carry out chromosome replication.

m. False. Reverse transcriptase does require a primer. In normal virus replication the primer is a tryptophan tRNA H-bonded to the viral genome.

n. False. The reaction requires NAD^+ not as an electron acceptor but rather as a source of phosphate-bond energy.

o. True

p. True

18.2 a. RNA, 5'

b. $5' \rightarrow 3'$

c. proofreading

d. leading, continuous; lagging, discontinuous

e. repair

f. displacement-loop (D-loop)

g. Rolling-circle

h. glycosylase, insertase

i. direct, indirect

18.3   The answer is d. See Figure 18.1. After three successive doublings, there will be two duplex molecules containing one parental strand for every eight total duplexes.

18.4   The answer is d. In rich medium, a second round of bidirectional replication begins at the origin when the first round is only half completed. This second initiation results in four new replication forks, making a total of six. Thus one round of replication is completed every 20 min and each daughter cell at division receives a chromosome that is already half replicated.

18.5   The *E. coli* chromosome is 1300 μm long (Table 17.2). Because the DNA double helix makes one turn every 3.4 nm or $3.4 \times 10^{-3} \mu$m, 1300 μm represents 3.8×10^5 helical turns. All these turns must be untwisted during one round of replication. If one round takes 38 min, a single DNA swivel would have to rotate at 10,000 rpm!

18.6   At 16 μm/min, each replication fork will travel 4800 μm or 4.8×10^{-3} m in 5 hr (300 min). To replicate the entire content of DNA (1.2 m) in this interval there must be

$$\frac{1.2 \text{ m}}{4.8 \times 10^{-3} \text{ m/replication fork}} = 250 \text{ replication forks}$$

18.7 a. Remember that the cell populations are growing *asynchronously* and that only cells in metaphase are analyzed for incorporation. The first mitotic cells to show labeled metaphase chromosomes are derived from those cells that were in the end of S phase when the thymidine was added. Similarly the last cells to show labeled chromosomes are derived from cells in the beginning of S phase at the time of the pulse. Using the 50% point on the curves for comparison, your results indicate that G_2 is about 2 hr long, S is about 7 hr long, and G_1 is about 3 hr long.

b. The dihydrofolate reductase genes are replicated during the first half of S phase.

18.8   If the densities of entire chromosomes were measured in such an experiment, the predicted results would not be the same as those found by Meselson and Stahl, except after an integral number of generations. After 0.5 generations all of the replicating structures should be at an intermediate density between those of ^{15}N and ^{14}N–^{15}N DNA. After 1.5 generations all should be at an intermediate density between those of ^{14}N–^{15}N and ^{14}N DNA. These results are not found, because it is technically impossible to analyze whole replicating chromosomes by equilibrium sedimentation without fragmenting them. In Meselson and Stahl's experiments the DNA was broken (inadvertently) to pieces about $\frac{1}{1000}$ the size of the chromosome. Hence the fragments containing the replication forks, which were of intermediate density, represented only 0.2% of the total and were not observed.

18.9 a. If replication is bidirectional, gene 4, which is closest to the origin, will be present in two copies per cell; genes 3 and 5 will be next most frequent, genes 2 and 6 next, and so on down to gene 10, which will be least frequent at one copy per cell.

b. If replication is unidirectional, gene 4 will be duplicated first and hence will be most frequent, gene 5 will be next, and so on down to gene 3, which will be least frequent.

      The expected distributions are shown in Figure 18.21. The two principal problems with such experiments were in measuring gene frequencies accurately enough and obtaining enough uniformly spaced genetic markers to distinguish between the

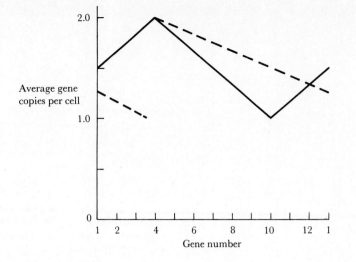

Figure 18.21
Gene-frequency distributions resulting from bidirectional (solid line) and unidirectional (dashed-line) chromosome replication in *E. coli* (Answer 18.9).

two possible distributions. However, careful experiments in *E. coli* clearly indicate that replication is bidirectional.

18.10　SV40 replication is bidirectional beginning in fragment C and terminating in fragment G. The key points for the analysis are (1) a random starting population of replicating molecules and (2) analysis only of those molecules that have completed replication. After short labeling times only those molecules that were close to completion when the label was added will be isolated and analyzed. These molecules will have relatively more label in the terminator region and little, if any, near the origin. For the two labeling times shown, the largest amount of label was in fragment G, which therefore must include the terminator region, and the least amount of label was in fragment C, which therefore must contain the origin. Because the origin and terminator are opposite one another on the circle, replication must be bidirectional. That conclusion is supported by the bidirectional gradient of increasing label from fragment C to fragment G.

18.11　Unlike the origin for replication there is no unique sequence at which replication terminates. Apparently, the normal terminus is simply the point at which oppositely moving replication forks fuse.

18.12　The amount of DNA present was large enough relative to the amount being synthesized so that incorporated radioactivity was trapped in the DNA pool, and lost at a negligible rate compared to the rate of synthesis. Thus the rate of uptake could be measured despite net loss of total DNA during the reaction.

18.13　The deoxyribonucleoside triphosphate, dITP, is never produced in the cell because there is no kinase that will catalyze the phosphorylation of dIMP. Thus it cannot be a substrate for DNA polymerases in vivo.

18.14　Remember that A must always pair with T and G with C, and that the two strands of the double helix have opposite polarity.
　a. ApA must equal TpT.
　b. ApG need not equal TpC.
　c. CpA must equal TpG.
　d. CpG need not equal ApT.
　e. CpT must equal ApG.
　f. GpT need not equal CpA.

18.15　a. The results show that every A is adjacent to T; none are adjacent to A. Likewise, all T are adjacent to A; none are adjacent to T. Hence the structure is

---A-T-A-T-A-T---
---T-A-T-A-T-A---

b. G is always adjacent to G; C is always adjacent to C. Hence the structure is

$$\text{---G-G-G-G---}$$
$$\text{---C-C-C-C---}$$

18.16 a. Because there is transfer of ^{32}P from dNT^{32}P to a ribonucleotide, the RNA must be in the 5′ direction from the DNA, hence on the 5′ ends of DNA strands.

b. The ribonucleotide linking the RNA tail to the DNA strand is always AMP.

c. Because three different deoxyribonucleotides transfer ^{32}P to the terminal nucleotide of the RNA tail, initiation of DNA synthesis must be occurring at a minimum of three different sequences.

d. It will be released, because its 2′-OH group will allow alkali cleavage of the phosphodiester bond to the first deoxyribonucleotide.

18.17 a. A type I topoisomerase will catalyze several reactions with single-stranded circles. It can interlink separate circles to form catenated circles or it can interlink separate parts of the same circle to form knots (Figure 18.22a). If the single-stranded circles are a mixture of complementary strands, a type I topoisomerase will catalyze formation of covalently closed, duplex circles.

A type I topoisomerase will relax supercoils in unit steps (Figure 18.22b), but will produce no change in catenated circles, if both circles are covalently closed. However, if the catenated circles contain nicks or gaps, a type I topoisomerase can unlink them.

b. A type II topoisomerase will not react with single-stranded circles. It will relax supercoils in steps of two (Figure 18.22c), and can unlink catenated circles. Additionally, it can tie duplex circles into knots. Some type II topoisomerases, such as DNA gyrase from *E. coli*, can supercoil duplex circles in the presence of ATP.

18.18 a. After the initial heteroduplex is replicated, each infected cell will contain one normal duplex and one mutant duplex. The normal duplex can supply all the gene products necessary for a productive infection. Thus 100% of the infected cells will produce progeny phage.

b. If the repair system has no preference for which member of the mismatched pair to replace, 50% of the molecules will be converted to fully mutant duplexes, and the other 50% to normal duplexes. Only the latter will yield progeny: therefore, 50% of the infected cells will produce phage. In practice, the repair process does not appear to be completely random with respect to strand selection; that is, the fraction of normal duplexes resulting from repair may be consistently greater than or less than 50% for heteroduplexes made with any particular mutant.

c. If repair occurs first, the progeny phage from a productively infected cell all will be normal. If replication occurs first, the progeny phage from a productively infected cell will be a mixture of normal and mutant phage.

18.19 Assuming that the enzymes found are the only ones involved in DNA synthesis, the organism must replicate its DNA by (1) conservative synthesis of an RNA single strand complementary to one DNA strand, catalyzed by the RNA polymerase, (2) stepwise reduction of each ribonucleotide of this RNA to a deoxyribonucleotide, catalyzed by the new enzyme, "RNA reductase," at the expense of NADPH (the deoxyribonuclease-insensitive, nondialyzable factor is the single-stranded RNA precursor), and (3) complementary copying of the resulting DNA strand by the single-strand-specific DNA polymerase to form a duplex DNA that is identical to the original parental duplex. Thus the overall replication process is conservative, and duplexes of intermediate density do not form.

18.20 a. RNA replication in f2 appears to proceed by formation of a double-stranded RNA (fraction 2), followed by production of a single-stranded RNA using the double strand as a template.

b. The finding that only 50% of the radioactivity in fraction 3 is single-stranded (released by pancreatic ribonuclease) suggests that there are equal probabilities of conservative

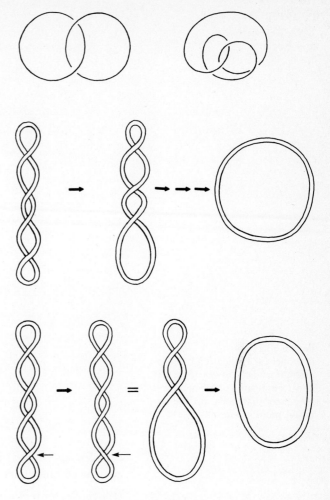

Figure 18.22
Products of topoisomerase action on DNA (Answer 18.17).
(a) Catenated circles and knots. **(b)** Stepwise relaxation of a supercoiled DNA by a type I topoisomerase. **(c)** Stepwise relaxation of a supercoiled DNA by a type II topoisomerase. The small arrows indicate the change in sign [right (−) to left (+)] that occurs at a crossover point when one duplex segment passes through another.

or semiconservative replication of the duplex. Therefore, replication can be diagrammed as in Figure 18.23.

c. Fraction 1 is parental RNA. Fraction 2 is the double-stranded template. Fraction 3 is most likely the double-stranded template in the process of replication, with single-stranded "tails" attached to it.

18.21 The 5′ ends of the new strands in the daughter duplexes cannot be completed. This problem exists because DNA polymerase requires a primer and can only extend chains in the 5′ → 3′ direction. If an RNA primer began at the end of the chromosome, a DNA polymerase could extend it. However, when the primer was removed, the nascent DNA strand could not be extended in the 3′ → 5′ direction necessary to

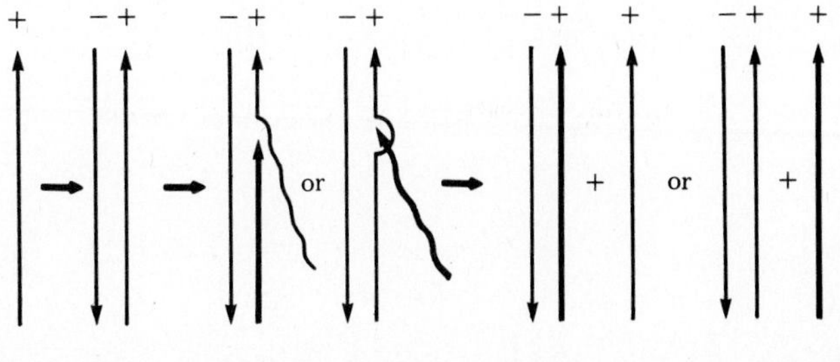

Figure 18.23
Stages in replication of f2 RNA (Answer 18.20). The RNA strand found in the virus is indicated by +, and its complement by −.

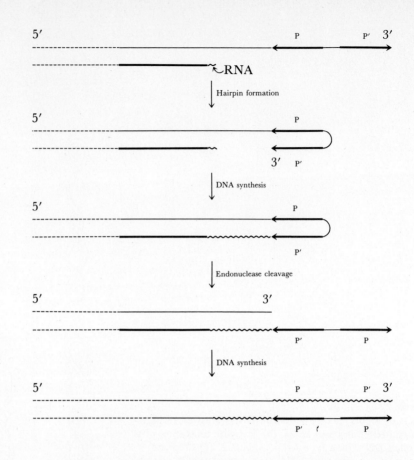

Figure 18.24
A model for replication of chromosome ends (Answer 18.22). P and P′ indicate complementary sequences that make up the terminal palindrome.

complete the strand. This problem exists only for duplexes with ends and not for circular chromosomes.

18.22   One model for replication of chromosome ends is shown in Figure 18.24. The actual mechanism by which the ends of eucaryotic chromosomes are replicated is not yet known.

19 Recombinant DNA and Genetic Engineering

The discovery of enzymes called **restriction endonucleases** led to the development of recombinant DNA techniques, which allow a DNA fragment from any source to be joined artificially with procaryotic or eucaryotic DNA molecules that replicate autonomously. Microorganisms carrying such recombinant DNA molecules can be cloned in large numbers, and the exogenous fragment can be reisolated easily in quantities sufficient for size and sequence analysis. Recombinant DNA techniques permit analyses of eucaryotic gene structure, organization, expression, and evolution that were previously impossible. These techniques also allow genetic engineering of microorganisms to produce the protein products of artificially introduced genes. This chapter considers current methods for constructing recombinant DNA molecules, propagating them in microorganisms, and analyzing their nucleotide sequences.

Concepts

19.1 **DNA molecules can be cleaved at specific sites with restriction endonucleases.**

A. Restriction endonucleases recognize specific short nucleotide sequences in double-stranded DNA and cleave both strands of the molecule. These enzymes are divided into two major classes, based on manner of cleavage, molecular weight, and cofactor requirements.

1. **Class I** restriction endonucleases bind to specific sequences but catalyze cleavage at variable sites up to thousands of nucleotide pairs from the binding sequence by a mechanism that is not well understood. These enzymes have molecular weights of about 300,000, consist of nonidentical subunits, and require ATP, Mg^{2+}, and usually S-adenosylmethionine as cofactors. Two examples are the enzymes *Eco*K and *Eco*B from the K and B strains, respectively, of *E. coli*. Because of the variability in their cleavage sites, these enzymes generally are not useful for the engineering or analysis of DNA sequences, and will not be considered further in this chapter.

2. **Class II** restriction endonucleases recognize specific sequences of four to six nucleotide pairs in length and catalyze double-strand cleavage of the DNA within or next to these sequences to produce specific fragments. These enzymes have two important features: They always cleave at the same nucleotide position relative to the recognition sequence, and they cleave virtually all sites at which the recognition sequence occurs. The recognition sequences for restriction endonucleases almost always include **inverted repeats** (see Table 19.1; also Problem 17.9), so that usually the same sequence is cut at the same point in both strands. Some of these enzymes catalyze coincident cleavage of the two strands so that the ends of the resulting fragments are fully base-paired (often referred to as **blunt ends**). Other restriction enzymes catalyze a staggered cleavage of the two DNA strands so that the resulting fragments have protruding, unpaired single strands, generally one to four nucleotides in length (**sticky ends**), which can reassociate by complementary base pairing (Figure 19.1). The class

371

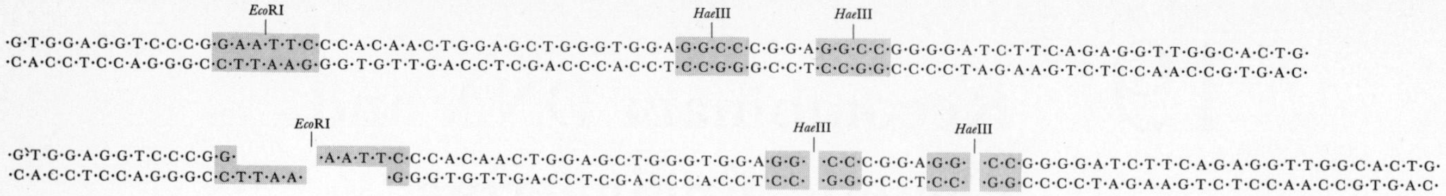

·G·T·G·G·A·G·G·T·C·C·C·G·G·A·A·T·T·C·C·A·C·A·A·C·T·G·G·A·G·C·T·G·G·G·T·G·G·A·G·G·C·C·C·G·G·A·G·G·C·C·C·G·G·G·G·A·T·C·T·T·C·A·G·A·G·G·T·T·G·G·C·A·C·T·G·
·C·A·C·C·T·C·C·A·G·G·G·C·C·T·T·A·A·G·G·G·T·G·T·T·G·A·C·C·T·C·G·A·C·C·C·A·C·C·T·C·C·G·G·G·C·C·C·T·C·C·G·G·C·C·C·C·T·A·G·A·A·G·T·C·T·C·C·A·A·C·C·G·T·G·A·C·

EcoRI   *Hae*III   *Hae*III

·G⁵'T·G·G·A·G·G·T·C·C·C·G·G·   ·A·A·T·T·C·C·A·C·A·A·C·T·G·G·A·G·C·T·G·G·G·T·G·G·A·G·G·   ·C·C·C·G·G·A·G·G·   ·C·C·G·G·G·G·A·T·C·T·T·C·A·G·A·G·G·T·T·G·G·C·A·C·T·G·
·C·A·C·C·T·C·C·A·G·G·G·C·C·T·T·A·A·   ·G·G·G·T·G·T·T·G·A·C·C·T·C·G·A·C·C·C·A·C·C·T·C·C·   ·G·G·G·C·C·T·C·C·   ·G·G·C·C·C·C·T·A·G·A·A·G·T·C·T·C·C·A·A·C·C·G·T·G·A·C·

EcoRI   *Hae*III   *Hae*III

Figure 19.1

Cleavage of DNA by two restriction endonucleases. The enzyme *Hae*III recognizes a four-nucleotide sequence and cleaves both strands at its center to produce fragments with blunt ends. The enzyme *Eco*RI recognizes a six-nucleotide sequence and catalyzes staggered cleavage of the two strands to produce fragments with sticky ends. Shading indicates enzyme recognition sequences.

II restriction endonucleases have molecular weights in the range of 20,000 to 100,000 and require only Mg^{2+} as cofactor.

B. A large number of class II restriction enzymes with different specificities have been purified from a variety of bacteria. The enzymes are named by the first letter of the bacterial genus and the first two letters of the species, followed by the serotype or strain designation if any and a Roman numeral if the bacterium contains more than one such endonuclease. For example, *Hin*fI and *Hin*fII are obtained from *Haemophilus influenzae*, serotype f. The characteristics of several class II restriction endonucleases are listed in Table 19.1.

Table 19.1

Recognition Sequences of Some Class II Restriction Endonucleases

Name	Recognition sequence[a]	Number of cleavage sites				Microorganism
		φX174	λ	SV40	pBR322	
*Alu*I	AG↓CT	24	>50	35	16	*Arthrobacter luteus*
*Bam*HI	G↓GATCC	0	5	1	1	*Bacillus amyloliquefaciens* H
*Bgl*I	GCC(N₄)↓NGGC	0	22	1	3	*Bacillus globigii*
*Bgl*II	A↓GATCT	0	6	0	0	*Bacillus globigii*
*Eco*RI	G↓AATTC	0	5	1	1	*Escherichia coli* RY13
*Hae*III	GG↓CC	11	>50	19	22	*Haemophilus aegyptius*
*Hha*I	GCG↓C	18	>50	2	31	*Haemophilus haemolyticus*
*Hinc*II	GTP$_y$↓PuAC	13	34	7	2	*Haemophilus influenzae* R$_c$
*Hind*III	A↓AGCTT	0	6	6	1	*Haemophilus influenzae* R$_d$
*Hinf*I	G↓ANTC	21	>50	10	10	*Haemophilus influenzae* R$_f$
*Hpa*II	C↓CGG	5	>50	1	26	*Haemophilus parainfluenzae*
*Mbo*II[b]	5′-GAAGA(N₈)↓-3′ 3′-CTTCT(N₇)↓-5′	11	>50	15	11	*Moraxella bovis*
*Pst*I	CTGCA↓G	1	18	2	1	*Providencia stuartii* 164
*Sal*I	G↓TCGAC	0	2	0	1	*Streptomyces albus* G
*Sst*I	GAGCT↓C	0	2	0	0	*Streptomyces stanford*
*Taq*I	T↓CGA	10	>50	1	7	*Thermus aquaticus*

[a] Note that most of these sequences are inverted repeats; that is, if the sequences of both complementary DNA strands are written, the sequence of each strand on one side of the midpoint is the reverse of the sequence of the opposite strand on the other side of the midpoint. In other words, these sequences are symmetric around a 2-fold rotational axis (Problems 17.9 and 17.11).
[b] *Mbo*II belongs to a rare group of class II restriction enzymes that recognize an *asymmetric* sequence and cleave at specific sites on one side of the sequence but several nucleotides away from it.

1. Different restriction enzymes that have the same recognition specificities are called **isoschizomers** ("same cleavage"). Some isoschizomers show different sensitivities to methylated bases in the cleavage site, and therefore are useful in studies of DNA methylation. Generally, however, isochizomers are functionally interchangeable so that the most stable and easily purified enzyme can be selected for use.

2. Restriction enzymes that recognize different sequences but produce identical sticky ends are called **isocaudamers** ("same tail"). If two enzymes are isocaudamers,

Figure 19.2
Restriction map of the DNA fragment in Figure 19.1, showing the distances in nucleotide pairs between restriction sites and the ends of the fragment. Lengths of fragments used to construct restriction maps are determined by electrophoresis in agarose gels (see Figure 19.3).

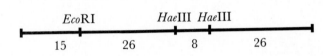

then fragments produced with one can be joined by base pairing to fragments produced with the other.

C.   A restriction endonuclease catalyzes the cleavage of large DNA molecules into a population of specific **restriction fragments,** which range in length from a few to thousands of nucleotide pairs, depending on the frequency and positions of the cleavage sequence in the original DNA. A **restriction map** may be constructed for a given DNA fragment by determining the number and locations of the sites for various restriction endonucleases (Figure 19.2). Restriction maps are useful for preliminary tests of relatedness between two DNA fragments and for ordering of small subfragments in preparation for nucleotide sequencing. Restriction fragments can be separated and purified on the basis of size by electrophoresis at neutral pH in slabs of agarose or acrylamide gel, as shown in Figure 19.3.

19.2   Unrelated DNA fragments can be joined enzymatically.

Recombinant DNA molecules are formed by enzymatically joining two or more DNA fragments. The fragments joined can be from any source; for example, restriction fragments of naturally occurring DNA, DNA molecules synthesized enzymatically using RNA as a template for reverse transcriptase (Concept 18.4), or completely artificial DNAs produced by combined chemical and enzymatic synthesis. Three general methods are used for DNA joining:

1.   Restriction fragments produced using an enzyme that catalyzes staggered cleavages can be joined noncovalently under annealing conditions, because fragment ends can associate by complementary base pairing (Figure 19.1). Subsequent covalent joining can be accomplished by nick closure with a DNA ligase (Concept 18.3).

2.   Any two populations of fragments can be made complementary by the addition of appropriate homopolymer extensions ("tails") at their 3′ ends, using an enzyme called **terminal transferase.** This enzyme will catalyze sequential addition of deoxynucleoside triphosphates to unpaired 3′-OH ends of DNA strands without any requirement for a template. For example, if polydeoxyadenylate (poly-dA) is added to

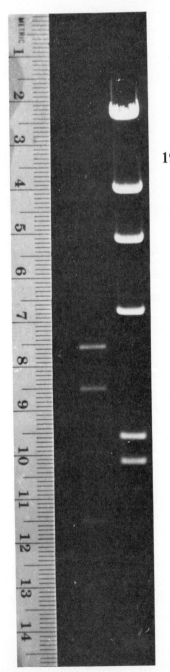

Figure 19.3
Separation of restriction fragments on the basis of size by electrophoresis in an agarose gel. Bands corresponding to fragments of a given length are visualized by staining with the fluorescent intercalating dye ethidium bromide and viewing under ultraviolet light. The migration rates of fragments through the gel are proportional to the logarithms of their lengths, so that distance traveled can be used as an accurate measure of fragment size. The right-hand lane of the gel shows separation of the *Hin*dIII digestion products of λDNA. These seven fragments, which range in size from 0.6 (very faint; at 14.3 cm) to 23.8 kb, often are used as standards for calibration of sizing gels. (Courtesy J. Files.)

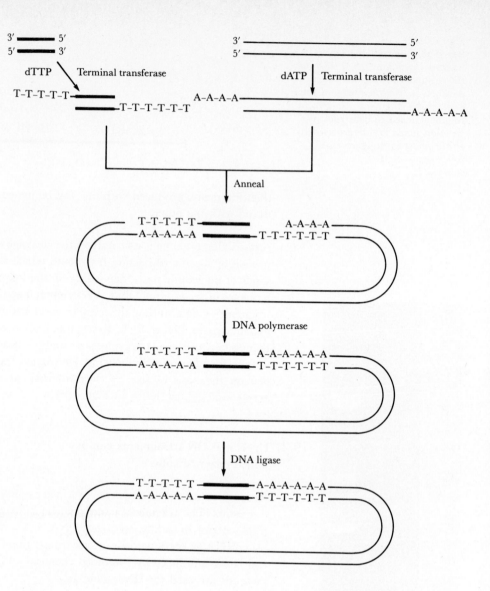

Figure 19.4
Homopolymer tailing and joining of two DNA fragments.

the ends of one fragment and polydeoxythymidylate (poly-dT) is added to the ends of a second, then the two fragments can be joined noncovalently by complementary base pairing. If desired, gaps resulting from length differences in the tails can be filled in using a DNA polymerase, and the two fragments then can be joined covalently using DNA ligase (Figure 19.4).

3.   Fully base-paired duplex fragments can be joined directly using high concentrations of bacteriophage T4 DNA ligase. Alternatively, blunt ends can be converted to sticky ends by joining them to short, chemically synthesized linker sequences, which carry a recognition site for a restriction enzyme that makes staggered breaks.

19.3   Recombinant plasmid or viral DNAs can be introduced into cells and replicated in vivo.

A.   If a DNA fragment is joined to an autonomously replicating DNA such as a plasmid or viral genome, and the recombinant molecule is introduced into an appropriate cell, it can replicate like a normal plasmid or virus. The autonomously replicating molecule is known as the **vehicle** or **vector** and the fragment it carries as the **insert**. The cell used to propagate a vector and its insert is called the **host**. Propagation of inserted

DNA sequences by this technique has been termed **molecular cloning**, because cells carrying single recombinant molecules can be isolated and propagated as individual clones. Some commonly used cloning vectors are listed in Table 19.2.

Table 19.2
Some Recombinant DNA Cloning Vectors

Vector	Type	Cleavage sites at which exogenous DNA may be inserted	Size (kb)	Other characteristics
pBR322	Plasmid (*E. coli*)	*Bam*HI, *Eco*RI *Hin*dIII, *Pst*I, *Sal*I	4.362	Carries genes that confer resistance to ampicillin (Ap^R) and tetracycline (Tc^R).
pJC720	Cosmid	*Hin*dIII	24	Carries rifampicin resistance (Rf^R) gene; can be packaged in vitro into phage λ particles.
Charon phages 1–16	Viruses	*Eco*RI, *Hin*dIII, *Sst*I	43–50	Accommodate inserts of 0–24 kb; insertion at *Eco*RI site inactivates *lacZ* (β-galactosidase) gene.
M13mp2	Virus	*Eco*RI	7.2	Single-stranded DNA virus; insertion inactivates *lacZ* gene.
SVGT5	Virus (eucaryotic)	*Bam*HI, *Hin*dIII	4.14	Fragment of SV40 virus; infects animal cells in tissue culture.
pYe(CEN3)41	Plasmid (yeast–*E. coli* hybrid)	*Bam*HI, *Bgl*II, *Eco*RI, *Hin*dIII, *Pst*I, *Sal*I	9.2	Can be propagated in *E. coli* or in yeast cells as a minichromosome with accurate mitotic and meiotic segregation.

B. **Plasmids,** particularly those of *E. coli*, are among the most widely used cloning vectors. A plasmid is a circular extrachromosomal DNA molecule that replicates autonomously.

1. Recombinant DNA techniques have been used to develop several *E. coli* plasmids that carry drug-resistance markers as well as single recognition sites for several restriction endonucleases. Treatment with one of these enzymes converts the circular plasmid DNA to a linear molecule. Annealing and ligation of the linear plasmid DNA in the presence of appropriately prepared foreign DNA fragments reconverts the plasmid molecule to a circular DNA that carries an insert at the point of the original cleavage. Circular plasmid DNA can be reintroduced into bacteria, treated if necessary to make them **competent**, that is, able to take up free DNA molecules at a low frequency. This process is known as **transformation** of the bacteria. Many if not all the progeny of a transformed cell will acquire the plasmid, to produce a clone of transformed cells.

2. Because the frequency of transformation is generally about 10^{-3} per cell, it is convenient to use conditions that select for cells that have acquired the plasmid. Furthermore, because not all reconstituted plasmids carry the desired insert, a screening procedure must be available to determine which transformed clones carry recombinant plasmids. A frequently used approach is illustrated by the following example. The *E. coli* plasmid pBR322 carries two genes that confer tetracycline resistance (Tc^R) and ampicillin resistance (Ap^R) respectively. The plasmid includes a single recognition site for the restriction enzyme *Bam*HI located within the Tc^R gene. To clone foreign DNA sequences at this site, the plasmid DNA can be cut with *Bam*HI, annealed with exogenous DNA fragments also cut with *Bam*HI, ligated, and used to transform bacteria that are sensitive to both ampicillin and tetracycline. Then the bacteria are incubated on agar plates in the presence of ampicillin, so that only cells carrying the plasmid can grow. Those that form colonies are tested with tetracycline. If the plasmid in cells of a particular colony carries an insert at the *Bam*HI site, the cells will be killed by tetracycline because the Tc^R gene is interrupted by the insert. If the plasmid carries no insert, then the cells will be resistant to tetracycline because the Tc^R gene

will be intact (Figure 19.5). Therefore, ampicillin-resistant, tetracycline-sensitive cells are likely to carry plasmids with the desired insert.

3.   Yeast plasmids provide useful vehicles for recombinant DNA propagation in yeast. This system promises to be particularly valuable for applications that require expression of eucaryotic genes, because yeast cells can carry out at least some of the necessary mRNA processing steps involved in eucaryotic gene expression (Concept 20.3) as well as post-translational modifications such as glycosylation that are not performed by bacteria. Particularly useful should be recently developed yeast–*E. coli* hybrid plasmids, which can replicate in either host and contain a yeast centromeric sequence so that they segregate autonomously as minichromosomes during yeast mitosis and meiosis.

C.   Several viral vectors are used for propagating foreign DNA sequences, not only in bacteria but also in eucaryotic cells.

1.   Among the most widely used viral vectors are the **Charon bacteriophages,** named for the boatman of Greek mythology who carried dead souls across the river Styx to the underworld. These vectors, derived using recombinant DNA techniques from the *E. coli* bacteriophage λ, carry appropriate restriction enzyme sites as well as the *E. coli* β-galactosidase gene, which allows recombinant bacteriophages that carry an insert to be distinguished from those that do not by the color of the plaques they produce on special indicator plates seeded with *E. coli* (Figure 19.6).

Use of a Charon bacteriophage as a cloning vector involves isolation of the linear DNA molecule, and then cleavage with an appropriate restriction enzyme to yield generally two arms and a smaller central fragment, which can be separated from the arms on the basis of size. The two arms are annealed with appropriately prepared exogenous DNA fragments and ligated. For efficient introduction into host bacteria, the DNA can be packaged into infectious virus particles by incubation with extracts of virus-infected cells that supply components necessary for encapsulating DNA into

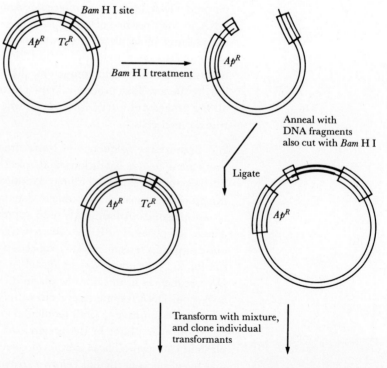

Figure 19.5
Production and selection for a recombinant plasmid DNA vector carrying an exogenous DNA insert. Drug-resistance genes are indicated by shaded boxes. Exogenous DNA is indicated by heavy lines.

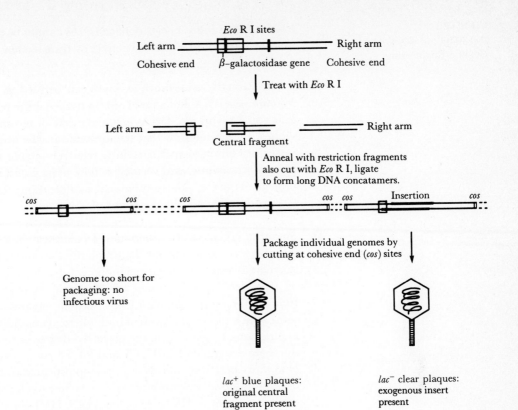

Figure 19.6
Production and selection for a recombinant Charon bacteriophage vector carrying an exogenous DNA insert. The two arms obtained by *Eco*RI digestion generally are separated from most of the central fragment DNA before ligation, to decrease the probability of reconstructing molecules that do not contain an exogenous insert but instead carry the original central fragment in the correct orientation (which will give *lac*+ plaques) or the reverse orientation (which will give *lac*− plaques). Exogenous DNA is indicated by the heavy horizontal lines.

viral heads and attaching viral tails in vitro. The viruses produced in the packaging reaction then are plated with sensitive bacteria on indicator plates, and clones with exogenous inserts are identified by plaque color (Figure 19.6).

Because only DNA in a certain size range can be packaged, this process selects for molecules with inserts in a certain size range. The Charon phages can carry relatively large inserts, from a few kilobases up to 22 kb in length and, accordingly, are useful in studies of chromosomal organization over large regions. By contrast, plasmids generally are used to carry much smaller inserts, from a few base pairs up to several kilobases. These smaller inserts are more useful for other purposes, such as DNA sequence analysis. An advantage of the λ-related vectors is that each phage particle has almost 100% probability of infection, whereas a plasmid molecule has about a 0.1% probability of transformation.

2. **Cosmids** are a special class of artificially constructed *E. coli* plasmids that carry the λ *cos* site, which allows them to be packaged into λ phage particles for efficient introduction into bacteria. Once introduced, a recombinant cosmid replicates as a plasmid in the bacterial cell. Cosmids are useful for replication of very large inserts, which can be up to 45 kb in size.

3. Filamentous single-stranded DNA phages such as M13 and fd also have been employed as cloning vectors. They are useful for applications in which a single strand of a particular insert is desired, as, for example, in DNA sequence studies. Recombi-

nant single-stranded bacteriophage DNAs cannot be packaged in vitro. Instead, they must be introduced into host bacteria by **transfection**: that is, the infection of competent bacteria with free DNA.

4. Eucaryotic viruses such as SV40 can be used as vectors for the introduction of recombinant DNA into animal cells in tissue culture by transfection. In addition, such cells will take up any DNA, including that of recombinant bacterial plasmids and viruses. By mechanisms that remain unclear, the exogenous DNA often is incorporated into chromosomal sites in a relatively stable manner, and sometimes is expressed. Eucaryotic viral vectors promise to be useful in the production of eucaryotic proteins requiring post-translational modifications that can be carried out only by eucaryotic cells, and in the study of the regulation of eucaryotic gene expression.

D. Since the initiation of recombinant DNA research, some scientists and nonscientists have been concerned about the possibility that introduction of exogenous genes into microorganisms could create environmental or health hazards. Although experiments on the safety of recombinant DNA techniques have mitigated these concerns, the funding of most recombinant DNA research remains subject to governmental regulations, which specify the levels of both physical and biological containment for various applications, depending on the perceived degree of risk. Physical containment procedures are designated P1, P2, P3, and P4; P1 corresponds to ordinary microbiological laboratory practices, and P4 requires sophisticated containment facilities available in only a few special laboratories. Approved host–vector systems are certified for biological containment as HV1, HV2, and HV3; HV1 corresponds to ordinary *E. coli* K12 bacteria, and HV3 uses specially developed mutant hosts that have virtually no chance of survival in natural environments outside of the laboratory.

19.4 Specific gene sequences can be isolated from libraries of cloned DNA fragments.

A. **A clone library** is a set of bacterial or viral recombinant DNA clones, including many of the sequences from a larger sequence set, such as the entire genome of an organism or the population of expressed sequences in a particular cell type. Two general kinds of libraries are useful for different purposes.

1. A **genomic library** is usually constructed by mechanically shearing genomic DNA or partially digesting it with a restriction endonuclease to generate a population of overlapping sequences, subjecting the entire population to joining with a vector DNA as described under Concept 19.3, and cloning individual bacteria or bacteriophages containing inserts. The resulting clone library represents a random sample of sequences from the original population (Figure 19.7). If the library is large enough, it will include most of these sequences. For example, starting with DNA from the mouse, which has a genome size of 3×10^6 kb, and using as vector a Charon bacteriophage that can accommodate inserts of up to 22 kb, a library of 10^6 recombinant plaques will include 99% of the sequences in the mouse genome, with individual sequences represented an average of five times.

2. For some purposes a **cDNA library** is more useful than a genomic library. A genomic library will include nontranscribed as well as transcribed and translated sequences. Most eucaryotic genes contain intervening sequences (**introns**) that are transcribed but not translated; they are removed in RNA processing reactions as the primary transcripts are transported from the nucleus to the cytoplasm to become mature mRNA molecules for translation (Concept 20.3). A genomic clone that includes a particular gene will contain any introns within that gene, and may also contain nontranscribed sequences adjacent to it. By contrast, a cDNA library will contain only transcribed and translated sequences. Such a library is constructed by

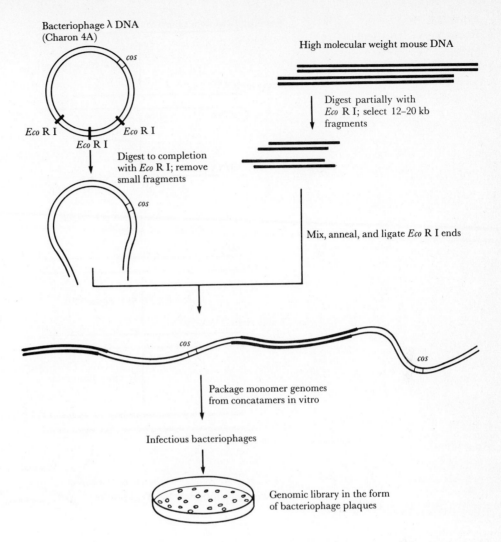

Figure 19.7
Construction of a mouse
genomic clone library using a
Charon bacteriophage vector.

making complementary DNA (cDNA) copies from a population of cytoplasmic
mRNA using the enzyme reverse transcriptase (Concept 18.4), converting the cDNA
single strands to double-stranded DNA using *E. coli* DNA polymerase I, tailing the
cDNA duplexes with homopolymers using terminal transferase, and then cloning as
described in Concept 19.3 using an appropriately tailed vector DNA (Figure 19.8).
Assuming that the copying of all mRNAs is equally efficient, a set of clones from the
cDNA library will represent a random sample of the sequences in the original mRNA
population.

B. A number of techniques are available for selection of particular gene sequences from a
clone library. For eucaryotic gene sequences it is generally easier to obtain a particular
sequence in the form of a cDNA or cDNA clone, and then if desired to use this DNA
as a **probe** to screen a genomic library for clones that contain the gene sequence.
There are several possible ways to obtain the cDNA corresponding to a desired gene
sequence.

1. If the corresponding mRNA can be purified, then cDNA can be produced directly by reverse transcription and inserted into a plasmid or bacteriophage vector.
The mRNA for a protein to which specific antibodies are available often can be
purified from cytoplasmic extracts by antibody precipitation of the synthetic complexes on which the protein is being made, because these complexes also contain the
corresponding mRNA.

2. If the mRNA corresponding to a desired gene sequence can be translated in vitro

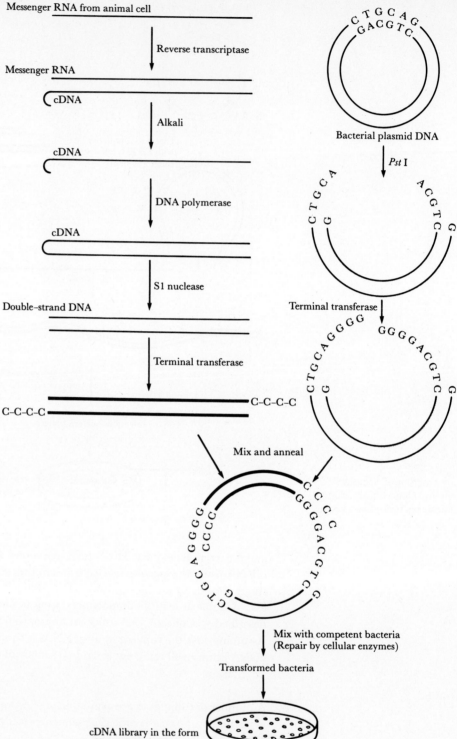

Figure 19.8
Construction of a cDNA library
from animal cell mRNA using
a bacterial plasmid vector.
(Adapted from W. Gilbert and
L. Villa-Komaroff, "Useful Proteins from Recombinant Bacteria," *Scientific American*, April
1980, p. 74.)

to produce an identifiable protein product, then clones from a cDNA library can be
screened for inserts that will hybridize specifically with the active mRNA and thereby
remove it from the rest of an mRNA population. Figure 19.9 shows how one such test,
called **hybrid-selected translation,** can be used to identify a desired cloned cDNA by
its ability to hybridize with and allow isolation of a translatable mRNA from an RNA
population. A similar test, called **hybrid-arrested translation,** depends on the ability
of the cloned cDNA to hybridize with and thereby remove a translatable mRNA from
the population, leading to disappearance of the corresponding polypeptide from the
pattern of in vitro translation products.

3. If a desired gene is expressed as a cloned cDNA insert, then clones carrying this gene sometimes can be selected for by the ability of the insert to complement a mutation in the host organism.

4. If a desired gene is expressed but selection by complementation is impractical, clones that produce the corresponding protein may be identified by immunological methods, or by functional tests if the protein has an activity that can be assayed. In this approach replicas of the library are produced by transferring colonies or plaques from the master plates to replica plates, in such a way that the spatial pattern is preserved. The replicas are screened for expression of the desired gene, and then used to locate corresponding colonies in the master library.

Once a cDNA (or mRNA) corresponding to a desired gene sequence has been obtained, it can be radiolabeled and used as a probe to identify clones that carry this sequence in any clone library (Figure 19.10). In this procedure clones in the form of

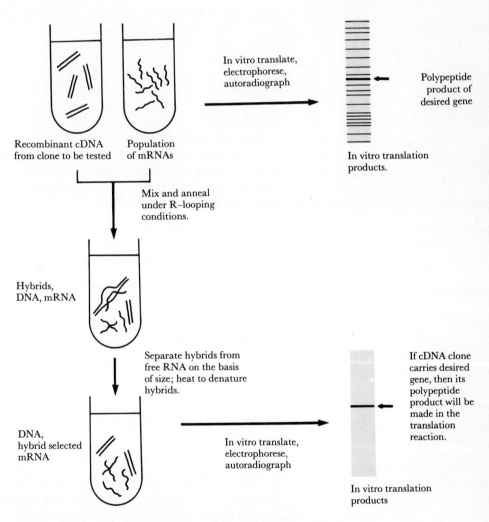

Figure 19.9
Testing a cDNA clone for presence of a desired gene by hybrid-selected translation. In vitro translation is carried out with radiolabeled amino acids so that the polypeptide products can be detected by autoradiography. R-looping conditions are explained under Concept 19.5, section 5. In practice, cDNA clones are tested first in sets of 10 or more, so that a larger number can be screened conveniently; clones in sets giving a positive result then are tested individually.

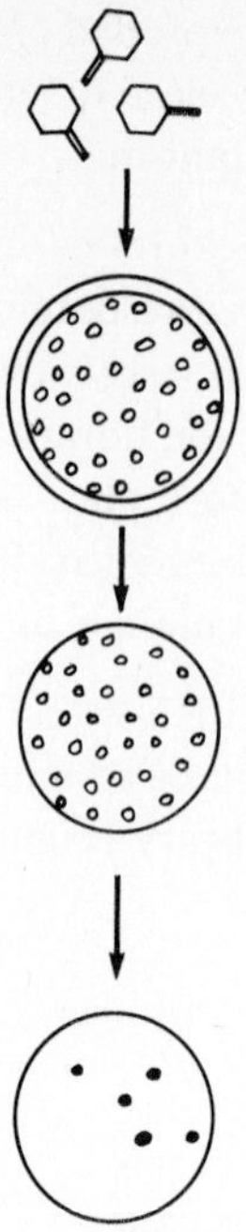

Library in the form of Charon bacteriophages
containing recombinant DNAs

Plate with *E. coli*

Bacteriophage plaques on agar plate

Press nitrocellulose sheet onto plate surface

Filter replica of individual plaques

Anneal nitrocellulose–bound DNA
with labeled probe

Autoradiograph nitrocellulose sheet; pick
corresponding plaques from agar plate

Figure 19.10
Screening of a library for clones
carrying a desired sequence using
a radiolabeled probe. The probe
can be purified mRNA, cDNA,
or another cloned DNA.

bacterial colonies or bacteriophage plaques from a genomic library, for example, are replicated from master plates onto nitrocellulose sheets, treated with alkali to denature their DNA, annealed with the radiolabeled cDNA probe, washed free of unannealed probe, and then autoradiographed (overlaid with x-ray film and left in the dark until radioactive decay of the labeled probe exposes the adjacent film). Clones carrying inserts that anneal to the probe produce dark spots on the film. The positions of these spots then can be correlated with those of the desired clones on the master plates of the library.

19.5 Cloned eucaryotic genes can be characterized by several techniques.

Cloned DNA sequences can be analyzed conveniently for size, primary structure, homology with other DNA sequences, frequency of occurrence in the genome, transcription in different cell types, homology with nuclear and cytoplasmic transcripts, and so on. Some of the techniques now available for such analyses are as follows:

1.   Cloned genes often are characterized initially by restriction mapping (Concept 19.1), which can be used to determine the size of a cloned insert and the order of subfragments bounded by restriction endonuclease recognition sites.

2.   Heteroduplex mapping (Problem 17.17) can be used to determine the extents and locations of homologous sequences in two cloned genes—for example, a cDNA clone and a genomic clone of the same gene.

3.   The **Southern transfer** technique allows estimation of the number of times a particular cloned sequence is represented in the genome (Figure 19.11). A sample of genomic DNA is digested with a restriction endonuclease and the resulting fragments are subjected to electrophoresis on an agarose gel to separate them by size. After denaturing with alkali, DNA from the agarose gel is transferred by blotting onto a sheet of nitrocellulose, to which the single-stranded DNA fragments adhere tightly, giving a replica of the separation pattern. Then the nitrocellulose sheet is incubated under annealing conditions with a radioactively labeled denatured sample of the cloned sequence. The radioactive probe associates with its complementary sequences on the nitrocellulose, which binds single-stranded DNA in a manner that allows it still

to anneal with complementary probe DNA. After annealing, the sheet is washed to remove unassociated probe, dried, and autoradiographed. DNA fragments that anneal with the probe show up as dark bands on the autoradiogram. A cloned sequence that is represented only once in the genome will show a single band if the sequence is included in only one specific restriction fragment (however, it will show more than one band if the sequence includes a recognition site for the restriction enzyme used for digestion of the genomic DNA). A cloned sequence that is represented several times will generally show several bands, because of the likelihood that different copies of the sequence will be found in different-sized restriction fragments.

4.   The transcription of a cloned sequence can be investigated by a similar technique termed a **northern transfer.** Isolated RNA is subjected to separation by gel electrophoresis and transferred onto nitrocellulose or chemically treated paper that covalently binds the RNA, to give a replica of the separation pattern. The replica then is annealed with the radioactive cloned DNA probe and autoradiographed. The position and intensity of bands on the autoradiogram provide information on the size and relative abundance, respectively, of RNA transcripts complementary to the cloned probe.

5.   **R-loop mapping** permits visualization of the extent of homology between a cloned gene and its corresponding mRNA (Figure 19.12). Because DNA–RNA duplexes are more stable than DNA–DNA duplexes under certain annealing conditions (**R-looping conditions**) hybrid structures can form in which intervening sequences present in DNA but not in mRNA are seen by electron microscopy as single-stranded deletion loops.

19.6   DNA fragments can be sequenced rapidly by chemical or enzymatic methods.

A.   The Maxam–Gilbert chemical method for sequencing DNA is diagrammed in Figure 19.13. In this procedure a single-stranded DNA fragment to be sequenced is end-labeled, usually by treatment with bacterial alkaline phosphatase to remove 5′ phosphates, followed by reaction with γ-^{32}P-labeled ATP in the presence of **polynucleotide kinase,** which attaches ^{32}P to the 5′ terminal nucleotide. Samples of the labeled fragment are treated under four different conditions with reagents that cause cleavage next to particular nucleotides. The four commonly used conditions are as follows:

1.   **Guanine cleavage.** DNA is reacted with dimethylsulfate, which methylates the 7-position of guanine and the 3-position of adenine. Subsequent treatment with piperidine base breaks the phosphodiester bond next to positions that were occupied by guanine.

2.   **Guanine–adenine cleavage.** DNA reacted with dimethylsulfate is treated with pyridinium formate at pH 2. Subsequent treatment of the acid-modified DNA with piperidine breaks the phosphodiester bond next to positions that were occupied by a purine.

3.   **Thymine–cytosine cleavage.** Hydrazine reacts with DNA to cleave thymine and cytosine bases, forming ribosyl urea and other products called hydrazones. Treatment of the hydrazinolysis products with piperidine catalyzes cleavage of the sugar phosphate backbone at exposed deoxyribose residues, thereby causing breakage of the DNA strand with about equal frequencies next to positions that were occupied by cytosine or thymine.

4.   **Cytosine cleavage.** Carrying out the hydrazinolysis reaction in the presence of $2M$ NaCl suppresses reaction with thymine residues preferentially. Therefore, subsequent cleavage with piperidine breaks DNA strands specifically next to positions that were occupied by cytosine.

CHAPTER 19
Recombinant DNA and
Genetic Engineering

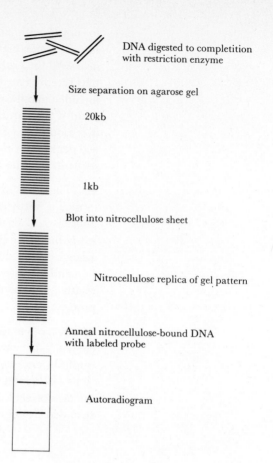

DNA digested to completion
with restriction enzyme

Size separation on agarose gel

20kb

1kb

Blot into nitrocellulose sheet

Nitrocellulose replica of gel pattern

Anneal nitrocellulose-bound DNA
with labeled probe

Autoradiogram

Figure 19.11
Detection and size determination of specific restriction fragments in a DNA digest by the Southern transfer technique. Fragments that contain sequences complementary to those in the probe RNA or DNA give rise on the autoradiogram to labeled bands whose positions indicate the sizes of the complementary fragments.

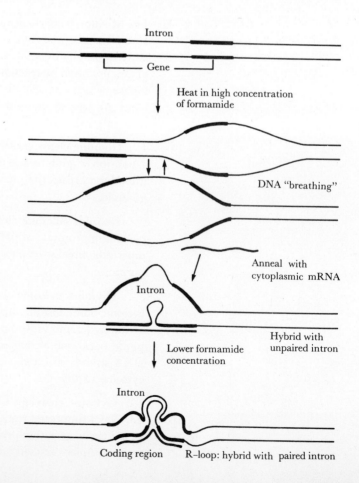

Intron

Gene

Heat in high concentration
of formamide

DNA "breathing"

Anneal with
cytoplasmic mRNA

Intron

Hybrid with
unpaired intron

Lower formamide
concentration

Intron

Coding region   R-loop: hybrid with paired intron

Figure 19.12
Visualization of homology between eucaryotic mRNA and its cloned gene by the R-looping technique. Heavy straight lines indicate two coding regions of a cloned gene separated by an intron sequence, which will be spliced out of the primary transcript and will be absent from the cytoplasmic mRNA (Concept 20.3). Medium-weight line represents cytoplasmic mRNA. At the higher formamide concentration, RNA–DNA hybrids are more stable than DNA duplexes, so that the hybrid with the unpaired intron will form as the mRNA anneals to the coding strand of the gene. When the formamide concentration is lowered, the unpaired intron loop pairs with its complementary sequence on the other DNA strand to give the R-loop structure. In electron micrographs of these structures, single-stranded regions can be distinguished from duplex, and the position of an intron within a gene can be mapped by measuring lengths of unpaired DNA on either side of the paired DNA loop.

Reaction conditions are chosen so that on the average one cleavage occurs every 50–100 nucleotides. Therefore, each of the four reactions produces a population of different-sized fragments, all of which terminate at nucleotides characteristic of that reaction.

The fragments from each reaction are separated on the basis of chain length by polyacrylamide gel electrophoresis, and the gel is autoradiographed to indicate the positions of radioactive bands. Fragments that differ in length by a single nucleotide can be separated. The products of each of the four reactions are run in parallel on adjacent lanes of the same gel. Because cleavage at every position in the DNA strand must have occurred in at least one of the reactions, every possible fragment length will be represented on at least one lane of the gel, with the result that the nucleotide sequence can be "read" directly from the pattern of bands in the four lanes. Determination of complementary sequences on each strand provides a check on the results. Study Figure 19.13 to convince yourself that this procedure works.

B. Sanger and his collaborators have developed various enzymatic methods for sequencing DNA, the most convenient of which is the **chain-termination procedure.** In this procedure a DNA strand to be sequenced is used as a template for *E. coli* DNA polymerase I, with a short complementary fragment as a primer. The primer is annealed to the template and then extended enzymatically for an average of 15 to 300 or more nucleotides in the presence of labeled deoxyribonucleoside triphosphates and the dideoxynucleoside triphosphate analogue of one of the four substrates. Dideoxynucleoside triphosphates lack both 2′ and 3′ hydroxyl groups on the pentose ring. Because DNA chain growth requires the addition of deoxynucleotides to the 3′-OH group, incorporation of a dideoxynucleotide terminates chain growth. Incorporation of the analogue in place of the normal substrate occurs randomly, so that each of the four reactions generates a heterogeneous population of labeled strands terminating with the same nucleotide.

After termination of synthesis, the DNA from each of the four reaction mixtures is cleaved with a restriction endonuclease to separate labeled strands from their primers, and then is denatured by heating in formamide. The resulting single strands are separated electrophoretically in parallel on adjacent lanes of a gel, which is then dried and autoradiographed. As described for the Maxam–Gilbert procedure, because every possible fragment length will be represented in one of the four lanes, the nucleotide

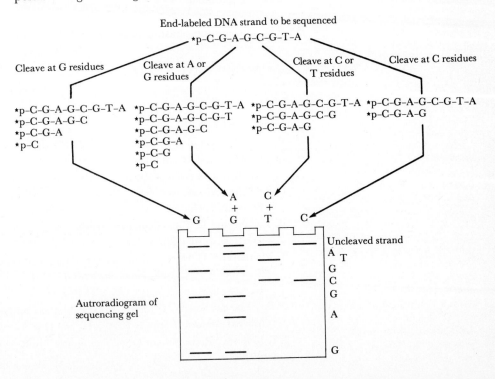

Figure 19.13
Sequencing of DNA by the Maxam–Gilbert chemical method. A DNA fragment generally is end-labeled as a duplex, then cleaved with a restriction endonuclease that gives a larger and a smaller subfragment, which are separated by size and denatured prior to beginning the procedure shown.

sequence of the labeled strand can be read from the pattern of bands on the auto-radiogram.

C. Because of the ease of sequencing DNA, the most convenient approach to sequencing RNA is to make a cDNA copy using reverse transcriptase and then to apply one of the methods described in the preceding paragraphs. Alternatively, a chemical approach similar to the Maxam–Gilbert procedure sometimes is used. Some of the specific cleavage techniques used in RNA sequencing are given in Problem 21.21.

19.7 Cloned DNAs can be used to synthesize desired polypeptides in bacteria.

In theory, the DNA sequence that codes for any desired polypeptide now can be either synthesized artificially or isolated from a cDNA library, inserted in a plasmid vector adjacent to an appropriate procaryotic promoter to allow efficient transcription, and then introduced into a bacterial host, which can be grown to produce large quantities of the polypeptide product. Bacteria have been engineered in this manner to produce human interferon, insulin, and somatostatin. This approach has great promise for the commercial production of medically and industrially important proteins.

19.8 Additional concepts and techniques are presented in the Problems section.

A. Construction of restriction maps. Problems 19.6, 19.9, 19.10, 19.11, and 19.18.

B. Analysis of Southern transfers. Problems 19.7, 19.8, and 19.9.

C. Transposable genetic elements (transposons). Problem 19.11.

D. Determination of a DNA nucleotide sequence by the Sanger–Nicklen–Coulson enzymatic method. Problem 19.13.

E. Determination of a DNA nucleotide sequence by the Maxam—Gilbert chemical method. Problem 19.14.

F. The nucleosome phasing problem. Problem 19.15.

References

COMPREHENSIVE TEXTS:

Lehninger: Chapter 31
Metzler: Chapter 15

Stryer: Chapter 31
White et al.: Chapter 25

OTHER REFERENCES

W. Arber, "Promotion and Limitation of Genetic Exchange," *Science*, **205**, 361 (1979).

L. Clarke and J. Carbon, "Isolation of a Yeast Centromere and Construction of Functional Small Circular Chromosomes," *Nature*, **287**, 504–509 (1980).

D. Freifelder, *Recombinant DNA*, Readings from Scientific American, W. H. Freeman, San Francisco, 1978.

W. Gilbert and L. Villa-Komaroff, "Useful Proteins from Recombinant Bacteria," *Scientific American*, April 1980, p. 74.

T. Maniatis, R. C. Hardison, E. Lacy, J. Lauer, C. O'Connell, D. Quon, G. K. Sim, and A. Efstratiadis, "The Isolation of Structural Genes from Libraries of Eucaryotic DNA," *Cell*, **15**, 678 (1978).

A. M. Maxam and W. Gilbert, "A New Method for Sequencing DNA," *Proceedings of the National Academy of Sciences* (*U.S.*), **74**, 560 (1977).

J. F. Morrow, "Recombinant DNA Techniques," in R. Wu (Ed.), *Methods in Enzymology*, **68**, 3 (1979).

Recombinant DNA issue, *Science,* **209**, 1319–1435 (1980).

F. Sanger, S. Nicklen, and A. R. Coulson, "DNA Sequencing with Chain-Terminating Inhibitors," *Proceedings of the National Academy of Sciences (U.S.),* **74**, 5463 (1977).

Problems

19.1   Answer the following with true or false. If false, explain why.

a. Class II restriction endonucleases require ATP and *S*-adenosylmethionine.

b. Some class II restriction endonucleases produce restriction fragments with sticky ends; others produce fragments with blunt ends.

c. Restriction fragments with sticky ends can associate by complementary base pairing only if they were produced using the same restriction endonuclease.

d. The restriction endonuclease *Hpa*II will cleave DNA at either CCGG or GGCC because these sequences, being inverted repeats, are indistinguishable in a duplex DNA molecule.

e. Most class II restriction endonucleases will catalyze cleavage of double-stranded but not single-stranded DNA.

f. Recombinant plasmids that have an exogenous DNA fragment inserted into the plasmid gene that confers ampicillin resistance can be obtained from a population of recombinant plasmid DNA molecules by transformation of a bacterial recipient and selection for ampicillin-resistant colonies.

g. Recombinant λ DNA can be packaged in vitro to produce infectious virus particles, but only if the DNA molecules are within the size range that can be accommodated in the λ bacteriophage head.

h. The current guidelines for handling of recombinant DNAs are based on perceived possible risks, not on known risks.

i. The rapid methods for chemical and enzymatic sequencing of DNA restriction fragments, like the methods for sequencing proteins, rely on determining sequences of many subfragments produced by specific chemical cleavage or specific replication termination.

j. The Sanger–Nicklen–Coulson enzymatic sequencing method requires single-stranded DNA and a fragment complementary to this DNA adjacent to the sequence to be determined.

k. An exogenous DNA fragment tailed with A's, which has been annealed to a plasmid DNA tailed with T's, can transform competent bacteria without prior in vitro ligation, because nicks will be closed by endogenous ligases in cells that take up the recombinant plasmid.

l. Eucaryotic genes can be cloned in procaryotic host-vector systems, and procaryotic genes can be cloned in eucaryotic host–vector systems.

m. A eucaryotic gene cloned from a genomic DNA library is more likely to be expressed in a procaryotic host–vector system than the same gene cloned from a cDNA library.

n. Clones of a particular gene in a genomic library cannot be identified by colony or plaque hybridization to a cloned probe of the same gene isolated from a cDNA library.

o. If a cloned and labeled genomic restriction fragment is used to probe a Southern transfer of a digest of genomic DNA made with the same restriction enzyme, then the number of labeled bands always will be equal to the number of times the cloned sequence is repeated in the genome.

19.2   a. The complementary single strands at the ends of DNA fragments produced by restriction endonucleases that catalyze staggered cleavage often are referred to as _____.

b. The first class II restriction endonucleases isolated from *Bacillus amyloliquefaciens* H and *Bacillus globigii* are named _____ and _____, respectively.

c. Restriction endonucleases that recognize the same cleavage sequence are called _____ ; restriction endonucleases that cleave at similar sequences to produce sticky ends that can associate by complementary base pairing are called _____.

d. A restriction enzyme will catalyze the cleavage of almost any large DNA molecule into a population of specific _____, which range in length from a few to several _____ nucleotide pairs.

e. Using the enzyme _____, cDNA copies can be made from mRNA templates.

f. DNA duplex fragments with fully base-paired ends can be joined directly using high concentrations of the enzyme _____ from _____.

g. In the cloning of recombinant DNA molecules, a bacterial plasmid often is used as the _____ or _____ for exogenous DNA _____.

h. When *E. coli* bacteria have been treated to make them _____, they can take up free plasmid or bacteriophage DNAs by processes that are called _____ and _____, respectively.

i. The Maxam–Gilbert chemical method for DNA sequencing employs _____ to cleave at purine nucleotides and _____ to cleave at pyrimidine nucleotides.

j. In the Sanger–Nicklen–Coulson chain-termination method for DNA sequencing, _____ serve as chain terminators, because they lack _____.

k. The _____ technique is useful for analyzing transcription of a cloned gene in different tissues or cellular compartments.

l. Labeling of the 5′ ends of a DNA duplex can be accomplished using _____ as a substrate for the enzyme _____.

19.3   Does the restriction endonuclease *Bam*HI cleave DNA into fragments with blunt ends or sticky ends? Diagram the ends of the DNA fragments produced by *Bam*HI cleavage.

19.4 a. If a homogeneous population of high-molecular-weight DNA molecules that contain 50% GC nucleotide pairs is digested with the restriction endonuclease *Hae*III, what will be the average fragment length, assuming that the DNA nucleotide sequence is random?

b. What will be the average fragment length if the same DNA is digested with *Hin*dIII?

c. What will be the average fragment length after *Hin*dIII digestion if the DNA contains only 40% GC base pairs?

19.5   A circular plasmid vector that contains two *Eco*RI restriction sites is cleaved with *Eco*RI and annealed with a purified *Eco*RI fragment from a different source. Diagram all the possible annealing products that contain two fragments or less and can replicate if introduced into a bacterium. Assume that the plasmid fragments produced by *Eco*RI cleavage are unequal in size and that the genes required for plasmid replication are on the larger of these fragments.

19.6   You have cloned a *Bam*HI fragment 3.0 kb in length that contains a gene you wish to sequence. In preparation for sequencing you wish to make a restriction map of the fragment, that is, to cleave it into smaller subfragments and determine their relative order. To begin this process, you digest three separate samples of the purified fragment with *Eco*RI, *Hpa*II, and a mixture of these two enzymes, respectively. The digests are subjected to electrophoresis on agarose gels and stained with ethidium bromide to visualize the banding patterns, which are shown in Figure 19.14. From these results, diagram a restriction map of the *Bam*HI fragment showing the relative positions of *Eco*RI and *Hpa*II cleavage sites and the distances in kilobases between them.

19.7   A gene for which you have a cloned, labeled cDNA probe occurs once in an organism's genome. The gene contains one *Eco*RI cleavage site near its center and has no intervening sequences. If you probe a Southern transfer of a complete *Eco*RI digest of the organism's DNA with your labeled cloned sequence, the number of radioactive bands you are most likely to find will be

a. 0

b. 1

c. 2

d. 3

e. 4

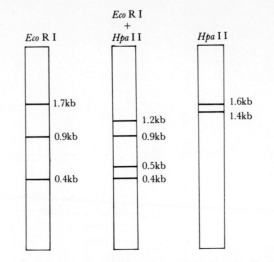

Figure 19.14
Electrophoretic patterns of DNA from digests of a *Bam*HI fragment with *Eco*RI and *Hpa*II restriction endonucleases (Problem 19.6).

19.8   Suppose that from the genomic DNA of the organism in Problem 19.7 you have cloned a *Bam*HI fragment that will hybridize with your original cDNA probe. When you now label the cloned *Bam*HI fragment and use it to probe a Southern transfer of an *Eco*RI digest as in Problem 19.7, you find that four bands are labeled. How would you explain this result? Diagram a possible arrangement of *Eco*RI and *Bam*HI sites relative to the ends of the gene represented by your original DNA probe.

19.9 a. A cloned *Eco*RI fragment 1.4 kb in length from a genomic library of housefly DNA is labeled and used to probe a Southern transfer of an *Eco*RI digest of the genomic DNA, with the results shown in Figure 19.15. From other evidence the cloned fragment is known to include at least part of a gene 1.3 kb in length. How many copies of that gene are present in the housefly genome, and how are these copies arranged?
      b. Diagram a possible arrangement of the gene copies in the genome and the *Eco*RI restriction sites in their vicinity.

19.10   Certain animal viruses transform cells to a neoplastic (cancerous) phenotype by stably integrating their DNA into one of the cell's chromosomes, as shown in Figure 19.16a for a virus with a circular double-stranded DNA. You are interested in studying the structure of the viral genome as it exists in the integrated state in the transformed cell. You digest samples of viral and transformed cell DNA with restriction enzymes that cut viral DNA at known sites. Subsequently you separate the fragments by electrophoresis·on agarose gels and obtain the patterns shown in Figure 19.16b. The fragments from viral DNA are visualized by staining with ethidium bromide; the viral fragments in the cellular DNA digest are visualized by Southern transfer to nitrocellulose, hybridization to a labeled viral DNA probe, and autoradiography. Figure 19.16c shows the positions of the five known, restriction sites in the viral DNA, which define five DNA segments. From the results in Figure 19.19b identify the segment in which the integration event occurs, and diagram the order of segments and restriction sites in the integrated viral DNA.

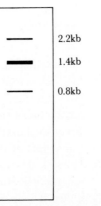

Figure 19.15
Pattern of labeled bands in a Southern transfer of a genomic *Eco*RI digest probed with a cloned *Eco*RI fragment (Problem 19.9). The intensity of the 1.4 kb band is three times that of the other two, which are approximately equal in intensity.

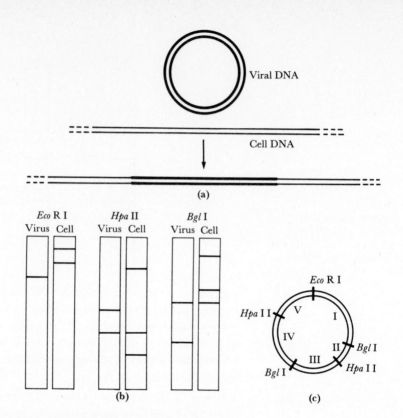

Figure 19.16
Diagrammatic representation of integration of a circular
viral DNA into a cellular genome and restriction enzyme
analysis of its free and integrated forms (Problem 19.10).
(a) Integration of viral DNA into host cell chromosomal
DNA by a reciprocal recombination event. **(b)** Electrophoretic patterns of viral restriction fragments after digestion of viral and cellular DNAs with restriction enzymes.
(c) Location of restriction sites on the viral DNA.

19.11   Transposons are genetic elements that have the ability to generate copies of themselves that can reinsert at another location, apparently randomly, by mechanisms that
are not fully understood. Because of this remarkable property they sometimes are
referred to as "jumping genes." Fluhardy Pharmaceuticals has isolated a pathogenic
bacterium that is resistant to their new antibiotic fluhamycin. They suspect that the
gene for resistance may be carried in the form of a transposon on a small transmissible
plasmid, and they are worried. They have contracted with you to investigate further
by restriction mapping the plasmid DNA from sensitive and resistant strains of bacteria. Sure enough, the plasmid from the resistant strain has an insert. You digest the
plasmid DNAs with four restriction enzymes, each of which alone cuts both DNAs at
least once, to obtain the data given in Table 19.3. From these data, construct restriction maps of the two plasmids showing the position and length (in kilobases) of the
insert and the distances (in kilobases) between all restriction sites.

19.12 a. You have cloned a gene for armadillo aldolase from a genomic library, and you wish
to study its expression in armadillo liver. You isolate RNAs from liver cell nuclei and
liver cell cytoplasm, separate them by gel electrophoresis on the basis of size, and carry
out a northern transfer, probing the gel replicas with your genomic clone, which you
have labeled radioactively. You obtain the results shown in Figure 19.17. What is a
likely explanation for the difference in size between the nuclear and cytoplasmic
transcripts of the cloned gene?

       b. Draw a structure consistent with these results that could be observed by electron
microscopy after hybridization of the cytoplasmic transcript to your cloned gene
under R-looping conditions.

Table 19.3
Sizes of Restriction Fragments of Plasmid DNAs Isolated from Drug-Sensitive and Drug-Resistant Strains of a Bacterium (Problem 19.11)

Restriction enzymes	Fragments obtained		Restriction enzymes	Fragments obtained	
	Plasmid from sensitive strain (kb)	Plasmid from resistant strain (kb)		Plasmid from sensitive strain (kb)	Plasmid from resistant strain (kb)
*Bgl*I	4.3	4.4	*Bgl*I + *Hae*III	1.8	1.8
		0.8		1.5	1.6
*Eco*RI	4.3	4.6		1.0	1.0
		0.6			0.8
*Bam*HI	3.4	4.3	*Eco*RI + *Bam*HI	3.4	3.9
	0.9	0.9		0.7	0.7
*Hae*III	2.5	3.4		0.2	0.4
	1.8	1.8			0.2
*Bgl*I + *Eco*RI	3.2	3.2	*Eco*RI + *Hae*III	2.1	2.4
	1.1	0.8		1.8	1.8
		0.6 (2×)		0.4	0.6
					0.4
*Bgl*I + *Bam*HI	2.5	2.5	*Bam*HI + *Hae*III	1.9	2.8
	0.9 (2×)	1.0		1.5	1.5
		0.9		0.6	0.6
		0.8		0.3	0.3

19.13   Figure 19.18 shows a DNA sequencing gel for a portion of the histidine operon control region. The labeled DNA fragments were obtained using the Sanger–Nicklen–Coulson chain termination method. Read the sequence of nucleotides from positions −200 to −120. (Negative numbers refer to nucleotide positions preceding the first structural gene of the operon.)

19.14   To investigate control of transcription in the herpes simplex virus, the viral DNA was digested with *Eco*RI. A fragment containing the origin of transcription was isolated, labeled, and chemically cleaved for sequencing by the Maxam–Gilbert method. Autoradiograms of two gels used for electrophoretic separation of the cleavage fragments are shown in Figure 19.19. The gels are of different agarose concentration to allow resolution of fragments over a broad size range. From the gel patterns shown, read as much of the sequence as you can, starting from the labeled 5′ end of the fragment.

19.15   Several studies suggest that nucleosomes (Concept 17.5) may be not just DNA packaging vehicles but also elements in controlling the functional states of genes. In this context a question of current interest is whether nucleosomes are located randomly with respect to a given nucleotide sequence or whether a specific relationship exists between nucleotide sequences and nucleosome location. This question is known as the

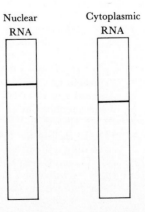

Figure 19.17
Northern transfers of nuclear and cytoplasmic armadillo liver RNAs probed with a labeled genomic clone (Problem 19.12).

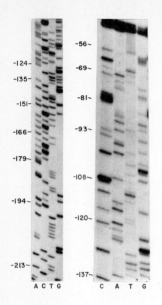

Figure 19.18
Autoradiogram of DNA sequencing gel of labeled fragments produced by the Sanger–Nicklen–Coulson chain-termination method (Problem 19.13). (Autoradiogram courtesy of Wayne M. Barnes, Washington University.)

nucleosome phasing problem. A description of a clever approach to the question of nucleosome phasing follows.

Tetramers of nucleosomes were isolated from chicken chromatin after limited digestion with staphylococcal nuclease, which preferentially cleaves DNA in the internucleosomal linker region. This random collection of tetranucleosomes then was enriched for those containing tRNA genes. The histones were stripped from these tetranucleosomes and the resulting 760-base-pair DNA fragments were treated in two ways. (The DNA associated with one nucleosome plus the adjacent internucleosomal DNA is about 190 base pairs long in the chicken.)

In one experiment the DNA fragments were cloned into an *E. coli* plasmid. Twelve clones were identified that contained the genes for one or the other of two lysine tRNAs. The tRNA genes then were positioned relative to the ends of the inserted DNA by restriction mapping (Figure 19.20a and b; Table 19.4).

In a second experiment the DNA fragments were digested with *Alu*I, which cuts DNA containing the tRNA^Lys genes only once. The cleaved DNA was analyzed in a way that detected either both fragments from a digestion or only the one containing the 3′ half of the tRNA^Lys genes (Figure 19.20c).

Do these experiments indicate that the tRNA^Lys genes are located randomly or nonrandomly with respect to nucleosomes? Explain your answer.

Table 19.4
Location of the 5′ End of the tRNA Gene Relative to the End of Cloned Tetranucleosomal DNA (Problem 19.15)

Bacterial clone	x^a	y^a
1	390	345
2	45	720
3	250	540
4	220	510
5	600	130
6	410	360
7	32	700
8	610	150
9	38	710
10	245	530
11	55	730
12	620	155

^{a} See Figure 19.20b.

Table 19.5
Mutant Mapping (Problem 19.16)^a

		Wild-type virus		
Experiment	DNAs	*Hpa*II	*Eco*RI	*Bam*HI
1	A + B	0	+	0
2	A + D	0	0	+
3	B + C	+	0	0
4	C + D			

^{a} The results in this table are to be read as follows, using experiment 1 as an example. Ligated mixtures of A and B DNAs when digested with either *Hpa*II or *Bam*HI yield no wild-type virus (0); however, when digested with *Eco*RI they yield many wild-type viruses (+).

Figure 19.19
Autoradiograms of DNA sequencing gels of labeled fragments produced by the Maxam–Gilbert method (Problem 19.14). Cleavages were carried out as described in Concept 19.6. In each of the two gels, the four lanes from left to right display fragments produced by cleavages at C, T + C, A + G, and G, respectively. **(a)** 20% gel run for 2 hr. **(b)** 8% gel run for 2 hr. (Fragments of a given size move faster through an 8% gel than through a 20% gel.)

(a)   (b)

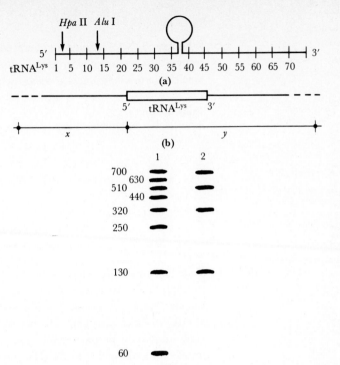

Figure 19.20
Phasing of tRNA^{Lys} genes (Problem 19.15). **(a)** Restriction map of the tRNA^{Lys} genes. The looped-out region represents an intron. **(b)** Position of tRNA^{Lys} genes in tetranucleosomes (see Table 19.4). **(c)** Electrophoretic separation of the *Alu*I digestion products of tetranucleosomal DNA. In lane 1 both fragments were detected. In lane 2 fragments containing the 3′ half of the tRNA^{Lys} genes were detected. Numbers indicate sizes of fragments in base pairs.

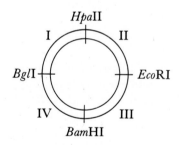

Figure 19.21
The closed circular, double-stranded DNA genome from an animal virus (Problem 19.16). The diagram shows the locations of four restriction sites and the DNA segments they define.

19.16   One of your fellow students, who enjoys a good joke, claims to have devised a quick method for locating mutations on the circular genome of an animal virus (Figure 19.21). Because he has fooled you before, you are understandably dubious. Out of curiosity you peek at his notebook. His procedure seems simple enough, but it is not immediately apparent how it works.

Quickie Mapping Procedure: Mix together equal amounts of DNAs from two different mutants. Digest them to completion with *Bgl*I and then ligate at very high DNA concentrations to promote formation of oligomers. Digest to completion with a second enzyme (*Hpa*II, *Eco*RI, or *Bam*HI). Finally, infect cells with the digested DNA and measure production of normal (nonmutant) virus.

Apparently he has already performed several experiments with DNAs from four different mutants, A, B, C, and D (Table 19.5). However, you can find no explanation of the procedure in his notebook. When you ask him directly to explain his procedure he challenges you to figure it out on your own. Furthermore, he claims that the data in Table 19.5 uniquely position the mutations into the segments of the genome indicated by Roman numerals in Figure 19.21. Finally, he challenges you to predict the results of experiment 4 in Table 19.5. Is he fooling you once again, or does he really have something this time?

19.17   Restriction enzymes that recognize different nucleotide sequences but leave identical single-stranded tails upon cleavage are termed isocaudamers. One set of isocaudamers is shown in Table 19.6.

a.   Of the possible combinations of DNA fragments generated by cleavage with the different isocaudamers in Table 19.6, how many can be joined together by DNA ligase?

b. Whenever DNA fragments generated by different isocaudamers are joined, a hybrid recognition sequence is produced. For the isocaudamers listed in Table 19.6, list the possible hybrid sites and indicate which of the isocaudamers will cleave them.

Table 19.6
A Set of Isocaudamers
(Problem 19.17)

Restriction enzyme	Recognition site[a]
1. BamHI	G↓GATCC
2. BclI	T↓GATCA
3. BglII	A↓GATCT
4. Sau3A	↓GATC
5. XhoII	U↓GATCY

[a] U and Y stand for purine and pyrimidine, respectively. Fragments produced by cleavage with these restriction enzymes have 5'-phosphoryl and 3'-hydroxyl groups.

19.18 a. Your first task as a newly arrived post-doc in the laboratory of Dr. Groucho Ursh is to analyze the structure of the shellase gene from the Bulgarian spotted grosbeak. Luckily, your predecessor, Dr. Klassik, has left you a small, but very pure preparation of mRNA for this protein. The mRNA is 9.5 kb in length. As the starting material for your study, you prepare whole genomic DNA from the spotted grosbeak. Using the restriction endonucleases BamHI, EcoRI, HindIII, and SalI, in all combinations, you digest the DNA and subject it to electrophoresis on an agarose gel. You then do a Southern transfer from the gel to nitrocellulose paper. As a probe, you take half of Dr. Klassik's mRNA preparation and incubate it with γ^{32}P-ATP and polynucleotide kinase to radioactively label the 5' end (Concept 19.6). You then hybridize the probe to the DNA on the nitrocellulose. After washing off unhybridized probe, you autoradiograph the filter. Table 19.7 lists the sizes of the bands seen after overnight exposure. You know from Klassik's former work that there are about 20 copies of the shellase gene per haploid genome. Diagram the restriction map of the gene.

b. What, if any, are the unusual features of the gene structure?

c. The boss is still not satisfied, and wants a better autoradiogram for publication. You leave another sheet of film on the filter—this time for 3 days. You are aghast at the results! Table 19.7 shows your data. How would you explain the extra bands?

d. Is the piece of DNA that carries this gene in the genomic DNA preparation circular or linear? Why?

e. Can you say how large this piece of DNA is? Why or why not?

f. Dr. Ursh has asked you to find out what the direction of transcription is on the restriction map. You are at a total loss as to how to do this until one of your colleagues suggests that you repeat your experiment and use RNase. How could you use RNase

Table 19.7
Sizes of Fragments
Identified by Southern
Transfer in Digests of
Grosbeak Genomic DNA
(Problem 19.18)[a]

Enzymes	Fragments (kb)	
	Overnight exposure	Three-day exposure[b]
EcoRI	10	10, 7*
EcoRI + HindIII	6, 4	7*, 6, 4
EcoRI + BamHI	9, 1	9, 6*, 1
EcoRI + SalI	6, 4	7*, 6, 4
HindIII	10	17*, 10
HindIII + BamHI	5 (dark)	7*, 5 (dark)
HindIII + SalI	8, 2	15*, 8, 2
SalI	10	17*, 10
SalI + BamHI	7, 3	7, 3
BamHI	10	10, 7*
EcoRI + HindIII + BamHI	5, 4, 1	6*, 5, 4, 1
EcoRI + HindIII + SalI	4 (dark), 2	7*, 4 (dark), 2
EcoRI + BamHI + SalI	6, 3, 1	6, 3, 1
EcoRI + BamHI + HindIII + SalI	4, 3, 2, 1	6*, 4, 3, 2, 1

[a] Restriction digests were probed with purified ^{32}P-labeled shellase mRNA.
[b] Asterisks indicate faint bands, less than 10% as intense as the main bands.

to help you determine the direction of transcription, given the manner in which your mRNA is labeled? Will an RNase experiment provide sufficient information?

☆ 19.19 A highly purified radioactive mRNA probe from one organism was hybridized to a Southern transfer of restriction fragments from another organism. The autoradiogram of the pattern showed five labeled bands. Give some possible reasons why more than one band was seen.

☆ 19.20 You have been given a homogeneous preparation of a small DNA molecule and asked to make a restriction map of sites recognized by the enzymes *Eco*RI, *Hpa*II, and *Hin*dIII. You cleave samples of the molecule with each enzyme and with all possible combinations of enzymes and determine the sizes of the resulting fragments as shown in Table 19.8. Diagram the restriction map. Is the molecule circular or linear?

Table 19.8
Sizes of Restriction Fragments Produced from a Small DNA Molecule Using Three Restriction Enzymes (Problem 19.20)

Enzyme(s)	Fragment sizes (kb)
*Eco*RI	1.3 (2×)
*Hpa*II	2.6
*Hin*dIII	2.6
*Eco*RI + *Hpa*II	0.5
	0.8
	1.3
*Eco*RI + *Hin*dIII	0.6
	0.7
	1.3
*Hpa*II + *Hin*dIII	1.2
	1.4
*Eco*RI + *Hpa*II + *Hin*dIII	0.5
	0.6
	0.7
	0.8

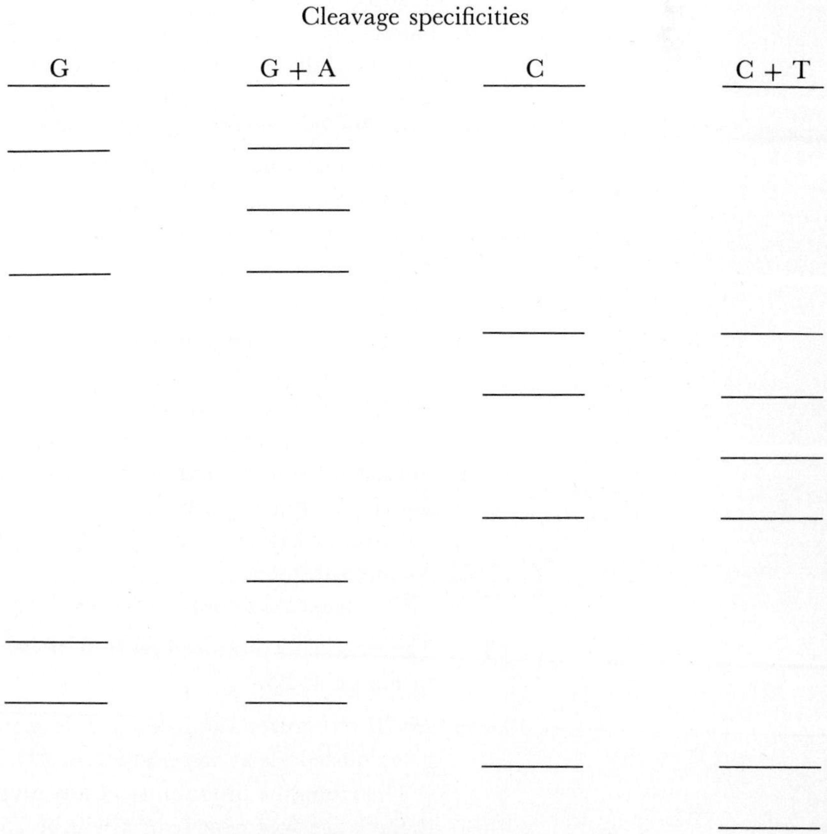

Cleavage specificities

G	G + A	C	C + T

Figure 19.22
Pattern of labeled bands on a Maxam–Gilbert sequencing gel (Problem 19.21).

☆ 19.21   You have just sequenced one strand of a 12-nucleotide-pair DNA fragment that you suspect includes the binding site for a dimeric regulatory protein. The pattern of labeled bands on your Maxam–Gilbert sequencing gel is shown in Figure 19.22. A colleague of yours glances at your results and concludes that 10 of the 12 nucleotide pairs are arranged symmetrically about an axis of 2-fold rotational symmetry. Is she correct? Write the nucleotide-pair sequence of the fragment.

Answers

19.1 a. False. Class II restriction endonucleases require only Mg^{2+} as cofactor. Class I restriction endonucleases require ATP and S-adenosylmethionine.
   b. True
   c. False. Fragments produced by two different enzymes can associate with each other if the enzymes are either isoschizomers or isocaudamers.
   d. False. *Hpa*II recognizes the sequence 5'-CCGG-3', which is distinct from the reverse sequence 5'-GGCC-3'.
   e. True
   f. False. Plasmids that have an insert in the ampicillin-resistance gene will no longer confer ampicillin resistance upon a bacterial host.
   g. True
   h. True
   i. False. The DNA sequencing methods rely on determining the sizes of fragments produced by specific cleavage or replication termination at a particular nucleotide.
   j. True
   k. True
   l. True
   m. False. Because the gene cloned from the genomic library is likely to contain intervening sequences, which the procaryotic host cannot process, expression is more likely with the gene cloned from a cDNA library, which will not include intervening sequences.
   n. False. A cDNA clone and a genomic clone of the same gene will have sequences in common (all those except for intervening sequences); therefore, one can be used to identify the other by hybridization.
   o. False. If a sequence is repeated in tandem, then many of the restriction fragments that include it may be of the same size, so they will produce only one band on the Southern transfer.

19.2 a. sticky ends
   b. *Bam*HI, *Bgl*I
   c. isoschizomers, isocaudamers
   d. restriction fragments, thousand
   e. reverse transcriptase
   f. DNA ligase, bacteriophage T4
   g. vehicle, vector, inserts
   h. competent, transformation, transfection
   i. dimethylsulfate, hydrazine
   j. dideoxynucleoside triphosphates, 3'-OH groups
   k. northern transfer
   l. $\gamma^{32}P$-labeled ATP, polynucleotide kinase

19.3   The fragments produced by *Bam*HI cleavage have sticky ends. They are diagrammed in Figure 19.23.

19.4 a. *Hae*III recognizes a four-nucleotide sequence, GGCC. The probability of finding any given nucleotide at any position in a DNA of 50% GC and random sequence is 0.25 or $\frac{1}{4}$. Therefore, the probability of any given four-nucleotide sequence is $(\frac{1}{4})^4$ or $\frac{1}{256}$, and the average fragment length will be 256 nucleotide pairs.

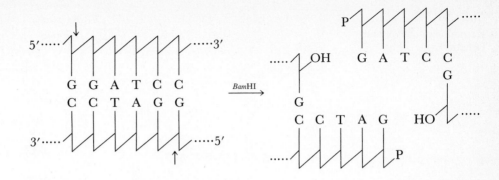

Figure 19.23
Diagram of the *Bam*HI cleavage site in a DNA duplex and the ends of the fragments produced by *Bam*HI-catalyzed cleavage (Answer 19.3).

b. *Hind*III recognizes the six-nucleotide sequence AAGCTT. By the foregoing argument, the probability of occurrence of this sequence will be $(\frac{1}{4})^6 = \frac{1}{4096}$, and the average fragment length will be 4096 nucleotide pairs.

c. If the DNA contains only 40% GC pairs, then the probability of a G or a C at any given position becomes 0.2, and the probability of an A or a T becomes 0.3. The probability of the six-nucleotide *Hind*III recognition sequence of 2 GC pairs and 4 AT pairs therefore will be $(0.2)^2(0.3)^4 = 0.000324$, and the average fragment length will be the reciprocal of this number, that is, 3086 nucleotide pairs.

In practice average fragment lengths may differ from such calculated values because the nucleotide sequences in naturally occurring DNAs are not random.

19.5   The plasmid, the fragments into which it will be cleaved by *Eco*RI (designated A and B), and the exogenous *Eco*RI fragment (designated C) are diagrammed in Figure 19.24a. To replicate, an annealing product must be circular and must contain plasmid fragment A. Because the sticky ends produced by *Eco*RI are identical, fragments can anneal in either orientation with respect to each other. Therefore, there are seven possible products that can replicate, as diagrammed in Figure 19.24b.

19.6   One approach to arriving at a restriction map is as follows. Draw a line of appropriate length on graph paper to represent the 3.0 kb *Bam*HI fragment. Because *Hpa*II cuts the fragment only once, the *Hpa*II site can be located unequivocally; mark its position on the fragment 1.6 kb from one end. *Eco*RI cuts the fragment twice. If you position an *Eco*RI site 1.7 kb from either end of the fragment, you will find that its distance from the *Hpa*II site cannot be reconciled with the sizes of bands from the double digest. Therefore, the two *Eco*RI sites must be 0.4 kb and 0.9 kb from the two ends, respectively. Only one of the two possible orientations is consistent with the fragment sizes from the double digest. Therefore, the map must be as shown in Figure 19.25 (reading either from left to right or from right to left).

19.7   The *Eco*RI digest will contain two fragments that include sequences within the gene and therefore are complementary to your probe. Unless they are fortuitously of exactly the same length you will see two labeled bands on the Southern transfer. Therefore, the answer is c.

19.8   The *Bam*HI fragment must include sequences that extend beyond the two *Eco*RI fragments identified with the cDNA probe. As a result the *Bam*HI probe can hybridize not only to those two *Eco*RI fragments, but also to two adjacent fragments. Two possible arrangements of the restriction sites are diagrammed in Figure 19.26.

19.9 a. The pattern of labeled bands indicates that there are three fragments containing sequences present in the probe, and that the 1.4 kb fragment is three times as abundant as the other two. This result suggests that the 1.3 kb gene includes one *Eco*RI restriction site, and that the gene is repeated in tandem, in such a way that the restriction sites within the tandem repeat are 1.4 kb apart. The two bands of lower intensity must represent the ends of the tandem repeat. The presence of three internal fragments per pair of end fragments indicates that the gene must be repeated four times. Therefore, the genome contains four copies of the gene, arranged in tandem, with 0.1 kb spacers separating the copies.

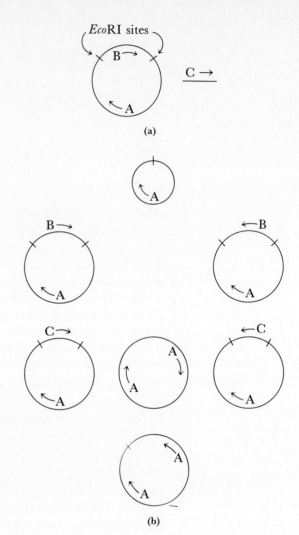

Figure 19.24
*Eco*RI restriction fragments from a plasmid and possible
products of annealing them with an exogenous *Eco*RI fragment (Answer 19.5). **(a)** Diagram of the original plasmid
showing sizes and orientations of the two *Eco*RI fragments
A and B, and the size of the exogenous fragment C.
(b) Diagrams of the seven possible replication-competent
annealing products containing two fragments or less.

b. One arrangement of *Eco*RI restriction sites that would be consistent with the observed
results is diagrammed in Figure 19.27.

19.10 The structure of the integrated viral genome can be deduced as follows: First, note
that the cell digests always contain one more band than the viral DNA. That is
because the integrated viral DNA is linear rather than circular and has cell DNA
attached to its ends. Second, note that the viral DNA segment that contains the site of

Figure 19.25
Restriction map of a *Bam*HI
DNA fragment (Answer 19.6).
Numbers below the line indicate
segment lengths in kilobases.

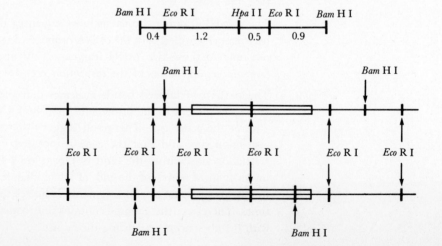

Figure 19.26
Two possible arrangements of
*Eco*RI and *Bam*HI restriction
sites around a gene (Answer
19.8). The extent of the gene is
indicated by the boxes.

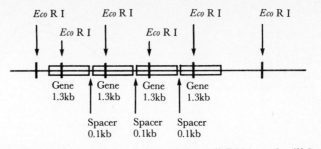

Figure 19.27
A possible arrangement of *Eco*RI cleavage sites in the neighborhood of a set of tandemly repeated genes (Answer 19.9).

integration will be missing from the digest of the cell DNA and will be replaced by two other bands. The sizes of the new bands cannot be predicted in advance because they depend on the proximity of the corresponding restriction enzyme sites in the adjacent cell DNA. The critical information is contained in the electrophoretic patterns of the *Hpa*II and *Bgl*I restriction digests. Note that the large *Hpa*II band and the small *Bgl*I band are missing from the cell digests. The overlap between these two segments on the viral genome is interval II, which therefore must contain the site of integration. The arrangement of restriction sites and numbered segments in the integrated DNA therefore must be as diagrammed in Figure 19.28.

19.11   You should proceed essentially as outlined in Answer 19.6. Both plasmid DNAs must be circular; however, it may be more convenient to construct the map as the linear sequence of fragments that would result if the circle were opened at one of the restriction sites. The maps you should arrive at are shown in Figure 19.29 as linear sequences opened at the *Bgl*I site on the plasmid from the sensitive strain.

19.12 a. The gene probably contains at least one intervening sequence (intron) that is transcribed in the nucleus but is removed from the RNA transcript by processing when it is transported into the cytoplasm.

       b. Under R-looping conditions, RNA–DNA hybrids are more stable than DNA duplexes. Because cytoplasmic mRNA lacks the intron, this sequence will be seen as an unpaired loop on the coding strand of the DNA, the rest of which will be base-paired to mRNA. A possible structure for the hybrid is diagrammed in Figure 19.30.

19.13   The A lane of the gel shows fragments that terminate with A; the T lane shows fragments that terminate with T, and so on. Therefore, the presence of a fragment n nucleotides long in the N lane of the gel indicates that nucleotide N must occupy position n in the sequence. The sequence from -200 to -120 can be read from the gel as:

```
    -200                -190                -180
     T T T A T G A C A C G C G T T C A A T T T
                        -170                -160
     A A A C A C C A C C A T C A T C A C C A
                        -150                -140
     T C A T C C T G A C T A G T C T T T C A
                        -130                -120
     G G C G A T G T G T G C T G G A A G A C
```

Figure 19.28
Restriction map of an integrated viral genome in host cell DNA (Answer 19.10).

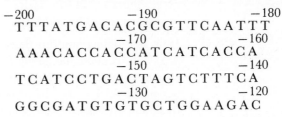

Figure 19.29
Restriction maps of plasmid DNAs isolated from drug-sensitive and drug-resistant strains of a bacterium (Answer 19.11). The circular DNAs are diagrammed as linear molecules that have been opened at the *Bgl*I site on the plasmid from the sensitive strain. Distances are indicated in kilobases. **(a)** Map of plasmid DNA from the sensitive strain. **(b)** Map of plasmid DNA from the resistant strain; box shows extent of inserted transposon.

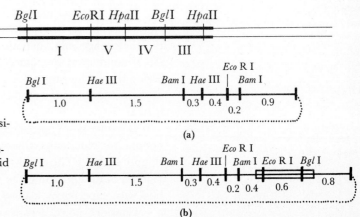

Figure 19.30
Structure of a possible hybrid of cytoplasmic armadillo aldolase mRNA with part of a genomic clone containing the aldolase gene (Answer 19.12). Heavy line represents mRNA.

19.14 To read the gels, remember that fragments that terminate with C will appear in both the C and C + T lanes; fragments that terminate with T will appear only in the C + T lane, and so on. The cleavages are not entirely specific; you can see that fragments terminating with G, for example, are darkest in the G and A + G lanes but can be seen in the other two lanes as well. The smallest fragment recovered will be nearest the bottom of the 20% gel; therefore, to read the sequence from the 5′ end of the labeled fragment, start at the bottom of the 20% gel and read up. You should be able to read about 45 nucleotides before the bands become difficult to resolve. Then go to the bottom of the 8% gel, which displays the same population of fragments except that the smaller ones will have run off the bottom and the larger ones will be better separated, and read upward again. You should find that the sequences read from the two gels overlap, so that you can determine a total sequence of about 80 nucleotides. The correct sequence is as follows:

```
1       5        10       15       20       25       30
G-C-A-G-A-T-G-C-A-G-T-C-G-G-G-G-C-G-G-C-G-C-G-G-T-C-C-G-A-G-
        35       40       45       50       55       60
G-T-C-C-A-C-T-T-C-G-C-A-T-A-T-T-A-A-G-G-T-G-A-C-G-C-G-T-G-T-
        65       70       75       80       85       90
G-G-C-C-T-C-G-A-A-C-A-C-C-G-A-G-C-G-A-C-C-C-T-G-C-A-G-C-G-A-
```

19.15 Both experiments indicate that the tRNA^{Lys} genes are located at special positions within the tetranucleosomal DNA. The 5′ end of the tRNA gene is located at about 50, 240, 430, or 610 nucleotides from one end of the tetranucleosomal DNA fragment. This spacing correlates well with the 190-base-pair nucleosomal repeat length of chicken chromatin. Thus the tRNA^{Lys} genes must be located nonrandomly with respect to nucleosomes. A random relationship between the tRNA^{Lys} genes and the nucleosomes would have yielded a wider range of distances in Table 19.4 and a smear of fragments in Figure 19.20c.

19.16 He is not fooling you this time. The oligomeric DNA created in the first step of his procedure contains tandemly linked mutant DNAs. Monomers derived from these oligomers contain complementary parts of the genomes that were adjacent in the oligomers. As described here, monomers derived from junctions between the two different mutants can be wild type. The pattern of wild-type monomer production in the series of crosses uniquely fixes the positions of the mutants.

Consider experiment 1. The two mutant DNAs can be linked in two ways in the oligomer (Figure 19.31a). If nonmutant monomers are derived from structure I by *Eco*RI cleavage only, then mutation A must be in region II and mutation B in region III. If nonmutant monomers are derived from structure II, mutation A must be in region III and mutation B in region II. Thus, at this stage in the analysis, the positions of these mutations are ambiguous; either A is in II and B in III, or A is in III and B is in II.

Consider now experiment 2. Regardless of whether A is in region II or region III, nonmutant monomers cannot be derived from structure II by cleavage with *Bam*HI (Figure 19.31b). Thus wild-type monomers must have come from structure I. If this is so, then mutation D must be in region IV and mutation A in region III. In conjunction with experiment I, these results locate mutation B in region II.

Consider now experiment 3. Because mutation B is in region II, wild-type mono-

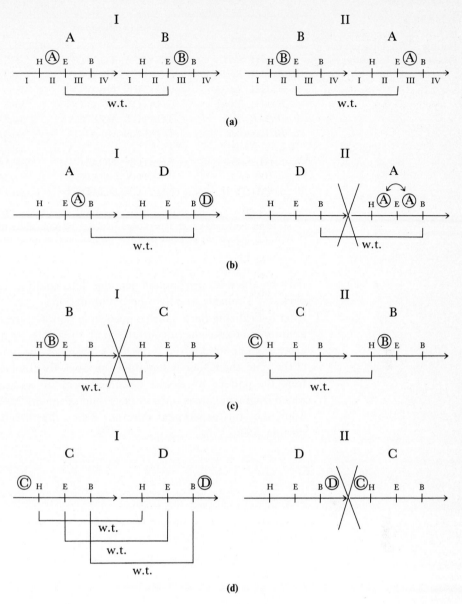

Figure 19.31
Analysis of mutant mapping procedure (Answer 19.16). See text for explanation of individual panels.

mers could not have come from structure I, but rather must have come from structure II (Figure 19.31c). If so, then mutation C must be in region I.

Thus, just as your fellow student claimed, these three experiments uniquely position all four mutations. Knowing the positions of mutations C and D, you can predict correctly that wild-type monomers will be produced by cleavage with any of the three restriction enzymes in Table 19.5 (Figure 19.31d).

19.17   a. All the possible combinations can be joined together by DNA ligase.
   b. See Table 19.9.

19.18   a. See Figure 19.32.
   b. The gene is present in about 20 copies, which are arranged in tandem.
   c. One of the repeats has a deletion of about 3 kb spanning the *Sal*I and *Hind*III sites.
   d. The piece is circular; there are no end fragments visible in the autoradiogram.
   e. One piece must be a circle of at least two repeat units, and the total number of genes

Figure 19.32
Restriction map of the shellase gene (Answer 19.18). Distances are shown in kilobases.

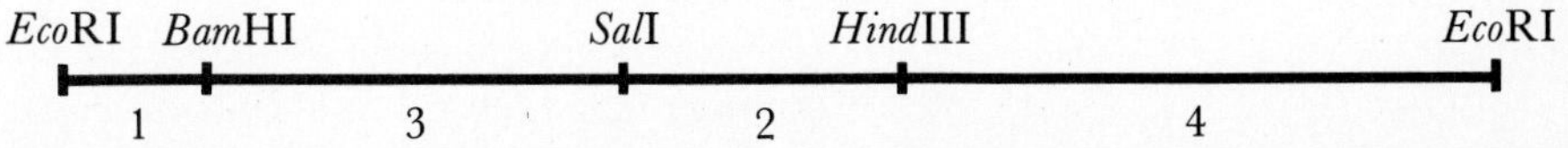

*Eco*RI   *Bam*HI   *Sal*I   *Hind*III   *Eco*RI

        1   3   2   4

Table 19.9
Hybrid Sites Generated by
Joining DNA Fragments
Produced by Isocaudamers
(Answer 19.17)

Combination of isocaudamers	Hybrid recognition sites[a]	Hybrid site sensitivity
1. *Bam*HI, *Bcl*I	GGATCA, TGATCC	*Sau*3A
2. *Bam*HI, *Bgl*II	GGATCT, AGATCC	*Sau*3A, *Xho*II
3. *Bam*HI, *Sau*3A	GGATCN, NGATCC	*Sau*3A, *Xho*II (50%), *Bam*HI (25%)
4. *Bam*HI, *Xho*II	GGATCY, UGATCC	*Sau*3A, *Xho*II, *Bam*HI (50%)
5. *Bcl*I, *Bgl*II	TGATCT, AGATCA	*Sau*3A
6. *Bcl*I, *Sau*3A	TGATCN, NGATCA	*Sau*3A, *Bcl*I (25%)
7. *Bcl*I, *Xho*II	TGATCY, UGATCA	*Sau*3A
8. *Bgl*II, *Sau*3A	AGATCN, NGATCT	*Sau*3A, *Xho*II (50%), *Bgl*II (25%)
9. *Bgl*II, *Xho*II	AGATCY, UGATCT	*Sau*3A, *Xho*II, *Bgl*II (50%)
10. *Sau*3A, *Xho*II	NGATCY, UGATCN	*Sau*3A, *Xho*II (50%), *Bam*HI (12.5%), *Bgl*II (12.5%)

[a] N stands for any nucleotide. Percentages indicate the probability that either of the hybrid sites will be cleaved. Percentages are calculated on the assumption that alternative nucleotides occur with equal frequency.

must be about 20 per haploid genome. This could mean 1 circle of 20 repeats or 10 circles of 2 repeats, or any other combination.

f. After hybridizing the 5′ labeled probe to a Southern transfer of DNA digested to give asymmetric fragments (for instance *Sal*I + *Eco*RI), treatment with RNase will digest away any unpaired RNA. If the DNA fragment does not contain the 5′ coding region of the gene, the RNase will remove the label. By observing which bands are removed from the pattern by RNase treatment prior to autoradiography, you can deduce which fragment corresponds to the 5′ end of the mRNA. However, because the DNA is circular, this experiment does not define the direction of transcription, only its starting point.

20 Expression of Genetic Information

During gene expression the linearly arranged information in DNA directs the formation of three-dimensional protein structure. Initially RNA is transcribed from DNA. The resulting messenger RNA nucleotide sequences then are translated into polypeptides, whose amino acid sequences determine their folding into the correct conformation. In addition to energy input, both RNA and protein synthesis require information, supplied by polynucleotide templates, to direct the polymerization of activated monomer units. This chapter considers the informational and energetic aspects of gene expression.

Concepts

20.1 Information flows from DNA to RNA to protein.

    A. The flow of genetic information in cells is shown in Figure 20.1. During gene expression, information is transcribed from DNA into RNA and then is translated from RNA into protein. This important generalization first was stated explicitly by Francis Crick, who called it the central dogma.

    B. During transcription the nucleotide sequences of mRNA (and tRNA and rRNA as well) are determined by complementary base pairing between the polymerizing nucleotides and the **sense strand** of a duplex DNA template. A stretch of DNA that is transcribed as a single, continuous mRNA strand is called a **unit of transcription.** A stretch of DNA that carries the information for a polypeptide chain (or an rRNA or a tRNA) is called a **gene** or **cistron.** A unit of transcription may include more than one gene. In procaryotes such **polycistronic** transcripts are common and can be translated to give more than one protein product. In eucaryotes most mRNAs are monocistronic and yield only the polypeptide chain encoded at their 5′ ends.

    C. During translation the amino acid sequences of proteins are determined by complementary base pairing between trinucleotide sequences (**codons**) in mRNA molecules and trinucleotide sequences (**anticodons**) in tRNA molecules, which are linked to the amino acids. As a polypeptide chain grows, its constituent amino acids interact with each other and their surroundings to reach a minimum-free-energy conformation. The amino acid sequence of a protein thereby uniquely determines its three-dimensional structure (Chapter 4).

20.2 RNA polymerase catalyzes transcription of DNA into RNA.

    A. RNA polymerase is the enzyme that catalyzes synthesis of RNA from a DNA template. In procaryotes there is one polymerase that synthesizes all classes of RNA. In eucaryotes there are three polymerases that synthesize rRNA (RNA polymerase I),

Figure 20.1
Flow of genetic information in cells. Arrows indicate the primary flow of information. Protein components are required to catalyze each step.

$$\text{DNA} \xleftrightarrow{\text{Replication}} \text{DNA} \xrightarrow{\text{Transcription}} \begin{array}{c} \text{rRNA} \\ \text{mRNA} \\ \text{tRNA} \end{array} \xrightarrow{\text{Translation}} \text{Protein}$$

mRNA (RNA polymerase II), and tRNA and 5S rRNA (RNA polymerase III), respectively. These three enzymes can be distinguished on the basis of their sensitivity to the antibiotic α-amanitin. All RNA polymerases are asymmetric complexes of several subunits. In procaryotes the composition is $\alpha_2\beta\beta'\sigma$. Eucaryotic RNA polymerases appear analogous in structure.

B. RNA synthesis takes place in four stages:

1. **Binding.** RNA polymerase binds to DNA at specific asymmetric sequences called **promoters** near the beginning of each transcription unit (Figure 20.2). The asymmetric interaction orients the polymerase on the sense strand in position to initiate transcription. In procaryotes a dissociable subunit of the enzyme, called **sigma** (σ), enhances specific binding at promoters. Binding at a promoter presumably is accompanied by local opening of the DNA duplex to expose H-bonding groups on each strand.

2. **Initiation.** The initiating ribonucleoside triphosphate (NTP), usually ATP or GTP, pairs with its complementary nucleotide on the sense strand of the enzyme–DNA complex. The next NTP pairs with the next DNA base and forms a phosphodiester bond to the 3′-OH of the initiating NTP, with elimination of PP_i. In procaryotes the formation of this first bond is sensitive to the antibiotic **rifampicin.**

3. **Elongation.** With formation of each succeeding phosphodiester bond the enzyme moves along the DNA sense strand from 3′ to 5′. Because nucleotide pairing is antiparallel, the mRNA strand grows in the 5′ → 3′ direction by addition of monomers at the 3′ end. The DNA duplex re-forms behind the enzyme, so that the 5′ end of the RNA is released as a free single strand. Propagation can be blocked by the antibiotic **actinomycin D,** which binds to GC dinucleotide sequences in DNA.

Procaryotic Promoters

              −35 region   −10 region

trp operon   AGC [TGTTGACAATTA] ATCATCGAACTAG [TTAACTA] GTACGCA ↓

spc operon   TTT [TCTACCCATATC] CTTGAAGCGGTGT [TATAATG] CCGCG ↓

Eucaryotic Promoters

            −25 region

Adenovirus major late   GGC [TATAAAA] GGGGGTGGGGGCGCGTTCGTCCTCA ↓

Chicken ovalbumin   GC [TATATAT] TCCCCAGGGCTCAGCCAGTGTCTGTA ↓

Figure 20.2
Promoter sequences in procaryotes and eucaryotes. The antisense (noncoding) strand of DNA is shown in all cases. Arrows indicate the nucleotides at which RNA transcription begins. Nucleotides to the left of the start site are given negative numbers. Boxed regions indicate conserved sequences important for RNA polymerase recognition. The eucaryotic promoters are both recognized by RNA polymerase II. Note the similarity between the −10 region in procaryotes and the −25 region in eucaryotes. The *trp* operon encodes several proteins involved in tryptophan biosynthesis; the *spc* operon encodes several ribosomal proteins.

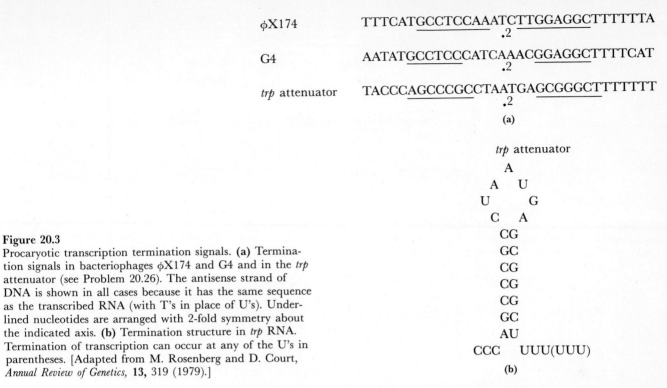

φX174   TTTCATGCCTCCAAATCTTGGAGGCTTTTTTA
.2

G4   AATATGCCTCCCATCAAACGGAGGCTTTTCAT
.2

trp attenuator   TACCCAGCCCGCCTAATGAGCGGGCTTTTTTT
.2

(a)

trp attenuator

A
A   U
U   G
C   A
CG
GC
CG
CG
CG
GC
AU
CCC   UUU(UUU)

(b)

Figure 20.3
Procaryotic transcription termination signals. **(a)** Termination signals in bacteriophages φX174 and G4 and in the *trp* attenuator (see Problem 20.26). The antisense strand of DNA is shown in all cases because it has the same sequence as the transcribed RNA (with T's in place of U's). Underlined nucleotides are arranged with 2-fold symmetry about the indicated axis. **(b)** Termination structure in *trp* RNA. Termination of transcription can occur at any of the U's in parentheses. [Adapted from M. Rosenberg and D. Court, *Annual Review of Genetics,* **13,** 319 (1979).]

4.   **Termination.** In procaryotes a hairpin structure in RNA followed by a string of U's signals termination (Figure 20.3). Some procaryotic termination events are assisted by an additional protein factor called **rho** (ρ). The termination signal in eucaryotes is still undefined.

20.3   RNA usually is modified after transcription.

Only mRNA in procaryotes appears to be an unaltered primary transcript. Other RNAs are modified by cleavage of phosphodiester bonds or by alteration of individual nucleotides. rRNA, tRNA, and many eucaryotic mRNAs are transcribed as longer precursors that subsequently are reduced in size. For rRNA and tRNA this processing generally occurs by trimming extra sequences from the ends. However, in eucaryotes many genes are interrupted by intervening sequences of DNA (introns) that are not represented in the final mRNA product. Introns are included in the primary transcript but are removed (spliced out) during processing. In splicing, the RNA chain is broken at two points and the terminal pieces are reunited. For mRNA the 5′ terminal dinucleotide of the intron is GU and the 3′ terminal dinucleotide is AG (Figure 20.4). The mechanism of the splicing process is unknown.

Several individual nucleotides in rRNA, tRNA, and eucaryotic mRNA are modified chemically after transcription. In eucaryotes RNA destined to become mRNA is capped on the 5′ end with a reversed 7-methyl G in 5′-5′ linkage, and usually is tailed on the 3′ end with a string of 100–200 A residues (Figure 20.4). Both modifications presumably protect mRNA from nuclease degradation. In addition the cap is important for alignment during translation, and the poly A tail may function during export from the nucleus. The sequence AATAAA is found about 20 nucleotides in front of mRNA polyadenylation sites and may be the signal for poly A addition.

20.4   Aminoacyl-tRNA synthetases link amino acids to their cognate tRNAs.

Each aminoacyl-tRNA synthetase catalyzes the linkage of one amino acid to the 3′-terminal hydroxyl group of a specific tRNA molecule, as shown in Figure 20.5. The

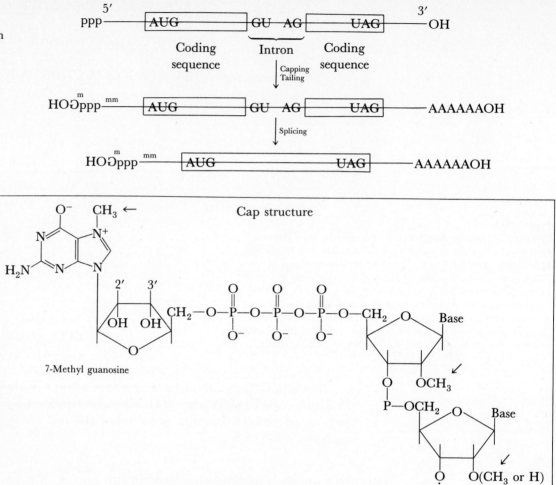

Figure 20.4
Processing of eucaryotic mRNA.
Processing occurs in the following
order: capping, tailing, splicing. Positions of methyl groups
(m) are indicated with arrows in
the detailed drawing of cap
structure.

reaction proceeds through an enzyme-bound aminoacyl-AMP intermediate. The
driving energy for this process, also called **amino acid activation,** is supplied by the
subsequent hydrolysis of PP_i to $2P_i$ ($\Delta G'_0 \simeq -6$ kcal/mol). Sufficient energy is conserved in the resulting aminoacyl ester ($\Delta G'_0$ of hydrolysis $\simeq -7$ kcal/mol) to drive
the formation of a peptide bond ($\Delta G'_0$ of hydrolysis $\simeq -4$ kcal/mol). The acceptor
specificity of a tRNA molecule is indicated by a superscript; for example, $tRNA^{Leu}$
symbolizes the set of tRNA molecules specific for leucine. The activated amino acid is
written as $Leu\text{-}tRNA^{Leu}$.

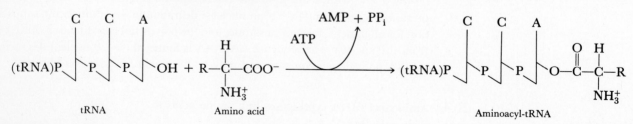

Figure 20.5
Amino acid activation. The $\Delta G'_0$
for this reaction is about
0 kcal/mol.

20.5 Translation of mRNA occurs on ribosomes.

A. mRNA-directed polypeptide synthesis is catalyzed by **ribosomes,** which are complex cytoplasmic particles each consisting of two ribonucleoprotein subunits. The subunits, generally referred to by their sedimentation coefficients, are 50S and 30S in procaryotes and 60S and 40S in eucaryotes. The smaller subunit contains 16S (procaryotes) or 18S (eucaryotes) rRNA, and about 20 proteins. The larger subunit contains 5S rRNA, 23S (procaryotes) or 28S (eucaryotes) rRNA, and more than 30 protein components. In addition, eucaryotic large subunits contain a 5.8S rRNA species. The smaller subunit carries the binding site for mRNA, and the larger subunit carries the binding sites for aminoacyl-tRNAs.

B. The major steps in translation are formation of an initiation complex, elongation of the polypeptide chain, and termination. These steps are similar in procaryotes and eucaryotes.

1. **Initiation-complex formation.** The sequence of steps in formation of procaryotic initiation complexes is outlined in Figure 20.6. In the first step an mRNA is bound by

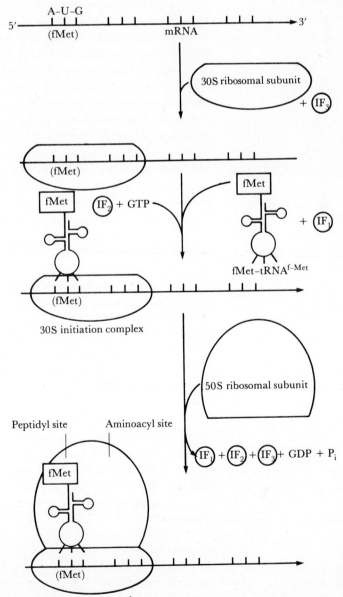

Figure 20.6
Formation of a 70S initiation complex in procaryotes. IF1, IF2, and IF3 refer to protein initiation factors that are required to catalyze initiation-complex formation.

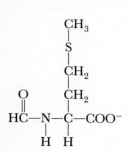

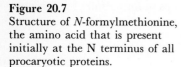

Figure 20.7
Structure of *N*-formylmethionine,
the amino acid that is present
initially at the N terminus of all
procaryotic proteins.

a small ribosomal subunit so that the initiating Met codon (AUG) is positioned correctly. Binding of mRNA requires participation of a protein initiation factor. In procaryotes a signal sequence (often AGGA), which usually is present 7–8 bases to the 5′ side of the initiation AUG, directs proper alignment by base pairing with a complementary sequence at the 3′ end of 16S rRNA. In eucaryotic mRNA such a matching sequence probably is not present. Eucaryotic small ribosomal subunits apparently bind to the cap structure and scan the mRNA from the 5′ end until they come to the first AUG.

The mRNA–small subunit complex then binds the special Met tRNA that is used only during initiation. In procaryotes the Met is modified by tetrahydrofolate-mediated formylation of Met-tRNA^{fMet} to produce *N*-formylmethionine (Figure 20.7). In eucaryotes the special initiator tRNA carries an unmodified Met. In the presence of GTP and protein initiation factors, the aminoacylated initiator tRNA recognizes and binds to the initiation codon AUG. The resulting complex then binds a free large ribosomal subunit to form the complete initiation complex, and releases all initiation factors with concomitant splitting of GTP to GDP and P$_i$. Initiator tRNAs are special in that they alone, of all the aminoacyl-tRNAs, can bind to the peptidyl site (**P site**) on the large subunit.

2.   **Chain elongation.** Peptide-bond formation proceeds via a cycle of three steps, repeated for each amino acid as shown for procaryotes in Figure 20.8. In each cycle a new aminoacyl-tRNA binds to the aminoacyl site (**A site**) in a reaction requiring a protein elongation factor and GTP. The growing chain, bound as a peptidyl-tRNA in the P site, then forms a peptide bond between its activated carboxyl terminus and the amino group of the aminoacyl-tRNA in the A site, thereby freeing the tRNA in the P site to dissociate. Formation of the peptide bond requires the enzyme peptidyl transferase, which is a component of the large ribosomal subunit. The new peptidyl-tRNA then is translocated from the A site to the P site in a reaction requiring a second elongation factor and GTP. In the process, the association between the tRNA and the mRNA is maintained, so that the mRNA moves three nucleotides relative to the small subunit. Thus a new codon is positioned at the A site to direct the binding of the next aminoacyl-tRNA. In this manner the ribosome moves along the mRNA in the 5′ → 3′ direction, with concomitant growth of the polypeptide chain from the N terminus to the C terminus. Additional ribosomes can initiate translation, one at a time, as the original ribosome moves down the mRNA, so that the same mRNA molecule can direct simultaneously the synthesis of many copies of the corresponding protein(s). Such an mRNA molecule with many ribosomes bound to it is called a **polyribosome** or **polysome**. The energy for peptide-bond formation presumably is provided by the high-energy aminoacyl-tRNA linkage. However, in addition, each cycle requires expenditure of two high-energy phosphate bonds. The binding of each incoming aminoacyl-tRNA to the A site is accompanied by cleavage of GTP to GDP + P$_i$, as is each translocation reaction. The coupling of these cleavages to binding and translocation is not yet understood.

3.   **Termination.** Hydrolysis of the final peptidyl-tRNA to release the completed polypeptide requires a termination codon (UAG, UAA, or UGA) in the A site, a soluble protein-release factor, and GTP. Under these conditions peptidyl transferase hydrolyzes the peptidyl-tRNA bond to release the completed polypeptide, and GTP is split to GDP and P$_i$. The ribosomes then run off the mRNA and dissociate into subunits ready to begin the cycle again. A few inhibitors of translation are listed in Table 20.1.

C.   Mitochondria contain ribosomes that have physical properties unlike ribosomes from eucaryotic cytoplasm but quite similar to those from procaryotes. As indicated in Table 20.1, mitochondrial ribosomes also resemble procaryotic ribosomes in their

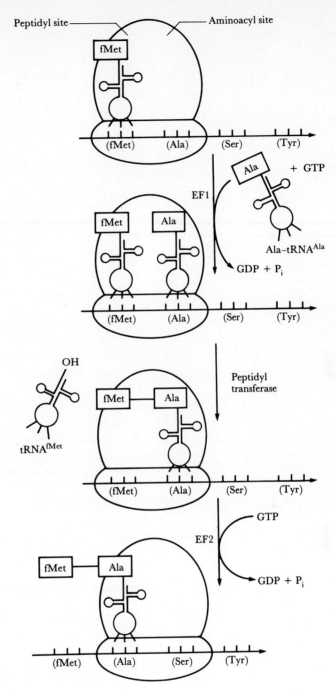

Figure 20.8
Peptide-bond formation.

sensitivity to inhibitors of translation. These and other similarities between mitochondria and procaryotes have fostered the speculation that mitochondria evolved from intracellular procaryotic symbionts.

20.6 **Exported proteins cross the membrane during translation.**

In both procaryotes and eucaryotes a number of proteins must be transported across the plasma membrane in order to function outside the cell. The mechanism for this transport process was described first for eucaryotes, as shown in Figure 20.9. Translation of a eucaryotic mRNA that encodes an export protein begins on cytoplasmic ribosomes. During translation a hydrophobic signal sequence of 15–20 amino acids,

Table 20.1
Inhibitors of Translation

Inhibitor	Procaryotes	Eucaryotes Cyto-plasm	Eucaryotes Mitochon-dria	Mode of action
Chloramphenicol	+	−	+	Binds to 50S ribosomal subunit; blocks chain elongation (mechanism not known)
Cycloheximide	−	+	−	Same as chloramphenicol, for 60S ribosomal subunit
Puromycin	+	+	+	Binds to A site of larger ribosomal subunit; causes premature chain termination
Streptomycin (and other aminoglycosides)	+	+	±	Binds to smaller ribosomal subunit; blocks both chain initiation and elongation
Erythromycin (and other macrolides)	+	−	+	Binds to 50S ribosomal subunit; blocks chain elongation (mechanism not known)
Tetracyclines	+	−	+	Bind to 30S ribosomal subunit; block A site
Sparsomycin	+	+	+	Blocks peptidyl transferase
Fusidic acid	+	+	+	Interferes with aminoacyl-tRNA binding
Aurintricarboxylic acid	+	+	+	Interferes with attachment of mRNA to ribosomes, blocking initiation

which is usually at the N terminus, attaches the translation complex to the membrane of the rough endoplasmic reticulum. Continued protein synthesis then pushes the nascent polypeptide through the membrane into the lumen of the endoplasmic reticulum. The protein exits the cell by cycles of vesicle formation and fusion that lead first to the Golgi apparatus and then to the external environment (Concept 6.7). The mechanism of transport appears to be similar in procaryotes, where synthesis occurs directly across the plasma membrane. A number of integral transmembrane proteins also are positioned in the membrane during translation by the same basic process. In these cases one portion of the protein is extruded through the membrane and another portion remains on the cytoplasmic side, so that the protein spans the lipid bilayer.

20.7 Proteins often are modified after translation.

Proteins can be modified after translation by cleavages of peptide bonds or by alteration of individual amino acid side chains. The formyl group of fMet and often one or more additional N-terminal amino acids are removed from most procaryotic proteins

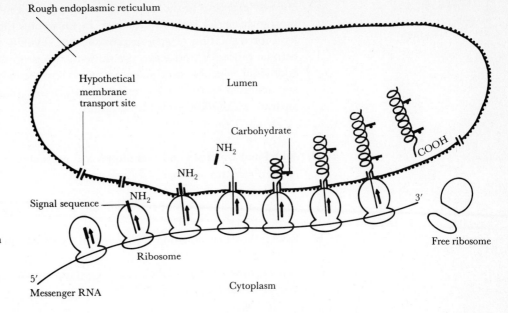

Figure 20.9
Synthesis of an exported protein in eucaryotes. (Adapted from H. F. Lodish and J. E. Rothman, *Scientific American*, January 1979, p. 48.)

following translation. The hydrophobic signal sequences of exported and integral membrane proteins usually are cleaved off as soon as they cross the membrane. In addition, internal cleavages can convert inactive or partially active proteins to their fully active form, as occurs in the conversion of proinsulin, trypsinogen, and chymotrypsinogen to insulin, trypsin, and chymotrypsin, respectively. Chemical alteration of specific amino acid residues occurs in some specialized proteins such as collagen, in which some Pro and Lys residues are converted to hydroxyproline and hydroxylysine. Reversible modifications, such as phosphorylation and methylation, play an important role in regulating enzymatic activities (Concept 10.3).

In eucaryotes most exported proteins and nearly all plasma membrane proteins that face the external environment are modified by the addition of carbohydrate "trees" to Ser, Thr, or Asn residues. One common "complex" carbohydrate tree attached to Asn residues is added in two stages. First, a stump is attached to the protein as it enters the lumen of the endoplasmic reticulum, and then in the Golgi the stump is trimmed and the final branches are added. Specific carbohydrate additions may be involved in **targeting** of membrane-associated proteins for transport from the Golgi apparatus to the plasma membrane or a specific organellar membrane.

20.8   Expression of genetic information is controlled at several levels.

Procaryotes and eucaryotes have two classes of genes: **Nonregulated** (**constitutive**) genes, whose products are made constantly at fixed relative rates, and **regulated** genes, whose products are expressed variably at different times or in different tissues. In procaryotes the synthetic rate of a constitutive gene product apparently depends only on the nucleotide sequence of the promoter. Different promoters compete for available RNA polymerase, thereby fixing the relative ratios of gene transcripts. For regulated bacterial genes, accessory proteins either alter the frequency of initiation by RNA polymerase or change the probability with which new transcripts are propagated past critical checkpoints, known as **attenuators.** In both cases the regulatory effect is to vary the level of translatable transcripts.

In eucaryotes the molecular mechanisms for control of gene expression are not yet known. Bacterial modes of gene regulation undoubtedly will be present in some form in eucaryotes. For example, synthesis of ovalbumin in chick oviduct is stimulated by exposure to the steroid hormone estradiol in a manner analogous in many ways to bacterial control. However, in eucaryotes there is probably another major level for regulation of gene expression that involves selection for which transcripts become processed and leave the nucleus, two processes that may be coupled. This additional level of control in eucaryotes is possible only because DNA and ribosomes are separated by the nuclear envelope. A primary function of the nucleus may be to separate translation from transcription.

20.9 Additional concepts and techniques are presented in the Problems section.

A. Role of σ in initiation of transcription. Problem 20.12.

B. RNA:DNA hybridization. Problems 20.13, 20.14, and 20.15.

C. Kinetics of polypeptide labeling during chain growth on ribosomes (the Dintzis experiment). Problems 20.17 and 20.18.

D. Involvement of small nuclear RNAs in splicing. Problem 20.21.

E. mRNA-independent synthesis of a polypeptide antibiotic. Problem 20.24.

F. Regulation of bacterial operons by regulatory proteins, variable promoters, and variable terminators (attenuators). Problems 20.25 and 20.26.

References

COMPREHENSIVE TEXTS
Lehninger: Chapters 32, 33, and 35
Metzler: Chapter 15

Stryer: Chapters 25, 27, 28, and 29
White et al.: Chapter 26

OTHER REFERENCES
H. F. Lodish and J. E. Rothman, "The Assembly of Cell Membranes," *Scientific American,* January 1979, p. 48.
M. Rosenberg and D. Court, "Regulatory Sequences Involved in the Promotion and Termination of RNA Transcription," *Annual Review of Genetics,* **13,** 319 (1979).
P. R. Schimmel and D. Söll, "Aminoacyl-tRNA Synthetases: General Features and Recognition of Transfer RNAs," *Annual Review of Biochemistry* **48,** 601 (1979).
J. D. Watson, *Molecular Biology of the Gene,* Benjamin/Cummings, Menlo Park, Calif., 1976, 3rd ed. Chapters 11, 12, and 14.
I. G. Wool, "The Structure and Function of Eucaryotic Ribosomes," *Annual Review of Biochemistry,* **48,** 719 (1979).

Problems

20.1 Answer the following with true or false. If false, explain why.
  a. Both mRNA and protein synthesis involve polynucleotide templates.
  b. The amino acid sequence of a protein is determined during synthesis by complementary interaction between amino acids and trinucleotide sequences (codons) in the mRNA template.
  c. One enzyme, RNA polymerase, catalyzes synthesis of the three major classes of RNA in procaryotes.
  d. Most mRNAs are initiated with a pyrimidine nucleotide.

e. Eucaryotic mRNAs have 3'-OH groups at both ends.

f. Many mRNAs in procaryotes and eucaryotes are polycistronic.

g. The drug rifampicin blocks initiation of mRNA synthesis by preventing RNA polymerase from binding to promoter sites.

h. During RNA synthesis, RNA polymerase moves along the DNA sense strand in the $3' \to 5'$ direction, thereby catalyzing RNA chain growth in the $5' \to 3'$ direction.

i. Eucaryotic ribosomes are somewhat larger and more complex than procaryotic ribosomes.

j. The formation of fMet-tRNA^{fMet} is catalyzed by an aminoacyl-tRNA synthetase specific for fMet.

k. To initiate a new polypeptide chain, fMet-tRNA^{fMet} binds to the A site on the ribosome.

l. Binding of each successive aminoacyl-tRNA to the A site requires the participation of an elongation factor and the expenditure of a high-energy phosphate bond of GTP.

m. During polypeptide synthesis, ribosomes move along the mRNA in the $3' \to 5'$ direction.

n. An mRNA molecule cannot begin to direct protein synthesis until it is completed, because the point of ribosomal binding for polypeptide initiation is always near the end of the mRNA that is synthesized last.

o. Formation of each peptide bond on the ribosome requires expenditure of two high-energy phosphate bonds in addition to those utilized in amino acid activation.

p. Termination of a growing polypeptide on the ribosome requires the presence of two adjacent stop codons in the message.

q. Judging from their response to inhibitors of protein synthesis, procaryotic ribosomes are similar to the ribosomes of eucaryotic mitochondria, but different from those of eucaryotic cytoplasm.

r. Carbohydrates are added to nascent proteins in compartments that are topologically outside the cell.

s. In eucaryotes transcription occurs in a compartment that is topologically outside the cell.

20.2 a. Each amino acid is positioned for polypeptide synthesis on ribosomes by base pairing between the _____ of an aminoacyl-tRNA molecule and a _____ on the mRNA.

b. Sufficient energy to drive peptide-bond synthesis is obtained at the expense of two high-energy phosphate bonds of ATP in the process of _____.

c. The sites on DNA at which RNA polymerase binds to initiate transcription are called

_____.

d. The antibiotic _____ blocks RNA polymerase–catalyzed propagation of RNA chains by binding to the DNA at GC dinucleotide sequences.

e. An RNA polymerase subunit known as sigma appears to play a role in recognizing the sites on DNA that specify _____ of RNA synthesis.

f. In procaryotes, all polypeptide chains probably are initiated with the amino acid

_____.

g. The _____ ribosomal subunit carries the binding site for mRNA.

h. The initiating codon for polypeptide synthesis is always _____.

i. The three termination codons are _____, _____, and _____.

j. The complex of many ribosomes attached to an mRNA molecule is called a _____.

k. At the end of each cycle of peptide-bond formation on the ribosome, the growing chain is left as a peptidyl-tRNA bound to the _____ site.

l. Following translation, the terminal _____ group is enzymatically removed from most polypeptide chains.

m. Eucaryotic mRNAs typically are _____ on their 5' end with a reversed G, _____ on their 3' ends with poly A, and _____ together with elimination of internal sequences from larger precursors.

20.3 If the following DNA duplex is transcribed from right to left,

a. Which is the sense strand?

b. What is the resulting mRNA sequence?

c. What is the informational relationship between the sequences in the mRNA and the antisense strand of the DNA?

$$5'\text{-A-T-T-C-G-C-A-G-G-C-T-}3' \qquad \text{Strand 1}$$
$$3'\text{-T-A-A-G-C-G-T-C-C-G-A-}5' \qquad \text{Strand 2}$$

Direction of transcription

20.4 Diagram a gene as a stretch of DNA duplex, and assume it is transcribed from left to right.

a. Will the 5' end of the DNA sense strand be on the left or the right?

b. Is the end of the gene corresponding to the N terminus of the protein for which it codes on the left or the right?

20.5 Give the number of high-energy phosphate bonds expended for the following:

a. Insertion of one nucleotide into a growing mRNA, starting from the nucleoside monophosphate

b. Insertion of one amino acid into a growing polypeptide chain, starting from the free amino acid

20.6 If the average $\Delta G'_0$ for hydrolysis of phosphodiester bonds is -4 kcal/mol, what is the approximate $\Delta G'_0$ for addition of one nucleotide to a growing mRNA in the RNA polymerase reaction?

20.7 The nucleotide sequence around the initiation site on the message for the coat protein of the RNA phage R17 is

$$5'\ldots\text{G-A-A-G-C-A-U-G-G-C-U-U-C-U-A-A-C-U-U-U}\ldots 3'$$

a. Which codon specifies the first amino acid of the protein?

b. Why does the trinucleotide sequence UAA toward the right end of the sequence not cause chain termination?

20.8 To investigate the mechanism of Trp activation, a student is carrying out exchange experiments (see Problem 15.15) with purified tryptophanyl-tRNA synthetase from *E. coli*, and the various combinations of reaction components shown in the first column of Table 20.2. Predict which of these experiments will give him the exchange reaction measured, shown in the second column.

Table 20.2
Exchange Experiments with Tryptophanyl-tRNA Synthetase (Problem 20.8)

Reaction components	Exchange measured
a. Enzyme + ATP + ^{32}PP$_i$	^{32}P into ATP
b. Enzyme + tRNA^{Trp} + ATP + ^{14}C-AMP	^{14}C into ATP
c. Enzyme + tRNA^{Trp} + ATP + ^{32}PP$_i$	^{32}P into ATP
d. Enzyme + Trp + ATP + ^{32}PP$_i$	^{32}P into ATP
e. Enzyme + Trp + ATP + ^{14}C-AMP	^{14}C into ATP
f. tRNA^{Trp} + ATP + ^{14}C-AMP	^{14}C into ATP
g. tRNA^{Trp} + ATP + ^{32}PP$_i$	^{32}P into ATP

20.9 A purified bacterial isoleucyl-tRNA synthetase will recognize no other tRNA besides tRNA^{Ilu}, but in the absence of tRNA it will catalyze ^{32}PP$_i$ exchange into ATP when supplied with either Val or Ilu (see Problem 20.8). The ratio of the two exchange rates is about 1:5. What would you predict will be the relative rates of Val-tRNA^{Ilu} and Ilu-tRNA^{Ilu} formation when the two amino acids are incubated separately with enzyme, ATP, and tRNA^{Ilu}? Carefully consider the consequences of your answer, and then explain it, justifying the experimental result described.

20.10 Suppose you are studying RNA synthesis in the presence of purified RNA polymerase and DNA. As substrates you use all four nucleoside triphosphates uniformly labeled with ^{32}P and ^{14}C of known specific radioactivities, so that by counting the two isotopes independently you can determine the ratio of phosphate groups to nucleoside residues. You incubate a mixture of the mono- and oligonucleotides present, and separate them from PP_i and each other using a column that fractionates on the basis of chain length. Give the ratio of phosphate to nucleoside you will find in the first four fractions from the column; that is,

    a. Mononucleotides
    b. Dinucleotides
    c. Trinucleotides
    d. Tetranucleotides

20.11   The material from fraction d of Problem 20.10 is digested with alkali and then fractionated by a chromatographic procedure that separates only on the basis of the charged phosphate group/nucleoside ratio.

    a. How many fractions will be obtained, and what is the general structure of each?
    b. Which of the four bases are likely to be found in the most negatively charged fraction?
    c. Which bases are likely to be found in the least negatively charged fraction?

20.12   When intact T4 phage DNA is used as a template, purified RNA polymerase "core enzyme" lacking the sigma subunit will not initiate RNA synthesis. Addition of purified σ ($\simeq$100,000 daltons) to the core enzyme ($\simeq$400,000 daltons) restores activity. Suppose that you have set up two experiments to study the role of σ in initiation, which you plan to assay by incorporation of ^{32}P from a mixture of the four γ-labeled nucleoside triphosphates (*pppN) into acid-precipitable RNA chains as a function of time. To reaction mixture 1 you add 0.4 μg of core enzyme and 0.1 μg of σ. To reaction mixture 2 you add 4 μg of core enzyme and 0.1 μg of σ. Both reaction mixtures contain excess T4 phage DNA and γ-labeled nucleoside triphosphates (specific activity 10^8 cpm/μmol), in a total volume of 1 mL. The results of these experiments are shown in Figure 20.10.

    a. Explain why the assay method is or is not a valid measure of chain initiation.
    b. What is the final number of initiation events per molecule of core enzyme and per molecule of σ in each reaction?
    c. What can you conclude from these data about chain initiation under your experimental conditions?

20.13   RNA:DNA hybridization experiments can be used to determine quantitative relationships between sequences in the genome and the transcribed RNA of an organism. For example, suppose you are studying the genes for rRNA and their expression in the

Figure 20.10
Experiments on the role of σ in initiation (Problem 20.12). Results are expressed as counts per minute (cpm) incorporated per milliliter of reaction mixture, as a function of incubation time at 30°C.

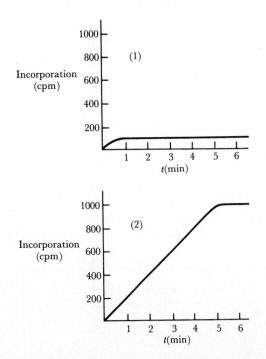

Martian microorganism of Problem 18.19. You have established that the organism has a genome size of 1×10^7 nucleotide pairs. Now you wish to determine (a) the percentage of total cellular RNA represented by the 22S rRNA of the larger ribosomal subunit, and (b) the number of copies per genome of the gene for this RNA. To answer these questions, you have prepared from the organism radioactively labeled and unlabeled DNA, uniformly labeled total RNA, and unlabeled rRNA from the purified larger ribosomal subunit, which you determine to be 3000 nucleotides in length. With these materials you carry out two experiments:

1. A sample of radioactively labeled DNA is sheared (mechanically broken) into fragments about 400 nucleotide pairs in length, denatured, and incubated with increasing amounts of unlabeled 22S rRNA. DNA:RNA hybrids then are separated from unhybridized DNA and assayed for radioactivity. You find that a maximum of 0.14 ± 0.02% of the input DNA radioactivity can be converted to hybrid in the presence of excess 22S rRNA.

2. A sample of unlabeled DNA is denatured, hybridized with excess 22S rRNA, and then digested with deoxyribonuclease under conditions where DNA complexed with RNA will not be attacked. The hybrid molecules then are isolated, denatured, treated with pancreatic ribonuclease, and reisolated, to give a preparation of single-stranded DNA sequences complementary to 22S rRNA. Samples of labeled total cellular RNA then are incubated with increasing amounts of this DNA preparation, and the resulting hybrids are separated from free RNA and assayed for radioactivity. You find that a maximum of 55% of the total RNA input radioactivity can be converted to hybrid in the presence of excess DNA.

What answers will you publish to the two questions asked at the outset? Does the answer to question a represent the percentage of number of RNA chains or percentage of total RNA mass represented by 22S rRNA?

20.14   Hybridization competition is a useful general method for comparing two populations of mRNA molecules derived from the same DNA under different conditions. One of the populations, radioactively labeled, is incubated in minute amounts with an excess of the denatured DNA and increasing concentrations of unlabeled RNA of the second population, under conditions where RNA:DNA hybrid molecules can form. The hybrid molecules then are separated from free RNA (usually by equilibrium sedimentation, chromatography, or adhesion to nitrocellulose filters) and assayed for radioactivity. Labeled molecules that cannot be prevented from hybridizing even by a large excess of unlabeled RNA are assumed to be absent from the unlabeled population.

Consider the following experiments comparing the mRNA produced by transcription to phage φC DNA in vitro, using *E. coli* RNA polymerase, with the mRNA produced in vivo during the first 5 min after infection of *E. coli* by phage φC. Two competition experiments are carried out with unlabeled, denatured φC DNA. In the first, the in vitro RNA is labeled and competed with unlabeled in vivo RNA; in the second, the reverse procedure is followed. For each experiment a control is performed also, in which the labeled RNA is competed by unlabeled RNA of the same population. The data shown in Figure 20.11 are obtained.

Figure 20.11
Hybridization–competition experiments (Problem 20.14). Experiment 1: labeled in vitro RNA, unlabeled in vivo RNA. Experiment 2: labeled in vivo RNA, unlabeled in vitro RNA.

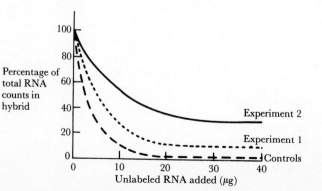

    a. What percentage of the total RNA sequences made in vivo also are transcribed by RNA polymerase in vitro?

    b. What percentage of the sequences transcribed in vitro do not represent sequences in the in vivo population?

       Suggest possible interpretations for each of your answers.

20.15   Describe a simple hybridization–competition experiment that would answer the question posed in Problem 20.13a.

20.16   In an in vitro protein-synthesizing system from *E. coli*, the polyribonucleotide AUGUUUUUUUUUUUU directs the synthesis of fMet-Phe-Phe-Phe-Phe (AUG is the codon for fMet, UUU for Phe). In the presence of farsomycin, a new antibiotic just perfected by Fluhardy Pharmaceuticals, this polymer directs synthesis of only fMet-Phe.

    a. What step in polypeptide synthesis does farsomycin inhibit?

    b. Will either the oligopeptide (uninhibited) or the dipeptide (inhibited) product be found attached to tRNA at the end of the reaction? Explain.

    c. What known inhibitor of translation appears to act at the same step as farsomycin?

20.17   A particular protein consists of one polypeptide containing five Leu residues, of which one is C-terminal and another is N-terminal. In a suspension of cells at 15°C the average time required to synthesize this polypeptide is 8 min. At time zero, radioactive Leu is added to five different suspensions of cells that are synthesizing the protein at the above rate. At $t = 2$ min, one suspension is chilled to 0°C, the cells are broken open, and the protein is isolated. In the isolation of this protein the incomplete precursor polypeptides are eliminated. The second, third, fourth, and fifth suspensions are treated similarly at 4, 6, 8, and 80 min, respectively. The protein from each suspension then is analyzed for C-terminal and total radioactive Leu. Assume that the rate of synthesis of this protein is the same and constant for each suspension. The ratio of C-terminal radioactivity to total radioactivity in the isolated protein should do which of the following?

    a. Increase to a final value of 0.2 with increasing time of exposure of cells to radioactive Leu

    b. Increase to a final value of 0.4 with increasing time of exposure

    c. Remain constant at 0.2 with increasing time of exposure

    d. Remain constant at 0.4 with increasing time of exposure

    e. Decrease to a final value of 0.2 with increasing time of exposure

    f. Decrease to a final value of 0.4 with increasing time of exposure

20.18   A suspension of rabbit reticulocyte cells is synthesizing hemoglobin under conditions where completion of the α chain (141 amino acids) takes 5 min. At $t = 0$ min you add to the suspension a mixture of all 20 ^{14}C-labeled amino acids of equal specific radioactivity (counts per minute per nanomole of amino acid). At subsequent times you take samples from the suspension, split each into two portions, purify ribosomes carrying attached incomplete hemoglobin chains from one portion and soluble hemoglobin from the other, and subject each to trypsin digestion and chromatography. You know from experience which spots on the chromatogram correspond to the α-chain N-terminal and C-terminal peptides; you also know that these contain 7 and 2 amino acid residues, respectively.

    a. Which of these two spots from the soluble hemoglobin will become labeled first?

    b. You find that at $t = 4$ min, four unidentified, internal α-chain peptides from the soluble hemoglobin have specific radioactivities of (1) 3900 cpm/nmol of amino acid, (2) 5700 cpm/nmol, (3) 270 cpm/nmol, and (4) 2500 cpm/nmol. What is the order of these peptides in the α chain, in the N- to C-terminal direction?

    c. At $t = 5$ min, what will be the approximate ratio of specific radioactivities of the C-terminal compared to the N-terminal peptides from the ribosome fraction?

    d. At $t = 5$ min, what will be the approximate ratio of specific radioactivities in the two peptides from the soluble hemoglobin?

20.19   The genes coding for the 10 enzymes required in His biosynthesis constitute a single transcription unit in *E. coli*. They are clustered on the genome in the sequence shown in Figure 20.12a, where each number represents a gene (the numbers also indicate the sequence of the corresponding enzymes in the biosynthetic pathway, with 1 catalyzing the first reaction, etc.).

Suppose that you isolate a mutant that somehow has undergone a perfect inversion of two genes by breaking and rejoining at the points shown by arrows, in such a way that the entire nucleotide sequences of genes 5, 7, 8, and 9 are preserved, but the order now is that shown in Figure 20.12b.

a. Would you expect this mutant to be His$^+$ (normal phenotype) or His$^-$ (requiring His for growth)?

Explain how, if at all, the inversion might affect

b. The transcription of gene 4

c. The translation of gene 4 message

20.20   The classic studies of Christian Anfinsen and his co-workers on the refolding of denatured, reduced ribonuclease proved that amino acid sequence alone can specify the unique three-dimensional structure of a protein (Chapter 4). However, in the course of this work they discovered an enzyme from mouse liver (MLE) that greatly increased the rate of ribonuclease refolding. MLE subsequently was shown to promote the renaturation of other proteins as well, and to do so by nonspecific catalysis of disulfide interchange reactions, that is,

$$\begin{array}{c}-S_1 \quad S_3- \\ \mid \quad \mid \\ -S_2 \quad S_4-\end{array} \rightleftharpoons \begin{array}{c}-S_1-S_3- \\ \\ -S_2-S_4-\end{array}$$

Such interchanges must occur in order that incorrect disulfide bonds formed initially upon reoxidation of the denatured protein can rearrange to form the correct disulfide bonds as the protein configuration reaches thermodynamic equilibrium.

Suppose you find that 20 randomly selected native mammalian enzymes, all with at least two disulfide bridges in their structures, fall into two groups based on their behavior when incubated with purified MLE. Seventeen of the enzymes (group 1) apparently are unaffected. The remaining three (group 2) lose their enzymatic activity, at rates proportional to the concentration of MLE in the incubation mixture.

a. What is the most likely general explanation for this result?

b. How would you expect synthesis of group 2 enzymes to differ from synthesis of group 1 enzymes?

c. Would you expect group 2 enzymes to be generally less stable than group 1 enzymes in the absence of MLE?

d. Name two mammalian proteins that you might expect to exhibit group 2 behavior with MLE.

e. Can you think of any advantages of group 2 proteins for the organism?

20.21   It has been suggested that base pairing between mRNA precursors and small nuclear RNAs (snRNAs) may align sites for correct enzymatic splicing.

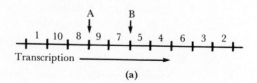

(a)

Figure 20.12
Order of genes for enzymes in His biosynthesis (Problem 20.19). **(a)** Normal order. **(b)** Inversion of genes 7 and 9 produced by breaking and rejoining at points A and B.

(b)

a. Which of the bridging structures represented in Figure 20.13a could provide the means for juxtaposing splice sites?

b. The sequence of the 5' end of the snRNA, U1a, and the sequences around two splice sites in the precursor to ovalbumin mRNA are shown in Figure 20.13b. Which, if any, of the permissible bridge structures in Figure 20.13a could form between U1a and the ovalbumin splice sites?

20.22 You have cloned two DNA sequences that code for a particular protein. One cloned sequence was obtained by copying mRNA for the protein into a double-stranded DNA (cDNA) using reverse transcriptase. The other cloned sequence is the natural gene encoding the protein. Both clones were generated from fragments produced by cleavage with the restriction endonuclease *Pst*I. Your analysis of the cloned cDNA indicates positions for a few other restriction sites (Figure 20.14a).

Several of your experiments have suggested that there are introns in the natural gene. In one experiment you compared electrophoretically the restriction digests of the cloned cDNA and genomic sequences (Figure 20.14b). In a second experiment you denatured and reannealed a mixture of the cDNA and genomic *Pst*I fragments to create heteroduplexes. You then digested the mixture with S1 nuclease, which is spe-

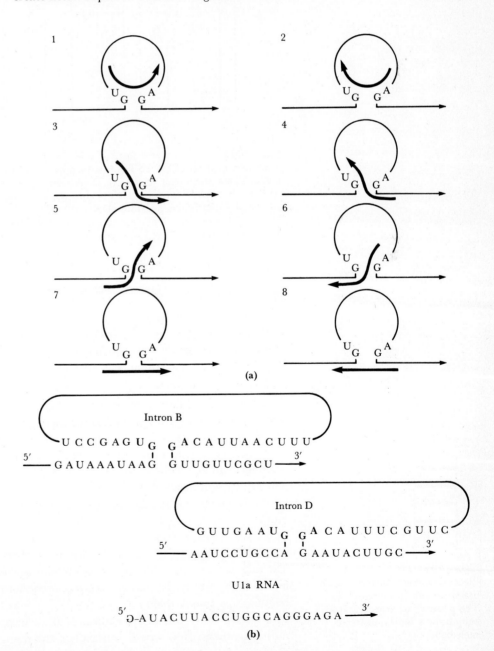

Figure 20.13
Bridging structures at RNA splice sites (Problem 20.21).
(a) Hypothetical bridging structures. Arrowheads indicate the 3' ends of RNA molecules. (b) Sequences around two splice sites in the precursor to ovalbumin mRNA and sequences at the 5' end of snRNA U1a.

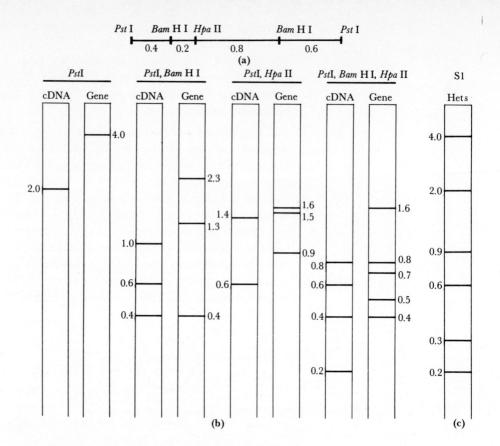

(a)

(b)

(c)

Figure 20.14
Restriction analysis of cloned DNA sequences (Problem
20.22). All numbers refer to sizes of DNA segments in kilobases. **(a)** Restriction sites in cDNA clone. **(b)** Comparison of restriction fragments from cDNA and genomic
clones. **(c)** Product of S1 nuclease treatment of heteroduplexes (hets) between cDNA and genomic *Pst*I fragments.

cific for single-stranded nucleic acid. An electrophoretic separation of the products is
shown in Figure 20.14c.

a. To the extent the data permit, describe the location, number, and sizes of the introns.
Also show positions for any new restriction enzyme sites.

b. Describe an experiment that will clear up any remaining ambiguities.

20.23 You have been studying a particular membrane protein. In a variety of experiments
you have observed four different electrophoretic forms of the protein (Figure 20.15).
You have determined that form A is the usual form associated with the plasma membrane. To study the synthesis of this membrane protein in more detail, you have
developed an in vitro protein synthesizing system in which the entire population of
ribosomes can be synchronized at various points during synthesis. The complete system, which synthesizes form A, consists of ribosomes, the mRNA for your protein,
soluble factors, and a membrane system derived from dog pancreas endoplasmic reticulum.

a. In one study you selectively disrupt the membranes at various points during synthesis
by adding detergent. (The detergent does not interfere with peptide-bond formation.)
The migration forms of the resulting proteins are shown in Table 20.3a. From this
information identify the various electrophoretic forms and describe the biosynthetic
relationships among them.

b. In a second study you add membranes to an incomplete system at various points
during synthesis. How would you explain the results in Table 20.3b?

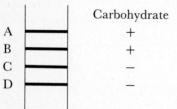

Figure 20.15
Electrophoretic forms of a membrane protein (Problem 20.23).
The presence or absence of carbohydrate is indicated beside
each band.

Table 20.3
Synthesis of a Membrane
Protein (Problem 20.23)

	Peptide chain length	Electrophoretic form			
		A	B	C	D
a. Detergent addition	0			+	
	75				+
	150		+		
	400	+			
	500	+			
b. Membrane addition	0	+			
	40	+			
	70	+			
	110			+	
	550			+	

20.24   The biosynthesis of polypeptide antibiotics such as tyrocidin appears to represent either an intermediate in evolution or an example of independent evolution that demonstrates the basic similarity of biologic solutions to polymerization problems. Tyrocidin biosynthesis bears a strong resemblance to both ribosomal protein synthesis and fatty acid synthesis, and points out the similarity of those two more common processes. Tyrocidin is a cyclic decapeptide that is synthesized on an enzyme complex without the use of mRNA. The amino acids for tyrocidin biosynthesis are activated much as in ribosomal protein synthesis. However, each aminoacyl adenylate intermediate is transferred to a thiol group of a specific enzyme in the complex instead of to a tRNA hydroxyl group. As in fatty acid synthesis, activated subunits (in this case amino acids) are added to the growing chain via the thiol group of a special shuttle protein, the peptidyl carrier protein (PCP).

a. In analogy to fatty acid synthesis, propose a sequence of steps for the transfer of activated groups to the growing chain.

b. Discuss the similarities to ribosomal protein synthesis.

20.25   Bacterial genes often are grouped in functionally related clusters, termed **operons,** which are regulated as a unit. The lactose operon in *E. coli* encodes two proteins that are necessary for transport and hydrolysis of the disaccharide, lactose. The gene products of the operon normally are induced only when lactose is present in the environment and glucose, the preferred energy source, is absent. The *lac* operon is regulated by a variable promoter. The binding of RNA polymerase, and with it the activity of the genes, is affected by the binding of two regulatory proteins: the *lac* repressor and the catabolite activator protein, CAP (Figure 20.16a). The *lac* repressor is said to exert *negative* control because its binding to DNA prevents transcription. CAP is said to exert *positive* control because its binding enhances transcription. In the absence of both proteins the native transcriptional activity of the promoter is very low.

a. CAP, which is a dimer of identical subunits, possesses C2 symmetry, whereas the *lac* repressor, which is a tetramer of identical subunits, possesses D2 symmetry (Chapter 5). The DNA binding sites for these regulatory proteins both have an approximate 2-fold axis of rotational symmetry. Is there matching symmetry between the regulatory proteins and their DNA binding sites? How many complete DNA recognition sites would you expect on each CAP dimer and on each *lac* repressor tetramer?

b. Predict the transcriptional activity of the operon when the regulatory proteins are bound as indicated in Figure 20.16b.

c. The DNA binding affinities of both regulatory proteins are affected by binding of specific metabolites that signal the presence or absence of lactose and glucose. The DNA binding affinity of the *lac* repressor is altered by allolactose, which is a metabolic derivative of lactose. The DNA binding affinity of CAP is altered by cyclic AMP, whose intracellular concentration is related inversely to external glucose concentration. For example, when glucose concentration is high, cyclic AMP concentration is low. In each case predict whether binding of the metabolite will increase or decrease the affinity of the regulatory protein for its DNA binding site.

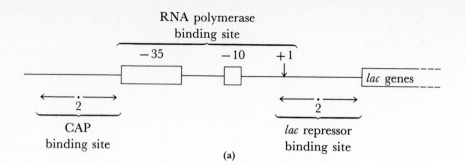

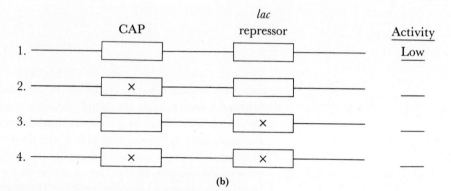

Figure 20.16
Regulation of the *lac* operon (Problem 20.25). **(a)** Schematic diagram of the promoter for the *lac* operon. The arrow at +1 indicates the start site for transcription.
(b) Four possible regulatory states for the *lac* operon. Boxes indicate the DNA binding sequences and *X*'s indicate the presence of the regulatory protein.

    d. Offer plausible molecular explanations for positive and negative control in the *lac* operon.

20.26   Bacterial operons concerned with amino acid biosynthesis typically are regulated not only by variable promoters, but also by variable terminators (attenuators) that lie between the promoter and the regulated genes. When the regulated genes are not required, the nascent transcript is prematurely terminated in a process termed **attenuation.** Attenuators operate on the principle of mutually exclusive RNA secondary structures. When the gene products are needed (when the amino acid is absent from the medium), the RNA forms a secondary structure that favors continued transcription through the decision point. When the gene products are not needed, the RNA forms a secondary structure that signals termination. These relationships are illustrated schematically in Figure 20.17.

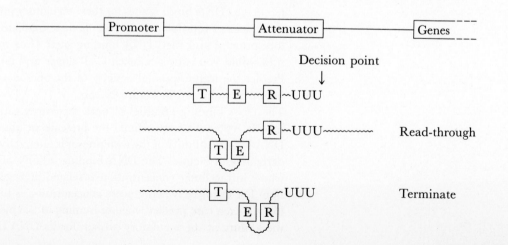

Figure 20.17
Gene regulation by an attenuator (Problem 20.26).

a. Write RNA sequences four nucleotides in length that would satisfy the pairing relationships among segments T, E, and R in Figure 20.17. Could T and R pair?

b. Long before the mechanism of regulation was understood it was known that transcription of the regulated genes was very sensitive to the cellular levels of tRNA charged with the regulated amino acid. Recently a stretch of DNA encoding a short nonfunctional polypeptide has been found just preceding each such attenuator. Typically this stretch of DNA contains several codons for the amino acid that is regulated. Using this information, speculate on how protein synthesis might influence secondary structure in the nascent RNA.

c. Is gene regulation by attenuators a likely mechanism for controlling gene expression in eucaryotes?

☆ 20.27 An overlapping triplet code originally was ruled out on formal grounds. Given present knowledge of ribosome function, explain whether or not the reading of a fully overlapping code would be possible given existing translation mechanisms, and if not, how these mechanisms would have to be altered to read such a code.

☆ 20.28 The light (L) chains of immunoglobulins are composed of an N-terminal variable (V) half and a C-terminal constant (C) half. Different L chains from a given organism show very few amino acid differences in the C portion, but several in the V portion. The pulse-labeling technique devised by Dintzis was used to study the synthesis of L chains. A brief pulse of radioactive amino acids was given to a system that was already synthesizing L chains with unlabeled amino acids, and L chains then were isolated from the system for analysis. A gradient of increasing specific radioactivity from the N to the C terminus was found in the completed labeled L chains. Which of the following hypotheses concerning L-chain synthesis was ruled out by this finding?

a. The L chain is coded by two genes, V and C, which fuse at the level of DNA.

b. The L chain is coded by two genes, V and C, which fuse at the level of mRNA.

c. The L chain is coded by two genes, V and C; the corresponding gene products fuse at the polypeptide level.

d. There is a single gene for the L chain. The diversity of sequences in V depends upon the action of a mutagenic polymerase.

e. There are a large number of genes for the L chain.

☆ 20.29 To investigate the control of transcription in the animal virus SV40, you examine the synthesis of viral RNA before and after SV40 DNA replication begins (early and late RNA, respectively). You have prepared unlabeled and radioactively labeled preparations of SV40 DNA, early RNA, and late RNA from SV40-infected cells. With these materials you carry out three experiments.

1. A sample of radioactively labeled SV40 DNA is sheared into fragments about 400 nucleotide pairs in length, denatured, and incubated with increasing amounts of unlabeled early or late RNA. DNA:RNA hybrids then are separated from unhybridized DNA and assayed for radioactivity. You find that a maximum of 25% and 50% of the input DNA radioactivity can be converted to hybrid by early and late RNA, respectively.

2. A sample of unlabeled DNA (in excess) is sheared and denatured as in part 1 and then incubated with a minute amount of radioactively labeled early RNA and increasing amounts of unlabeled early or late RNA. You find that 100% of the labeled early RNA is competitively inhibited from hybridizing by both early and late unlabeled RNA.

3. Another hybridization–competition experiment is carried out, this time with labeled late RNA and increasing amounts of unlabeled early or late RNA. You find that the labeled late RNA can be completely inhibited from hybridizing by unlabeled late RNA but only partially by unlabeled early RNA.

a. How many distinct classes of RNA does SV40 synthesize?

b. At what time during infection is each class of RNA synthesized?

c. What fraction of the SV40 coding capacity does each class represent?

Answers

20.1 a. True

b. False. Amino acids do not show complementary interaction with polynucleotides. Amino acid sequence is determined by complementary interaction between mRNA and tRNA adaptors that carry amino acids.

c. True

d. False. Most mRNAs are initiated with a purine nucleotide, ATP or GTP.

e. True

f. False. In eucaryotes mRNAs normally are monocistronic.

g. False. The drug does not inhibit binding of RNA polymerase to DNA, but blocks one of the subsequent steps in initiation—binding of the first two triphosphates to the enzyme–DNA complex and formation of the first phosphodiester bond.

h. True

i. True

j. False. f-Met-tRNA^{fMet} is produced by formylation of Met-tRNA^{fMet}.

k. False. f-Met-tRNA^{fMet} binds to the P site.

l. True

m. False. Ribosomes move in the $5' \rightarrow 3'$ direction along mRNA.

n. False. The initiator codon for ribosome binding is usually toward the 5' end of the mRNA. Because this end of the mRNA is synthesized first, translation of an mRNA in procaryotes begins before its synthesis is completed.

o. True

p. False. A single termination codon, arising by mutation in the middle of a message, is sufficient to cause chain termination.

q. True

r. True

s. False. In eucaryotes transcription occurs inside the nucleus, a compartment that is topologically continuous with the cytoplasm.

20.2 a. anticodon, codon

b. amino acid activation (or aminoacyl-tRNA synthesis)

c. promoters

d. actinomycin D

e. initiation

f. fMet

g. smaller (or 30S, or 40S)

h. AUG

i. UAA, UAG, UGA

j. polysome (or polyribosome)

k. P

l. formyl

m. capped, tailed, spliced

20.3 a. mRNA is synthesized $5' \rightarrow 3'$; therefore, the direction of movement along the DNA template is $3' \rightarrow 5'$. Because synthesis proceeds from right to left in this example, the answer is strand 1.

b. The mRNA sequence is simply the complement of the DNA sense strand sequence, with U replacing T. Hence the resulting sequence is

3'-U-A-A-G-C-G-U-C-C-G-A-5'

c. Both are complementary to the DNA sense strand sequence; consequently, they are informationally identical.

20.4 a. The right end (see Figure 20.18). Remember that the messenger is synthesized $5' \rightarrow 3'$, and that its template, the DNA sense strand, must have opposite polarity.

b. The left end (see Figure 20.18). The messenger also is read $5' \rightarrow 3'$, so that the 5' end carries the information for the N-terminal portion of the protein.

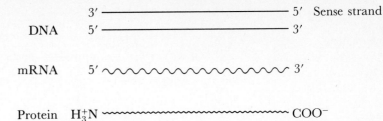

Figure 20.18
Sequence relationships between DNA, mRNA, and protein (Answer 20.4).

20.5 a. Two for conversion of $NMP \rightarrow NTP$, and two more $[(NMP)_n + NTP \rightarrow (NMP)_{n+1} + PP_i; PP_i + H_2O \rightarrow 2P_i]$ for incorporation. The total is four.

b. Two for activation of the amino acid by conversion to amino acyl-tRNA at the expense of $ATP \rightarrow \rightarrow AMP + 2P_i$, and two more for aminoacyl-tRNA binding and translocation on the ribosome, each at the expense of $GTP \rightarrow GDP + P_i$. The total is four.

20.6 The driving energy comes from two reactions:

$$NTP + H_2O \rightarrow NMP + PP_i + H^+ \qquad \Delta G'_0 \simeq -7\,kcal/mol$$
$$PP_i + H_2O \rightarrow 2P_i + H^+ \qquad \Delta G'_0 \simeq -6\,kcal/mol$$

These reactions must overcome the $+4$ kcal/mol needed to reverse phosphodiester-bond hydrolysis, that is, to form the bond by removing the elements of water. Therefore the approximate $\Delta G'_0$ is -9 kcal/mol.

20.7 a. Reading of the message begins at the 5′ end. The first codon read for any protein will be AUG, which specifies the initiating amino acid N-formylmethionine. In this case, the AUG triplet begins six nucleotides in from the left end of the sequence shown.

b. Following initiation, the sequence of codons read will be AUGGCUUCUAACUUU... The sequence UAA will not be read as a codon. It is said to be *out of phase* with the *reading frame,* which is established by the initiation codon AUG as shown (see Concept 21.4).

20.8 Aminoacyl-tRNA synthesis occurs in two steps, as shown in Figure 20.19. Reaction 1 results in formation of enzyme-bound aminoacyl AMP with release of PP_i. In the absence of tRNA the reverse of reaction 1 leads to incorporation of added $^{32}PP_i$ into the ATP pool. Because there is no ATP cleavage in the absence of Trp, or in the absence of enzyme, experiments a, b, c, f, and g will give no exchange. Exchange could be observed in e only if reaction 1 formed

$$RCH-C{\overset{\displaystyle O}{\underset{\displaystyle O\,\text{(PP)}}{<}}} + AMP$$
$$\underset{\displaystyle NH_3^+}{|}$$

rather than the products shown. Therefore only experiment d will give exchange.

20.9 It is certain that the enzyme will not catalyze net Val-tRNA^{Ilu} formation, because this would result in the incorrect incorporation of Val into protein in response to an Ilu codon. Therefore, the answer is 0. The experimental results could be explained as follows: The active site of the free enzyme is sufficiently nonspecific to allow occasional formation of the enzyme [Val-AMP] complex, but this complex does not have the configuration necessary to react with tRNA^{Ilu}. Hence only the correct complex, enzyme [Ilu-AMP], will participate in the second step of the reaction.

20.10 The first fraction contains only the NTP substrates. The next three are the early products of mRNA initiation. The 5′ triphosphate of the initiating nucleotide remains intact and is still present on finished mRNAs. Therefore, the general structures and ratios for the four fractions will be

a. pppN $\qquad\qquad$ 3:1
b. pppNpN $\qquad\quad$ 2:1
c. pppNpNpN $\qquad$ 5:3
d. pppNpNpNpN $\quad$ 3:2

(1)

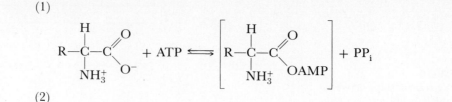

(2)

Figure 20.19
Mechanism of Trp activation
(Answer 20.8). The enzyme-
bound intermediate is enclosed
in brackets.

20.11 a. Alkaline hydrolysis occurs between each intrachain phosphate and the adjacent 5'-position on the ribose to yield nucleoside 2'- and 3'-monophosphates except at the two ends of the chain (Concept 17.1, part B; Problem 17.20; Table 21.6). Therefore, three fractions will be obtained: pppNp, Np, and N.

b. Only A and G, the bases of the two nucleoside triphosphates used in chain initiation, should be found in the pppNp fraction.

c. All four bases, A, G, C, and U, should be found in the nucleoside fraction, which represents the fourth position in the mRNA.

20.12 a. Because only the 5'-terminal nucleotide will retain its γ phosphate upon incorporation into an RNA molecule, the conversion of ^{32}P label to acid-insoluble form measures initiation independently of chain elongation. Therefore, the assay method is valid.

b. 100 and 1000 cpm incorporated represent 10^{-12} and 10^{-11} mol of RNA chains initiated, respectively. 0.4 μg and 4 μg of core enzyme correspond to 10^{-12} and 10^{-11} mol of enzyme, respectively, and 0.1 μg of σ corresponds to 10^{-12} mol. Hence the final numbers of chains initiated are 1 per molecule of core and 1 per molecule of σ in reaction 1; 1 per molecule of core and 10 per molecule of σ in reaction 2.

c. These results indicate that σ can dissociate from an enzyme complex that has initiated and then can activate another molecule of free core enzyme for initiation. The rate of initiation is rapid until the number of initiations is the same as the number of σ molecules added (10^{-12} mol); then the rate decreases. Therefore, σ exchange from one core enzyme complex to another must be the rate-limiting step during the latter part of the reaction. Finally, a core-enzyme molecule that has once initiated apparently cannot reinitiate. This result suggests that RNA chain termination with release of free core enzyme does not occur under the reaction conditions.

20.13 a. Experiment 2 indicates that 22S rRNA represents 55% of the total cellular RNA. This figure represents the mass percentage of total RNA, because in a uniformly labeled RNA population, the radioactivity per nucleotide will be constant for all RNA chain lengths.

b. Because the total number of nucleotide pairs is 1×10^7 per genome, the total number of nucleotides in the population of denatured DNA sequences is 2×10^7 per genome. Therefore, the value of $0.14 \pm 0.02\%$ hybridized in experiment 1 represents $28,000 \pm 4000$ nucleotides per genome complementary to 22S rRNA of length 3000 nucleotides. Therefore, there are 8 to 10 copies of the gene per genome. If your answer was 4 to 5, you probably forgot the factor of 2 explained in the first sentence. This factor arises simply because 22S rRNA will hybridize with only one of the two DNA strands (the sense strand) of the corresponding gene.

20.14 a. Because an excess of unlabeled in vitro RNA fails to prevent 30% of the labeled in vivo RNA from forming hybrids in experiment 2, it follows that the in vitro population contains only 70% of the sequences made in vivo. This result could be because new promoter sites, not recognized by the RNA polymerase from uninfected cells, become active in vivo during the first 5 min after infection.

b. From experiment 1, by the same reasoning as in part a, 10% of the sequences transcribed in vitro are not present in the in vivo RNA. This result could occur because some in vivo mRNA molecules made immediately after infection have been degraded by 5 min, or because the RNA polymerase in vitro is making 10% of its RNA at initiation sites that do not serve as promoters in vivo during the first 5 min after infection.

Note that two reciprocal experiments are necessary to define the overlap of two RNA populations by this method. Interpretation of hybridization–competition experiments is intrinsically confusing, and even experienced investigators require practice. If you had difficulty with this problem, go through the answers carefully to make sure that you understand how the data lead to the conclusions.

20.15　　The simplest experiment for answering this question would involve incubation of labeled total RNA with excess denatured DNA and increasing amounts of competing unlabeled purified 22S rRNA. From the results obtained in Problem 20.13, the unlabeled RNA would be expected to decrease the amount of hybridized label by 55%.

20.16　a.　Farsomycin inhibits the last step of each cycle of reactions on the ribosomal surface— translocation of peptidyl-tRNA from the A to the P site with concomitant movement of the mRNA. Inhibition of any earlier step would prevent formation of the first peptide bond.

　　　　b.　Both products will be made as peptidyl-tRNA, because there is no chain-termination signal present to activate a release factor.

　　　　c.　Fusidic acid (see Table 20.1).

20.17　　The answer is e. If the reasoning behind this answer is unclear, see Answer 20.18.

20.18　　You may find it helpful in understanding this and the preceding problem to draw diagrams such as those in Figure 20.20 for various times after addition of label.

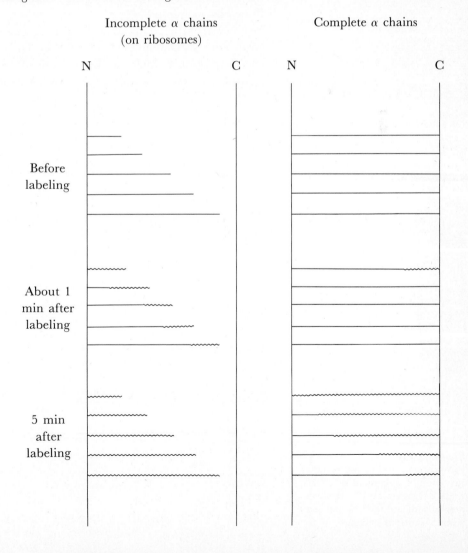

Figure 20.20
Distribution of labeled amino acids in complete and incomplete polypeptides at different times after addition of label (Answer 20.18). Straight and wavy lines represent unlabeled and labeled sequences of polypeptide, respectively.

Convince yourself that in the ribosomal population, all peptides will become labeled approximately simultaneously, and the specific radioactivity ratio between any two peptides will reach a constant value of 1 when all the incomplete chains present at the time of addition of label have been completed and released from the ribosomes. However, in the completed α-chain population (soluble hemoglobin), the C-terminal peptide will become labeled first, and the specific radioactivity of internal peptides will increase from the N terminus to the C terminus. To answer part d, consider that out of 141 new labeled chains at $t = 5$ min, on the average, $\frac{141}{141}$ will be labeled at position 141; $\frac{140}{141}$ will be labeled at position 140. Likewise only $\frac{1}{141}$ will be labeled at the N-terminal position, $\frac{2}{141}$ at the next position, and so on. The average degree of labeling in the first 7 amino acids (the N-terminal peptide) will be $\frac{4.0}{141}$ compared to a value of $\frac{140.5}{141}$ for the C-terminal peptide. Therefore, the correct answers are as follows:

a. The C-terminal peptide

b. 3, 4, 1, 2

c. 1

d. 35

20.19 a. If the stretch of DNA corresponding to genes 9 and 7 is inverted and reinserted as described, the antisense strand of this segment must become connected to the sense strands of genes 8 and 5 to preserve polarity, as shown in Figure 20.21. Because no new promoter is present in the mutant, the entire cluster will continue to be transcribed from left to right into a single mRNA, in which the segment corresponding to genes 7 and 9 will carry not the normal message, but its complement in reverse order instead. Therefore, the enzymes coded by genes 7 and 9 will not be produced, and the mutant will be His⁻.

b. The reversed antisense strand of the 9 + 7 region, which is not normally transcribed, may fortuitously contain the sequence that signals chain termination for mRNA synthesis. If so, gene 4 would not be transcribed.

c. Regardless of how it is read in the mRNA molecule, the reversed complementary message transcribed from the 9 + 7 segment is almost certain to include, by chance, one or more of the termination codons UAG, UAA, or UGA. Premature polypeptide-chain termination often has a polar effect on expression of downstream genes, because of premature termination of RNA transcription by cryptic termination signals. Normally these silent signals are "hidden" by actively translating ribosomes (see Answer 20.26).

20.20 a. Group 2 enzymes appear to be thermodynamically unstable structures requiring disulfide bonds to maintain their active configurations, whereas group 1 enzymes are thermodynamically stable structures in which the disulfide bonds simply confer added stability.

b. All proteins attain their three-dimensional structure by folding to a minimum-free-energy state. No *direct* mechanism is known that allows a polypeptide chain to be folded and fixed by disulfide bonds into a thermodynamically unstable structure. However, it is possible to create such a structure by peptide-bond cleavages after folding and disulfide cross-linking of a stable precursor. Consequently, it is expected

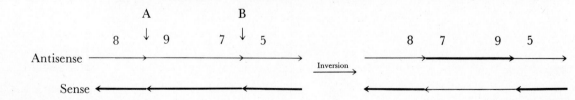

Figure 20.21
Strand relationships following inversion of a segment of DNA duplex (Answer 20.19). Heavy arrows indicate the original sense strand before inversion.

that synthesis of all group 2 proteins will include this kind of post-translational modification. (Because modifications will not *necessarily* decrease thermodynamic stability, they may occur occasionally in group 1 proteins as well.)

c. Group 2 proteins will be more unstable in the presence of sulfhydryl reagents, which inefficiently catalyze disulfide interchange. Otherwise, they should be as stable as group 1 proteins. However, their stability is not thermodynamic but kinetic, depending upon the large activation energy of disulfide interchange in the absence of a catalyst to prevent a finite rate of refolding.

d. Two well-characterized examples are insulin and chymotrypsin. Any other protein produced by proteolytic cleavage of a precursor structure is a likely candidate.

e. There are at least two advantages. (1) Such proteins can be stored in the precursor form and then activated rapidly by proteolytic cleavage when needed. (2) Such proteins will self-destruct in the presence of free sulfhydryl groups or enzymes such as MLE and therefore can be cleared easily from the system. It is probably no accident that a hormone and a potent hydrolytic enzyme are both of this type.

20.21 a. Only structures 1 and 8 in Figure 20.13a show antiparallel base pairing between nucleotide chains. In principle either structure could align splice points.

b. Structure 1 could form at both ovalbumin splice points (Figure 20.22). In both cases 14 of 20 bases can pair. Structure 8 could form with pairing at only 8 or 6 positions, respectively.

20.22 a. See Figure 20.23. The first experiment (Figure 20.14b) identifies the restriction fragments that are interrupted by introns and the overall sizes of the inserted sequences. This experiment yields a minimum estimate of the number of introns (2) but does not fix the end points of the introns. The second experiment (Figure 20.14c) defines the number of introns but gives no information about intron size. Together the experiments define the size and location of intron 1; the location but not the size of intron 2; and neither the size nor the exact location of intron 3. The sum of the sizes of introns 2 plus 3 is 1.7 kb. The new *Hpa*II restriction site is located 1.6 kb from the right-hand *Pst*I site.

b. Examination of the heteroduplexes in the electron microscope would resolve all the ambiguities listed.

20.23 a. The enzymes required to remove the signal sequence from the nascent protein and to add carbohydrates to it function only inside intact membrane compartments. The order of appearance of the various electrophoretic forms after membrane disruption suggests the biosynthetic relationship C → D → B → A. If the membranes are disrupted before protein synthesis has begun, form C results, suggesting that it is the unmodified translation product with the signal sequence still attached. Form D has had the signal sequence removed but no carbohydrate attached. The different mobilities of forms A and B suggest that there are a minimum of two carbohydrate attachment sites: one that becomes accessible after synthesis of residue 75 but before synthesis of residue 150, and one that becomes accessible after synthesis of residue 150 but before synthesis of residue 400.

b. The results in Table 20.3b indicate that at some point after synthesis of 70 residues and before synthesis of 110 residues, the nascent chain loses its capacity to be inserted through the membrane and thus is not processed at all. There are several possible explanations. The signal sequence may fold with additional residues in the nascent chain to become inaccessible to its membrane attachment site. Alternatively, significant structure in the nascent chain itself may prevent attachment of ribosomes to the membrane or prevent passage of the chain through the membrane.

20.24 a. A diagrammatic representation of tyrocidin synthesis is shown in Figure 20.24. The similarities to fatty acid synthesis are apparent.

b. The similarities between tyrocidin synthesis and ribosomal protein synthesis are not so obvious. However, if the enzyme carriers of the activated aminoacyl groups are replaced by tRNA (essentially only a change from a thioester linkage to an ester link-

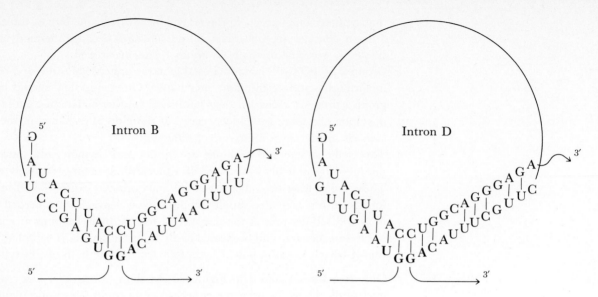

Figure 20.22
RNA pairing between U1a and
ovalbumin mRNA precursors
(Answer 20.21).

age), the analogy is apparent. The two systems have evolved different mechanisms for specifying the order of addition of subunits and for bringing activated groups together. The tyrocidin biosynthetic system carries the information for the order of addition not in the mRNA, but rather in the structure of the enzyme complex whose subunits carry the activated amino acids. To bring activated groups together this system uses a special protein, PCP, which can accept the activated monomer from one enzyme and transfer it to the next. In ribosomal protein synthesis the two activated groups are bound in closely enough so that they can interact directly without an intermediate.

20.25   a. Both multimeric regulatory proteins possess an axis of 2-fold rotational symmetry. Therefore there is matching symmetry between the regulatory proteins and their DNA binding sites. From symmetry considerations one would expect the CAP dimer to possess one complete DNA recognition site and the *lac* repressor to possess two complete DNA recognition sites. (It is a property of isologous tetramers that each surface is represented twice on the aggregate. This property can be visualized most readily by building an isologous tetramer with dice.) Quasi-equivalence among the subunits of the *lac* repressor could reduce the number of functional binding sites to one (Concept 5.5).

  b. Configuration 2 in Figure 20.16b is maximally active, because the negative control protein is not bound and the positive control protein is bound. Configurations 3 and 4 are transcriptionally inactive because of the bound repressor.

  c. Binding of allolactose to the repressor decreases the affinity of the repressor for its DNA binding site. Thus in the presence of lactose the repressor does not bind to DNA and transcription is enhanced. Binding of cAMP to CAP increases the affinity of CAP

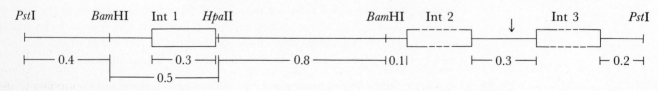

Figure 20.23
Natural gene containing introns
(Answer 20.22). The arrow indicates the alternative site for intron 3.

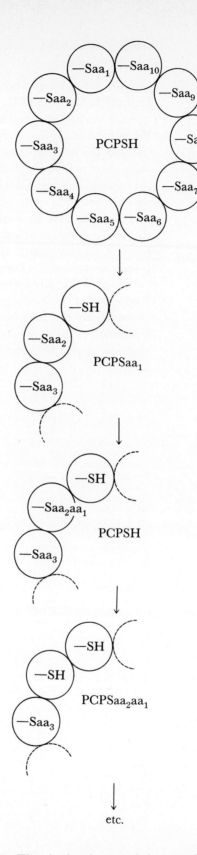

Figure 20.24
Tyrocidin biosynthesis (Answer 20.24).

for its DNA binding site. Thus in the absence of glucose, when cAMP concentration is high, CAP binds to DNA with increased affinity, thereby enhancing transcription.

d. Negative control by the *lac* repressor seems relatively straightforward. Binding of the repressor blocks binding by RNA polymerase so that transcription cannot be initiated. Positive control is not so well understood. It could be that CAP binding alters the stability of the DNA in the RNA polymerase binding site to facilitate entry of RNA polymerase. Alternatively CAP may provide an additional binding surface for recognition by RNA polymerase, thereby increasing the affinity of RNA polymerase for the promoter.

20.26 a. One set of RNA sequences that would satisfy the pairing relationships indicated in Figure 20.17 is UACG(T), CGUA(E), and UACG(R). Note that the T and R sequences are identical and thus could not pair.

b. When the cellular concentration of the regulated amino acid is adequate, ribosomes translate the nonfunctional polypeptide. In so doing the ribosomes cover the T segment, thereby favoring E:R pairing and termination. If the cellular concentration of the regulated amino acid is low, a ribosome will stall at the codons for that amino acid during translation of the nonfunctional polypeptide. Because the exposed T segment and the E segment are synthesized before the R segment, they pair with one another, thereby favoring read-through. Implicit in this description is the idea that ribosomes follow RNA polymerase very closely. Measurements of rates of synthesis indicate that translation normally is faster than transcription, supporting the notion that ribosomes "tailgate" RNA polymerase.

c. Regulation of eucaryotic genes by variable terminators is possible. However, because ribosomes are excluded from nuclei, such terminators could not be linked directly to translation as they are in bacteria. The likelihood of such a mechanism is difficult to evaluate, in part because the transcription termination signal in eucaryotes is undefined.

21 Genetic Language

Genetic information is stored as nucleotide sequences in chromosomes. The genetic machinery of the cell interprets specific sequences as molecular signals, which together constitute a **genetic language.** One well-defined aspect of this language is the **genetic code,** which describes the informational relationship between the 20 amino acid alphabet of the proteins and the 4 nucleotide alphabet of the nucleic acids in all organisms. Genetic language also includes signals that regulate the transmission and expression of genetic information. This chapter considers what is known about genetic language.

Concepts

21.1 **Genetic signals control the transmission and expression of genetic information.**

   A. All genetic signals are stored in nucleotide sequences within the genetic material, but they may function at the level of DNA, RNA, or protein. Genetic signals may function as nucleotide sequences or conformations, or as amino acid sequences or conformations. The correct functioning of genetic signals requires interaction with other specific molecules, which are often proteins.

   B. Genetic signals in DNA that function during transmission of genetic information include replication origins (Concept 18.2) and sites for chromosomal segregation at cell division. In eucaryotes segregation sites appear as chromosomal constrictions (**centromeres**) with associated **kinetochores** to which spindle fibers attach for proper chromosomal segregation at mitosis and meiosis (see Figure 5.9).

   C. Genetic signals that control expression of genetic information may function in DNA, RNA, or protein. Signals in DNA include transcription promoters (Concept 20.2) and binding sites for regulatory proteins that modulate transcription (Concept 20.8). There may also be special signals for defined gene rearrangements, such as have been demonstrated to occur during the development of the immune system in vertebrates.

      Signals in RNA that function during expression of genetic information include transcription terminators (Concept 20.2), RNA processing signals (Concept 20.3), translation alignment signals (Concept 20.5), and translation start and stop signals (Concept 21.4). Signals in protein include protein processing signals (Concept 20.7) and hydrophobic N-terminal sequences that are used to position proteins for extracellular transport and for membrane insertion (Concept 20.6).

   D. Unlike the genetic code, the signals that control transmission and expression of genetic information are not universal. Although similar, the specific sequences that serve as a certain signal may vary between species and even between different sites within the genome of a single organism.

433

21.2 **Nucleic acids are related to proteins by the genetic code.**

A. The rules relating nucleotide sequence in mRNA to amino acid sequence in proteins appear to be the same in all living systems, with minor exceptions. Each amino acid in a protein is specified by an mRNA sequence of three nucleotides (a triplet), which is called a code word or **codon.** Sequential codons in mRNA are contiguous; they do not overlap and are not separated by spacers. The genetic code dictionary is shown in Figure 21.1.

B. The code is **degenerate;** that is, more than one codon can specify the same amino acid. However, all codons are **unambiguous** in that each specifies no more than one amino acid.

C. The only known exceptions to the universality of the genetic code are found in eucaryotic mitochondria, which have been studied in detail in fungal and mammalian cells. All use the opal triplet UGA as a codon for Trp rather than a termination signal. Mammalian mitochondria apparently use the triplet AUA as a second codon for Met instead of Ilu. Finally, yeast mitochondria use the CUN family of codons to specify Thr instead of Leu.

21.3 **The structure of the code minimizes the effects of mutation.**

Changes in the third base of a codon often cause no change in the amino acid specified. Such mutations are **silent.** Changes in the first base of a codon generally lead to insertion of the same or a similar amino acid.

The second base of a codon is related most consistently to the chemical nature of the corresponding amino acid. All amino acids with strongly nonpolar side chains have codons with a pyrimidine as the second base, whereas all amino acids with strongly polar side chains have codons with a purine as the second base. Therefore, in general only purine ↔ pyrimidine substitutions in the second position of a codon lead to major changes in amino acid side chains.

21.4 **Four codons serve special functions.**

A. AUG near the beginning (5′ end) of an mRNA codes for fMet in procaryotes or Met in eucaryotes and signals the start of translation. This AUG also fixes the **reading frame,** that is, the starting point that determines which groups of three bases in the mRNA sequence are interpreted as codons by the protein-synthesizing machinery (see Figure 21.2a).

B. UAG, UAA, and UGA signal termination of translation and release of the growing polypeptide from the mRNA–ribosome complex. These triplets often are referred to as the **amber, ochre,** and **opal codons,** respectively.

21.5 **Amino acid changes caused by mutation are consistent with the code.**

A. The nucleotide sequences of codons initially were determined biochemically (see Problems 21.9, 21.10, and 21.11). Analysis of amino acid differences between mutant and normal proteins provided the first check that the biochemically deduced code was valid in living organisms. In general, amino acid replacements resulting from sponta-

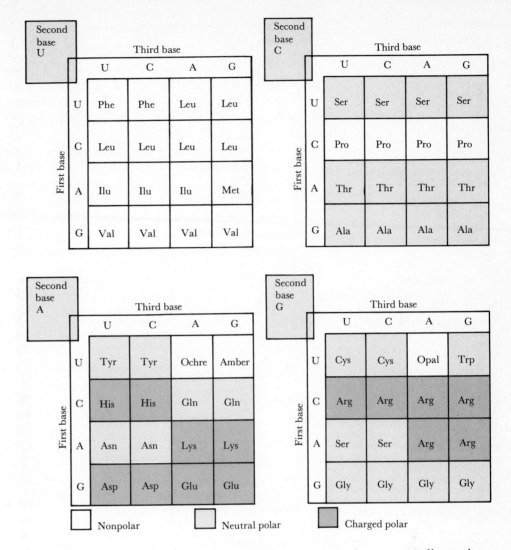

Figure 21.1
The genetic code dictionary.
(Adapted from R. E. Dickerson
and I. Geis, *The Structure and
Action of Proteins,* Benjamin/
Cummings, Menlo Park, Calif.
© 1969 Dickerson and Geis.)

neous mutation are consistent with single base changes in the corresponding codons. Moreover, mutagens known to induce certain kinds of nucleotide alterations in DNA or RNA produce the expected kinds of amino acid replacements in mutant proteins. More recently, comparisons of known nucleotide and amino acid sequences have provided direct proof of codon assignments.

B. There are two principal kinds of mutation:

1. One nucleotide or nucleotide pair can be substituted for another. Replacement of one purine or pyrimidine by the other is called a **transition** mutation; for example, GC → AT in DNA or C → U in RNA. Replacement of a purine by a pyrimidine or vice versa is called a **transversion** mutation; for example, GC → TA in DNA or C → A in RNA. Nucleotide-substitution mutations can cause either **missense,** by converting the normal codon to one that specifies a different amino acid, or **nonsense,** by converting the normal codon to a termination codon. Nonsense mutations lead to

Normal . . . AGC̲A̲U̲G̲G̲C̲U̲U̲C̲U̲G̲C̲G̲C̲A̲G̲A̲U̲U̲A̲G̲G̲C̲A̲C̲ . . .

(a)

Mutant . . . AGC̲A̲U̲G̲G̲C̲U̲U̲A̲C̲U̲G̲C̲G̲C̲A̲G̲A̲U̲U̲A̲G̲G̲C̲A̲C̲ . . .

Sense   ↑ Missense   ↑ Missense

Insertion   Nonsense

(b)

Figure 21.2
Reading frames in **(a)** a normal
and **(b)** a frameshift mutant
mRNA.

premature release of the mutant protein from the ribosome as an incomplete polypeptide fragment.

2. One or more nucleotides can be added or deleted. Such additions and deletions are called **frameshift mutations** if they cause displacement from the correct reading frame, as shown in Figure 21.2b. Frameshift mutations often lead to both missense and nonsense in the region of mRNA following a substitution or deletion.

C. Some common mutagens and their mutagenic effects are listed in Table 21.1. **Base analogues** exert their effects by mispairing either during their incorporation into DNA or during subsequent replication. **Chemical mutagens** and **ionizing radiation** alter DNA bases directly, thereby changing their H-bonding properties and causing nucleotide substitutions in the opposite strand during subsequent replication. **Intercalating dyes** become sandwiched between the stacked bases in DNA, thereby causing additions or deletions upon subsequent replication.

Table 21.1
Common Mutagens and Their Predominant Mutagenic Effects

Mutagen	Mutagen type	Basis for mutagenic action	Predominant mutagenic effect
2-Aminopurine	Base analogue	Adenine analogue; mispairs with cytosine	GC $\rightleftharpoons$ AT transitions
5-Bromouracil	Base analogue	Thymine analogue; mispairs with guanine	GC $\rightleftharpoons$ AT transitions
Nitrous acid	Chemical	Deamination; converts cytosine to uracil, adenine to hypoxanthine	GC $\rightleftharpoons$ AT transitions
Hydroxylamine	Chemical	Converts cytosine to hydroxylamino cytosine; mispairs with adenine	GC $\rightarrow$ AT transitions
Nitrosoguanidine	Chemical	Alkylation of guanine	GC $\rightarrow$ AT transitions
Ethyl methane sulfonate	Chemical	Alkylation of purines followed by depurination	GC $\rightleftharpoons$ AT transitions, and transversions
Ultraviolet irradiation	Ionizing radiation	Pyrimidine dimer formation	GC $\rightarrow$ AT transitions, frameshifts
Proflavin	Intercalating dye	Intercalation	Frameshifts

21.6 Codon–anticodon pairing exhibits "wobble."

A. Transfer RNA recognizes its complementary codon in mRNA by antiparallel pairing between the bases of its anticodon and those of the codon. There is a certain amount of ambiguity or "wobble" in the pairing of the first base (5′ end) of the anticodon with the third base (3′ end) of the codon. A normal tRNA anticodon may be able to pair with up to three different codons for the same amino acid. The rules for third-position pairing are given in Table 21.2.

Table 21.2
Rules for Third-Position Pairing Ambiguity (Wobble) in Codon–Anticodon Recognition

Anticodon (first position)	Codon (third position)	Anticodon (first position)	Codon (third position)
U	A,G	G	U,C
C	G	I	U,C,A
A	U		

As a result of wobble, fewer than 61 species of tRNA are required to translate the 61 sense codons. Nevertheless, there are about 60 tRNAs found in *E. coli*.

B. In mitochondria, additional ambiguity in third-position pairing results from lack of certain modified nucleotides in tRNAs. The mitochondrial translation machinery includes only about 24 species of tRNA.

21.7   Some mutations can be suppressed by mutational alterations in tRNA.

Nonsense mutations and some missense and frameshift mutations can be suppressed—that is, compensated for to produce a functional protein by alterations in tRNA. Nonsense and missense suppressors are tRNAs carrying nucleotide substitutions in the anticodon that allow insertion of acceptable amino acids in response to nonsense or missense codons. The properties of a few bacterial nonsense and missense suppressors are summarized in Table 21.3.

Table 21.3
Bacterial Nonsense and Missense Suppressors

Suppressors	Codon recognized	Amino acid inserted
Nonsense		
Su 1 (amber)	UAG	Ser
Su 2 (amber)	UAG	Gln
Su 3 (amber)	UAG	Tyr
Su 4 (ochre)	UAA, UAG	Tyr
Su 9 (opal)	UGA, UGG	Trp
Missense		
Su 36	AGA, AGG	Gly

Because a suppressor tRNA interacts with normal as well as mutant codons, suppressors cause abnormalities in protein synthesis. However, bacterial strains carrying amber or opal suppressors grow normally, suggesting that the normal termination signal may consist of more than a single termination codon. In several sequenced procaryotic genes the primary termination codon is followed by a backup termination codon, either in tandem or several codons distant but in phase. Bacteria carrying ochre suppressors, which suppress both amber and ochre termination codons, grow more poorly than normal strains, indicating that these suppressors interfere with normal protein synthesis.

21.8   Additional concepts and techniques are presented in the Problems section.

A. Synthesis of random polyribonucleotides in the polynucleotide phosphorylase reaction. Problem 21.9.

B. Deduction of codon compositions from protein-synthesis experiments using random polyribonucleotide messengers. Problems 21.9 and 21.10.

C. Deduction of codon sequences from protein-synthesis experiments using polyribonucleotides of defined sequence as messengers. Problems 21.11 and 21.22.

D. The Brenner proof against a fully overlapping code. Problem 21.12.

E. Frameshift suppressors. Problem 21.18.

F. Determination of mRNA nucleotide sequences from amino acid sequence analysis of the corresponding proteins from wild-type and frameshift mutants. Problems 21.19 and 21.20.

References

COMPREHENSIVE TEXTS

Lehninger: Chapter 34
Metzler: Chapter 15

Stryer: Chapter 26
White et al.: Chapter 26

OTHER REFERENCES

F. H. C. Crick, "Codon–Anticodon Pairing: The Wobble Hypothesis," *Journal of Molecular Biology,* **19,** 584 (1966).

F. H. C. Crick, "The Origin of the Genetic Code," *Journal of Molecular Biology,* **38,** 367 (1968).

"The Genetic Code," *Cold Spring Harbor Symposia in Quantitative Biology,* **31** (1966).

M. Rosenberg and D. Court, "Regulatory Sequences Involved in the Promotion and Termination of RNA Transcription," *Annual Review of Genetics,* **13,** 319 (1979).

J. D. Watson, *Molecular Biology of the Gene,* Benjamin/Cummings, Menlo Park, Calif., 1976, 3rd ed. Chapter 13.

Problems

21.1 Answer the following with true or false. If false, explain why.

a. Genetic signals control the correct transmission and expression of genetic information.

b. Codons for nonpolar amino acids generally contain a pyrimidine base in the second position of the codon, whereas those for charged amino acids contain a purine base in that position.

c. One of the tRNAs that recognizes Ilu codons contains an inosine (I) nucleotide in its anticodon.

d. Considering only the predominant effects of the following mutagens, one would expect that all 2-aminopurine-induced mutations could be mutated back to the original nucleotide sequence (reverted) by 5-bromouracil, whereas only about half could be reverted by hydroxylamine, and none by proflavin.

e. Within a single gene, nucleotide additions and deletions that sum to any multiple of three will restore the correct reading frame, thereby yielding a functional protein.

f. Mutation of the codon AGA to the codon CGA will lead to missense.

g. Nitrosoguanidine-induced mutations can be reverted by a second treatment with nitrosoguanidine.

h. The tRNA^{Met} anticodon could be either pUpApU or pCpApU.

i. Conversion of a codon for a nonpolar amino acid into one for a charged polar amino acid usually must occur by transition mutation.

j. Within a gene the same codon always is used for a given amino acid.

21.2 a. Replication origins and transcription promoters are genetic signals that function in _____; RNA processing signals and translation alignment signals function in _____; protein processing signals and transport signals function in _____.

b. The two unidirectional chemical mutagens are _____ and _____.

c. _____ signals the start of translation and _____, _____, and _____ signal the termination of translation.

d. According to the "wobble" rules, only tRNAs with anticodons beginning with _____ or _____ can read single codons.

e. A termination codon can arise by transition mutation only from the codons for _____, _____, and _____.

21.3 a. There are _____ amino acids that are each specified by six different codons; they are _____.

b. There are _____ amino acids that are specified by five different codons.

c. There are _____ amino acids that are each specified by four different codons; they are _____.

d. There is _____ amino acid that is specified by three different codons; it is _____.

    e. There are _____ amino acids that are each specified by two different codons; they are _____.

    f. There are _____ amino acids that are each specified by only one codon; they are _____.

21.4   Write the tripeptide sequences encoded in the following polyribonucleotides and polydeoxyribonucleotides. (Remember that DNA sequences first must be transcribed into RNA.)

    5'   3'

    a. A-C-U-C-A-A-U-G-G

    b. G-C-T-A-C-G-C-C-T

    c. G-A-G-G-C-U-U-A-A

    d. A-U-G-A-U-C-G-U-G

    e. T-T-T-A-C-C-A-G-G

    f. A-T-G-C-A-A-G-C-A

21.5   Which of the following amino acid changes can result from a single nucleotide change?

    a. Met ↔ Arg

    b. Pro ↔ Ala

    c. Glu ↔ His

    d. Cys ↔ Trp

    e. Val ↔ Tyr

21.6   Which amino acids might be found in the place of Met as a result of

    a. Transition mutations?

    b. Transversion mutations?

21.7   The following amino acid changes have been observed in the β chain of human hemoglobin. In each case describe the possible codons involved and indicate whether the mutation is a transition or a transversion.

    a. Glu ⇗ Val ⇘ Lys

    b. Gly ⇗ Arg ⇘ Asp

    c. His ⇗ Tyr ⇘ Arg

    d. Val ⇗ Glu ⇘ Ala

21.8   In a collection of mutationally altered proteins you find the following amino acid substitutions at three sites that normally contain Arg:

    1. Gly ↙ Arg ↓ Trp ↘ Pro

    2. Thr ↙ Arg ↓ Ilu ↘ Lys

    3. Met ↙ Arg ↓ Trp ↘ Thr

    Deduce the codons that are used for each Arg in the wild-type protein.

21.9   Polyribonucleotides of random sequence can be constructed by the action of the enzyme polynucleotide phosphorylase on mixtures of ribonucleoside diphosphates, where m and n can be any numbers:

$$n\text{UDP} + m\text{CDP} \xrightarrow{\text{polynucleotide phosphorylase}} \text{poly UC} + (n + m)\,\text{P}_i$$

When used as mRNA in a protein-synthesizing system, such a random-sequence poly-ribonucleotide will direct the incorporation of amino acids according to the molar ratio of its constituent nucleotides.

a. Which amino acids will be incorporated under the direction of a random copolymer of U and C in which the molar ratio of U to C is $4:1$?

b. What will be their relative rates of incorporation, assuming that mRNA is rate-limiting?

21.10   You are investigating the genetic code in the Martian organism of Problem 18.19. From it you have prepared a crude extract that will incorporate ^{14}C-labeled amino acids into protein when polyribonucleotides are added. You have prepared high-molecular-weight polyribonucleotide by incubating polynucleotide phosphorylase with a mixture of CDP and ADP in the ratio of $2:3$. You find that the resulting polymer stimulates the incorporation of the seven amino acids listed in the first column below. Their relative rates of incorporation ($\pm 5\%$) are listed in the second column, in which the rate of Ala incorporation has been set equal to 1.00. The background rate of incorporation, determined in control experiments without added poly-nucleotide, has been subtracted in obtaining these values.

Ala	1.00
Arg	0.44
Cys	0.29
Leu	0.68
Phe	0.65
Ser	0.46
Tyr	0.70

a. What are the nucleotide compositions of the seven corresponding codons?

b. Cite three possible sources of error in the interpretation of such data and describe experiments that should be done to check for them.

21.11   Polyribonucleotides of defined sequence can be constructed from small H-bonded polydeoxyribonucleotides, as illustrated in the following example:

$$\begin{array}{ccc}
\text{CAG} & & \\
\vdots\ \vdots\ \vdots & \xrightarrow[\text{polymerase I}]{\text{DNA}} & \left(\begin{array}{c}\text{CAG} \\ \vdots\ \vdots\ \vdots \\ \text{GTC}\end{array}\right)_n \\
\text{GTC} & &
\end{array}
\quad
\begin{array}{c}
\xrightarrow[\text{RNA polymerase}]{\text{+CTP, ATP, GTP}} (\text{CAG})_n \\
\xrightarrow[\text{+GTP, UTP, CTP}]{} (\text{GUC})_n
\end{array}$$

Consider the defined polyribonucleotide $(\text{UCAU})_n$. What is the maximum number of different amino acids expected to be incorporated under the direction of this polymer for a nonoverlapping (a) two-letter code, (b) three-letter code, (c) four-letter code? Describe the kinds of polypeptide products expected for each.

21.12   Before the genetic code had been deciphered, one hypothesis suggested that it was a fully overlapping triplet code. Several variations of such a code were proposed. All contained the following general propositions:

1.   The coding triplets are composed from four nucleotides.

2.   Coding is fully overlapping, each triplet sharing two nucleotides with the succeeding triplet in a sequence. Thus the sequence GCACA codes for three amino acids: GCA for the first, CAC for the second, and ACA for the third.

3.   An amino acid may be represented by more than one triplet.

Such overlapping codes place restrictions on amino acid sequences. For example, the amino acid coded for by GCA can be followed only by an amino acid that has a codon beginning with CA. Calculate the maximum number of different dipeptide sequences that can occur with a hypothetical, overlapping triplet code and for the code as we know it.

21.13 One of the codons recognized by a tRNA^Ala is GCC. The sequences pCpGpG and pIpGpC both occur in the tRNA structure. With no further information, which of these two triplets would you pick as the anticodon? Why? What other codons will be recognized by this tRNA?

21.14 What is the minimum number of tRNAs required to recognize all 61 sense codons without ambiguity?

21.15 Decide which, if any, of the following anticodons might be expected among tRNAs purified from *E. coli*. (I pairs only with C in the first two positions of a codon.)
a. UAU
b. CCI
c. IUG
d. GCU
e. CUA
Which amino acids would the anticipated tRNAs accept?

21.16 a. Assuming that a nonsense suppressor arises by a nucleotide change in the anticodon of a tRNA, predict which amino acids might be inserted in response to UAA in the different ochre suppressors that can arise by single-base changes.
b. Six different amino acids theoretically could be found inserted in response to UGA in single-base-change opal suppressors. Consider the hypothetical situation of an organism in which you know the nucleotide sequences for all the anticodons of the tRNAs that accept these six amino acids (Table 21.4). Which of these tRNAs would you expect to be altered in the various opal suppressors that can arise in this organism? Which of these alterations would result in ambiguity in translation?

Table 21.4
Anticodon Sequences in the tRNAs of an Imaginary Organism (Problem 21.16)

Amino acid accepted	Anticodon	Number of different tRNA species	Amino acid accepted	Anticodon	Number of different tRNA species
Arg	CCU	1	Leu	GAG	1
	CCG	1		UAG	2
	GCG	2		UAA	1
	UCU	1		CAG	1
	UCG	1		CAA	1
Cys	ACA	1	Ser	GCU	2
	GCA	1		UGA	1
Gly	ACC	1		CGA	1
	ICC	1		ACU	1
	UCC	1		AGA	2
	GCC	2		GGA	1
			Trp	CCA	1

21.17 Dr. Franklin Stein, a classical anatomist by training, has developed an interest in genetic engineering and directed evolution. In a preliminary investigation of specific amino acid conversions, he has been studying a protein of unknown function from the bacteriophage λ. Using hydroxylamine, he isolates mutant *a*, which makes only a fragment of the wild-type protein. Upon treatment of mutant *a* with 2-aminopurine he is able to isolate two additional mutants, *b* and *c*, which also make only fragments of the wild-type protein. Mutants *a*, *b*, and *c* are nonviable on most bacterial strains, but can be propagated and distinguished by their growth on suitable nonsense-suppressing strains of bacteria, as indicated in Table 21.5. When mutant *a* is mated to either mutant *b* or *c*, no recombinants that will grow on an Su⁻ host are produced. However, viable recombinants are produced in a mating of mutants *b* and *c*.

What one amino acid difference exists between the protein from the wild-type bacteriophage and that from a viable recombinant from the mating of mutants *b* and *c*?

Table 21.5
Growth of Three
Bacteriophage Mutants on
Nonsuppressing and
Suppressing Bacterial
Strains (Problem 21.17)

	Su⁻	Su 2	Su 4	Su 9
Mutant *a*	−	−	+	−
Mutant *b*	−	+	+	−
Mutant *c*	−	−	−	+

21.18   A few suppressors of frameshift mutations have been isolated. They have the following properties:

1. They suppress very few frameshift mutations. All the suppressible mutations are single-nucleotide-addition mutants.
2. The suppressors themselves were created by mutagenesis with proflavin.
3. The suppressors are altered tRNAs.

Can you suggest a proflavin-induced alteration of a tRNA that could lead to frameshift suppression?

21.19   You have isolated a series of proflavin-induced mutants. From one mutant you are able to purify the inactive protein made by the defective gene. Comparison of the fingerprints of trypsin digests of the normal and the mutant proteins indicates only a *single* difference. You determine the amino acid sequences of the relevant peptides and find the following:

Met-Val-Cys-Val-Arg   Normal peptide
Met-Ala-Met-Arg   Mutant peptide

a. What is the position of this peptide in the protein?
b. What is the mutation that leads to the altered amino acid sequence?
c. Deduce the normal and mutant mRNA nucleotide sequences that can account for the observed peptide difference.

21.20   To obtain evidence for the validity of the genetic code in vivo you are working with a bacteriophage T4 enzyme that is easy to purify from phage-infected cell extracts. The enzyme is not detectable in extracts made with a proflavin-induced mutant, J74, but is found in two proflavin-induced revertants of this mutant, J74R1 and J74R2. With considerable effort you have isolated and sequenced the corresponding decapeptides from the purified enzymes made by the wild type and the two revertants. However, in your excitement you spill cleaning solution on the sequence data for wild type. All that can be salvaged is the molar ratio of amino acids in the wild-type decapeptide.

Wild type: (Asp,Ilu₂,Leu₂,Lys,Met,Phe,Ser,Val)
J74R1:   Met-Arg-Phe-Pro-Ser-Met-Lys-Ser-Ilu-Val
J74R2:   Met-Arg-Phe-Pro-Ser-Asp-Glu-Lys-Gln-Val

Despite this setback,
a. Describe the nature of the original mutation and each of the revertants.
b. Write the nucleotide sequence of the mRNA that codes for the wild-type decapeptide.

21.21   In the absence of tRNA, procaryotic ribosomes will bind to mRNA and protect the initial codons of the cistron from enzymatic digestion. Assume that such an experiment has been carried out using the RNA message from an RNA bacteriophage. Following digestion of the unbound portion of the message with pancreatic ribonuclease, an oligonucleotide is isolated. Results of the following analyses are expressed per mole of the oligonucleotide (see Table 21.6 for enzyme specificities). Alkaline hydrolysis yields 1 pAp, 2 Ap, 2 Cp, 2 Gp, and 2 Up. Ribonuclease T₁ digestion yields 1 Cp, a trinucleotide, and a pentanucleotide. Upon treatment with alkaline phosphatase followed by snake venom phosphodiesterase, the pentanucleotide yields 2 pA, 1 U, 1pG, and 1 pC. When the original oligonucleotide is subjected to alkaline phosphatase followed by limited digestion with snake venom phosphodiesterase, a pentanucleotide can be isolated, which upon alkaline hydrolysis yields 1 A, 1 Ap, 1 Gp, and 2 Up.
a. What is the most likely nucleotide sequence of the original fragment?
b. What are the first three amino acids of the protein for which this cistron codes?

Table 21.6
Specificity of Cleavage Procedures Useful in Nucleic Acid
Manipulations (Problem 21.21)[a]

Procedure	Substrate	Type of enzyme or reaction	Specificity of cleavage	Predominant reaction products
Terminal cleavages				
1. Snake venom phospho-diesterase	RNA, ssDNA	Exonuclease	At b where N_2 is the 3' terminus and carries a 3'-OH group	pX
2. Spleen phosphodies-terase	RNA, ssDNA	Exonuclease	At c where N_1 is the 5' terminus and carries a 5'-OH group	Xp
3. Alkaline phospha-tase	RNA, DNA	Phosphatase	At a where N_1 is the 5' terminus; at d where N_2 is the 3' terminus	P_i and oligonucleotide with 3'-OH and 5'-OH groups
Internal cleavages				
1. Ribonuclease T_1	RNA	Endonuclease	At c where N_1 is G or I	Xp---Gp, Gp Xp---Ip, Ip
2. Ribonuclease T_2	RNA	Endonuclease	At c where N_1 is usually A, sometimes G	Xp---Ap, Ap
3. Ribonuclease U_2	RNA	Endonuclease	At c where N_1 is a purine	Xp---Pup, Pup
4. Pancreatic ribonuclease	RNA	Endonuclease	At c where N_1 is a pyrimidine	Xp---Pyp, Pyp
5. Alkali	RNA	Esterolysis	At c where N_1 is any nucleotide	Mixture of 2' and 3' nucleotides
6. Deoxyribonuclease I	DNA	Endonuclease	At b where N_1 and N_2 are any nucleotides	Nucleotides and small oligonucleotides pX---X, pX
7. Deoxyribonuclease II	DNA	Endonuclease	At c where N_1 and N_2 are any nucleotides	Nucleotides and small oligonucleotides X---Xp, Xp

[a] I indicates inosine, and X indicates any nucleoside. Pu and Py denote purine and pyrimidine nucleosides. A dashed line between two nucleotides indicates an unspecified number of additional nucleotides; ss stands for single stranded.

21.22 Consider the following sequence of reactions. The enzyme specificities are listed in Table 21.6. CMC is a carbodiimide, which adds to uridine and protects it from attack by pancreatic ribonuclease. CMC can be removed by treatment with NH_3.

1. ADP + UDP $\xrightarrow{\text{polynucleotide phosphorylase}}$ product 1

2. Product 1 $\xrightarrow[\text{ribonuclease}]{\text{pancreatic}}$ $\xrightarrow{\text{DEAE cellulose chromatography}}$ product 2

3. Product 2 $\xrightarrow{\text{KOH}}$ equimolar Ap and Up

4. Product 2 $\xrightarrow[\text{phosphatase}]{\text{alkaline}}$ product 3

5. Product 3 + ADP $\xrightarrow{\text{polynucleotide phosphorylase}}$ $\xrightarrow{\text{chromatography}}$ product 4

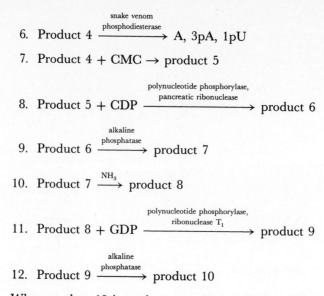

6. Product 4 $\xrightarrow{\text{snake venom phosphodiesterase}}$ A, 3pA, 1pU

7. Product 4 + CMC → product 5

8. Product 5 + CDP $\xrightarrow{\substack{\text{polynucleotide phosphorylase,} \\ \text{pancreatic ribonuclease}}}$ product 6

9. Product 6 $\xrightarrow{\substack{\text{alkaline} \\ \text{phosphatase}}}$ product 7

10. Product 7 $\xrightarrow{NH_3}$ product 8

11. Product 8 + GDP $\xrightarrow{\substack{\text{polynucleotide phosphorylase,} \\ \text{ribonuclease } T_1}}$ product 9

12. Product 9 $\xrightarrow{\substack{\text{alkaline} \\ \text{phosphatase}}}$ product 10

When product 10 is used as a synthetic mRNA in vitro, what peptide will be produced?

21.23 Nitrous acid, HNO_2, can be used to induce mutations in free virus particles. It acts by deaminating cytosine and adenine, thereby converting them respectively to uracil and hypoxanthine (which pairs like guanine). An analysis of the amino acid changes in the coat protein of HNO_2-induced mutants of TMV (tobacco mosaic virus, a single-stranded RNA plant virus) confirms this action of HNO_2.

Amino acid changes in TMV coat protein	Expected nucleotide changes in TMV RNA
Pro → Leu	C → U
Ser → Phe	C → U
Ilu → Val	A → G
Pro → Ser	C → U
Glu → Gly	A → G

Recently you have isolated a large number of HNO_2-induced coat protein mutants of a previously uncharacterized DNA virus X. All the amino acid changes are of the following type:

Arg → His
Leu → Ser
Tyr → His
Met → Ilu
Gly → Asp
Val → Ala

Are these changes consistent with the action of HNO_2? What can you deduce about the genome of the unknown virus?

21.24 The N-terminal portion of the *rIIB* gene of bacteriophage T4 has been the focus of many genetic studies. Although the protein itself is essential for growth of T4 in certain bacterial hosts, the N terminus of the protein is not essential under any conditions. Apparently the *rIIB* protein can function normally with virtually any amino acid substitution in its N-terminal section.

a. You have isolated seven new frameshift mutations that map in the N-terminal section of *rIIB*. Six of these mutations are single-base deletions (−), and one is a single-base insertion (+). Which of these mutant bacteriophages will grow in a host that requires *rIIB* protein?

b. You have mapped the (−) mutations and numbered them sequentially beginning with the one closest to the N terminus. You also have created a series of double mutants containing the (+) mutation paired with each of the (−) mutations. The

Restriction enzyme	Recognition sequence
*Alu*I	AGCT
*Sau*96I	GGNCC
*Hin*dIII	AAGCTT
*Bgl*I	GCCNNNNNGGC

(a)

Ilu · Lys · Leu · Gly · Pro · Arg · Ala · Ser · Phe · Ala

(b)

Figure 21.3
(a) Restriction enzyme recognition sequences, and (b) a decapeptide (Problem 21.25). Only one strand of DNA is shown. N stands for any nucleotide.

growth properties of the double mutants are shown in Table 21.7. Offer an explanation for the growth patterns of the double mutants on nonsuppressing (Su⁻) and suppressing hosts. Also position the (+) mutation as precisely as the data allow.

Table 21.7
Growth of Bacteriophage T4 Mutants on Three Host Strains (Problem 21.24)

Double mutant	Host strain			Double mutant	Host strain		
	Su⁻	Su 1	Su 9		Su⁻	Su 1	Su 9
+,1	−	+	−	+,4	+	+	+
+,2	−	+	−	+,5	−	−	+
+,3	+	+	+	+,6	−	−	+

21.25   The recognition sequences for four restriction enzymes are shown in Figure 21.3a. Can it be stated with *certainty* that any of these restriction enzymes will cleave the DNA segment that encodes the decapeptide in Figure 21.3b?

☆ 21.26   From your knowledge of tRNA structure deduce the identity of the two tRNAs that are contained in the dimeric precursor tRNA shown in Figure 21.4. This precursor tRNA, which is synthesized by the bacteriophage T4, normally is cleaved as indicated by the arrows and further modified into two mature tRNAs. Can you suggest one modification that must be made in each tRNA?

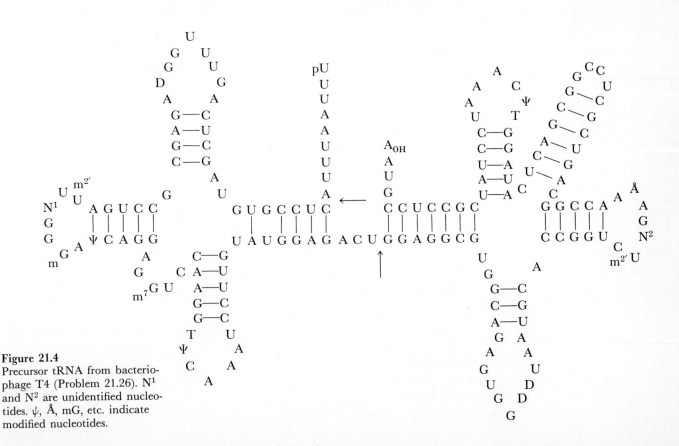

Figure 21.4
Precursor tRNA from bacteriophage T4 (Problem 21.26). N¹ and N² are unidentified nucleotides. ψ, Å, mG, etc. indicate modified nucleotides.

☆ 21.27 Deduce the nature of the mutations in two proflavin-induced revertants of the same frameshift mutant, given the following sequence of codons in the wild-type mRNA and the amino acid compositions of the two corresponding revertant peptides.

...AGU CUG GUU CAU CCC GAU... Wild-type mRNA

1. Asp, His, Leu, Ser$_3$ Mutant peptide 1
2. Asp, His, Ilu, Pro, Trp, Val   Mutant peptide 2

☆ 21.28 The protein you are interested in contains Met at position 12. By mutagenesis with 2-aminopurine you have isolated two mutant organisms that produce proteins with new amino acids at position 12. Among the recombinants produced by mating the two mutants, you find a new strain that produces a protein containing an amino acid at position 12, which is not present in the original parent or in either mutant. If you assume that each mutant differs from the parent by a single base-pair change, you can deduce the identity of the new amino acid in the recombinant. What is it?

Answers

21.1   a. True
     b. True
     c. True
     d. True
     e. False. The correct reading frame will be restored; however, the protein will function only if acceptable amino acids have been inserted in the "out-of-phase" portion of translation, that is, the translation between the first and last frameshift mutation.
     f. False. AGA and CGA are both codons for Arg.
     g. False. An AT base pair that arose in the first treatment with nitrosoguanidine cannot be converted back to GC by a second treatment, because nitrosoguanidine promotes only GC → AT transitions.
     h. False. pUpApU would recognize both AUG (Met) and AUA (Ilu), thereby leading to the insertion of Met in response to an Ilu codon.
     i. False. Conversion of a codon for a nonpolar amino acid into one for a charged polar amino acid must occur primarily by transversion mutation.
     j. False. In a given gene more than one codon generally is used to specify any amino acid for which the code is degenerate.

21.2   a. DNA, RNA, protein
     b. hydroxylamine, nitrosoguanidine
     c. AUG, UAG, UAA, UGA
     d. C, A
     e. Arg, Gln, Trp

21.3   a. three; Leu, Ser, and Arg
     b. no (or zero)
     c. five, Val, Pro, Thr, Ala, and Gly
     d. one; Ilu
     e. nine; Phe, Tyr, His, Gln, Asn, Lys, Asp, Glu, and Cys
     f. two; Met and Trp

21.4   a. Thr-Gln-Trp
     b. Arg-Arg-Ser
     c. This sequence codes for the dipeptide Glu-Ala
     d. Met-Ilu-Val
     e. Pro-Gly-Lys
     f. Cys-Leu-His

21.5   a. a, b, and d

21.6 a. Transition mutations:

GUG	Val
ACG	Thr
AUA	Ilu

b. Transversion mutations:

UUG	Leu
CUG	Leu
AGC	Arg
AAG	Lys
AUU	Ilu
AUC	Ilu

21.7 a. $\text{Glu}\left(\text{GA}_\text{G}^\text{A}\right)$
$\nearrow \text{Val}\left(\text{GU}_\text{G}^\text{A}\right)$ A → U   transversion
$\searrow \text{Lys}\left(\text{AA}_\text{G}^\text{A}\right)$ G → A   transition

b. $\text{Gly}\left(\text{GG}_\text{C}^\text{U}\right)$
$\nearrow \text{Arg}\left(\text{CG}_\text{C}^\text{U}\right)$ G → C   transversion
$\searrow \text{Asp}\left(\text{GA}_\text{C}^\text{U}\right)$ G → A   transition

c. $\text{His}\left(\text{CA}_\text{C}^\text{U}\right)$
$\nearrow \text{Tyr}\left(\text{UA}_\text{C}^\text{U}\right)$ C → U   transition
$\searrow \text{Arg}\left(\text{CG}_\text{C}^\text{U}\right)$ A → G   transition

d. $\text{Val}\left(\text{GU}_\text{G}^\text{A}\right)$
$\nearrow \text{Glu}\left(\text{GA}_\text{G}^\text{A}\right)$ U → A   transversion
$\searrow \text{Ala}\left(\text{GC}_\text{G}^\text{A}\right)$ U → C   transition

21.8   Arg (1) CGG
Arg (2) AGA
Arg (3) AGG

21.9 a. The codons present in the copolymer will be UUU (Phe), UUC (Phe), UCU (Ser), CUU (Leu), UCC (Ser), CUC (Leu), CCU (Pro), and CCC (Pro). Therefore, four amino acids, Phe, Ser, Leu, and Pro, will be incorporated.

b. To predict the relative rates of incorporation one first must calculate the frequencies of individual codons in the random copolymer. Because the molar ratio of U to C is 4:1, the frequency of U is 0.80 and the frequency of C is 0.20. Therefore, the frequencies of U_3, U_2C, UC_2, and C_3 codons will be as follows:

U_3 codon:	UUU(Phe) = (0.80)(0.80)(0.80)	= 0.51
U_2C codons:	UUC(Phe) = (0.80)(0.80)(0.20)	= 0.13
	UCU(Ser) = (0.80)(0.80)(0.20)	= 0.13
	CUU(Leu) = (0.80)(0.80)(0.20)	= 0.13
UC_2 codons:	UCC(Ser) = (0.80)(0.20)(0.20)	= 0.032
	CUC(Leu) = (0.80)(0.20)(0.20)	= 0.032
	CCU(Pro) = (0.80)(0.20)(0.20)	= 0.032
C_3 codon:	CCC(Pro) = (0.20)(0.20)(0.20)	= 0.0080

The relative rates of amino acid incorporation will be equal to the relative frequencies in the copolymer of codons for the four amino acids:

$$Phe = 0.51 \quad + 0.13 \quad = 0.64$$
$$Ser \ = 0.13 \quad + 0.03 \quad = 0.16$$
$$Leu = 0.13 \quad + 0.03 \quad = 0.16$$
$$Pro = 0.032 + 0.0080 = 0.040$$

Thus the ratio of incorporation rates will be 16 Phe : 4 Ser : 4 Leu : 1 Pro.

21.10 a. Calculations analogous to those detailed in Answer 21.9 yield the answer.

Codon composition	Codon frequency	Normalized frequency	Codon assignments
A_3	0.22	1.00	Ala
A_2C	0.14	0.67	Leu, Phe, Tyr
AC_2	0.096	0.44	Arg, Ser
C_3	0.064	0.30	Cys

The inability to account for one codon of the AC_2 class suggests that it may code for an unidentified amino acid or for nonsense.

b. Three possible sources of error in the interpretation of such data are:

1. The C to A ratio in the polyribonucleotide is not $2:3$. This possibility should be checked by determining the nucleotide composition of the polymer.
2. The polyribonucleotide is not a random sequence of C and A. This possibility should be tested by determining the nearest-neighbor frequencies (Problem 18.14).
3. The relative rates of incorporation do not reflect codon frequencies, but rather some other limiting factor. This possibility should be checked by determining that the added polyribonucleotide template is the rate-limiting component in the reaction mixtures.

21.11 Because the number of different codons is four in each case, the maximum number of different amino acids expected to be incorporated is also four in each case. The nature of the polypeptide product distinguishes the three types of codes.

a. . . .$aa_1aa_2aa_1aa_2$. . . + . . .$aa_3aa_4aa_3aa_4$. . .

b. . . .$aa_1aa_2aa_3aa_4aa_1aa_2aa_3aa_4$. . .

c. $(aa_1)_n + (aa_2)_n + (aa_3)_n + (aa_4)_n$

21.12 In an overlapping triplet code, a sequence of 4 nucleotides codes for 1 dipeptide. Therefore, the maximum number of different dipeptide sequences equals the number of unique tetranucleotide sequences, which is $(4)^4 = 256$. In a nonoverlapping triplet code there are no restrictions on the sequence of triplets, so that each amino acid may be followed by any one of the 20 amino acids. Thus the number of different dipeptide sequences equals $(20)^2$ or 400. These relationships were pointed out first in the late 1950s by Sidney Brenner, who proved the impossibility of a universal overlapping triplet code by showing that more than 256 dipeptide sequences had been reported already in known proteins.

21.13 Because recognition between codon and anticodon is antiparallel, pIpGpC must be the correct anticodon. According to "wobble" rules, this tRNA also should recognize GCU and GCA.

21.14 One approach to this problem is to determine the minimum number of anticodons necessary to recognize the codons for each amino acid by applying the wobble rules in Table 21.2. A more general approach is possible if you realize the following:

1. The set of codons for each of the amino acids specified by one, two, or three codons can be recognized by one anticodon. There are 12 such amino acids (Problem 21.3); these require a total of at least 12 anticodons.
2. The set of codons for each of the amino acids specified by four codons requires at least two anticodons. There are 5 such amino acids (Problem 21.3); these require a total of at least 10 anticodons.

3. The set of codons for each of the amino acids specified by six codons requires at least three anticodons. There are three such amino acids (Problem 21.3); these require a total of at least nine anticodons.

By either approach, the minimum number of anticodons required to recognize all 61 sense codons without ambiguity is 31.

21.15 Only CCI (Arg) and GCU (Ser) would be expected to occur in wild-type *E. coli*. Both UAU and IUG would lead to ambiguity and consequently would not be expected. CUA would recognize the amber codon and might be expected among the tRNAs from a strain of *E. coli* carrying an amber suppressor.

21.16 a. The anticodon of an ochre-suppressor tRNA must be UUA (this suppressor will recognize the amber codon UAG as well as the ochre codon UAA). The anticodons that can mutate to UUA by single-base changes are CUA, GUA, AUA, UAA, UGA, UCA, UUG, UUC, and UUU. Two of these (CUA and UCA) recognize nonsense codons and should not occur in the tRNA population. The remaining seven would be expected to occur among tRNAs for Gln, Glu, Leu, Lys, Ser, and Tyr. Hence the amino acids inserted in response to UAA by different ochre suppressors most probably will be among these six.

b. Some potential suppressors (e.g., the tRNA^{Arg} with anticodon UCG) cannot arise because the necessary anticodon alteration would leave an amino acid codon without a tRNA to recognize it—a lethal condition. Such restrictions in tRNA alteration have been demonstrated in *E. coli*. Nine of the anticodons shown in Table 21.4 could mutate by a single base change to one of the two possible opal suppressor anticodons, UCA or ICA. However, six of these changes would be lethal, because they would result in untranslatable codons. Only two of the nine potentially mutable anticodons [ACA (Cys) and ICC (Gly)] are superfluous, in that the codons they recognize also can be recognized by other anticodons that correspond to the same amino acid. A third anticodon [CCA (Trp)] can mutate to UCA without losing its ability to recognize the Trp codon, UGG. Therefore, only three tRNA species would be expected to give rise to opal suppressors in this organism:

1. ACA (Cys) → UCA   Ambiguous; will insert Cys in response to Trp codons

2. ICC (Gly) → ICA   Ambiguous; will insert Gly in response to Cys codons

3. CCA (Trp) → UCA   Unambiguous; will insert Trp in response to opal and Trp codons

Whether the mutations leading to ambiguity actually would be found is an unanswered question. The degree to which an organism can tolerate ambiguity is not known.

21.17 From the growth patterns on the nonsense-suppressing strains of bacteria you can deduce that mutant *a* must carry an ochre codon, mutant *b* must carry an amber codon, and mutant *c* must carry an opal codon. Because mutant *a* was produced by mutagenesis with hydroxylamine, it must have arisen by a GC → AT transition. The only codon that can mutate to the ochre codon by a GC → AT conversion is CAA, a codon for Gln. Only recombination between mutants *b* and *c* can produce a sense codon. (The recombination shown is depicted in terms of ribonucleotide sequences for simplicity.)

```
                              -U-G-G-   Trp
                            ↗
            -U-A-G-  ⟋
            ----˅--
            ----˄--
            -U-G-A-  ⟍
                            ↘
                              -U-A-A-   Ochre
```

The recombinants from this cross that will grow on an Su⁻ host must carry the codon for Trp. Consequently, the one amino acid difference between wild type and recombinant is a Gln to Trp change.

21.18 Current evidence favors the idea that proflavin causes a one nucleotide addition to the anticodon of the tRNA, thereby allowing it to pair with four bases instead of the usual three. Such altered pairing could restore the correct reading frame in suppressible one-base-insertion mutants.

21.19 a. Because this peptide is the only one affected in the frameshift mutant, it must be at the C terminus.

b. A correlation of the possible codons for the amino acids in the normal and mutant peptides indicates that the mutation results from the insertion of C between G and U of the first Val codon.

c. To account for the single difference between the normal and mutant peptides, there must be a termination codon immediately following Arg in the new reading frame. The Arg codon and the second Val codon shown below will cause the appearance of UAG in the new reading frame. Thus the wild-type amino acid and nucleotide sequences must be;

$$\text{Met - Val - Cys - Val - Arg} \qquad \text{Wild-type amino acid sequence}$$

$$\text{AUG GUA UGC GUU AG}^\text{A}_\text{G} \qquad \text{Wild-type nucleotide sequence}$$

$$\downarrow$$

$$\text{AUG GCU AUG CGU UAG}^\text{A}_\text{G} \qquad \text{Mutant nucleotide sequence}$$

21.20 a. The original mutation is insertion of G. Mutants J74R1 and J74R2 result from deletions of G and U, respectively.

b. The mRNA sequence for wild type and the positions of the insertion and deletions are

+G original   −G J74R1   −U J74R2

↓   ↑   ↑

$$\text{AU}^\text{C}_\text{A}\text{ GAU UUC CUU CUG AUG AAA AGC AUA GU}^{\substack{\text{U}\\\text{C}\\\text{A}\\\text{G}}} \qquad \text{Wild-type mRNA sequence}$$

Ilu - Asp - Phe - Leu - Leu - Met - Lys - Ser - Ilu - Val   Wild-type decapeptide

21.21 a. The experimental data yield the sequence

$$\text{pApUpGpUpAp(ApC)pGpC}$$

in which (ApC) indicates that the relative order of these two nucleotides is unknown. However, it is unlikely that the initiation codon AUG would be followed immediately by the termination codon UAA. Therefore, the most likely sequence is

$$\text{pApUpGpUpApCpApGpC}$$

b. The first three amino acids would be Met-Tyr-Ser.

21.22   Product 1   = poly AU
Product 2   = ApUp
Product 3   = ApU
Product 4   = ApUpApApA
Product 5   = ApU(CMC)pApApA
Product 6   = ApU(CMC)pApApApCp
Product 7   = ApU(CMC)pApApApC
Product 8   = ApUpApApApC
Product 9   = ApUpApApApCpGp
Product 10 = ApUpApApApCpG

Ilu-Asn is the only peptide that can be made.

21.23   All changes in the X virus coat protein are either U → C or G → A. For these altera-tions to be consistent with the mode of action of HNO_2, the virus must contain single-stranded DNA, which is the sense strand for the coat protein. HNO_2 induces C → U and A → G changes in the DNA single strand. In the mRNA transcribed from this strand these changes become G → A and U → C, respectively.

21.24   a.   None of the frameshift mutants will grow in a host that requires the *rIIB* protein. Even though the mutations themselves are located in the nonessential N terminus, they alter the entire downstream amino acid sequence.

      b.   Because the mutations are located in the nonessential N terminus, it might be ex-pected that all combinations of (+) and (−) mutations would restore the reading frame to normal and thus yield a functional *rIIB* protein. Some combinations do not grow because nonsense codons occur in the new reading frame between the (+) and (−) mutations. The (−) mutations 1 and 2 activate an amber codon that precedes the (+) mutation. Similarly, the (+) mutation activates an opal codon that precedes the (−) mutations 5 and 6. Only the (+) mutation and the (−) mutations 3 and 4 are not separated from one another by nonsense codons and thus can grow on an Su⁻ host. The (+) mutation thus maps on the C-terminal side of mutation 2 and on the N-terminal side of mutation 5.

21.25   Only *Sau*96I definitely will cleave the DNA sequence that encodes the decapeptide. The amino acid sequence Gly–Pro is encoded by the nucleotide sequence GGNCCN and thus will be cleaved by *Sau*96I. Codon degeneracy makes cleavage by the other restriction enzymes uncertain. [Note that because each recognition sequence has 2-fold symmetry, the mRNA encoding the polypeptide has the same 5′–3′ nucleotide sequence as the restriction sequence shown in Figure 21.3 (with U's in place of T's) regardless of which DNA strand is the sense strand.]

Appendix: Analysis of Nucleic Acid Association Reactions

Kinetic analysis of nucleic acid association by base pairing is a valuable technique for determining the complexity and relatedness of sets of nucleotide sequences. Various applications of this technique provide information on the genetic content, sequence organization, and expression of eucaryotic genomes. Similar methods can be used to study DNA–DNA, DNA–RNA, and RNA–RNA association reactions. This appendix considers the basic theory and some applications of nucleic acid association kinetics.

Concepts

A.1   Separated complementary strands of DNA can reassociate to form base-paired duplex structures.

A.   The rate at which two complementary sequences reassociate depends on four parameters:

1.   The concentration of cations, which decrease the intermolecular repulsion of negatively charged DNA strands

2.   The incubation temperature, which is optimal for reassociation at about 25°C below the melting temperature (T_m) of the original duplex DNA (Concept 17.3)

3.   DNA concentration, which determines the frequency of intermolecular collisions

4.   The size of the DNA fragments

B.   Reassociation studies generally are carried out as follows:

1.   Purified DNA is sheared into small fragments by passage through a small orifice at high pressure, by high-speed blending, or by sonication. Uniform fragment sizes of 3×10^2 to 10^5 nucleotide pairs can be produced by controlled shearing.

2.   The fragments are denatured by heating briefly to 100°C and then cooling rapidly. This procedure separates complementary strands without breaking a significant number of internucleotide bonds.

3.   The dissociated fragments are incubated in a standard phosphate buffer (generally 0.18N monovalent cation) at a DNA concentration and temperature that will give an appropriate rate of reassociation (annealing conditions; Concept 17.3).

4.   The extent of reassociation as a function of time is measured by one of the three following techniques, which distinguish between double- and single-stranded DNA:

    a.   Nuclease digestion. Using a nuclease that catalyzes hydrolysis of single-stranded but not double-stranded DNA (such as S1 nuclease from the mold

This appendix is adapted from Leroy E. Hood, John H. Wilson, and William B. Wood, *Molecular Biology of Eucaryotic Cells*, Benjamin/Cummings, Menlo Park, Calif., 1975.

Aspergillus), samples can be digested to completion and the amount of nuclease-resistant material determined.

b. Hypochromicity. Because double-stranded DNA absorbs less ultraviolet light than single-stranded DNA at the same concentration, the degree of reassociation is directly proportional to the decrease in absorbance of 260 nm light (hypochromicity) as the reaction proceeds.

c. Hydroxyapatite chromatography. Because double-stranded DNA adsorbs to hydroxyapatite under conditions where single-stranded DNA does not, reassociation can be followed by passing samples through a column and determining the fraction of the DNA that adsorbs. Hydroxyapatite chromatography is useful also as a preparative technique for separating rapidly reassociating from slowly reassociating fragments.

A.2 Reassociation follows bimolecular reaction kinetics.

DNA reassociation is a bimolecular second-order reaction. The rate of disappearance of single strands is given by the expression

$$-\frac{dC}{dt} = kC^2 \tag{A.1}$$

in which C is the concentration of single-stranded DNA in moles of nucleotide per liter, t is time in seconds, and k (liters per mole second) is a second-order rate constant. The value of k depends on cation concentration, temperature, fragment size, and the sequence complexity of the DNA population (Concept A.3). Equation A.1 can be rearranged to

$$-\frac{dC}{C^2} = k \, dt$$

and integrated from initial conditions $t = 0$ and $C = C_0$ to yield

$$\frac{1}{C} - \frac{1}{C_0} = kt$$

or

$$\frac{C}{C_0} = \frac{1}{1 + kC_0 t} \tag{A.2}$$

Because at $t = 0$ all the DNA is single-stranded, C_0 is equal to the total DNA concentration.

Equation A.2 shows that the fraction of single-stranded DNA remaining in a reassociation reaction (C/C_0) is a function of $C_0 t$, the product of the initial concentration and the elapsed time. Therefore, the time course of a reassociation reaction is plotted conveniently as shown in Figure A.1, to give a so-called "Cot" curve.

Figure A.1
$C_0 t$ curve of an ideal second-order reassociation reaction. Note that 80% of the reaction occurs over a two-log interval of $C_0 t$. [Redrawn from R. J. Britten and D. Kohne, *Science,* **161,** 529 (1968).]

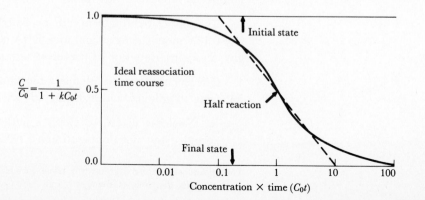

$C_0t_{1/2}$ is defined as the value of C_0t at which the reaction has proceeded to half-completion ($C/C_0 = \frac{1}{2}$). Substitution into equation A.2 shows that $C_0t_{1/2}$, which can be determined experimentally as shown in Figure A.1, is the reciprocal of the second-order rate constant:

$$C_0t_{1/2} = \frac{1}{k}$$

A.3 $C_0t_{1/2}$ is proportional to the sequence complexity of a DNA preparation.

The **complexity** (X)* of a sheared DNA preparation is the length in nucleotide pairs of the longest nonrepeating sequence that could be produced by splicing together fragments in the population. For example, a preparation of repeating dAT copolymer (. .ATATAT. .) has a complexity of 2; a preparation of a repeating tetramer of the form $(ATGC)_n$ has a complexity of 4; and a preparation made from identical but internally nonrepeating DNA molecules 10^5 nucleotide pairs in length has a complexity of 10^5.

$C_0t_{1/2}$ is related directly to complexity. Consider the reassociation of two populations of denatured DNA fragments, one derived from identical nonrepeating molecules 10^5 nucleotide pairs in length such as the DNA of a bacteriophage ($X = 10^5$), and the other derived from identical nonrepeating molecules 5×10^6 nucleotide pairs in length such as the DNA of a bacterium ($X = 5 \times 10^6$). If the fragment size is 500 nucleotides, then in the first population the fragments representing any particular sequence and its complement make up 0.005% of the total DNA. In the second population, each 500-nucleotide sequence represents only 0.0001% of the total DNA. Therefore, if both populations are adjusted to the same *total DNA concentration*, the concentration of each 500-nucleotide sequence will be 50 times greater in the first population than in the second. Therefore $t_{1/2}$ for the first population will be $\frac{1}{50}$ of $t_{1/2}$ for the second. Or, if the DNA concentrations are unequal, $C_0t_{1/2}$ for the first population will be $\frac{1}{50}$ of $C_0t_{1/2}$ for the second.

The proportionality of $C_0t_{1/2}$ to complexity means that

$$X = KC_0t_{1/2} \tag{A.3}$$

in which the proportionality constant K will depend on reaction conditions (cation concentration, fragment size, and so on). Under the standard conditions generally employed ($0.18N$ cation concentration, 400-nucleotide fragment size), $K \simeq 5 \times 10^5$ (liters $\times$ nucleotide pairs)/(moles of nucleotides $\times$ seconds), or

$$X = (5 \times 10^5)(C_0t_{1/2}) \tag{A.4}$$

nucleotide pairs.

For organisms whose DNA contains no repeated sequences, X is simply the genome size (N) in nucleotide pairs, and N can be determined directly from measurements of $C_0t_{1/2}$ using equation A.3 or A.4. All procaryotic genomes examined so far fall into this category. The reassociation of sheared DNA from these organisms goes to completion over about a two-log interval of C_0t (see Figure A.1), indicating that the concentration of all sequences in the population is the same.

A.4 C_0t curves reveal the presence of repeated nucleotide sequences in eucaryotic genomes.

Most eucaryotic DNA preparations reassociate over a C_0t range that is much greater than two logs, indicating that different sequences in the population are present at

*In the literature complexity often is denoted by C. In this treatment X is used, to avoid confusion with the symbol C for DNA concentration.

different frequencies, and therefore reassociate at different rates. Consider a hypothetical example of an organism whose genome consists of 50% repeated sequences of total complexity 10^5 nucleotide pairs, each repeated 10^4 times per genome (component a), and 50% nonrepeated (unique) sequences of total complexity 10^9 nucleotide pairs (component b). N, the haploid genome size for this organism, is 2×10^9. If the DNA fragments representing these two components could be separated and reassociated independently, they would give the C_0t curves shown by dashed lines in Figure A.2, with $C_0t_{1/2}$ values that differ by a factor of 10^4. When reassociated together, the two components behave *independently* to give the biphasic C_0t curve shown by the solid line in Figure A.2. The following information can be obtained from such a curve:

1. **Genome fraction of each component (f).** The fraction of the genome represented by each component can be determined by extrapolation from the end point of each component of the reassociation curve to the ordinate. In the example, $f_a = f_b = 0.5$.

2. **$C_0t_{1/2(\text{pure})}$ for each component.** The $C_0t_{1/2}$ value for each component in the mixture can be determined by extrapolating from the midpoint of each component of the reassociation curve to the abscissa. In the example, $C_0t_{1/2(\text{mixture})}$ for a = 2×10^{-1} mol sec/L and $C_0t_{1/2(\text{mixture})}$ for b = 2×10^3 mol sec/L. Note that these values are different from those determined from the C_0t curves of each component alone (Figure A.2, dashed lines). This discrepancy arises because for the mixture C_0 is taken to be the *total DNA concentration*, whereas for an isolated component C_0 is taken to be the *concentration of the component*. To determine the complexity of a component, it is necessary to know the $C_0t_{1/2}$ value that the component would exhibit alone ($C_0t_{1/2(\text{pure})}$). This value can be obtained by multiplying the observed $C_0t_{1/2(\text{mixture})}$ by the fractional contribution of the component to the genome:

$$C_0t_{1/2(\text{pure})} = fC_0t_{1/2(\text{mixture})} \tag{A.5}$$

In the example, the $C_0t_{1/2(\text{pure})}$ values for components a and b are 10^{-1} and 10^3 mol sec/L, respectively.

3. **Repetition number (R).** The *relative* frequencies of sequences in the various components of a mixture are inversely proportional to their $C_0t_{1/2(\text{mixture})}$ values. If the most slowly reassociating class is known to be unique ($R = 1$), or if the genome size, N, is known, then the absolute frequency or repetition number of the sequences in a component can be calculated. For any component, i, R_i is related to f_i, N, and X_i by the expression

$$R_i = \frac{f_i N}{X_i} \tag{A.6}$$

This relationship also can be used to calculate the complexity X_i of a component if R_i, f_i, and N are known.

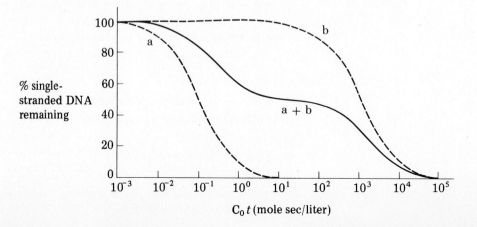

Figure A.2
C_0t curves for whole DNA (solid line) and isolated frequency components (dashed lines) from a hypothetical eucaryotic organism.

A.5 **Simple $C_0 t$ curves provide no information on arrangement of sequences or degree of complementary matching.**

A. The analysis described here provides no information on the lengths of unique and repeated sequences as functional units in the genome, or on the organization of these units. The question of organization and an experimental approach to it are considered in Problem A.10.

B. Complications in the analysis of $C_0 t$ curves arise when the members of a family of repeated DNA sequences are similar but not identical. The extent of mismatching in a component isolated after reassociation (using hydroxyapatite chromatography) can be determined from its absorbance–temperature profile in a thermal denaturation experiment (Concept 17.3). DNA duplexes that contain mismatches have a lower thermal stability than perfectly complementary duplexes of the same nucleotide composition. Generally, a drop of $1\,°C$ in the melting temperature (T_m) of a DNA duplex indicates about 1% mismatching. Some examples of mismatching and the complications that arise from it are considered in Problems A.6 through A.8.

A.6 **Complementary RNA and DNA molecules can associate to form hybrid duplexes.**

A. RNA–DNA association often is referred to as hybridization. This technique provides a valuable approach to determining relationships between DNA sequences in the genome and the RNA products of their transcription. Two conditions for hybridization are considered here: association reactions in which DNA is in large excess over RNA (**DNA-driven** reactions) and reactions in which RNA is in large excess over DNA (**RNA-driven** reactions). These two conditions yield different but complementary information.

B. RNA–DNA hybridization generally is carried out using the procedures described for DNA reassociation in Concept A.1. Either the RNA or the DNA is labeled radioactively to facilitate the analysis. Extents of hybridization reactions are measured by one of the following techniques:

1. Under the appropriate conditions pancreatic ribonuclease (RNase) will catalyze hydrolysis of single-stranded RNA, but not of RNA in the form of an RNA–DNA hybrid duplex. Thus samples containing labeled RNA can be digested to completion and assayed for nuclease-resistant RNA.

2. Hydroxyapatite chromatography can be used to separate hybrid duplexes from single-stranded RNA and DNA under partially denaturing conditions. Single-stranded RNA often binds to hydroxyapatite under conditions where single-stranded DNA does not (Concept A.1), because of the tendency of RNA to form intramolecular duplexes. However, in the presence of urea, formamide, or high concentrations of NaCl, single-stranded RNA does not bind, but duplex molecules still are retained. Under these conditions, association can be followed by passing samples through a hydroxyapatite column and determining the fraction of labeled RNA or DNA that is retained.

3. Nitrocellulose filters retain DNA molecules, which aggregate and remain at the filter surface. RNA molecules in RNA–DNA duplexes are retained as well, whereas free RNA passes through the filter. Thus reaction mixtures containing labeled RNA can be analyzed by filtration and analysis of RNA remaining on the filter. Treatment of the filter with RNase before analysis removes uncomplexed portions of RNA molecules that are only partially in the duplex form.

C. Another convenient procedure for hybridization is carried out by immobilizing denatured DNA on nitrocellulose filters *prior* to the reaction and then incubating the filters with labeled RNA. Hybridization is measured as filter-bound radioactivity after RNase treatment and washing to remove unreacted RNA. Because the DNA molecules are not free in solution, this technique gives results that are quantitatively less reliable and more difficult to analyze kinetically than those of solution hybridization reactions. Filter hybridization therefore is not considered in the following discussion.

A.7 DNA-driven reactions can be used to determine which frequency classes of DNA sequences are represented in an RNA population.

A. In a DNA-driven (DNA-excess) association reaction, the RNA is present in minute quantities as a radioactively labeled tracer. Two reactions are occurring under these conditions:

$$DNA + DNA \xrightarrow{k} DNA:DNA$$

$$RNA + DNA \xrightarrow{k} RNA:DNA$$

in which k (liters per mole second) is a second-order rate constant that varies with reaction conditions, as discussed in Concept A.2. To simplify the following derivations it is assumed that k is the same for the two association reactions, although this equivalence is only approximate in practice.* The rate of disappearance of single-stranded DNA is given by equation A.1,

$$-\frac{dC}{dt} = kC^2 \tag{A.1}$$

in which C is the concentration of single-stranded DNA in moles of nucleotide per liter and t is time in seconds. As shown in Concept A.2, this expression can be integrated from initial conditions $t = 0$ and $C = C_0$ to yield equation A.2:

$$\frac{C}{C_0} = \frac{1}{1 + kC_0 t} \tag{A.2}$$

or

$$C = \frac{C_0}{1 + kC_0 t} \tag{A.7}$$

The rate of disappearance of single-stranded RNA is given by an expression analogous to equation A.1:

$$-\frac{dR}{dt} = kRC \tag{A.8}$$

in which R represents the concentration of single-stranded RNA. Substitution of equation A.7 into equation A.8 gives

$$-\frac{dR}{dt} = kR \left(\frac{C_0}{1 + kC_0 t} \right) \tag{A.9}$$

or

$$\frac{dR}{R} = -kC_0 \left(\frac{1}{1 + kC_0 t} \right) dt$$

This expression can be integrated from initial conditions $t = 0$ and $R = R_0$ to yield

$$\ln \frac{R}{R_0} = \ln \frac{1}{1 + kC_0 t}$$

*For a more rigorous and detailed treatment of this subject, see G. A. Galau et al., *Proceedings of the National Academy of Sciences* (*U.S.*), **74**, 1020 (1977), and G. A. Galau et al., ibid., **74**, 2306 (1977).

or

$$\frac{R}{R_0} = \frac{1}{1 + kC_0 t} \qquad (A.10)$$

A comparison of equations A.10 and A.2 indicates that the RNA sequences in a DNA-driven reaction associate at the same rate as the DNA sequences. Because the rate of association depends only on the initial DNA concentration, C_0, hybridization reactions with excess DNA are called DNA-driven reactions.

B. Because RNA tracer sequences associate with the same kinetics as the corresponding DNA sequences, the $C_0 t_{1/2}$ for a species of RNA indicates the frequency class of the DNA sequence from which the RNA was transcribed. As an example, consider the hypothetical eucaryotic genome discussed in Concept A.4. One half of this genome consists of sequences with a total complexity (X) of 10^5 nucleotide pairs, each repeated 10^4 times, and the other half consists of unique sequences with a total complexity of 10^9 nucleotide pairs. Analysis of DNA reassociation kinetics gave $C_0 t_{1/2(\text{mixture})}$ values for these components of 2×10^{-1} mol sec/L and 2×10^3 mol sec/L, respectively. If radioactively labeled RNA from embryonic cells of this organism were isolated and used to perform a DNA-driven hybridization reaction, the results shown in Figure A.3 might be found. Reassociation of the bulk DNA is followed by hypochromicity (Concept A.1), and hybridization of the labeled RNA is monitored by analysis of RNase-resistant radioactivity. The results indicate that 25% of the RNA sequences are transcribed from repeated DNA sequences, and 75% of the RNA sequences are transcribed from unique DNA sequences.

C. Using a combination of hydroxyapatite chromatography and RNase resistance to analyze hybrid formation, it is possible to distinguish between RNA molecules that are transcribed completely from one DNA frequency class and molecules that contain sequences of two classes, as the result of transcription from adjacent repetitive and unique sequences in the genome. For example, analysis of the hybridization reaction of the preceding paragraph by these two techniques might give the results shown in Figure A.4, which indicates that although only 25% of the RNA *sequences* are transcribed from repetitive DNA, 100% of the RNA *molecules* include sequences transcribed from repetitive DNA.

D. The properties of specific RNA transcripts often can be studied most conveniently by synthesis of a highly labeled complementary DNA sequence (cDNA) with reverse transcriptase, followed by association analysis of the cDNA. For experimental purposes, a cDNA tracer behaves identically to an RNA tracer in a DNA-driven association reaction, so that the frequency class of a cDNA species can be determined from its $C_0 t_{1/2}$ using hydroxyapatite chromatography as in the preceding example.

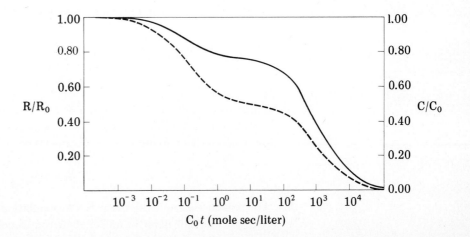

Figure A.3
Association kinetics of tracer RNA (solid line) and bulk DNA (dashed line) in a hypothetical DNA-driven hybridization reaction.

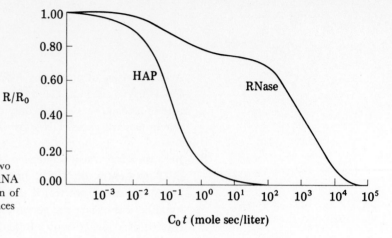

Figure A.4
Analysis of the RNA hybridization in Figure A.3 by two methods. The hydroxyapatite (HAP) column retains RNA molecules that are hybridized to DNA over any portion of their sequence. The RNase assay measures only sequences that actually base-pair to DNA.

A.8 RNA-driven hybridization can be used to measure directly the complexity of an RNA population.

A. In an RNA-driven (RNA-excess) association reaction, the following two reactions occur:

$$RNA + DNA \xrightarrow{k} RNA{:}DNA$$

$$DNA + DNA \xrightarrow{k} DNA{:}DNA$$

However, because the DNA is present in very low concentration as a radioactive tracer, the DNA–DNA reaction usually can be neglected. Under these conditions, the rate of disappearance of single-stranded DNA is given by the equation

$$-\frac{dC}{dt} = kRC \qquad \text{(A.11)}$$

Because the RNA is present in large excess over DNA, the concentration of single-stranded RNA will not change appreciably during the reaction, that is, $R = R_0$. Equation A.11 becomes

$$-\frac{dC}{dt} = kR_0C$$

or

$$\frac{dC}{C} = -kR_0\, dt \qquad \text{(A.12)}$$

Integration of this expression from initial conditions $t = 0$ and $C = C_0$ yields

$$\ln \frac{C}{C_0} = -kR_0 t$$

or

$$\frac{C}{C_0} = e^{-kR_0 t}$$

Thus an RNA-driven hybridization is a pseudo first-order reaction, in contrast to the second-order association reactions discussed so far (Figure A.5). The value of $R_0 t$ when the reaction is half-complete $(R_0 t_{1/2})$ is given by

$$R_0 t_{1/2} = \frac{\ln 2}{k} \qquad \text{(A.13)}$$

B. The sequence complexity of an RNA population can be determined from either the $R_0 t_{1/2}$ or the end point of an RNA-driven association reaction.

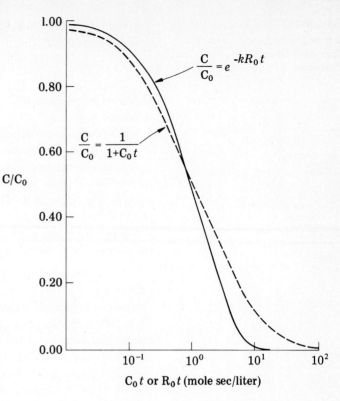

Figure A.5
Kinetics of single-stranded DNA disappearance in pseudo first-order and second-order reactions. Solid line represents C/C_0 as a function of $R_0 t$ in an ideal pseudo first-order RNA-driven hybridization reaction in which the DNA tracer contains sequences of only one frequency class, all of which are present in the RNA population. Dashed line represents C/C_0 as a function of $C_0 t$ in an ideal second-order DNA reassociation reaction.

1.   In a DNA reassociation reaction, the sequence complexity (X) is related to $C_0 t_{1/2}$ by a proportionality constant, K, whose value depends on the reaction conditions (Concept A.3):

$$X = K C_0 t_{1/2} \tag{A.3}$$

The rate constant for DNA–DNA reassociation is related to $C_0 t_{1/2}$ by the expression

$$k = \frac{1}{C_0 t_{1/2}} \tag{A.14}$$

(Concept A.2); the rate constant for RNA–DNA association is related to $R_0 t_{1/2}$ by equation A.13. Under equivalent conditions, assuming equal rate constants, these two expressions can be equated if a factor of 2 is included to account for the fact that for a given set of sequences, the concentration of nucleic acid molecules from a single-stranded RNA preparation will be only half the concentration of the molecules from a double-stranded DNA preparation. Accordingly, equation A.13 must be modified to

$$R_0 t_{1/2} = \frac{1}{2}\left(\frac{\ln 2}{k}\right)$$

or

$$k = \frac{\ln 2}{2 R_0 t_{1/2}} \tag{A.15}$$

Then, equating the two expressions for k,

$$\frac{1}{C_0 t_{1/2}} = \frac{\ln 2}{2 R_0 t_{1/2}}$$

or

$$C_0 t_{1/2} = \frac{2 R_0 t_{1/2}}{\ln 2} \tag{A.16}$$

Substitution of equation A.16 into equation A.3 gives a relationship between RNA complexity and $R_0t_{1/2}$.

$$X = \frac{2KR_0t_{1/2}}{\ln 2} \tag{A.17}$$

Under standard association conditions, $K \simeq 5 \times 10^5$ liter nucleotides per mole second (Concept A.3).

2.   RNA sequence complexity can be determined more directly from the amount of tracer DNA that has associated to form hybrid duplexes at the end of an RNA-driven hybridization reaction. To simplify interpretation, such experiments generally are carried out using an isolated DNA frequency component (e.g., unique DNA from a eucaryotic genome) as the DNA tracer. At the completion of the reaction, the fraction of DNA that has associated with RNA indicates the fraction of the DNA sequences that is present in the RNA population. If the complexity of the tracer DNA is known, the complexity of the RNA population can be calculated from the extent of reaction.

As an example, consider an experiment in which a large excess of mRNA from cells of the hypothetical eucaryote of Concept A.4 is associated in an RNA-driven reaction with radioactive tracer DNA representing the unique fraction of the genome ($X = 10^9$ nucleotide pairs). A possible result is shown in Figure A.6. Because mRNA is transcribed asymmetrically, that is, from only one of the two DNA strands for any given sequence, a maximum of 50% of the DNA could hybridize if the complexities of the mRNA (in nucleotides) and the DNA (in nucleotide pairs) were the same. Thus the 1% of DNA hybridized at the end of the reaction represents 2% of the DNA complexity, and the complexity of the RNA population is at least $0.02 \times 10^9 = 2 \times 10^7$ nucleotides. This figure is a minimum value, because the RNA population also may contain sequences that are not present in the tracer DNA from the unique fraction. This possibility can be checked using the kinetic approach described in the preceding paragraph.

A.9   Homologies between RNA populations can be determined by hybridization competition under DNA-excess conditions.

In a DNA-driven hybridization reaction with radioactive RNA, formation of labeled hybrids will be prevented by the addition of sufficient unlabeled RNA that contains sequences in common with the labeled tracer. This technique, called **hybridization competition,** can be used to measure the relatedness of two RNA populations—for

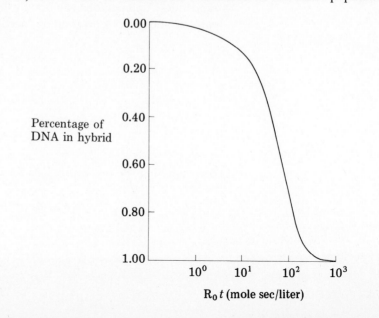

Figure A.6
Determination of RNA sequence complexity from the final extent of tracer DNA association in an RNA-driven hybridization reaction. Hybrid is measured as radioactive tracer DNA retained by a hydroxyapatite column.

example, labeled tracer RNA from one cell type and unlabeled competitor mRNA from another cell type. The fraction of the tracer RNA that can be prevented from hybridizing by increasing amounts of the competitor indicates the fraction of the tracer sequences that also is present in the competitor RNA population. For some examples of this technique, see Problems 20.13 through 20.15.

References

R. J. Britten, D. E. Graham, and B. R. Neufeld, "Analysis of Repeating DNA Sequences by Reassociation," in L. Grossman and K. Moldave (Eds.), *Methods in Enzymology*, Vol. 29, Academic Press, New York, 1974, p. 363.

R. J. Britten and D. Kohne, "Repeated Sequences in DNA," *Science*, **161**, 529 (1968).

G. A. Galau, R. J. Britten, and E. H. Davidson, "Measurement of the Sequence Complexity of Polysomal Messenger RNA in Sea Urchin Embryos," *Cell*, **2**, 9 (1974).

G. A. Galau, R. J. Britten, and E. H. Davidson, "Studies on Nucleic Acid Reassociation Kinetics: Rate of Hybridization of Excess RNA with DNA, Compared to the Rate of DNA Renaturation," *Proceedings of the National Academy of Sciences* (*U.S.*), **74**, 1020 (1977).

G. A. Galau, M. J. Smith, R. J. Britten, and E. H. Davidson, "Studies on Nucleic Acid Reassociation Kinetics: Retarded Rate of Hybridization of RNA with Excess DNA," *Proceedings of the National Academy of Sciences* (*U.S.*), **74**, 2306 (1977).

J. Wetmur and N. Davidson, "Kinetics of Renaturation of DNA," *Journal of Molecular Biology*, **31**, 349 (1968).

Problems

A.1 Answer the following questions with reference to Figure A.7.

  a. How many of these DNA preparations contain more than one frequency class of sequences? Explain your answer.

  b. If the genome size of *E. coli* is taken to be 4.5×10^6 nucleotide pairs, what is the genome size of T4?

  c. What is the complexity of mouse satellite DNA?

  d. Mouse satellite DNA represents 10% of the mouse genome. What is the repetition number for mouse satellite sequences, given that the haploid genome size is 3.2×10^9 nucleotide pairs?

  e. The calf genome is the same size as the mouse genome. What fraction of the calf genome is composed of unique sequences?

  f. The reassociation curve for *E. coli* DNA, shown in Figure A.7, shows a $C_0t_{1/2}$ value of 8 mol sec/L. How will this value change if *E. coli* DNA is allowed to reassociate in the presence of a 1000-fold excess of calf thymus DNA?

A.2 The reassociation curves for calf thymus DNA and an internal standard, *E. coli* DNA, are shown in Figure A.8.

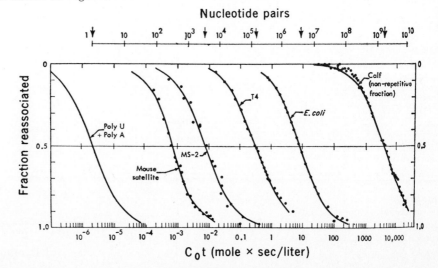

Figure A.7
Reassociation of nucleic acids, sheared to 500-nucleotide fragments, from various sources (Problem A.1). [From R. J. Britten and D. Kohne, *Science*, **161**, 529 (1968).]

464

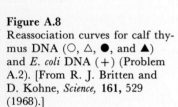

APPENDIX

Analysis of Nucleic
Acid Association
Reactions

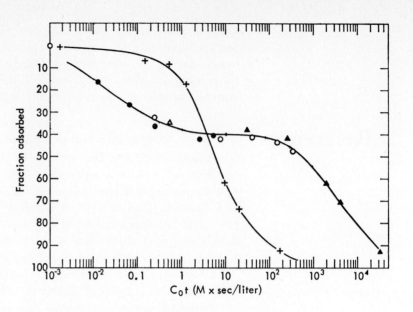

Figure A.8
Reassociation curves for calf thymus DNA (○, △, ●, and ▲) and *E. coli* DNA (+) (Problem A.2). [From R. J. Britten and D. Kohne, *Science,* **161**, 529 (1968).]

a. How many frequency classes of DNA are present in the cow?
b. What fraction of the DNA does each class represent?
c. What is the $C_0t_{1/2(\text{mixture})}$ of each class?
d. How many times are the most rapidly reassociating sequences repeated with respect to the most slowly reassociating sequences (S fraction)?
e. Given that the *E. coli* genome size is 4.5×10^6 nucleotide pairs, what is the complexity of the S fraction?

A.3 A small five-legged creature called a cloewg, which resembles the terrestrial cow, is brought back from an early morning expedition to Disneyland. The reassociation curve of its DNA is shown in Figure A.9.

a. How many frequency classes of sequences are present in this DNA?
b. What fraction of the total genome does each class represent?
c. Explain how you might isolate the fastest (F) and the slowest (S) classes of DNA.
d. If you were to rerun C_0t curves on these isolated classes, what $C_0t_{1/2(\text{pure})}$ values would you obtain?
e. What is the complexity (X) of the S class of DNA, assuming that the reassociation was carried out under standard conditions (as defined in Concept A.3)?
f. Given that the haploid genome size of the cloewg is 2.5×10^9 base pairs, how many copies of each sequence are present in the S class (i.e., what is the repetition number R)?
g. What is the repetition number for the F class?

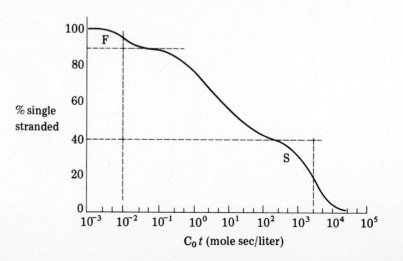

Figure A.9
The reassociation curve of DNA fragments from the cloewg (Problem A.3) (F = fastest, S = slowest).

h. What is the complexity of the F class?

i. How do the frequency classes of the Disneyland cloewg differ from those of the ordinary cow?

j. From the data presented, what can you determine about the organization of these sequences?

A.4 **Polytene chromosomes** are found in certain tissues of several organisms. These chromosomes arise from the chromosomes of diploid nuclei by successive duplications that differ from those of the normal mitotic cycle. Following replication, daughter chromosomes do not segregate but remain paired with each other. The nuclear membrane remains intact following replication, and there is no cell division. Nine to ten cycles of such replication result in a nucleus containing giant polytene chromosomes, each composed of 1000–2000 identical extended DNA molecules in a multistranded cable. The duplication process for polytenization appears to be complex, in that different portions of the genome are duplicated to different extents. The presence of polytene chromosomes is referred to as **polyteny.**

a. A C_0t curve for DNA from a fly embryo is shown in Figure A.10a. Would you expect a C_0t curve of polytene chromosomal DNA from this insect to be identical? Why?

b. Suppose that you obtain the C_0t curve shown in Figure A.10b for the polytene DNA. How does this C_0t curve differ from the preceding one, and how would you interpret this difference?

A.5 The most slowly reassociating fraction of the DNA from *Amphiuma*, an amphibian, gives a $C_0t_{1/2(\text{mixture})}$ value of 1.6×10^5 mol sec/L. Assuming that the reassociation was carried out under standard conditions and that $R = 1$ for the most slowly reassociating fraction, calculate the genome size of *Amphiuma*.

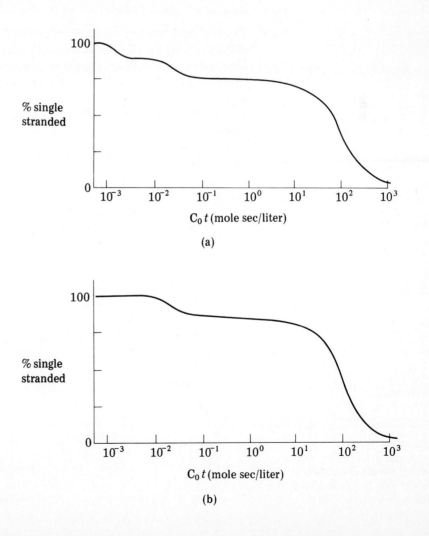

Figure A.10
Hypothetical C_0t curves for
(a) fly embryo DNA and
(b) DNA from polytene nuclei
(Problem A.4).

APPENDIX
Analysis of Nucleic
Acid Association
Reactions

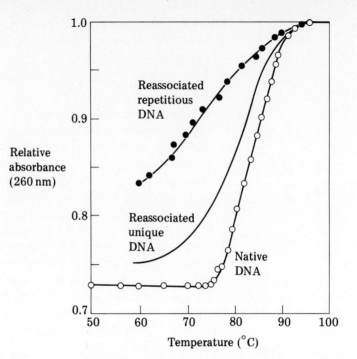

Figure A.11
Absorbance–temperature profiles
of various calf DNAs. Native
DNA is high-molecular-weight
(Problem A.6). [Adapted from
R. J. Britten and D. Kohne, *Science,* **161**, 529 (1968).]

A.6   Figure A.11 shows absorbance–temperature profiles for various calf DNAs.
   a. How would you explain the large difference in the melting profiles of the reassociated repetitious and unique DNAs?
   b. What is the significance of the difference between the profiles of native and reassociated unique DNA?

A.7   Thermal denaturation experiments can yield valuable information about the evolutionary relatedness of various frequency classes from different animals. In one such experiment, a mixture of denatured ^{3}H-mouse DNA (290 μg/mL) and ^{14}C-rat DNA (0.086 μg/mL) are incubated together to a C_0t value sufficient for reassociation of the repeated sequences but not the unique sequences. Because of the difference in concentration of mouse and rat DNA there is essentially no self-association of the rat sequences. The mixture then is passed over a hydroxyapatite column. About 55% of the added DNA is bound to the column. The bound material is eluted by passing a phosphate buffer through the column while increasing its temperature linearly with time. The fractions then are assayed for acid-precipitable radioactivity. The results are shown in Figure A.12.
   a. Which column fractions correspond to the reassociated sequences with the least mismatch?

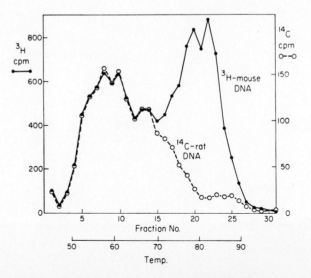

Figure A.12
Thermal denaturation of
reassociated repeated sequences
of mouse and rat DNA (Problem
A.7). [From N. Rice in H. H.
Smith (Ed.), *Evolution of Genetic
Systems, Brookhaven Symposia in
Biology,* Vol. 23, Gordon and
Breach, New York, 1972.]

b. The repeated sequences of the mouse can be divided into two general categories, middle-repetitive and highly repetitive. Which column fractions correspond to each class?

c. Which of these frequency classes shows more homology with rat DNA?

d. The rat and mouse evolutionary lines diverged about 10^7 years ago. From this experiment, what can you say about the relative times of evolution of the middle- and highly repetitive sequences of DNA in the mouse?

A.8   Consider the data in Table A.1.

Table A.1
Effect of Reassociation Temperature on Apparent Percentage of Repetitious DNA (Problem A.8)[a]

DNA	Temperature of reassociation (°C)	Percentage of genome as repetitious DNA
Human	51	43
	60	34
	66	25
Mouse	51	53
	60	34

[a] From D. Kohne, *Quarterly Review of Biophysics,* **33,** 327 (1970).

a. Why does a change in the reassociation temperature affect the percentage of the genome classified as repetitious DNA?

b. What does this temperature effect indicate about mammalian DNA?

c. How would you expect the melting curves of DNA reassociated at 60°C and 51°C to differ?

A.9   Differential polyteny has been suggested to account for large differences in DNA content per nucleus within certain taxonomic groups that do not show corresponding differences in chromosome number. According to this hypothesis, the larger genomes evolved from the smaller ones by lateral duplication of the entire genome to produce multistranded chromosomes.

Vicia faba contains five times as much DNA per nucleus as *Vicia sativa,* but both these species of the pea genus have a haploid chromosome number of 8. Because the two species are closely related, it has been argued that the additional DNA of *V. faba* is unlikely to represent new genetic loci not present in *V. sativa.* Moreover, studies of chromosome structure using trypsin digestion have indicated that *V. faba* has more lateral strands in its chromosomes than does *V. sativa.* Thus *V. sativa* and *V. faba* would appear to be likely candidates for differential polyteny.

The differential polyteny hypothesis can be tested using DNA reassociation kinetics. An increase in polyteny increases the frequency of each sequence by the same amount and thus leaves the concentration of each sequence per gram of DNA unchanged. Because the rate of DNA reassociation is concentration dependent, differential polyteny will not change the rate of DNA reassociation. However, if new sequences are responsible for the increase in DNA content, the concentrations of individual sequences will be lower, and their rate of reassociation will decrease.

With these considerations in mind, the reassociation kinetics of *V. faba* and *V. sativa* DNA were studied, with the results shown in Figure A.13. Under the conditions used, sequences present once per haploid genome would be half-reassociated at $C_0 t$ values of 3000 and 15,000 mol sec/L for DNA from *V. sativa* and *V. faba,* respectively. Therefore Figure A.13 represents the reassociation curves of repeated DNA only. Do the results support the differential polyteny hypothesis or not? Explain.

A.10   In an important series of experiments with *Xenopus laevis* DNA, hydroxyapatite chromatography was used to assay the reassociation of labeled fragments of various lengths with a 10,000-fold excess of unlabeled 450-nucleotide fragments. Figure A.14 shows the fraction of labeled fragments reassociated sufficiently to bind to the column as a function of labeled fragment length (L), at $C_0 t = 50$ mol sec/L. Under these conditions, only repetitive sequences associate.

In a separate experiment, larger quantities of 450-nucleotide and 1400-nucleo-

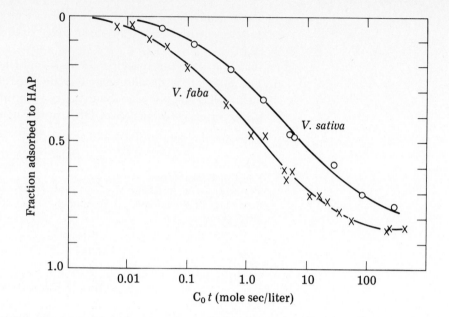

Figure A.13
Reassociation kinetics of isolated
repetitive DNA from *V. faba* and
V. sativa monitored by adsorption
to hydroxyapatite (Problem A.9).
[From N. Straus, *Carnegie Institution Year Book,* **71**, 258 (1972).]

tide fragments each were reassociated independently to $C_0t = 50$ mol sec/L. The
reassociated fractions then were isolated by hydroxyapatite chromatography and analyzed by thermal denaturation. The hyperchromicities observed were 17% and 10%,
respectively, where hyperchromicity is defined as the increase in optical density from
60°C to 98°C expressed as a percentage of the 98°C value. The hyperchromicity of
native *Xenopus* DNA is 27%.

a. When *Xenopus* DNA is sheared to an average chain length of 4000 nucleotides, what
fraction of the fragments consists entirely of unique sequences, based on the data in
Figure A.14?

b. From the data in Figure A.14, what fraction of the *Xenopus* genome is made up of
repetitive sequences? Is your answer more, or less, reliable than the value for this
fraction that would be obtained from a standard C_0t curve?

c. Propose an interpretation for the change in slope of the curve in Figure A.14 at
$L \simeq 800$ nucleotides, and for the continued slow rise beyond this point.

d. Based on the hyperchromicity experiment, what are the average lengths of repetitive
sequence in 450-nucleotide and 1400-nucleotide fragments, respectively? How would
you explain the differences in these lengths?

e. Suggest an alternative and more direct experiment that would answer the first question in part d, using methods that you have encountered in this Appendix.

A.11   Hybridization experiments using labeled 28S rRNA and unlabeled DNA from *Xenopus laevis* demonstrate that at saturation 0.070 μg of 28S rRNA (molecular weight
1.6×10^6) is bound for each 100 μg of DNA. *Xenopus* somatic cells contain 3.6×10^{12}

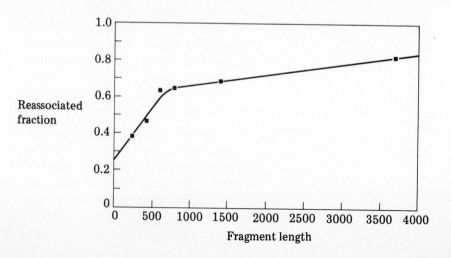

Figure A.14
Reassociation of *Xenopus laevis*
DNA at $C_0t = 50$ as a function
of fragment length (Problem
A.10). [Adapted from E. H. Davidson and R. J. Britten, *Quarterly Review of Biology,* **48**, 565
(1973).]

daltons of DNA. Calculate the number of 28S rRNA genes per diploid genome of *Xenopus*.

A.12   Ovalbumin is produced in large amounts in chick oviduct tissues after stimulation with estrogen, which increases the synthesis of ovalbumin mRNA. Because ovalbumin mRNA (2000 nucleotides long) constitutes such a large fraction of the mRNA in a stimulated cell, it can be purified relatively easily. It is transcribed from unique DNA. Design an experiment to determine whether ovalbumin mRNA is transcribed from unique DNA that is contiguous with a repetitive DNA sequence.

A.13   5-Bromodeoxyuridine (BrdU) is incorporated readily into DNA in place of thymidine by all cells. If incorporated into determined but undifferentiated cells, BrdU inhibits the appearance of the differentiated functions that they normally would express, but exerts little influence on their proliferation rate or their general viability. For example, erythroid stem cells that have been transformed into leukemic cells by Friend leukemia virus will synthesize hemoglobin if exposed to dimethylsulfoxide (DMSO). However, if BrdU is added to these cells prior to addition of DMSO, the synthesis of hemoglobin is inhibited. BrdU does not seem to affect the rates of total RNA, DNA, or protein synthesis. To study the molecular basis for the BrdU inhibition of hemoglobin synthesis in Friend leukemia cells, you prepare normal mouse globin mRNA and transcribe it with reverse transcriptase to produce ³H-cDNA. You then prepare total cellular RNA from DMSO-treated and BrdU-DMSO-treated Friend leukemia cells. The results of hybridization of ³H-cDNA with globin mRNA and total cellular RNAs are shown in Figure A.15a and b, respectively.

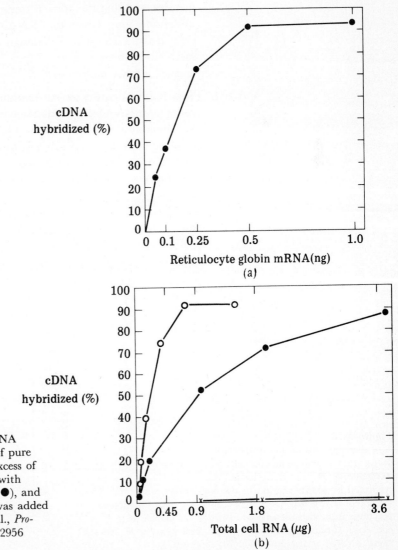

Figure A.15
Hybridization of ³H-cDNA with mouse globin mRNA (Problem A.13). **(a)** Hybridization with an excess of pure mouse globin mRNA. **(b)** Hybridization with an excess of total cell RNA from Friend leukemia cells treated with dimethylsulfoxide (O), BrdU + dimethylsulfoxide (●), and BrdU alone (×). The same amount of ³H-cDNA was added to each mixture. [Adapted from H. D. Preisler et al., *Proceedings of the National Academy of Sciences (U.S.)*, **70**, 2956 (1973).]

a. What are the relative concentrations of globin mRNA sequences in the total RNA from DMSO-treated and BrdU-DMSO-treated cells?

b. Did the BrdU treatment lead to a preferential loss of any subset of the globin mRNA sequences normally present in DMSO-treated cultures?

c. The size distributions of the globin mRNAs from inhibited and noninhibited cultures are given in Figure A.16. Did the BrdU treatment affect the length of the mRNA?

d. In view of these results, how can you account for the inhibition of hemoglobin synthesis by BrdU?

A.14 Consider an organism whose total haploid genome consists of 2×10^9 nucleotide pairs, of which 10^9 nucleotide pairs are unique DNA. In a DNA-driven hybridization experiment, all the mRNA from this organism is shown to be transcribed from unique DNA sequences. When radioactively labeled mRNA from this organism is hybridized at different DNA:RNA ratios to a C_0t of 10^5, the end of the kinetic reaction, the data shown in Figure A.17 are obtained. Two classes of mRNA are apparent, designated class 1 and class 2 in the figure.

a. What is the sequence complexity of the two classes of mRNAs?

b. How many different mRNA molecules are there in each class? Assume that each mRNA is 10^3 nucleotides long.

c. Calculate the number of molecules per cell for each of the different mRNAs in each class, if there are 4.4×10^{-13} g of mRNA per cell.

A.15 Certain data suggest that each mRNA molecule from *Xenopus laevis* embryos is transcribed partly from unique DNA sequences and partly from repetitive DNA sequences, and that the portion transcribed from repetitive sequences is about 50 to 60 nucleotides long. Given that RNA molecules can be labeled chemically or enzymatically at the 5' end with ^{32}P, design an experiment that will demonstrate whether the mRNA sequences transcribed from repetitive DNA generally are located at the 5' or 3' ends of mRNA molecules.

A.16 Several investigators have attempted to measure how much of a eucaryotic genome codes for mRNA by hybridization of labeled DNA with an excess of polysomal RNA (presumably mRNA). Initially, such studies were done under conditions that allow only the more common mRNAs to hybridize. Messengers made in only a few cells in the organism, made only during a brief period during development, or made by all cells but at a very low level would not have hybridized with DNA at the RNA:DNA ratios used.

In one such study, mRNA was isolated from sea urchin embryos at the gastrula stage (600 cells), and was hybridized in excess with labeled unique DNA. At a R_0t of 10^3, about 1% of the DNA was hybridized. Assuming asymmetric transcription, the authors concluded that about 2% of the unique DNA is used to code for gastrula message. Is this estimate likely to be an accurate one? Calculate the number of copies of an mRNA that would have to be present in each embryo in order to be half-hybridized at $R_0t = 10^3$. Assume an average of 1200 nucleotides per mRNA, 7.2×10^7 mRNA molecules per embryo, and a K of 5×10^5 liter nucleotides per mole second.

Figure A.16
Size distributions of globin mRNA present in total cell RNA from Friend leukemia cells treated with dimethylsulfoxide alone (●) and dimethylsulfoxide + BrdU (×) as determined by sedimentation in sucrose density gradients (Problem A.13). mRNA was measured by hybridization of fractions from each density gradient to ^{3}H-cDNA as in Figure A.15. [From H. D. Preisler et al., *Proceedings of the National Academy of Sciences (U.S.)*, **70**, 2956 (1973).]

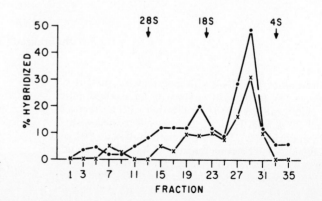

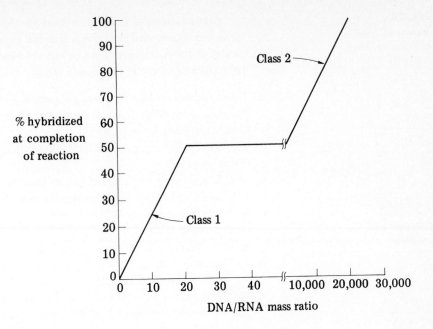

Figure A.17
Extent of mRNA hybridization
as a function of increasing
DNA/RNA ratio (Problem A.14).

Answers

A.1 a. None of the preparations contains more than a single frequency class of sequences, because each shows about 80% reassociation over a two-log interval of C_0t. If more than one frequency class were present, the C_0t curves would be broader.

b. Genome size for procaryotes is equal to complexity, which is proportional to $C_0t_{1/2}$. From the curves in Figure A.7, the $C_0t_{1/2}$ values for *E. coli* and T4 are 8 and 0.3, respectively. Therefore the genome size of T4 is $(4.5 \times 10^6)(0.3/8) = 1.7 \times 10^5$ nucleotide pairs.

c. The $C_0t_{1/2}$ value for mouse satellite DNA is 7×10^{-4}. Therefore its complexity is $(4.5 \times 10^6)(7 \times 10^{-4}/8) = 400$ nucleotide pairs.

d. Mouse satellite DNA comprises $(0.10)(3.2 \times 10^9) = 3.2 \times 10^8$ nucleotide pairs. If the complexity of the repeating sequence is 400 nucleotides, this sequence must be repeated 8×10^5 times.

e. From Figure A.7, the complexity of the calf unique sequence fraction is $(4.5 \times 10^6)(4 \times 10^3/8) = 2 \times 10^9$. Because these sequences are present only once, they comprise $2 \times 10^9/3.2 \times 10^9 = 60\%$ of the calf genome.

f. The $C_0t_{1/2}$ value for *E. coli* DNA will not be affected significantly. The complementary sequences in a mixture appear to associate independently; their rate of association is dependent only on their concentration and is independent of the concentration of noncomplementary sequences. This independence must be assumed in order to interpret any C_0t curve involving more than one frequency class of DNA sequences.

A.2 a. Two frequency classes are present because there appear to be two second-order transitions in the reassociation curve. For convenience, these classes are designated the fast (F) and slow (S) classes.

b. The fraction of the DNA in the F class is 0.4; the fraction in the S class is 0.6.

c. $C_0t_{1/2(\text{mixture})(F)} = 0.03$; $C_0t_{1/2(\text{mixture})(S)} = 3000$.

d. The concentration of sequences that reassociate rapidly is $C_0t_{1/2(S)}/C_0t_{1/2(F)}$ or 10^5 times the concentration of sequences that reassociate slowly. If the S fraction is made up of unique sequences, each of which occurs only once in the calf genome, the sequences of the F fraction must be repeated 10^5 times on the average.

e. This question can be answered in either of two ways. Complexity is proportional to $C_0t_{1/2(\text{pure})}$, which for the calf S fraction is $(3 \times 10^3)(0.6) = 1.8 \times 10^3$ mol sec/L. From the curve shown in Figure A.8, $C_0t_{1/2}$ for *E. coli* = 5. Therefore the complexity of the calf S fraction is $(4.5 \times 10^6)(1.8 \times 10^3/5) = 1.6 \times 10^9$ nucleotide pairs.

Alternatively, if you know that the haploid genome size of calf is 3.2×10^9 nucleotide pairs, and that the S fraction represents single-copy DNA, then the complexity of the S fraction must be equal to its portion of the genome, which is $(3.2 \times 10^9)(0.6) = 1.9 \times 10^9$ nucleotide pairs.

A.3 a. There are at least four frequency classes. F and S appear to be single-frequency classes, but the intermediate fraction must contain more than one class, because it reassociates over a three-log interval of C_0t.

b. The fastest class represents 10%, the intermediate class 50%, and the slowest class 40% of the genome.

c. The F class can be isolated by incubating the reassociating mixture to a C_0t of 10^{-1} mol sec/L, adsorbing the double-stranded DNA to hydroxyapatite, and eluting with buffer containing a high concentration of salt. The S class may be isolated by incubating the mixture to a C_0t of 2.5×10^2 mol sec/L, passing it through a hydroxyapatite column, and collecting the material that does not adsorb.

d. In general, $C_0t_{1/2(\text{pure})} = fC_0t_{1/2(\text{mixture})}$. Therefore, $C_0t_{1/2(\text{pure})(\text{F})} = 0.1 \times 10^{-2} = 10^{-3}$ mol sec/L, and $C_0t_{1/2(\text{pure})(\text{S})} = 0.4 \times 0.25 \times 10^4 = 10^3$ mol sec/L.

e. Under standard experimental conditions, complexity is related to $C_0t_{1/2(\text{pure})}$ by the proportionality constant 5×10^5 liter nucleotides per mole second. Hence, for the S class, whose $C_0t_{1/2(\text{pure})}$ is 10^3 mol sec/L, $X = 5 \times 10^8$ nucleotide pairs.

f. The S class represents 40% of the total genome, or 1×10^9 nucleotide pairs. The complexity of the S class is half this value; hence there must be two copies of every sequence per genome, that is, $R = 2$.

g. The ratio of R values for different frequency classes in the population can simply be read off the original C_0t curve as the ratio of $C_0t_{1/2}$ values. For the S and F classes, this ratio is $2.5 \times 10^3/10^{-2} = 2.5 \times 10^5$. Because the repetition number for the S class is 2, the repetition number for the F class is 5×10^5.

h. The complexity of this class can be obtained as in part e from the $C_0t_{1/2(\text{pure})}$ for the F class (10^{-3} mol sec/L). The complexity of the F class is $(5 \times 10^5)(10^{-3}) = 500$ nucleotide pairs.

i. In marked contrast to all earthly creatures, the genome of the cloewg contains no unique sequences. Forty percent of its genome is composed of sequences repeated only twice, and 10% is composed of short sequences of complexity 500 that are present in half a million copies. The remainder of the genome consists of two or more classes of DNA with intermediate repetitiveness.

j. This analysis tells you nothing about the arrangement of sequences within the genome. For example, the F class might represent 5×10^5 copies of a sequence of 500 contiguous nucleotide pairs, or 5×10^5 copies each of 5 different sequences of 100 contiguous nucleotide pairs. The repeated sequences could be in tandem, or interspersed between nonrepeating sequences. Other kinds of experiments are required to distinguish among these possibilities.

A.4 a. The curve in Figure A.10a is about 10% highly repetitive, 15% middle-repetitive, and 75% unique. A C_0t curve for polytene DNA should be identical to that of embryo DNA only if the C_0 for each frequency class does not change upon polytenization.

b. The polytene C_0t curve suggests that highly repetitive DNA is lost upon polytenization. This would suggest that the highly repetitive (centromeric) DNA present in most chromosomes has not been amplified. The fruit fly *Drosophila*, in fact, shows this behavior; its four polytene chromosomes are closely associated at their centromeric regions in a highly heterochromatic structure called the **chromocenter.**

A.5 Under standard conditions, $X = (C_0t_{1/2(\text{pure})})(5 \times 10^5)$. $C_0t_{1/2(\text{pure})} = fC_0t_{1/2(\text{mixture})}$. Therefore $X = (fC_0t_{1/2(\text{mixture})})(5 \times 10^5)$. X is related to N by the expression $X = fN/R$. Equating the two expressions for X gives $N = (C_0t_{1/2(\text{mixture})})(5 \times 10^5) = (1.6 \times 10^5)(5 \times 10^5) = 8 \times 10^{10}$ nucleotide pairs.

A.6 a. The smaller relative absorbance change, shallower slope, and lower T_m of the rapidly reassociating DNA indicates the presence of single-stranded regions and considerable mismatching in the reassociated sequences.

b. The unique fraction would be expected to reassociate almost perfectly if each sequence finds its complement. Thus the difference between these profiles probably is due in part to the small fragment size of the reassociated DNA rather than to mismatching.

A.7 a. The sequences with the least mismatch melt at the highest temperature. Therefore fractions 22 to 27 represent the least mismatched sequences.

b. Because the highly repetitive mouse sequences (satellite DNA) are nearly identical ($\leq 6\%$ mismatch), the reassociated duplexes will have a high melting temperature. The less similar middle-repetitive sequences form duplexes with more mismatches that melt at a lower temperature. Therefore fractions 5–12 are middle-repetitive sequences, and fractions 16–26 are highly repetitive sequences.

c. The middle-repetitive sequences show more homology.

d. The satellite DNA must have evolved in the mouse *after* its divergence from the rat evolutionary line. Thus the appearance of the mouse satellite DNA is a recent evolutionary event. In contrast, the middle-repetitive sequences apparently existed prior to divergence. Other satellites also appear to have evolved in recent times.

A.8 a. The fraction of DNA that reassociates rapidly increases as the temperature is lowered because sequences with more mismatches become able to form stable duplexes.

b. This effect indicates that mammalian repetitious DNA contains related sequences that have varying degrees of homology.

c. The 60°C temperature imposes a higher *criterion* for reassociation; only well-matched duplexes are stable enough to form at this temperature. At 51°C, more mismatching is permitted. Therefore duplexes formed at 60°C will give melting curves with greater total increase in absorbance, higher melting point, and steeper slope than those of duplexes formed at 51°C.

A.9   The reassociation curves show that the average renaturation rate of DNA from *V. faba* is *faster* than that of *V. sativa*. This result suggests that if the genome of *V. faba* grew from a genome very much like that of *V. sativa*, it did so by multiplying some sequences more than others. Therefore the results rule out the hypothesis that *V. faba* is a simple polytenic derivative of the present-day genome of *V. sativa*.

A.10 a. At $C_0 t = 50$, labeled fragments that contain both repetitive and unique sequences will reassociate partially and be retained by the column, but fragments that consist entirely of unique sequences will not. The reassociated fraction of 0.8 at a fragment length of 4000 nucleotides indicates that 80% of these fragments contain at least one repetitive sequence. The remaining 20% must consist entirely of unique sequences.

b. As the length of the labeled fragments decreases, the probability becomes higher that each fragment consists entirely of unique or entirely of repetitive sequences. At $C_0 t = 50$, only repetitive sequences will reassociate. Therefore, extrapolation of the curve in Figure A.14 to $L = 0$ gives a value for the fraction of the genome that consists of repetitive sequences. This value of 0.25 is more reliable than that obtained from a standard $C_0 t$ curve analysis, in which the fragments are generally 400 to 500 nucleotides in length and have a higher probability of including both unique and repetitive sequences.

c. The change in slope suggests that in 60% of the genome, there is an average of one repetitive sequence and one longer unique sequence per 800 nucleotides, and that in the remaining 40% of the genome repetitive sequences are much less frequent. At $L = 800$ almost all of the fragments from the 60% portion of the genome contain at least one repetitive sequence. Further increases in L beyond 800 simply produce fragments from this portion of the genome with two or more repetitive sequences, and therefore do not increase the fraction of these fragments that can partially reassociate. However, as L increases up to 4000, more of the fragments from the remainder of the genome contain a repetitive sequence, so that the curve continues to rise gradually.

d. Native *Xenopus* DNA, which is 100% duplex, gives a hyperchromicity of 27%. The hyperchromicity of 17% for reassociated 450-nucleotide fragments indicates that the population is $\frac{17}{27}$ or 63% duplex. The duplex DNA represents repetitive sequence; therefore the average amount of repetitive sequence per fragment is $0.63 \times 450 = 280$ nucleotides. A similar calculation for the 1400-nucleotide fragments yields a value of 530 nucleotides of repetitive DNA per fragment. The latter value is greater because at $L = 1400$ most fragments contain more than one repetitive sequence.

e. Each of the fragments isolated in the hyperchromicity experiment will contain duplex repetitive DNA and single-stranded unique DNA. If the population of fragments is digested with a single-strand-specific nuclease, such as the S_1 nuclease from *Aspergillus*, only the duplex regions of each fragment will remain. The size distribution of these regions then can be estimated directly by zone sedimentation, gel filtration, or polyacrylamide gel electrophoresis.

A.11   If 0.070% of the DNA sequences code for 28S rRNA, then, considering the complementary DNA strands for these regions, 0.14% of the DNA consists of 28S rRNA genes of molecular weight 3.2×10^6. Thus the diploid genome of *Xenopus laevis* must contain

$$\frac{(3.6 \times 10^{12} \text{ daltons/genome})(1.4 \times 10^{-3})}{3.2 \times 10^6 \text{ daltons/rRNA gene}} = 1600 \text{ rRNA genes/genome}$$

A.12   Long segments of DNA that contain repetitive sequences can be isolated by shearing chick DNA to fragments of 2000–3000 nucleotide pairs in length, denaturing, and then reassociating to a C_0t value just sufficient to anneal repetitive sequences. Fragments containing repetitive sequences can be recovered from this reassociation mixture by passing it over hydroxyapatite and isolating the fraction that is retained. Given labeled ovalbumin mRNA, a DNA-driven hybridization experiment with the isolated DNA fraction will indicate whether it contains unique sequences complementary to the mRNA.

A.13 a. The 50% saturation points of the hybridization curves in Figure A.15b show that the globin mRNA content of the DMSO-treated cultures is about three times greater than that from cultures treated with DMSO and BrdU.

b. Because the RNA from inhibited and noninhibited cultures reached the same maximum hybridization value, all of the globin mRNA sequences must be present after BrdU-DMSO treatment, but at lower than normal concentration.

c. Because the distributions of hybridizable RNA obtained from inhibited and noninhibited cultures were very similar, there must have been no appreciable change in the length of the mRNA.

d. The effects of BrdU on globin mRNA synthesis are quantitative rather than qualitative because similar transcripts are present in both cultures. Thus BrdU appears to affect only the rate of transcription of the gene. It has been reported that the rate of dissociation of *lac* repressor from BrdU-substituted *lac* operator DNA in *E. coli* is 10 times slower than normal. Conceivably, BrdU could have a similar effect on the dissociation of some regulatory protein in eucaryotic cells.

A.14 a. The class 1 mRNA is hybridized completely at a DNA:RNA mass ratio of 40:1. At this point the mass ratio of unique DNA, which contains all of the mRNA sequences, to mRNA, is 20:1. Assuming transcription of only one DNA strand, the ratio of total unique DNA sequences in nucleotide pairs to RNA sequences in class 1 is 10:1; that is, one-tenth of the unique DNA sequences are represented in the class 1 mRNA population. Given that the complexity of the unique DNA is 10^9 nucleotide pairs, the complexity of the class 1 mRNA is 10^8 nucleotides. By similar reasoning, the complexity of the class 2 mRNA is 10^5 nucleotides.

b. If the average mRNA molecule is 10^3 nucleotides long, there must be $10^8/10^3 = 10^5$ different mRNA molecules in class 1 and $10^5/10^3 = 10^2$ different mRNA molecules in class 2.

c. The total number of mRNA molecules per cell is

$$\frac{(4.4 \times 10^{-13} \text{ g/cell})(6.02 \times 10^{23} \text{ nucleotides/mol of nucleotides})}{(330 \text{ g/mol of nucleotides})(10^3 \text{ nucleotides/mRNA molecule})}$$

or 8.0×10^5 mRNA molecules per cell. For the 50% of the mRNA that represents 10^5 different kinds of mRNA molecules (class 1), there are

$$\frac{(0.5)(8.0 \times 10^5 \text{ mRNA molecules/cell})}{10^5 \text{ kinds of mRNA}}$$

or 4 mRNA molecules of each kind per cell. For the 50% of the mRNA that represents 10^2 different kinds of mRNA (class 2) a similar calculation shows that there are 4×10^3 mRNA molecules of each kind per cell.

A.15 There are several ways to determine the location of the repetitive portion of the mRNA. One possibility is to isolate intact mRNA that is uniformly labeled with ^{3}H-uridine and label it with ^{32}P at the 5′ end. The ^{32}P-labeled mRNA then could be fragmented into small pieces and analyzed in a DNA-driven hybridization reaction. Treatment of the hybrids with ribonuclease should show that the ^{3}H-mRNA reacts with two DNA components. A small fraction should hybridize with the $C_0 t_{1/2}$ of repetitive DNA, whereas the majority should hybridize with the $C_0 t_{1/2}$ of unique DNA. By contrast, the ^{32}P label should hybridize entirely with either the $C_0 t_{1/2}$ of repetitive DNA or unique DNA. If the portion of mRNA transcribed from repetitive DNA is located at the 5′ end, ^{32}P label will hybridize entirely with repetitive DNA. If the repetitive portion is located internally or on the 3′ end, ^{32}P label will hybridize entirely with unique DNA.

A.16 The average complexity of any single mRNA species will be equal to its chain length; that is, $X = 1200$ nucleotides. The $R_0 t_{1/2}$ for a pure preparation of such an RNA can be calculated using equation A.17 as follows:

$$R_0 t_{1/2(\text{pure})} = \frac{(X)(\ln 2)}{2K}$$

$$= \frac{(1200 \text{ nucleotides})(0.69)}{2 \times 5 \times 10^5 \text{ L nucleotides/mol sec}}$$

$$= 8.3 \times 10^{-4} \text{ mol sec/L}$$

If this same RNA is present as some fraction, f, of the total RNA population, its $R_0 t_{1/2}$, in terms of total RNA concentration, will be higher by the factor $1/f$, that is,

$$R_0 t_{1/2(\text{mixture})} = \frac{R_0 t_{1/2(\text{pure})}}{f}$$

or

$$f = \frac{R_0 t_{1/2(\text{pure})}}{R_0 t_{1/2(\text{mixture})}}$$

For an RNA species to be half-hybridized at $R_0 t = 10^3$ mol sec/L, f must be $8.3 \times 10^{-4}/10^3 = 8.3 \times 10^{-7}$. For the organism in the problem, this fraction represents $(8.3 \times 10^{-7})(7.2 \times 10^7 \text{ mRNAs per embryo}) = 60$ copies per embryo, or 0.1 copies per cell. Therefore hybridization to $R_0 t = 10^3$ should detect any mRNA that is common to all the cells of the gastrula or that is made in at least 60 copies by a subpopulation of gastrula cells. Hybridization to this value of $R_0 t$ will not detect an mRNA that is made in less than 60 copies by a subpopulation of gastrula cells. Thus the conclusion that 2% of the unique DNA is used to code for gastrula mRNA may be an underestimate of the true value.

INDEX

Note: Page references in italics denote illustrations.

solubility properties, 126, 127, 133, 138
in structural hierarchy, *8*
structure, 16
subunit, 54
techniques for separation, 127
thermodynamics of folding, 53
thermophilic bacteria, 69, 77
three-dimensional structure, 57
transport, 111, 261
unwinding protein, 347
Protein kinase, 197
Protein processing
genetic signals, 433
Protein sequenator
data analysis, 43, *44,* 50, 51
description, 35, 36
sequencing strategy, 30
Protein sequencing
data analysis, 37, 38, 39, 40, 41, 42, 46, 47, 48, 49
identification of Gln and Asn, 39–40, 48
by partial acid hydrolysis, 38, 47
peptides, 35
strategy, 30
unfractionated mixtures of peptides, 40, 42, 48
Protein synthesis. *See also* Translation
classes of RNA involved, 323–325
Dintzis experiment, 417, 427, 428
information flow, 403, *404*
inhibitors, *410,* 417
in vitro, 417
kinetics, 417, 427, 428
relation to tyrocidin synthesis, 421
tRNA, 324–325
Proteolytic cleavage *See* Post-translational modification
Protoplasmic membrane, 108
Protomer
definition, 80
microtubule, 86
point group symmetries, 82
quasi-equivalence, 83
Proton gradient. *See also* Proton translocation
chemiosmotic coupling, 231
two components, 231, 236
Proton translocation
chemiosmotic coupling, 231
in chloroplasts, *245*
in mitochondrial electron transport, *232*
in photosynthetic bacteria, 245
topology in mitochondria, *231, 245*
Protozoa, *90,* 101
Proximal convergence
in stereo viewing, *63,* 64
possible size format of stereo pictures, 64
Pseudo first-order kinetics
of RNA driven RNA-DNA association, 460, *461*
Pseudomonas lindneri
alcoholic fermentation, *202, 203,* 208
Pseudoscopic
images in stereo viewing, 65
Pseudosymmetry
hemoglobin, 99

IgG, 99
Pseudouridylate
tRNA, 325
PTH-amino acids. *See* Phenylthiohydantoins
Purines
biosynthesis, 295, *296,* 304
isotope tracer experiment, 305
nucleic acid component, 315, *316*
regulation of biosynthesis, *299*
salvage pathway, 295
structure, *6, 316*
Puromycin, 410
Pye, 205
Pyridine
nucleotide, 181
ring, 216
Pyridoxal phosphate
analogues, 216, 221, *222,* 225
mechanism, *216*
Pyrimidine dimer, 436. *See also* Thymine dimer
Pyrimidines
ATP requirement in biosynthesis, 305, 311
biosynthesis, 295, *298*
isotope tracer experiments, 305
nucleic acid component, 315, *316*
regulation of biosynthesis, *299*
salvage pathway, 295
structure, *6*
Pyrophosphate (PP$_i$)
composition, *197*
transfer, 275
Pyrrolidone carboxylate, *33*
Pyruvate
amino acid biosynthesis, *293*
amino acid catabolism, 216
bacterial transport, 264
catabolism, 192, *193*
electron transport, *230*
Entner-Doudoroff pathway, *202, 203,* 208
gluconeogenesis, *277*
glycolysis, *194*
nutritional consequences, 218
standard half-cell potential, 178
TCA cycle, *217,* 218
Pyruvate carboxylase
gluconeogenesis, 222, 226, 276, 277
regulation of carbohydrate synthesis, 276, *277*
regulation of TCA cycle, 222, 226
TCA cycle, 218, *219*
Pyruvate decarboxylase, 201, 208
Pyruvate dehydrogenase, 218, *219*
Pyruvate kinase
glycolysis, *194,* 195
phosphoketolase pathway, 203, 208, *209*
standard free energy change, 195
relation to gluconeogenesis, 276, *277*
regulation of glycolysis, 277

Q

Quantum, 242
Quasi-equivalence
definition, 83
insulin dimer, *96,* 97

Quaternary structure
determination, 94, 95
level of protein organization, 54
Quinone, 230

R

R (gas constant), 176
rIIB gene
frameshift mutations, 444
Racemization
amino acids, 216
Radiation
electromagnetic, *242*
Radical
paramagnetic nitroxide, 116, 122
Radioactive tracer experiments. *See* Isotope tracer experiments
Ramachandran diagram, 71, *73*
Random coil
nucleic acids, 318
proteins, 53
Rare nucleotides
tRNA, 325
Rate constants, 133–134, 138–139, 144
Rate equation, 133–134, 138–139
Reaction
equilibrium, 127
rate, 145
rate constants, 133–134, 138–139, 144–145
Reading frame, 414, 425, 434, *435,* 436
Reassociation of DNA. *See* DNA reassociation
rec genes
recombination-repair, *354*
Recombinant DNA
and genetic engineering, 371–386
cloning vectors, 375
joining of DNA fragments, 373
molecular cloning, 374, 375
perceived risks and containment procedures, 378
Recombination
genetic recombination, 322
mechanism, *323, 324*
Recombinational repair, 353, *354*
Redox couple, 176, 177
Redox reactions, 176–178, 184, 185, 231–232
Reducing end
glycogen, *196*
Reducing power
biosynthesis, 180, 181, 276
phosphogluconate pathway, 192, 198
photosynthesis, 246
Reduction
disulfide bond, 30, *31*
reactions, 176–178, 184, 185, 231–232
Regulated
gene expression, 411
Regulation
adenylate control, 205, 210, 211
amino acid biosynthesis, 292, 293, *294*
biosynthesis, 276
Calvin cycle, 278, *279*
deoxyribonucleotide biosynthesis, 295, *299*
fatty-acid biosynthesis, 290, *291*
feedback inhibition, 276